TRUE LOVE SWEET WESTERN TALES OF ROMANCE

KATIE WYATT   BRENDA CLEMMONS
ELLEN ANDERSON   KAT CARSON   ADA OAKLEY

RoyceCardiff
Publishing House
WHOLESOME INSPIRATIONAL ROMANCE

RoyceCardiff
P u b l i s h i n g   H o u s e
WHOLESOME INSPIRATIONAL ROMANCE

Dear Reader,

It is our utmost pleasure and privilege to bring these wonderful stories to you. I am so very proud of our amazing team of writers and the delight they continually bring us all with their beautiful clean and wholesome tales of, faith, courage, and love.

What is a book's lone purpose if not to be read and enjoyed? Therefore, you, dear reader, are the key to fulfilling that purpose and unlocking the treasures that lie within the pages of this book.

CONTENTS

THROUGH THE STORM DANIEL'S COURAGE

DISAPPOINTED HEARTS

ETHAN'S FAITH

BECKY'S WINTER

MARY & JOHN

MARIA'S DESTINY

JENNY'S UNEXPECTED

RAYNE'S MEADOW

GOLDEN COLORADO

OKLAHOMA DESTINIES

FLOSSIE'S MOUNTAIN

JOSEPHINE

BE MINE, VALENTINE

ANNABEL AND ERNEST

LOVING THE WRONG BROTHER

A PERSONAL WORD FROM AUTHORS

WE WANT TO THANK YOU FOR ALL YOUR CONTINUED SUPPORT FOR ALL OF OUR bestselling series. We wouldn't be where we are now without all your help. We can't thank you enough!

We had a lot of fun writing this series about adventures, hardships, hopes, loves, and perseverance. Writing these Historical Western and Contemporary Romance was a magical time.

Sixteen sweet romances books from multi authors. They can be read as standalone, every book is complete on its own that you're sure to fall in love with all the other available series, don't wait!

Thank you for being a loyal reader.

Katie

HANNAH'S HEART

Mail Order Bride Western Romance

RoyceCardiff

Publishing House

WHOLESOME INSPIRATIONAL ROMANCE

Dear Reader,

It is our utmost pleasure and privilege to bring these wonderful stories to you. I am so very proud of our amazing team of writers and the delight they continually bring us all with their beautiful clean and wholesome tales of, faith, courage, and love.

What is a book's lone purpose if not to be read and enjoyed? Therefore, you, dear reader, are the key to fulfilling that purpose and unlocking the treasures that lie within the pages of this book.

🕮

NEWSLETTER SIGN UP FREE BOOKS!

http://katieWyattBooks.com/readersgroup

🕮

THANK YOU FOR CHOOSING A INSPIRATIONAL READS BY ROYCE CARDIFF PUBLISHING HOUSE.

Welcome and Enjoy!

A PERSONAL WORD FROM ADA

I LOVE WRITING BOOKS ABOUT THE HARDSHIPS AND STRUGGLES OF WOMEN WHO turn around their hopeless situations and in the end found true love and happiness is something that she enjoys bringing to the readers.

I wishes that the readers will once again learn to believe in love and develop trust through reading her books, and be inspired by the characters in her novels who through perseverance, in spite of very tough harsh obstacles that tested their faith, overcame the hurdles in the end.

If you love Western Romance and Mail Order Bride stories about the courageous women who traveled alone to the Wild West with nothing but hope and strong faith in God. Now's the time to grab it!

Thank you for being a loyal reader.

Ada ..

CHAPTER 1
JUNE 1893

Hannah Buchanan shook the reins and clicked her tongue, urging Daisy, the cart horse, into a trot. It was quite a way into town and she needed to be there and back before lunch.

Buc, her husband of two months, stood on the porch and waved. She loved him so, it was a pain to leave him, but the farm wouldn't take care of itself. Anyway, it was silly for them both to ride into town to get a few things and Hannah was more than capable of going on her own. She had always been fiercely independent. Buc understood that about her and didn't try to stop her, saying it was one of the things he loved most about her.

It was so early, only just light, the sun was still climbing up the horizon. With the wind out of the south, it would be a hot summer's day. Hannah found the heat would get to her and she preferred to get as much done early in the morning as possible. That included the supply run to Bear Claw.

Bear Claw, Montana, was a tiny town. It had sprung up not more than ten years previously as a way station between the outlying farms and Great Falls itself. Nestled in the foothills next to a lake, there was great fishing, water all year round, and the biggest, endless view of the sky anywhere. It was a picturesque place to live. Or so the eighty-five people who lived in the town itself told anyone and everyone who came by.

In her first week there, more than ten people had told her all about the virtues of living in Bear Claw, including Mrs. Henrietta Cromwell, who owned and ran the local general store. It was lovely. As far as Hannah could see, there was only one blemish on the town, and it was the constant animosity between the townies and the miners.

With their houses clustered up on the rolling hills just north of the town proper, the coal miners were a poor lot. Their children were underfed, their dogs almost feral, and no matter how they scrubbed, they were always gray from the dust in the mine. It was a pathetic little mine that hardly seemed worth the cost of running it, however, it supplied jobs, and so Hannah guessed it was a necessary evil. Her heart broke for those poor people, though very few "decent" folks would listen when she tried to talk about it. To most townies, the miners were a waste of good land.

As she rode towards the town, Hannah went through her shopping list. They were out of salt, sugar, coffee, and rice. She also wanted to see if Henrietta had any new cloth in. Buc needed a new shirt badly. He'd all but worn through his favorite and she couldn't have the man of her dreams in tatters. Absorbed as she was in her thoughts, Hannah didn't notice the smell of smoke, at first.

It was only after the third sneeze that she noted it and looking up, saw the smudge of black right over the town. The smoke stretched in a severe straight line across the blue sky and filled her heart with dread. There was only one way that much smoke got into the air.

"Get on, Daisy!" she said, urging her horse to go faster. Daisy was young and strong and she obliged, carrying Hannah the last few miles in record time.

Even though she had seen the smoke, Hannah was still shocked as she rode into Bear Claw. The air hung thick with smoke, blown down so it hung like fog between the buildings. Daisy snorted and whinnied.

"It's all right, girl," Hannah said. "We're just going to see if anyone needs help."

It was dim in the town, the smoky air not letting a lot of sunlight through, and Hannah covered her nose and mouth with a handkerchief from her pocket. No one was on Main Street. She turned the cart onto West Street and rode along to where the air seemed less deadly. Up a little rise and she reached the churchyard.

Here there was the clamor of voices and sharp metal sounds. The air shifted and she saw a scene that made her eyes go wide in shock. The churchyard, an open square of grass between the church itself and the house Pastor Ashby and his wife lived in, was often used for market days and church picnics. Now it was a makeshift hospital. People lay on the grass in a long row, many crying, some so silent and still, Hannah feared they were dead.

"Hannah!"

She looked down and found Henrietta, her face soot-blackened and smudged, looking up at her.

"Oh, thank heaven you're here. The cart has slipped its wheel and there's no way to get the water buckets up to the fire now," Henrietta babbled.

"Are you all right?" Hannah asked. "What happened?"

Henrietta touched her dark brown hair as it blew in wisps about her face and seemed close to tears. "It started up in Miners' Town," she said. "We don't know how, and with this blasted wind it's just rampaging through the town. Oh, Hannah, this might be the end of Bear Claw!"

Reaching down, Hannah squeezed her friend's hand reassuringly.

"You'd better get the buckets ready," Hannah said. "I can take them to where they're needed."

A man, smoke stained and sweating, holding two buckets of water, shook his head. "No, ma'am. Begging your pardon, but I'll drive the cart up."

"You most certainly will not," Hannah exclaimed. "Daisy will be afraid. But if I'm with her, things will go better."

Henrietta shook her head. "No! Hannah, you can't!"

Though they tried, Hannah wouldn't be swayed. She was going to help, and that was final.

The man, his name was Ben Farthing, got on the driver's seat next to Hannah and, once the back of the cart was full of buckets dripping water, he urged the horse out of the churchyard and back into the street. They headed up towards Miners' Town.

It wasn't a long ride and as they approached, Hannah could hear the roar of the fire, see the orange and yellow tongues as it leapt into the air, and feel the intense heat on her skin. It was eating its way through the clusters of houses, built so close together that often, one roof overlapped another. It was a warren of small spaces, alleyways, and nooks and crannies and they were all burning.

Ben jumped down.

"Hold her steady, if you can," he ordered Hannah as he began to off-load the buckets. Men appeared out of the stinging smoke that made eyes and nose water, and grabbed the buckets. She slid off the driver's seat and held Daisy's reins. The horse fidgeted, wanting to run, so Hannah made soothing noises.

One man, so singed and fire blackened he was practically the color of midnight, turned shockingly blue eyes on her and spoke over her head to Ben.

"This section is done for," he said. "There's no way in. We'd do better clearing the next few streets. It might stop the spread."

Another man grabbed a bucket and said, "We should burn a firebreak down there ..." he pointed down the way they had come. "This beast is hungry and the water ain't doing diddly. Tearing down will take too long. A controlled burn will—"

"Tearing down is the only way. We can wet the houses, stop the spread before it gets down there."

"Burning a firebreak—"

"More fire? How you going to control that one?"

Hannah tuned out as the men fought. She coughed and moved herself and Daisy to the side a little, where the air seemed clearer. It was then that she heard the small voice.

"Help!"

Standing stock-still, Hannah pricked up her ears and listened.

"Help!"

It was coming from down a little smoke-filled alley. Here the houses had a narrow walkway between them, thick with gray, billowing smoke. Hannah looked at Daisy and the horse seemed to nod her head.

"Okay," she said and dipping her handkerchief into one of the buckets of water on the cart, she replaced it over her nose and mouth and headed into the alley.

The smoke stung her eyes, making them water so badly she could hardly see where she was stepping. Hannah held out a hand, running it along the wall. This was stupid. She should have alerted one of the men and let them come. But she could still hear them fighting by the cart. What would the point have been?

"Help!"

Her heart was beating far too fast and her fingers felt prickly, like she had pins and needles. She wasn't getting enough air. Bending double was a little better, though not much, and soon Hannah dropped to all fours. She was hardly any way into the alley but she could hear someone coughing.

"Help me, please!"

Hannah dug deep and, crawling on the hard-packed dirt, she made her way further into the smoke.

"Hello ..." she called, removing her handkerchief for a moment. "Hello ... is anyone there?"

"Help me!" came the reply. It was faint.

She crawled on, reaching out with her right hand to the place where she thought the voice had come from. Suddenly her hand touched something. It was clammy. Then something grabbed her wrist and Hannah screamed.

CHAPTER 2

Ben Farthing materialized out of the smoke with the other two men on his heels. Hannah coughed and spluttered. The grasp on her arm disappeared as she was lifted into the air.

"Someone ..." she said coughing. "In the smoke ..."

"We'll get them," Ben said, nodding to the other two men behind him.

In a few quick strides, Ben had her out of the alleyway and on her cart. Hannah coughed and spluttered, doubling over as the smoke clung to her lungs. A moment later, two people, a woman and a little girl, were deposited on the back of the cart with her. Ben turned the cart around and rode out of the smoke.

As the air cleared and Hannah found the tightness in her chest easing, she looked at her fellow passengers. The woman was coughing and the rag she held to her mouth was bloodstained. She was pale, weak, and her brow was beaded with sweat, though she shivered and shook like a leaf in a gale.

Hannah knew what it meant. She placed her own wet handkerchief on the woman's brow. She grabbed Hannah's arm and, with blood-flecked lips said, "Help Rosie. Take care of her ..."

Her eyes slid shut and she stopped breathing all together.

Hannah and the child stared at each other for a horrible moment that lasted a year and a second at the same time. It shattered when Rosie screwed up her little soot-blackened face and screamed.

"Mama!"

There was nothing she could do. Hannah pulled herself into a sitting position and hammered on the woman's chest, in the vain hope that it might force her lungs to give it one more try. But nothing happened. The woman was gone.

"What's going on back there?" Ben asked, turning in the driver's seat.

"She's gone," Hannah said, a hollow feeling in her gut. "She didn't make it."

Rosie wiped her streaming eyes and nose with a grubby hand and laid her head on her mother's chest. She wouldn't be moved. Hannah didn't try very hard. She could understand.

Not even two years previously, Hannah's father and sister had both fallen victim to a terrible fever that ran through her hometown like the fire was running through Bear Claw. So many fell to the disease that Hannah and her mother had begun to think they were sure to fall ill, too. However, they never had.

Hannah was certain she would never forget the day her father died. She had lain next to him on his bed with her head on his chest, despite the doctor's warnings it might make her catch the fever, too. If she was honest, Hannah would have said in that moment, she didn't care if she fell ill and died right alongside him.

Jolting in the cart on the way to the churchyard, Hannah wondered if Rosie felt that way too. She was terribly quiet; the only sound she made was a cough now and then.

When they reached the yard, Rosie and her dead mother were offloaded by helping hands, the pastor's among them.

"Mr. Farthing," Hannah said. "Thank you for saving me."

He smiled, showing white teeth in a blackened face. "My pleasure."

"Perhaps it would be wise to take the cart back up again and see if there are any more injured folks that need moving?" Pastor Ashby suggested.

Ben nodded. Hannah was about to get back on the cart when a gentle hand stopped her. The tall, gray-haired minister shook his head. "I have another place for you, better suited to your skills," he said.

He put Hannah to work in the makeshift hospital, while Daisy and another horse took turns pulling the cart and gathering up as many survivors as possible. Hannah found herself treating wounds, burns, gashes, and boiling water for an herbal mixture that the pastor's wife made up.

"It eases the breathing and clears the lungs," she said, directing Hannah to hold a towel over a man's head and let him breathe in the fumes.

What had started as a quick supply run turned into a full day and by the time the sun sank westward, the blaze finally put out, Hannah and all the other helpers breathed a little more easily. More than half the town was lost. People were homeless, separated from family, and lost. Through it all, Hannah kept an eye on Rosie.

"What will happen to her?" she asked Henrietta.

"I don't know," she said, in a manner that made Hannah wonder if she cared at all.

"Does she have family?"

Henrietta shrugged. "She's a miner's child. Who knows?"

"Henrietta, where is your Christian charity?" Hannah exclaimed, and walked off to find the pastor and his wife.

They were converting the church into a hostel for the displaced people to stay in.

"Oh, Hannah," Mrs. Ashby said, smiling. "I'm so glad you're here. This little girl, Rosie, needs a place to stay. Do you think you and Buc could take her in for a few days? Poor little thing has no family left, what with ..."

"I'll do it ... yes, of course she can stay with us as long as is needed," Hannah said hastily.

Things moved quickly then. Rosie was bundled up in a blanket and placed on the driver's seat next to Hannah and in no time, they were on the road back to the ranch.

It was a quiet ride. Rosie stared at the grassland and the odd Ponderosa pine tree, or snowberry, that stood sentinel along the way. Hannah fretted and wondered if it wouldn't have been better to leave Rosie with Pastor and Mrs. Ashby. She had seemed more talkative there.

"Are you all right?" Hannah asked. It was a stupid question.

Rosie sighed and wiped her nose on the blanket. "Guess so."

"Where's your father? Is he a miner?" Hannah asked. She didn't want to ask a possibly painful question. However, if there was a father out there looking for his little girl, she had to know.

"Ain't never met him," Rosie said. "We lived with my uncle Roger. He's dead. Part of the roof fell on him when it was burning."

Hannah bit her lip. So much pain in this little one's life and she was so matter-of-fact about it all. Perhaps it hadn't sunk in properly yet.

"Well, you're safe now. Buc and I live in a big house on a lively ranch. We have cows and grow wheat and sometimes barley," Hannah told her.

"Can I milk a cow?" Rosie asked, sitting up straight, a sudden light in her eyes. They were the palest blue Hannah had ever seen.

"Sure," Hannah said.

"I've always wanted to milk a cow," Rosie said.

The rest of the ride home Hannah told Rosie about the farm and all the chores there were to do on it. She had expected Rosie to say she wanted to play. However, the little girl bounced excitedly on her seat, saying she was good at collecting eggs, but not good at carrying water from the pump, taking an excited interest in the work.

"The water gets too heavy," Rosie said. "But I can learn ..."

She smiled up at Hannah.

"Thank you, Mrs. Buchanan, for taking me in. I know it's probably a great burden."

Hannah felt her throat constrict with tears. She sucked her bottom lip and wrapped an arm around Rosie's shoulders. "It's my pleasure to have you to stay."

There was a tall stand of lodgepole pine trees at the gate to the Buchanan land and as they approached it, a horse came galloping out of the gate. It skidded to a halt in front of the cart and Hannah looked into her husband's face.

"Hannah! My goodness, where have you been? I was worried sick!" Buc exclaimed. He reached across the space between them, grabbing her right arm. "What happened? You're covered in soot and ash!" His eyes left Hannah's dirt-smeared face and landed on Rosie. His large green eyes grew even larger and rounder. "And who on earth is this?"

"Buc, this is Rosie, and she's coming to stay with us for a while," Hannah said. "There's a lot to explain, I know."

Buc's face grew red, went pale, and reddened again as he chewed his cheeks and stared at her.

"We'd better discuss this inside," he said and, turning the horse around, galloped back through the gate.

Hannah could see he was annoyed. Buc didn't like her making decisions without him. It would take careful words to calm him. Her heart beat fast with nerves, though she smiled at Rosie nonetheless and steered the cart down the drive towards the house.

CHAPTER 3

"How many are hurt?" Buc asked when Hannah finished her story of the fire in town. "Do they know how it started?"

Hannah shook her head. "Not that I heard. Oh, Buc, there are so many homeless and burnt, others with smoke in their lungs. It's terrible."

He hugged her. "It's okay. Doc Washington is going to have his hands full. They will need to rebuild. We can send some supplies, I'm sure."

Hannah smiled up at him.

"So, what's the plan with our young guest? Is someone looking for her family?" Buc asked.

"Pastor Ashby said he would send out word to Great Falls and a few other places and see if anyone knows her and her mother," Hannah said. "There's not much hope."

He nodded and, releasing her, rubbed his chin thoughtfully. "What were you thinking of doing with her in the meantime? Can she help you around the house or something?"

"She's just a little girl who lost everything and everyone she had in the world," Hannah said, her voice calm and quiet. "I was thinking she might need some time to work through that. If she wants to help me, she can, but I'm not forcing her."

Turning from him, she moved to the window through which she could see Rosie sitting under a thimbleberry tree, eating the bread and cheese she had given her. "She's so young to have suffered so much. Do you know her father never stuck around to meet her? Isn't that awful?"

"Well, maybe he can get his chance now," Buc said. He picked up his pipe and fiddled with his tobacco box next to it, thumbing a ball of the dried leaf into the bowl. "Do we know who he is, or where he is?"

Hannah shook her head. "Her mother didn't have a chance to tell anyone anything. By the time we found her, the smoke was deep in her lungs. I think she had consumption as well. She was coughing up blood." She sighed sadly, hearing Buc strike a match. The room filled with the smell of his smoke and she wrinkled her nose. She hated the pipe. "I doubt there's a person alive who knows who Rosie's father is. She's as close to an orphan as she can be."

They were silent for a while, both lost in their thoughts.

"Perhaps the asylum at Great Falls would be a good place for her, then," Buc said, breaking the silence. "We can't keep her indefinitely."

"No!" Hannah turned and frowned at her husband. How could he say something like that? Rosie wasn't some stray dog. She was a lovely little girl who already had a very special place in Hannah's heart. "Pastor and Mrs. Ashby asked that we keep her a while, and I think we should." Her pulse was racing as her cheeks flushed. Hannah teetered on the verge of losing her temper. "Buc, we can't send her off. I promised."

"Do you mean you want to keep her?" Buc asked, astonished. He puffed his pipe. "I assumed we would send her off ... I mean, she's not blood, Hannah. You never know what you're getting when you bring strangers into your home. Do you really think it's wise to keep her? The asylum will train her to work. She'll have a future."

"Not a better one than we can give her," Hannah said. She walked to him and grabbed his arms, looking into his face beseechingly. "Please, Buc, say you'll give it more thought. Say you'll at least get to know her before you decide something so permanent."

His face was reddening as he puffed his pipe. He didn't like this idea. Hannah could see it on his face as though it was written there. Buc came from a traditional family and new ideas took time to grow in the not-overly-fertile soil of his opinions. "Hannah, you should have spoken to me first before promising the pastor we would take Rosie in."

"I know, but where would she be sleeping tonight if I had?" Hannah demanded. "There was no quick way to reach you. The church is full of people who have lost their homes and every earthly possession they had. Every house that is still standing in Bear Claw is packed to the rafters. There was no space, except here."

Buc held her gaze, looking for something, she wasn't sure what. She held his gaze steadily, without blinking. Eventually, he nodded and sighed. "You're determined to have her stay, aren't you?"

Cocking her head on one side, Hannah made a gesture that was somewhere between a nod and a shrug.

Buc sighed again. "You drive a hard bargain, Mrs. Buchanan," he said. "She can stay ..."

Hannah bobbed up and down, her heart racing as she clapped her hands.

"BUT ..." Buc continued. "It's not definitely forever. She can stay while the pastor tries to find her family. We'll take it from there."

"Oh, thank you, Buc," Hannah said, rising on tiptoes and kissing his cheek. "You are the best, and I do love you so."

He wrapped his arms around her and held her to him. Hannah felt his warmth and strength fill her and she squeezed him in her arms.

They parted and Buc looked at her questioningly. "Well, what happens now?"

"I think I should get her cleaned up," Hannah said. "And then she and I can make us a bit of dinner. You don't mind a cold one, do you? It's just a little late to get something hot made."

"That sounds great," Buc said. He sat down in his favorite arm chair in front of the grate. It wasn't lit, the evening being very warm. With a book on his lap, and his reading glasses on his nose, Buc looked more like a professor than a farmer. Hannah kissed the top of his head and went to fetch the newest addition to the household.

Rosie came in when she was called.

"Is it okay if I stay?" she asked, nervously fiddling with the hem of her dress.

Hannah nodded. "He just had to understand the situation."

"You're not in trouble for bringing me home, are you? I got in trouble with Uncle Roger for bringing home a stray dog once."

"You're not a stray dog," Hannah said. "And no, I'm not in trouble. Buc just wanted to know what happened, is all. I think you'll find he's strict but fair. He's a very good man, really, he is. I'm sure you two will get along when you get to know each other." She smiled nervously, her left cheek twitching slightly. "Now, we are both filthy, and there's no dinner on the table."

"I can help," Rosie said eagerly.

"First, we get clean," Hannah said.

She drew water from the pump outside and filled the big pot on the fire in the kitchen. Luckily, Buc had kept it burning. When the water was hot, she sloshed it into the big metal bath and told Rosie to undress and get in.

Then she went upstairs to her trunk. It had come with her on the train from Maine. Opening it, she moved some clothes aside and found what she was looking for: a blue dress and pinafore she had worn as a child. Hannah had kept it, thinking one day her daughter might wear it, if she had one. She looked at the dress and sighed. Well, phantom children were all well and good, but there was a living, breathing girl downstairs with nothing to wear. This would have to do.

When she came back down, Rosie was scrubbed pink and washing the soot out of her hair.

"You managed on your own?" Hannah asked, an incredulous smile on her lips.

Rosie nodded. "Yup. Been taking care of myself a while now. I'm a big girl anyway. I'm almost six."

"Are you now?" Hannah asked as she helped the clean Rosie out of the tub and wrapped her in a towel.

"Uh-huh. Mama said I was born at the end of summer, just before the leaves start to turn."

"So, August then," Hannah said.

"I guess so," Rosie said. "I don't know which day." She looked sad.

Hannah rubbed her dry. "Don't worry. I'm sure someone will know."

Rosie slipped the blue dress on over her underthings. She twirled in it. "It's beautiful."

"It was mine when I was little," Hannah said. "I kept it ..."

"It's lovely," Rosie said. "It looks brand-new."

"It was my Sunday best and I grew so quickly that year that my mother had to make me a new one almost straightaway," Hannah said, smiling at the memory. "It's a bit big for you. Well, at least you'll have room to grow."

Rosie smoothed the fabric. "Thank you so much."

"It's a pleasure," Hannah said.

When Rosie was finished dressing, and Hannah had washed her own face and hands, they went into the kitchen and began to make a quick dinner. There was leftover chicken from the night before, fresh bread, and some preserves in the pantry. It took no time to put it all together and get a pot of tea on the boil for Buc.

When he came into the kitchen, he sat down to a feast.

Hannah watched in fascination as Rosie ate and spoke at a rapid pace. The bread and cheese from earlier seemed to have had no effect on her appetite. She was ravenous. She also had a lot to say for one so young. Even Buc seemed mesmerized and watched the child eating. Hannah was relieved when he chuckled at a few of Rosie's comments. She had a sharp wit for one so very young and it was clearly making an impression on her husband. That was good. She hoped it would continue.

When she was done, Hannah took Rosie up to the spare room and got her settled. She helped her brush and braid her long dark brown hair that fell in coils down her back. Hannah hadn't noticed how thick and lovely it was until now.

"Thank you, Mrs. Buchanan," Rosie said as Hannah tucked her up in bed.

"Call me Hannah, okay?"

Rosie smiled.

"You're very welcome," Hannah said, and kissed her forehead.

After clearing the dishes, Hannah washed properly and went up to bed. She was exhausted and couldn't keep her eyes open any longer. Buc didn't fuss, but sat downstairs alone reading in the parlor.

Hannah drifted off peacefully, feeling her life was greatly improved with the addition of lovely Rosie.

⚜

SCREAMING WOKE HER.

Hannah sat up in bed. It was still dark and she couldn't, for a moment, place the source of the scream. The day filtered into her mind and she fumbled for a match to light her bedside lamp. When it was lit, she blinked in the light.

Buc looked at her a frown on his face. "What was that?"

"I'm not sure," Hannah admitted.

The scream came again and was accompanied by sobbing.

"Rosie!" Hannah cried and shot out of bed. She ran along the passage to Rosie's room, flinging the door open. Rosie tossed and turned in her bed, still asleep.

"Mama!"

Hannah placed the lamp on the bedside table. She hesitated. She'd heard terrible stories of what happened when people were woken from nightmares. The child was writhing, sobbing. She had to do something.

Laying a gentle hand on the little girl, Hannah shook her to wake her, hoping for the best. Rosie's eyes popped open and she drew in her breath sharply.

"You were only dreaming," Hannah said, trying to soothe her. "It's all right, you're safe."

Rosie blinked and sat up looking around. Her blue eyes focused on Hannah.

"I dreamed a big fiery monster ate my mama," Rosie sobbed. "He gobbled her up like a duck eating bread."

"It's okay," Hannah said, sitting on the bed and holding Rosie to her. She rocked the little girl as she sobbed. When she was quiet, Hannah smoothed her hair and looked into her face.

"Will you stay with me?" Rosie asked.

Hannah nodded and slipped under the covers. They lay down together, Rosie saying she doubted she would ever sleep again. Hannah agreed, but offered to sing a lullaby anyway. Rosie agreed and as Hannah sang a song her mother had sung to her, Rosie's breathing slowed. When she was certain Rosie was deeply asleep, Hannah stopped singing and with her arms around the small girl, she drifted off.

CHAPTER 4

HANNAH WAS UP EARLY, BEFORE THE BREAK OF DAY, AND WAS MILDLY SURPRISED half an hour later to find Rosie dressed and ready and in the kitchen. They made a breakfast of porridge. Buc seemed in better spirits in the morning, and spoke to Rosie politely over the breakfast table. Hannah listened as they spoke, hardly daring to breathe. If he could see how wonderful Rosie was, he would love her too, she was sure of it.

After finishing his food, Buc smiled at Rosie and kissed Hannah's cheek before leaving to do his work in the fields.

With him gone, Hannah and Rosie turned to all the household chores. There was cleaning to do, which Rosie was surprisingly good at.

"Mama cleaned houses for the old folks and the ones too sick to manage," Rosie said cheerfully, dusting the parlor. "She took me with her." Her little chin wobbled and a tear ran down her cheek.

"You can take a break if you like," Hannah said. She was polishing the coffee table.

Rosie shook her head. Dressed in the blue dress and white apron, she looked so sweet. "Mama wouldn't want me to take your kindness for granted. She always said people had to earn their bread."

"You're a child," Hannah said kindly. "You can play, too."

She stood up and stretched her back. Her chest was tight today. That meant the work would get done, but it would be slow going.

"Maybe later," Rosie said.

She sang and spoke as she worked. At first it got on Hannah's nerves a little. She was used to working in silence. It saved energy, and meant she could get more done. However, having the child prattling on about everything and nothing was comforting in a way Hannah had never thought it could be. She stopped seldom, and almost never needed Hannah to participate in the conversation at all.

By the end of the day, all the chores were done, Rosie having done more than her fair share. She even helped with dinner, cutting the carrots and potatoes for the stew herself, very carefully with a sharp knife.

"How did you learn to do all this?" Hannah asked. "I wouldn't expect an almost six-year-old to be able to cook and clean. You didn't stop to play once today."

"Play?" Rosie asked, frowning.

"Don't you ever play with your dolls or something?" Hannah asked.

Rosie looked thoughtful. "It would be a waste of time. There was always a lot of work to do."

Hannah blinked back tears. What kind of world allowed such a life for a little girl? A life with no dolls, no time to play ... Placing her own knife on the table, she looked Rosie in the eyes.

"Rosie, I want you to do something for me," Hannah said.

"Of course," Rosie said. "What is it?"

"Today is the last day you will ever spend working from sun up to sun down, until you're all grown up."

Rosie's face fell. "Did I do something wrong? Aren't you happy with my work? I can do better. I promise I can work harder ..."

Hannah moved around the large wooden table in the kitchen and took the child's hands. She was standing on a stool to reach the tabletop and was only a little shorter than Hannah herself.

"Rosie," Hannah said and sighed. "I don't want you to work at all. I want you to play. I want you to have fun, to dance and sing in the summer sun. Please ... leave the work to me."

Rosie frowned and shook her head. "But Mama said ..."

"Mama was right," Hannah said hastily. "But she forgot a bit of that saying. You see, children should help out around the house, but they should also have time to learn and time to play. It's terribly important."

"I don't know how," Rosie said, her blue eyes enormous and her bottom lip wobbling as though she was about to burst into tears.

"We'll find someone to help you," Hannah said. "The farm across the way has two children around your age living there. Perhaps we can see if they'd like to be friends." She wrapped her arms around the child. "You're safe here, and you can be a child. You don't have to try and be so grown up. I'm here to look after you."

"And Mr. Buchanan?" Rosie asked.

Hannah let her go and smiled. "Him, too."

Dinner that night was good and loud. Rosie told them everything that popped into her head, and there was a good deal of that. Hannah could see her husband was tired and Rosie's chatter was getting on his nerves. He looked down at his plate a lot more than usual, until it was too much.

"A moment's peace, Rosie, please!" he exclaimed, making an annoyed gesture and knocking over his tea. "Oh, for heaven's sake!"

Rosie's face crumpled and tears streamed down her cheeks in seconds. She dashed out of the kitchen door and ran off into the dusk.

Buc, dripping tea as it sloshed onto his lap, stood up, saw her leave, and his face fell.

Hannah raised her eyebrows at him.

"I didn't mean ..." he began. "I'm sorry. I'm not used to someone who talks so much all the time," Buc said gruffly. Shaking his head, he threw his napkin on the table. "I didn't mean to upset her."

Pursing her lips, Hannah shook her head. "I'll see to her." She stood up and followed Rosie into the garden.

The child was around the back of the barn on her haunches, staring at the setting sun. The sky was a lovely orange with delicate pink clouds lying like streaks across it.

Hannah sat on the ground with her back against the warm wood of the barn. She could smell the cows and horses and the dust as the hot summer's day drew to an end.

"He's not normally like that," Hannah said as Rosie sniffed and sobbed beside her. "He's just used to quiet. It's a big change, having you here ... a really good one, but a big one, too."

Rosie shifted, but stayed silent.

"We're all adjusting," Hannah said. "Before yesterday, we'd never met each other and now we're living together ... it's a big change for all of us. So, perhaps we just need to take some time to get to know each other, and you never know what could happen. I think we all just need to consider each other's feelings."

Rosie raised her head. Her eyes were bloodshot and her face was tearstained. "I miss my mama."

"I know you do," Hannah said, letting the little girl lie on her lap and cry. She stroked her hair gently.

Rosie cried for a while and as the first stars came out, she stopped and looked at the sky. "Will you be taking me back to town now?"

"No," Hannah said, frowning. "Why would I?"

"Because Mr. Buchanan ..."

"Mr. Buchanan feels terrible for yelling at you. Though I would suggest you talk a little less around him. Let him get a word in now and then," Hannah said. "Come on. You haven't finished your dinner and it's sad to let it go to waste. Especially since you helped make it."

"That is true," Rosie said.

Back in the house, they found Buc at the table. He'd cleaned up the tea and made more and was spooning fresh bowls of stew out for them. "The food got cold," Buc said as they entered through the back door. He turned to Rosie. "I'm sorry I yelled. Can I ask that you speak a little less, please? I'm not used to not being able to hear myself think."

"It's no problem," Rosie said. "I can be as silent as the grave."

"I don't think you have to be that quiet," Buc said, handing her a bowl. "Careful, it's hot."

Rosie took the bowl carefully and went back to her place at the table.

Hannah smiled at Buc. He looked sheepishly at her, his dark bangs falling in his eyes. She kissed him as he handed her a bowl.

Buc smiled and Hannah's heart skipped a beat. That was the man she had crossed the country for; the man she had fallen in love with. He shrugged. "We've got some adjusting to do for while you're here."

"Speaking of which," Hannah said. "I think you two should spend some time together tomorrow. I have to go back to Bear Claw, and you can get to know each other better."

Buc suddenly looked panicked. "I don't know anything about children ..."

"You'll be fine," Rosie said. "Neither do I."

Hannah chuckled.

"But ... my work isn't good for a little girl," Buc protested.

"Can I milk a cow? Oh please ...?" Rosie begged.

In the face of his wife's expectant smile and Rosie's pleading, Buc seemed to have no choice but to agree to look after Rosie for the morning.

When they got into bed later, Buc complained. "She'll talk me to death," he said.

Hannah sighed. "If she's going to be here a while, you might want to spend more time with her than meals only."

"You *are* planning on asking about her family when you're in town tomorrow, aren't you?" he asked pointedly. "I haven't changed my mind, Hannah. This isn't permanent."

"What's the point? She doesn't have anyone, Buc. Not a soul in this world, as far as she knows," Hannah said. "It may take a long time for anyone to find her kin, if she has any."

He sighed. "I understand. But what about our family?"

"We can have her and our own children," Hannah said dismissively. "There's no reason we can't have both."

"Won't she feel out of place when we have a baby of our own? It's not easy to adjust. I'm just thinking of how she'll feel, knowing she's not ours. It's not a situation a child should be in," he said.

Hannah watched him in the moonlight streaming in their bedroom window. She sighed and laid a hand on his chest. "I'm not even pregnant, Buc," she said. "You're worrying about something that hasn't happened yet."

"But it will," he said.

"And we'll deal with it then. Rosie may not care that she's adopted. Why would she, if we give her as much love as we would a child of our own?"

He was silent a while.

"But we don't know what we're getting. She's an orphan," Buc said. "She could be crazy or violent. She could burn the house down. You hear stories about things like that happening with orphans. You've heard the stories too. Henrietta is always going on about that orphan her Uncle Chester took in who burned the barn down."

Hannah snorted. "Chester is an idiot who ran a moonshine still in his barn. I doubt that poor boy had anything to do with the barn burning down. And as for what we're getting ... we're being blessed with a beautiful, smart, strong, capable little girl."

"I'm not comfortable with this, Hannah. I think she should go to the asylum, before ..."

Hannah felt her pulse quicken as anger rose in her chest. "You can't be serious! I can see you like her. You've been laughing at her jokes and smiling at her and ... How can you say something like that?"

"I think we have to face facts," he said. "She's not ours. She can't stay. The longer she does, the more attached you get. And then what if Rosie's father turns up some day and demands to have her back? Then what? It'll break your heart and I can't have that. Better to let her go now ..."

Hannah felt as though she was going to explode with anger. "Are you sure it's my heart you're worried about?" She threw the bedclothes off and stood up. "Are you sure it's not your image with all your narrow-minded friends? You've been speaking to Jackson Smith again and the others, haven't you?"

He had the sense to look guilty.

She headed for the door.

"Where are you going?" he asked.

"I'm sleeping in Rosie's room," Hannah said hotly. "I won't share a bed with someone who has no heart and no backbone!"

She stormed out of the room, leaving Buc alone and confused.

CHAPTER 5

Hannah rode into town the next day.

The Cromwells' general store was untouched by the fire and open for business.

"I see they're starting the cleanup," Hannah commented as she stood at the counter.

Henrietta nodded. "I hope they do it quickly. I have the Simons in my house and it's packed to the rafters. How is your little ward doing?"

"Rosie is fine," Hannah said. "I was wondering if you had a bolt of cloth in a blue or green? I have to make Buc a new shirt and a dress for Rosie. She only has an old one I wore as a child. I don't think any amount of scrubbing and patching will fix the rag she was wearing."

Henrietta went into the back to fetch the cloth. It was a lovely sea green.

"And speaking of Buc," she said. "How's he taking to her?"

Hannah had to admit that things weren't peaceful. Buc wasn't adjusting well to Rosie staying with them. "I have them spending the morning together in hopes he'll realize how much he likes her. I'm sure with a little time they'll find some common ground."

"You'd better get back quickly," Henrietta said, sounding unconvinced.

She added up Hannah's purchases and while Hannah was taking out her money from her purse, she leaned on the counter. "Listen, Hannah," she said her face stern. "You need to think carefully about this girl. She's not blood, and it's not always wise to let that into your home, especially when you're young and recently married. You and Buc should be free to start making your own family ... if you know what I mean?"

Hannah drew her lips into a straight line. "I'm getting really sick of people saying things like that when they don't even know Rosie."

"Fact is, neither do you!"

Hannah slammed her money onto the counter and with her chest tightening and pins and needles sliding down her arms, she strode out of the store. A young boy had loaded her sacks of sugar and salt, the coffee, and the fabric on the back of the cart for her, and she rode off in a huff, up to the church to see the pastor.

Pastor Ashby was tending the sick. They were fewer now, most having recovered enough to be allowed to stay with friends. There were still some who were homeless and staying in the church, along with the burnt and those suffering from the smoke. The air above the town was clear, with a brisk wind from the south chasing all the smoke away.

Hannah found the church hot and stuffy with so many bodies, some none too clean, all living in the space. Pastor Ashby, though his shirt was sweat stained, seemed in good spirits when she greeted him.

"Hannah, my goodness, you look flushed. Are you ill?" he asked, taking her hand.

"Not ill, Pastor," she said. "I'm annoyed. But don't worry about that. I came to see if you needed anything? We have some supplies at the farm, good timber and the like. If you think it would help, we can bring it through."

His old face wrinkled into a smile. "That would be most generous of you, my dear. How is little Rosie getting on? I'm afraid we've had no time to track down her kin."

"She's settling in nicely," Hannah said. "Buc is taking some convincing ... He's been listening to unwise counsel. I don't understand why everyone seems to be against her staying with us. She's just a little girl. She's had such a hard life ... do you know she doesn't know how to play? She said she's never had time."

Pastor Ashby shook his head sadly. "Not all children are lucky enough to enjoy childhood, Hannah. If it's any consolation, I think Rosie is a perfect fit for your family. I've known her since her mother moved them here about two years ago. She's a good little girl, and I would love to see her in a good, solid family. I believe the Lord has a plan for everyone and this little girl was meant to cross your path. She has ignited a light in you that I never thought I'd see."

"You think so?"

"Oh yes. Would you like me to speak to Buc for you? I can pop by tomorrow, perhaps, and have a word. Perhaps he just needs to have his eyes opened to God's plan," he asked.

"Would you? That would be amazing," Hannah said.

"It would be my pleasure," he said, patting her hand. "How are you feeling? I've noticed you looking a little pale these last few weeks."

Hannah shrugged. "It's the heat. I've never been good with it."

"Perhaps it will rain soon and we can all get some relief."

Hannah stayed an hour, helping clean wounds and change dressings. Then she rode back to the farm. When she arrived home, it was to the wonderful sound of children at play.

It seemed the neighbors' children, Annabella and David, had come over with their father, Jackson. He and Buc were standing in the yard while the children, all around the same age, ran about playing a game of tag.

Rosie was clearly It, and she charged after the brother and sister.

Jackson was a tall man, with fair hair he'd passed on to his two children. He nodded when Hannah arrived.

"Hello, Jackson," Hannah said, a small chill in her voice, as she climbed down off the cart. "What brings you by?" If he was filling her husband's head with nonsense, she was going to have a word with him.

"Afternoon, Hannah," Jackson said. "Came to see if you folks can spare anything for the poor folks caught in the fire in town. My wife is on some town committee to find supplies to help rebuild."

"I'm sure we can spare something," Hannah said.

"I've taken care of it," Buc said, kissing her cheek in greeting. "How is the town?"

"It's going to take a lot of work to rebuild," Hannah said. "But Pastor Ashby is hopeful it can get done quickly."

"What did he say about Rosie?" Buc asked.

He and Jackson shifted. Clearly, they'd been discussing her.

"Only that she's lucky to have us," Hannah said, "As are we to have her."

"You aren't keeping her, are you? Not as a part of your family?" Jackson asked.

"We're considering it," Hannah said. "Aren't we, Buc?"

Buc sighed. "She's a lovely little girl."

"But she's not yours! Buc, you can't keep her," Jackson said. "You don't know her family or anything."

"Pastor Ashby has known her family for two years and he says she's good people," Hannah said hotly. "If he says so, that's good enough for me."

She turned and picked up a sack of rice to carry into the house.

"Okay," Buc said, raising his hands in a placating gesture. "Clearly, we have a lot to talk about."

"I would kick her out, before she makes trouble," Jackson said.

Hannah turned on him, her pulse racing as pins and needles rushed down her arms. "You are a heartless, horrible man! She's just a little girl! Tell him to keep his long nose out of our business, Buc!"

"Hannah!" Buc exclaimed. "He's my friend."

"And I'm your wife!"

Buc visibly ground his teeth. He looked at Jackson and then at Hannah, his hands balling in fists and releasing as he tried to get a handle on himself. Eventually, he turned to her. "Hannah ..." he said.

She felt the tears burn her throat and her eyes. "How could you?"

Her chest was terribly tight. Hannah panted as she stormed up the steps, sack in hand, and burst into the kitchen. She laid the sack on the table. Sweat dripped off her brow. She had to sit down for a minute, but Buc was right behind her.

"Hannah, listen ... Jackson was just trying to help," Buc said. He held out his hands to her. She slapped them away. "You shouldn't have spoken to him like that."

"He fills your head with nonsense," Hannah said. She was finding it hard to breathe. Her heart was rattling in her chest. "Always has, from the sound of it."

"You're not being fair. He's my oldest friend and I value his opinion."

"Even though he's not willing to give her a chance? Even though he can't see how wonderful she is when we both can? Don't deny it. You like her, too."

Buc sighed and nodded. "I do. She's a great kid."

"Then what's the problem?"

He shrugged. "I just want to make sure we do the right thing for her and for us and our own flesh and blood children ..."

It was too much. Buc was so hung up about phantom children somewhere in the future that he was struggling to see the one right in front of him now. Hannah felt her chest tighten even more as her pulse raced. She wasn't getting enough air. Spots danced before her eyes. She staggered to the side, reached for the corner of the table, and missed.

As she crashed to the floor, she heard someone calling her name, but they were very far away.

CHAPTER 6

Hannah opened her eyes. Her head ached, and she felt as though an anvil was pressing down on her chest.

"Hello there."

"Buc? What happened?" she asked.

Buc's eyes were red and his hair stood in messy tangles on his head. He was growing a beard.

"You've been asleep for four days," he said.

"How?" Hannah asked, trying to sit up, but he gently pushed her back down.

"Dr. Washington's been, and said you had a heart attack," Buc's voice broke and his eyes filled with tears. "I almost lost you ..." he stared at her blinking and shaking his head. "It was ..."

Hannah absorbed the news. A heart attack? How could she possibly have a heart attack? She was young and healthy. Unbidden, her mind filled with times all through her life when her chest grew tight, her breathing labored, and she felt weak.

Smiling weakly at Buc, she said, "It's okay. You didn't lose me."

"I could have," he said. "The doc said it was touch and go there for a bit. Luckily, Jackson knew he was visiting the Jones' over the hill and it didn't take long to call him. Rosie and Jackson's David ran the whole way to fetch him."

"So, am I still at death's door?" she asked, hoping she sounded more jovial than she felt. She'd almost died. Somehow, that knowledge was floating up in a big cloud of things Hannah was certain she couldn't deal with right now. It felt far away and she was tired.

"I was being so stupid, going on and on at you ... like that ... about having children ..." his voice broke again.

There was something there in the room. Something big hanging over them that she couldn't quite see, but she could feel.

"What aren't you telling me?"

Buc sighed and wiped his face. "The doc says ..." he hesitated and held her hand. "He says you're going to be fine. You need rest, and when you're up to it, you can carry on with your chores and things around the house. We have to get you help. No heavy lifting ..."

"Okay."

"He also said ..." He ran a hand through his hair and swallowed.

Hannah wanted to reach inside him and pull out whatever he wasn't telling her.

"It's nothing. I'll let you rest ..."

"And you think I will, with something you can't tell me hanging over my bed?" she asked, raising her eyebrows. She could sleep; it was stealing up on her. Still, anything this big had to come out, and the sooner, the better.

Buc smiled a watery smile at her and nodded. "Okay. The doc said it wasn't a good idea for you to have children."

"What?" Hannah asked, all tiredness evaporating from her like early morning mist. "Why?"

"It's your heart, honey," Buc said. "Doc said you probably wouldn't live through the pregnancy and certainly not through the strain of giving birth. I'm sorry. I've been such a boor going on and on about having babies ..."

Hannah held up a hand, stopping him in his tracks. She shouldn't have children. Shouldn't, not couldn't. That was probably a good thing. Although, trying to see the silver lining in this situation was proving difficult. "I'm tired," she said, feeling the tears welling up in her throat. "I'd like to get some sleep. You should, too."

Buc nodded, kissed her cheek, and left the room.

Hannah rolled on her side, gripped her pillow, and cried until she fell asleep.

When she woke much later, the light had shifted and there was a person next to her. She looked up into a little serious face.

"How are you feeling?" Rosie asked.

Hannah smiled and took Rosie's little hand in hers. "Just fine now, thanks."

Rosie smiled. "You don't need to worry about a thing, Hannah. I've tended the garden, made the meals, cleaned the house, and I did some of the laundry. Buc had to help with the buckets. I still can't carry them."

"You did all that?" Hannah asked.

Rosie nodded proudly.

"And how have you been getting on with Buc?" she asked.

Rosie shifted and wiped her nose on her sleeve. Hannah would have to put a stop to that habit, though it could wait. "He's all right with me, I guess. Mostly he's been up here with you. I brought some soup. It's the same I made for Mama when she was ill. It's cold now, though."

"That's all right," Hannah said. "Help me to sit up and I'll be happy to taste it and let you know what I think."

Rosie helped her up and insisted on spooning some of the brown liquid into Hannah's mouth. It was a little too salty, but very tasty.

"You know, I think this soup is so good, it being cold makes no difference at all," Hannah said.

Rosie beamed, spooning more into Hannah's mouth. After a few spills, Rosie agreed to let Hannah feed herself.

CHAPTER 7

HANNAH GREW STRONGER AS THE SUMMER ROLLED ON. THE WHEAT BEGAN TO ripen and the rains came, rolling in and out of the hills on a regular cycle. Everything was green and lush. Hannah spent her afternoons on the porch sewing, while Rosie played. It was their time off, and mandated by the doctor, who came by regularly.

Buc was around the house a lot more and helped with carrying anything he deemed too heavy for her, which was just about everything. Hannah was pleased to hear Buc and Rosie talking more and more. She would stand in the kitchen and listen to them in the garden just outside the door. She even heard them laughing as they harvested the fresh vegetables for dinner and pulled out the weeds that never seemed to stop growing.

It was midway through July before the doc would let Hannah travel into Bear Claw again. By that time, she was chomping at the bit to get out of the house.

They chose a Sunday and rode into town for the morning sermon.

When they arrived, the first one over was Henrietta Cromwell. She bustled up to Hannah.

"Oh, my dear! How are you? It's been so long. I'm sorry to hear you weren't well," she said, taking Hannah's hand.

"Henrietta," Hannah said. "I'm much better, thank you. The town is looking like new. I'm so impressed with the work. But I see that Miners' Town is still in a shamble."

They looked up the hill.

"Yes, well ... priorities, dear. We can't rebuild everything all at once ..." Henrietta said. She wrinkled her nose when she spotted Rosie in a lovely green dress Hannah had made, climbing down off the cart with Buc's help. Hannah was proud of the little girl and the dress. Heaven knew she'd had the time to spend on both lately, and both had turned out quite well.

"I see she's still hanging around," Henrietta said out of the corner of her mouth. "I suppose you'll be sending her to the asylum in Great Falls any day now?"

Hannah stopped and turned, her eyes wide in disbelief. "What did you say?"

"Only that I'm sure you'll be sending what's her name to the asylum ... you can't be thinking of keeping her?"

"Actually, Henrietta," Buc said, taking Rosie by the hand and offering Hannah his arm, "We're adopting her."

Hannah's heart leapt in her chest and she almost fell over. Her knees gave in and Buc turned worried eyes on her.

"I'm all right," she said as she recovered. "But it might be wise not to surprise me like that too often." She smiled at her husband. "Are you serious?"

Buc looked down at Rosie as she beamed up at him. "Yes. You were right. I just had to get to know her and now we're good friends, aren't we, chicken?"

"Chicken?" Hannah asked.

"You got a problem with her nickname?" Buc asked.

"Oh no," Hannah said. "I'm just wondering how she got it."

"Want to tell her?" Buc asked Rosie.

Rosie shrugged and smiled. "Nah. Later, maybe," she said.

Hannah realized there had been a lot going on in her own house she'd missed. Being so sick had taken a toll on her and she frequently had to nap in the day. She supposed it was only natural that Rosie and Buc would develop a bond. She was so happy. The more she looked at the two of them together, the more Rosie looked like Buc. She had the same dark hair, the same-shaped face. It was uncanny.

At the door to the church, Pastor Ashby welcomed them back warmly and his wife embraced all three of them. "I'm so glad you could come today," she said. "We have all missed you terribly."

"Thank you," Hannah said. "I missed you all. In fact, if Doc Washington hadn't let me out of the house today, I think I would have disobeyed doctor's orders and come through anyway."

"Then I'm glad it didn't come to that. Howard has a special little something in his sermon. So, keep your ears open," she said and, smiling, let them take their seats.

"That sounded ominous," Buc said, smiling.

The sermon began. Howard Ashby was a very plain-spoken pastor. He certainly never softened the blow, nor did he mince his words, and it was clear from the start there was something on his mind.

"I'm so glad we have everyone here today," he said, standing in the pulpit with his hands clasped in front of him. "I've been a member of this community since the beginning of Bear Claw. My darling wife and I have watched all of you come and build your houses here and raise your children, and it pains me to say you have raised your intolerance right along with them."

There was a sharp intake of breath. Hannah shifted in her seat.

"Doesn't the Bible tell us in John 13:34 that the Lord said, 'Love one another, as I have loved you'?

"Did our father say, only love those who are like you? Did He say you should only love those who make you happy, make you feel good? No! He said love one another ... He wasn't specific about the another but I take it to mean everyone you meet."

"This intolerance of one another, this judging each other based on a stupid belief that just because people are different they are less, has to stop. Bear Claw is a beautiful place to live. The lake is wonderful; the trees and mountains around this area are some of the most beautiful I have ever seen. But sometimes, I wonder if we deserve such beauty around us, because if we can't love each other, how can we love anything around us?"

Pastor Ashby nodded at the congregation, who sat in stunned silence.

"And now for the hymn ..."

Hannah sang the hymn "All Things Bright and Beautiful" along with everyone else and smiled. Finally! Perhaps now people would change their attitude towards the miners. It was about time.

When the service ended and everyone found themselves out on the lawn in the sunshine, people's shocked expressions told Hannah that her hopes were well founded. She smiled when she saw Mrs. Ashby walked over to them.

"Well, that kicked some folks in the pants," Mrs. Ashby said and chuckled. "This place has been a powder keg since the fire. A few hotheads took it on themselves to beat some miners not three nights ago. It took Ben Farthing and a few others to pull them apart. This is a small town. Either we all stand together or we should go our separate ways."

"Was that the bit we had to listen for?" Hannah asked, shocked. She thought she had always done her best to live by that particular command.

"Oh no, not like that," Mrs. Ashby said. "I meant it's to make things easier for you, since you're adopting young Rosie here. People can be thoughtless and cruel. It will take time for them to forget where she came from. We'll be here to help you as much as we can." She took Rosie's hand in hers. "Would you like a cookie, young lady?"

"Oh yes," Rosie said nodding vigorously.

Hannah watched her go and smiled.

"That is a very pretty dress," she heard Mrs. Ashby say.

"Hannah made it for me," Rosie said. "Look, she even gave it ruffles. I've never had ruffles before."

They disappeared into the house.

Hannah turned to Buc. "I can't help getting the feeling that everyone knows we're adopting Rosie except me."

"It was meant to be a surprise for you. I thought you'd like it," Buc said. He smiled sheepishly in the way that made her want to kiss him. "Surprise!"

"You most certainly have surprised me," she said and, standing on tiptoes, gave in to her desire.

It had been a while since they'd been this close, what with their fighting and then her illness. Hannah realized she had missed him terribly, as her friend and her husband.

"Let's try not to fight again," she said.

"We can try," Buc said, not sounding as though he held out much hope of success.

She shrugged. "Well, we'd better go and sign whatever we need to. I think I might need to rest soon."

Buc escorted her into the house, where Mrs. Ashby had a set of papers all laid for them. It was a simple matter of filling in a few details, signing, and it was all done. Rosie was now Rosie Buchanan. The little girl cried and hugged them, and then cried some more. She screamed, ran around, and when David and Annabella came over to see what was wrong, Rosie hugged them both before gushing about how happy she was.

On the ride back to the farm, Hannah and Rosie sat in the back of the cart where they had piled cushions and blankets to make it comfortable for Hannah.

"You know what?" Rosie asked. "I think I know when I want my birthday to be."

"Oh?" Hannah asked.

"I want it to be August fifteenth," Rosie said, and nodded. "Yeah. It sounds good."

"What made you choose that date?" Buc asked from the driver's seat.

Rosie's blue eyes sparkled. "I like the sound of the word fifteenth, don't you? It sounds ..."

"Perfect," Hannah said. "August fifteenth it is."

Rosie snuggled up to Hannah and, though it was hot again, she didn't mind. "I think I'm going to like being a Buchanan. We have big hearts." She wrapped her arms around Hannah, who didn't think she could be happier if she tried.

When August fifteenth rolled around, Hannah and Buc surprised Rosie with a party. They held it outside in the yard, under the thimbleberry tree, and all the neighborhood children came. There were treats and games and a huge cake with berries on it.

Rosie was so happy, she beamed at everyone. Even Henrietta, who brought her daughter Judy to the party.

Hannah was less welcoming. Henrietta had been cruel, and she wasn't sure she was ready to just let it all slide under the carpet.

"Lovely party," Henrietta said as the mothers sat on the porch watching the children play. "Rosie looks lovely. Did you make that dress for her?"

"No," Hannah said. "It's a gift. We bought it in Great Falls."

"Pink is her color and no mistake," Henrietta said. She shifted. "Look, Hannah. I know I've been a fool. I can admit when I'm wrong. Seems your Rosie is a good girl after all."

"Thank you, Henrietta," Hannah said stiffly. "Nice of you to notice."

"Hannah!" her friend exclaimed. "I'm sorry. I didn't think, and I let nasty ideas that had no right to be there into my head. I didn't mean any harm."

"Yes, you did. If I'd listened to you, I would have missed out on the greatest gift God has ever given me," Hannah said.

Henrietta looked mortified. She hung her head.

Hannah sighed and took her hand. "Luckily for us both, I'm terrible at taking advice."

"Does this mean I'm forgiven?" Henrietta asked.

Hannah hugged her. "Of course. Now have some cake."

⚅⚄

As the weeks rolled by and summer came to an end, the town of Bear Claw grew back out of the ashes. Like the phoenix, it resembled the parent town that had died to bring it to life. However, there were subtle changes. Miners' Town was better built, the houses still small, but not ramshackle. They were properly built, with space between them. The locals even sank a pump or two to make getting water to the houses less of a chore.

People greeted each other in the streets and when Ben Farthing found out his daughter Mary had been stepping out with a young miner named Todd Jones behind his back, he didn't overreact at all. The young man, newly scrubbed and wearing his best, was invited over to dinner.

"And he didn't shoot the boy," Henrietta told Hannah when she came to the store.

"Pastor Ashby must be so proud of him," Hannah said, smiling.

They watched Rosie and Judy playing on the porch. They were swinging around the poles that held the roof up and laughing fit to burst. Two other children joined in. They were scruffy and dusty, but it didn't seem to bother the two girls at all.

Things were changing. No one had said anything to her or Buc about adopting Rosie since Pastor Ashby's sermon. Hannah was grateful. She loved the little girl more than she could explain.

They stayed in town a while longer and then rode home. Rosie dozed quietly, her head on Hannah's lap, and when they reached the ranch, Buc was waiting. He took Rosie off the cart, helped Hannah down, and hugged them both.

"I'm so glad my ladies are home," he said. "I missed you both."

As he held her and Rosie together, Hannah's heart was so full, she thought it might burst.

❧

THANK YOU SO MUCH FOR READING MY BOOK. I SINCERELY HOPE YOU ENJOYED EVERY bit reading it. I had fun creating it and will surely create more.

Your positive reviews are very helpful to other reader, it only takes a few moments. They can be left at Amazon.

https://www.amazon.com/Ada-Oakley/e/B01FTGKL62

❧

WANT FREE BOOKS EVERY WEEK? WHO DOESN'T!

BECOME A PREFERRED READER AND WE'LL NOT ONLY SEND YOU FREE READS, BUT you'll also receive updates about new releases.

So you'll be among the first to dive into our latest new books, full of adventure, heartwarming romances, and characters so real they jump off the page.

It's absolutely free and you don't need to do anything at all to qualify except go to.

PREFERRED READ FREE READS

http:/katieWyattBooks.com/readersgroup

ABOUT THE AUTHOR

ADA OAKLEY IS AN AMERICAN-BORN ITALIAN, WHO HAS LIVED MOST OF HER life in Dallas Texas and has traveled to many countries. She has been an avid reader and a lover of western movies since her teenage years, so she decided to pursue a writing career. Ada loves writing Western Romance and Mail Order Bride stories about the courageous women who traveled alone to the Wild West with nothing but hope and strong faith in God.

Writing books about the hardships and struggles of women who turn around their hopeless situations and in the end found true love and happiness is something that she enjoys bringing to the readers.

Ada wishes that the readers will once again learn to believe in love and develop trust through reading her books, and be inspired by the characters in her novels who through perseverance, in spite of very tough harsh obstacles that tested their faith, overcame the hurdles in the end.

MOLLY'S STORY

Contemporary Western Romance

RoyceCardiff
P u b l i s h i n g   H o u s e
WHOLESOME INSPIRATIONAL ROMANCE

Dear Reader,

It is our utmost pleasure and privilege to bring these wonderful stories to you. I am so very proud of our amazing team of writers and the delight they continually bring us all with their beautiful clean and wholesome tales of faith, courage, and love.

What is a book's lone purpose if not to be read and enjoyed? Therefore, you, dear reader, are the key to fulfilling that purpose and unlocking the treasures that lie within the pages of this book.

A PERSONAL WORD FROM BRENDA

Dear Readers,

You read about the Wild West because of the romance, the adventure, the spirit of possibility that filled those frontier days. I write these books for the same reasons. I love the stories of the pioneer women who crossed the country to build new lives in what must have felt like a totally foreign land. With courage, faith, common sense, and a good dose of humor, many of these courageous women married their true loves and became the Old West's literal founding mothers!

Many of my books draw directly from history, using the real-life stories of those women to tell the story of the birth of the western half of our nation. As I look around my southwest backyard, I often take a moment to think about what it might have looked like before we all moved in. These stories are my attempt to share that wonderful adventure with you.

Happy reading,

Brenda

CHAPTER 1

"MOLLY, DO YOU HAVE A MINUTE?" CAROL, MY BOSS, CALLED TO ME AS I TRIED to sneak past her office unnoticed.

Don't get me wrong, I liked Carol, and I loved my job at the Knightsdale Community Center, but I didn't really have time for any of the extra duties that Carol was likely to drop in my lap at any given moment. There already were forty kids in the gym having free time and we needed all hands on deck there.

I let out a sigh, checked to make sure that my face didn't reflect my annoyance, and stepped into the musty, wood-paneled room that Carol used as an office. "What do you need?" I asked with false cheer.

"Bill just radioed that the boys' locker room is flooded again. You'll have to have the boys use the staff bathroom on the second floor." Carol's curly hair was frizzing extra high today, a sure sign that her stress level was equally elevated.

"Did Bill replace the light bulb in there? I doubt they can use the bathroom in the dark."

Carol paused. "I forgot about the light bulb. I hate to pull him away from the locker room to change it right now."

After three years, I knew that my boss was about to reach the critical level where she would stop being useful and start panicking. Fortunately, I had a ready solution. "We'll just cycle the boys through the girls' locker room. It'll take longer, but we'll be fine."

My boss wilted slightly. "Thank goodness you're here, Molly. I don't know what I'd do without you. Oh, can you stay late tonight? I've got a report that has to go out today and I still haven't gotten around to payroll."

"Sure, I can stay," I forced a half smile and headed back towards the gym. There was no point in hoping that I'd get paid overtime. I was considered a part-time employee, but I typically worked a full-time schedule as it was. It was a good thing that I had few needs and fewer ambitions.

As I reached the gym and stood watching the kids, I pursed my lips. This was why I worked so hard to keep the community center afloat. Knightsdale was a small town surrounded by sheep ranches. Most of the children in our program had parents who worked long hours at the ranches. If it wasn't for our after-school program, they would be unsupervised until their parents came home, sometimes after dark. I also knew that many of the parents of kids in our program were migrant workers, here for the winter and headed south when spring arrived. The migrant camps where these families lived throughout the growing season were often unstable and sometimes dangerous. These kids had already been through so much, they desperately needed a safe place to have fun.

Nothing would make me give up on kids who needed me. After all, I'd been abandoned when I was six. My mother had gone to work one night and then had never come home. I'd been placed with a foster family where I lived until I was eighteen and aged out of the system. The Dorians had been good parents to me, but it had never stopped me from longing to find a forever family.

Toby, one of our after-school counselors, drifted over to me. "How's it going, Molls?"

"Looks like the boys' locker room has flooded."

"Again?" He sighed. He looked around the gym and shook his head. "It's amazing that this place is still standing."

My eyes swept over the old wooden bleachers that were roped off with yellow caution tape, the basketball hoops that bore chipped paint, the worn floorboards, and the cracked window we had yet to replace. The building was one of the oldest in Knightsdale and, between its advanced years and small maintenance budget, it was in rough shape.

I patted the door frame and said, "She's a good girl and we're grateful for her."

Toby raised an eyebrow at me.

"You have to be nice to her or she's liable to fall over." I gave him an impish grin then swept the kids again with my eyes. "Why is Miles sitting alone?"

Toby glanced towards where the new boy sat cross-legged and glum against the wall. "I saw Miguel invite him to play basketball earlier. He might just be shy, which is definitely your department."

I rolled my eyes at my coworker, who laughed.

"You didn't say two words to me for the first month that I worked here," he reminded me good-naturedly.

"I can't help it," I shrugged. I hated my shyness. It made everything in life so much more challenging. No matter how often I told myself that I would get over it, I froze whenever I met new people.

Scratch that. I froze whenever I met new adults. I could talk to kids all day long. As I made my way over to where Miles sat, I wondered yet again why kids were so much easier than grownups.

"Do you mind if I sit here?" I asked Miles.

He shrugged one shoulder without looking up. I slid down beside him, pulling my knees up to my chest to avoid tripping any of the enthusiastic basketball players who might go scampering past at any moment.

"You're Miles, right? I'm Molly." I watched him out of the corner of my eye. Since I'd handled his application paperwork, I actually knew a lot about him. Miles was ten, in the fifth grade, and lived with his single dad. I also knew that they had moved to town recently. "Where did you live before you came to Knightsdale?"

"Colorado Springs," the boy mumbled.

"Oh, that's cool. Are you into skiing?"

The head that rested on his fist nodded.

"I've only been once and I was terrible," I admitted. "It was really fun, but I fell over just about every thirty seconds."

"I've been skiing since I was about three," Miles said. I noted the touch of pride in his voice.

"I'll bet you're good then. Have you ever tried snowboarding?"

He sat up, leaning against the wall. "Yeah, I love snowboarding. It's not hard."

"It's not hard for you. I'd probably fall over and squish some little kid."

Miles laughed at that. He began an involved explanation of what I needed to do to make sure I didn't fall as much next time I went skiing. I noted the use of technical terms, meant to impress me, as well as his careful explanation of them, meant to help me. As he talked, I found myself liking the kid more and more.

"Do you want to play basketball? Or would you rather just sit here?" I asked when he finally came to the end of his instructions.

Again, the one-shouldered shrug.

"Do you like playing basketball?"

Another shrug.

"I always think it's hard to play with kids I don't know very well," I tried.

"I know Miguel from school. He's cool." Miles' eyes found the other fifth-grade boy in the throng.

"Just not in the mood?"

He sighed as though the weight of the world was dragging him down. "I don't know if my dad is going to let me keep coming to the center after school."

"Oh yeah?" I asked carefully. The last thing I wanted to do was insult Miles' dad or make false promises I couldn't keep, though both were tempting.

"He wants to find a babysitter to stay with me instead."

"That could be fun," I hedged. "But I see why you don't want to be too friendly with everyone. It would be hard to know you're missing out on a fun time."

Miles nodded. "Yeah."

"Of course, you could look at it a different way." I waited for him to look at me before going on. "You could just be glad you get to hang out today and have as much fun as you can. It would be pretty disappointing to miss out on a good time today. Besides, your dad might not find you a babysitter for a while."

The little boy thought that over, his eyes watching the other kids. Finally, he said, "I guess I could play basketball for little bit."

"Great idea. We've got another fifteen minutes before snack time. Go tear up the court."

Miles flashed me a grin before pushing to his feet and making his way towards Miguel. I watched as the other boy assigned Miles a team and the kids around him explained the rules of their game. I smiled to myself as I went in search of the boxes of chips we'd be handing out, very pleased with the situation at hand.

CHAPTER 2

MILES NOT ONLY HAD A FABULOUS TIME PLAYING BASKETBALL, HE ALSO MADE A new friend during snack time when he traded his Doritos for the less-desirable Fritos, helped a kindergartener glue her project together in arts and crafts, and got told off for having a water fight with Miguel. In short, I knew he'd had a red-letter day. He even made sure to give me a hug before being shepherded off to the parent pick-up spot.

Once things quieted down, Carol kept me busy until after nine o'clock. The report wasn't the only thing that desperately needed work. As I vacuumed the hallway carpet, I mulled over the fact that I liked being needed like this. Sure, I would never make millions, but I was making a big difference. The center would never find someone else who was willing to both plunge toilets and monitor the youth lock-ins.

I had an associate's degree from the community college where I'd grown up. My foster parents, the Dorians, had helped me complete the paperwork for financial aid, found me an affordable apartment, and aided in the purchase of my battered Ford Escort. I'd seen them regularly while I'd worked on my dental hygiene degree. However, once I'd finished, the idea of cleaning teeth for the next thirty years depressed me. I'd scoured job websites until I'd stumbled across the Knightsdale Community Center position.

One of my friends from school, Bailey, had moved to Knightsdale to work at the local nursing home and was only too glad to have me move in. Knightsdale was only thirty minutes from Casper, where I'd grown up, and seemed like the right mix of adventure and safety.

Bailey was already working on getting a more advanced degree and moving up in the world of nursing. She talked occasionally about the house she wanted to buy and the garden she would plant. I, on the other hand, talked of no such thing. The future was a hazy place that I was vaguely aware of, but not a reality that I felt needed actual work. Working long hours at the center for little pay was fine with me. I knew that Kermit, as I had christened my green-under-the-rust-colored car, would need replacing eventually. One day Bailey would marry and move off and I would have to figure out new living arrangements. But, for now, I was happy to push those thoughts away and nestle into the life that I was living now.

Of course, when I reached Kermit and saw that my front tire was flat, I was immediately far less content with my life.

"No!" I moaned. I unlocked the car, wrestled the dented back door open, and tossed my backpack inside before turning my attention to the tire.

I became aware of a dog sniffing at my shoes at just about that exact moment. Surprised, I looked down to see a puppy that was in the lanky, long-legged stage. From there, my eyes found the leash attached to his collar and followed the length of red nylon up to the person holding it.

My stomach clenched and my eyes grew wide. The man attached to the puppy was quite possibly the most attractive guy I had ever seen in real life. Between his square jaw, warm eyes, and muscled physique, I was awed. Which didn't help the shyness I would have been experiencing even if his looks had fallen in the fair-to-middling range.

Later, as I thought back over the evening's events, I had to admit that I must have looked pretty crazy. There was no doubt that I had stared, wide-eyed and open-mouthed, at the man. Add to that the messy bun that had developed over hours of dealing with a large group of children, the four layers of sweatshirts and jackets I was using in lieu of an actual coat, and the fact that I'd been talking to my car, and I was very surprised that the poor man didn't cross to the other side of the street and act as though he hadn't seen me.

"Do you need a hand with that tire?" he asked instead.

I think I nodded mutely.

"Do you have a jack?" The inexplicably attractive man tied his dog to a handy signpost and turned back to me expectantly.

"Er ..." was all I managed to say. I shrugged one shoulder and gestured inanely in the general direction of Kermit.

My knight in jeans and a military jacket took that to mean that he should help himself to whatever he could find in his car. Since my brain wasn't working, I was happy with that interpretation.

"I'm Daniel, by the way," he paused to say once he'd found the jack.

My frozen brain scrambled for the appropriate response. "Molly," I finally blurted.

He gave me a half smile that was unfairly dreamy. "Nice to meet you, Molly. Any chance your spare tire is in good shape?" He waited for my guilty expression and then laughed. "Don't worry about it. Cars that are this ... experienced don't always have all the pieces they're supposed to."

Kneeling down, he began to whistle while he did whatever mysterious things one did when changing a tire.

"I just moved to town and was hoping to get to meet a few interesting people. Lucky for me, Turk there needs regular walks," he nodded towards the dog.

"Turk?" I asked without thinking.

Daniel flashed me a full-on grin and I almost fell over. "I'm hoping he grows into it."

I watched as Turk tangled himself in his leash and began to whimper. I reached down and lifted the puppy loose. Turk rewarded me with enthusiastic kisses and I gave him a good cuddle.

"Have you had him long?" I asked, braver when I didn't have to look Daniel in the eye.

"About two weeks. My old neighbor's dog had puppies and she wanted to give me one as a going-away gift. Of course, the thing you need when you start a new job in a new town is a puppy, but one look at the little guy and I knew he was a keeper."

He saved women from flat tires and loved dogs. Was this guy too good to be true or what?

In less time than I would have imagined possible, Daniel had the spare tire in place and muscled the damaged one into Kermit's hatchback. He handed me the tire iron and I handed him Turk.

"Thanks so much," I forced myself to say.

"No problem. I'm glad I could help." Daniel smiled at me, and even the smudge of grease under his eye seemed adorable. "Have you lived in Knightsdale long?"

My brain flopped around for an answer and I ended up shaking my head lamely. I could feel an embarrassed flush heating my cheeks as I called myself all sorts of names. Why did I have to be so dang shy?

Daniel's smile turned kind and understanding in a way that made me mentally kick myself all over again. He probably thought I was socially inept and would now back away slowly and hurry away. And, while I wanted desperately to escape the awkwardness of the moment, I hated the idea that I would have to stop staring at his gorgeousness.

"Well, I hope to see you around, Molly," he said cheerfully.

I waved goodbye and then sighed dreamily, climbed into Kermit, and drove home with my mind a long way off.

CHAPTER 3

KNIGHTSDALE WAS A SMALL TOWN TUCKED INTO THE HILLS OF WYOMING, surrounded by sheep ranches and farms. One of the very best things about it was that it had a hundred cool things to do outside. Bailey and I had already found our favorite hiking trails, gone white-water rafting, and signed up to become search-and-rescue volunteers.

I also had taken a second job at a horse farm about fifteen minutes out of town. The Buckles' farm offered trail rides, corporate bonding experiences, and kid camps. When Bailey and I used a Groupon to get a discounted afternoon of horsiness, I'd fallen in love with the place. Luckily, Hal Buckle was hiring a part-time employee and had taken a liking to me.

So, after stopping to get my old tire patched and put back in place the next morning, I headed to work. We'd been enjoying a mild spring so far. It had snowed a few times, but nothing significant. The cold weather had even taken things down a notch lately.

I wore my oldest work jeans and a pair of secondhand boots that were more scuff than anything else. Since I'd stopped growing as a sophomore in high school, I was wearing my regulation PE T-shirt under a grungy flannel.

I parked in my usual spot next to the Buckles' big pickup, grabbed my work fleece and an enormous scarf Bailey had knitted me for Christmas, and headed into the barn. The twenty or so horses that called it home kept the barn warm. It always had the same smell and I breathed it in, feeling that all was right in the world.

"Morning, Deb," I called at the small office.

The farm's foreman, Deb, waved at me without taking her eyes off her computer. "Morning, Molly."

I waited for her to finish whatever she was doing and wandered over to Star, my favorite horse. I rubbed her velvety nose and told her how beautiful and good she was. I was fairly confident that I was her favorite too, though she was too much of a lady to tell anyone.

Deb came out of the office with her usual long-legged strides. She checked her watch and said, "We've got a corporate group coming in at eleven. Trail ride, cleaning the stalls, that sort of thing."

I nodded. Various corporations in the area liked using the Buckles' farm for team-building activities. The business people would trade in their suits and fancy shoes for the day and come out here, ride horses, and then work together to clean the stalls. Some would then have a meeting in the picnic shelter with a catered lunch. Others would climb back in their ritzy cars and hurry home to their showers.

"Kyle's daughter has the flu, so he won't be in today. Are you okay riding in the rear?" Deb speared me with her eyes.

"You bet," I grinned.

The first weeks that I'd worked here, I'd been terrified of Deb. She was a large woman who had a complete lack of fluff. However, once I realized that she loved horses and liked me well enough, I stopped being afraid of her gruffness and started appreciating her capable management of the farm.

We got to work saddling the horses. The company was bringing eight employees and then Deb and I both needed horses, too. We talked over which horses to use and I wheedled my way into getting to ride Star.

The first cars began to arrive and out climbed the corporate folks, who were wearing older designer jeans and very classy shoes. I rolled my eyes and turned back to finishing saddling Honey. Deb would handle the spiel we gave at the beginning of each trail ride. While she talked, I focused on bringing the horses out of their stalls and into the corral, where everyone would mount up.

It was as I was returning after my second trip when I looked over the group standing in front of Deb and my eyes met Daniel's. He smiled and waved at me. I promptly gulped and turned my ankle slightly, bumping into Midnight. Smooth.

I made a point not to look back over at the group and instead put laser focus into getting the horses tied up properly without falling or doing something else embarrassing. Then I went back for my red Buckle Farm fleece, once-black-now-more-brown-somehow baseball cap, and wrapped Bailey's scarf around my neck. I was warm from working, but knew that if the wind picked up, I'd be glad for the extra layers.

Just about then, Deb was wrapping up the talk with the business people and began steering them towards where I stood in the coral.

"This is Molly," she called when the group got closer. I waved mutely and tried to smile. "She'll help you mount up and make sure your stirrups are the right length. Why don't we start with you, miss? We'll have you ride Sam, here."

Thankfully, I didn't have to say anything as I helped people who had never ridden horses mount and settle into the saddle. One woman dropped the reins four times in a row until I showed her how to wrap them loosely around her wrist.

Daniel was last and when I looked up into his beautiful brown eyes, my heart began galloping instantly.

"We meet again," he said easily. "You work here? That is really neat."

Really? He was wearing jeans that fit perfectly, a new gray hoodie over a crisp T-shirt, and very expensive boots. This was not the picture of someone who thought that horseback riding was cool.

"Have you ever ridden a horse before?" I croaked.

"Twice. But it's been a while, so you should probably walk me through it."

I held the stirrup and instructed him to put his left foot into it. Then I told him how to hold the pommel and swing his right leg over. His first attempt was bad and I felt my nerves loosen as he laughed at his mistake. What would it be like to be so confident that I could laugh at myself when I goofed up? It made me like him even more.

Daniel's second attempt was better. Once he was sitting looking like he belonged on a horse, I let out the stirrups a little and reminded him to keep his heels down as he rode.

I made my way to Star and pulled myself up smoothly (thank goodness). Deb was calling instructions from the front about how to steer the horse to the left or right and how to stop without hurting the horse. Truth be told, these horses had walked this trail so many times they would need little steering. But people liked to feel that they were in control.

Then Deb was leading the way out of the corral and down towards the trail. The other horses fell into line easily and I took up the rear, noting that Daniel was in the middle of the pack. While I would have enjoyed it, I was glad that I didn't have to stare at his back the entire time we rode.

It was a great day for a trail ride. The wind was a bit brisk, but I adjusted my scarf so it covered my chin and lower ears and fell into the sway of Star's back and the beauty of the world around us.

I almost forgot about Daniel and the butterflies he stirred up in my stomach. That is, I did until his horse, Midnight, began limping and I had to pull him over to the side of the trail.

CHAPTER 4

AFTER CHECKING MIDNIGHT, I RODE UP TO DEB AND LET HER KNOW THAT I'D need to take the horse back to the barn. One of his horseshoes was looking like it needed fixing. I knew Midnight could handle the walk back, since we weren't more than two miles down the trail, but he shouldn't carry a rider.

Which meant that I would have to walk back to the barn with Daniel. The butterflies began to feel more like rhinos.

Daniel was a great sport about it. He took Midnight's reins and I took Star's and we began the trek back to the barn. The silence stretched and I tried to force myself to begin a conversation. If he felt awkward, Daniel didn't show it.

"Man, what a view," he said. "This is my favorite part of living in Wyoming. Sure, the cell-phone reception is spotty and there aren't any pro-sports teams, but the view can't be beat."

I laughed. "I love it too."

"Where did you live before this?" Daniel asked, remembering our previous encounter.

"Casper. I grew up there," I forced myself to say. "Where were you?"

"Colorado."

I swallowed the nervous lump in my throat. "They have beautiful views, too, I hear."

"That's true. Of course, I lived in the city, so it wasn't quite the same as this. Is your family still in Casper?"

"That's a complicated question." I glanced at him and read interest in his expression. It gave me the courage to say, "My mom took off when I was six and I grew up in foster care."

"Wow, that's tough." His tone seemed earnestly sympathetic. Too often, when I told people about my family situation, they often grew awkward and didn't know what to say. Daniel's response was refreshing.

I shrugged. "I stayed with the same foster family for ten years, so that was great. There aren't as many foster homes in this part of the world. Kids out here don't always move around as much, especially if their parents aren't in the picture."

"Still, it couldn't have been easy."

"No, you're right about that." I noticed that, somehow, my nerves had fallen away as we walked.

"So, you work here at the farm?" Daniel queried.

"Just a couple mornings a week and every other weekend. I also work at the Knightsdale Community Center." I looked back at Midnight and checked that he was still doing okay.

"What do you do there?"

I marveled at how easy it was becoming to talk to this crazily attractive man. "My official job is as the head of the after-school program. However, I think I've done just about every other job they have over there. I work in the office when needed, help the janitor, and fill in when the adult ed teachers have to cancel. I've even taught the senior aerobics class, if you can believe it."

Daniel's laughter burst out, echoing off the rocks around us. "Sorry. It sounds like a great workout."

I laughed too. "It's pretty low impact. Which is why I could fill in. I'm not much of a workout gal."

"That's one thing I miss here. No gym."

"Ah, I see. I should have known you were athletic. What are you, a runner? Swimmer? Don't tell me you're one of those horrible CrossFit guys," I teased.

"Wow, that's harsh, Molly," he joked back. "There are a lot of nice people who do CrossFit."

I shot him an unrepentant grin.

"I will confess that I have done CrossFit before. Mostly, though, I like to run and do some weights."

From the look of him, I wasn't surprised to hear it. He was in seriously good shape. It was one more thing that we didn't have in common.

We walked in companionable silence for a few minutes before I asked, "How's Turk?"

"He loves to eat shoes," Daniel said dryly.

I grimaced in sympathy.

"Yeah, it's the worst. Luckily, he seems to like shoes that smell really bad, so he's left my nice ones alone."

"Remind me not to offer to dog sit," I quipped. "My shoes wouldn't stand a chance."

Daniel raised an eyebrow at me. "Are you admitting to some sort of foot problem, Molly?"

I blushed a little. To hide my embarrassment, I said, "I can only take partial credit for any shoe odor. I tend to buy all my shoes secondhand."

"What?" He looked truly surprised. "You actually buy other people's old shoes? And wear them?"

"It's the only way I can afford them." I took in his mildly horrified look and laughed. "I've gotten some really good shoes that way. Besides, it's hardly worth paying a lot of money for new boots when I'm just going to wear them here and clean stables."

"What about when you get dressed up or go out or to church or something?"

I shrugged again. "I don't get dressed up very often. I'm more a jeans-and-T-shirt kind of girl. It's possible that I'm allergic to skirts and high heels."

If I'm completely honest, I have to admit that it hurt a little to admit that to Daniel. I could easily picture him going on dates with an equally gorgeous woman wearing a slinky dress and sky-high heels. It was almost as though I felt compelled to show him all the things about myself that would guarantee that he would never form romantic attachments to me. If I could show him the worst parts of myself, I could protect myself by keeping him away. Still, a tiny part of me really, really wanted there to be some sort of miracle in which he would be interested in me.

"I see," he said, and dropped into quiet contemplation that lasted until we came in sight of the barn.

I went in search of Hal and told him that Midnight needed his shoe fixed. Then I made my way to the barn and talked Daniel through unsaddling his horse and cleaning out his stall. We were finished just about the time that the others arrived back. I was extremely impressed when Daniel went ahead and helped the others with unsaddling and cleaning their own stalls.

His group went off to the picnic shelter and I got busy with other tasks Deb barked at me. I was just coming around from one of the outbuildings when Daniel's coworkers left the shelter and headed towards their cars.

"Molly!" Daniel called, and loped towards me.

"All done?" I asked, my shyness beginning to creep back up my legs and making my fingers tingle.

"We're headed back to the office. Listen, would you be interested in going to the movies with me this Saturday?"

I took a step back, stunned. His face was completely sincere, though his trademark confidence wasn't shining quite as brightly. It was so endearing that my heart melted a little.

His eyes searched my face and the corner of his mouth tipped up adorably. "I'll even throw in burgers and fries. It will strictly be a T-shirt-and-jeans type of thing."

I tried not to smile, but it broke through despite my best efforts. "Sounds fun."

As Daniel pulled out his phone and added my name and number to his contacts list, I couldn't shake the feeling of unreality that this beautiful man was interested in me. It seemed too good to be true.

CHAPTER 5

MY FOSTER MOM, DIANE, WAS A STUDENT OF SAFETY. WE HAD GROWN UP BEING taught all her adages about looking both ways, putting toilet paper on the seat, and not letting men you just met know where you lived. Therefore, I suggested meeting Daniel at the theater for the afternoon matinee, rather than having him pick me up at the apartment.

We texted back and forth throughout the week. He was really good at asking every afternoon how my day was going. I was amazed at his attentiveness. The few guys I'd dated had been determined to prove how aloof they were by never calling when they said they would. Daniel, though, had no such qualms.

Bailey helped me pick an outfit and did one of her fabulous French braids in my hair before our date. Since I'd made a big deal out of it, I had to wear a T-shirt and jeans, but Bailey insisted on choosing just the right shirt and lent me her cute jeans without any holes or worn cuffs.

Daniel was waiting when I arrived and looked ridiculously wonderful as always. He smiled his fabulous smile at me and I melted a little. I swore that man could have put his smile to work for the military. It would have knocked down any person he flashed it at.

We sat through an action film with lots of explosions and over-the-top car chases. Then Daniel steered me towards the one chain restaurant in town, where we ordered hamburger meals and triple-thick milkshakes.

Once we were seated with tiny ketchup cups and piles of napkins, Daniel paused to pray silently and we dug in.

"I feel like I don't know much about you," I said, barely remembering to swallow before I spoke. "What should I know about you?"

He took a sip of his milkshake and thought that over. "Well, I'm thirty-one. I'm a lawyer. I have one son. And I guess you need to know that I'm divorced."

My eyebrows lifted in surprise. What woman would give up this man? Was she crazy? Or were there things about him that had yet to make it onto my radar? Like being overly jealous or refusing to do household chores or absolutely vile body odor.

"My ex-wife's name is Kelly. We met in college. You need to know that in my college days, I was determined to be as a big a jerk as possible. I thought I was the coolest guy ever. God's gift to women. I'm sure you know the type." He shook his head in disgust.

I, on the other hand, nodded slowly. I definitely knew the type. It was the type of guy I avoided. And it also was the exactly the type of guy I'd first guessed Daniel was. He was too good looking to be kind and considerate. In my experience, guys who were as attractive as he was were used to women fawning all over them and took advantage of it. It made sense that Daniel had been that way at one point, though I was a tad disappointed to hear it.

"I joined the fraternity on campus with the reputation for having the biggest players. I wanted to be a lawyer and make huge amounts of money. Money and girls, that's all I wanted for my life back then." He dipped two fries in ketchup thoughtfully. "When Kelly and I got together, I thought it would just be a fling. Then she got pregnant."

I sipped my milkshake, riveted.

Daniel's eyes met mine and I felt him assessing me. Was he worried that this story would scare me off? I wished I had an answer to that question for myself.

He went on. "That's when things started to change. For me, at least. I went to a church on campus and talked with the pastor. He invited me to come to Sunday service and to join their men's group. It was like I suddenly realized that I had this big empty hole inside myself that I thought girls and money would fill. The more I went to church, the more that hole shrank.

"Kelly and I started dating exclusively and I asked her to marry me." He pursed his lips and looked out the window. "To be honest, I think she only said yes because she was eight months pregnant and beginning to realize that she couldn't be a mom all on her own. That same pastor married us a week later and we moved in together.

"We had a rocky start. Over the years, we had a few good patches, but mostly we were miserable. We tried to make things work for our son, but when he was five, Kelly had had enough and moved out."

I keenly felt the shock of what that would mean for both Daniel and his son. "Did she stay in the picture or did she take off?"

"She's still around. We have joint custody of our son. However, she got remarried about eighteen months ago and now she only sees him every other weekend. That's one of the reasons we moved here. Her new husband took a job in Casper and I didn't want to be too far away." Daniel took a bite of his hamburger, chewed, swallowed, and sighed. Then he raised an eyebrow and speared me with his eyes. "Have I scared you off yet?"

I trailed a fry through the ketchup and pondered that. "No," I said, surprising myself. "Not yet."

Daniel looked relieved and clapped his hands together. "Okay, no more serious talk. Tell me your favorite movie."

We spent the next hour laughing and talking and slurping the dregs of our shakes. By the time we parted ways, I was thoroughly smitten with Daniel and extremely glad we were meeting for coffee later that week. I didn't know if I could have walked away from that date if we didn't have another planned.

CHAPTER 6

I WAS NOT A MORNING PERSON. IT WAS ONE MORE REASON WHY MY JOB AT THE community center was ideal: I didn't report until afternoon. Meeting someone for coffee at 7:00 a.m. seemed criminal to me. However, for a man like Daniel, I was willing to go against the laws of nature.

So, I was up and showering before the sun came up, which was admittedly refreshing. I resisted the urge to make coffee before my coffee date, for fear of being too jittery. Instead, I applied the little makeup I owned, blow dried my hair, and chose a casual-yet-cute outfit from my roommate's closet.

I arrived at Della's Diner at five minutes to seven. Daniel was already seated at the counter reading over the menu. I walked over to him and was thrilled when he got up from his stool, leaned forward, and gave me a quick hug. He smelled like heaven. It would be rude to cling to him and go on sniffing his neck, so I kept it short, settling instead for a smile and a seat on the stool next to him.

"What's good here?" he asked, eyes back on the menu.

"Della's is famous for waffles," I said as I picked up my own menu.

"Sounds good." Daniel shut his menu and gave me that adorable half smile again.

Soon Patsy, the middle-aged waitress, was taking our order while eyeing Daniel and no doubt wondering what he was doing there with plain old Molly Doyle. She waddled off to the kitchen and nerves threatened to swallow me whole.

"What do you do for work?" I asked into the quiet. Even though I'd spent time with his coworkers, I had realized that I didn't actually know what his job was.

Daniel began to explain something about being a lawyer and the sort of law he practiced. It was mostly over my head, but I sure enjoyed watching him talk.

"I didn't realize there was more than one law firm here in town. Oh no, you don't work for Ernie Shankton, do you?" I grimaced and then wished I'd bit my tongue. What if he did work for Ernie?

Instead, Daniel laughed, his eyes almost closing. "I do not work for Ernie Shankton. My firm is Watkins and Montoya. They're based in Casper, but recently opened an office here."

"How old is your son?" I asked, changing the subject. Last night, I'd had plenty of time to think over our conversation and found that I was very curious about his son.

"Miles just turned eleven and is in the fifth grade."

I snapped out of my swoony state. "Miles? Does he go to the community center's after- school program?"

I'd forgotten what Miles had told me about his dad not liking him going to the program, but Daniel's momentary frown of disapproval snapped all the pieces together. In that instant, a horrible sense of dread thudded into my stomach.

"He's going there for now," he said delicately.

"You don't like having him in an after-school program?" I tried not to sound accusatory.

Daniel let out a little sigh. "I'm sure those programs are great for the kids who really need them, but I'd prefer that Miles had a babysitter."

His words rankled me. I felt my dread growing. We'd really hit it off and I hated that Daniel disapproved of the place that I loved. I tried to keep my voice even as I said, "The program is a really good one. Miles can spend time with other kids which will help him to make friends faster. He gets exercise, homework help, and lots of adult mentoring. I think most parents would be glad to have their kids in such a great environment."

Daniel looked surprised. His eyebrows rose as he said, "I'm sure it has its merits. I've just never liked day cares. And I've heard that this center has a lot of kids who come from rough homes. I'm not sure that's who I want my son having for friends." He paused. "I'm not trying to insult what you do, Molly. Miles has had a good experience so far. I just want him to be somewhere else."

I tried to tamp down my crushing disappointment. For reasons I didn't want to delve into, I was taking Daniel's disapproval of the center extremely personally. "I can tell you that I've seen firsthand that your son has started to make friends with a lot of those kids you're so worried about. They welcomed him to the program and have treated him really well. Miles is enjoying being there."

"I'm sure that what you do for the community is very valuable. I just don't think my son needs that sort of help," Daniel said with his hands raised defensively.

I knew that I was probably overreacting. A lot of people saw the ragtag bunch of kids who came to the center each day and made the same judgments about them. Maybe I had formed my own bias about Miles' dad when the boy had first told me he might not stay. Maybe I was disappointed that this incredibly attractive man didn't fall over in wonder at my selfless work.

Either way, I couldn't resist getting up from my stool or saying, "I think this was a mistake. I'm not the sort of girl you're looking for. I hope you'll keep Miles in the program." Then I made my way to the checkout, paid for my mostly untouched coffee, and stomped out to my car.

I huffed and growled all the way home, using all the insults that came to mind as I drove, choosing anger over heartache. Looked like I would have to bury all the hopes I'd begun to have for my relationship with Daniel.

CHAPTER 7

I WAS A FIRM BELIEVER THAT CRAWLING INTO BED, EATING CHOCOLATE, AND reading mindless romance novels was one of the best ways to deal with a bad day. However, despite polishing off a Dove bar and a pack of Reese's peanut butter cups, as well as reading an entire battered paperback, I was still grouchy when it was time to go in to work.

If I'd taken the time to analyze my feelings, I'm sure that I would have identified my embarrassment at having gorgeous Daniel think so little of my work and the awesome kids we helped. Unfortunately, I had no intention of doing that and so my brain only had room to fume at his narrow-minded superiority. I was in such a funk that I didn't even pause on my top step to admire the mountain view as I did most days. Head down and feet stomping, I made my way to Kermit and made a point not to look at the spare tire that a certain someone I didn't want to name had changed.

Over the years, it had become a habit for me to first stop in Carol's office whenever I arrived at the center. We were friendly, though we weren't friends. Carol did everything she could to keep the center running. While I appreciated her commitment, I didn't always agree with her methods. We'd butted heads on more than one occasion, though she didn't know it since I never said anything.

Today, Carol was as harried as ever, though I could immediately tell that something was very wrong. Her hair was curling frantically and she'd misplaced her glasses next to the plant on the bookshelf, but this was nothing out of the ordinary. In fact, what alerted me to the problem was the fact that the files on her desk were organized into neat piles. The typical layers of paperwork that formed a strata on her desk were neat and tidy.

I sank into the battered chair opposite her desk and demanded, "What's wrong?"

Carol sat back in her own chair and sighed, uncharacteristically still. "I had a meeting today with Stan Lawrence. He told me that the board has decided to sell this building."

"Who would buy it?" I burst out without thinking.

"Property developers. They've purchased the entire block and intend to create a trendy shopping area with apartments on the upper floors." Carol seemed entirely too reasonable about the whole thing.

"Did you tell them about all the good the center does for the community? Did you tell him about all the kids we take care of every day? About the free adult education classes? About the soup kitchen we run at the end of each month?" The anger from my meeting with Daniel was clearly rekindling and pouring out onto the stupid board of directors.

Carol blinked at me in surprise. She was used to me being quiet and calm. This was surely the first time I'd ever exploded in front of her.

"The board has already made the decision. They've signed paperwork. I don't think there's anything more to be said."

My boss handed me a manila envelope. I opened it and pulled out the thick sheaf of legal paperwork. My eyes took in the name of the firm and my ire grew exponentially. The letterhead clearly read "Watkins and Montoya." I knew where I'd heard that name before.

"Daniel," I hissed, and forcibly handed the paperwork back to Carol before I could give into the urge to throw it on the ground and stomped on it. I settled for pacing in the small, crowded office. It was nowhere near as satisfyingly dramatic, but would probably prove wiser in the long run.

Please tell me that Daniel didn't work out this deal because of his dislike of the center. It wasn't exactly a prayer, since I was long out of practice praying. I'd spent too many years as a kid praying that the Dorians would adopt me. Any God who was worth following surely would work out that sort of a request for an abandoned child. Unfortunately, since I no longer was on speaking terms with Him, I didn't have anyone to whom I could run to when things got hard.

And boy, was this hard. Closing the center was bad enough. Why did it have to be Daniel's company who was behind the sale?

"Molly, I'm sorry," Carol said lamely.

I turned furious eyes on her and she shrank back. "We're just going to have to fight to keep the center open. We can't give up. The people who use this place are the ones who most need help. Trading the center for a stupid shopping center is despicable!"

"I agree, but it's already decided."

"Are they going to rebuild somewhere else? Is there any talk of what we're supposed to do to continue the vital work we do for this community?" I grabbed the edge of her desk and loomed over her.

Carol's eyes widened. "I don't think so."

"We're going to lose our jobs, Carol, do you understand that? We'll be out of work, not to mention all of the people who depend on the center losing the aid they receive here. We can't just sit back and let this happen."

"I'm as angry as you are, Molly, but we have to face reality. This building is very old and the necessary repairs are outside our operating budget. It wouldn't have been long before it would have closed anyway because it's unsafe."

I ground my teeth. It was a fair point, but I didn't have to like it. "Maybe we can move somewhere else. Surely there's another building nearby that could be reno-vated. We don't have to have a fancy place, just the bare minimum to get started."

"It would cost close to a million dollars to purchase such a building and put in even the most basic of renovations. If the city had that kind of money, they would have fixed up this old place long ago." Carol did, indeed, look crushed. "We have to face the truth: the center is going to close."

Despite the fact that I knew Carol was as upset as I was, she was the only person around I could take my anger out on. I shot her my most furious scowl, grabbed my bag and coat, and left the room, huffing angrily all the way to the after-school room.

CHAPTER 8

BEFORE YOU START IMAGINING THAT I WAS JUST SOME UNSTOPPABLE FLAMING ball of rage, I must tell you that being surrounded by the after-school kids soothed my frustrations. Jacquelyn gave me a hug and showed me the book she was reading. Little Jesús grinned at me with his big dimples and then refused to sit down until I talked to him in Spanish. Even Miles readily joined in the kickball game that Toby organized for the older kids.

During arts and crafts time, I pulled Tessa into my lap and helped her cut out the elephant pictures for her project. When we sat down to enjoy our snack, I put an arm around Aiden, even though he usually drove me crazy with his talking. I watched the kids and staff throughout the afternoon with fresh eyes and a heavy heart. It wasn't until about a half hour before parents were due to arrive that a lightbulb flashed on in my brain. This was my family. Sure, we bugged each other and argued and griped. It didn't matter that many of the kids were transient and could be gone without a moment's notice. The center was a home and the people there depended on each other. This was the way community was supposed to be.

Maybe I was always going to react badly to a threat to my family due to my growing-up-with-a-foster-family issues. I grudgingly had to admit that that was probably why Daniel's dislike of the center had hit me in such a personal way. And now he was a part of the group that was determined to take away my home and my family. Even if I knew I'd overreacted to Daniel's disapproval of the center, I couldn't get over the fact that he was in any way associated with losing this place that I loved so much. Especially because Miles so obviously loved it here.

Even with all the love from our kids, one sight of Daniel at parent pick-up ratcheted my anger right back up. The moment I saw him handing Miles his backpack, I was instantly annoyed. There was no point in telling myself to leave Daniel alone.

I completely forgot my usual shyness. I was seeing red, and heaven help anyone who got in my path.

"Can I talk to you privately?" I hissed in Daniel's ear.

He looked up in surprise and blinked at me in what would have been a very adorable way had circumstances been different. To his credit, he took in the steam that was surely pouring from my ears and still agreed to follow me as I stalked off to a quieter corner of the gym.

"I need to apologize for this morning," he began.

With a swipe of the hand, I cut him off. "I just found out that this property has been sold. Tell me you aren't involved in that deal."

But I knew instantly that he was very much involved. Daniel's mouth formed a small "O" and he rocked back on his heels, scratching his chin and looking like he wanted to be anywhere else.

I raked furious fingers through my hair. "I know you don't like the center, but why are you trying to shut it down? Miles is making real friends here, even if they're not the sort of kids you approve of. This place is a home for so many people. Yes, many of the kids here come from rough families, but they're just kids. They desperately need a place where they can come and play and have fun and be safe. Some of them will only be here a few weeks before their parents move on to the next job. Who knows where they'll be next. It might not be a place where they can just be kids for a few hours a day. And your company wants to shut this place down!" I paused for breath, panting and most assuredly looking like I'd lost my marbles.

Daniel held up his hands defensively. "Molly, your compassion for the people of this town is admirable."

I snorted.

"This building is old and in need of repairs the city can't afford. It doesn't matter how good the programs are here or how many people are being helped, because the building is no longer safe. Something has to be done about it. When faced with the overwhelming costs to bring the center up to code, the board decided it would be best to sell before someone is seriously injured." Daniel's voice was infuriatingly calm and logical.

"It isn't that bad," I scoffed, even though I knew it was a lie. "It's better to have a rundown building offering help to our community than to have nothing at all. No one else offers what we do. If you get rid of the center, you eliminate a source of help for dozens of families in the area."

"I'm not saying that the programs aren't good," Daniel argued. "That's irrelevant. The building is too expensive to maintain and is becoming unsafe."

I pointed out Aiden as he ran by. "Are you suggesting that little boy is going to care more that he has to keep his coat on inside during winter or that he has a place to play so that he doesn't have to follow his parents to work on the sheep ranch?"

A pained look passed over Daniel's face. He clenched his jaw, hands on hips for a moment before turning serious eyes to mine. "How would you feel if that little boy was seriously injured because the roof collapsed or the plumbing exploded?"

"It's not that bad," I dismissed him with a snort.

The gravity in his voice drained away my derision. "It is that bad, Molly. This place cannot continue to operate safely."

While I'd been arguing with Daniel, the heavy rock that had dropped into my stomach had been lighter. Now, it plunked down again, taking away my breath for a moment. Tears sprang to my eyes that I couldn't bear for Daniel to see. I threw up a hand, turned on my heel, and hurried away before I burst into tears.

CHAPTER 9

I MADE IT HOME AND MANAGED TO CHANGE INTO MY FAVORITE FLANNEL PJ pants and worn T-shirt before crawling into bed for a good cry. When my tears were spent, I lay in my nest and stared up at the ceiling, trying not to think about the future. After a while, the front door opened and my roommate, Bailey, arrived home. She was humming to herself as she put away groceries and divested herself of her outside garments.

"Molls, are you home?" she called.

I tried to decide what to say. My grief would be obvious. Was it better to try and sound upbeat and confident that everything would work out? Or to be more honest and admit that I was in the depths of despair.

Before I could make up my mind, Bailey's face appeared around the door. Her enormous curly hair always looked like a dark halo to me. Her warm brown eyes crinkled when she saw me and her cheerful freckled face and gap-toothed smile evaporated as she took me in.

"What happened?" she asked, coming in without invitation and sinking onto the bed next to me.

Bailey was one of my favorite people in the entire world. She already had a sister, but they didn't get along, and she always swore that the two of us were more like sisters. I'd never met anyone else who knew how to listen without giving advice when none was needed. She just lay next to me on the bed, holding my hand and rubbing my wrist in that way that always calmed me down.

I poured out the story of my disastrous date with Daniel, learning that the center was closing, and my confrontation with him at the end of the day.

"The worst part is that he's right," I sniffled. "We can't keep the center open if people are in danger."

Bailey sighed. "It's a bummer, though."

"No kidding."

"It's a good thing I bought some fudge brownie ice cream at the store today."

I turned to look at her. "Did you really?"

She nodded sagely. "I think God directed me to the ice-cream aisle, knowing it would be on super sale and that you would need some."

I only had the enthusiasm to lift one corner of my mouth. Bailey was a devout believer in God's goodness and personal interest in our lives. She didn't go on and on about it, but neither did she hide what she believed. And I had to admit, it was semi-miraculous that my very favorite kind of ice cream, which never, ever went on sale, would be half-off.

Nothing short of fudge brownie ice cream would have gotten me out of bed. But soon we were sitting on our slightly itchy brown plaid couch, wrapped in old quilts and eating right from the carton.

"You know, there might be other places that would allow you to run an after-school program in their buildings," Bailey mused.

I raised an eyebrow at her and licked my spoon thoughtfully. "Do you really think so?"

She lifted one shoulder. "It's possible. Lots of schools and churches have that sort of thing in place. I don't know of any here in Knightsdale, so there are probably a few places that might be available and interested."

"What would I do to find a place?" I wondered.

"Call them and talk to people." Bailey's eyes challenged me.

I hated that sort of thing. Meeting new people was always terrifying. Having to meet new people and ask them for a favor was ten times worse.

Bailey knew me too well. "Is it worth it for you to keep the program running?"

I gulped. Of course it was worth the horror of asking strangers for help. I just had to gather my courage and make it happen.

Bailey pulled out the phone book which had been long ago delivered and never used. She flipped to the list of churches and together we wrote out the addresses and hours for the likely candidates. It became apparent that speaking with one representative for the school system would be enough to get an answer as to whether or not we'd be allowed into the middle or elementary schools which were both in town. The local high school was in the next town over and wouldn't really work for our needs.

With much trepidation and hope, I started out the next day. I wore my nicest dress pants and cleanest sweater and hoped that I looked capable despite my nerves. However, how I looked didn't seem to matter. Every single place refused to let us use their facilities.

The reasons why were varied. Some places didn't have the space, some were sure they couldn't get board approval. One pastor looked as though I'd asked him to saw off his left arm and couldn't get rid of me fast enough.

So, by the time I sat in the final pastor's office on my list, and listened to him turn me down, I was crushed.

The middle-aged man, who insisted I call him Pastor Brian, looked at me over the top of his reading glasses and said, "You are working for a very noble cause, Miss Doyle. The work the community center does is vital to our town. You must trust that God will work it all out."

Normally, I would have mumbled an excuse and exited as fast as I could manage. Today, though, I was so discouraged I boldly said, "I don't think God is interested in working things out for me."

Pastor Brian's expression, rather than looking offended, took on an understanding gleam that I hadn't expected. "It sounds like you've been disappointed in the past."

"I was in foster care for a long time," I explained quickly. I shrugged as if it wasn't a big deal. "I prayed for a family, but it didn't work out."

"Would you mind if I read you a verse from the Bible?" Pastor Brian reached for a battered book and flipped through it for a moment. "Here it is. Ephesians 1:5 says 'In love he predestined us for adoption to sonship through Jesus Christ in accordance with his pleasure and will.'"

I pursed my lips, not sure of what to say.

"Don't you see? God already has a family for you. He wanted you to be His child so badly that He gave His own son in exchange for you. You can trust Him to provide for your needs, Miss Doyle."

I thanked him hastily and hurried out of the building, Pastor Brian's words following me as I went, refusing to leave me alone.

CHAPTER 10

YOU WOULD HAVE THOUGHT THAT AFTER SO MUCH REJECTION I WOULD BE IN A bad mood. Of course, I was disappointed that I hadn't found some place to host our after-school program. It was a real blow. On top of that, I'd had to face my worst fear of repeated rejection from strangers all day. It was enough to put me in a place where even fudge brownie ice cream couldn't help. Yet, I couldn't even get my brain to think about all that because I couldn't shake Pastor Brian's words.

I'd always assumed that there was something wrong with me because I wasn't adopted. To hear that God wanted to adopt us all into His family was new to me and I couldn't stop thinking about it. Questions I'd never considered swirled through my mind. What if not being adopted had really been the best thing for me for some unknowable reason? What if closing the center was really a good thing? What if God did love me and had cared for me all along?

I was distracted as I moved through the day. It was our Fun Friday and Toby had set up equipment stations around the gym that the kids rotated through. I observed everything with only semi-focused attention. A group was making use of the hula hoops in one area, another bunch skipped rope nearby, and several kids were generally missing the basketball hoop as they took turns shooting.

It wasn't until one of the basketballs bounced up into the bleachers that I snapped to full attention. Despite the old yellow caution tape we'd used to rope them off, Miles was climbing up to where the ball was wedged.

I knew that the bleachers weren't in very good shape, but I'd always believed that the reason they were out of bounds was because of the very real danger of splinters. After speaking with Daniel yesterday, though, my heart began pounding as I watched Miles high-stepping his way upwards. I didn't like the way that the supports shook with each step he took.

Before I realized it, I was dodging kids and hurrying to the bottom of the bleachers. I don't know if anyone else noticed Miles in the midst of the chaos around us. Most of the staff was busy keeping the fun from devolving into chaos, and so I was the first to notice when Miles jerked, his foot stuck in a gap.

"Don't move, Miles!" I called, and ducked under the caution tape without weighing the consequences.

I reached him quickly, though I felt the shaking of the bleachers with every nerve in my body.

"Molly, my foot's stuck," Miles said, as though it was a mere annoyance.

"I see that." My voice was nonchalant. "We'll have to be careful on these old bleachers, though. Did you notice the yellow tape?"

He looked around as I reached for his foot and I glanced up just as his eyes registered the caution tape.

"Nope," he replied with a shrug of his shoulders.

Of course not. I almost chuckled at his boyish focus on his basketball when the outside door opened and Daniel strode in looking very handsome in his well-cut suit. I groaned instead. Great. The last thing we needed was Daniel witnessing this situation.

"Does your foot hurt?" I asked, pushing aside this newest problem. Miles' safety mattered far more than his father's disapproval.

"Not really."

"Okay, I'm going to try and wiggle it loose. Let me know if it hurts at any point."

I grasped his ankle in one hand and his heel in the other and began to carefully push and pull. With relative effort, the foot popped free and Miles' arms pinwheeled before he grabbed the bleacher seat in front of him.

"Whoa," I cautioned. "Let's get down from here."

"What about the ball?" Miles whined.

"It's not safe up here. Forget the ball."

Miles paused, longing on his face. "But I bet you can reach it from here if you stretch."

I raised an eyebrow at him. "If you head down right now, I'll try and reach it one time."

Clearly that was not what he wanted, but he nodded grudgingly and began to climb down. Once he was on solid ground again, I turned and stretched out my hand. My fingers could just reach the ball. I stretched out a little further, one hand on the bleachers, one leg in the air for balance.

That was when there was a cracking sound and the bleachers collapsed around me.

⚜

I LAY IN MY HOSPITAL BED A FEW HOURS LATER AS THOUGH I WAS LYING IN A pool of defeat instead. My leg was in a cast from foot to thigh from where it had broken in two places. I had a broken collarbone and a sprained wrist.

All of that was bad enough. But the worst part was that everything else was broken, too. My job at the center didn't provide insurance and so I could only imagine the medical bills I was racking up. Besides that, I was about to be out of work with no way to pay for them. And my accident only proved that Daniel and the board were right to close the center since it was clearly unsafe.

Which made me think of Daniel, and my heart clenched painfully. We'd hit it off and had had an amazing week together. I'd pushed away thoughts about him as much as I could, but there was no escaping them now. I was devastated that things hadn't worked out with him.

I'd been asking God to provide for me and this was what happened? I ended up in the hospital with no way to pay for my bills and with a broken heart on top of it all. Everything I'd ever believed about God not caring for me seemed to stuff itself into the room with me. Surely I was unlovable. Maybe God wanted other people, but He couldn't want me. Here was further proof. I felt too hopeless to even bother to cry.

I was about to indulge myself in a real pity party when the door opened and Bailey entered like a coffee-colored ray of sunshine.

"Molly! I can't believe this!" Her dark eyes swept over me and she dropped her bags on the other bed. She moved to hug me then froze. "Can I give you a hug? Or would that hurt too much?"

"Just be careful of my collarbone," I said, needing a hug more in that moment than I'd ever needed one before in my life.

As my wonderful friend maneuvered her arms around me so that she could hold me close, my tears let loose in a torrent of fear and worry, gratefulness and love.

"Oh sweetie," she crooned. "It'll be okay."

"No, it won't," I sobbed. "I don't have insurance and they're going to close the center, so I won't have a job. They'll probably close it even faster, now that this happened."

Wisely, Bailey pulled up a chair next to me and took my hand while I cried.

"I don't know what to do. I thought God would take care of me, but now ..." my voice trailed off and I sank further into the open arms of hopelessness.

Bailey sat up straighter. "What do you mean?"

I let out a snotty laugh of derision. "Look at me. How can you say that God's taking care of me?"

"Whoa." Bailey's eyes were growing fierce. "Did you think that if God's taking care of you that nothing bad will ever happen to you?"

I shrugged, refusing to meet her eyes. That was exactly what I thought, but suddenly it didn't seem right.

"Molls, God takes care of His children, but that doesn't mean everything goes the way we want it to. Sometimes really hard things happen in our lives."

She bit her lip and I knew she was thinking of her mom, who had died when Bailey was eleven. Her voice trembled as she said, "God never promises to make our lives easy. He does promise to use the hard things to glorify His kingdom, to help others, and to help us trust Him more. We don't always get to know why hard things happen in our lives, but we can trust that God is there for us and will never leave us."

"That takes a lot of faith," I said slowly. "I can't see any good purpose in this."

Bailey squeezed my hand gently. "I see a good purpose already."

"You do?" I asked in surprise.

"You are the one who was hurt and not that boy. It could have been him and it wasn't. I know you never would have forgiven yourself if one of your kids got injured."

I bit my lip. It was true, and I hadn't thought about it. I was suddenly incredibly thankful that it had been me and not Miles.

By the time Bailey left, my spirits had lifted a bit, though I still wasn't certain where God and I stood.

⚜

WHEN I SHOWED NO SIGNS OF A CONCUSSION, I WAS ALLOWED TO LEAVE THE next morning. Bailey filled my pain prescriptions and helped me collapse into her car so she could drive me home. The stairs up to our second-floor apartment almost did me in, but Bailey helped with one arm around my waist and we managed it in the end.

She handed me the crutch I could use with my unsprained wrist and stepped over to unlock the door. I tried not to envision myself losing balance and tipping back down the stairs as I fumbled my way into our apartment.

I stopped as soon as I entered the door. Bouquets of flowers and handmade cards were everywhere. My mouth hung open as I looked around our small living room and dining room.

"What is this?" I gasped.

Bailey stepped forward with a wide grin. "Everyone at the center wanted to do something nice for you. I told them to send everything here as a surprise. Flowers and cards have been arriving since last night."

Tears again sprang to my eyes, but this time it was because my heart was so warm. The people who came to the center had so little and they had wanted to do something nice for me. That fact alone touched me deeply.

"Sit on the couch and let's go through your cards." Bailey directed me to the couch, wrapped me in my quilt, and then bustled about collecting all the cards.

We spent twenty minutes reading every one. Some of the cards were in broken English from grateful parents. Many were handmade and I had a feeling that someone at the center had provided supplies for the kids. The flowers were from the staff, as well as some community members I never would have believed would even know my name.

One particular bouquet of bright Gerber daisies came with a card from Pastor Brian. It read, "I'm praying for a speedy recovery and that God will use this situation in mighty ways." I tucked that one into my hoodie pocket and fingered it occasionally as the day went by.

I was incredibly sore for the next few days and grew tired of the couch. Still, I had only to look over at the cards and flowers to know that I'd been adopted into a sort of family after all. While I didn't have a solution for paying my bills, finding a new job, or relocating the center, I was wrapped in a sense of peace that was every bit as comforting as my quilt.

CHAPTER 11

"THIS DRESS LOOKS COMPLETELY STUPID WITH MY CAST," I COMPLAINED.

"Don't be silly. You look adorable," Bailey scolded from behind me.

I looked myself over in our bathroom mirror as my roommate worked to coax some curl into my hair. She'd also done my makeup, chosen one of her dresses to lend me, and was fixing my hair. Normally I avoided dressing up if I could help it, but Bailey had convinced me that I needed to get out and this would be perfect. I had to admit that it was fun to get dolled up for a girls' night out. The navy-blue dress Bailey had chosen from her closet for me was young and flowy and I felt pretty for the first time since before my accident.

"Okay, I think this is as good as it's going to get," I finally said.

Bailey grinned her gap-toothed smile at me. "You look fabulous. Go wait in the living room."

I reached for my crutches and swung my way expertly down the hall. After nearly a month of practice, I felt that I was almost on an Olympic level with them.

The doorbell rang and I changed course, aiming for the door instead of the couch. I didn't have any idea who could be on the other side, but guessed that it was one of our neighbors with misdirected mail or a college kid selling magazines.

To my complete surprise, Daniel was standing on the other side. I gaped at him, not registering the bouquet in his hand or his very trendy jeans and button-up shirt.

"What are you doing here?" I asked, surprise making my words sharper than I'd meant for them to be.

Bailey came into the living room then and one look at her extremely self-satisfied expression made my stomach sink.

"I'm taking you to dinner," Daniel said, and handed me the flowers.

I didn't know what to say. Bailey took advantage of the moment to step forward and accept the flowers on my behalf.

"Yellow roses are Molly's favorites. How on earth did you know?" She gave Daniel a cheeky wink before turning towards the kitchen. "Have fun, you two!" she called over her shoulder.

Short of flatly refusing to go to dinner with him, I didn't see a way out, so I hobbled forward and Daniel awkwardly helped me down the stairs and then handed me into his very classy car. He pulled out of the parking lot smoothly and headed towards the highway.

"Where are we going?" I asked, once my curiosity got the better of me.

"Considering that there are only fast food restaurants open after seven in Knights-dale, we'll have to go to Casper for supper."

I swallowed that information and fell silent. I began thinking of the exact words I'd have with my so-called best friend when I got home later. The quiet stretched and Daniel reached for the radio knob. The car was suddenly filled with soothing music.

He cleared his throat and said, "I wanted to thank you for saving Miles."

Instantly, I relaxed. If this was his attempt to thank me, I could handle that. My still-mending heart would be in no danger. "Oh well, I'm glad he's okay." I chewed my lip for a moment before forcing myself to admit, "After you pointed out the repair problems, I started noticing them more. I might not have gone up there so carefully if I hadn't been thinking about what you said. So you really saved Miles just as much as I did."

I glanced at him and he flashed me a worried look.

"I would have liked to have been wrong about that. I've been hearing a lot about all the work the center does for the community. So many people depend on it. And everyone agrees that you're a major player in that work."

I watched his handsome profile and felt the weight in my stomach loosen. My heart even gave a tentative flutter at his praise. I quickly got it back under control with a stern, but silent, talking to.

"It's easy to do work that matters so much, you know?" I shrugged. "We all have such big needs and it's vital that there's a place for people to go when they need help. Even if that's just a place for a little boy to go and make some new friends." Immediately, I wished I could take that back. Did it sound like I was trying to push Daniel's buttons?

Instead, he nodded thoughtfully. "Miles really loves going there. He invited another boy, Miguel, to come get pizza with us. I was impressed with how fun Miguel was."

I smoothed my skirt over my knees and said, "Miguel's parents are migrant workers. They tend to disappear in the summers, but Miguel always comes back in the fall. I can't believe how nice and funny he is, considering how unstable his life can be."

Daniel flashed me a smile. "I know! It's amazing what these kids go through. No wonder they depend on the center so much."

"I'm hoping to find somewhere else for the after-school program to meet. I was asking around at various churches and schools. I'd hate to have to stop running the program when the center closes." It felt a little funny to be telling this to one of the people involved in closing it down, yet Daniel seemed to now understand why the center mattered so much.

"I'm glad you're fighting for it. Let me know if there's anything I can do to help. I know Miles would love to continue participating."

I looked over at him and saw that he'd changed his mind about the program completely. A knot in my stomach loosened.

From there, the conversation roamed to an array of topics. By the time we arrived at the restaurant, we'd both talked about our families and our childhoods, and where we'd gone to college. Even with my crutches, the rest of the evening was comfortable and enjoyable. Daniel insisted on ordering dessert and second cups of coffee before we went home.

He saw me upstairs to the apartment and gave me a warm hug, thanking me for a wonderful evening. I closed the front door behind myself and leaned against it. Going to dinner with Daniel had been like going on a date with a movie star. Even if it was just a "thank you for saving my son" dinner, it was one I'd always treasure.

I checked my phone before heading towards the bedroom and saw that I'd missed a call from Carol. I dialed voice mail and put in my password as I held the phone to my ear.

"Hi, Molly, this is Carol. I wanted you to hear the news from me. The board met today and decided that with the bleacher incident, it would be best if they closed the center right away. So, as of today at five, we're officially closed. I'll call you tomorrow when I know more."

My heart thudded painfully. Even knowing it was coming, learning of the center's closing was a blow. For the first time, though, I remembered that God could work even difficult things out for the best.

"Okay, God, let's see what you do with this," I whispered before swinging myself towards Bailey's room for a late-night chat.

CHAPTER 12

MY HEART POUNDED AS I LISTENED TO THE HOSPITAL'S OPTIONS, MY SWEATY hand making it hard to hold the phone in place against my ear. I hit the number for patient accounts and then waited through the questionable music selection until a voice answered.

"Yes, my name is Molly Doyle and I need to talk to someone about my hospital bill." I tried to sound as though I wasn't about to beg for mercy. I had yet to receive a bill, but it felt right to go ahead and face the facts.

The woman on the phone asked for my particulars. I waited, nerves humming, as she clicked her way through to my account.

"Miss Doyle, you don't have a balance," she said briskly.

"That can't be right," I explained in my calmest voice, sure she was mistaken. "I don't have any insurance and I was in overnight. There must be a bill."

"There was a bill, but it was paid in full two weeks ago."

My mind went blank. It absolutely refused to come to terms with this news. "Oh. Thank you." I hung up. It was only much later that I began to wonder who had paid my bill. Would the receptionist have told me if I'd asked? I doubted it and decided not to call back.

It wasn't the only surprising event of my day. Not twenty minutes later, my phone rang and a man with a very polished voice asked if I'd be available for an appointment at the firm of Watkins and Montoya the next day. I agreed, and barely remembered to ask what the appointment was in regards to.

"I'm afraid I don't have that information," the man said smoothly.

I gulped. "Am I in trouble? Like, am I being sued or something?"

He laughed as though I'd made a mildly funny joke. "I don't believe it's anything like that. Tomorrow at 9:30, then?"

"Sure," I mumbled.

Later that night, Bailey and I sat and marveled at these odd turns of events. We didn't know what to make of the appointment with Daniel's law firm. But Bailey had plenty to say about my mysterious hospital bill.

"God is taking care of you. It's what fathers do for their children," she nodded knowingly.

Just a few weeks ago, I would have argued with my friend. Now, I wasn't so sure. I'd never felt so much peace of mind in the midst of turmoil before in my life. I didn't have a job, yet I wasn't afraid. Daniel had been very kind to me over the past week since he'd taken me to dinner. He called and texted daily, asking how I was feeling and telling me funny things that Miles said or did, proving that he was determined to be my friend at the very least. People from the community kept bringing us casseroles and loaves of homemade bread and far too many desserts to be good for my waistline.

It was the only thing that allowed me to walk calmly into the meeting the next morning. I say walked, but I was really hobbling along on my crutches. I feared that they quite ruined the effect of my best blouse and a borrowed skirt from Bailey.

"Miss Doyle, it's nice to meet you," a sleek Hispanic woman in a tailored pantsuit greeted me. "I'm Estafani Montoya. My partner, Mr. Watkins, won't be joining us today, although I do believe you know Mr. Arias."

I looked at the door just as Daniel walked in. He flashed me his perfect white smile, which always made my stomach wobble. Luckily, Ms. Montoya suggested we sit and then asked if I needed anything to drink. It was so hospitable that for the first time, I began to truly doubt that I was in any kind of trouble.

"I'll cut right to the chase," Ms. Montoya said. I doubted that she'd be able to do anything less than dive right into whatever problem came in front of her. "Our company has a large amount of money to be used for charitable projects. Mr. Arias has talked to us at length about the good that is being done by the Knightsdale Community Center. We are interested in helping to fund the building of a new center."

My mouth dropped open and my eyes flew to Daniel, who was grinning at me. "That's wonderful," I spluttered. "Thank you!"

Ms. Montoya gave me a very genuine smile and I warmed to her instantly. "We'd like you to to work with our designers to help create a center that will best meet the needs of the community. And we'd like you to run the center when it's built."

I sat back into my chair with a thud. "Me?" I gasped. "What about Carol Beaumont? She's been running the center for the past fifteen years."

"We considered Carol," Daniel explained, "but she has decided to retire. Besides, we believe that the center needs someone who cares passionately about it and will have the energy to help it run at its very best."

"That's why we chose you, Miss Doyle." Ms. Montoya's fiery eyes seemed to challenge me. "Mr. Arias has told us a great deal about your caring for the people of the community who are served by the center. We've spoken with Ms. Beaumont, as well as many other people, and your name is the unanimous choice for administrator."

"I'm only twenty-two years old. That's a lot of responsibility to take on." I wasn't sure whether or not I was up to the challenge.

"We'll be appointing a board of directors," Daniel said, his voice soothing.

"And Mr. Arias will be working closely with you," Ms. Montoya added.

They went on to discuss the benefits package and salary that I would be paid. It was all too much. I'm pretty sure that my eyes glazed over as I listened. My brain refused to absorb any more information. The center was going to reopen! They were going to build a new building! I would get to direct it and help make it great!

"What do you say, Miss Doyle? Will you take this position?"

I looked from Daniel to Ms. Montoya and gaped wordlessly. The pair exchanged a worried look and then Daniel asked to speak with me alone. Ms. Montoya nodded and left the room, promising to return in five minutes' time.

"Daniel, I can't believe all of this! It's so much," I shook my head, eyes wide. "I don't know if I can do it."

"When I first learned of the center, I didn't like it," Daniel said calmly, taking my hands in his. "Then I saw how much the staff there cared for the children and their families. I watched the change in Miles and I knew that something extraordinary takes place there. The more we looked into how to make the new center a reality, the more we learned that it wouldn't work without you. You are incredible, Molly."

I sat there with his thumbs rubbing the backs of my hands and had a sudden flash of insight. "It was you, wasn't it? You paid my bill."

"You were protecting my son. You give everything to this community and ask very little in return. It was no trouble." His eyes grew tender. "Molly, I rushed into my first marriage. We were young and foolish and we made a lot of mistakes. As much as I want to believe that I know what God has in store for us, I want to take things very slowly with you. I care very deeply for you and I want to do everything right this time around."

Tears welled in my eyes. "Really? You care about me?"

He leaned forward and kissed me gently. "More than you can guess."

A smile spread slowly over my lips and I whispered, "Oh, I have an idea what you might be feeling," before kissing him again.

Thank you so much for reading my book. I sincerely hope you enjoyed every bit reading it. I had fun creating it and will surely create more.

Your positive reviews are very helpful to other reader, it only takes a few moments. They can be left at Amazon.

https://www.amazon.com/Brenda-Clemmons/e/B07CYKVVRT

WANT FREE BOOKS EVERY WEEK? WHO DOESN'T!

Become a preferred reader and we'll not only send you free reads, but you'll also receive updates about new releases.

So you'll be among the first to dive into our latest new books, full of adventure, heartwarming romances, and characters so real they jump off the page.

It's absolutely free and you don't need to do anything at all to qualify except go to.

PREFERRED READ FREE READS

http://brendaclemmons.gr8.com/

ABOUT THE AUTHOR

On a college road trip down the "Mother Road," Route 66, Brenda Clemmons fell in love with the beauty of the southwest and promised herself that one day she'd return. After graduating with a history degree, Brenda fulfilled that promise and moved to Arizona, where she met her future husband, who was teaching literature in the classroom several doors down from her own social studies class.

Today, she, her husband, and their two kids love to explore the Southwest's beautiful mountains and deserts every chance they get.

Brenda's habit of pulling over at every historical marker eventually led to her husband suggesting that she combine her love of romance novels with her in-depth historical knowledge. She put pen to paper and has been writing ever since, filling her stories with the landscapes, legends, and unique local characters that she wants everyone else to share in!

THROUGH THE STORM
DANIEL'S COURAGE

Mail Order Bride Western Romance

RoyceCardiff
P u b l i s h i n g   H o u s e
WHOLESOME INSPIRATIONAL ROMANCE

Dear Reader,

It is our utmost pleasure and privilege to bring these wonderful stories to you. I am so very proud of our amazing team of writers and the delight they continually bring us all with their beautiful clean and wholesome tales of, faith, courage, and love.

What is a book's lone purpose if not to be read and enjoyed? Therefore, you, dear reader, are the key to fulfilling that purpose and unlocking the treasures that lie within the pages of this book.

A PERSONAL WORD FROM KATIE

I LOVE WRITING ABOUT THE OLD WEST AND THE TRIALS, TRIBULATIONS, AND triumphs of the early pioneer women.

With strong fortitude and willpower, they took a big leap of faith believing in the promised land of the West. It was always not a bed of roses, however many found true love.

Most of the stories are based on some historical fact or personal conversations I've had with folks who knew something of that time. For example a relative of the Wyatt Earp's. I have spent much time out in the West camping hiking and carousing. I have spent countless hours gazing up at night thinking of how it must been back then.

Thank you for being a loyal reader.

Katie

CHAPTER 1

SARAH WAITED PATIENTLY OUTSIDE OF HER FATHER'S ROOM. HER MOTHER, JANE, was talking to him privately. It was an odd request that her father had made, to talk to each of them in private, and it didn't portend a hopeful prognosis. He was dying. Had been for years. But now it was gravely serious, and he seemed to be more aware of it than anyone else.

Jane came out of the room with tears in her eyes and took in a deep breath, clearly trying to keep strong in the face of what was going on. "Sarah, it's your turn to see your father. It is good that we can be so close as a family at a time like this."

Upon entering the room, Sarah looked upon her father with loving eyes. Gaunt and gray though he had become, lines of pain tightening his once-strong jawline, she could still see the man he had once been. The great man, as far as she was concerned. He always did what was right, no matter what, never compromising on his morals. And his devotion to his principles had ultimately led to his injury; a gunshot wound inflicted during the Civil War (ended eight years ago) while he was tending to a fallen comrade. He lay dying now of that long-ago, never-fully-healed wound.

Sarah knew that his mind was at peace and he could enter into eternity with a clean conscience before God, having done his duty on earth. His eternal position was not the issue. The issue was how would she go on in life without him, the man that had always set an example for her, who had always given her courage to go on, to face an unknown future with certainty.

"Sarah, come near to me." He stretched out a frail hand before dropping it on the checked bedcover and coughing weakly. "I fear I don't have much time left on this earth. So I wanted to talk to the most precious people in the world to me."

"I'm right here, Pa," said Sarah with tears in her eyes. She sat down in the chair beside his bed and folded her fingers around his cool hand, seeking to reassure him in this difficult time.

His voice was low and soft and his eyes, usually closed in exhaustion, occasionally blinked open to gaze into her own blue gaze, so like his. "You must not spend the rest of your life grieving me. Don't look towards the past for anything except guidance. I have to know, before I leave this body, that you will go forward into this world, that you will do everything in your power to thrive. Life is far too precious to spend it mourning the dead. Do you understand?"

He asked the question with sincerity mixed with kindness that was underscored by his wizened face, aged beyond his years from the trials of life. He had taken his time on earth seriously and, Sarah knew he wanted to make certain that she would do the same, seeking after God with all her heart.

Sarah shook her head, tears overflowing and spilling down her cheeks. "Why talk about that right now? You aren't going to die. You have many years left." She started crying harder now, sobbing. "I don't know what I would do without you ... I can't even face that possibility."

"But that is the Lord's will. My dear child, life is not just for us to enjoy; it is to teach us lessons that we may grow. This is one of those lessons. I've done everything I can to guide you and teach you, and now you must rely on God." He pressed her fingers lightly but intently, driving home his point as best he could in his weakened state.

"Why would God allow this? I don't want any of this. It's too hard. I don't trust God. Why would a good God do something like this ... it makes no sense."

Her father smiled gently. "Live your life the best you can, and you will always find peace ..." After he said those words he closed his eyes and didn't open them again. Sarah grabbed his hand, her heart constricting.

"Pa!" His pulse continued, as did his breathing, but it was clear that he was deeply asleep, perhaps never again to wake. "I will go on and find joy," she whispered through her tears, promising him, hoping he could hear, hoping for a last word, anything more. But she knew it was the end, that his brief time had passed, and a new era in her life had begun.

She went outside and hugged her mother. They wept together, consoling one another.

"I will let you know if he wakes up," said Jane, hoping for such an occasion as she stepped back, smoothed her worn dress, and moved toward the sickroom, to keep vigil over her husband in his last hours.

Sarah nodded and went to her room to cry on her own. Nothing was fair about life; that much she had figured out already. But she was determined to make her father proud. She thought about all of the things that he had taught her. It made her tear up even more. She had been his only child, his pride and joy, so he had poured everything into her. Sometimes he had even made her go through difficult times just for the sake of it, telling her to embrace the difficulty, to enjoy hardship, for doing so was the very essence and joy of life. And now the ultimate test was in front of her. To make him proud would be to endure, to press on, and to be able to live her life with energy and joy ... to flourish.

Sarah woke up the next morning with the news of her father's passing. It was no surprise to her, but that didn't lessen her grief or the feel that her heart had split clean in two. Throughout the next painful days of the wake and the funeral, she stayed close to her ma, making sure to be there for her through the pain of her loss. And in truth, Sarah needed to be close to someone as well.

Because of how much time she had spent taking care of Pa the past few years, she had lost touch with most of her friends, and sometimes she felt isolated. But as she had gotten older, she had realized more and more the necessity of having other people around. Other people were a way to anchor yourself in a turbulent world. Sarah hadn't grown up with the type of wealth that secured one against misfortune. She needed other people in her life not just emotionally but financially, however crass and shallow that thought felt whenever it crossed her mind. But life in Virginia was hard, and most people were too concerned with their own interests. She felt like there was nothing there for her.

"What am I going to do, Ma?" she asked as she and her mother sat in the kitchen, hands cupped around steaming mugs of tea "I just don't see anything here for me, and I want so badly to do something to make Pa proud of me."

Jane looked at Sarah with understanding in her eyes. "It's not what you can do that will make him proud, but who you can become. Think of it in those terms. What kind of woman would your father want you to become?"

Sarah nodded. Both of her parents were so smart ... so wise. They were great role models, but now she was reaching an age—twenty-three—where having great role models was not enough, where her potential was not enough; now she had to become who she was supposed to be.

"I feel like I am called to marry. But after the war, there are so few men. And I am not cut out like so many others who grew up to be ladylike." It was true. Sarah had had great parents, but they'd been focused on survival, since they'd never had much money, and had not taught Sarah the proper etiquette of a lady. Sarah thought that stuff was superficial, anyway, but it didn't matter what she thought, those kinds of things mattered—mattered a lot—when it came to attracting and keeping a good husband.

Her mother hugged Sarah in understanding, knowing how sensitive the subject was, how no girl would ever want to admit to feeling like she couldn't find a suitable man. "I've thought about this too," she said. "As much as I love having you around, you are young and you need to live a full life."

"What are you saying?" asked Sarah, wondering what her ma was getting at.

"Well," Jane began, stirring her tea slowly, "You are at an age where it's no longer proper to sugarcoat things. You will find out what I mean if you have kids one day. I just want you to understand full well the gravity of our situation, that life can be difficult, and that there are not great prospects for marriage here."

"And so, since you are not sugarcoating it ... what exactly are you saying?"

Jane sighed. "I'm saying that you should consider putting out an ad for a husband out west. I hear glowing reports about it. You can make a new life for yourself. And at the very worst, at least you can give yourself a chance for any life at all."

Sarah sat back, not knowing exactly how to react. "Mail order bride," she repeated slowly. She trusted that her mother always had her best interests at heart, of course. And she had heard about the mail order bride business. But it was like her mother was agreeing that Sarah wouldn't be able to find a suitable husband right here in town. Wasn't she supposed to disagree with her, to tell her that of course she could find a good man, and that she would be happy and have a wonderful family?

"It's not you," Jane said softly, reaching over to touch her only daughter's hand. "You're a catch for any good man, Sarah. There simply aren't any such men in these parts any longer. The war has left us bereft in more ways than one."

They sat quietly for a long spell as Sarah absorbed everything before finally speaking. It was the truth, and, she was grateful that her mother hadn't shied from it. "I will consider it," she said finally.

"I'm glad," said Jane. She got up and wrapped her arms around Sarah's slender shoulders. "It is always difficult, becoming an adult. I remember being your age. You want so badly to be a child forever. But that is not the way of the Lord. He has called us to put away childish things as we reach maturity. There is no greater test in life. But I know you are up for it." Jane looked at Sarah with so much love in her eyes that her words were in no way harsh, but rather uplifting and encouraging.

⚜

SARAH SPENT THE REST OF THAT DAY IN DEEP THOUGHT. HERE SHE WAS FACED with the biggest decision in her life, and she had to make that decision in a fragile emotional state— grieving her father's death. It was almost too much to handle, and so she cried out to God.

God, please hear me. I want to do what is right, but it is hard for me to trust you. I don't know why you would take my father. I can't understand any of it. I can't see the meaning of it. He was good and followed you, and yet he knew so much suffering. And now I feel empty and lost. I need you, God. I need your guidance in my life.

When Sarah finished praying, she looked around the room. There was no bolt of lightning, no sudden epiphany. There was, however, assurance from her father as his words came into her head. "Do what you believe is right, and the world will step in line."

Sarah knew then that she couldn't just live in Virginia forever. Adventure was out there; truly living was out there. She had made her father a promise. She had to fulfill it.

CHAPTER 2

"How can I improve the sanitation of my house?" he asked the store clerk, leaning across the counter. "No matter how often I sweep, the weather seems to seep in as snow or rain or dust."

Daniel lived about half an hour from town on horseback and didn't like to ride in often. So when he did, he had to make it count. He had to make good use of this time, something he practiced diligently, since he had learned so many hard lessons about the importance of being steadfast.

Harold, the clerk, nodded at some building materials nearby. "First thing is you gotta seal in the sod. Make it smooth and tight so's not to allow matter to seep in, no matter how bad conditions are outside."

"Cover it with wood," said Colt, another customer who was perusing the feed supplies. "Shore it up real solid."

Daniel didn't have that kind of money, unfortunately. "How about some newspapers?"

"Sure thing," said Harold. "You can get you some right over there." He pointed. "Won't be as good as wood, but it'll help some."

It cost Daniel nearly all the money he had, and it wasn't much of an improvement. But at least the newspapers would provide some form of insulation, and hopefully that would keep out some the insects and snakes. It better, because he wanted his house in good condition. He was no longer working just for his own comfort.

There were a few reasons he worked so hard. Partly, it was just his nature. He was a good-hearted man who wanted to do what was right. He came from a background that had taught him hard work was the measure of a man. But more than that, he wanted to be thought of as more than just good, but also honorable, and worthy of respect and admiration even. He longed for the love of a woman, but because of what had happened to Amy (though intellectually he knew it wasn't his fault) he imagined he wasn't worthy. That, he had to fix, and he prayed earnestly to God to give him the fortitude to do what was right.

Another reason that he worked so hard was that he had to "prove up" his land. This meant showing that his land was improved upon over a five-year period. He had no doubt that he had done so. But he also didn't want to feel like he had taken advantage of the government in any way. So he worked as hard as he could to be a good steward of the property.

As he came to believe he was in a good enough position to take care of a woman, Daniel finalized his house preparations as best he could and put an ad out for a wife. Sarah Conrad had she accepted, after a brief correspondence, bringing him joy, but also a giant sense of responsibility. He wanted to make sure that he did everything in his power to give her the best life possible.

"Let me know if you have any more questions," said Harold with honesty in his gaze. He had his own family to protect, Daniel knew, and was a square dealer. "I know how hard it can be out there, and I have collected quite a few tidbits from customers over the years."

"Sure will," said Daniel. He didn't interact with the people of the town too often since he spent so much time working the land by himself. The work was endless and basically impossible. But when he did, he made sure he was genuine. He knew that was how you earned respect. And he found there were many in town deserving of a lot of his respect in return.

DANIEL'S NEXT STOP AFTER THE STORE WAS THE TRAIN STATION, WHERE HIS fiancée, Sarah, would be arriving. They had exchanged only a few letters to each other. He had been honest with her, but not necessarily open about himself and his life. He'd told her the truth, but withheld anything that he didn't deem pertinent. It was just part of his reserved nature. And besides, there was only so much you could convey by writing anyway. You couldn't convey the difficulty of living as a homesteader, or the type of culture that you found out west. It was completely different than life on the East Coast, where there was safety in numbers.

Out here, you were on your own. You had to struggle and fight every single day to survive. Daniel knew that that mentality had eaten away at his joy for living, especially since his wife had passed two years ago. And as much as he felt anxious about what his new wife would think of him and his struggles, he was also hopeful that he could find someone to love again, a kindred spirit to share life with. But that was not always the experience one found with a mail order bride. More often, simple respect would have to suffice.

Daniel arrived at the train station merely a few minutes before the train appeared in the distance—perfect timing— and started to get nervous. He didn't have much of an idea of what to expect appearance wise or anything else. It was in God's hands, but that was okay in his book, for he was a man of faith. He said a quick prayer, asking for the courage to do what was right. In spite of her cordial, engaging letters, he knew that his new bride might be quarrelsome, a nag, and impossible to live with. But she could also be delightful and beautiful. He hoped for the latter, of course.

And as the train came into the station, in all its glory as a symbol of the expansion of the country, his optimism returned, and he smiled, waiting in nervous anticipation to meet the person that would change his life in one way or another.

CHAPTER 3

I AM A HARD WORKER, A KIND MAN, DISCIPLINED, AND ABOVE ALL I SEEK TO PLEASE God. I am resolved to do what is right, no matter what. I know that my words and promises can only mean so much. What really matters is that I act in a way that is upright and honorable. I believe you will find me to be so.

Your journey out west will not be in vain, Sarah, I promise you that much. Out here you will find much work. I can promise you that as well. But through the work, and in the cultivating of the land and our building a relationship together, we can create a new life for ourselves. It is a lot to hope for. But if you are willing to make this trip, without ever having met me, then I believe you are a dreamer too.

– Daniel Murphy

Sarah read his last letter over and over again. It was beautifully written, she thought. But much more than that, it sounded sincere, as if he had been through something that had taught him the importance of speaking the truth no matter what. Or maybe that was just how he had been raised. Or maybe, admittedly, it was all a lie. But, like Daniel had said, she had to dream and had to believe that he would be faithful to his promises so that her life with him would be everything she hoped for.

The train reached the station, and Sarah's nerves reacted accordingly; her heart rate spiked, her palms became sweaty, and she feared making a fool of herself. It was as if her strength immediately left her, and she knew she couldn't rely on herself any longer.

"Please, God. Guide me. Give me the strength to always do what is right." *Yes,* she thought to herself. *Doing what is right will be the key.* For no matter what happened, no matter what Daniel was like, she could control herself and how she reacted to any situation.

She looked at herself in her pocket mirror for a last-minute inspection. Her blue eyes were her best feature, she thought. And despite the hardship of life, she imagined that they shone with a brilliance that belied her otherwise plain appearance. She was a few pounds too skinny, and otherwise unremarkable looking. *But beauty is vain,* she reminded herself.

The train pulled into the station and Sarah made her way to the exit, nodding at passengers she had spent days beside. As she stepped onto the platform, Sarah looked around in amazement. Not because of the amazing sights, but because of the lack of anything of note to see. The town was practically a blank canvas, and beyond the town there was nothing but grasslands. The smell in the air was that of dust mixed with sweat, a testament to the hard work it took to live on the frontier. The few people she saw looked exhausted, including the horses as well. The difficulty of life was evident, but there was also an element of excitement. In this town she also sensed a spirit of determination; people who chose to live here were building the lives they wanted for themselves. And that was why Sarah had come so far in the first place.

"Hello ... are you Sarah Conrad?" asked a man from behind her.

The first thing Sarah instinctively thought was, *how does he know who I am?* Then realization set in and she knew the voice must belong to Daniel. When she turned and saw him, she breathed a sigh of relief. He was a rugged-looking man, not overtly attractive, but not ugly; no doubt he was a few inches above average in height, wearing plain clothes, boots, and had a utilitarian look. He had an air of respectability that was immediately apparent, and perhaps also a sense of industriousness. His strong build seemed to corroborate this inclination. And he had stunning blue eyes that were kind and gentle, exuding honesty so she was put at ease.

"I am," she replied.

"I'm Daniel." He shook her hand awkwardly, clasping it in his large rough palm, so unlike her own small and soft hand. "I'm glad you made it here safely. I hope the trip wasn't too bad."

"It was wonderful," said Sarah, looking down at their interlaced hands until he released her abruptly. "I enjoyed seeing the country and things I've never looked upon before."

"I'm happy to hear that. Let me help you with your luggage. I know how big of a change all of this must be for you, and I don't want you to have any extra burdens to weigh you down."

It was a double entendre, and Sarah found it amusing and was glad to know Daniel had a sense of humor. She smiled slightly and relaxed further. It would take a while for her to become completely at ease around him, but this was a good start.

"I must say that I am happy to finally be here, as nice as it was to see the country," said Sarah. She was nervous and tried to make small talk, maybe to let him know that she approved of him so far.

"I'm glad you are here too," replied Daniel. He looked nervous. "It's not too far to my place from here." He kept pausing, creating awkward silences. His nerves seemed to belie his strong outward appearance. In another way, however, Sarah found it endearing, for she felt instinctively that he was a gentle man. After a little more awkward conversation, he put her luggage in a carriage, and they left for what she presumed was his house.

CHAPTER 4

ON CLOSER INSPECTION, SARAH NOTED THAT DANIEL WAS MORE ATTRACTIVE than she had initially thought. He was tall with high cheekbones. And those blue eyes continued to stand out. But it was more than just that. It was the way that he carried himself. She thought about how to define it (she enjoyed classifying things) but found it difficult, and reasoned that she would have to get to know him more to be able to tell fully what it was she liked about him so much.

Perhaps it was the fact that she was there on her own, with nobody else ... and needed someone to protect her.

"How was the trip?" asked Daniel, as they made their way to his house. Sarah could tell he wasn't sure if he was repeating questions. He was stiff, trying to act normal. As was she, in all likelihood.

"It was long, and there wasn't much to do other than read. But I quite like reading, so it ended up being a very enjoyable time."

"Well you should have told me you enjoyed reading." Daniel smiled and breathed in heavily, as if his whole body was relaxing. Sarah hadn't even realized that he was so tense.

"Why should I have told you?" she asked curiously, settling further back into the carriage seat and watching the bleak landscape out the window.

"Because I enjoy writing here and there. Nothing serious. And I do love to read myself. Nothing like getting lost in a book. Though I haven't had any time lately. More of a hobby I had when I was younger. Still, I try to write here and there when I can."

Sarah was very happy to have something to talk about and something to bond over so soon into their interaction. "What kinds of things do you write?"

He cleared his throat, seeming a little shy. "Mainly I try to write down my goals for the future, what I want my life to look like. Who I want to be. Sometimes I try to put it in story form. But I think that our lives our stories, so it's hard to make it up … at least that's what I find."

"That's an interesting perspective," admitted Sarah. She thought about her own life, and how it did appear to her as a story, how she'd grown up learning so many lessons from such a wonderful father, and how she was now here, being tested, seeing if those lessons would hold up.

"And what is it that you're aiming for?"

"Mainly I just want to be a good man," said Daniel. He looked towards the horizon, seemingly in deep reverie. "There is so much in this world, good and bad. I want to understand it, but I don't think that's my place. I aim just to be a good person … maybe that's all I can do."

Sarah thought she understood what he meant. To her surprise, part of her wanted to hold his hand or at least touch him somehow, perhaps reassure him that she already felt the beginning of a kinship with him, but she didn't think it would be proper. Not yet, when they were not wed. But at least they were able to have some kind of real connection. For a mail order bride, she assumed, anything would be better than nothing; friendship would be better than an ice-cold man. But love, she knew, could be elusive. Of course, Sarah hoped for true love, but she didn't want to get her hopes up too high. Right now, she just wanted to build some trust.

"So, tell me more about yourself?" suggested Sarah.

Daniel still looked almost looking wistfully towards the mountains. "Well, there's not much I want to say right now. I think we will get to know each other in time. I guess I'm coming off as somewhat reserved for now. I hope you can understand that."

Sarah nodded, disappointed as the feeling of connection immediately evaporated between them. She turned fully toward the window and they sat in silence the remainder of the way to his homestead.

It was nothing special, that was for sure. He lived in a sod house, something she knew of, but didn't know much about. It was a common house on the frontier, made primarily from grass, roots, and dirt found on the prairie. Wooden beams were used sparingly, probably to make the house sturdier. From the looks of it, Daniel's house was on the sturdier side, even though expensive lumber wasn't used all over the sod exterior. Sarah knew that on the frontier people had to make do with what they had, and she had an immediate respect for the innovation required.

He helped her down from the carriage, not seeing to notice the warmth that Sarah did when their hands touched again. "Tomorrow we will go into town and meet some of the town's people and see about gettin' married."

At least that's still going to happen, thought Sarah. The last thing she would want was to be sent back home packing. It could happen: there was never any guarantee for a mail order bride.

Inside Daniel's house, Sarah appraised it the best she could. It was small and clean, divided into a space for a kitchen, near a wood-burning stove, a sitting area with a rough table and two chairs that looked hand-carved, and a bedroom toward the back, behind a partition so she couldn't see clearly inside beyond a hint of a large bed. She wondered briefly where her place would be—surely they would not share a bed yet? The thought made her flush nervously.

It was all so different from what she knew that it was hard to assess, and all she could go by was the fact that it looked sturdy and orderly. The orderliness was what most stood out to her. Everything was in its place. This was a positive sign to Sarah, for it spoke of Daniel's character. The state of the house must be a manifestation of the state of his heart.

"Daniel," she said, smoothing her hands nervously over her dress, "Tell me what you are thinking about all of this. I know that you are reserved. But we are going to be getting married soon, and I still hardly know anything about you. Does that concern you?"

Daniel sighed, and they took a seat at the table. "You know, you are right. I am reserved, but I owe it to you to try and open up. I know how hard all of this might be for you. In fact, maybe this will make you feel better, but my friend James, he had a bride come all the way from Georgia, and it took her an entire year to get acclimated."

Sarah laughed on the inside, but didn't feel comfortable enough yet to do so audibly. "What do you mean by acclimated?"

"I mean that for a year she would just lie in bed most of the day and despair over her situation. It was like she was a fish out of water, always acting strange when they were in public. But after enough time passed, her new life sort of became her new normal and she adjusted. I tell you that so you don't think you have to adjust and feel comfortable right away. I don't expect you to. I am just hoping to provide you with a safe place and take care of you and maybe eventually you will feel at home."

Sarah wanted to somehow express her approval at what he had said. It was such a noble thing to say. She had been trying to make out what kind of a man he truly was, and now it seemed like she had good evidence to say that he was a truly good man. And what more could she ask for, besides a man with her best interests at heart?

"I could love a man like that," said Sarah quietly, deciding that honesty was best even if it made her blush slightly.

He also flushed and looked down at his rough hands. "Well ... I'm hoping. We are getting married after all. I wouldn't want to be in a loveless marriage."

"Oh?" She felt a flare of surprise—and hope. "You are also looking for love?"

"Why shouldn't I be?" Daniel looked back up at her and the intensity in his gaze left her heart fluttering.

"Well ... I don't know," said Sarah. "I thought that quite a few men sent for brides just for companionship. I guess I never wanted to get my hopes up too high."

"It's best to temper expectations," said Daniel, clearly understanding where she was coming from. "But I think that you also have to have a high aim for your life. If you don't aim for the best, then you will end up living a life you don't truly want."

Sarah nodded in agreement. "So how long have you lived in this house?"

Daniel seemed to like the question, and it put him in a more talkative mood. "For around four years now. I need to be here five to get the full title from the government. It's the Homestead Act of 1862. I'm sure you've heard of it."

"Of course."

"So I'm working hard to have it ready, to show improvement." He nodded at the walls. "I still need to insulate those more. I'll be using the newspapers you saw me carryin'."

So that's what those were for! "There is a lot of improvement already, I'm sure," Sarah complimented him and he appeared pleased.

"I agree," said Daniel. "But I can't rest on my laurels. Every day I must do as much work as I can."

"That is really commendable. Do you ever have time for pastimes outside of work?

"Mainly work." He got up and walked over to a shelf laden with an assortment of kitchen staples. "Like some coffee?" When Sarah nodded and he began to methodically prepare their drinks, he went on, "Like I said, I write here and there. Sometimes I get a chance to read. But it's mainly work in these parts."

They talked a bit more over coffee, getting along well, then Sarah asked him more about his past. Not just about how long he had lived here, but more personal questions concerning who he was and where he came from.

That killed any comfort they'd managed to establish between one another. "I don't want to reveal everything about who I am just yet," said Daniel bluntly. "I think the best way for this to work is we just live day to day together."

Sarah blinked in dismay. "Okay ..."

"I think it is time for bed," said Daniel, getting up and collecting their mugs. "I will sleep on the ground, and you can sleep in my bed as we are not married yet."

"That's kind of you," said Sarah, relieved, though saddened at the abrupt end to their conversation.

THAT NIGHT, AS DANIEL SLUMBERED ON THE FLOOR BEYOND THE CURTAIN partition and she lay in his big comfortable bed, she thought through the past few days. She found Daniel to be a bit of an enigma so far. At times they got along well, and at other times there was a wall between them. But maybe he was right. Maybe the best thing for them to do would be to just live their lives together and after a while they would naturally learn to trust each other.

CHAPTER 5

"THIS IS THOMAS," SAID DANIEL AS HE INTRODUCED SARAH TO HIS FRIENDS. "And this is Tyler. He is the pastor in town and will be performing the ceremony." Both men were rugged looking, a theme in the town. Sarah figured that you had to be to survive. Even the pastor looked like he could survive in the wilderness on his own. That was oddly comforting. In such an unknown place, Sarah didn't want to be surrounded by weak men.

She observed the church they were in, and noticed its utilitarian design. There were, the odd parts that were embellished, such as the scrolled backs of the pews, signifying the creative spirit. But for the most part, everything in town, with the church being no exception, existed for function. Of course, that was because life was hard. But Sarah hoped she could add some more life. Indeed, she felt that was the specialty of women, and the idea of being useful in that capacity made her feel warm inside. She hoped to meet others that felt the same way, that wanted to add a feminine touch to the ruggedness of the town.

"Hello, dear, you must be Sarah," said an older woman, walking over. She had a sweet countenance and was slightly rotund, but with enough grace to easily compensate.

"I am indeed," replied Sarah.

"My name is Susan. I'm basically the town mother." She motioned for the men that were present to leave, to give them a few minutes of private conversation. Daniel and the others obliged, stepping a fair distance away "My husband passed away over a decade ago," Susan explained, "and now it's just me out here. I try to build relationships with anyone new that comes into town. That way they have a starting point, a place to build their foundation. I know how hard it can be with a new man." The presence she had about her was indeed what one would expect from a mother. She was tender with her words and movements, both soothing Sarah's soul and easing the natural tension that had built up from being so far from home.

"Things seem like they are going well so far," said Sarah. She thought that was honest—it was as good as she could hope for so far. But that didn't mean there weren't plenty of doubts. How could there not be? She didn't know almost anything about Daniel, and he wouldn't reveal much about himself.

"I am glad to hear that," said Susan. "I just wanted to reassure you that Daniel is a really great man of God. He comes to church every single Sunday and is very involved. Is your faith important to you?"

Sarah looked slightly confused. "Yes ... but why do you ask?"

The motherly woman touched her arm earnestly. "Because that is the most important thing to know about a person. Especially out here."

"What is so different about life out here?"

"It's a hard life," Susan warned, "and you must have faith to make it through."

Sarah nodded, thinking deeply, and wondering what she had gotten herself into. "Well, I made a commitment to come here and marry Daniel, and that is what I am going to do. I believe that we are nothing without our commitments."

"I couldn't agree more," agreed Susan. "Remember what I said. He is a good man. You have to remember that when life gets tough ... and it will."

"I will do my best," said Sarah, truly meaning it. "Daniel has talked about how he tries to live for God, and it touched my heart. I just want him to open up more about his life and his faith."

"He will," said Susan. "You have never been married before, have you?"

Sarah shook her head.

"I bet you have lived a sheltered life."

"I guess so. But my pa was sick and died not long ago. But other than that, I've basically taken care of him and just helped around the house."

"I'm sorry about your pa," said Susan. "You are so young. And you haven't gone through enough life yet to truly understand relationships. I want you to ask Daniel about his past relationships. I'm not sure if he will open up. But it's important that he does so you can understand where he is coming from."

"Thank you." Sarah pressed Susan's hand warmly and watched her bustle away.

Inside she felt warm and happy to know there was someone in the town that truly cared for her and wanted to get to know her—a kindred spirit. That was important, and as she thought more about what Susan said, she realized she'd had a good point. Sarah had never really been far from her house, never been seriously courted by a boy, and for the past few years, had spent all of her time taking care of her pa. With that kind of life, she didn't have much experience with getting to know new people and building new relationships.

Suddenly she felt scared. *What if I don't know how? What if the reason that I never built a lot of relationships back home was because I simply don't know how ... or am not cut out for it*. Sarah always tried to trust God, but there were times when self-doubt crept in and crippled her.

She went in search of Daniel, but couldn't find him. He had to be somewhere. Her insecurities were beginning to multiply. Being so far from her family was surely to blame, but Sarah was in no state of mind to think rationally. She started to think that he was trying to get away from her, wanting to spend time with his friends rather than with her. On the surface, this was irrational. But the difficulty of being on her own really started to weigh on her.

Sarah wondered why she was feeling the way she did, and realized it was more than just being scared of being on her own, being so far from home. It was a desire to be loved. And though she had never known true love in her life, with Daniel she felt some kind of possibility for it. And she hoped he felt the same way. She regained her composure and told herself, "I must believe this man is who he says he is."

CHAPTER 6

"SARAH, WHAT ARE YOU DOING?" ASKED DANIEL. AFTER BEING CHIDED BY Susan for not paying more attention to his fiancée he had felt guilty and gone in search of her. He had found her sitting on a bench outside the church, crying into her hands. The sight filled him with as much fear as it did worry. Fear that she was unhappy at the vows they were going to exchange. And worry that she might be having regrets already at having joined him out west.

"It's not your fault," she said with a soft voice, barely looking up, and Daniel hesitantly sat down beside her. He was glad when she didn't draw away. "It's just being out here on my own, away from my family. It's a lot to handle. I just felt alone. I know I shouldn't put this on you. You were just visiting with your friend."

Awkwardly, Daniel touched her elbow. When she looked up at him with tear-filled eyes, his heart turned over. She was beautiful. And also soft and warm in ways he had not been for so long since his first wife's death. Somehow he had to reach inside to give his bride-to-be something more than he even knew he had within him.

"I was just talking to some of the men about the storm that's coming through," he explained. "It's a serious matter. I wasn't trying to evade you. And don't worry about being a bit ... emotional." He coughed and finally thought to offer her his hanky to wipe her cheeks.

"Thank you," she mumbled, dabbing at her face.

He controlled the urge to draw her into his arms. After all, they were not yet wed. And also, he ... just wasn't ready yet, however lovely Sarah was, truly. "Remember how I told you it can take a while to adjust. You are doing just fine. We both are. We are in this together."

"I know," said Sarah, seeming to gather herself quite quickly, which impressed Daniel. She was genuine, rather than hysterically seeking attention. "But I just got to thinking about how we don't really know anything about each other ... and I don't even know what it's like to be married. Do you?"

The question caught him by surprise. "Do I what?"

"Do you know what it's like to be married?"

Daniel wanted to be able to comfort Sarah. But at the same time, he didn't want to talk about his former life. That part of him was history; it didn't matter anymore. But he knew that if he was honest with himself, he spent much of his private time thinking about his first love, Amy. She had been full of optimism and cheer, always spurring him on to good works and to be a better man. Since she'd passed away, life had changed dramatically. But he wanted to move on ... he had to move on.

"I have been married," admitted Daniel finally. "But it's not something I want to talk about."

"Why? Do you still love her?" asked Sarah.

He was relieved that she didn't start to cry again. She did seem very honest, rather than attention seeking. It was only normal that she had questions. "No ... it's not like that at all. I mean, it was a good marriage. But in life you have to move on ... you have to be able to forget the past and forge forward. Do you understand what I mean?"

Sarah's features softened. "Yes ... I too came here because I had to let go of the past ..."

Compassion filled Daniel's eyes and with it another edge of guilt as he realized he had neglected to learn almost anything about his new bride. "What happened? You can tell me anything, Sarah." Cautiously, he rested his hand over her knee. "That's why I sent for you, so we can be stronger together."

She looked at his hand for a long moment before gently, carefully covering it with her own. The tender touch eased an ache in Daniel's chest that had been present so long, it had come to feel as normal as breathing.

"My father passed away, not long before I applied to be a bride. It was one of the most difficult things that ever happened to me. I truly loved him unconditionally, truly believe that he shaped my life in every way possible, and that I am here because of him. And yet ... I have to live now without him. How is that even possible?"

"I know what you mean," said Daniel, getting to his feet with his hand still in hers. It felt right, somehow. "Come, let's take a walk together." They walked down Main Street and up a hill, both wanting to get away from town. They had such a difficult task ahead of them, and only Daniel knew the full measure of it.

"It really is pleasant out here," said Sarah. Daniel looked to the sky, agreeing with her words, but also noticing the horizon and the ominous signs of a storm coming their way. The consensus in town was to be extra prepared. Could be a light rain, or could be a twister, and there was no way to know.

"Are you okay?" asked Sarah, clearly wondering why Daniel was being silent once more.

"It's just that ..." he fumbled, realizing that his long silences would need to lessen or at least be explained from here on out. "I don't know ... just thinking."

"You can tell me anything," said Sarah. "Remember, that's why I'm here, so we can be stronger together."

"As good as that sounds, it's just hard for me to believe," he admitted. "I know that I need to lead by example, and so I will. But it's going to take time."

"You told me about your first wife," said Sarah. "That takes a lot of courage. We need to be one hundred percent honest with each other. Can we do that?"

Daniel nodded and they stood beside one another watching the sunset together before going back home.

CHAPTER 7

"Sarah, we are going to figure this thing out together," said Daniel.

Sarah looked over at him. He'd gotten quiet again during the carriage ride. "What do you mean?"

"Everything. How we are going to be together. What kind of life we will have. What we are going to do to get through this storm. It's hard, but all we have to know right now is that we are both in it together."

"I like the sound of that." She nodded. "I can get emotional ... I guess women often are. Men don't understand, of course."

Daniel laughed and she found she liked the deep, rumbling sound as much as the realization that he was relaxing slightly. "Oh ... well I can be stubborn and reserved. Sometimes I don't want to talk to anyone. We all have our foibles. That's the point. We can't let that get in the way."

"We can be a team," Sarah agreed. "I like that."

Daniel seemed to be in a great mood for the first part of the ride home, talking freely. Then as they got closer to home, he started to get quiet yet again, keeping to himself, so Sarah felt distance between them, rather than a comfortable silence. It wasn't that she wanted him to talk constantly. She was just confused about how they could feel completely united one second and then the next it would feel like they were strangers.

She wondered if it was all in her head, however. Maybe that's just what marriage was like. Or not even marriage (since that wouldn't be for a few days) but just any kind of real relationship. But she was resolved to depend on God for her happiness, and not on Daniel. She remembered her father talking about that; how if you depended only on your spouse, they would always let you down.

That was turning out to be harder to put into practice than she had thought.

"Daniel ... thanks for a really nice evening," she said hesitantly.

Daniel looked over at her and smiled slightly, then turned his head back to the road.

Sarah reached her arm over towards Daniel, tentatively, and then lowered her arm again. She wanted to express affection, to be feminine, but it was hard for her, and she was nervous. So she let her words do the work. "I ... think you're going to be a really good husband."

He looked back at her, confusion written visibly on his face, so much so that she was dismayed. "Why are you saying all of this right now?"

"Because I want to be a good wife for you and to support you." But she never knew how to act around men. It hadn't been part of her upbringing, so she was clumsy and awkward, saying and doing all the wrong things. Sarah respected Daniel, and she was attracted to him, but she didn't know how to let him know how she felt.

"You need to just let it grow on its own." His tone had turned terse and perhaps a little impatient. "We spent the evening together. That was really nice. But I don't think I can emphasize enough how much hard work it is going to take living out here. Tonight we are going to have to do nothing but work on the house. There is a storm that could come tonight. I want to be prepared for it."

His words, though undoubtedly not couched with ill intent, still stung. Sarah wished with all of her might that she could comfort Daniel in his worry about the storm, but he seemed uninterested. She secretly began to wonder if he was everything that Susan had said he was.

When they got home, they worked on the house. Daniel put wood over the sod where he could, and newspaper in the other areas. Every inch was as clean as possible. He gruffly explained to Sarah that if it rained very hard, the water that got inside would bring a lot of vermin to scurry around. This could lead to infections. While he worked, Daniel had Sarah organize the kitchen, making sure that anything with a bowl was available to catch the water that would surely drip from the roof. She got buckets ready, soup cans ready, anything she could.

"You have done a good job making sure the house is sound," said Sarah, as she swept the floor around where she had organized. "I am impressed."

"Thanks," said Daniel, as he hammered cloth over some sod. "No need to be. Just my job." He didn't look like he truly believed her compliment. From what Sarah could tell, he had spent a great deal of time on the house, making sure that it was sturdy, that the roof wouldn't leak—or would leak as little as possible—and that the sod was sealed. In fact, she swore that their house was in better condition than a lot of the houses back in Virginia, and those were made of wood. But why wouldn't Daniel accept that she was proud of him?

"Well, I think we've done everything we can." He dusted his hands off and finally stopped moving around restlessly. "Now it is in God's hands."

"Tell me about your faith in God," said Sarah, taking the opportunity to learn something else about him. "I trust him in every situation. But sometimes my faith is weak."

He spoke slowly but very steadily. "I believe God puts us in difficult situations to test our faith."

It felt awkward to just be standing there, doing nothing, so Sarah looked around for something to do, something out of place, or anything at all to clean. But the hose was above reproach in its cleanliness. "I think you are right. Being tested is hard sometimes."

"Of course. And I believe we are supposed to do everything in our power to be prepared, and then trust in God. That is what the parable of building your house upon a rock is all about. It's not just about the afterlife. It's about the here and now. God doesn't want us to be ignorant of the world. But rather, he wants us to be able to prosper, and the Bible tells us how to go about it."

"I like how you lay that out," said Sarah. "You have definitely been tested. And I can tell it has refined you."

Daniel seemed to appreciate this compliment, at least. He shuffled his feet and flushed a little, but didn't bat it away.

"You are a hard worker as well," she pressed on clumsily, wanting badly for him to know that she admired him.

The tension in his shoulders sagged suddenly and he raked his fingers through his hair. "Sarah ... I really appreciate your support," he said quietly." I'm sorry that I have been acting the way I have. It's just that there are so many things going on in my life. So many memories. And I've been single for a while now. I'm not used to all of this."

Taking a chance, Sarah walked over and grabbed Daniel's hand, pressing it firmly. "I'm not used to this either."

He looked away and when he looked back, there was a glimmer of ... something in his eyes. "I have to admit, you are really opening my eyes to a lot of things about life. It feels good to have your hand in mine. It's a closeness that I haven't felt in years; I imagined that I would never feel it again. Maybe you are more than just a companion. I don't know if I dare say more ..." He paused in mid-sentence.

Sarah looked at him. She was young and scared, so far from home for the first time. But she hoped in him. It wasn't trust yet, and definitely not love. But she knew that she could hope in him. "I'm giving us the best shot I know how," she said honestly. "And I know that I am going to overreact a lot. I know that I will get scared and mad sometimes ... mostly scared. Right now, I don't feel scared, though. And right now, I love holding your hand."

The rain began to fall on the house, interrupting their moment. It started off gradually, but then fell harder and harder, louder and louder.

"This is what has me worried," said Daniel, closing off again and dropping her hand.

"What?"

"I don't want to talk about it now … I just want to get through this."

"You can't close yourself off," she protested. "Now you're scaring me. Is this supposed to be a huge storm? Should I be worried?"

"No. It's fine."

But Sarah didn't believe him. Now, just as had happened many times before, she felt a distance between them. The rain was heavy on the roof, and water started to drip. They both started placing buckets around the house to make sure there wasn't any extra damage. The leaks grew bigger, but manageable. Sarah looked over at Daniel, and he was just standing in the middle of the house, frozen.

"What's the matter?"

"If we get through this, Sarah," said Daniel, and there was a new urgency in his tone, "I will tell you everything."

CHAPTER 8

THE RAIN CONTINUED DAY AND NIGHT. AS DANIEL AND SARAH SPENT TIME together just doing daily things, finding a gradual rhythm to their togetherness, things grew less strained, though Daniel never relaxed fully. Sarah could see how tense he was every time the rain picked up and wondered what it was that unnerved him so. But she didn't press, choosing instead to bring him a cup of coffee or touch his shoulder quietly in passing. And in turn, he seemed to be able to breathe just a little more easily.

The storm kept going for so long that Sunday came and it was still raining. Fortunately, as if by divine providence from God, the rain was light enough in the morning that the church service was able to take place. There were only a few in the congregation, and they served as the only witnesses to Daniel and Sarah's wedding. They'd thought about postponing the marriage, but Sarah enthusiastically told Daniel she wanted to get married no matter what, even if the pastor had to come to their house to do the wedding. There was something about the security of knowing they would be bound together.

The wedding was small, as expected, but still beautiful, with the purity of the vows being what Sarah treasured most of all.

"That was beautiful," said Susan, walking over after they were swiftly and simply wed. "I'm so happy for you two."

Daniel stepped away, allowing them privacy, and Sarah looked down at her wedding gown, white, though without much embellishment. Daniel wore almost the same thing he always did, though this time it was cleaner looking. Sarah thought it was at least an attempt to look good for the wedding, and maybe it was his idea of a suit. But she didn't care. She understood that it was the character of the person you were with that mattered, not the style of the wedding. This was especially true in the frontier

"Thank you." She looked around, letting it sink in that she was now forever bound to another person. "What do you think about all of this rain we are having?"

"Well ... it's not normal," admitted Susan. "Normally it's very dry here. I think it's unheard of for it to rain for days on end. It can easily lead to flooding. That's why it's surprising anyone came to the service at all. But thank God they did!"

"I am glad people came," Sarah agreed. "But that never mattered to me. I have gotten to know Daniel somewhat by now, and he is all I care about. Though he is acting strange, which has me slightly concerned." She looked over at him, and he was now talking to the pastor. She trusted him and knew that he would do anything to protect her, that surely he was trying to figure out the severity of the storm. But Sarah couldn't help but feel uneasy.

"Well, he has reason to," Susan replied bluntly.

"What?" Sarah's head jerked back toward her friend. "What do you mean?"

Susan shook her head. "It shouldn't be me that tells you. It's something you must learn from Daniel."

Sarah didn't like the sound of that at all. Her mind went through a million different possibilities, none of them good. Finally, she asked, "How is your place holding up with all the rain?"

"Well, to be honest, I live on the part of town closest to the river. And it's frightening. I have seen the water rising," Susan told her. "Living alone makes it harder. But I pray to God that everything will be okay. I have a lot of faith. I think that you have to have a lot of faith when you are a widow."

"I believe you," said Sarah. She hugged Susan and Susan returned the hug with enthusiasm. They went to a reception area that had a few things to eat and have some coffee while Daniel was still in conversation with the pastor.

"You are a really great soul, Susan," Sarah said warmly. "I appreciate you wanting to get to know me when I felt so alone that first day. And I want to make sure that you know you can come to me too."

"Thank you," said Susan, as she sipped on some coffee. It was necessary in the cold, damp environment. "Not many people care about an old widow. I just want to follow God and be a blessing in other people's lives. I think that is what I was called to do in this world. You know? If think you think about yourself too much, you will become bitter."

Sarah thought about what she said and wondered if she agreed. "But don't you think we need to look after our own interests? To see that we are treated right and that we don't get the short end of the stick?"

"Well, I'm not saying we need to be dumb," Susan replied. "The Bible calls us to be wise as serpents but innocent as doves. What I'm saying is that when we look out for others, God blesses us and it enriches our lives and the lives of others. People that only think about themselves get caught up in the most trivial things. They never forget the past, never forgive themselves, and their mind is relentless in thinking pointless thoughts. I should know. I live alone with all day to think about my lot in life. But I can't let myself do that. I must get out of the house and help others."

Sarah found a whole new appreciation for Susan, and gave her another, even tighter hug. "You are an amazing woman. Any advice for me?"

"Always be in prayer."

That was all Susan said, and Sarah thought that it was all she would ever say. "Thank you so much again." She looked over at Daniel. They had only known each other a few days, but she could read his look well enough to know that he wanted to leave. "I have to get home with my husband."

"You do," said Susan. She smiled and waved goodbye.

CHAPTER 9

"I do believe that God is smiling on us," Sarah said to her husband as they were leaving.

Daniel looked over at her, his face somewhat obscured by the suddenly renewed rain. "Why's that?"

"Because the rain lightened up just long enough for us to get married."

"That is true." He smiled. "And it was a lovely wedding. Sarah, I'm glad to have you as my wife."

She reached for his hand, and this time there was no awkwardness between them. "I'm glad to have you as my husband." Now they were man and wife, and they had built up some hard-earned trust. They still weren't exactly where she wanted to be in terms of their relationship, but it was going in the right direction.

"I'm glad we got married," said Daniel. "Tonight is supposed to be the worst night of the storm. And I want to be a protector for you, not someone who makes you nervous."

She frowned. "What do you mean nervous?"

"I mean that I've had a lot of trepidation about the weather, and isn't good for either of us. I want to make sure that tonight we are only concerned with our new love."

"Love?" Sarah felt warmth all the way to her toes.

"Well ... it will grow into that."

She looked up into his eyes as they made their way home and saw a man whom she cared deeply for. She could work on building love with this man.

"It's really coming down," said Sarah. The rain was pouring harder than it had in the past few days since they'd been wed. All the buckets and pans and bowls they had were put in the appropriate places to catch all of the leaking water.

"Yes ... but God will see us through. And besides, we have each other," said Daniel. "You know, I'm really starting to believe in us."

"What do you mean?" She finished mopping up a particularly large puddle and dropped the cloth in a bucket, wiping her hands on her skirts.

"Well ... it's just that having a true relationship built on trust is not common. Most of the time it is built on convenience; maybe the man can provide a place to live and the woman can provide some companionship. But when you have someone that really supports you no matter what ... that's what makes life worthwhile."

He had grown more open since their wedding, though part of that wall still remained and they had not ... fully become man and wife yet.

Sarah smiled and walked over to him. "I have been waiting for you to say something like that." She looked up at him and then moved her face close to his, peering into his eyes. She could see in him a strength that was far behind any physical ability. It was a kind of internal fortitude, the kind that can only be grown through trial and tribulation. Sarah started to breathe heavier, her heart pounding.

"You are the most beautiful girl in the world," said Daniel. "Maybe I should have said that earlier. But I wanted to wait until after we were married; until after I knew that we would be together forever. You see, that is what is important to me, the commitment, not just the feelings."

Sarah moved her lips close to his, hesitantly, but with the confidence that it was right. Daniel retreated and her heart sank like a stone. Her dismay surely registered on her face.

"I'm sorry." Daniel shook his head and awkwardly brushed his fingers over her hair. "All of this rain ... this weather. It has got me really thinking a lot lately. That's why I've been acting strange. I know I told you I would tell you all about it once we got through it. But I can't wait any longer. I have to tell you now." Daniel was now visibly distressed, but Sarah could tell that her presence offered him comfort. That comforted her.

"You can tell me anything." She took his hand. "I'm here for you no matter what."

"It's just a lot to tell you." His fingers tightened on hers. "But I think it is appropriate. You are my wife and I don't want to hide anything from you. That is not a good precedent to set."

"I know you are honorable," said Sarah, as she moved her thumb against Daniel's hand, trying to reassure him the best way she knew how.

"The reason that I have been acting the way I have been is that my wife—" he stumbled over the word and tried again, "My first wife, Amy, she died of an infection that she got during a period of bad weather. It was cold and damp, right in the middle of winter, and she caught something, I'm not sure what, and passed away." There was such anguish on his face that Sarah didn't dare interrupt, not even to offer words of comfort.

"I have never been able to forgive myself for it," he rasped. "And since then, I have done little but make sure that this house is ready for another storm. I want it to be able to withstand anything Mother Nature can throw at it. Then when I knew you were coming out here, I worried about it. I want this place to be safe for you, a sanctuary away from the cold of the outside world."

Daniel was now pacing the room. No longer holding his hand, Sarah felt like he was distancing himself again.

"You don't have to blame yourself anymore," said Sarah. She wished he would just believe her. Believe that she was there for him no matter what. But she sensed that he felt he had something to prove. "It wasn't your fault. You did the best thing that you could to keep her safe. The frontier is a difficult place. Tragedies happen. People are lost. And you are doing an amazing job in keeping me safe. I feel it, not just in the house, but in you. When I look at you, I know that you care for me."

"And I know that you care for me too," said Daniel. Suddenly the rain started falling even harder, and they could hear water rushing outside. "Fortunately, we're at a slightly higher elevation than the rest of town, so we don't have to worry about severe flooding."

His words triggered an abrupt, horrified realization. "Susan!" exclaimed Sarah.

"What do you mean?"

"She lives close to the river, all by herself. We have to help her!" Sarah rushed for her coat.

"No." Daniel walked over. "I have to help her. You wait here, and I'll see to it that she is safe. If there are flood waters, you shouldn't be subject to them." Obviously seeing the argument in Sarah's eyes, he took both her hands and pressed them hard. "I cannot lose you too, Sarah. You must let me do this."

The thought of losing him made her almost physically ill. "Be careful," said Sarah, looking up intently into his eyes. "You must come back to me, Daniel. You are all that I have out here. And ... I care about you deeply."

"I promise I will come back." Leaning down, he touched his lips very gently to her cheek. "I have done nothing but prepare myself for a moment like this. And, Sarah, I also care about you very much."

CHAPTER 10

As Daniel prepared to go after Susan, he looked at his Sarah. She was so good to him, better than he could have ever imagined his mail order bride would be, and he wanted to give her the world. He resolved to do what he could and to show her finally that he was leaving Amy behind.

Finished with buttoning his coat, Daniel drew his wife into his arms for the first time. As she looked up at him trustingly, he put his hand behind Sarah's head and pressed his lips against hers. He hadn't planned it, but he felt compelled to kiss her and the tenderness between them told him yet again that this was right, as did the way she instinctively leaned in and sighed just a little, quietly happy. Sarah meant more to him in that moment than he could put into words. As he rode off to make sure Susan was all right, he turned the right words over in his mind so later he could express his heart.

Sarah waved goodbye with tears in her eyes. Daniel left with tears in his. His heart ached with love for Sarah. But he was a man of duty and discipline. That always came first in his life, before any kind of emotional experience. He had learned what it meant to be a man in life from his father first, and then through experience. He knew that what a woman needed most was courage. The sweet kisses, the kind words, those could come later, after she was protected. For if there was no courage, no fortitude of will, then any amount of kindness was worthless, the empty deeds and words of a weakling. Even though Amy's death had not been Daniel's fault, it had made him question himself. He still wondered if he was weak, if he had done everything he could to be a protector of women and a steward of the strength God had given him.

There had never been an answer before to those questions. But those questions would be answered tonight. For now he was called into action again. Not by Susan or even by Sarah, but by his own conscience. For it bore witness to him and commanded he obey it, that he be the man God created him to be.

He rode with determination through town. The mud was deep, and his horse only made progress with great difficulty. But an animal can sense the will of its master, and it knew Daniel's was iron strong. Soon the sound of the rushing river was clear and loud. Daniel looked around with keen eyes, making sure that nobody was in need of aid. He might be just a simple homesteader, but on this night he was more. He had to be. He came to Susan's house at last and found waters rushing all around it, roaring, bringing destruction.

Daniel looked again at the neighboring houses in town, wondering why nobody else was trying to do any good. He met eyes with a man, younger than himself, who looked despondent. Not because of fear for his own safety, but because he knew that he lacked the will to act.

That was what Daniel was equipped with: the will to act. He didn't need any special gear, just his person and his fortitude. Something within him let him know that Susan was in need of help. He didn't know what it was. He sent up a prayer to God, and went towards the house and the roaring waters. It was situated only a few hundred yards from the river, but because of the rain and the flood waters, the house had a few feet of water surging around and through it.

Daniel approached as close as he could before the water started to get deep, then he dismounted, nodding at the frightened young man to hold his horse as there was nowhere to tie it He scanned the area, searching for anything that would indicate Susan was there. After all, he knew she might be someplace else. Maybe in another person's home. But he was going with his gut. He believed she was still there and in need of rescue.

Lord, please guide me as I try to do your will.

Daniel waded into the water, and as soon as he did, he heard a cry from the house. It was weak and weary but blessedly still full of life. He battled through the rushing water, dodging piles of flotsam and debris as they surged downstream. When he finally got to the house, he was relieved that the door wasn't bolted and was easy to pull open, even though it stuck some because of the water-swollen wood

Setting foot in the small home, he immediately saw Susan stuck underneath a fallen beam in the kitchen with just her head sticking out the water.

"Daniel," she whispered, amazingly not appearing frightened or even surprised.

"Don't worry, I'm here for you." He sloshed over and knelt in the muddy water, feeling around the beam to determine how best to lift it without crushing her further.

"I knew you would come," said Susan. She seemed to be in peace, not given over to her fate, but accepting of whatever the Lord had in store for her.

Daniel didn't know why she would have thought that. But this was not a time to pick apart her motivations. "How long have you been like this?" When she didn't answer, he looked up and saw that she had sagged into unconsciousness, barely remaining above the water by propping her head on some storm debris.

Using another piece of wood as leverage, he lifted away the fallen beam that was on top of her and picked her up, wincing at how light the usually robust woman felt in his arms. She must have been trapped for several days, with no one thinking to help the old widow woman.

With Susan raised high in his arms, he waded through the rushing waters once more toward higher land. His adrenaline gave him strength, and his desire to see Sarah's smile steeled his will against fatigue. It kept him upright as the current fought to knock him to his knees.

CHAPTER 11

SARAH PRAYED WITHOUT CEASING FOR HER HUSBAND. HE WAS OUT IN THE MIDST of the storm, and it scared her to death. But she knew it was his duty, and that made her proud. For deep in her heart, she desired a man with strength and honor, not just a man that would take care of her, but one that would stand up for his duty.

She paced around the house, tidying up anything she could. She swept a bit in one corner and adjusted the position of a bucket in another. As much as she worked, her mind continued to race. She was consumed with love for her husband, remembering the strength of his embrace and tender kiss, and his safe return became the only thing she could focus on.

She continued to pray. It made her glad to know he was a selfless man. But that sentiment wasn't alone. For there was another part of Sarah that wanted her husband to be selfish, to stay indoors, to stay with her. If he did that, they would be safe, and they would live together, for a long time. *But what kind of a life would that be?* wondered Sarah. It would be a life of cowardice, she knew, ultimately. And she'd had the option of cowardice when she was back in Virginia. But she hadn't taken that option. She had decided to choose adventure, to choose to try and make her life the best it could be, fulfilling her promise to Pa.

And when she came to Nebraska, she'd also had a choice to be a coward, to not try and get closer to Daniel. He had been hard at first, but Sarah had been committed to trying to understand him. And that commitment has paid off. And so now definitely was not the time for cowardice. She resolved to remain bold in pursuing what was good, and believed that Daniel would soon return.

So far the Lord had sent her in the right direction, giving her no reason not to trust in him. But as time went on, she began to become nervous. It would take a heroic deed to make it through such a storm. And what if Susan wasn't even there?

Maybe she was just at a friend's house? Or maybe she was totally fine and without need of assistance ...

Suddenly the door opened and there stood her husband, drenched to the bone, looking completely exhausted. He carried Susan, who looked limp over Daniel's shoulder, pale, and near death.

"My heavens," exclaimed Sarah, feeling the rush of utter relief at seeing his beloved face all right and stronger than ever, along with dismay at her friend's weakened condition. "Put her here, quickly."

She guided Daniel to where she had prepared their bed for Susan, believing that he might be bringing her home just as he had. She hurried to strip Susan of her wet garments, wrapping her in heavy blankets instead, while Daniel boiled hot water that, when it was ready, Sarah would use to dress Susan's head wound.

She stepped back, feeling helpless now that there was nothing more she could do until the water heated. Daniel stepped behind the curtain and slid his arm around her waist. Even though he was soaking wet, Sarah leaned immediately into him. He bowed his head and kissed her hair, pulling her closer than they'd ever been previously.

"She'll be all right, Sarah," he murmured. "We'll take care of her. And as soon as the rain lets up enough, I'll find a doctor. But I have to ask you a question. How did you know that Susan was in trouble?"

She pressed her cheek to his wet jacket and closed her eyes, thanking God silently for his safe return. "It was something she said to me after we got married. How she lived close to the river and that it was scary. When it started to rain so hard, I got scared, and then I remembered her and I just got a feeling that something wasn't going right. Maybe it was just a prick in my conscience from the Lord. I don't know, but you have to act on your impulses."

"That you do," said Daniel, tipping her chin up and kissing her very gently before slipping away and returning with the kettle of hot water.

Sarah gently bathed Susan's head wound and bandaged it, fretting when her friend barely stirred. She stepped back, now with nothing else definitive to do, and Daniel came to her side again. He opened his arms and she walked into them tentatively at first, then all at once, feeling that he was the safest thing in the world.

"I worried so about you," she whispered, holding onto him tightly. "I don't know what I would have done without you."

"I worried about you too," said Daniel, smoothing the hair back from her face. "And that is why I had to go save Susan, beyond just neighborly Christian concern. I had to show you that I am capable of protecting you. I had to redeem myself. You deserve to be with a man that can stand tall in his community and be a protector of the weak."

Boldly, Sarah laced her fingers behind her neck and kissed him. "I can't believe I'm married to you." She had gone from being physically attracted to him, to being intrigued by his character and his dreams, to respecting him, and now, to loving him.

"I can't believe it either," said Daniel, murmured into her lips. "You make me more than I could otherwise be. And for that I love you."

"I love you too," she whispered.

They kissed and kissed, Daniel's soaked clothes dripping all over Sarah. She didn't care. They continued to kiss until a coughing sound drew them abruptly apart and Sarah rushed to Susan's side as the older woman struggled to sit up.

"Stop, stop. You'll injure yourself." She eased Susan back down.

"What happened?" asked Susan, clearly confused.

"You were trapped in your house, in the middle of the flood," explained Daniel. "I came and rescued you."

"Now I remember. I remember I knew you would come." Susan looked over at Sarah, her words broken by deep, worrisome cough. "I told you he was a good man."

"He is," Sarah agreed. "Good man, put the kettle on again, please, this time for tea. Susan needs something to warm her from the inside."

And with a smile, her good man did just as he was bid.

CHAPTER 12

After the worst of the rain stopped (it lasted a total of six days), the town slowly started to return to normal. A doctor that Daniel located was able to treat Susan and she was able to go to a neighbor's house after a few days, one with two beds, so Daniel and Susan didn't have to huddle on the wet floor beside the fireplace.

Sarah checked on her friend every few days and smiled every time neighbors praised her brave husband.

Daniel, who had been respected before for being a hard worker, was now praised for being brave, for saving Susan's life, but also for being the most prepared for the rain and the floods. There were many repairs that needed to be done to the houses after the storm, and Daniel was hired to do the most expensive and most difficult repairs. It took him away from some of the stuff he needed to do on the farm, but with the extra money he was earning, he could hire others to do that work.

Life was indeed good for Daniel and Sarah Murphy, both in their finances and in their new relationship as devoted, full husband and wife, sharing one bed and one heart. Before long they would surely be able to prove up their land to the government and got full title.

"Can you believe all this?" asked Sarah one day, a few weeks after the flood.

"What do you mean?" replied Daniel. He was busy making his schedule for the next few days. He had a lot of repairs to make and meetings to go to. And as a humble man, he didn't think much of it.

"Just what has happened since I got here. You are so well respected here now, you might as well be mayor. It's like I'm married to a totally different person. Not that you weren't respected before—"

"Now, don't start talking like that," Daniel interrupted with amusement. "I told you that I write down my goals and values. I value doing what is right at all times no matter what, wherever it leads. This time it happened to lead to me gaining a certain level of prestige in the community. But there could be another time where doing what is right would lead to us being publicly mocked. Would you stay with me then?"

"Of course," said Sarah firmly. "As long as you are living out your convictions, I will always be proud of you."

"I know you would," said Daniel. "And that's one of the many reasons that I love you so much."

"What are some of the others?" she teased, walking over to the table and leaning down for a slow kiss.

"Well, you are beautiful, that's obvious." His long fingers played tenderly through her hair. "Another one is that you are supportive. I really appreciate that about you; that's probably my favorite thing. I know that no matter what trial I face, you are going to be there with me through the end."

"I can promise you that I will," said Sarah.

And Daniel smiled and kissed her again, whispering, "As will I, wife. As will I."

EPILOGUE

"You were conceived during the harshest storm in memory," said Sarah softly to her baby. "If it were not for a man as strong as your father, this house would not have been enough to keep it at bay. But it was, and now you are here."

Tears fell liberally from Sarah's eyes. Her baby boy, less than a year old, was beautiful, with the same blue eyes that her and Daniel had. How could God have known that she loved blue eyes so much? It wasn't that she wouldn't have loved a man if he didn't have blue eyes ... but she loved Daniel's so much, she could hardly put it into words.

They were trustworthy and kind and always honest. That was the main thing, honesty. Sarah knew that whatever he said, he was going to do. He didn't mess around when it came to his word.

And so, when he had promised that her mother could come and stay with them, she had believed him wholeheartedly. This was the day she was to arrive, and Sarah waited in anxious anticipation, as Daniel had gone to pick her up so Sarah could stay home with the baby, rather than packing their son up for the long ride to the train station.

The door opened suddenly and her mother came in. Ever tactful, Daniel took the baby and moved aside so the two women could embrace. Sarah ran to her mother with open arms and held her tight.

"It is amazing to see you," said her mother, teary eyed. She looked older than Sarah remembered. The stress of the separation had clearly weighed on her.

Sarah was crying too hard to properly answer. "Mother ... I have missed you so much."

"And I've missed you," Jane replied, sniffling. "And I felt guilty for the longest time."

"Why would you feel guilty?" asked Sarah, guiding her mother to the kitchen for something to drink. She was so excited to see her, she had almost forgotten to be a good host.

"I felt that I sent you out of the house, like I was telling you that you weren't good enough unless you were married," Jane explained, taking the mug of tea. "I imagined all the bad things that could happen to you. Seeing you here, happy, is the best gift I could ever have. You could never know how much this means to me, how much your heart burns to see your child happy."

"I am starting to learn," said Sarah, nodding at Daniel. He joined them and she took baby Luke. "Isn't he beautiful?"

"Yes," said Jane as she reached for the baby and cuddled her grandson close. "The eyes ... the life is always in the eyes." She held Luke in front of her and smiled, seeing the resemblance to his grandfather.

"And they are full of life," said Sarah. "Just as Daniel's are. They are full of a life affirming energy. I know that Luke will grow up to be a protector of the weak, someone that cares about those that can't care for themselves. That is what I want for him. I think that every wife should be able to say this: I want Luke to grow up to be just like his pa!"

The three of them ate together and enjoyed conversation and laughter. None of them could believe how much their lives had changed in the past few months. It showed Sarah how much God loved her and that he always had a plan for her life. She now could fully trust Him, for she had found joy, and she had found peace!

◌⁂◌

THANK YOU SO MUCH FOR READING MY BOOK. I SINCERELY HOPE YOU ENJOYED EVERY bit reading it. I had fun creating it and will surely create more.

Your positive reviews are very helpful to other reader, it only takes a few moments. They can be left at Amazon.

www.amazon.com/Katie-Wyatt/e/B011IN7AF0

◌⁂◌

WANT FREE BOOKS EVERY WEEK? WHO DOESN'T!

BECOME A PREFERRED READER AND WE'LL NOT ONLY SEND YOU FREE READS, BUT you'll also receive updates about new releases.

So you'll be among the first to dive into our latest new books, full of adventure, heartwarming romances, and characters so real they jump off the page.

It's absolutely free and you don't need to do anything at all to qualify except go to.

PREFERRED READ FREE READS

http:/katieWyattBooks.com/readersgroup

ABOUT THE AUTHOR

KATIE WYATT IS 25% AMERICAN SIOUX INDIAN. BORN AND RAISED IN Arizona, she has traveled and camped extensively through California, Arizona, Nevada, Mexico, and New Mexico. Looking at the incredible night sky and the giant Saguaro cacti, she has dreamed of what it would be like to live in the early pioneer times.

Spending time with a relative of the great Wyatt Earp, also named Wyatt Earp, Katie was mesmerized and inspired by the stories he told of bygone times. This historical interest in the old West became the inspiration for her Western romance novels.

Her books are a mixture of actual historical facts and events mixed with action and humor, challenges and adventures. The characters in Katie's clean romance novels draw from her own experiences and are so real that they almost jump off the pages. You feel like you're walking beside them through all the ups and downs of their lives. As the stories unfold, you'll find yourself both laughing and crying. The endings will never fail to leave you feeling warm inside.

DISAPPOINTED HEARTS

Mail Order Bride Western Romance

RoyceCardiff
Publishing House
WHOLESOME INSPIRATIONAL ROMANCE

Dear Reader,

It is our utmost pleasure and privilege to bring these wonderful stories to you. I am so very proud of our amazing team of writers and the delight they continually bring us all with their beautiful clean and wholesome tales of, faith, courage, and love.

What is a book's lone purpose if not to be read and enjoyed? Therefore, you, dear reader, are the key to fulfilling that purpose and unlocking the treasures that lie within the pages of this book.

৩২৩

NEWSLETTER SIGN UP PREFERRED READ

http://katieWyattBooks.com/readersgroup

৩২৩

THANK YOU FOR CHOOSING A INSPIRATIONAL READS BY ROYCE CARDIFF PUBLISHING HOUSE.

Welcome and Enjoy!

A PERSONAL WORD FROM KATIE

I LOVE WRITING ABOUT THE OLD WEST AND THE TRIALS, TRIBULATIONS, AND triumphs of the early pioneer women.

With strong fortitude and willpower, they took a big leap of faith believing in the promised land of the West. It was always not a bed of roses, however many found true love.

Most of the stories are based on some historical fact or personal conversations I've had with folks who knew something of that time. For example a relative of the Wyatt Earp's. I have spent much time out in the West camping hiking and carousing. I have spent countless hours gazing up at night thinking of how it must been back then.

Thank you for being a loyal reader.

Katie

CHAPTER 1

DISAPPOINTED HEARTS

"JAMES, PLEASE," MARGARET SAID. IT SEEMED TO BE HER MOST COMMONLY USED phrase.

James, please don't go out again.

James, please don't speak to me that way.

James, please can we just spend some time together?

James, please don't talk to her anymore.

This time, though, *James, please,* was far more urgent. Her husband of two years, whom she had married when she was just eighteen years old, whom she had promised to love with all her heart and dedicated herself to serving day in and day out, was turning her out of their house.

Except that it was his house, of course. She had no claim over anything that they had built together during their marriage. It was his banking salary that afforded them their upscale Boston home. It was his same salary that allowed them to purchase the high-end furniture they had, and all of her costly clothing. Margaret didn't care about any of that and she never had, but James liked a certain lifestyle.

Just the way he liked a certain kind of woman—a high-society, glamorous woman who he would be proud to have on his arm as he donned his top hat and walked about the town with his head held high.

Margaret didn't know how to be that woman. She was a simple girl at heart, plain in her ways, but her mother had always told her she had captivating eyes. Apparently, James was immune to their powers, because he was standing before her, in the foyer of their house, looking at her with utter disdain.

"Oh, stop saying 'please' all the time!" he snapped, his hands moving to his hips as he took a step closer to her. "I'm not opening this for discussion, Margaret. This is just the way things are."

"But we took vows!" Margaret protested, tears forming in her eyes. She desperately tried to keep them from sliding down her cheeks, not wanting to humiliate herself any further than James already had. "We promised before God and witnesses that we would love and be faithful to each other forever."

He sighed, rubbing his forehead as though her antics exhausted him. "We were young then."

"It was two years ago!"

"Enough!" James glowered at her, his patience clearly up. "I am still the man of this household, and I still have the power to make decisions. And my decision is that I am serving you with a script of divorce. You're not going to change my mind, Margaret."

The tears did spill down her cheeks now, fear and desperation overtaking her. Where would she go? What would she do? A single woman had no power, no options, and no hope for herself. He was throwing her out into the streets. "I've tried so hard to be good to you," she whispered. "Everything you've ever asked of me, I've done. I've kept the house, cooked, attended any function you wanted to go to. I've learned how to sew dresses in the fashion you like ... I've tried to be the woman you want."

He seemed to soften, walking to her and putting his hands on her shoulders. James looked down into her eyes and sighed, shaking his head as though they were both in this unfortunate situation together. "I know, Margaret. But you just don't have it in you. When we were younger, it might have been all right. But you never know what life will bring you, and it's brought me a great deal of success. I didn't plan for it, but here I am."

"And haven't I helped you achieve that success?" she asked, her voice cracking.

"Of course not." He seemed almost amused as he stepped back. "You don't have the head for these kinds of things. Emily is far more suited to my lifestyle, and we're in love, Margaret. There's nothing more to say. She's the woman I need."

Margaret wanted to continue arguing in the hopes that, somehow, she could make him see what he was doing, but all the wind went out of her sails when he said he was in love with Emily, one of the many glamorous Bostonian women he enjoyed spending time with when they were out on the town. So many nights, Margaret had suffered in shame while her husband had abandoned her at social engagements to flirt with other women who better lived up to his standards. Now she was cast out of his house, forever shamed.

She couldn't fight it any longer. She had no recourse if he wanted to put her away, and they both knew it. Her shoulders sagged and she stared at the floor. "What am I to do?"

James took her hand, and she felt him place something in her palm. When she looked up, it was a packet filled with bills.

"There," he said, as though he was being generous. "It's one hundred dollars. More than enough to make a new life for yourself. But it has to be somewhere else."

One hundred dollars was more money than she had ever dreamed of seeing, much less holding in her hand. She stared at it, not wanting to take it, given that it was a payment for her cooperation, but knowing that if she didn't take it, she would have nothing.

"Somewhere else," she repeated, testing the words out on her tongue. "Somewhere outside of Boston."

"Yes," James said quickly. "Absolutely. Anything else would be simply uncomfortable, don't you think?"

Lifting her head, Margaret mustered what little pride she had left and looked him in the eye. "I should hope that the wrong you've committed against me would make you uncomfortable, yes. This will not make you happy, James. The man I married two years ago has been lost, replaced by a man overly confident in his own ability and success. What you had in me was a true wife who would have supported you through anything and everything. When your success fades, as success always does, I hope your glamorous new wife will comfort you."

Without waiting for a response, Margaret walked out of the house. She didn't take anything with her, because none of what was in the house was hers—not in property and not in spirit. Nothing about her life with James was what she had wanted or chosen. If she was going to start over, she would do so with the clothing on her back and the money in her hand.

CHAPTER 2

A NEW BEGINNING

MARGARET SAT ON THE TRAIN, TRYING EVERYTHING SHE COULD NOT TO LOOK out the window or notice the landscape rushing by at twenty-two miles an hour—faster than she had ever gone in her life. Instead, she focused on the newspaper in her hands, flipping through the articles that mostly dealt with the House of Representatives' recent decision to award the presidential election to Republican candidate Rutherford B. Hayes over Democrat Samuel J. Tilden. Mary had no opinion on such things, but it occurred to her that James would be pleased. Hayes, apparently, had a better plan for the economy.

The thought of James threatened to trigger the motion sickness she had been dealing with through the entirety of the trip, so Margaret put aside the newspaper, instead retrieving out of her reticule the letter that she had already read so many times.

It was from her cousin, Jane, to whom Margaret had written the day after James had turned her out of the house. Jane had moved to the Arizona territory with her husband not long after the end of the Civil War—about ten years ago. She was the only family Margaret had left. An epidemic had taken Margaret's two younger siblings many years ago; her father had been killed in the Civil War; and her mother, whose constitution had always been weak, had died shortly after Margaret had married James. In a way, Margaret was glad that her family was not present to see what had become of her.

When she had written to Jane, she had only told her of her desire to move west, not providing her with any details. She would, of course, tell her older cousin about James' treatment and the destruction of their marriage, but she wanted to do so in person, after she and Jane had some time to reacquaint themselves. They had been close once, but distance had prevented their relationship from flourishing.

Margaret was eager to rekindle the relationship and desperately thankful for Jane's willingness to let her come out and stay with her family.

The train ride across the country had been long and arduous, and had taken up most of the one hundred dollars James had given her. She had only thirty dollars left to her name, no skills of any kind, and no idea what she would now do with her life. All she knew was that she didn't want to marry again. She had promised her heart, her loyalty, and her being to a man once, and he had abused all of it. In the West, it was more acceptable for a woman to be single, and she would somehow find a way to carve a life for herself there, independently.

The town of Tombstone appeared ahead of them, and Margaret, seeing the other passengers craning their necks to look, risked a glance out the window. The landscape was still rushing by at high speeds, and she quickly looked away again, pressing a hand to her stomach. She was only too grateful that the trip was nearly over and that soon she would be in the welcoming embrace of her only family.

It was with great relish that Margaret stepped off the train, feeling the firm, solid ground beneath her feet. She had almost no luggage, though she had purchased a small bag and some basic items during her stay at the Boston boardinghouse. Holding her small bag tightly, she looked around for Jane's familiar face, but almost didn't recognize her cousin when Jane finally walked up to her.

"Margaret?"

"Jane!" Margaret stared in surprise at the woman, who appeared much older than she had expected. Jane's once lovely face looked haggard and lined, her eyes dim and tired. Not far behind her, a crowd of five children huddled, their clothes ragged and their hair mussed. Trying not to react in her surprise, Margaret moved forward to hug Jane. "Cousin! I'm so glad to see you."

Jane just patted her back, offering her a tired smile. "Yer trip all right, then?"

The twang to Jane's voice was another surprise for Margaret, whose Northern, educated accent seemed suddenly out of place. "Ah, yes," she said, stretching the truth a bit. "It was fine. Thank you. Are these your children?"

"That's the lot of 'em," Jane said, waving a hand toward the group. "Hank, Harry, Hannah, Hope, and Harrison."

"Oh my."

"Yeah, it's a lot of 'em." Jane motioned for Margaret to walk with her. "Welcome to Tombstone, then. You and everyone else are comin' out here these days. Town struck silver not so long ago, and you'd think everyone had heard about it."

Margaret's eyes widened. "That must be exciting."

"A pain in the neck is what it is," Jane told her, shaking her head. "Miners comin' in every which way, lookin' to strike it rich."

"Where is Thomas?" Margaret asked, realizing that the children were scurrying along behind them but that Jane's husband was nowhere to be seen.

"Dead," Jane said, her voice respectfully sad but also matter-of-fact. "Two years now."

Margaret gasped, grabbing Jane's hand in hers. "Oh, Jane! That's terrible!"

Her cousin looked almost amused. "I almost forgot about those fancy Eastern ways. You have that nice accent, and I bet ya have some smellin' salts in yer bag."

Unsure as to whether she should be offended, Margaret dropped Jane's hand. "I suppose I stick out here."

"Sure and you do, dressed like that," Jane agreed. "Anyway, the kids and I are makin' do, but we don't have any room at the house, so I made arrangements for you."

Margaret felt a flicker of disappointment and anxiety, but she stifled the feeling, knowing that Jane had been through so much and didn't need to be burdened by Margaret's misfortune too. "Oh, certainly. I'm sure there's a boarding house around here that I can stay in?"

"No, nothin' like that," Jane said, waving a hand again. "Everythin's full, what with the miners. But I got you a better deal. Robert Preston just settled in town, and he was wantin' a bride from out east. You know how these western men do. They advertise, and some Eastern beauty comes travelin' west to keep 'em company. Well, since you were comin' anyway, I told him all about you, and he's agreed to marry you first thing."

CHAPTER 3

QUITE THE SHOCK

MARGARET COULD HARDLY CATCH HER BREATH, STANDING THERE IN THE unfamiliar, crowded, loud streets of Tombstone, Arizona. Jane was nothing like she had expected, and there was no place for her in Jane's home. There was no place for her anywhere in town except as the wife of one of the local ranchers.

Please, God, no. I can't go through this again. I can't marry him.

"Jane," Margaret managed. "There's been some mistake. I didn't come out here to get married."

"Well, yer not married anymore, are you?" Jane asked, crossing her arms. "You'd hardly be comin' out here alone if you were."

"I'm not," Margaret agreed, trying to steady herself. "But there's a reason for that, Jane. You can't just promise my hand in marriage! I don't even know Robert Preston. I'm not going to marry him. I can't."

Jane shrugged a shoulder, grabbing one of her kids by the arm to stop him from running off. "Well, I don't know what yer gonna do out here, then. This town is overrun right now and there's no good place for ya to stay. There's not a spare inch of room in my house, I'll tell ya that. And no money for the food. So if yer not gonna marry Robert, you'll have to find yer own way."

Margaret thought she might faint, and she actually swayed where she stood, the last few weeks of tragedy catching up to her all of a sudden. "Jane ..."

"Look, there he is now, ready to meet you." Jane gestured down the street toward a building that appeared to be the local church. Outside of it, a man waited, his hands shoved in his pockets, a wide-brimmed hat pulled down over his eyes, and broad shoulders that stood out even amongst a crowd of broad-shouldered men.

Margaret just stared at him from a distance, and beside her, Jane eventually sighed.

"Listen, Margaret. Somethin' bad must have happened to you. I figured that much out. But out here, there's no time or space to dwell on anythin'. You gotta keep goin' or you'll get yerself run right over. Marriage is how a woman protects herself out here, and Robert's a good man and a good catch. He'll do right by ya, and he'll keep a roof over yer head. I'm tellin' you, as family, that this is your future."

Somewhere deep inside, Margaret knew that there was a great deal of truth to what Jane said. A woman was always safer under the protective umbrella of a marriage, at least financially and physically, if not emotionally. It was the natural place for her, in a home with someone to care for. But Margaret was still reeling from the divorce script she had received from James, and she didn't know how to face another marriage.

God, this is not what I wanted. It's not what I'm looking for. Please help me. What am I supposed to do?

"He isn't gonna wait around, ya now," Jane added. "He's in the market fer a wife. If it's not you, he'll find someone else. Like I said, he's a catch."

God wasn't answering, and Margaret felt lost, lightheaded, and out of options. Somehow, she found her way over to the church. She was never exactly sure how. The man, Robert, her husband-to-be, said something. Barely registering his words, she somehow had a conversation with him, introducing herself and confirming what Jane had said—that she had come out west to marry.

And then they were in the church. The preacher stood before them, asking them to repeat promises to each other. They were promises that Margaret had already made, but to James. Promises that had been broken. Dissolved. Ruined. She had never imagined making such promises again, preferring loneliness to heartbreak, but there she was, promising to love and serve a man she didn't know, in a town she wasn't familiar with, surrounded by the only family she had, who were also complete strangers to her.

As soon as the preacher proclaimed that Robert and Margaret were man and wife, Margaret concluded the ceremony by slumping rather unceremoniously the floor, darkness washing over her even as she welcomed it.

CHAPTER 4

THE ROAD TO RECOVERY

MARGARET WALKED ALONG THE FENCE THAT FRAMED THE PROPERTY OF HER NEW home, her hand trailing along the wooden slats that were so foreign to her. There was so much brown in Arizona, large expanses of it that stretched further than she could see. She had never known that there could be so space in the world, with so little apparently in it. Boston had always been busy, crowded with buildings, factories, and people on every corner. Arizona couldn't have been more different, lacking anything that felt familiar to her.

It was one more adjustment to make to her new life, though it was a far easier one to accept than the situation she suddenly found herself in.

It had been two days since she had fainted right after promising herself to Robert Preston. He had been kind about it, admittedly. He seemed like a gentle person with a good heart, but so had James at the beginning. Robert had taken good care of her, insisting that she take some time to rest and recover from a long journey. She hoped that she had been pleasant in return, but her memories were blurry, hazy with distress.

God, would I have come out here if I had known? Would have I chosen this marriage? I don't think I would have. God, show me what I'm supposed to do here. How am I supposed to manage this?

"Margaret?"

For a brief moment, she wondered if it was God responding to her personally. She started, then turned, realizing that Robert had ridden up behind her on horseback and she hadn't even heard him, so lost was she in her own thoughts.

"Oh," she said, attempting a smile. "Hello."

"Hi there." His own smile was warm and nonjudgmental. "It's good to see you out and about. Yer feelin' better then?"

She nodded. "Yes. Thank you. I'm sorry that I've been so ... useless so far."

"Don't apologize," he told her, loosening the reins on the horse and sitting back on the animals bare back, relaxing. "Everyone reacts to change differently. I just hope you'll find the place to yer likin'."

"It's very different from where I came from," she said, touching the fence again. "Very."

"Suppose it would be," he agreed, looking off into the distance. "I'm glad I happened on ya, though. Yer gettin' a bit too close to the cattle herd. They don't always take kindly to strangers, ya see."

Her eyes widened. Jane had told her that he was a rancher, but she hadn't fully processed what that meant. The last thing she wanted was to stumble upon a herd of huge animals.

"I'll turn back," she said quickly, backing away toward the house that sat in the distance.

"No, no." He turned his horse, stopping her retreat. "Come on. I'll show ya."

He reached his hand down to her, smiling as though he expected her to take it and join him on the horse. Margaret recoiled, horrified at the thought.

"Oh no. I couldn't."

"Sure ya can. You can ride sidesaddle. Silver here is gentle at heart. He won't scare ya."

But the truth was that Silver was scaring her even just standing there. She had seen horses among the streets of Boston, but she had never ridden one. And those horses had seemed far more civilized than this wild horse in front of her now.

But Robert was holding his hand out, expecting her to join him. Margaret took his hand, letting him pull her up even as she realized that she had a terrible habit of going along with whatever anyone told her to do. *James must have taught me that.*

Suddenly upon the horse, Margaret could feel the tension in her body. But Robert was right behind her, his chest pressing up against her back and one of his arms encircling her waist. His presence, surprisingly, gave her enough of a sense of security that she could take a deep breath and shift into a more comfortable position, both of her legs draped over the horse's left side, her skirts arranged carefully.

"Not so bad?" Robert asked her.

"It's manageable," she agreed, trying to sound confident.

Then Silver began to walk and Margaret grabbed onto Robert's arm, holding on tightly as they picked their way over the rough terrain, heading further out to pasture. Just as she started to get comfortable with the walking pace, Silver picked up, seeming to trot along the ground.

Margaret closed her eyes, focusing on keeping her body in place, and then Robert's lips were right at her ear. "Look."

She cautiously peeked her eyes open, then openly stared at the herd of cattle that was in front of her at a distance. They were like nothing she had ever seen before. They stood in a group, meandering around, chewing at the grass, and occasionally shaking their large heads. Margaret watched them in fascination, her lips parting as she drank the whole scene in, the mountains that bordered the town setting the whole scene perfectly.

"Oh my," she finally murmured.

"You like it?"

"I do," she said, surprising herself. "I wouldn't want to be any closer, but yes, I do."

"It's all ours," Robert told her. "Yours now, too, since we're married."

She looked over her shoulder at him, not trusting his generous words. James had never made her feel like anything they had belonged to both of them. She had always been very clear that she lived in his world, and that she was privileged to do so. "Oh, not really," she protested. "It's yours. I mean, I just got here."

"But you're my wife." He smiled at her. "I haven't had a chance to tell you that I'm glad about that. The day you arrived, you seemed a little distracted. I wondered if you even really knew what was going on. Maybe I should have delayed the wedding, but there was part of me that wanted to snatch you up while you were still available."

Margaret blushed at his implied compliment and the notion that he might find her appealing. What would a man like him see in her? James had always made sure she knew exactly how plain she was, even though Margaret thought she had a nice smile and warm eyes. "I'm afraid I wasn't expecting a wedding," she admitted nervously.

"But Jane said ..."

"Jane didn't tell me she had arranged for me to be married." Margaret felt relief just in saying the words out loud. "I had no idea, until I met you."

Robert looked horrified, and he pulled back from her, seeming to shut down. "Why didn't you say anything?"

"I didn't know what to do," Margaret said, hating to hurt this nice man's feelings but desperate for someone to understand where she was coming from. "Jane was so different from what I expected, and she said she had no space for me in her home. I didn't want to be a burden, so I said I would stay in a boarding house, but she said they were all full. She said my only option was to marry, and so ... I did."

"The boarding houses are not full," Robert said stiffly. "The miners stay in encampments. Everyone knows that."

She stared at him, not sure how to read the change in his mood or how to deal with the fact that Jane had given her misinformation. "Perhaps Jane was confused."

"She would have known that." Robert swung down off the horse with no warning, then reached up and lifted her off as well, setting her on the ground. Suddenly formal, he tipped his hat to her. "Please accept my apologies, ma'am. It seems we've both been fooled. I won't hold ya to promises ya didn't mean."

Then, before she could respond, he was back on Silver, riding off into the distance much too quickly for her to protest or have a hope of catching up to him.

She had wanted to be honest, but now yet another husband was turning her away. Margaret bowed her head, putting her face in her hands as she let the tears flow.

God, where are you?

CHAPTER 5

ALL OVER AGAIN

WHEN ROBERT ARRIVED BACK AT THE HOUSE THAT EVENING, MARGARET WAS waiting for him, sitting stiffly in the kitchen with dinner on the small stove. When he walked in, she avoided his eyes, clearing her throat awkwardly.

"I had no way to get to town," she told him, her voice too formal. "I know you would prefer I was gone, but I'm sorry—you'll have to take me to town. I'll find my way from there."

"What will you do?"

His voice was soft again, almost gentle. Somehow that only made the situation worse. "I have not yet decided."

"Margaret ..." he walked over, sitting down with her at the table. "I was rash earlier. I got my pride up. Pride goeth before the fall, ya know. Well, I sometimes fall a lot. I didn't like the idea that I married a woman who didn't want me, but I don't want to let pride cause more troubles than we already have."

She dared a look up at him, unaccustomed to a man being so forthright. "I was too blunt in what I said."

"The truth can't always be softened," he told her, looking into her eyes. "I've been thinkin' all day, and I know that you didn't come out here with marriage in mind. But we did marry. Is there any part of you that thinks you could want this?"

Again, Margaret wanted to be honest with him, but she didn't know how to tell him what she was really feeling. Not without telling him about James. She just wasn't sure she was ready to confess her failed marriage and rejection to him yet, though. He was still a stranger.

"That's a long pause," he said, sighing and sitting back in the chair. "I'm not gonna force ya."

"I do want to try," she said quickly, surprising herself with the words. "I don't want to just walk away after making promises. It's just that I need to adjust mentally. I want to try."

The smile that lit up his face touched her scarred heart. "Then we'll try. There isn't any rush."

She studied him, trying to separate him from James in her mind. "You really want this, then? You want a wife. A wife ... like me."

"Would I have married ya otherwise?"

Margaret gave him a look. "Men sometimes think they know what they want, until life changes and they realize they want something completely different."

He nodded. "That can happen, sure. It's happened to me. See, I used to think I never would marry. Where I lived before, back in Oklahoma, I always had lots of family 'round me. But then I moved out here to get in on the ground floor of this town, get me some land of my own, and make a place for myself. Everythin' changed, and it turns out I got downright lonely. I realized how important it was to have someone with ya. Someone you can talk to. Care for. Support."

The words coming out of his mouth sounded good, but Margaret couldn't shake her skepticism. So she avoided replying directly. "How long ago did you move out here? You sound like you've always been here."

Chuckling, he shrugged a shoulder. "The western twang is easy to pick up. Give it a few years and you'll be talkin' like the rest of us. I haven't been here in Tombstone long at all. Just arrived last season, actually. Took over the ranch belongin' to a guy who realized all he really wanted to do was go be a doctor. But in Oklahoma, we talk this way too. So I've grown up with it. To tell the truth, you sound downright fancy, ma'am." He winked and tipped his hat to her.

It was hard not to smile, so Margaret gave in to the impulse. "I sound out of place, you mean."

"Nothin' wrong with bein' a little different," he promised her, sitting forward again. "I know you probably had reasons for movin' out here. Probably big ones, especially since you didn't even come out here to get married. You came out here all on your own, probably to start a new life fer yerself. You still can, Margaret. I'll be a part of it, but if this is a new beginnin' fer you, then you take it. And I'll support you."

"Why are you being so nice to me?" she asked, shaking her head. "You don't know me. You have no idea what my background is or what issues I might have. And since I've been here, I've barely spoken to you, fainted at our wedding, and spent most of the first two days in bed, ill."

"Hasn't anyone ever just been nice to ya because you're a person?"

She stared at him for a long moment before shaking her head. "Not ... really. Not just because I'm me. A lot of people tend to overlook me."

"Then there's somethin' wrong with a lot of people's eyes."

CHAPTER 6

RECONNECTING

Margaret gingerly sat down on the rickety chair that sat near the table in Jane's kitchen. The children were running around in the small yard outside, and Margaret could hear their shrieking through the walls. She wasn't entirely sure whether or not they were having fun, but Jane seemed content to let them do what they wanted to as long as they were outside.

"Here," Jane said, walking over with two tin mugs of weak coffee, one of which she handed to Margaret. "Have some."

Sipping the pale brown liquid, Margaret watched her cousin, finally, after several days in town, in a place where she could really focus on what had happened to Jane in the ten years that she had been in the West.

"Jane, are you all right?"

"'Course. Why do you ask?"

"Because you don't seem all right," Margaret said carefully. "Your husband passed away, and you have these five children to raise. It's a lot. How are you making any money?"

Jane's eyes narrowed. "Who told you to ask me that?"

"Nobody!" Margaret was shocked, setting her cup down on the table as she stared at Jane. Her cousin's tone was suddenly furious, her eyes blazing. "Nobody told me —I just—I know it must be hard!"

"Yeah, well, don't judge me."

"I ... wasn't," Margaret said, deeply confused. All the connection she had once felt to Jane was gone. It was as though the woman was a complete stranger to her. And, yet, somehow, she was compelled to confess to Jane. Perhaps it was her mind's way of trying to find that connection between them again, because surely Jane would have sympathy for Margaret's situation, and they could bond over their troubles. "Jane, there's something I haven't told you."

"I figured there would be."

Margaret nodded, pressing on past Jane's continued sharp tone. "You know that I married James."

"And he got rich, yeah."

"Yes," Margaret agreed slowly. "And when he became so successful, he decided that he didn't want to be married to me after all. I was too plain, too slow, and too boring for him. He fell in love with a beautiful, high-class, glamorous woman, and he served me with a divorce. He told me, essentially, to get out of town so he wouldn't have to be bothered by seeing me while he enjoyed his new life."

Jane took a long sip of her coffee and set the cup down. "Men can be the worst kinda creatures."

Margaret waited a moment for Jane to continue, but that was all her cousin seemed to have to say, and Margaret felt affronted. How could Jane have such little sympathy?

"I suppose so," she said slowly, frowning. "Jane ... perhaps it was wrong of me to ask you for help. Clearly the familial connection between us ..."

"Is it true yer gonna leave Robert?"

Margaret blinked, again taken aback. "No. Where did you hear that?"

"I have sources," Jane said. "Because you would be a fool, Margaret. And if you do it, I want nothin' to do with you."

"I'm not leaving Robert!" Margaret stood up, at her wit's end with Jane. "And frankly, I'm not sure I want much to do with you, given how you're speaking to me."

Jane didn't apologize, or even look up at Margaret. "Don't leave him. And when the time comes, remember who got you that husband in the first place."

"Yes, thank you for promising my hand in marriage without my permission," Margaret said icily, picking up her reticule and dusting off her skirts. "Excuse me. I'll take my leave."

Without waiting for Jane to protest, Margaret stalked her way out of her cousin's house. The children all called to her, and she managed a wave and a smile for them as she made her way off the property and began the walk home. Robert's ranch was not far from Jane's house, which was really more of a shack than anything else. It was about three miles, which was a longer walk than she was used to. When she had told Robert of her plans to visit Jane that day, he had wanted her to take the horses and wagon instead of walking, but she didn't feel comfortable driving along the rough roads in such an unfamiliar vehicle. Walking was, at least, a safe option.

And it gave her plenty of time to stew over the encounter she had just had with Jane. She walked the first mile at an energetic pace, her muscles still rigid with tension and anger. Jane had no right to treat her the way that she had! Margaret didn't deserve that, just like she hadn't deserved it from James. She had thought Jane would be trustworthy, but it was growing clearer all the time that no one was trustworthy.

The thought lodged in her brain. If nobody—including the man she had been married to and the only family she had left—was worthy of her trust, then how could she possibly think that Robert, whom she didn't know at all, would be worthy of it? He had seemed harmless and even kind and generous, but people always did at the beginning.

She was the fool Jane accused her of being if she let her guard down with a man who had no reason to do right by her.

God, why are people this way? How am I supposed to get by if I can't trust anyone? Are you there, God?

As Margaret was saying her silent prayer, movement to her left caught her eye and she lifted her eyes from the path in front of her, staring off into the distance.

She didn't know, at first, what she was looking at. There seemed to be a mass moving on the horizon, and it was moving quickly. As it grew closer, she began to be able to differentiate between the shapes, and ice filled her veins.

There, in front of her, heading directly for the place she was headed, was a group of natives on horseback, bows and arrows strapped to their backs.

She had read of such things, but never, even in her wildest imaginings of the West, had she envisioned herself caught in the middle of something like what was before her. And yet, there was no retreat.

CHAPTER 7

FIGHTING FOR SURVIVAL

Margaret was frozen in place, not knowing if she should run back to Jane's house for shelter, or if she should run toward her new home to be with Robert. Her heart was pounding in her chest, and her eyes were fixed on the seemingly never-ending line of men on horseback charging toward Tombstone. They would pass directly by Robert's house, and there was no telling what they might do to the property or to him.

That thought made her decision for her. Without another moment's hesitation, she ran toward her new home, desperate to get there before the natives and try to warn Robert. There was no chance she was going to make it in time, but she had to try.

Her shoes were not made for running, and she had never run a long distance before. It was not long before she was out of breath, her lungs aching with the need for air, and her legs heavy and slow. Margaret pushed on, praying again and again as she ran.

Lord, please. Please. Please. Let me get to Robert!

In the distance, she could just see the edge of the fence that marked Robert's property, but the natives had disappeared from her sight, the varied terrain creating patches of cover where she couldn't see them. She had no idea of knowing which direction they had taken or how close they were, and the unknowable nature of the situation only increased her panic.

She had to stop for a moment, doubling over and gasping for breath as she clutched her chest. It seemed almost impossible for her to run any further, but she knew she had to. So she straightened up, willing her body through sheer determination to move forward. But as she straightened and her eyes looked to the horizon, she saw the natives again. This time they were rounding the bend of a mountain, not nearly as far from her as she had thought. In fact, they were heading directly for her, only moments away by horseback, and she was standing there in the road, vulnerable, out of breath, and a perfect target.

"O Lord, please help me," she whispered, stumbling backward and desperately searching around her for cover. She made it to the side of the road, clutching her stomach as she tried to imagine hiding behind the collection of cacti there or somehow pressing herself so close to the ground that she would be invisible, and then the sound of hooves thundered behind her, a hand snatched at her, and she was lifted into the air before being clutched against a hard body.

Margaret screamed, flailing against her captor, but it was no use. His arm only tightened around her, making her so frantic that she forgot to be afraid of the fact that she was at the mercy of an enormous horse thundering across the terrain.

"It's me!"

The voice that had been speaking to her the whole time suddenly registered with Margaret as the horse sharply changed direction, running back toward Robert's house.

"Margaret, it's me! Calm down. I've got you. I promise—I've got you."

Her whole body went slack when she recognized his voice, tears of gratitude springing to her eyes. But they weren't tears for her and her own safety.

"I was so worried," she croaked, emotion clogging her throat. "I was trying to warn you. To get to you."

"I was terrified," Robert said back. "To think of you out here all alone. I never should have let you walk. I'm a fool, Margaret. Look at what could have happened to you."

They were riding too fast to keep up a conversation, and in no time at all, they were past Robert's fence and on their own property. Moments later, Robert stopped Silver outside his log cabin and swung down, pulling Margaret with him.

"Get inside," he told her, pushing her toward the door. "Hurry."

"Come with me," she urged, not wanting to separate. It suddenly felt as though if she let him out of her sight, she might never see him again.

He shook his head. "No. They're headed for Tombstone. They'll burn the town to the ground. Someone has to get there first."

"Don't leave me here!" she pleaded. "Let me come with you."

"Margaret ..."

She could see the indecision on his face, and knew her own was desperate. It was suddenly imperative that he not leave her.

"Fine, but help me," he told her, hurrying to the cart and getting it hitched to Silver and another of his horses. Everything flashed by in a blur, and she tried to help him get the wagon ready as quickly as she could, then got in herself, staying low and holding on tight.

When Robert cracked the reins, sending the horses running, Margaret thought she might be sick at first. But she was the one who had insisted on joining him, so as they rocketed along the rough terrain, the wagon tossing this way and that, she hunkered down, kept her mouth shut, and held onto the wooden slats with every bit of strength she had.

When Robert glanced down to check on her, she nodded, reassuring him that she was going to be just fine.

And the fact that he had first—before warning the town—ridden out in search of her in case she was in the natives' path made her believe that everything really was going to be okay, as long as she had Robert.

CHAPTER 8

RAISING THE ALARM

MARGARET AND ROBERT ROARED INTO TOMBSTONE, THE HORSES RAISING UP ON their hind legs as Robert jerked them to a stop and leaped down from the wagon. He started to hurry away, but stopped and turned, reaching up to help her down.

"You doin' all right?" he asked, searching her face.

"I'm fine. Go. Hurry," she urged him.

He touched her cheek, then ran down the street, shouting as loudly as he could. "Indians on their way in! Indian raid! Everyone! Get the women and children to safety! Men—grab your weapons. Now! Move now!"

The town broke into a frenzy, people running all over the place as they tried to get some to safety and the rest put together a battalion. Margaret tried to help, running toward a woman who was herding a large group of children into the church, where many were taking shelter.

"Let me help," Margaret said, taking two of the kids' hands to hurry them along.

The woman glanced hurriedly at her, nodded, and kept herding the children until they were inside the church, the door shut heavily behind them. Together, the two women ushered the children into the pews, then stood back, both pushing their hair out of their faces as sweat dripped down their necks.

"I'm going to head back out and see what else I can do," Margaret told the woman. "Stay here with them."

"Are you Jane's cousin?" the woman blurted out. "The new woman from out east?"

"That's right," Margaret said, wondering at the look on her face. "Why?"

"You better help your cousin, while someone still can," the woman said, even as she was ushering Margaret out the door of the church. "She got desperate after

Joseph died. There's only one thing for a desperate woman with five children to do out here."

Margaret stepped back outside the church, staring as she tried to comprehend what the woman was telling her. She was confused at first, but then it hit her in a rush of horror, and she clasped her hands over her mouth, everything about Jane's anger and bitterness now making sense to her. Sympathy for her cousin crashed over her, as well as a determination to save her from the life she was living. But before she could voice either impulse, chaos broke out behind her.

She whirled just in time to see the natives on the edge of the town, facing down a line of townsmen who were armed with guns. The immediacy of the situation took over, and she began to look desperately for Robert, her eyes scanning back and forth even as people shouted, screamed, and gunfire whistled through the air.

"Robert!" she couldn't help but call out to him when she finally spotted him crouched at the edge of the local saloon, gun poised at his shoulder as he took aim again and again. Margaret hadn't meant to shout, but the relief at seeing him had overcome her.

How was it possible to feel such a connection to a man she had only known for a few days and whom she had been determined to resist?

Even as her mind questioned her feelings, she knew the answer. He had put her above everything else. He had risked his life to come after her when he saw the natives approaching. James would never have done that, and it wasn't something Robert could have faked with smooth words and nice smiles. His life and the life of the townspeople had been on the line, and he still had chosen her.

That made him her husband in the truest sense of the word.

Even as she stood on the church steps, hands up at her face, watching her husband fight to protect all of their lives, he paused in his shooting and turned to look at her, as though he could feel his eyes on hers. He took his hand off his gun, motioning for her to get back in the church—to stay safe.

She shook her head. She couldn't leave him. She couldn't hide herself away while he risked his life again to protect her. In the past, she had always stayed in the shadows, never willing to put herself out there and get rejected, but Robert had inspired her to take a risk and invest—and it was time for her to invest in this town.

Hurrying forward, Margaret picked up the gun that was lying beside an injured townsman who was being seen to by the doctor. It was already loaded and ready to fire, so she took aim, pulling back the trigger on the gun.

The kickback sent pain shooting through her shoulder, but she didn't stop. She shot again and again, doing her part to help protect her new home and her new husband. Vaguely, she could hear Robert calling to her, and she turned to look at him. Their eyes met and for a moment everything stopped. They smiled at each other, her smile a bit smug and his a bit incredulous. Then, side by side, they worked to keep the natives at bay.

Margaret felt a strange sort of high—an empowerment that was taking over her. She thought there was no way that they would not win against the band of natives, equipped primarily with bows and arrows. They would never be able to withstand the gunfire. But she was a newcomer to the area, and she wasn't prepared when one of the natives—one of the last remaining of the group that had arrived—pulled out an arrow, lit it on fire, and shot it over their heads.

The arrow landed in the building behind Robert and Margaret, and the dry wood immediately caught fire. Townspeople began running and shouting again, a few steady men maintaining their place at the front line while the others ran for water. The fire behind her caused Margaret to turn around, and it was only then that she saw the destruction of the town that had already begun to take place. Several people were lying in the streets, injured or dead. Arrows littered the ground and the buildings, and now a fire raged as the natives sent flaming arrow after flaming arrow past the line of defenders.

Margaret turned to Rodger, her face sweaty and red with exertion. "What do we do?" she asked, standing with him as people began to run. Another group of natives on horseback could be seen in the distance, backup for those who had already fallen. Townspeople were scattering, buildings were being abandoned, and within mere moments the battle that had seemed almost won had turned on them.

Robert grabbed the back of her head, hauling her to him until their lips met in a fierce kiss that stole her breath away.

"We run," he told her, taking her hand and pulling her away from the front lines.

CHAPTER 9

LAST DITCH EFFORT

Margaret ran as fast as she could behind Robert, her hand caught in his. He pulled her to their wagon and then let go of her as he tried to calm the frantic horses there. "Get in," he urged. "The town is lost, but our ranch doesn't have to be. The ranch hands will already be standing in defense, but we have to get back there."

As she climbed into the wagon, he talked to the horses, somehow managing to calm the huge animals. When he swung up into the wagon, she gripped his arm hard, knowing that they were about to tear down the rocky road again.

"Robert, thank you," she shouted above the sound of warfare and wind. "Thank you."

"What?" he called back, urging the horses to run faster back to the ranch. "Thank you for what?"

"For coming after me," she said, the wind whipping her hair out of what remained of her up-do. "For finding me. For putting me first."

He risked a glance over at her. "Yer my wife, Margaret! Yer always gonna be first for me, darlin'. Get used to it."

"I want this," she told him, gripping his arm harder. "More than anything, I want to be married to you."

He grinned over at her, his boyish eyes lighting up even in the midst of the terror they found themselves in. "Then I'm a lucky man," he shouted. "Just hold on tight, darlin'. The only way yer husband can provide for ya is if that ranch is still standin'."

Margaret kissed his cheek as he drove. "Even if it's not, I won't mind being poor with you."

It didn't take them long to get back to their property, and Margaret let out a sigh of relief when it looked untouched. But a ranch hand met them at the gate, armed and obviously ready to defend the property.

"There you are, boss. What's the word?"

"Tombstone's being raided. We fought back for as long as we could hold 'em, but they were usin' flamin' arrows."

"The town is destroyed, then?"

Robert shook his head. "It's not lookin' good. How's things here?"

"Lots of Indians ridin' by. Couple of shots, but they haven't stopped. They've got a mission—Tombstone."

"That's in our best interest," Robert said, lifting Margaret down from the wagon. "Get in the house," he told her, touching her cheek. "You were somethin' else out there today, but I can't put you at risk again. Please, this time go inside."

She was covered in dirt, soot, and grime, but Margaret put her arms around his neck, lifting onto her toes and kissing him again. "I'll go inside," she murmured. "But what are you going to do?"

His hands lifted to frame her face, his eyes looking down into hers. "I'm going to ask God what I ever did to deserve you, and while I do that, I'm going to check the fence line of the property and make sure everythin' is in order. Then I'll be in. I promise."

Margaret nodded. "Hurry."

"Be safe," he told her. "Noah, stay with her and defend the house."

Then, with just one more look back at her, Robert was unhitching Silver and mounting him bareback. He rode off, two of his other ranch hands following behind him. Margaret watched him until she couldn't see him anymore, then let Noah lead her into the house because she had promised Robert she would stay out of sight.

But as soon as she was in the house, with its dirt floors, wooden slats, and large, bulky furniture, she found that she couldn't stop pacing, worrying about what Robert might face out on the property. The minutes ticked by like hours, and she kept going back to the window, her hands twisting together as she watched and waited.

"Ma'am, it could be a while," Noah said politely from his place by the door. "It might be best to settle somewhere."

She turned to look at him, knowing that she was making him, and probably herself, nervous with her pacing and whispered prayers. Margaret attempted a smile. "Sorry. I need to focus on something else."

"Good idea."

"Do you know if there is a ... soiled doves business in this town?"

Noah choked in surprise, trying to cover his reaction by pounding his chest and coughing into his hand. "'Scuse me, ma'am?"

"I think I know someone who got herself into a bad situation," Margaret said, her cousin returning to the forefront of her mind as she tried to think of anything but Robert and the danger he was in. "Would you know anything about that?"

Noah's eyes widened and he coughed again. "Uh, reckon not, ma'am. I don't fool with that."

"That's a good man," she told him, nodding. "But how do I find out? I don't want to ask her, in case I offend her."

"I think she'd get over the offense if ya helped her," Noah said, his face red and his eyes averted.

Margaret thought about that for a moment. "Yes, I suppose she would, wouldn't she?" She sank down into the large rocking chair that sat by the fireplace, her mind going in every direction. The ruined town, Robert's heroism, Robert's danger, and Jane's misery. There were so many problems ahead of her, and yet, for the first time in her life, she felt like she had purpose. She was useful. She could make a difference.

Robert had given her that gift just by thinking she was important, and now all she wanted was for him to come back to her and for the two of them to work as a team to help the town and save Jane.

CHAPTER 10

A NEW BEGINNING

IT WAS AFTER DARK WHEN ROBERT FINALLY RETURNED. MARGARET WAS SITTING in a chair by the door, and when it opened, she leapt to her feet, her arms moving around him before he could even step all the way inside.

"I've been so worried," she told him, easing back to look him over. Before her was an exhausted, filthy man with haggard eyes and blood staining the left shoulder of his shirt. Margaret touched his face, so glad to have him back close to her that she could hardly speak. How had he become so important to her in such a short amount of time?

"Are you all right?" he asked, tucking her hair behind her ear even as he leaned heavily against her.

She nodded. "I'm fine. I'm more concerned about you. You've been gone for so long. What happened?"

He led her the rest of the way inside, closed the door, and sank into the chair she had been sitting in. Reaching out a hand, he pulled her to perch on his knee, his hand rubbing her back gently. Margaret was stunned at the simple gesture of intimacy and the way it warmed her from somewhere deep within.

"It was a battle out there," he said, leaning back and closing his eyes. "There were groups of them everywhere, some big and some small. The town was overrun ... burned down in huge sections."

"Oh, Robert." Margaret rested her head against his shoulder, aching for him and all the people she didn't know but whose lives had been devastated. "I'm so sorry."

He kissed her forehead. "It's the way of things out here, Margaret. We have battles to fight every day. Some we win, and some we don't."

"Did we win this one?"

"You and I did," he promised her, putting his arm closer around her. "Because our home is safe. But the town ... no, the town didn't win this one, darlin'."

"We'll help rebuild," she said, looking up into his face. "God will bring something good from it. He brought something good for me out of the darkest moment of my life, and I want to tell you about it and finally be honest. But maybe this isn't the time."

He gave her a tired smile. "Tell me."

And she did. She told him about James, about her doubt, and her misery. "He just cast me aside," she whispered at the end of her story. "And I swore I would never let a man be able to do that again. But when you rescued me earlier, I knew ... you never would."

Robert touched her cheek, stroking the skin softly. "Never. I was nervous about you comin' out here, but the moment I saw you standin' beside Jane, I knew you were the one for me. Somethin' about you fits me. I know that we're goin' to love each other."

"I'm falling in love already," Margaret whispered, looking up at him. "For real this time. But I need you to do one more thing for me, Robert."

"You've found out about Jane."

Margaret sat up, surprised. "You knew?

"I suspected, yes," Robert said, sighing. "A woman with five kids would have trouble finding a husband. She had no other choice, perhaps. Or at least she felt she didn't."

"But we can give her that choice," Margaret said, with some hesitation. It was still early for her to be assuming, but Robert made her feel so safe that she took the risk. "Can't we?"

"Of course," Robert said. "I knew Jane was not the woman for me to marry, but even if you hadn't asked, I'd want to find a way to help her somehow. We will." He kissed her softly. "We'll help rebuild the town and we'll help rebuild Jane, because I have a feelin' that we make a really good team."

She stared into his eyes, amazed at how much had changed in just a week. "Somehow, you make me feel hopeful. I've never felt that way before. I think God gave you to me for a reason."

"And here I thought you were my gift from God," he said, his sentiments light but his voice heavy with emotional and physical exhaustion.

Margaret stood up, taking his hand in hers and helping him to his feet. "Let's get you cleaned up, and then to bed. You've had a long day. I've got some soup warming for you, and I'll draw up a bath."

"You really are a gift from God," he said, leaning on her as she helped him back to the bedroom that she had been staying in. They'd had separate rooms since she'd arrived, but she was ready to move past that now and really start their life together. As she led him into her room, he smiled down at her, the gesture not lost on him.

"You and me," Margaret told him, kissing him before she went back to the kitchen to warm some water and get his soup ready. As she fussed over her husband, she sent up a prayer of thanks.

Lord, thank you for second chances and for men with good hearts.

EPILOGUE
A BREATH OF FRESH AIR

MARGARET STOOD BETWEEN ROBERT AND JANE AS THEY, ALONG WITH MANY OF the other townspeople, stood in front of the new school building. It was one of the first buildings the town had worked together to restore after the Indian raid, and Margaret and Robert had both had a hand in the project from the beginning. Margaret had worked with the other women on collecting new books and other materials, and Robert had helped to rebuild the frame of the building in the areas where it was damaged. Together, they stood in front of the building, hand in hand, proud of their work. As the doors opened and the crowd applauded, Margaret and Robert looked at each other, sharing a smile.

She was proud of the work they had done together, but she was even more proud when the mayor of the town gestured for Jane to step up and join him. Margaret watched as her cousin hesitantly stepped up in front of the school, her hands twisting together nervously. Jane was afraid that the town was judging her, but Margaret gave the people the benefit of the doubt. Jane had made some mistakes, but when Robert had helped arranged the opportunity for her to become the new schoolteacher in Tombstone, Jane had dedicated herself to the idea.

Now, her life was going to be completely different, and Margaret felt tears spring to her eyes as she watched the crowd applaud Jane after the mayor's speech. She pressed Robert's fingers, amazed at all that had happened in the last two months.

"I love you," she whispered to him, her head resting against his shoulder.

"I love you too, darlin'," he said back, kissing the top of her head. "One day our babies are gonna go to that school. And Jane is goin' to teach 'em."

She smiled up at him, knowing that this was the moment. "It won't be that long from now, Robert. Not with our first one on the way."

His eyes widened, and then, right there in the center of town, he scooped her up and spun her around, laughing. When he set her down, he kissed her softly. "My gift from God is giving me another gift. Thank you, Margaret. Thank you for changing my life."

"Thank you for changing mine," she whispered back, leaning into his embrace and knowing that she had finally found her place in the world.

⛤

THANK YOU SO MUCH FOR READING MY BOOK. I SINCERELY HOPE YOU ENJOYED EVERY bit reading it. I had fun creating it and will surely create more.

Your positive reviews are very helpful to other reader, it only takes a few moments. They can be left at Amazon.

www.amazon.com/Katie-Wyatt/e/B011IN7AF0

⛤

WANT FREE BOOKS EVERY WEEK? WHO DOESN'T!

BECOME A PREFERRED READER AND WE'LL NOT ONLY SEND YOU FREE READS, BUT you'll also receive updates about new releases.

So you'll be among the first to dive into our latest new books, full of adventure, heartwarming romances, and characters so real they jump off the page.

It's absolutely free and you don't need to do anything at all to qualify except go to.

PREFERRED READ FREE READS

http:/katieWyattBooks.com/readersgroup

ABOUT THE AUTHOR

KATIE WYATT IS 25% AMERICAN SIOUX INDIAN. BORN AND RAISED IN Arizona, she has traveled and camped extensively through California, Arizona, Nevada, Mexico, and New Mexico. Looking at the incredible night sky and the giant Saguaro cacti, she has dreamed of what it would be like to live in the early pioneer times.

Spending time with a relative of the great Wyatt Earp, also named Wyatt Earp, Katie was mesmerized and inspired by the stories he told of bygone times. This historical interest in the old West became the inspiration for her Western romance novels.

Her books are a mixture of actual historical facts and events mixed with action and humor, challenges and adventures. The characters in Katie's clean romance novels draw from her own experiences and are so real that they almost jump off the pages. You feel like you're walking beside them through all the ups and downs of their lives. As the stories unfold, you'll find yourself both laughing and crying. The endings will never fail to leave you feeling warm inside.

ETHAN'S FAITH

Contemporary Western Romance

RoyceCardiff

P u b l i s h i n g   H o u s e
WHOLESOME INSPIRATIONAL ROMANCE

A PERSONAL WORD FROM BRENDA

Dear Readers,

You read about the Wild West because of the romance, the adventure, the spirit of possibility that filled those frontier days. I write these books for the same reasons. I love the stories of the pioneer women who crossed the country to build new lives in what must have felt like a totally foreign land. With courage, faith, common sense, and a good dose of humor, many of these courageous women married their true loves and became the Old West's literal founding mothers!

Many of my books draw directly from history, using the real-life stories of those women to tell the story of the birth of the western half of our nation. As I look around my southwest backyard, I often take a moment to think about what it might have looked like before we all moved in. These stories are my attempt to share that wonderful adventure with you.

Happy reading,

Brenda

CHAPTER 1

ETHAN

ETHAN STARED OUT THE WINDOW OF THE FOUR-SEATER SINGLE-ENGINE CESSNA Skyhawk, as always marveling at the beauty of the northernmost Rockies and millions of acres of pine forest spreading out below. The aircraft flew through a bright blue, cloudless sky. The noise of the propeller discouraged conversation, which was just fine with him. He wasn't much in the mood for talking.

Oliver Jespersen piloted the plane, pushing it close to its maximum cruising speed. Oliver had piloted Ethan to the wilderness landing strip numerous times in the old training craft, suitable as a "puddle-jumper" commonly flown short distances throughout the region. After letting him off at the airstrip, the plane would continue west over the mountains.

Sixty-three-year-old Oliver wore aviator glasses, bubbled headphones, jeans, long johns, and a flannel shirt. He looked perfectly comfortable at his controls, handling the craft with ease, as always. Ethan had known Oliver for years, though not well, one of the few pilots who had the skill and coolness to guide and land the Cessna between two massive mountain ridges in the oblong meadow at the base of Johnson Peak, nestled in the northern edges of the Kootenai National Forest near the Canadian border.

Two other passengers had climbed aboard back in Billings: a woman who appeared to be in her mid-twenties, close to Ethan's age, although the haunted look in her eyes had caught his attention the moment she boarded. Behind her came an older man with wispy white hair, a bald pate, and a friendly smile. Not related. No words were spoken between them as they boarded. Ethan offered a polite nod and then stared out the window. He looked forward to the two- to three-day hike to the secluded cabin in the middle of nowhere. Which was exactly why he had purchased it when he'd turned twenty-one, using inheritance money left to him by his grandfather.

He rearranged himself on the worn cushioned seat tucked up against one side of the plane behind the pilot, the woman and the older man also seated single file on the opposite side. No one attempted conversation, which suited him just fine. He wasn't in the mood for chitchat.

The aircraft shook slightly as a gust of wind caught it from below, lifting the nose up. As always, his heart skipped a beat and he instinctively clutched at the seat, but he didn't white-knuckle it. Not yet. He hated flying. Unfortunately, it was the quickest and easiest way to reach his secluded property. The aircraft flew over pine-studded foothills and green valleys, rounding thirteen-thousand-foot peaks covered with forests of pine, aspen, and birch trees. The tops of the higher mountain peaks still wore a veil of snow even this late into summer. Though the higher elevations maintained cooler temps, the lower elevations basked in the mid- to high eighties.

The aircraft banked slightly portside, another gust of wind again buffeting the metal, causing Ethan's heart to pound. His stomach turned an uneasy somersault as he closed his eyes and tried to find his equilibrium, swallowing his unreasonable fears. How many times had he taken this flight with Oliver? How many times over the past seven years had he taken off and landed safely?

So he was afraid of flying. No big deal. No one was perfect, right?

He glanced at the woman sitting across from him. Her long blonde hair was carefully woven into a French braid that cradled the back of her skull and fell to her shoulder blades. She too looked out her window as she leaned against the side of the aircraft. Despite the vibrations of the plane and the turbulence, the up-and-down dipping and rising that startled Ethan so terribly, she appeared to be sleeping, her face expressionless. The man sitting behind her also looked to be sleeping, head tilted back against the seat, mouth open. Probably snoring, but Ethan didn't hear it due to the whir of the propeller.

He shook his head, amazed at their calm demeanor, opposite his trepidation. He unconsciously lifted his hand to his throat and felt for his collar beneath his tee and buffalo-check flannel shirt. Not there. He had tucked it into his backpack. With a surge of impatience and frustration, he leaned forward and unzipped his backpack, checking to make sure it was there. Almost reverently, he touched it, and then with a sigh, zipped the pocket back up and returned to staring out the window.

Maybe he hadn't made such a good decision after all—he clutched at his seat as the Cessna took another brunt of wind against its portside, sweeping off the mountain looming to their left. As the aircraft banked right, he stared down at the treetops, the jagged mountainsides, the sheer rock faces that interrupted those vast green carpets. This was the area that was almost always turbulent, the drafts rising up from the mountains buffeting the aircraft, constantly challenging Oliver's skill at keeping the plane level.

Ethan shook his head in growing self-recrimination. Nothing to be afraid of. They weren't going to crash. He was not afraid of much, but flying, well, flying was different. He didn't pretend to know anything about aerodynamics, the physics of how the heavy metal aircraft could float and fly through the air.

The plane's altitude dropped suddenly and his stomach lurched into his throat. This was the worst it had ever been ... the jostling of the plane grew rougher and he clutched his seat with both hands. From the corner of his eye he saw movement and glanced toward the woman. She sat upright in her seat now, eyes wide, not panicked, but concerned. The older man behind her still slept. Ethan's heart pounded hard in his chest and the pulse throbbed in his throat. His stomach tightened into a hard knot as he fought back nausea and attempted to adjust his equilibrium.

The Cessna caught another crosswind that precipitated another alarming drop in altitude. The craft shuddered. Ethan glanced at Oliver and saw the tension in his shoulders, his tight grip on the steering wheel or whatever you called it in an airplane ... he glanced at his instrument panel, out the windows, and back again.

The wings rocked as they rolled slightly to starboard and the nose of the small aircraft dipped up, leveled out, then shot down again. Sharply. The woman uttered a startled cry of alarm while the man behind her finally woke and immediately reached for the back of her seat. Ethan clutched his seat with one hand, the other braced against the back of Oliver's seat, his own knuckles white as Oliver corrected and lifted the nose, bringing the craft level again.

Ethan caught his breath with relief but the next moment yet another gust of wind pushed the nose even higher. The plane rolled to the right. No one had to tell Ethan how dangerous these mountains were, filled with craggy outcroppings, deep canyons, tall mountain peaks, and erratic wind currents.

He automatically began to mouth a silent prayer, then grimaced. *Hypocrite!* He should never have—

A loud, pulsing buzzing sound filled the aircraft. It took him a few seconds to realize what it was, especially when he heard Oliver curse. An alarm. The Cessna pitched and yawed, vibrating more forcefully. Then, even more alarming, the tail of the plane yawed hard to the right. No ... no, not a spin—

The alarm, the vibrations, the tremulous wobbling had all three passengers frightened now. The older passenger grasped at his seat for support, eyes wide as he stared out his window, face pale, a trickle of sweat appearing on his brow.

"Oliver!" Ethan shouted above the noise. "What's happening? Can you—"

A loud bang cut off his words, followed by the sound of a grinding, metallic thump. No, not a thump. Shearing. Metal screeching and ripping. The Cessna shook violently and the nose dropped again.

"Hold on!" Oliver shouted. "I've lost the rudder!"

Ethan stared at the back of Oliver's head, dismay warring with a growing sense of panic. Then, for just an instant, he almost smiled. Par for the course, wasn't it? How else should a new pastor struggling with his faith be tested? *God, if this is your idea of a joke, it's not funny!*

At that point, the Cessna began to rock and bounce every which way, struggling to find equilibrium, nose up one moment, tail up the next. Ethan clamped his jaws shut to prevent himself from yelling at Oliver to do something, to save them, to get this plane down on the ground ASAP. Ethan glanced at the woman, her face drained of color, the dark circles under her eyes amplified by that lack of color, and from somewhere inside him, he found the strength to provide her with a modicum of comfort.

"It'll be all right!" he shouted. "Oliver's the best pilot!"

Oliver did his best to maintain control of the Cessna, but an invisible force prevented him from succeeding in leveling the plane or even maintaining a consistent altitude. The aircraft continued to drop, zooming ever closer to the treetops on the side of a mountain that loomed incredibly and fearfully close.

"Hold on!" Oliver shouted.

No responses were needed or required. The Cessna rolled at such a steep angle that Ethan's torso slammed against the side of the plane. He banged his head against the metal and winced in pain, but barely registered more than that before the Cessna rolled to the opposite side. The right wing clipped something and shuddered again, followed by the horrid sound of crunching metal. Everything went topsy-turvy then, so fast he barely absorbed one before something else happened.

His seat belt fastened him in his seat, but still his body flung this way and that as the Cessna rolled. The woman uttered a bloodcurdling scream while the older man shouted at Oliver. Then, for just a moment, the aircraft righted itself. Ethan stared in horror out the windshield. Trees approached ever closer, their upper branches scraping against the bottom of the Cessna. Nothing now but the sound of screeching, ripping metal, the whine of the engine, the screams and shouts of the passengers, the roaring of the propeller blade ... he didn't want to die like this. Not without—

A jolt and then the small aircraft spun sideways, like a merry-go-round spun off its axle. The left wing shattered and a good chunk of the left side of the plane ripped free. Cold, crisp air buffeted Ethan as he stared out into space. Trees blurred past, branches, then a rock face. Mouth open, trying to scream, no sound coming from his throat, he only observed as the plane ripped apart.

Oliver and the cockpit disappeared. The cabin, now torn to shreds, slid about fifty yards, then slowed to an abrupt halt. He and the female passenger, still buckled snugly into their seats, turned to stare at one another. Amid the destruction, Ethan turned to find the older man had disappeared too, the tail of the plane gone.

The remnants of the Cessna's fuselage had come to a halt on a rocky slope of the mountain side, cleared by years of landslides, settling slightly on its right side against a stand of ancient pines.

Silence. Incredible, peaceful silence encompassed him. Was he dead? Was this it? Was this how it was all going to end, before he even had a chance to—

A low moan broke into his thoughts and only then did he realize it had come from his own throat. The dust settled. Slowly, the silence was broken by the sound of a bird, then another. The scent of mountain pine and chokecherry and fresh mountain air wafted into his nostrils. He watched dumbly as a yellow jacket hovered nearby, then settled on a chunk of metal nearby before buzzing off.

"Oh my God ..."

He turned to find the female passenger sitting wide-eyed in her seat, half the seat tilted precariously, two of the seat bolts sheared off. Her hands, tightly clasped together in prayer against her chest, trembled wildly. Tears glistened in her eyes as she turned to him.

"Are we alive?" she asked softly.

The question jarred him but he nodded. Somehow, they were. They had to get out of here, find Oliver and the other passenger. Maybe they had survived. He smelled smoke, the acrid stench of seared wiring, plastic and electronics ... and fuel.

Before he attempted to release his seat belt, his hands also trembling so badly he could barely manage that, he took a deep breath, looked up into the bright blue sky above, and prayed. Yet even while he sent that prayer of thanks upward, he felt its emptiness, it's lack of conviction, and he cursed himself for his lack of faith in the very moment he should be counting his blessings.

CHAPTER 2

FAITH

How could one's heart pound so hard without bursting? It was the first thought that came to Faith when the noise, the vibrations, and the terror stopped. Her pulse raced but she froze, afraid to move, afraid to break that bubble of silence, afraid that one wrong move would propel the aircraft into yet another descent, only to tip what remained of the fuselage downward to crash against rocks or fall into a gorge to be dashed into infinitesimally small pieces against the rocky mountainside below.

Tilted precariously in her seat, only her half-torn seat belt holding her in, she gazed across the narrow span of aisle between the seats and watched the man sitting as frozen as she, his expression dazed. He wasn't handsome in a traditional model-handsome sense, but his profile displayed a high forehead, straight nose, and strong chin. He turned to her again and she noted his eyes were blue, the lightest blue she'd ever seen, almost gray. The color might have frightened her if not for the compassion she saw in them as his worried glance swept her from head to toe and back again. A day's worth of stubble grew on his cheeks. He wore a blue buffalo-check long-sleeved shirt over a dark blue T-shirt and olive-green cargo pants with leg pockets. Sturdy hiking boots on his feet. Broad shoulders, lean torso, and long legs also registered in her brain.

"Oh my God... are we alive?"

He nodded. "You okay?"

Before she could answer, he looked out the front of the plane, where the cockpit and the pilot used to be. She saw nothing but forest in front of them. Oh no ... the pilot ... what had happened to him? Carefully, Faith also peered around, stunned to find that the Cessna had been reduced to the maybe eight-foot length where she and her fellow passenger still sat, buckled into their seats.

No wings, no cockpit, no tail ... she caught her breath. The older man who had sat behind her ... he was gone too. She dangled sideways at an angle, not complete sideways but enough to orient herself. The fuselage had landed on a steep slope. She didn't recall much of the past few seconds and supposed she should be grateful for that.

For a second, a very brief one, she thought she might laugh. Just her luck, wasn't it? To escape one horrible situation only to find herself in another? What was that old saying? Don't jump from the frying pan into the fire? Well, looked like she had done just that. Now what?

Hands trembling wildly, Faith carefully reached for her seat belt, her hands shaking so badly she could barely grasp the metal flap to lift it. As she did, she dared to look around again, this time noting the sharp edges where the cockpit had been savagely torn from the fuselage. Behind them, jagged strips of metal were all that remained of the fuselage in which the two of them had made their precarious landing.

Her stomach was in a hard knot, nausea roiling as reality settled. The pilot and other passenger were likely dead. She swallowed back the bile and turned to the man now looking straight ahead, into a dense forest of trees.

"Are they dead?" Her question jolted him from his thoughts and he turned to her, resolve replacing the blank look that had been on his face moments ago.

"Probably, but we can look for them. Maybe they were as fortunate as we are. Maybe they're still alive."

Fortunate. She was fortunate? Sure, she was alive, but was she *fortunate*? She didn't think so.

"You all right?" he asked again.

Was she? For the first time, she assessed her condition. Other than her heart still pounding and the trembling in her hands and body caused by adrenaline, she felt okay. She moved her feet and her legs, shrugged her shoulders, and nodded. "I don't think I have any broken bones. You?"

He shook his head and carefully unlatched his seat belt. He grabbed a backpack nestled at his feet with one hand and reached for a handhold as he, hunched nearly in half due to the crumpled fuselage, extended his hand toward her. After a brief moment of indecision, she gave him her hand.

He waited as she unlatched her belt with the other and as carefully as he, stood. He moved to the rear of the plane, ducking low, watching where he placed his feet. She followed suit as they stepped out of the demolished aircraft, eyes wide, gazing at the scenery around her as if she just landed on a different planet.

He glanced back at her with a lifted eyebrow. "You don't have a backpack?"

She shook her head. She had left with nothing but the clothes on her back. A pair of jeans, tennis shoes, and a long-sleeved tee. His look prompted an excuse. A lame one. "I wasn't expecting a delay ..." She didn't want to say more.

The fuselage had come to rest on the slope of the mountain, as she'd thought, but the images she saw now made her heart skip a beat. Maybe they had been fortunate at all. The fuselage teetered precariously against the base of a massive cliff of rocks rising above, dotted sparsely with pine. Snow clung stubbornly to its peak. The air smelled of pine and dirt with a hint of oil and gasoline. Around and below them the landscape dipped sharply, blanketed with miles upon miles of evergreens reaching toward the horizon.

"Where are we?" she whispered, awestruck.

"Somewhere in the Kootenai National Forest near the Canadian border," the man said grimly.

He released her hand and turned to look toward the east. She followed suit, but the hump of the mountain slope prevented her from seeing any remnants of the plane, their pilot, or the other passenger.

"How long do you think it'll take someone to find us?"

He took a few wobbly steps, then straightened as he turned toward her, his expression grim. "I don't know if Oliver got off an SOS call." He swept his arm over the expanse. "This forest spans over two million acres."

Faith's heart sank as she gazed around the panoramic view spread before her. It was wild, beautiful and awesome, and scary. Slope after slope, craggy peak after craggy peak, ridge after ridge, the mountains spread out before them. In the distance, a taller mountain climbed high above the rest.

The man turned toward her, extending a hand. "I'm Ethan. Ethan Seidel."

She gave him her hand, enveloped once again in his warm, strong, hand and noted his calloused fingers. A carpenter? Builder? "Faith. Faith Chalmers."

They eyed one another for several moments. Did he have the same questions swirling through his brain that she did? How had they survived? Why? Looking back at the piece of fuselage that remained of the Cessna, she couldn't believe it. She didn't understand. And now ... what were they supposed to do now? How far away was rescue or...

Without a word, Ethan moved away, traversing the rocky, scrub-sided slope of the mountain upon which they had landed, walking east, the direction from which the plane had traveled.

"Wait!" she cried out, startled by his abrupt movement. "Where are you going? You—"

"Looking for signs of wreckage," he explained.

She felt foolish as she followed. Her initial panic of being left out here alone ebbed as she followed him, carefully placing her feet on the rock-strewn slope. And all the while, she asked herself why she followed him so willingly. Especially after what she had just been through. Before the plane crash. The incident ... the reason she had been on that Cessna in the first place.

She pushed the memory behind her and followed Ethan as they searched for signs of wreckage, signs that perhaps the pilot and their fellow passenger had also survived the crash. Bit by bit, they found it. Faith swallowed hard as she spied a three-foot chunk of wing half caught in a pine tree maybe fifty yards away. Another thirty feet downslope, she saw the remains of the cockpit that had been sheared from the fuselage, crumpled around the base of a huge pine.

"Wait here," Ethan said as he quickly scrambled downward.

Faith waited with bated breath as Ethan reached the cockpit, the propeller blades crumpled and curled upon themselves. He briefly peered inside and turned away, shaking his head. She knew. The pilot was dead. Ethan returned to her side, his gaze taking in the vast wilderness.

"Shouldn't we bury him?"

He turned to her with a look she couldn't describe. Jaw tight, eyes looking at her but not really *seeing* her ... and then, with a sigh, shook his head.

"With what?"

They continued searching. Over the next hour, they searched for the older male passenger. They found bits and pieces of the plane, but they never found him. The vastness, the emptiness, the aloneness of this place inspired awe and fear. To die out here ... no one the wiser ... it was a sobering thought.

Perhaps to break the silence, perhaps in an effort to put her more at ease with him, or perhaps merely to hear the sound of his own voice in the emptiness around them, Ethan gave her a surprisingly thorough yet brief lesson on the Kootenai National Forest. About the rugged terrain, its ranges: Bitterroot, Salish, Whitefish; its two major rivers, the Kootenai and Clark Fork, which branched into yet ever smaller rivers and tributaries; about the animals and birds that called this place home. The white-tail and mule deer, elk, the big-horned sheep, black and grizzly bears, sometimes a mountain lion, and rarely, if you were lucky enough to see them, moose. Hawks and eagles also called the forest their home, as did bobcats, beaver, coyotes, and mink. He identified several tree species, pointing to one, then another; lodgepole pine, aspen, cottonwood. He pointed out wildflowers: Indian paintbrush, Columbine, and something called fairy slipper orchids.

Faith said nothing as they walked, half interested in the wildness around her, the other half wondering how they were going to get out of there. Finally, he sat down on an old, fallen tree trunk, a huge ball of roots exposed at its upper end, a splintered mass of bark on the other.

"Struck by lightning," he said, gesturing at the shattered end, then for her to sit. "Better rest for a minute. We'll have to find a good spot for camp soon."

It was only then that she noticed that deepening shadows, the sun hanging low to the west, soon to dip behind the mountains. Fear once again took hold and she turned toward him. She'd never spent a night outdoors in her life.

"How do you know so much about this place?" she asked.

He offered a slight shrug. "I spent much of my youth up here in these forests, not just here, but in Glacier, the Bitterroot and the Big Horns."

She almost smiled. Almost. "You some kind of outdoor enthusiast or survivalist or something?"

He grunted a laugh. "No." He shrugged out of his backpack and placed it on the ground between his feet. He unzipped it, dug around inside and pulled out a package of dried meat. He ripped the plastic wrapper open with his teeth, then reached in and withdrew a strip. "Elk jerky." He handed her a piece. "Rip slivers off with your teeth. It's chewy but packed with protein."

Elk. Dried meat. She'd never eaten wild game before. At the moment, she didn't care. At the sight of food, even dried, her stomach rumbled. When had she eaten last? She couldn't remember. She nibbled at one end, realizing that he'd been serious. She dug in her teeth and tore off a sliver. It tasted delicious. He pulled out a strip for himself, balanced it on his knee as he tucked the package into the pocket of his backpack, unzipped the top and dug his hand back inside, then pulled out a bottle of water.

"Only a liter, so we'll have to make this last until we find some water." He unscrewed the lid, took a sip, then another, and handed it to her. "Just a sip or two." He gestured toward the jerky. "We can have some more when we make camp."

It was at that moment that reality struck home. No one was going to find them out here, at least not today. She gazed at the miles and miles of wilderness and then once more at Ethan. "Are we lost?"

A strange look crossed his features as he slowly nodded. "I suppose you could say that we are."

CHAPTER 3

THE FALL

Ethan nibbled on his jerky, chewing thoughtfully, taking his time, his gaze passing over the wilderness. The terrain here was unfamiliar, but physically, he didn't feel lost. He knew north from south, east from west. He knew their chances of rescue to the south were greater than any other direction. To the east, beyond the mountains, lay the open plains of Montana, sparsely populated. To the north, hundreds of miles of wilderness to the Canadian border. To the west, extremely rugged mountain ranges, canyons, and ravines as the forest spread into northeastern Idaho.

It was rough country all around, and though he wasn't sure exactly where they were, he also knew that his cabin lay south. At least there, they could find shelter. With every stay, he always laid in a good stock of water and canned and dried goods before he left. Plenty of chopped firewood, though warmer nights would soon prevail as they headed into the lower valleys. Eventually, he would recognize landmarks, familiar ridges, river bends, mountain peaks ... but traveling with a woman ill-equipped for survival in the wilderness gave him pause.

His spiritual state was another matter. He tried to pray but it just didn't *feel* right. Nothing had *felt* right in a long time ... his prayers, his thoughts, his conversations with God ... they'd seemed empty of late, like he was engaged in a one-way conversation on the phone. His prayers felt more out of habit, rote, but without the depth of emotion, that invisible *connection* he usually felt. It wasn't there anymore ... at first, he'd just been confused, not understanding what was wrong. Now he knew what was missing. God was missing in action. He felt lost, ignored, if you will. Adrift and without an anchor to guide him back to port. Clichéd analogy, he knew, but apropos.

While doubts assailed him, he also realized that this time it wasn't just himself that he needed to worry about. Faith also looked to him for guidance. If she only knew ...

Would it be better for them to return to the remnants of the fuselage or to strike out on their own? He had no idea whether Oliver had managed to transmit an emergency signal, but he had seen nothing flashing on the remnants of the burnt-out cockpit control panel, had heard no telltale beep of a GPS locator or transponder. Oliver had still been strapped to his seat, hands still clutching the wheel ...

He shook the image away. Did he dare strike out through the wilderness with a woman wearing only a pair of jeans, tennis shoes, and a long-sleeved T-shirt? He only had a flannel shirt, but he was used to roughing it. She appeared so dainty, barely five-foot-seven and maybe weighing one-twenty soaking wet. Still, he had noticed that her jeans weren't designer jeans. Her shoes looked study and sensible, with good tread. Her fingernails were short. She wore no makeup. He didn't get the impression that she was high-maintenance.

Ethan glanced at her; eyed her pale skin, the dark circles under her eyes, the strain in the slight grimace of lips tilted downward in a frown. She had beautiful features; high cheekbones, finely arched eyebrows, a straight, small nose, and full lips. Her green eyes were the color of spring grass. He hadn't taken much notice of her when she'd scrambled aboard back in Billings, so deep had he been in his own thoughts.

"You from Billings?" he asked, thinking that some light conversation might ease the tension from her shoulders.

She didn't answer right away. A slight breeze rustled through long grasses and the cottonwoods that grew in clumps along the slope. In the distance he heard the scree of a hawk searching for dinner, the soft breeze carrying the scent of pine and rich earth. At any other time, he would have felt perfectly at ease, at peace with himself and the land.

"No," she said softly, turning to him. "You?"

He shook his head. "No, me either."

So much for conversation. That was fine with him. Still, he should offer her some comfort. Even with the somber thoughts swirling through his head? Was this yet another test? His faith was already on the edge, and this didn't help. Not one bit.

"What are we going to do?"

He looked at her and answered without doubt. That he could do. "First, we need to find shelter and a water source. I have a few supplies," he said, gesturing to his backpack. "It's warm enough now, but the temperatures dip at night up here. We'll get some rest, and then strike out in the morning."

"Strike out where?" She gazed at the miles of wilderness spread out before them. "Should we stay put? Isn't that a Boy Scout rule or something? If you're lost, stay put?"

"For a camper in a relatively popular area, yes," he smiled. "And if someone knows you're missing." He paused. "Is someone waiting for you? Will your arrival be missed?"

She said nothing for a moment and then shook her head. "No. What about you?"

What about me? While he had told his superior that he planned a retreat in his cabin in the mountains, he didn't recall telling him exactly where it was located or how he would be getting there. He never had before, either. Finally, he shook his head. "No."

"Great," she muttered and crossed her arms over her chest, shaking her head. "I should've known. Par for the course."

Curious. A woman traveling alone; traveling with nothing but the clothes on her back. No suitcase, no supplies, no one waiting for her. Who was she? What was she doing on that Cessna? Where was she headed? Plenty of questions, and every one of them none of his business.

He popped the last piece of jerky into his mouth, chewed thoughtfully, and then finally shrugged. He knew how she felt. Nothing to do about it now though, so he stood, slid his arms into his backpack straps, then gestured downslope. "We'll look for a campsite down there. It'll be too cold up here on the slope, with nothing to block the wind."

"We shouldn't start a fire or something? Something to signal a rescue plane?"

He glanced up into the breadth of the sky and then back down at her, speaking softly. "Do you see any?"

Without waiting for her reply, he started down, already having visually traced a zigzag pattern down the rocky slope dotted with knee-high pine saplings and an occasional boulder that ranged from head-sized to car-sized. He spoke over his shoulder. "Step carefully, follow my path, and take your time."

She said nothing, but followed him as he proceeded down, stepping sideways, his right shoulder facing the mountain slope. This way would be slower, but much safer. A minute later, he glanced over his shoulder to make sure she was following. Unlike him, she kept her toes pointed down the rocky slope, her back facing the mountainside. "You shouldn't walk like—"

His cautioning words broke off as he watched gravity take over. She lost her footing and physics took over. Her off-balance momentum carried her forward. With a startled cry, her torso bent forward, scrambling downward, right past him. He reached out to grab her arm but she was already going down, sliding on the loose shale. Ethan stood in dismay as she fell and then began to tumble, head over heels, leaving a trail of rising dust and grunts of pain drifting on the air behind her.

He quickly hurried after her, still keeping his feet parallel to the mountain, scrambling down sideways, arms outstretched for balance as he followed her pell-mell catapulting until, with a pained cry, she crashed into the base of an aspen tree. She didn't move.

"Faith!" He eyed her still figure crumpled against the base of the tree for several seconds and then continued downward, watching where he put his feet. She had landed about fifty yards down, slightly to his right. His breath escaped his chest in harsh gasps as he quickly hurried toward her, anger, despair, and frustration whirling in his brain as he finally reached Faith's prone, unconscious figure. He couldn't tell if anything was broken as carefully, he turned her over, his heart sinking when he saw the blood on her forehead. He noted the steady throb of a pulse in her throat and sighed with relief. A good sign, and at least she was alive. A bad sign because if she were seriously injured, they were up the proverbial creek without a paddle.

CHAPTER 4

THE WILDERNESS

PAIN.

She tried to focus, assess where it came from. Her head ... throbbing and deep. She opened her eyes and blinked several times, startled by the darkness surrounding her. She saw only odd sparkles of light and then realized she was gazing up into a black night sky, carpeted with millions of stars. A crackling sound a short distance away prompted her to turn her head, but she regretted it instantly, groaning with pain that throbbed anew.

She saw a campfire, mesmerized by the dancing flames, and beyond that, a shadow of movement. Where was she? What—and then she remembered, all in a flash, accompanied with a renewed pounding of her heart and a knot of dread in her stomach. The plane crash. Ethan, the only other survivor besides her, their search for a pilot and the other passenger, one dead, one still missing.

"Oh good, you're awake."

Ethan paused on the other side of the fire and placed the armload of sticks he had gathered in the forest, keeping them a short distance from the fire. He approached and crouched down beside her.

"How are you feeling?"

"My head hurts," she said simply.

He nodded. "You've got quite a goose egg on your forehead, but as far as I can tell, nothing's broken."

He retreated to the other side of the fire and sat down cross-legged. She followed his movements with her eyes, moving her head more slowly. "Where are we?"

"Same place we were this afternoon, except at the bottom of the slope," he shrugged. "Think you can sit up so you can drink some water and have something to eat?"

Could she? She'd better. The thought of being injured out here prompted her to try. Without his help, she managed a sitting position, wincing at the renewed pain throbbing in her skull and a sharp wrenching along the side of her knee. He saw her wince.

"Your leg?"

"Yes," she said tremulously. "My knee ... I think I twisted it." She reached a hand up to gently touch the tight, swollen bump at the hairline of her forehead. The throbbing eased after several moments and she gingerly explored her range of motion with her arms and legs. Other than her injured right knee, which protested movement but moved nevertheless, she felt she was okay. She was able to bend the knee a bit, biting back a moan of pain, but she didn't think it was broken. Her muscles ached, and she was likely bruised, not surprising given the tumble she had taken. She supposed she should count her blessings, but—

"Try not to force the knee," Ethan said. "Better to rest it for the night, because tomorrow morning, we're going to have to walk out of here."

Faith said nothing, her heart sinking as she watched Ethan put another small branch on the fire. She watched the flame curl under it, then started as one of the other small chunks of pine bough popped. The rising flames illuminated only part of him, his face still fluttering shadows. He would leave her. She would slow him down, delay rescue, she felt sure of it. He wouldn't wait for her, not with her injured knee holding him back. He couldn't possibly. But then she reconsidered. Here she was, stuck in the middle of nowhere with a stranger, and yet, oddly enough, she felt perfectly safe around him. Something about his calm demeanor, his soft-spoken words, his confidence out here in the wilderness.

"You seem perfectly comfortable out here."

He offered her a half smile. "I am." He looked up from the fire and gazed into the darkness. "You might say I'm an outdoorsy type, and I spend much of my time off, when I get it, camping, fishing, or hiking." Another snap of sap and small embers shot upward as he glanced at her. "And you? Did you grow up around here?"

"No," she said. She hesitated to tell him what she was doing out here. She didn't want him to know that she was on the run. Not that she had done anything illegal, but she had seen something that she shouldn't have. Everybody wanted a piece of her now; the cops, the bad guys, even the U.S. marshals after she'd been placed in the witness protection program. That's why she had been on that small plane, flying under an assumed name, her false Nebraska ID card costing her a pretty penny...

He watched her, waiting for more of an explanation. "I'm starting over," she said, knowing it sounded lame. "At least I'm trying to. What's that they say about Murphy's Law?" She gestured into the darkness surrounding them, but the glow from the fire only reached maybe five feet outward, with everything beyond that in shadows, unknown and unfamiliar to her.

"We'll get out of this," he said. He reached for his backpack and began to dig around again. Her mouth watered as she thought of another piece of jerky. Something thin, stiff, and round fell out. Ethan reached for it as her eyes widened in dismay. She looked from the object that he held in his hand and then up at him. He didn't move, staring down at the pack, not looking at her. He knew that she'd seen it. She frowned, wondering why he'd hidden it.

"You're a priest?" Her voice cracked with dismay. No wonder.

He gently fingered the collar and then tucked it back into his pack, carefully, and then turned to look at her. "Newly minted pastor," he said softly. He pulled the packet of jerky from the pack, slid out a piece and handed it to her.

"Congratulations," she said, taking the strip of meat. "I'll bet your family is proud."

He offered a shrug and another smile that didn't reach his eyes. "I come from a family of law enforcement officers and military men. To say they were surprised when I announced my calling to the church is an understatement." He pulled out a piece for himself and then tucked the package back into the pack. "I have a brother, younger than me. He's in the army now, stationed in Afghanistan ..."

"Any calling is a good calling," she said softly.

She didn't want to be nosy, but now her curiosity was running full speed ahead. "You have a congregation out here?"

He shook his head, took a bit of his jerky, and chewed.

"I have a congregation in South Dakota ... but I was headed for my cabin before I take over my duties there. It belonged to my great-grandfather. Been in the family ever since. You might say I'm on a short ... retreat."

Retreat? Her curiosity grew, but it was something else that he had said that captured her attention even more. "Your cabin. It's out here somewhere?" She gestured into the darkness. Hope surged.

He nodded. "South of here. That's where we're heading tomorrow. I think we can reach it in a couple of days."

Her hope waned at the distance, but she needed to keep her spirits up. Maybe she wasn't going to die out here in the wilderness after all. "We will."

"You have a lot of faith ... in me, and in fate, don't you?"

She shrugged, regretting the instinctive movement when her shoulder muscles protested. "To tell you the truth, Ethan ... or pastor—"

"Just Ethan."

She nodded. "After everything I've been through in the past year, I'll tell you, if it wasn't for my faith and my firm belief that things will work out better—in spite of this ..." She again swept her hand into the darkness beyond the light of the campfire. "I'd lose my mind." He said nothing but off in the distance, she heard the sound of howling. Eyes wide, she looked at Ethan, who seemed unconcerned. "What's that? Wolves?" A shiver of dread swept through her.

"Coyotes," he said, placing another stick on the fire. "Finish eating, and then you should try to go to sleep. We have a long day ahead of us tomorrow."

CHAPTER 5

FACING THE TRUTH

ETHAN LAY ACROSS THE FIRE FROM A SLEEPING FAITH FOR QUITE SOME TIME, not moving other than to occasionally glance up at the stars to watch the tail of the Draco constellation between the Big and Little Dipper slowly make its way across the night sky. He contemplated what she had told him, about starting a new life. What had prompted it? A breakup? His thoughts drifted to darker places. An abusive relationship? Illegal activities?

She'd had some bad luck, he thought, but she was starting over. How had she ended up on that Cessna plane with him? Without anything more than the clothes on her back and the determination to, as she said, start over. She was pretty.

He admired her bravery, her willingness to take a chance, to just jumpstart a new life. He was not the impulsive sort, quite the opposite. No, Pastor Ethan Seidel carefully weighed all the pros and cons before making a decision. Except this one, which had compelled him to take a leave of absence between finishing seminary school and starting at his new parish in South Dakota.

Off in the distance, a coyote howled up at the moon, followed several moments later by the yip of another. The night was still and calm. Normally, he would've reveled in it. Instead, he frowned and turned toward the dying fire, thinking of his family. About his decision and the tragedy that had compelled him to ask for this brief retreat before he fully devoted himself to his duties as a pastor.

The truth—the truth that his superiors didn't know, that he hadn't revealed to anyone, not his family, not a supervisor, and certainly not to Faith—was that he was having a crisis of faith. The tragedy that had occurred three months ago, just before he completed his training, had done a number on his psyche. He questioned God, the age-old question: *why do bad things happen to good people?*

Why did three-year-old Gabbie Stands Tall have to suffer such a horrible, violent death? Why did Jessica, the baby's mother, have to endure such suffering before she was killed? And, in heaven's name, why had Jake Washington, the perpetrator of such horrible things, been given what Jessica and her baby had not? Protection, three square meals a day, and if not freedom—the chance to at least live. Why did so many innocent bystanders have to die, to suffer a life of physical limitations and traumas because of Jake's drunken rage?

After he had murdered his family, in a drunken rage, Jake had sped away in his car, and that car had struck a bus full of youngsters traveling across the reservation to compete in a tournament with their school rivals ... they'd been laughing, boasting, and teasing each other one minutes and the next ... Ethan had been in that bus. He'd gotten out without a scratch while others ... the screams, the cries of pain, and then later, the shrieks of anguish from their parents, their friends, their schoolmates when they got the news at the hospital ...

He knew the common answers that a person with a deep and well-grounded sense of faith would reply. The devil was at work in this realm. People had freedom of choice—the freedom to do good and the freedom to do evil.

There were no easy answers. There was suffering in this world and he realized that. He wasn't naïve. He didn't expect everything to be perfect. But when he had seen what had been done to that baby ...

He shook the horrible memory from his mind, looked up again at the stars, his lips moving silently as he sought answers.

Silence.

CHAPTER 6

THE WILDFIRE

FAITH WOKE UP JUST BEFORE DAWN, STIFF FROM THE CHILL THAT PERMEATED her clothing during the night. At first, she felt confused, not understanding where she was, but then she remembered. The plane crash. The pastor. Falling down and then waking up at the campsite Ethan had made. The fire at Ethan had built the previous evening was gone now, the heavy scent of burnt wood and wood smoke in the air, a faint wisp of smoke curling upward from the gray, charred remnants. She began to sit up, then winced in pain as her knee protested. She froze, looking for Ethan. Where was he?

She was just about to call out, worried that he might have left her to fend for herself out here in the wilderness, and then realized that he wouldn't do that. Why was she so convinced of that? She didn't know him. For all she knew, he could've been lying about being a pastor. But she knew he was. Not only had she seen the collar, but she believed him.

She found him then, maybe fifty feet away, standing in a small clearing in the midst of a growth of pine trees and low-lying shrub, the forest floor covered with dry pine needles. He stood, his face turned upward. His lips moved, but she didn't hear what he said. She studied him a moment, finding him intriguing. Even though she'd only known him for a few hours, she liked him. He seemed prepared for anything; from the bottle of water and jerky in his backpack to understanding the mountains, for which she was incredibly grateful. If she had been left out here alone, the only survivor of the crash, she didn't think she'd ever have been able to find her way back toward shelter or civilization. Or light a fire, or find food ... she had been unprepared.

But Ethan, he blended into the wilderness, comfortable with his surroundings. It was like he was one of those people who belonged in a different place in a different time. Gazing at him, she sensed he would easily fit into the landscape in an earlier century. She smiled at the thought, shaking her head. *And you?* She thought about that. Where did she fit in?

Why did she have to leave, to run and hide, to start over, because of someone else's wrongdoing? It wasn't her fault that she'd been in the wrong place at the wrong time. Long ago, one of her friends had told her that life was an adventure. Forget adventure. All she wanted was to live her life, mind her own business, and do what she loved best. Teach. But then the incident ... followed first by threats on her life and then an actual attempt to silence her.

The police had wanted to put her in a safehouse from the get-go but she had scoffed, told them that no one was going to scare her into hiding. It wasn't until that first attempt on her life that she had eaten a piece of humble pie and realized that there were some things that she couldn't overcome. How could she fight against something or someone she couldn't see? She'd wake up in the morning, find a threatening note under her doormat. Another one in her mailbox ...

It was then that she'd finally agreed to discuss the witness protection program. She was assured she could give a videotaped deposition and could appear in court via short-circuit or digital, whatever it was, without having to physically appear in court. The man she was testifying against belonged to a group of very bad people. Some South American cartel or such craziness, and it was then that a shiver of fear had prompted her to agree.

It wasn't like she had a lot to lose. Her parents had died years ago in a car accident. She'd lost them in her senior year of college. She'd lived in an apartment in a pleasant enough neighborhood on the outskirts of Dallas. No pets. While she'd had to give up her job as an elementary school teacher there, she had been told that when provided with a new identity, new paperwork and documentation, she would be able to teach again.

She sighed, watching Ethan. She knew why she'd been on a Cessna. A puddle-jumper, as they called it, on her way to Seattle, taking the scenic route, as her case agent told her. She appreciated the caution and the care with which the U.S. marshals had arranged her transfer and her disappearance from her old life and her rebirth in a new one. She should tell Ethan that yes, someone would notice her missing. Her case agent.

As she gazed at Ethan, she couldn't help but wonder what had put him on that Cessna. She was remotely aware that a few small towns dotted the slopes and peaks in this region, but as far as she knew, her journey on the Cessna took her over the mountains. She had to learn to mind her own business, hold her cards close to the chest, be extremely cautious to say nothing that would reveal the truth or expose her new life and her new identity to scrutiny. Might as well start now.

With a heavy sigh, she watched Ethan shift his position, hands clasped together as he bowed his head. When was the last time she had prayed? Really prayed? She believed in God, she believed ... but she was not a churchgoer, had never been. Now, in the middle of this wilderness, she felt incredibly small. She was nothing more than a speck in the wilderness. At this moment, stronger than she had felt in years, she felt that something bigger and better than herself was out there, compelling her to turn this way, make that decision, whatever the case may be. Like a leaf blown on a breeze, she often felt that her decisions came from something deeper than herself. Maybe—

"Faith! Get up! We have to go!"

She jolted out of her reverie with eyes wide with surprise to find Ethan careening toward her. Her heart skipped a beat as she sought the source of his obvious concern. "What's the matter?"

He grabbed his backpack with one hand and pointed over his shoulder toward the northeast. All she saw was thousands of acres of forest and mountain ridges and peaks. "What—"

She stared, blinked, and then turned to Ethan, sliding his arms through the backpack straps, kicking dirt over the remnants of the fire. His alarm caused her heart to lurch as she struggled to get to her feet. The pain that shot through her knee caused her to gasp and he quickly hurried over to help her to stand. It was then that she saw the rise of billowing smoke in the distance.

"Forest fire," he said.

She didn't understand. "But it's so far away ..."

He paused to gaze at the campsite, making sure nothing was left behind. "The wind's blowing southwest, toward us." Abruptly, he grabbed her arm, on the same side as her injured knee. He draped her arm over his shoulder, holding firmly onto it while his other hand snaked around her waist.

A forest fire ... a cold, hard knot of fear tightened her stomach. "What started it? The plane crash? A campfire?"

"This time of year, anything is possible, but there's not too many hikers or anglers this deep into the mountains this time of year. I'd venture to say it was probably a lightning strike."

Lightning strike? But she hadn't seen any lightning. Then again, she had slept most of the night. "It stormed last night?"

He shook his head. "Don't need to have a rainstorm to have lightning out here. Wouldn't be the first time." He looked over her shoulder, then back down at her. "Come on, let's go. I'll find something that you can use as a crutch."

She looked again at the grayish smoke rising in the far distance. It looked so far away! Why was he so worried? Before she could decide what to do, he made the decision for her. He stepped forward, forcing her to hop along, wincing as she gingerly placed weight on the ball of her right foot.

She felt his strength, inhaled the scent of manly sweat, dirt, and pine permeating from his clothing.

"The national forest service monitors these mountains, doesn't it?"

"Sure, but like I said, this is a pretty remote area, and they may not see it right away. I'd venture to say that we're much further north than the bulk of the fire watch stations more common around the more popular camping and recreational areas."

"What do you mean they won't see it?" How was that possible? With today's technology, you'd think—

"They'll see it, eventually. But in many cases, they let naturally caused forest fires burn. If populations, structures, or even towns aren't threatened—"

"How can they just let it burn?" she asked in dismay. "All that land, all the trees, the animals ... it's all going to be destroyed."

"Such is the way of life, isn't it?" he said quietly, then gestured toward the south. "Fires move pretty fast. While you may think it looks far away, it's only about twenty to thirty miles away. We've got to get moving."

"But—"

Ethan paused to stare at her, his expression somber. "Faith, with enough fuel, a wildfire can move as fast as twelve miles an hour. Winds behind it? Even faster. In grasslands, a wildfire can make headway at about fourteen miles an hour."

She stared at him, heart pounding. "Can we outrun it?"

He shrugged. "If we head downhill, we might be able to. Fires tend to move faster uphill because that's the way the wind flows and it generates more heat, which causes them to move faster. But I'm not going to lie to you. If the smoke doesn't overcome us, the heat will."

She stared in horror over his shoulder. "It's going to catch up to us?" She barely got the words out, her voice cracking with strain. She glanced down at her leg and then up into Ethan's face, who saw her hesitation.

"We can do this, Faith," he said calmly.

"I'll slow you down." It was the truth. She couldn't move fast on her injured knee, much as she wanted to.

"Then we better get moving, don't you think?"

CHAPTER 7

THE RACE

THE FIRST HOUR WAS THE HARDEST. ETHAN HELD FAITH CLOSE, ONE ARM wrapped around her waist, the other hand holding her arm down over his shoulder and chest. Every step she took, every bit of weight she placed on her injured leg, caused her to wince in pain. She bore that pain silently, spurred on by the urge to outrun that fire. Problem was, they were moving much too slowly. He resisted the urge to glance over his shoulder, to gauge the distance between the spreading wildfire and their own position.

He knew they would never reach his cabin in time, not that the cabin would provide any shelter from a raging forest fire. No, their best chance was to keep heading downhill as quickly as they could while he continued to cast about for some type of shelter, any possible shelter from the firestorm behind them. A river that might serve as a firebreak. A cave ...

Was this punishment for his loss of faith? No, he hadn't lost it; it had been taken from him, the aftermath of a senseless tragedy. Senseless pain and suffering and death. That's what had jarred his faith.

But Faith depended on him and he would do his best not fail her. For that reason, he prayed. Angrily, with resentment, and with more than a little desperation, he prayed. He *wanted* to feel that connection again. He yearned for it, more than he yearned for anything in his life. He felt empty without it, without that deep sense of belief that had been with him forever. He didn't want to be this way, didn't want to *feel* this way. One minute there, the next minute gone. How had it happened? How had he allowed it to happen?

"How are you doing?" he asked Faith, both of them now scrambling down a slight slope, for a moment hiding the cloud of billowing smoke rising behind them, growing larger and larger.

"I'll make it," she gritted. "I'm actually ... getting used to the pain."

He heard her low laugh and marveled that she could find humor in a moment like this. He used to be able to do that, before the tragedy. He missed that. Usually it was he and his faith that gave others comfort and strength, the desire to push ahead. At this moment, it was this stranger, this woman, who had been thrust into this situation, at this given time, as desperate as he.

"So why were you on that plane, Ethan?" she asked, breathing heavily from exertion.

He knew what she was doing. She was trying to fill the silence between them, to ignore the danger from behind, to encourage a sense of camaraderie, of companionship ...

"Like I said, heading for my cabin."

"For a retreat."

It wasn't a question, but a statement. He grunted an affirmative.

"But you're a new pastor, right?"

Again, he grunted.

Watching for shrubbery on the slope they navigated and then glancing at him before looking downward again, she asked him *the question*. The question that he asked himself a hundred times a day.

"So what happened to you, Pastor Ethan? What was so bad that you needed a retreat? Are you questioning your faith?"

The question, though he was expecting it, startled him. He paused, turned his face toward hers, noticed the fine sheen of sweat glistening on her skin, her flushed cheeks, the wince of pain in her eyes. He felt torn between a shrug and an explanation. Considering their situation, he felt she deserved the explanation. As he continued helping her down the slope, he told her his story, his tale only broken when he had to literally lift her over rocks strewn in the path, or when she stumbled, biting back the pain that hobbled her movements. By the time they reach the bottom of the slope, both breathing hard, her fingers tightly grasping his forearm, she turned to him, her expression kind and compassionate, one that ignored her own fears to allay his.

"You are a pastor, Ethan, but you're also a human being. A man." She frowned, gazing upslope, a relieved sigh escaping her lips as the burgeoning cloud of smoke was momentarily hidden from them. "You do know what most people would say, don't you? What most pastors or priests would say to a parishioner after a tragedy? A loss? And even senseless death?"

He nodded, his gaze taking in her features, for the first time noticing the flecks of gold in her hazel eyes, a smattering of freckles across the bridge of her nose, her white teeth. She offered a smile and squeezed his arm.

"Why do you doubt yourself so? Why do you doubt your faith? You know the truth."

He said nothing, merely stared at her for several moments, and then he nodded. "I do," he said softly. "But for some reason, I just can't *feel* it. I haven't felt that since ..." he sighed. "I don't know how to explain it."

"You don't have to," she said, giving his arm another squeeze. "You're human, just like the rest of us. Believe me, I have times when I want to ... well, let's just say there are times when I want to shout at God too. *Why me*? Why do bad things always seem to happen to *me*? Why can't I ..." she paused and offered another smile. "I'm sure you've heard it all before, from your parishioners ..."

"We better keep moving," he said, gesturing. "That way."

They continued on, Ethan trying to get her to move a little faster. She tried, really, she did. Despite the pain she must be experiencing, she was trying, and in the face of that courage, that determination, how could he feel sorry for himself? That feeling grew tenfold as she told him *her* story. Simply, matter-of-factly, with hardly any emotion.

Like him, she had experienced something bad, very bad, something that had prompted— no, *compelled*—her to become someone else, in a strange place, starting over, born again. She was doing it, not just because circumstances had forced her to, but because she wanted to live. She wanted a second chance.

So did he.

CHAPTER 8

TAKING A STAND

IT SEEMED LIKE DAYS HAD PASSED SINCE THEY HAD SET OUT EARLY THIS morning after she'd seen that cloud of gray smoke rising up against the horizon. It couldn't have been more than a few hours. Hard to tell, with the smoky haze gradually filling the sky above them, the wind gusting the smoke overhead, ahead of the fire. She glanced back once and then refused to do it again, her heart racing, her fear growing.

"Pastor ... Ethan," she had said more than once. "Go! We'll never make it! I'm slowing you down too much!"

He had replied calmly every time, tightening his grip around her waist. "I'm not leaving you, Faith, and that's all there is to it. Quit asking."

She admired him for that, finding it rather chivalrous, if foolish. While he seemed to think that he was the odd duck in his family, the black sheep, so to speak, he was more like his brother than he realized. He might not be a trained soldier, but he was courageous and loyal. She had never met anyone quite like him. Though they had only known each other for a very short time, she felt things for him that she'd never felt for any man. Respect. A desire to do better ... to be better, not just for herself, but for that someone. She didn't know how things would turn out, and while she certainly hoped they survived, she realized and understood that their chances were not that great.

After traversing a thankfully relatively flat meadow and reaching the other side, they paused to catch their breath. She was glad for the opportunity, and in that moment, standing beside Ethan, she impulsively lifted her face to give him a quick kiss on the cheek. A wordless thank you. A wordless gesture of her heartfelt appreciation for his support, for his determination to get them to safety.

Except at the very moment, he turned his head toward her and instead of her lips landing on a whiskered cheek, her lips met his own. He froze for the briefest of seconds, but with a sigh, his lips moved gently on hers. Was this one of those moments when two people, afraid of dying, clung to one another, adrenaline prompting them to do something they normally wouldn't do? Just this brief moment of contact, this wordless sharing of humanity, a desire for compassion, fears and hopes, and everything in between?

After several seconds, Ethan slowly lifted his head, gazing down at her, a small smile turning up the corners of his mouth. No words necessary. She smiled up at him as well, and then once again they were off, both of them struggling to stay on their feet, to hurry without stumbling, while the sound of the fire building, growing, and devouring behind them grew ever louder.

Despite her determined efforts not to, she cast a quick glance over her shoulder and cried out in horror. The fire was a lot closer than she had expected. She had heard it, yes, but the sound had almost become natural, a part of the environment. Her startled cry captured Ethan's attention, and he, too, looked behind them. It was if with that one look, they had ignited an even greater fury inside the fire. It seemed to breathe, to inhale and exhale, billowing a gust of smoky ash toward them, burning embers surging toward them, the air filled with ash that wanted to choke her. The heat tickled her skin, and then grew warmer, as if enveloping her in its fury. She felt—

"Come on!" Ethan shouted, tugging her along after him as he dashed down slope. "I see a stream down there! If we can make it—"

He didn't waste another breath. She couldn't think, couldn't feel. The only thought racing through her brain was escape from the pursuing fire. That one glimpse had been enough, the fire not just behind them, but reaching out to either side, north, east and west, a wall of fire. How deep? She had no idea. How hot? Hot enough. She focused on keeping her balance, on preventing a stumble that would take them both crashing to the ground. The river. The river. *The river!*

Heart pounding, Faith scrambled with Ethan, her terror growing, the sound of the fire roaring behind them ever closer. She cried out in startled dismay as a flash of movement on her left prompted her to turn in stupefied wonder as three deer crashed through the underbrush and ran right past them, eyes wide with terror, mouths open with silent screams. Birds too, flying overhead, flying south, trying to escape the wrath of the fire tearing through the trees. Rabbits skittered this way and that, ears up, racing by so fast they were little more than furry blurs.

"Come on, Faith, we can make it! We've got to make it to the river!"

Her heart pounded with fear and hope. Her brain sizzled with pain. The smoke in the air, the flying ash, how could this be happening? For a second, and a brief second only, the fire didn't matter. Ethan did. She didn't want him to die, not for her sake. She didn't want to know what it felt like to be burned alive. She didn't want to hear herself screaming in pain, or Ethan suffering through the same pain. A horrid thought surfaced that she needed to push him away, to yell at him to run, to get away while he still had a chance.

"Go, Ethan, please!" she begged. She blinked back tears that filled her eyes, already burning from the heat and the ash in the air. Her lungs felt like they were burning from the inside out, choking on that ash, the swirling dirt, the embers that danced through the air on the wind, looking like millions of bright red fireflies.

"We can make it," he grunted. "Just another hundred yards and we'll be there. You can do it!"

Every step shot pain through her body, but she gritted her teeth to halt the cry of pain that threatened every time her foot made contact with the ground. Her pain was nothing compared to what it would feel like if those flames caught up with them ...

Suddenly, she felt herself falling, held tightly in Ethan's arms as he propelled them down the steep slope toward the river bank. They fell to the ground, but Ethan quickly regained his feet, crouched over her, literally dragging her by her arms the rest of the way toward the river. Nearby, a huge elk splashed through the water, snorting with terror before it was gone, bounding up the opposite shore maybe twenty feet away. In that moment, she also noticed something else. The water wasn't deep. She heard splashing, and then felt surprisingly cold water on the back of her head, then her shoulders, and then the rest of her body, mostly submerged as Ethan dragged her toward the middle. It never got much deeper. Not a river, not even a stream, more like a creek, meandering in a lazy S-curve around the bottom of the hill.

As Ethan dragged her into that creek, she stared in horror at the wall of fire looming above them, flames darting at least thirty feet high, swirling up tree trunks while pine needles singed and curled upward, the sound of popping as the sap caught fire. The crackling, the wind gusting down along the ravine, angry and red, drove every living thing in front of it.

Ethan collapsed beside her, holding her close, arms wrapped protectively around her waist.

"Hold your breath!"

Before his words fully settled in her brain, he was pushing her under, splashing water on her. She grabbed a mouthful of air as he submerged her head. He let her up then and she gasped for air. She was wet now, from top to toe. He, too, dunked himself, rolled, tried to saturate his clothing. One little flame was all it would take, or choking to death on the ash in the smoke.

"Ethan, you should have—"

His voice in her ear now, his lips so close she felt his breath.

"Don't try to talk, Faith," he murmured. "Cover your mouth and your nose with your hand."

"I don't want you to die ... I don't want you to die, Ethan," she cried. "You should've ... you should've gone." And only then, after the words had left her mouth, did she do as he bade. At least, if she had to die, here, she wouldn't die alone. And yet the heavy shroud of guilt that lay over her shoulders would go with her to the grave.

"We're not going to die, Faith," he said. "You're not going to die."

She wanted to believe the conviction in his voice. He sounded so sure of himself, invincible. Watching the fire grow closer, witnessing the fury with her own eyes, she might've laughed if she'd had the energy or the strength. How could a human being withstand that wall of fire coming ever closer? The color of the flames shimmered on the water's surface, turning it into an underling cacophony of orange, red, and burnt ombre.

How could they possibly survive? An impossibility, trapped as it were, only a shallow stream that barely covered them, protecting them from how many thousands of degrees of heat, from burning embers that landed on her face, stinging her skin even though it still dripped with cool water. Animals continued to race across the forest. A fleeing deer landed so close to her that she thought for sure its hooves would strike her head.

She hoped that the animals, driven by instinct, would make it out of the forest fire, but it was moving so fast ... so fast. She didn't know how it was possible, but the roar of the consuming flames grew even louder, like a freight train rushing past the station. She watched in horrified awe as the fire whipped around the trunk of the tree not forty feet away, like a tornado, curling around the trunk, surging upward, a living, breathing thing. The pop and crackle of flames grew ever closer, the heat more intense. The wind, kicked up by the heat of rising flames, battered the surface of the water. Everything shimmered, glowed, and wavered.

She focused on breathing. Take a short breath in, exhale. Every few seconds, she dipped her face into the water, terrified that her hair would catch fire, lit by a burning ember. Her thoughts jumped erratically from one horrifying thought to another. She coughed, felt like she was choking, like she couldn't draw air into her lungs. She dipped her face into the water again, a brief reprieve, and holding her nose barely above the surface of the water, tried not to breathe in the smoke, the ash ...

Would that be the last sound she ever heard? The snapping of branches, the popping of sap? Would her screams, or those of Ethan, echo in her ears as she died? Oh Lord. For the first time in years, she closed her eyes and prayed, but even so, the glowing light of the fire coming ever closer was visible through her eyelids. Heart thundering, every muscle in her body trembling from exhaustion, from fear, with terror of the unknown, she closed her eyes and prayed like she'd never prayed before.

CHAPTER 9

SURVIVAL

Ethan held Faith close, trying to offer what comfort he could. The heat grew intense, the sound of the roaring fire drowning out the sound of his own heartbeat, the sound of their occasional cries of protest at the heat, the fear. He heard Faith gasping for breath. His chest burned as it grew increasingly difficult to breathe. In spite of the comfort he tried to provide Faith, he felt an overwhelming surge of fear. Was this what it was like to die?

Lord, your will be done.

At that moment, while he accepted his fate, he also experienced a resurgence of faith. He needed to believe. He needed to trust that he and Faith would survive this. Even as he fought against the urge to grab Faith and run, to follow the animals across the stream and into the forest beyond, he knew that this was the safest place. He cupped Faith's face in his hand, keeping her mouth and nose just above the surface of the lapping water. If she passed out, she would likely drown. He squinted against the smoke, his eyes burning with it, watching as thousands of glowing embers blew across the stream. He didn't turn his head to see where they landed. Didn't turn his head to see if they were catching the other side on fire, or if they were, how bad it would be.

No, they would stay where they were. They couldn't outrun those flames. He felt bad for Faith, that this might be the end for her. Would their bodies be found? Or would they lay in the middle of this river and slowly decompose? *Ashes to ashes, dust to dust.* Maybe someday their skeletonized remains would wash downstream. Perhaps they would sink into the soft, silky silt to the bottom. Maybe, after autumn rains and winter snow, their remains would be swept downstream in a torrent of water, to be separated, pushed this way and that, pieces of himself scattered throughout the wilderness.

Through it all, he felt the heat, heard the hiss as a burning branch dropped into the water next to his head, the flames licking along its length extinguished as it sank into the water. Incredibly, the waters submerging them grew warmer. For several moments, he closed his eyes and imagined himself in a heated swimming pool, at a roadside motel, one of many he'd visited as a child with his family on their annual summer camping trips. He tried not to worry about what might happen if he drifted off into unconsciousness.

He forced his eyes open again, only to see nothing but blackness. Then the wind shifted, and he saw the glow of the fire again. He felt Faith next to him, shifting her position, so he loosened his grip, but only a little, concerned that like him, she might succumb to the overwhelming desire to jump up and flee. With her injured leg, she wouldn't make it far.

The heat grew even more intense. Every exposed piece of skin not submerged in the water tingled with the heat. For a second, he wondered if it was possible to self-combust, if that was nothing more than a myth or if there was some truth behind it. Would the water become so hot that they would boil alive?

Stop it! He must have faith. He must! Not just for his sake, but for Faith's. If she saw him surrender, if she believed that he felt their deaths were imminent, she would give up. She would allow herself to slip into oblivion. He couldn't allow that. He wouldn't.

"Hang on, Faith," he said, his face close to hers. "Hang on ..."

Surrounded by the wrath of the wildfire, Ethan wrapped his arms around her, closed his eyes, and prayed. He poured his heart and soul into his prayers, for Faith to be saved. He didn't pray for himself, but for her. She deserved her second chance. She deserved to live. Her faith was strong, and unlike his, had never wavered. He felt humbled, shamed, but ... suddenly, despite the heat, the flames licking at one side of the river bank, sending embers flying to the other side, the roaring, crackling, and popping all around him, he suddenly felt the greatest sense of calm. Of peace.

Was he dying? Was this what it felt like the moment before your heart stopped beating and your lungs stopped expanding? Did the brain experience this soothing sense of serenity? He felt Faith's hands tightly clutching his, fingers intertwined around her waist, her face so close to his neck that he felt her moist breath against his skin. No, this wasn't death. This was love ... surrounded by fire and certain death, it was at that moment that Ethan's heart felt an overwhelming outpouring of love. For Faith. Not only the woman in his arms, but for God, for Christ, for his savior, who, in His good grace, had seen fit to restore Ethan at his lowest moment, the moment when life could very well cease to exist for him on this earthly plane.

He felt wetness on his cheek and lifted his head, thinking that he had allowed his face to drop too close to the water. Then he realized that they were tears. Silent tears. His prayers had been answered. In the midst of his greatest fears, his faith had been restored.

CHAPTER 10

THROUGH THE FIRE

TIME STOPPED. ETHAN WASN'T SURE HOW LONG THE TWO OF THEM LAY IN THE water while the fire raged around them. Breathing grew increasingly difficult, but clinging to one another, Ethan took comfort in the fact that if they were to die, he wouldn't die alone. He would die with someone he respected and admired, someone who had given him the strength to come this far.

How much time had passed? A few hours? A day? Only minutes? It felt like forever, but lying there, his arms trembling from the effort to keep Faith's head above the water line, fighting the increasingly painful stiffness in his neck to hold his head just so, enough to occasionally submerge it to keep his hair wet while still able to breathe, he continued to pray, to talk to God. He had a conversation, really, like old friends catching up. He was at peace. If he was destined to die out here in the wilderness, consumed by the wildfire, so be it. He just asked that Faith not suffer, that if they were going to die, that it would be quickly, perhaps with them both drifting off to sleep, preferably at the same time ...

From a distance, he heard a different sound, something separate from the fire. He opened his eyes, shifted his head slightly, and stared in amazement. The fire had jumped the river, but in the direction from which they had come the flames seemed smaller, the charred tree trunks with twisted, spindly naked branches extending outward, smoke twirling upward, several trunks glowing with the heat still eating away at their insides. But what was that sound?

And then, looking up into the sky, he saw a swath of fluorescent pink ... maybe not pink, but a reddish pink. And then the sound and sight brought realization. He turned his face toward Faith, tried to speak, but coughed instead. He dipped his face toward the water, took a drink, swallowed painfully, his throat scorched from inhaling smoke and ash, and tried again.

"Faith!"

She shifted in his arms, lifted her face toward his, squinting, blinking, eyebrows lifted in question.

"Faith, look!" He rolled onto his side, urging her to look up, to follow his arm as he pointed upward.

He shifted his gaze from her blank expression up to the sky and back again. Now, only a slight tinge of that reddish pink fluorescence floated on the air. Then the sound dissipated. "It's fire ..." he coughed, tried again, his voice hoarse and scratchy. "Fire retardant! I heard a plane!"

Still clinging tightly to him, Faith stared at the devastation around them, then turned to Ethan, eyes wide, trying to speak. Raw embers continued to float in the air, but it wasn't nearly as bad as it had been. He dared to sit upright, pulling Faith up with him. He cupped his hand, scooped water from the river, and lifted it to her lips. She drank greedily, and then twisted, bending her head toward the surface of the water, taking several gulps on her own before sitting upright next to him.

"Are we alive?" she croaked, her voice raspy as well. "Is it over?"

He held her close, his left arm wrapped around her waist, both of them sitting in the middle of the creek bed as if it was the most natural thing to do. Once again, he heard the rumble of an aircraft, once again watched in amazement as a swath of pinkish red fire retardant was released into the hills. He braced his weight against his right hand, submerged in the water, his fingers idly tracing the outline of several pebbles amidst the silty bottom. He turned to face her, lifted his hand, and caressed the side of her face, a smile lifting the corners of his mouth.

"We're alive, Faith, and while it's not quite over, it will be. Soon."

He looked back into the ruins of the forest from which they had emerged, racing for their lives, stunned to find a young buck standing on the edge, his hide slightly singed. To Ethan's amazement, the buck stepped toward the water, lowered his head, and drank. Then the buck took several more steps into the creek, heading right toward Ethan and Faith, who sat unmoving, watching, not wanting to frighten him. He came close, eyeing them, but not with fear. Like them, the young buck had escaped an even greater fear. Slowly, Ethan lifted his hand. His heart thumped and his eyes grew damp as the young buck lowered his head, sniffed, and then nuzzled at his moist palm before moving off.

"Did you see that?" he said in wonder, turning toward Faith.

Her face had lost its fear as she gave him a heartwarming smile and nodded. "I did."

Then, to his surprise, she shifted once more, placed both her hands on his shoulders and then brought her face closer to his. Her lips touched his. Whether that kiss was born of adrenaline or not, it didn't matter. For Ethan, it marked a new beginning. It marked a renewal of his faith, from which he knew at that moment he'd never falter again. With that kiss, he felt hope renewed.

He kissed her back.

EPILOGUE

ETHAN SAT QUIETLY IN THE LOBBY OF THE HOTEL IN BILLINGS, WAITING FOR Faith to come downstairs with the US marshal. Since the fire a week ago, he and Faith had shared their days, and a few late evenings, building on their relationship, grown from the very basis of survival instincts.

Even as the fire had waned on one side of the creek and moved onto the other, they'd been spotted by a helicopter, huddling in the middle of the creek, waving their arms. During those hours of waiting to be rescued, Ethan had had an unshakable sense that the two of them were destined to be together. They had survived together, just as they would survive whatever the future brought their way. Together.

After being rescued and evacuated to a small town with no name, given dry clothes and food by volunteers and then transported to a slightly larger town to the north and a motel they could stay, he had called his immediate supervisor and relayed the incident. He had been told to take a couple more weeks to recuperate before he was to report to his new parish at in a small town on the edge of the Standing Rock Indian Reservation, in a small town, ironically enough, called Faith, located approximately a five-hour drive north of Rapid City.

The following morning, they'd been evacuated further east, back to Billings. There, Faith had also contacted the US marshal's service. Her case agent had told her to stay put until he arrived in Billings yesterday afternoon.

While Ethan's immediate future had been decided, hers had not. She wanted to change the plan. She wanted to stay closer to Ethan, to see how their relationship developed. The only hindrance to that plan was the US marshal's service, her protected witness status, and of course, the importance of maintaining her new identity.

Ethan knew that despite his growing feelings for Faith, her safety was more important than anything. If the US marshals refused to agree to her suggestion, he knew he would have to let her go, no matter how difficult that would be. In Faith he had found a companion, a friend, a confidant, a woman with whom he had shared his deepest fears. They had learned much of each other since the fire, since that fateful trip aboard the Cessna. While he hoped and prayed that she could convince the marshals that she'd be safe here, well, he ...

The elevator dinged and he automatically turned toward it, standing as Faith emerged and quickly glanced around the lobby before her gaze finally latched onto him. She smiled and quickly walked toward him, wrapping her arms around his waist, resting her head against his chest, where it belonged. She liked doing that, he had learned over the past few days. She told him that she loved listening to his heartbeat, the steady thud that she found supremely comforting.

The marshal followed, gazing somberly at both of them. Ethan's heart sank. Then Faith released her grip on his waist and looked up at him, tears glistening in her eyes. At that point, he knew. He resolved to take the news bravely. Her words took him by surprise.

"I can stay," she said, a catch in her throat.

He glanced at her, then at the marshal, who nodded.

"They've already got me a teaching position on the reservation. Ethan, I can *stay*."

Everything fell into place. Everything right with his world. His faith restored. Falling in love. Starting over. They both had a second chance. His heart tugging with excitement in his chest, he extended a hand and shook that of the marshal. "Thank you," he said, knowing that the words weren't enough, but they were all he could offer.

The marshal gestured toward Faith. "She's quite convincing. Determined. When she sets her mind to something, good luck trying to change it."

Ethan chuckled, gazed down at Faith, looking up at him with joy. Maybe his crisis of faith, his presence on that Cessna, his race for survival with Faith had not been just chance. It had been meant to be. Because, without that crisis of faith, he never would have met this woman, this woman he was learning to love with all his heart and soul. He also understood now that while bad things might happen to good people, and while the ultimate purpose was not always easy to find, he knew one thing for sure.

Never again would he allow his faith to lapse. Not with this woman by his side. Without caring who was watching, ignoring the grin on the US marshal's face, he bent his head, wrapped his arms around Faith, and kissed her. She kissed him back, both of them expressing through that kiss their confidence that, together, they could endure anything.

THANK YOU SO MUCH FOR READING MY BOOK. WE SINCERELY HOPE YOU ENJOYED every bit reading it. We had fun creating it and will surely create more.

Your positive reviews are very helpful to other reader, it only takes a few moments. They can be left at Amazon.

https://www.amazon.com/Brenda-Clemmons/e/B07CYKVVRT

WANT FREE BOOKS EVERY WEEK? WHO DOESN'T!

BECOME A PREFERRED READER AND WE'LL NOT ONLY SEND YOU FREE READS, BUT you'll also receive updates about new releases.

So you'll be among the first to dive into our latest new books, full of adventure, heartwarming romances, and characters so real they jump off the page.

It's absolutely free and you don't need to do anything at all to qualify except go to.

PREFERRED READ FREE READS

http://brendaclemmons.gr8.com/

ABOUT THE AUTHORS

ON A COLLEGE ROAD TRIP DOWN THE "MOTHER ROAD," ROUTE 66, BRENDA Clemmons fell in love with the beauty of the southwest and promised herself that one day she'd return.

After graduating with a history degree, Brenda fulfilled that promise and moved to Arizona, where she met her future husband, who was teaching literature in the classroom several doors down from her own social studies class.

Today, she, her husband, and their two kids love to explore the Southwest's beautiful mountains and deserts every chance they get. Brenda's habit of pulling over at every historical marker eventually led to her husband suggesting that she combine her love of romance novels with her in-depth historical knowledge. She put pen to paper and has been writing ever since, filling her stories with the landscapes, legends, and unique local characters that she wants everyone else to share in!

KATIE WYATT IS 25% AMERICAN SIOUX INDIAN. BORN AND RAISED IN Arizona, she has traveled and camped extensively through California, Arizona, Nevada, Mexico, and New Mexico. Looking at the incredible night sky and the giant Saguaro cacti, she has dreamed of what it would be like to live in the early pioneer times.

Spending time with a relative of the great Wyatt Earp, also named Wyatt Earp, Katie was mesmerized and inspired by the stories he told of bygone times. This historical interest in the old West became the inspiration for her Western romance novels.

Her books are a mixture of actual historical facts and events mixed with action and humor, challenges and adventures. The characters in Katie's clean romance novels

draw from her own experiences and are so real that they almost jump off the pages. You feel like you're walking beside them through all the ups and downs of their lives. As the stories unfold, you'll find yourself both laughing and crying. The endings will never fail to leave you feeling warm inside.

BECKY'S WINTER

Mail Order Bride Western Romance

RoyceCardiff

P u b l i s h i n g   H o u s e

WHOLESOME INSPIRATIONAL ROMANCE

Dear Reader,

It is our utmost pleasure and privilege to bring these wonderful stories to you. I am so very proud of our amazing team of writers and the delight they continually bring us all with their beautiful clean and wholesome tales of, faith, courage, and love.

What is a book's lone purpose if not to be read and enjoyed? Therefore, you, dear reader, are the key to fulfilling that purpose and unlocking the treasures that lie within the pages of this book.

NEWSLETTER SIGN UP PREFERRED READ

http://katieWyattBooks.com/readersgroup

THANK YOU FOR CHOOSING A INSPIRATIONAL READS BY ROYCE CARDIFF PUBLISHING HOUSE.

Welcome and Enjoy!

A PERSONAL WORD FROM KATIE

I LOVE WRITING ABOUT THE OLD WEST AND THE TRIALS, TRIBULATIONS, AND triumphs of the early pioneer women.

With strong fortitude and willpower, they took a big leap of faith believing in the promised land of the West. It was always not a bed of roses, however many found true love.

Most of the stories are based on some historical fact or personal conversations I've had with folks who knew something of that time. For example a relative of the Wyatt Earp's. I have spent much time out in the West camping hiking and carousing. I have spent countless hours gazing up at night thinking of how it must been back then.

Thank you for being a loyal reader.

Katie

PROLOGUE

Dear Becky,

I am writing this missive to inform you of my inability to move forward with our wedding plans. I wish you the best for your future and hope that you understand,

Charles

THE SMALL SQUARE PIECE OF PAPER ESCAPED BECKY'S LOOSE GRIP, FLUTTERING to the floor as the bustling activity of the servants in the house drowned out everything else. Her mind raced as she tried hard to comprehend what had happened and why, but nothing made sense.

"Miss, where would you like these?" One of the workmen jerked her out of her thoughts, bringing her attention to the flowers in her hand, flowers she had chosen for her wedding. The sight of them made her sick.

Without uttering another word, she picked up her skirts, turned around, and bounded up the stairs, ignoring everyone as tears streamed down her face. She couldn't think about facing anyone at the moment, not the servants, and especially not her father, who had so many expectations from her marriage.

He will be devastated, was the thought that kept circulating in her head but she tried to forget everything. She needed to be alone for some time, needed to get herself together and bear all the scorn that would be directed her way as her grand wedding was cancelled just a week before it was supposed to take place. She had no idea why Charles had rejected her so. After all, she was not some lowly peasant girl. Her father was one of the richest in the state of Louisiana and she was perfect in every way a young girl was trained to be.

The coming months were her answers to almost all her questions.

CHAPTER 1

"Are you sure this is going to be okay?" Linda asked Becky in a whisper, who was busy scanning the newspaper laid out in front of them on the table. They were whispering in hopes of being as invisible as they could as their employer made rounds. Becky was concentrating hard on the ceramic pot she was painting, wincing as the side of the pot hit the sore spot where she had cut herself two days back when a plate had slipped out of her hand.

"I sure do hope it will be. You know as well as I that I have no other option," Becky replied, trying not to sound too bitter about the fact. She had had the most unexpected and toughest year of her life. Things she had never thought could happen to her had taken place and had ended up making her question her sanity, but she had held herself steadfast and not let anything break her or her spirit.

"I do know that, but maybe there could be some way out of it? Can you not ask for time from those debtors?" Linda asked.

"No, Linda. They have already given me so much more time than I thought they would. My father owed them a huge chunk of money. It's a wonder that they have been willing to take payments in installments so far," Becky replied.

"I know, I know. It's just that you're my only friend, and I feel sad that you would have no choice in such an important matter of your life," Linda argued and Becky felt the wave of grief and anger resurfacing. Anger at everything she was going to have to give up and grief over everything she had lost already.

"This is the choice I'm making, Linda. I was so relieved when you told me about this option. I could never in a million years have guessed that such a thing happened."

"You might be glad, but I'm regretting ever telling you about it. I wish Charles could have been a better man," Linda sighed wistfully and Becky's back straightened over the mention of her ex-fiancé.

"He was a good man. He just couldn't marry me after the bankruptcy," Becky told Linda for the hundredth time.

"He was marrying you, not the money. It shouldn't have mattered that your father's business incurred such a huge loss," Linda argued aggressively.

"It would have happened sooner or later, my friend. This is our society. A person is how much money he has, especially in the upper circles," Becky replied, remembering how everyone had turned their backs on them once they had lost the money.

"They are not human. How could they treat a young girl like that, a week away from her wedding, after she had lost her mother just a short time ago?!" Linda exclaimed and Becky smiled weakly at her friend's outrage.

She knew why Linda was angry, but she had worked so hard to forget everything that had happened to her in the short time of two years between 1936 to 1937: her father losing the business after investing heavily in cotton, her mother's death, and her fiancé's refusal to marry her. It felt like everything had happened in such a short span.

"It is the way of the world. My father should have been more responsible when investing everything and taking loans for that year's cotton business," Becky responded.

"How could the man have known? You do remember how the cotton industry flourished the previous year? Everyone who invested in cotton got rich. No one could have known that everything would fare so badly," Linda reminded her and Becky remembered. She remembered how happy her father had been, ecstatic more like it. He had told her and her mother repeatedly of how they were going to get richer than ever. He wanted to take them to England and show them the world. For a moment, Becky was glad that her mother had died before she could see what had followed. She knew her frail mother wouldn't have been able to stand the humiliation and parting with her beloved things.

"I remember, Linda. That very disaster cost my father his life. He couldn't stand what he had done to us. Those were his exact words in his suicide note," Becky related coldly. She remembered it vividly, how the letter had felt, how much of a shock it had been, and the stab of betrayal still felt very real.

Linda was the only one who had been there for her, a relative stranger, their neighbor in the down-trodden cottage they had had to move to. The very cottage she was going to have to sell now to pay the last of the debts.

"Becky?" Linda shoved her lightly, jerking her out of her thoughts.

"Huh?" she replied, still disoriented due to the direction her thoughts had taken. Her father's face flashed before her eyes and she did everything to hold her tears in check.

"Are you okay?" her friend asked, sympathy and understanding in her eyes as she guessed what Becky might have been thinking about.

"Of course," Becky answered, and she was. She had just blinked once in shock when she had been told of her father's death, because she did not have the privilege to let it all go and cry her heart out. There was so much to do. There were debts to be settled and a funeral to be arranged. By the time she was done with both, she'd had nothing left for herself, save for the barren cottage. At that moment, she had learned how useless the kind of education she had received really was. She was hungry, and managing a household did not put food on the table, especially if she had no experience of ever working. Linda had been her neighbor and confidant and her rock. She had helped her through everything, finally finding her a job in the ceramics factory she worked at, painting all kinds of items. Becky had a good hand with a brush and that was what had finally saved her.

"It will be okay. He might be a very nice man," her friend consoled, and Becky tried to smile through it. She knew Linda was just trying to cheer her up but she had no great expectations when it came to the man she was going to marry. She had answered the first advertisement she had read in the newspaper and talked with the man twice through letters. He sounded reasonable and educated and was ready to take her as his wife without any dowry or any other stipulations. That was enough for Becky. After all, she really had no other option if she wanted to pay back her father's last debt by selling the cottage. She had everything lying in the balance and however hard life in the West was, it couldn't be worse than the horror she had already experienced in the last two years.

CHAPTER 2

JOHN SWORE AS THE SOUND OF HOOFBEATS APPROACHED THE BARN HE WAS working in. He calmed his temper, knowing that it wouldn't do him any good to lose it. This was not the first time this was happening and even though he should have been used to all this by now, it still rubbed him raw every time the collectors came.

"John Dawson!" The rough shout echoed across the barn as a man dismounted from his horse, adjusting his Stetson before grinning in that outrageous way of his.

"Rocky," John muttered, controlling the urge to roll his eyes. Rocky brought out the worst in him. John was not usually a very violent person, preferring logical discussions over any other means of disagreements, but with Rocky he couldn't control his baser instincts.

"Do you have it?" Rocky asked, not wasting any time and getting right to the business. John gestured to the man's left with a swift jerk of his head, wanting to be done with this and get back to his work. Rocky turned to look at where he had pointing, whistling as he picked up the small bundle of cash from the small work-table John had installed in his barn just a few days ago. Rocky counted the money, taking his time while John bristled at the leisurely action. It pained him to see his hard-earned money in the man's hand but Rocky's obvious distrust in John, even after such a long time, insulted him.

"All good." He spoke up once he was done, using the money to offer John a mocking salute and a grin as he turned back towards his stallion. He was almost to the horse but turned back to look at John as if suddenly remembering something.

"I heard you placed that announcement about a bride in the paper," Rocky stated, and John simply nodded.

"Well, well. This place does need a woman's touch." He grinned, surveying the barn and letting out a laugh as John clenched his fists. "I hope the woman finally calms this temper of yours. It'd make our dealings far easier," Rocky announced and climbed on his horse, not waiting for a reply.

It took John almost an hour to put the encounter behind him and calm down and forget the money he could've used for the progress of his farm, to answer the latest letter he had received from Becky, the only woman who had written back to him. He opened her letter for the fourth time, skimming the contents as he thought of his own reply.

He was looking forward to Becky's arrival. He had not thought that he would actually find anyone suitable when Sylvester, the town's barber, had suggested that he find a bride for himself through the paper, but Becky's first letter had managed to intrigue and interest him in the strangest way. She had been very polite and straightforward and he, being educated as an attorney of law, had liked her direct style. But what had really impressed him was how different she was from the women he had known.

The woman was no damsel in distress and had not once written anything that could be looked upon as silly or impractical, and that might just be her best quality because he knew that any impractical woman would not be able to survive life in the West, especially given how the situation was with him. A small part of him felt guilty that he had not told her the entire truth about his own situation, just letting her know that he was a farmer who needed a wife to help out with his work and provide companionship. It was all true, but there was the whole thing with Rocky that he had decided to keep to himself, justifying that it wasn't anything big and she would find out about it once she arrived. But he had promised himself that he would let her go back if she was even a little alarmed with the situation.

He hoped to God not, because he actually liked conversing with her and was sure that they would get along well if she was as practical and sensible as she sounded in her letters.

Taking out his pen from the top drawer of the table in his bedroom, he folded out a fresh page and started writing his response.

Dear Becky,

I hope you really are fine with everything I've told you, like you've stated, because I would love to ...

It took him less than half an hour to write everything he wanted to say and once he was done, he sat back and looked down at the paper. This was it. He had told her how she was going to travel and was also going to attach the required sum of money for the journey along with the letter. If everything went well, he would have a bride in a week or more. The notion surprised him but he also felt it was right. It was high time he got married, since every other farmer his age now had children running around their farms. He, himself, had wanted to wait until he'd earned enough before he settled down and got married. He had traveled West chasing the dream of escaping poverty, owning a piece of land he could call his own.

He now had a farm that paid him well enough to sustain a family and would even give him enough to expand and grow, if he didn't have to make those payments, but it wasn't time to think about all that. He had a bride arriving soon enough and he needed to make sure that he didn't scare her away as soon as she arrived.

CHAPTER 3

To say that Becky would run the other way if she ever saw a stagecoach in her life again would be no understatement.

She had received John's letter and enclosed within had been all the information and money she needed for the journey west. She had been grateful because, after selling her cottage and paying off the debtors, she didn't have much left.

Becky looked out of the coach's small window as the scenery outside changed rapidly, the weather heating up as they drew closer to their destination. Her small trunk bounced on her lap, hitting her knee and making her wince as the woman sitting next to her glared at Becky. It had been the same way ever since they had started the journey.

When people talked about stagecoaches and how they were helping people in traveling long distances, no one mentioned how people were sitting almost right on top of each other as the moving vehicle bumped and shoved everyone together, the massive amounts of luggage from every traveler almost flying around inside the enclosed space. While Becky had been almost sad to see that she had nothing but a small trunk from her life of twenty-one years in Louisiana, she was now glad for the very same reason. Her small trunk had caused her such nuisance; she shuddered to think what would have happened if she was not traveling light. The glaring woman would probably have killed her, she thought.

Along the journey, Becky had realized that many of the people traveling alongside her were regular travelers, as they kept updating the others on where they were and how long it was going to take them to reach their destination along with tales of their own various and exciting adventures on the same journey.

"We will be there by noon!" a middle-aged man, whose name Becky had learned was Samuel, announced. Even though marrying this way was the option she had chosen and she was ready for everything mentally, butterflies fluttered inside her stomach as her childhood dreams of finding her prince, like every other girl, came up to the forefront of her mind.

She unconsciously prayed that her groom would be a decent man at least and crossed her fingers. It was a habit she had developed when she was child. Her father had been the one who had introduced her to the method of twisting her forefinger and her middle finger together when she hoped for something to go a certain way. It had just been a childhood game but the practice had never left her, even when she grew up.

The next few hours seemed like years as her heart beat a staccato inside her chest and she took deep breaths to calm the nervousness that seemed to have taken root inside her stomach. Finally, the stagecoach slowed and then it stopped, stopping her breath right along.

Everyone started jumping out of the vehicle, relieved to finally have reached their destination, but her own legs seemed to be stuck in the position they had been for the past so many days. Taking one last deep breath, Becky adjusted her bonnet and her skirt the best she could, trying to straighten as many of the creases out as possible before finally stepping out of the coach.

The hot air hit her face as the bustle of the street they were on reached her ears. She looked around to find that they were in the middle of a crowded street and small shops and businesses surrounded the cobbled road. The marketplace, as she guessed it to be, was such a contrast from the big shops she was used to that it took her a moment to take it all in.

"Excuse me?" A deep voice called out from right behind her, giving her a start as she pivoted around instantaneously.

She came face-to-face with a man who looked to be almost a head taller than her with a strong angular face, one that couldn't be called handsome but also couldn't be ignored easily with its high cheekbones, wide lips, and eyes that were such a startling blue that you couldn't help but look deep into them. Paired with the dark blond hair, the face wasn't something that you would forget for a while. Becky was so busy examining the man's face that she almost forgot that he had said something.

A faint blush started to move up her neck as she realized that she had been rudely staring at the man without having said even a single word. He must have noticed her blush because a small smile graced his lips, softening his whole countenance.

"Becky?" he asked, and she was sure that her heart had stopped beating.

"John?" She answered the question with one of her own and inhaled sharply as he nodded. She had no idea why she was reacting the way she was, but the truth was that John was far more of a handsome man than she had been expecting. It puzzled her why a man like him would need to order a bride.

"How was your journey?" John asked her as he took the small trunk from her hand, his calloused fingers brushing hers. It was a good thing that he had taken the handle from her because she might just have ended up dropping the thing on her very own toes after the small brush of fingers.

Get a grip, Becky, she scolded herself and replied,

"It was fine and uneventful." She tried to be as honest as possible without complaining about everything that she had suffered.

"That's good." John smiled at her and she found herself smiling back.

"So, how do you want to do this?" he asked as they started walking side by side.

"What do you mean?" she asked, confused.

"We could wait a few days until you get to know me and the area before going to the pastor," he replied, and she panicked. She had thought that they would get married right away but now with John wanting to wait a few days, a hundred thoughts formed in her head. Maybe he didn't like the way she looked or had expected someone elegant and beautiful instead of her plain self. Those were the less alarming thoughts as doubts flittered through her mind about everything.

Her face must have showed everything she was thinking because John suddenly halted, rushing to explain everything.

"I did not mean anything by that. I just thought ..." he started, but then shook his head. "Never mind. We can go to the pastor right now.

Becky finally breathed a sigh of relief. "I think that would be best," were her last words before 'I do.'

CHAPTER 4

JOHN COULD NOT BELIEVE HIS LUCK. WHEN HE HAD WRITTEN THE advertisement about finding a bride, not even in his wildest thoughts could he have imagined someone like Becky. So far, the woman was perfect. She wasn't beautiful in the classic way, but her auburn hair that shone almost red in the sunlight, paired with her olive complexion and those big green eyes, was in no way just average.

Becky was pretty in an unconventional way and with her practicality, she was the perfect wife he could've wanted. It hadn't escaped his notice that while all the other women in the coach had been laden with huge amounts of luggage, his new bride had had just a small trunk. If that didn't tell him about how sensible she was, he didn't know what would. He had traveled on the stagecoach from the South as well and knew how bad the journey could be and how advantageous having little luggage could be.

"Is your house close?" She spoke for the first time since they had gotten into the hack he had hired to get them to his farm.

"Yes, just a few more minutes," John replied, turning his head to look at her fully. Currently, she was worrying her plump bottom lip between her teeth and her stiff posture indicated that she probably wasn't at ease.

"It will be fine." He couldn't help reassuring her, knowing how nerve-wracking the whole experience must be for her, but he was glad that they had gotten married right away. He didn't know what might have happened in the next few days or if she would've changed her mind after seeing where she was to spend the rest of her life, since she was from a big city and his small farm would be a huge change for her.

She smiled in response to his reassurance and just at that moment, the hack stopped. He jumped off immediately and took hold of her small trunk. He had spent the past few days preparing the house for her arrival, making sure that everything was the best it could be. He silently let her take everything in as he moved ahead of her, leading her to the house.

"I will give you a detailed tour of everything later," he promised her, holding open the door to the house for her to enter.

John tried to look at everything from her eyes, seeing the small foyer that led to an open kitchen at the back of the house and another hallway that led to the two bedrooms. The house was clean and orderly, but he knew that it looked a little barren.

"Is it satisfactory?" he asked, unable to hold himself back.

"It is really nice. Better than my cottage back home," she replied, taking a turn around the small area as John thought through her words. He wanted to ask her why she had answered his ad instead of marrying a nice man back home, saving herself all the trouble of traveling such a long way, but held back.

You have a lot of time to get to know her, he consoled himself as she moved towards the bedrooms.

"You can have the one on the right," he told her, and she swung her wide-eyed gaze towards him.

"We aren't going to share a bedroom?" she questioned, sounding shocked, and he shook his head.

"Eventually, yes, but I think we need to take things slow. We need to be friends and confidantes before we become husband and wife," he explained, knowing he was right when Becky visibly relaxed in front of him.

"You're right, of course. I just didn't expect this," she confessed, and he was intrigued.

"What did you not expect?"

"For you to be so understanding. And for everything to be so normal," she answered, and John laughed.

"Normal? I really don't think anything about this place is normal in any way," he all but warned her, but she smiled.

"Relatively normal," she amended her sentence, and he was impressed.

"You're educated," he announced and she blushed again. The whole thing was very endearing to him.

"Yes, I had a governess when I was young. You seem to be educated yourself," she said.

"I studied to be an advocate of law before moving here," he told her, and enjoyed the shock on his face.

"Why did you move here?" she asked directly, a perplexed expression on her face.

"I wanted more than what life there had to offer," he answered simply and she looked amazed.

He ended up telling her everything over coffee as he heated the lunch he had prepared for her.

"I would've invited a few people over for our wedding feast if I had known it was going to take place today," John told her.

"It's good you didn't. We got some time to ourselves, and I don't know if I would've been able to entertain anyone," Becky replied and John remembered how tired she must be.

He hurried up and served the roasted chicken and mashed potatoes he had made and smiled the whole time as she couldn't eat fast enough or praise often enough. They talked a little about food and her cooking when he noticed that she was yawning every few minutes.

"You need to rest," he told her as she got up and cleared the plates with him.

"When do you sleep?" she asked, looking out the window in the kitchen to see that it was almost twilight.

"Just a few hours later than this." He grinned at her half lidded and tired eyes. She was adorable.

"I can stay up and help you," she offered and John felt warm inside. He couldn't remember the last time anyone had offered to help him with anything. He was glad that he had decided to get married.

CHAPTER 5

THE FIRST TIME BECKY FELT THAT SOMETHING WAS WRONG WITH JOHN WAS A week later when she saw him putting away all of the month's earnings in a jar labeled 'X' and keeping only the minimum required for them to tide over. She was confused when she knew how the farm and the house could use that money, but she was sure that John must be saving it. Her guesses proved wrong when John took the money out of that jar one day and went to town for the evening. Becky had expected him to come back with a lot of things they needed but instead, he returned empty handed.

She wanted to ask him about it but he seemed so worried after it that she decided against it. The same thing happened the very next month and by now Becky was sure something was up with John. The only thing she could come up with was that he was a gambler. She still wanted to be sure before she just assumed anything, so she decided to talk to him first.

He was just back from the field one day when she put forth her question.

"John?"

"Hmm," was the only reply as he continued to wash his hands and feet at the hose outside the house.

"Do you gamble?" she asked, deciding not to beat around the bush. His movements stilled instantaneously as he looked up at her, shock evident on his face.

"Why would you think that?" he asked, shaking his head slowly as if unable to believe her words.

"The money in the jar ..." were the only words she had gotten out of her mouth when his whole expression changed. His eyes became hard and turbulent while his jaw clenched as he avoided her eyes.

"Did you cook dinner?" he asked instead and Becky was confused. She was just about to open her mouth to ask him about the money again when he cut her off with a look.

"I will tell you what I want you to know. Try and focus on things that concern you," he said, and Becky was shocked. Not only had he reminded her to not delve in his business again, but he had also told her that she was supposed to focus only on her 'work' in the kitchen. It was the highest form of insult for Becky. It was obvious that John had probably only needed a wife who could share the burden of the kitchen and not someone he could share everything with.

Becky wanted to say quite a few things but kept silent, tears gathering in her eyes. She did not know why his rejection stung her that much, but she had started to look forward to their talks and considered him a good friend, if nothing else. But with his statement, John had established the roles they were supposed to have in the house and she was hurt, to say the least.

The next few days passed in extreme tension as Becky kept quiet and avoided extended contact with John, but if she expected him to be upset by it, she was wrong. Her husband gave no indication that he minded her distance and difference in demeanor, carrying on as if everything was just dandy.

He even stopped talking to her as if he was the one who was angry and that angered Becky even more. She had started working on some curtains and drapes for the house on an old sewing machine she found in the attic, using old pieces of fabric and spending almost all the day in her room. The only time she came out was for dinner, a silent affair as both of them ate their meals and retired to their respective rooms. John had always praised her cooking and any new changes she made to the house but he kept quiet now, not even saying anything as she put up the new curtains she had made.

His jar habit continued but she ignored it and he said nothing as well. As the days passed, Becky was sure that she had made a mistake by coming to the West and getting married to a man she barely even knew. It was apparent that her husband didn't trust her and would rather sever all contact than talk to her about whatever he was doing. She had never really had high expectations about the marriage, but their start had been really nice and her hopes of a happy, normal marriage had risen. Sick of the silence and the loneliness, Becky missed her friend Linda the most. The solution to that problem came to her one day. They were eating their dinner in relative silence like every other day when she brought up her question.

"John?"

Her husband looked up from his meal, surprised that she had decided to talk after all those days.

"Yes?" His voice was hesitant but hopeful.

"Do you know who lives on the farm next to ours?" she asked, avoiding thinking about the hope in his voice.

John's eyebrows furrowed but he answered easily, "Yes, Mr. and Mrs. Dominic live to our east while Mr. and Mrs. Headey with their children live to our west."

"Do you know them?" she asked immediately, excited about the prospect of getting to know more people.

"Sure, we meet in the fields or in town every few days as our paths cross," he replied and Becky beamed at him.

"So, I can pay them both a visit?" She posed the question that had been on her mind since the start. John smiled at her happiness and a small butterfly fluttered inside her stomach at the way her husband looked at her then.

"Why not?" he replied and she grinned.

The very next day, she started with her mission of getting to know her neighbors. She woke up early in the morning and started preparing the lemon cake her mother had taught her when she was a child. It was an old recipe that was easy but always turned out delicious. She had yet to make the cake for John and, deciding to surprise him with it, made three of them.

The aroma of the sweet treats wafted in the house. Her husband hummed his way out to the fields after tasting the cake. Satisfied that the cakes must have turned out all right after John's reaction, she packed the rest of them up and left for her neighbors' house.

She went to the Dominics' household first and was pleasantly surprised by how welcoming and nice Mrs. Dominic, whom she later called Susan, was. They became friends quickly as she came to know that Susan was also a mail order bride. They talked for a long time about where they came from and how their lives had changed, until it was time for lunch. Becky excused herself then but Susan didn't let her go without the chicken pie she had made for lunch that day.

Getting home, Becky picked up the pie and took it to the fields to share with John as they ate lunch together. They didn't talk much but it was still one of the better times that they had spent together and Becky was glad for the break. She had started to accept that John was still her husband, even if he had a gambling problem he didn't want to share with her, and they would be happier together if she put the issue aside and focus more on making their lives pleasant with whatever meager resources they had.

After lunch, she set out for the Headey farm. The Headeys were a pleasant family and their children, ages twelve to almost two years old, were respectful but a naughty bunch. Becky had a great time with Emily, Mrs. Headey, who was a shy but sweet person. Emily was glad that Becky had come over and told her so.

"No one ever really visits each other over here and I think it's great that you decided to. We can help each other out and stick together for so many things," she told Becky.

"You're right. I visited Susan before you and she said the same thing," Becky replied.

"Susan? Mrs. Dominic?" Emily asked and Becky nodded.

"I've met her a time or two in town; she seemed a very nice woman," Susan responded and Becky had an idea.

"We should all regularly get together every week. I know Susan would like the idea," Becky suggested, the idea taking root in her head. With a little persuasion, Emily agreed and they decided upon a mutual time on Wednesday every week for their small get-together.

Life in the West seemed a lot better to Becky as she headed home that evening.

CHAPTER 6

JOHN WAS FRUSTRATED AS HE COUNTED THE MONEY FOR THE THIRD TIME. HE had been sure he would be able to put aside enough to buy Becky a ring this month but it looked like he had been wrong. It had been almost three months since their marriage and he had yet to buy her an actual wedding ring instead of the steel band he had bought in haste on their wedding day. He had been working extra hours so that he could save some extra money for that, but the expenses had increased with two people instead of one. On top of that, Becky had been needing some fabric for the new tablecloths she had made and he hadn't had the heart to refuse her, so some money had been spent on that along with some other small things.

He hadn't yet told her about Russell or the payments he made and even though her assumption that he gambled still irked him, he was not yet ready to let her know everything. He didn't know why, but it embarrassed him.

She was finally getting happier, with her new friends and their small get-togethers, and he didn't want to dampen her spirit. They were back on speaking terms and their conversations were the best part of his day. He relived her words and her smiles as he worked in the fields or with the animals and usually couldn't wait to get back home at dinner. The house was warmer than it had been before her, with her small changes, but more so because of her presence.

Not once had Becky whined or demanded anything more than what he was willing to give or share and he was grateful for that. He knew that he needed to tell her everything, but every time he thought he should, something inside him wouldn't let him, which was why he had been making the trips to town to deliver the money, instead of waiting for Russell's goons to visit his farm.

He was deep in thought when he first heard the sounds of hoofbeats. For a moment, he was confused, but then everything cleared up. Rocky, Russell's right-hand man, was here to collect the payment.

In his work, he had forgotten to take into account what Russell would be thinking about his visits. The man had obviously assumed that John was hiding something from him, which was why he was delivering payments instead of waiting for Rocky like he used to. So, he had sent his men earlier than usual to see what was going on.

He wasn't worried about the money because he had it all, but rather about the fact that Becky could come out of the house any time and see what the whole thing was about.

"John, my man!" Rocky announced grandly as he got off his stallion near the entrance of the barn.

"Rocky," John grunted in acknowledgment, standing up with the cash in his hands, willing to thrust the money at the man and be done with it all.

"I see you have the payment ready, ahead of time too. Russell will be glad," Rocky commented, eyeing the wad of cash in John's hand.

"I would've delivered it myself," John replied tersely, eyeing the door of the house every few moments for any sign of Becky.

"Yeah, I heard about that but I just wanted to visit you myself, friend, since it has been a few months since we last met." Rocky grinned, and John controlled his anger. Rocky was one of the most infamous men in town after Russell. The man was arrogant, misbehaving, and irritating to the boot.

John had just moved forward to hand the cash to Rocky when the door of the house suddenly opened and out came Becky, a tray of lemonade balanced in her hands. John all but groaned as Rocky turned to look at the very same time, a lecherous smile coming over his lips.

"Well, well. So, this is what you have been hiding," Rocky muttered, his grin widening as Becky moved forward.

"John, I brought some lemonade for your friends," Becky announced and John all but closed his eyes at the disaster enfolding in front of him. This was the last thing he needed because at that moment, with Rocky standing next to him looking at Becky as if she was prey, he realized that the real reason he had been going into town to deliver the money was because he had wanted to save his young wife from the likes of Rocky and Russell.

"You did a good thing, sweet pea," Rocky crooned, raising his hand and dragging his filthy fingers over Becky's rosy cheek. It took everything inside John to not break every bone in Rocky's finger at the contact. He saw Becky's eyes widen in alarm just before she took a step back, moving away from Rocky and his hand.

Rocky was too stupid, or just enjoyed her discomfort, because he took another step forward, closing the distance between her and Becky. As he raised his hand again, John had had enough.

He swung him around and landed a square punch to the man's nose. He felt the crunching bones underneath his fist as Rocky howled in pain, his hand rising to cover up his bleeding nose.

"You'll pay for this!" Rocky growled, moving towards him, but John was prepared. He ducked as Rocky's fist came towards him and landed another punch to the man's stomach. As Rocky moved back from the force of the punch, John wasted no time in delivering a few more to his face and probably wouldn't have stopped if Becky's shouts hadn't registered in his head.

He moved away as Rocky limped his way to his horse, uttering threats and warnings the whole time.

"What was that?" Becky asked in a shaken voice once the man had disappeared.

That was when John told her everything about Russell, how he ruled their small town and village and the payments everyone had to make to him. Becky bandaged his bruised hand but said nothing. He felt like a huge burden had been lifted off him as he told his wife the truth, but he couldn't have been more wrong. Their fields were flooded the very next morning.

CHAPTER 7

IT TURNED OUT THAT SOMEONE HAD DIVERTED THE CREEK TO THE FIELDS THAT night and even though John had been able to save most of his hard work, a lot of it had been damaged as well. Becky knew that it wasn't just a coincidence. She had been unable to comprehend everything John had told her about Russell but when the very next day after the water incident, their hens and chicken were left out in the open, due to a broken barn door, she knew that John had not exaggerated.

The next few days became a challenge as John decided to stay awake at night and keep an eye on things. Becky couldn't sleep when she knew that he was awake and so tense, so she made him coffee and kept him company but that made both of them so tired that they were unable to do much work the next day. Their levels of exhaustion reached a plateau on the seventh day and John decided that they should sleep since nothing else had happened, but the worst was yet to come.

The barn was set on fire.

They barely saved the animals amongst all the chaos but Becky was thankful for their neighbors who all came to help them control the fire and even offered help in building a new barn. John refused at first, but knowing that he would never be able to build one all by himself, agreed later.

"We need to do something about this," John spoke up one day at dinner and Becky nodded. She was exhausted; her whole body ached due to the constant work; and neither of them had slept in a number of days.

"Maybe you should talk to Russell?" she suggested, hoping something could be solved by that because both of them knew that they wouldn't be able to take any more of the constant crises.

John laughed bitterly at that.

"That would never help and I don't even want to," he answered.

"But why?" Becky asked, exasperated at his reaction. At that point, she was willing to do whatever it took to have some measure of peace in their life.

"Because despite everything that has been happening, I feel free for the first time in years. I didn't come here to work day in and out for some tyrannical dictator. I came here to change my life and that of my children. I don't want to spend my whole life like this, Becky, working from one month's payments to the next. I want to be able to grow, to bring up a family to, and live freely. If Russell thinks that he can break me and let me stand by as one of his goons mistreats my wife, then he has another thing coming," John finished his speech as anger vibrated within every word.

Becky was astounded. She had not even once stopped to think about what the payments and how Rocky's action made John feel but now that she knew, she felt warm all over. Her husband was not only brave but also an upstanding man who was not willing to let a few goons change his ideals.

"You're right. You should not have to, but we cannot just sit and let them do this. Who knows what they might set on fire the next time," Becky said, her fear and apprehension clear in her eyes. John scooted forward in his chair, moving closer to Becky as his hands cupped her face lightly. Surprise, along with another emotion, shone in her eyes as she looked at him and he placed his forehead against hers.

"I know things are difficult right now, but I am trying, and you won't ever have to be scared like that again," he whispered and Becky gulped. They were so close and with him looking into her eyes, she forgot everything that had been going inside her head, just nodding at whatever he said.

When he moved away a minute later, she felt the loss of his warmth and of his gaze looking into hers. She felt incomplete and realized then that she had unknowingly fallen in love with her husband, the man who had ordered a practical bride without any idea of how she looked, the man who had kept her safe even when it had cost him so much, but most importantly, the man who was willing to fight for their future with everything he had.

"What do you have in mind?" she asked, once she had her heart under control.

"There is a new marshal in town and everyone is hoping that the man will be able to resolve some of the problems regarding Russell. I am going to go and file a complaint tomorrow," John explained.

"Why didn't you do it all that time ago?" she asked, confused.

"The marshal before this one was one of Russell's many men. There was no use going to him or filing a complaint. The produce is almost ready for this season and I don't want Russell to cause any more problems with the sale," John replied and Becky nodded. They stayed awake that night, too, and next morning, John filed a complaint.

CHAPTER 8

THE NEWS OF RUSSELL STEALING JOHN'S PRODUCE SPREAD LIKE FIRE. AS HE HAD gone through town to the marshal's office that day, the people had looked at him with either sympathy or as if he had lost his mind. He should have figured that Russell would never allow someone new to come to an important post before making sure that the new man would cause no problems for him. He did have to give Gunther, the new marshal, points for acting as he had when filing the complaint. He had not even once let him know that he worked for Russell and John hadn't suspected anything until it was too late.

Now, his whole season's hard work was in Russell's hands and there was nothing he could do. He was more or less done. He had spent the night thinking about what more he could do but nothing had come to mind. A small part of him had known that this might be the result of what he was doing, but he was still disappointed over the fact that he had let Becky down. He had wanted so badly for all this to work and hadn't planned on what they would do if it didn't, but now he knew what he had to do.

He could go talk to Russell and let the man set a price as punishment for Rocky and get back to paying him a higher rate of payments. Or he could accept that there was no way he could continue working in the conditions that were plaguing him and leave, like many of the other farmers had. His whole being rebelled at the thought of giving up but there was no way he could go back to working for Russell.

After the visit with the marshal, John reached home to see Becky on the front porch wringing her hands and pacing the length of the porch. Looking at her, he felt a burst of adoration and warmth rising in him. His wife was one of a kind. Where other women might have run the other way, she had stuck next to him, hadn't slept nights, and had kept him company as they went through everything. He knew that he should've told her firsthand the situation she was going to face instead of keeping her in the dark at the time of their marriage. She might have changed her decision of marrying him but it would've been for the good. She deserved better than the life he could give her and she might have ended up with someone better. The thought caused an ache in his chest.

Becky looked up at the same moment, as if sensing his distress. She all but ran the small length until she reached him and he was expecting anything other than what she did next.

She threw her arms around him and hugged him tight. He stood immobile for a minute, not sure what to do as Becky squeezed her arms, letting him know that she was waiting for him to reciprocate the action.

"You're not disappointed?" he asked, enveloping her and placing his chin on top of her head.

"I am, but I know how difficult it must be for you," she replied and he groaned inwardly. He didn't need this. He didn't deserve her understanding and her selflessness. She was thinking about him even now.

He got out from the circle of her arms, placing a finger underneath her chin to make her look at him.

"I'm sorry, Becky. I shouldn't have done this to you. I should've let you go after telling you the truth, but I was too selfish. You have every right to leave if you want," he finally said, the words burning as they came up his throat.

"I will," she replied quietly and he felt as if all the breath had whooshed out of him. His shoulders drooped but he said nothing, not wanting to elongate the conversation.

"But not without you." She spoke again and he looked up, shocked.

"What do you mean?" he asked, confused by her opposing statements.

"What I mean is that you taught me to fight, whatever the circumstances. I left my home to come here, hoping to make one with you, and I won't be going anywhere this time around," she answered.

"Then what?" John queried, still not understanding what she was saying.

"I have an idea of something we could do to keep Russell at bay, but I will need some time. If that doesn't work, we can leave together."

"You'd leave with me?" he asked, hope rising in him again.

"Yes, I would. You're my husband," she said, as if that explained everything.

"And you're my wife," he said, taking her back in his arms. Later that night, she told him everything she had planned and even though he didn't believe it would work, he knew that they didn't have any other option.

CHAPTER 9

Becky was nervous. It was payment day and Russell's man was bound to be here any moment. She had planned everything but she was still not sure if everyone would go along with it all. They would not know the results until a few more days and she couldn't wait. The plan could backfire, but they had nothing left to gamble upon.

In her time of living at the farm, she had made quite a few close friends with many of the neighbors, including Emily and Susan. Their circle had grown until they were now at least ten women and all of them were under Russell's pressure. They had all been helping her and John as they had undergone everything Russell had done to them and they were her final hope.

The idea had first come to her when every lady present at their small gathering had told her own tale of how Russell had treated her badly one time or the other and nobody had helped. It had planted the first seeds in Becky's mind. Russell was a man who depended upon his image and his fear in the masses. He benefitted because people were scared of what he would do to them if they didn't perform his bidding. If they ever wanted to be rid of him, they needed to stop that fear once and for all and there was only one way to do so. They were going to rebel. There would be no more payments made to him and his goons would not scare anyone any longer. All the farmers had armed themselves in preparation for those very goons and if everything worked fine, there wasn't much Russell would be able to do to so many men, as long as they were united.

She worked in the kitchen most of the day, trying to shed the tension that plagued her as she waited for John to come back with some news.

"Becky!" John called out as he entered the house and she rushed to his side to know what had happened.

Her heart was beating loud and fast as her breaths came in small pants.

"Did it work?" she asked, unable to contain her curiosity.

"Oh, it worked. It worked so well that there are ten farmers out there waiting to thank you!" John replied, swooping her in his arms and circling around the area as she squealed and laughed.

"Are you serious?" she asked when he let her down after a minute, a wide smile on his lips.

"More than I've ever been. I can tell you firsthand that I've never seen Rocky that scared as every other farmer pulled out a gun and threatened to kill him if he ever came near a farm again. He didn't even go to the last three farms, running back to his master," John told her.

"But Russell?" Becky asked worriedly.

"Russell alone cannot do anything to all these farmers. Even he knows not to mess with such a large number, as people here are so fed up with him that they wouldn't hesitate in using those very guns on him."

"I really hope so," she replied, worrying her bottom lip still.

"You'll see," John answered, taking her hand and urging her to go to all the men and women, people she called friends.

"Becky, dear, you were right." Emily was the first one who came towards her, her toddler balanced on her hip.

"Yes, you were." Susan joined the other woman. "We should have done this a long time ago. If we had, Russell wouldn't have survived in this town all these years. You united us all and made us realize what power we held."

"I did no such thing. I just pointed out something we all knew but were too scared to do," Becky smiled in response.

"And it's good that you did. No Russell or Rocky should be able to instill such fear or control people that way." Eleanor, another lady in their circle, chimed in as they all hugged and celebrated their victory well into the night.

CHAPTER 10

A HIGH-PITCHED CRYING SOUND RENT THE AIR AS BECKY GROANED IN HER sleep. She was just about to get up when John stilled her with his hand from the other side of the bed.

"You sleep. I'll get him," he told her in his deep voice and Becky smiled.

She had the best husband in the world. The man spent his days working hard and had turned the small farm into heaven for them. They were now producing vegetables and breeding cows for milk. The business end of the farm was doing really well and over four years, he had expanded the house to include another story as well as more rooms.

As for the rest, he helped her with all the household work even though they now had servants to help her with cooking and everything else. But he never balked from his own responsibilities, whether it was keeping his family safe and well-fed or changing his one-month-old's diaper.

Becky stayed awake, hearing as John sang a lullaby to their baby until he stopped crying. He was back after a few more minutes of putting their baby, Alexander, whom Becky had named after her father, to sleep.

"You're awake?" John asked as he got into bed.

"Yes. I couldn't help but think about how lucky I am," she replied, turning to smile at her handsome husband.

"And why is that?" John asked, kissing her atop her forehead.

Becky closed her eyes to savor the moment, opening them as love for John brimmed over in her eyes.

"Because I got you for every other thing that happened in my life. God gave me you to compensate for all the hardships. The perfect husband and the perfect father," she replied, tears of happiness clogging her eyes.

"You're wrong. I got you instead. You were there for me when no one else would have been and it was you who gave me the courage to stand up for myself and for you. If it wasn't for you, I don't think I'd have ever stood up to Russell. You were my inspiration and my reason for everything, and now our son is too," he told her, kissing her tears away and taking her face in his hands like he had so many years ago and like he did every day now.

"You taught me love, Becky. I don't think there's a grander cause in the world," John spoke, his voice thick as he embraced her. Becky smiled through it, sending up a silent prayer of thanks to God for giving her everything she had ever wanted in the form of one man whom she would spend her life loving.

☙❧

THANK YOU SO MUCH FOR READING MY BOOK. I SINCERELY HOPE YOU ENJOYED EVERY bit reading it. I had fun creating it and will surely create more.

Your positive reviews are very helpful to other reader, it only takes a few moments. They can be left at Amazon.

www.amazon.com/Katie-Wyatt/e/B011IN7AF0

☙❧

WANT FREE BOOKS EVERY WEEK? WHO DOESN'T!

BECOME A PREFERRED READER AND WE'LL NOT ONLY SEND YOU FREE READS, BUT you'll also receive updates about new releases.

So you'll be among the first to dive into our latest new books, full of adventure, heartwarming romances, and characters so real they jump off the page.

It's absolutely free and you don't need to do anything at all to qualify except go to.

PREFERRED READ FREE READS

http:/katieWyattBooks.com/readersgroup

ABOUT THE AUTHOR

KATIE WYATT IS 25% AMERICAN SIOUX INDIAN. BORN AND RAISED IN Arizona, she has traveled and camped extensively through California, Arizona, Nevada, Mexico, and New Mexico. Looking at the incredible night sky and the giant Saguaro cacti, she has dreamed of what it would be like to live in the early pioneer times.

Spending time with a relative of the great Wyatt Earp, also named Wyatt Earp, Katie was mesmerized and inspired by the stories he told of bygone times. This historical interest in the old West became the inspiration for her Western romance novels.

Her books are a mixture of actual historical facts and events mixed with action and humor, challenges and adventures. The characters in Katie's clean romance novels draw from her own experiences and are so real that they almost jump off the pages. You feel like you're walking beside them through all the ups and downs of their lives. As the stories unfold, you'll find yourself both laughing and crying. The endings will never fail to leave you feeling warm inside.

MARY & JOHN

Mail Order Bride Western Romance

RoyceCardiff
Publishing House
WHOLESOME INSPIRATIONAL ROMANCE

Dear Reader,

It is our utmost pleasure and privilege to bring these wonderful stories to you. I am so very proud of our amazing team of writers and the delight they continually bring us all with their beautiful clean and wholesome tales of, faith, courage, and love.

What is a book's lone purpose if not to be read and enjoyed? Therefore, you, dear reader, are the key to fulfilling that purpose and unlocking the treasures that lie within the pages of this book.

৩৯২৩

NEWSLETTER SIGN UP PREFERRED READ

http://katieWyattBooks.com/readersgroup

৩৯২৩

THANK YOU FOR CHOOSING A INSPIRATIONAL READS BY ROYCE CARDIFF PUBLISHING HOUSE.

Welcome and Enjoy!

A PERSONAL WORD FROM KATIE

I LOVE WRITING ABOUT THE OLD WEST AND THE TRIALS, TRIBULATIONS, AND triumphs of the early pioneer women.

With strong fortitude and willpower, they took a big leap of faith believing in the promised land of the West. It was always not a bed of roses, however many found true love.

Most of the stories are based on some historical fact or personal conversations I've had with folks who knew something of that time. For example a relative of the Wyatt Earp's. I have spent much time out in the West camping hiking and carousing. I have spent countless hours gazing up at night thinking of how it must been back then.

Thank you for being a loyal reader.

Katie

CHAPTER 1

SETTLER'S CREEK, CALIFORNIA 1851

THE TOWN WAS SMALLER THAN SHE EXPECTED, IN FACT, MUCH SMALLER, MARY Williams thought as she scanned up and down the short main street. Over the last six months she had seen most of the new world on the back of a stagecoach and had painted a picture in her mind of what her destination would look like.

She hadn't envisioned anything like the dusty, rural Main Street she was now contemplating, consisting of nothing more than about six buildings. Mary took a deep breath, rolling her travel-weary shoulders. She still couldn't believe she had finally arrived in California, come all the way from Baltimore to start life anew. As she stood surveying her new home, she couldn't help but wonder if her parents would be proud or disgraced by her decision to come west, as a mail order bride, no less.

The decision wasn't one she'd ever anticipated making, but it had been thrust upon her by circumstances. Major Hank Remi had been a dear friend of her father's and had fought alongside him in the Mexican-American War. When Hank had returned from the war with the grievous news of Mary's father's passing, the scarlet fever had taken hold of Mary's mother so suddenly that Mary suspected she been weakened by the terrible shock, almost to the point where she lost the will to live. Mary could still remember the fever that had almost immediately bedridden her mother. After a week of suffering, her mother's heart had finally given out, probably a combination of the fever and heartbreak.

Major Hank Remi had been kind enough to offer Mary a home with him and his family. At first, Mary had been overjoyed. Then she had started to see his true colors. Mary had been treated by his daughter as nothing more than a servant, but her problems had truly started when Hank's threats did.

Hank had made it clear that she was a burden to his family and that, if it hadn't been for his vow to her father to take care of her, she would have been long gone.

When his daughter had gloated to Mary that Hank planned on selling Mary to the highest bidder for marriage, that was when she had known she needed to leave and seek a new life for herself.

Hank's friends were cruel, always reeked of alcohol, and glared at Mary in a way that made her wish she was invisible. Late one evening, while he and his friends were drinking, Hank had called Mary into the parlor and announced that she was available for a good price.

The humiliation of that night still burned her cheeks. The following morning, she had promptly visited the agency in town, the one advertising men in the West who were seeking wives. Mary had had the opportunity to read letters from three viable candidates before she chose one.

John Whitlock.

Something about John Whitlock had made her heart skip a beat even though she had yet to meet him. His first letter was engraved in her memory.

Dear Mary,

Thank you for writing me.

I think it is best we approach this agreement as honestly as possible, and so I will tell you that I do not seek a romantic relationship. I seek a partner with whom I can make my life in the West. I intend to apply for land shortly.

I am a man of few words but can assure you will be taken care of. The work required by owning our own land will often be hard, and sometimes not even fruitful, but it will be ours. Together, I think we can build a life on mutual respect and understanding, and possibly even become friends.

For a long time I have dreamed of owning my own land. I have dreamed of finding a place where I can live out my years in peace whilst earning an honest living. I have traveled and fought for many years and believe the time has come for me to lead a quiet life, bountiful with rewards from the land. I am seeking someone who is seeking the same rewards and quiet life.

The West offers many challenges of which I am thoroughly aware, but it also offers a new beginning. As you mentioned in your own letter, I, too, look forward to starting anew. Maybe we could start anew in the West and build a life together.

I know coming west must be a big decision for you and I can assure you I will do all in my power to make it worth your while. You will never suffer by my hand or another's as long as you are my wife. At first it might be a little hard finding our own routine but I will try to be as accommodating as possible.

If you accept my offer of marriage, I will be graciously honored and will look forward to your arrival. I trust your journey will be safe and will be praying for God's protection for the duration.

Yours sincerely,

John Whitlock

Mary had replied instantaneously and agreed to marry John. That evening she had returned to Hank's home to announce her departure to the West. The complete and utter shock on his face had been more reward than the new life she would have, free of his hand. Once the shock had dissipated, Hank had insisted on hiring a guard to accompany Mary on the stagecoach, as a last favor to her father.

Of course, Mary knew hiring a guard was just his way of assuaging his guilt for the way he treated her.

Now, here she was in Settler's Creek, at long last. The only problem was she had no idea what John Whitlock looked like.

Shouts and curses from the saloon across the dirt road drew Mary's attention. She could hear furniture breaking even as the proprietor shouted for the fight to stop. Mary clutched her small valise, aware of the curious glances directed her way, clearly wondering about the newcomer. She looked up and down Main Street, wishing she had asked John Whitlock for a description of himself. In her mind she had pictured him as a handsome man with blond hair and blue eyes, a strong chin, and broad shoulders. She didn't see anyone fitting that description as the fight in the bar escalated.

Suddenly the saloon doors opened and three men were tossed out. One fell on the steps, the other a few yards from Mary, and one landed right at her feet, kicking up enough dust to make Mary cough.

She carefully took a step back, trying to brush the dust off her traveling robes.

"Good day, ma'am. My apologies for the mess." The man closest to her slowly got to his feet and tipped his hat. "Some men are just sore losers." His voice was deep and rich, sending a shiver down Mary's back. She had to crane her neck to look up at him. He was at least six two with an imposing face that had been weathered by life or the sun; Mary couldn't be sure which. His eyes were as dark as his hair, his face dominated by a regal nose. The stubble of a few days made his face seem even more imposing. Mary took another step back.

She looked up and down the street again, hoping John Whitlock would come to her rescue.

"You lookin' for someone?" he inquired.

"Yes." Mary cleared her throat nervously. "I'm looking for a Mr. John Whitlock."

The man laughed in obvious surprise, shaking his head as he slapped his hand on his knee. "Well, I'll be. I didn't expect you to be right pretty."

"Excuse me?" Mary stammered, taking another step back to put more distance between her and the brawler.

Instead, he held out his hand with a smile that caused two dimples to appear in his cheeks. "John Whitlock at your service. You must be Mary Williams?"

Mary's eyes widened as she looked him up and down. He was nothing like the picture she had in her mind. He wasn't attractive; he was more roguish, more ... dangerous. Suddenly the whole idea of coming west seemed like a bad idea. She had used her last money to buy supplies for the trip. Now, here she was, destitute and looking at a brawler who claimed to be her fiancé.

"There must be a misunderstanding," she started in a small voice.

"Nah, no misunderstanding. I'm the man you're looking for. Like I said, I apologize for my ... um ... entrance. I was waiting for you in the saloon over there when I made a bet. The loser didn't like his odds."

Mary straightened her back. She wanted to run back to the stagecoach and ask the driver to take her back to Baltimore immediately, but she knew she couldn't. She didn't have money to pay the fare and going back would only mean returning to Hank Remi and his horrid family. She thought of the letter John had written her and decided to judge him on that and not on how they had first met.

Lord, let me make the right decision here, please ...

She nodded, barely perceptibly, and held out her hand. "Mary Williams. Pleased to make your acquaintance."

CHAPTER 2

JOHN LOOKED DOWN AT THE TINY HAND THAT WAS OFFERED TO HIM. IT WAS soft and small, the color of ivory. He took it in his and felt a protective instinct so strong rush into him that he actually took a step back.

After years of only seeing the ugly in people, it was hard to imagine he was going to be married to such a beautiful woman. He had never thought he would approach an agency to find him a bride, but when the Donation Land Claim act had come through, he'd known it was the only way for him to finally own some land of his own. It was well-known that family men had far better luck when acquiring land, as opposed to bachelors. The government wanted people to build families for generations to come, guaranteeing the land would never lie fallow.

As a Texas Ranger serving under Captain McCulloch during the Mexican-American War, John had seen enough bloodshed to last him a lifetime. When the war had ended, unlike many of his counterparts who had sought to become sheriffs and lawmen, John had become a guard for wagon trains headed west. After three years, he had decided it was time to acquire a land—and a home—of his own. And a wife.

Shortly after visiting the mail order bride agency, he had received a letter from Mary Whitlock.

Dear Mr. Whitlock,

I know you must find it strange to receive a letter from a woman you have never before met in your life. It's equally strange for me to be writing this letter.

I am aware you are seeking a wife to join you in the West. I myself am seeking a new beginning. My father died during the war and my mother passed shortly after from scarlet fever. At this moment I am living at the hand of a friend of my father's who is seeking to wed me to the highest bidder.

I know I should be grateful for his efforts but his friends aren't the type of men I feel I can marry.

I am not expecting a romantic relationship but merely a partnership, and possibly, a friendship.

Mr. Whitlock, let me be frank. I have no prospects in Baltimore besides being auctioned to one of Hank's friends. I have no friends and, except for the few dollars I keep tucked away for emergencies, no money. I am seeking a new life, a new beginning, somewhere I can start fresh from all the hardships I have suffered in Baltimore.

I am a hard worker, a fair cook, a good seamstress, and have little need for worldly luxuries. If given the chance, I can assure you I will be a good wife to you. I believe we could build a good life together, God willing.

Yours truly,

Mary Williams

John dragged a hand through his hair, suddenly feeling unworthy of the beautiful woman in front of him. In her letter she had been so honest, so frank, that John had mentally pictured someone perhaps a little matronly. Now John was simply blown away by her decidedly youthful beauty, even if she was travel weary and had dark circles beneath her eyes.

He had saved enough money to build them a cabin once they received their land claim but until then they would need to stay in his home on the edge of town. His home, he thought, shaking his head; it was barely more than a shack with a bed and a small stove. It had served its purpose during the months John had waited for Mary's arrival but now he felt ashamed of taking his bride home to it.

"I've arranged for a priest for today, unless you want to rest for a day or two. I can arrange a room for you at the boarding house," John said, stuffing his hands in his pockets awkwardly.

A frown creased her brow at his suggestion. "No, I'd rather we get it over with."

John flinched at her words. "Ever the romantic."

Mary sighed and lifted her nose into the air. "As I said, Mr. Whitlock, I'm not seeking romance, merely a new beginning."

"Well then, let's get to that new beginning." John reached for her bag and looked around for any other luggage.

"There is only one," Mary informed him. "Hank wouldn't let me take my other belongings. He said he owned them, given that he'd paid for my room and board." Her voice broke slightly and John couldn't help but wish he had the time to make his way to Baltimore to teach Major Hank Remi a lesson in good manners.

"Not to worry, we'll get you more garments or whatever else you might need." He lifted the small bag and nodded across the street. The chapel was only a few yards from the saloon and they quickly arrived, introducing themselves to the priest, who was waiting.

The ceremony went by so quickly that it was a mere blur. When the time came for John to say the vows, he couldn't help but hesitate. Even during the war, he had held onto his faith, and making promises with God as his witness wasn't anything he took lightly. He said the vows looking into Mary's eyes, whispering a prayer that he could do right by this beautiful, brave woman God had placed by his side. When Mary repeated the vows back to him, he said another prayer, that they would build a good life together.

After the short ceremony, John turned to his new wife and tried to smile. It was an unusual situation and he wasn't sure what was expected; he just wanted to delay taking her to his shack at the edge of town. "Would you like to go the land claim office now?"

Mary nodded, barely meeting his gaze. "Yes. Thank you." Her voice was barely audible as she looked away shyly.

They crossed the street and John felt as if he had just won the lottery, the most beautiful bride in the world. The land claim office was thankfully quiet and they quickly received their deed, for which John had applied months back.

"Are we going home now?" Mary asked as they stepped back out. John could see she was tired and wished once more that he had somewhere better to take her than to his shack.

"Yes, but about that ..." John started with a sigh. "I'm going to build us a house on the land we just got, but until the house is ready ... my place isn't much."

Mary smiled and it lit up all of Main Street, such that John felt a flicker of hope in his chest. "If it has a bed, I won't even notice the rest."

John returned her smile. "It does."

Together they started towards his wagon. After helping Mary climb on, John took the reins and drove his new wife to their temporary home.

CHAPTER 3

ONE WEEK LATER

OVER THE LAST WEEK, MARY HAD WORKED HARDER THAN SHE HAD WORKED IN her entire life. Every morning she woke up before dawn to pack food for John before they took the horse and cart to their new land. They worked from sun up till sun down, building a new house on their new land.

Her hands were blistered, her face was burned by the sun, and her back was aching in a million different places. Mary had known that it would be hard work to rebuild a life in a strange town with a strange man—she just hadn't counted on quite how physical that work would be.

Her only consolation was that the home they were building was as much hers as it was John Whitlock's.

Mary Whitlock, she thought as she lay in the small bunk in the shack where John had been living before she'd arrived. John had taken to sleeping on the floor since the first night they'd arrived at the shack and Mary hadn't argued. She was grateful that he was willing to give them time to get to know one another.

Over the last week she had learned two things about John Whitlock: he was respected in town and he was a quiet man. He never wasted his words, only spoke when spoken to, and barely ever initiated a conversation.

John softly snored on the floor only a few feet away from her bed as she closed her eyes. She couldn't help but wonder if coming west had been a good idea. She had left everything behind in Baltimore only to live in a shack with a stranger.

She had been frank in her letters, not expecting a romantic relationship from John, but now that the deed was done and she was officially his wife, Mary wondered if love would ever come her way. Would she ever fall in love and have a family of her own, or would she simply survive in the West alongside John?

It seemed everything in the West was a danger to her life; from the Indian raids, the rattlesnakes, the scorpions, the unrelenting sun, to the gun-slinging men that frequented the saloon in Settler's Creek. She might not have been happy in Baltimore, but at least she'd been safe.

Sleep eluded Mary as she stared into the dark, wondering what was to become of her life, when a piercing scream startled her. Mary threw off the covers, ready to defend herself against anything outside the door, when she realized the scream was coming from John.

After lighting a candle, Mary saw the grief-stricken expression on his face. His arms flailed as if he was fighting an attacker and the guttural moans coming from the depths of his chest made Mary pull her legs against her chest in fear. Another scream ripped through the air and Mary's heart clenched.

She didn't know why but she found herself moving towards him. "John," she whispered, kneeling beside him. "John, wake up. It's just a bad dream."

He screamed again and Mary knew she had to do something. She placed her hand over his forehead and gently stroked it over his head. "John dear, wake up."

John's eyes flew open and he looked around the room in obvious distress before his eyes sought Mary out. She saw the anguish and the pain in them and wished she could take that look away. "You had a bad dream; you were screaming."

John sat up, his breaths coming in shallow pants, and nodded. "Yeah, I tend to get them." He dragged a hand through his sleep-tousled hair before meeting Mary's gaze again. "Sorry if I woke you."

"It's no problem. I couldn't sleep anyway." Mary tugged her bottom lip between her teeth. In the past week they had barely spoken of anything but the house and now she wanted to know more about the man she had married. What could possibly have happened in his life to make him dream such horrid things? "What are the dreams about?" she found herself asking.

John looked at her; his usually light brown eyes were dark with grief as he sighed. "The war."

Mary's brow furrowed. "The war?"

"I used to be a Texas Ranger, Mary. I know I should've told you, but I couldn't see what good it would do. I fought in the Mexican-American War. Some nights ... the things I saw there ... they're not the type of things you just forget."

Mary clasped her hands tightly together, whispering a prayer. She had never met a Texas Ranger, but back east they were spoken of frequently. They were the men that could end a war with a single battle; men that were as ruthless as they were skilled. They were dangerous lawmen, the kind called in when no one else could gain victory. Texas Rangers were always victorious. In her mind they were bearded men with guns slung around their hips as they sought trouble far and wide. Looking into the eyes of her husband, a dreadful feeling overwhelmed Mary. Yes, the Rangers were heroic figures, but the lives they led were anything but peaceful or quiet. What on earth had she gotten herself into?

Hank Remi had taught her that some military veterans, perhaps because of all the horrors they had undergone, had violent streaks. While Mary was certain this wasn't true of most—she fervently believed her father would have been different, had he lived—Hank's bullying had nevertheless scarred her.

"I'm sorry ..." She cleared her throat, suddenly afraid of John. "I'm sorry the dreams bother you. Good night." Mary quickly pushed up and scurried towards the bed. She climbed in and pulled the covers over her as if it were protection. Nothing John had done in the last week had given her reason to be afraid, but then she'd thought him merely a poor man, trying to make a living in the West. Not once had it crossed her mind that he was a retired military man, fighting the demons of his past.

CHAPTER 4

JOHN STOOD ON HIS PORCH AS THE SUN SET OVER THE MOUNTAINS IN THE distance. His body was weary from work, and sweat dotted his brow, but a more contented feeling he had never experienced before. Today they had moved into the cabin.

For a month they had worked every day from sun rise till sun set to get everything done. Over the last week, Mary had even started a vegetable garden beside the house. The sprouts were slowly starting to push through the fertile Californian soil and John knew that, in a few months, they would have vegetables from their own garden.

Mary ...

A smile tilted the corners of his face as he thought of his wife. He had never seen himself as married, or even in love, but something about Mary stirred something deep inside him. When she had arrived, John had thought her to be a beautiful Baltimore socialite; how wrong he had been. His wife was anything but. Mary worked as hard, if not harder, than John on some days. She sanded logs, hauled wood, and hammered nails into the timber as much as he did. The determination to make something of their cabin was clear in her sky-blue eyes.

In the distance you could hear the lowing of cattle, bringing a smile to John's face. He shielded his eyes against the setting sun and glanced towards the paddock he had built for the animals. He knew they still needed a lot of things for the cabin, but it had been a worthwhile investment to start his operation with the five cattle he had bought from a friendly neighbor at a discount.

The rich scent of beef stew drifted toward him from inside the cabin. He turned and glanced through the door to see Mary crooning to herself as she stirred the stew. He wasn't sure what he had done right to deserve such a beautiful, hard-working wife, but John knew she was more than he had expected.

Much more.

He headed into the cabin and Mary turned to him with a smile that set him alight, much like the setting sun was lighting up the horizon. "There you are. Dinner's ready if you're hungry."

"It smells good," John said with a smile as he took a seat at the table.

The cabin was built in a large rectangle. The kitchen and living room were in the center of the rectangle. On one side were two bedrooms and on the other side there was a large fireplace with more seating for when the winter came.

Mary had chosen her room first and John had taken the other room. He had no intention of pressing his marital privileges, fully mindful of their agreement to keep things platonic. However, though he hadn't married Mary for love, watching her move around their new cabin, John couldn't help but wonder if they would ever be more than friends. Ever since she had woken him from the nightmare, they had settled into a more comfortable manner around each other. She'd seemed nervous the first day or two afterwards, and he'd managed to glean enough from casual conservation to learn about Hank Remi's cruelty. Enough that he'd hopefully put Mary's mind at ease about John's own military past definitely not having had a similar kind of impact in the way he treated others.

It felt natural, John mused as Mary served the stew into two plates. As though they'd always known one another.

"Well, don't that beat all," John said, amazed at the bountiful supper on his plate.

Mary laughed, her smile lighting up the cabin as dusk fell over the hills. "It's just a stew, John; surely you've had one before."

John laughed. "Yep, I have. Can't say it smelled as good as this though."

Mary blushed lightly, shaking her head as she took a seat at the table.

"Let us pray," John said, holding his hand out to Mary. It was their first dinner on their own land and they had much to be thankful for.

"Yes, please." Mary said, taking John's hand. Her hand was small and warm in his. John looked up and met her gaze for a moment.

"Dear Lord, thank you for all the blessings you have bestowed upon us. Thank you for bringing Mary to me, and thank you for giving us the strength to build our new home. We ask you to bless this house and our lives on this farm. Let us honor your name with our lives together. Amen."

As soon as he was finished, Mary sighed. "John, that was perfect."

John smiled as he took a first bite of his stew. "Just like this stew." He put down his fork and looked at Mary again, unable to hold his thoughts to himself any longer. "I have a good feeling about this, Mary; about this home, about this land. About our lives together."

Mary's smile widened. "Me too, John."

John wondered if she also had a good feeling about their marriage. Did she also feel something when she looked at him?

"I think the few cattle we have will fetch a good price in a few months. Then we can buy even more."

"Are you just going to raise them and sell them?" Mary asked, interested.

"For now, yes. Until we can start building our own herd." John took another bite of stew and watched as Mary took one as well. The air in the cabin seemed thick with the sense of contentment. Sitting across from his wife, in his own home, John realized that something was changing between him and Mary.

Their marriage no longer felt like a business deal, a way to get land out of the government, or even a safe haven for both of them; it was starting to feel like more. John took a deep breath, allowing his train of thought to continue into the future where he imagined a few young'uns running around the yard. He glanced at Mary and felt something spark in his chest.

Could it be possible that he was starting to fall in love with his wife? Mary glanced at him right at that second and when their eyes met, John knew it wasn't just possible; it had already happened.

CHAPTER 5

Two months later

MARY WEEDED THE VEGETABLE GARDEN THAT NOW BOASTED NUMEROUS seedlings. She glanced towards the road leading to Settler's Creek for the thousandth time, watching for John's return.

A frown creased her brow as she realized she had been watching out for him since lunchtime. Sitting back on her heels, Mary wiped the sweat from her brow, wondering why that would be. She and John had become friends over the last few weeks, something she could admit freely, but that didn't explain why butterflies took hold of her tummy, twisting into tight coils whenever he smiled at her.

In the two months since she had arrived in Settler's Creek, she had worked her hands to blisters. Her back consistently ached from cleaning and gardening, and her skin had been colored to a deep tan by the sun. If her Baltimore friends saw her now, they would be repulsed, Mary laughed at the thought.

How far removed she was from the social conventions she had grown up with. She could never imagine her mother working in a garden or hauling lumber and yet Mary had never been more content in her entire life. It was hard work, but it was rewarding. The best part of every day was sitting down to dinner with John. They would share the events of the day of with each other, like the day John had encountered his first rattlesnake, or the day Mary had been attacked by the rooster in the chicken coop.

A smile formed on her face at the thought. A few weeks ago, John had arrived home with a box and a pile of lumber. After working in the relentless sun all day, he had called her out to open the box. It turned out he had bought them a few chickens and had built a coop.

Mary had insisted on collecting the eggs in the morning, until the day the rooster had attacked her. John couldn't stop laughing, and Mary had been so embarrassed, but it had felt so good to laugh with him.

So much had changed between them since the day he had fallen at her feet when she had arrived in Settler's Creek. John made easy conversation with Mary, as if she was a good friend, and the nightmares that had haunted him in the beginning were now few and far between. They'd talked enough that all of her previous fears had long since dissipated.

She held onto a secret dream of having a horse of her own, but she and John hadn't discussed finances since she arrived, and she wasn't going to ask him for one. His horse was a kind and gentle beast and Mary longed to have her own. She could see the two of them riding over their property, talking at the end of another long day.

With the new house, the cattle, and the chickens, they had enough expenses for the moment. Maybe in a few months Mary would be bold enough to ask him. She glanced towards the road again, wondering when he would return.

The realization hit her hard in the chest. It twinged and burned at first before it turned into a warm feeling right in the center of her heart. She missed John. Mary shook her head at the thought; when had she started to care for him beyond a friend? Mary remembered her mother's favorite Bible verse, one she had often repeated to Mary when she was a child. *Be completely humble and gentle; be patient, bearing with one another in love.* It was from Ephesians and as Mary remembered the verse, she couldn't help but think how it applied to her and John.

They had come together as strangers and yet, somehow, she had started to care for him more than she had ever anticipated. She glanced at the garden and wondered whether humility and patience would lead to love for her and John. Was that even possible?

When had she started so looking forward to seeing him every minute of the day? She headed into the house when she heard horse's hooves in the distance. Not wanting to seem as if she had waited for him, Mary quickly grabbed a potato and started peeling. A few seconds later she heard the thump of his boots on the stairs as he hurried into the house.

"There she, is the beautiful blossom from Baltimore," John said with a wide smile.

Mary turned, her heart fluttering at his compliment. Every time she saw him, he was even more handsome than the day before.

"Hello, John."

"Come, I need to show you something," John urged, almost giddy with excitement. Mary hurriedly set down the potato and the knife; she had never seen John this way and his excitement was contagious.

"What is it?" she asked curiously.

"Not telling." John laughed as he walked towards Mary. For a moment she thought he was going to pull her into his arms; instead, he moved around her and placed his hands over her eyes. His rough hands were warm on her skin and Mary felt a blush creep into her cheeks as she felt his breath on her neck.

"Walk, I'll guide you," John urged.

Mary took a deep breath as she started walking. John guided her out of the house, down the steps towards the paddock he had made for the cattle. He finally stopped and whispered in her ear, "Surprise."

He removed his hands and Mary couldn't help but gasp as she saw her surprise. A beautiful painted horse stood beside his horse. It was a mare with large, gentle eyes. She whinnied, shaking her head as Mary took a step closer. She turned, mouth agape, shaking her head. "John?"

John laughed with the bubbly exuberance of a child. "I've seen the way you take care of Amigo. I could be wrong, but I thought you'd like a horse of your own. Her name is Betty and I've been guaranteed she's gentle and a good horse for a lady."

"Betty," Mary whispered, still reeling from the heartfelt surprise. She turned, overwhelmed, and hugged John without a second thought. As soon as his strong arms wrapped around her waist, Mary knew that John was much more than a partner to her. The feelings she had for him were not the feelings of a mere partner.

Embarrassed at her display of affection, Mary stepped back and turned to the horse. For a moment, she thought she imagined John hesitating before letting her go.

CHAPTER 6

Preparations were in full swing for the winter to come in Settler's Creek. It was only the beginning of August but the days were still hot. John and Mary had fallen into an easy routine, each with their own chores and their relationship, stilted at first, had turned into a fully-fledged friendship.

John had never thought he would enjoy a woman's company again, especially not after being hurt by a long-ago girl in Tennessee, but the more time he spent with Mary, the more he realized how much he cared for her. Every time she did something thoughtful, or said something kind, John knew he was fighting a losing battle. It was hard to allow himself to love again, but God seemed intent on making that happen.

He stood in the field in the midday sun, working with the cattle, when a sudden scream sent a cold shiver running down his back.

Mary!

Without hesitation, John jumped over the paddock fence and ran towards the vegetable garden where he had heard the scream come from. Mary held her leg, pain clearly etched on her face.

"John! Help!" Mary clutched her leg tightly, her face white with agony. "It bit me!"

John rushed forward, kneeling beside her. Glancing at her leg, he didn't even need to ask what had bitten her. The two puncture marks were clear, the swelling already starting.

Dear God. Settler's Creek doesn't even have a doctor yet. Help me take care of my wife!

"What snake, Mary?" John asked frantically as he tugged his belt loose. He wrapped the belt just above her knee, hoping to stop the poison from spreading. Fear tasted vile in his mouth as his hands worked quickly. He had treated snakebites before, during the war, but somehow, with Mary, it was different. He'd cared for his soldier friends, of course. But Mary ... Mary was Mary.

Lord, save my wife. I beg you.

"A rattler," Mary whispered, so brave in the face of agony that it made John's stomach clench.

Swiftly, he scooped Mary up and started jogging towards the house.

He set Mary down on a chair carefully. Forgetting all propriety, he lifted her dress to above her knee, and pulled off her socks and shoes. He went for his rifle and quickly emptied a little gunpowder into his hand. He grabbed the jar of salt and an egg from the basket before kneeling in front of Mary again.

As he worked, he realized he didn't just care for Mary; he loved her. Deeper than he had ever expected to love. Just the thought of something happening to her made his heart ache like there was no tomorrow. He pressed the gunpowder into the puncture wounds, followed by ample amounts of salt and the yellow of an egg. After making sure the pumice had penetrated into the wound, he bandaged her leg with infinite care, murmuring his apologies when Mary cried out in pain.

The bruise was already swollen and had an angry red color. John prayed silently, hoping he had applied the poultice in time to save her life. Once he had completed his task, he scooped her up again and carried her to her bed. He placed her carefully on the down mattress and checked her forehead for fever.

"That worked in the war. I have faith it will work for you as well."

She stared up at him, her face flushed, her eyes glazed. Needing to comfort her, to assure them both that she would be all right, John reached for her hand. He squeezed it softly and, unthinking, pressed his lips to it. "Just rest, Mary. I'm right here with you. I won't go anywhere. I promise. I'm here."

Slowly, her eyes closed, and John knew she was trying to forget the burning pain in her leg. The fierce grip on his hand told him she was fighting screams of agony with everything she had. He closed his eyes as well and started to whisper a prayer.

"Dear Lord, please wrap Mary with your love during her time of recovery. Please watch over her and strengthen her as you heal her body. Breathe your healing power over her dear Lord and keep her safe. Amen."

Then he sat down beside his wife and kept his promise, watching over her all the long night, bathing her brow with cool compresses and praying all the while, whispering words of comfort to the woman he now knew he loved desperately.

CHAPTER 7

One week later

AFTER A WEEK OF BEING BEDRIDDEN, MARY WAS FINALLY UP AND ABOUT AGAIN. Her leg was still sore when she moved too much, but John's quick work had saved her life. She still wondered what had happened that day. One minute she had been kneeling in the garden, tugging at weeds, and the next moment she'd heard the tell-tale rattle before the fangs had struck her leg. The aftermath was all a bit of a blur.

She shook her head as she washed the dishes, confused. Vaguely, Mary remembered him staying with her all night long, and the next day, too. Quiet man though he was, he'd told her story after story, talking her through the worst moments of pain. Then, when she'd finally begun to rally, he'd suddenly gone quiet and contemplative once more, barely saying a word to her any longer. It hadn't changed in the days that had passed since.

Mary couldn't help but wonder if he was angry because she hadn't been more careful or because she hadn't been able to do chores for days. Even now, standing up was painful and required careful maneuvering. Today was the first day when she was feeling at least somewhat more like herself again.

She looked at the large meal that was simmering on the stove and hoped it would make up for the trouble she had caused. John had left for town early this morning to get supplies and attend a stock auction. Mary knew he usually returned by four o'clock in the afternoon on auction days. It was already almost eight o'clock now, however, and there was still no sign of John or Amigo on the horizon.

Her heart contracted in her chest as she stared into the darkness. Would John be angry enough to drown his sorrows in the saloon? The thought made tears burn the back of Mary's eyes. The realization that she loved her husband had initially come as a shock, but there was no denying it. Especially not after the memory, however fuzzy it might be, of how tenderly he had cared for her in the days immediately following the snakebite.

It pained her to think he would prefer the company of a bottle to her, but Mary shoved the thought aside as outside the clouds darkened and a roar sounded through the night air. She brusquely wiped the tear from her face when she heard the first crack of thunder in the distance. Betty whinnied outside, startled by the sudden storm. Mary glanced outside and noticed the vast cover of clouds that had gathered while she had cooked. The moon was hidden behind a thick barrier of storm clouds and the only light on the farm was the piercing bright light of lightning whipping through the sky.

When she heard the first fat drops of rain fall against the roof, Mary glanced outside once more, only to see the start of a downpour unlike one she'd ever seen before. Fear clogged her throat as the fields started to glimmer with the wet puddles of rain, then disappeared behind the veil of rain.

Betty whinnied again and the cattle lowed in fear even as Mary wondered how long such a downpour could last. She poured herself a cup of tea, hoping it would settle down by the time she was finished. Instead, the rain grew heavier, falling with the might of a waterfall from the heavens above.

The thunder and lightning created a deafening sound, making it clear the heavens still had more rain to bring. After an hour, Mary stood up and opened the front door. A chill of dread ran down her spine at the sight before her. The rain had come down too fast for the hardened soil. Instead of penetrating the fertile ground, it had created a dam on top of it. She carefully walked down the steps, wanting to test the depth of the small valley their land was in, and was shocked to find the water already reaching her mid-calf.

Adrenaline surged through her veins as she realized she needed to abandon their house. If the rain continued, it would only be a matter of time before the house was underwater. She heard the animals complain in the distance and knew she had no choice but to take drastic measures.

Mary scurried into the house, moving as fast as her leg allowed, and within minutes she had packed her most important belongings, along with some of John's clothes, and as much food as she could carry. She pulled on her boots, ignoring the pain in her injured leg, and gave their new home a last glance before heading to Betty.

The horse whinnied in distress, treading through the water. Mary didn't bother to try to reach the newly built barn, to get the saddle. She could barely see the barn as it was.

"Where's John?" Mary mumbled fervently as she climbed onto the horse with the reticule of belongings on her back. Grateful both for the riding lessons John had given her and for Betty's generally calm temperament, Mary urged the horse out of the paddock. The cattle followed, just as Mary had hoped, and she turned the mare around to ride out to the cattle. Mary fervently whispered a prayer for strength and guidance. She needed all the help she could get in the next few hours, and if God had healed her from a rattlesnake bite, Mary was certain he would stand by her during this storm.

They might lose their home and their chickens, but Mary was going to do everything it took to save their livestock.

CHAPTER 8

THE FOLLOWING MORNING, JOHN STEPPED OUT OF THE BOARDING HOUSE, shocked by the sight before him. The clapboard fronting of the stores had been ripped away from the buildings by the storm. The streets were nothing but rivers of mud now, any veneer of civility thoroughly washed away by the flood.

After the auction, John had been in a hurry to get home. Not only was he worried about how Mary was coping with her still-healing leg, but he missed her and knew he had been skirting around his feelings long enough. It was time for him to tell her he loved her. Then the rain had abruptly begun and John had known it wouldn't be safe to travel with the horse in the dark. Much as he longed to reach his wife, him getting hurt wouldn't help either of them.

He knew the house was sturdy and that Mary would be safe if she stayed inside, so he'd decided to stay the night in town. He'd barely slept a wink, beset by the roar of the storm and his relentless worry for his wife.

Now he climbed onto Amigo and started towards their home as fast as he could, the pools of deep water slowing his pace considerably. Two hours later, John arrived at the small creek that ran through their farm. It wasn't a creek anymore. It was a monster of a river. Fear clutched John's heart as he looked at the large body of water racing downstream. What usually only took a slow walk to cross now seemed insurmountable.

John jumped off the horse and guided his terrified mount to the other side, whispering prayers continuously, more for Mary's safety than his own. As they trotted towards the house at last, he urged the horse to go faster and faster until, finally, the house came into view. With the haste of a man in love, he jumped off the horse and ran into the house.

She wasn't there. John checked but found that most of her things were gone. Disappointment, shock, and grief filled him as he sank into one of the chairs.

She had left him.

John felt the familiar wrenching pain of heartache fill his heart as he shook his head. He should've taken better care of her, been kinder, more attentive ... but nothing he thought of now would bring her back. She was a Baltimore debutante, not a farmer; had John really expected her to become one simply because he loved her?

With a heavy heart, he finally headed outside to see what other damage the storm had done. There wasn't anything else to do; heartbroken as he was, he had to survive somehow. That was when he noticed all the livestock was gone. He had about twenty-five head of cattle and all his life savings had been used to buy them.

My wife has left me, Lord. And now all I own, except for this house, is gone. What am I to do?

He climbed atop Amigo and started towards the hills, praying the animals had been smart enough to head to high ground. As they climbed higher and higher, John found himself praying that Mary was all right. Surely she hadn't gone near the creek.

Please, God. No.

He blamed himself for her leaving; if only he hadn't stayed the night in town. She must have felt so frightened during the storm. So abandoned and alone. The horse stumbled as the climb grew steeper and its hooves slid a few times before gaining purchase. Adamant and determined, John urged him forward.

The horse whinnied in refusal but kept stumbling higher. When the horse's hoof slipped again, he tumbled, sending John flying off, straight into a large boulder.

John heard a crack as he landed, and the sharp pain that followed enticed a guttural moan from his chest. He glanced at Amigo, who was already pulling himself upright, glad to see the horse hadn't been injured before he looked down at his leg. There wasn't blood, but the pain was so overwhelming that John welcomed the dark fog that dragged him under.

As he closed his eyes, the image that flashed before his eyes was one of Mary smiling at him from their kitchen widow.

Mary. My Mary. How did I lose you?

CHAPTER 9

MARY WOKE AFTER BARELY TWO HOURS OF SLEEP. SHE HAD PULLED HER LEGS against her chest in the early morning hours when the rain had finally stopped, and succumbed to sleep after the most difficult night of her life.

Betty had struggled heading to the hills until Mary had finally climbed off and guided her on foot. She had managed to keep all twenty-five head of cattle with them and made sure they were grazing close by before she'd let sleep come. Looking around, shivering in her sodden clothing, Mary felt a vague satisfaction at seeing her animals all milling about, albeit lowing nervously. Then a cry in the distance caught her attention.

A frown etched her brow as she tried to figure out if it was an animal or a man. She poured the water out of her boots and pulled them on, then set off on foot towards the sound. Her leg ached and she shivered from head to toe, but she didn't let that slow her pace as she headed towards where the sound had come from. As she moved over the edge of the hill, she noticed a figure lying against an outcrop of rocks.

A man.

She quickened her pace as she rushed towards him, hoping he wasn't too badly hurt. A few paces from the figure, recognition made fear pool in the pit of her stomach, deep as some of the waters she'd forded yesterday.

"John!"

She rushed towards him and dropped to her knees, only to find him unconscious. For a moment there was sheer panic in her heart until she determined that he was very definitely still breathing. Mary knelt beside him, pressing a kiss to his forehead. "My dear John," she whispered as she checked him for injuries. "What happened to you, my love?"

As she palpated his oddly bent left leg, wondering whether it was broken, John moaned and his eyes fluttered open.

Thank you, God!

"Mary?" John asked in a strangled voice.

"Yes, John, it's me." She reached for his hand and pressed it tightly. "I'm here. I'm going to get you home."

"I thought you left ..." John whispered as his fingers reached for her rain-tousled hair.

"What?" she said in surprise. "I would never ..." The words trailed off. They could have that conversation later. "Come, let me help you up. I don't know if your leg is broken or sprained, but either way, we need to get you on a horse and home."

Somehow, with God's help, Mary managed to get John on his feet, shivering more from sympathy than from cold, this time, when he groaned in obvious pain. They made their way painfully back to her tiny encampment, leaving Amigo tethered to a tree.

"You brought the cattle up?" John murmured, clearly surprised as they reached the top of the small hill, where the cattle were still milling about.

"The storm, John," Mary tried to explain, as they stumbled over to the boulder she'd slept curled against. She helped ease her husband down, watching the pain diminish at least slightly when the weight was off his injured leg. "It was terrible. The water was surrounding the house, the animals ... oh John, we couldn't lose them. The only thing I could think of was to head into the hills."

John shook his head slowly, his eyes weary but bright. "What did I do to deserve you?"

A tear slipped over her cheek as she looked at him. "John, you deserve more than I can ever give you."

John took her hand and drew her gently down beside him. "Mary ... these last few months ... I never wanted to love again, you see. I loved a woman once, long ago, but when I returned from the war so broken, she was afraid and she left me. I thought I'd always be alone ... but then I met you."

Mary felt her heart swell in her chest as his words, but kept quiet, waiting for him to continue.

"I didn't want to love you Mary, I didn't want to give a woman that power ever again. But then you came into my life. You were beautiful and strong and more hardworking than most men I know. We've built so much together, Mary; it just made me scared of what would happen if I allowed myself to love again."

Mary nodded, smoothing away a smudge of mud from his cheek, unthinking, and then letting her fingers linger on the stubble of his jaw. John reached a hand and covered hers with his.

"I don't just want to be your partner, Mary. I love you. I love you like a man loves a wife. Last night, I wanted to come home, but the storm had already started. Amigo was giving me such trouble that I decided to stay in the boarding house. This morning I was awake even before dawn, wanting to come back to you. I'm so sorry I left you alone. Can you ever forgive me? Or maybe even ... one day ... come to love me?"

A smile tugged at the corners of her mouth. "John, I've loved you for weeks, but I wasn't sure you felt the same. Last night when you didn't come home, I was certain you went to the saloon because you were unhappy with me. Ever since the snake ... it felt like you were angry."

John pressed a tender kiss against Mary's forehead. "Why would I be mad? You're so brave, so strong. Just look at this; you saved our livestock. You herded them up a steep hill in the dark, with a storm raging, and then you saved me. How could I ever be angry at a woman like that? You're more than I expected, Mary, so much more."

"John," Mary scooted closer, leaning lightly into his uninjured side and sighing a little with contentment when his arm wrapped around her waist, drawing her close. "You're not what I expected either. Truthfully, I didn't know what to expect. But you've always been more, from the very first day. And I love you. I truly do."

John smiled wearily, joy lighting his beautiful eyes. "I love you, Mary. I'll never break your heart or hurt you in any way. I swear it."

Mary smiled, leaning her head against her husband's chest and not caring that it was soaking wet. "I promise."

With the sun sliding over the hills, lighting up the aftermath of the treacherous storm, Mary slowly dozed off in her husband's arms.

Nearby, the cattle grazed, Betty whinnied, and Amigo called up to them from lower on the hill. John smiled in spite of the pain in what he now was fairly certain was just a bad sprain. They weren't a conventional couple, but then, conventions weren't for people who dared to live in the West.

Thank you, God.

EPILOGUE

Four years later

THE BABY KICKED AS MARY FOLDED THE LAUNDRY, STANDING OUTSIDE IN THE spring breeze. A little over four years ago, she and John had arrived on this piece of land with nothing more than dreams. Now their small herd of twenty-five head of cattle was over a hundred strong. Their chicken coop was equally blessed, and the foal grazing beside Betty and Amigo in the field heralded the start of a different kind of herd.

Mary heard the laughter of her son and glanced towards the barn they had built the summer before. Today, John was helping him learn to ride the pony he had recently bought at the stock auction.

Mary's handed lowered to her swollen belly as she felt her baby kick. She hoped this one was a girl. A little girl for John to fall in love with all over again.

She still struggled to comprehend what she had done right to be so blessed. Not only had a single letter led her to the man of her dreams, but to a life she never thought she would lead. Settler's Creek was now a booming town. Mary and John attended church every Sunday and spent their days working on their very own farm.

A man she had struggled to warm to in the beginning was now the love of her life. John was a wonderful man, a fantastic husband, and a better father than Mary had ever dreamed anyone could be.

What had been a hard few months shortly after their marriage had cemented their relationship. Mary still couldn't believe that the ruffian that had landed at her feet

288

on the day of her arrival was now the man she was happily spending the rest of her life with.

On a whim, she set aside the laundry basket and headed to John and little John.

"Mama!" Little John yelled with excitement. "Look, I'm riding a pony."

Mary laughed at his exuberant smile. "You sure are." Mary smiled as she watched John lead their son around before he met her gaze.

"You can relax," her husband teased. "The pony is as tame as a lamb. I know you're fretting about whether or not he'll stay on top."

Mary's brow creased even as she shook her head. John knew her better than she'd care to admit. "I'm not fretting," she lied. "I'm simply wondering if you've named the pony yet."

"Yes, Mama, we have; we're naming him Settler, because he's settling with us right here in Settler's Creek."

Mary smiled at the name. Five years ago, she hadn't even known such a place existed; she'd only known of Baltimore and cruel men like Hank Remi. Now she knew of so much more; she knew the love of a husband that would give his life for hers. She knew the love of a child. And she knew the peace of their valley. How could she ever have doubted her decision to come west?

She glanced up at the sky and thanked the Lord for all her blessings. She thanked him for bringing her to Settler's Creek as a mail order bride, for giving her a kind and loving husband, for blessing them with a beautiful boy and another baby on the way.

Her eyes met John's over the pony and she knew God had many more blessings in store for their family.

Thank you, God.

⚜

THANK YOU SO MUCH FOR READING MY BOOK. I SINCERELY HOPE YOU ENJOYED EVERY bit reading it. I had fun creating it and will surely create more.

Your positive reviews are very helpful to other reader, it only takes a few moments. They can be left at Amazon.

www.amazon.com/Katie-Wyatt/e/B011IN7AF0

⚜

WANT FREE BOOKS EVERY WEEK? WHO DOESN'T!

BECOME A PREFERRED READER AND WE'LL NOT ONLY SEND YOU FREE READS, BUT you'll also receive updates about new releases.

So you'll be among the first to dive into our latest new books, full of adventure, heartwarming romances, and characters so real they jump off the page.

It's absolutely free and you don't need to do anything at all to qualify except go to.

PREFERRED READ FREE READS

http:/katieWyattBooks.com/readersgroup

ABOUT THE AUTHOR

KATIE WYATT IS 25% AMERICAN SIOUX INDIAN. BORN AND RAISED IN Arizona, she has traveled and camped extensively through California, Arizona, Nevada, Mexico, and New Mexico. Looking at the incredible night sky and the giant Saguaro cacti, she has dreamed of what it would be like to live in the early pioneer times.

Spending time with a relative of the great Wyatt Earp, also named Wyatt Earp, Katie was mesmerized and inspired by the stories he told of bygone times. This historical interest in the old West became the inspiration for her Western romance novels.

Her books are a mixture of actual historical facts and events mixed with action and humor, challenges and adventures. The characters in Katie's clean romance novels draw from her own experiences and are so real that they almost jump off the pages. You feel like you're walking beside them through all the ups and downs of their lives. As the stories unfold, you'll find yourself both laughing and crying. The endings will never fail to leave you feeling warm inside.

MARIA'S DESTINY

Mail Order Bride Western Romance

RoyceCardiff
Publishing House
WHOLESOME INSPIRATIONAL ROMANCE

Dear Reader,

It is our utmost pleasure and privilege to bring these wonderful stories to you. I am so very proud of our amazing team of writers and the delight they continually bring us all with their beautiful clean and wholesome tales of faith, courage, and love.

What is a book's lone purpose if not to be read and enjoyed? Therefore, you, dear reader, are the key to fulfilling that purpose and unlocking the treasures that lie within the pages of this book.

NEWSLETTER SIGN UP PREFERRED READ

https://katcarsonbooks.getresponsepages.com

❦

THANK YOU FOR CHOOSING A INSPIRATIONAL READS BY ROYCE CARDIFF PUBLISHING HOUSE.

Welcome and Enjoy!

A PERSONAL WORD FROM KAT

I LOVE WRITING ABOUT THE OLD WEST AND THE TRIALS, TRIBULATIONS, AND triumphs of the early pioneer women.

With strong fortitude and willpower, they took a big leap of faith believing in the promised land of the West. It was always not a bed of roses, however many found true love.

Thank you for being a loyal reader.

Kat

CHAPTER 1

MARIA

"Timothy is turning eighteen," Maria told her sister, though there was no doubt that Hannah was well aware. "I can't believe it, honestly. It seems just yesterday that he was born in Mama and Daddy's bedroom."

Hannah smiled, reaching into the tub of soapy water and grabbing another garment to rinse and wring out for the clothing line. "I know. He's so grown up. We're all adults now, the three of us. The Smith kids made it, against all odds."

It was true. Maria, better than either of her two siblings, remembered the day that both of her parents had died in a terrible riding accident out in the North Carolina hills. They had been celebrating fifteen years of marriage with a horse-carriage ride out to the spot where her father had proposed to their mother with his grandmother's wedding ring, and as they were driving the carriage had broken down, tumbling both of her parents into a nearby ravine.

Days had passed before Maria had been able to enlist the help of a family friend to locate her parents, and by the time they were found, both were dead. She could still remember the pain that had enveloped her as she had sunk to her knees, her face buried in her hands as she sobbed for the loss of her parents.

The grief, however, had to be quickly pushed away by fear over what would happen to the three children now that their parents were dead. The last thing she had wanted was to be separated from Hannah and Timothy on top of losing her parents, and because she had been the oldest at sixteen, she had decided to take the matter into her own hands.

For the past five years, through the grace of God, hard work, and the help of her family friend who had found her parents for her, she had managed to keep all three of them surviving in small-town North Carolina. The fact that she'd had to keep them away from society as much as possible, to avoid being found out, had meant sacrificing her own life, and she was quite officially an old maid at twenty-three, with no husband or even any prospects. But the sacrifice had been well worth it, and she would do it all over again.

She called to mind her mother's favorite Bible verse, Psalm 103:17-18, one she'd carried close to her since that terrible day five years back: *But the steadfast love of the Lord is from everlasting to everlasting on those who fear him, and his righteousness to children's children, to those who keep his covenant and remember to do his commandments.*

"You're musing again," Hannah said, smiling over at Maria as she clipped a dressing gown to the line. "Are you thinking of party plans for Timothy?"

"Actually, I was thinking about the past five years," Maria admitted. "Everything we've all been through together. And now everything is going to change. Timothy is going to take his apprenticeship with Paul, and you, I'm sure, will be getting a marriage proposal from John any day now." She smiled at her beautiful younger sister. "And you'll be very happy."

Hannah flushed prettily, turning away shyly to clip another piece of linen to the clothing line as the afternoon sun warmed their faces. "Oh, perhaps."

"Perhaps," Maria said, laughing. "That man dotes on you like no other, Hannah Smith. And you dote on him just the same."

"He's a good man," Hannah agreed.

"That he is, and I'm happy for both of my siblings to be starting new chapters in their lives. I just wonder, suddenly, what I'm going to do with my new chapter." Maria stopped her work and stretched her back, looking around the small property that she had worked so hard to maintain over the past five years. Her parents had never had much, choosing to live a simple life on the outskirts of a small town. The small plot of land and the little house they had called their own were still in good condition, thanks to the hard work of all three of the Smith children.

But Maria was realizing that she didn't have much of a life outside of that house. She was so busy being both parents, trying to manage the small inheritance her parents had left behind, and worrying about someone finding out that she was the custodian to two children that she didn't devote much time to friendships or pursuits of her own. They went to church as a family but were viewed as slightly odd as they kept to themselves and avoided a lot of questions about what it was they did out on this small property by themselves.

Timothy had only found good work through their family friend, Paul, who regularly came by to check on them and help however he could. And it was Paul's son, John, who had begun to woo Hannah just a few months ago. But Maria herself had nothing in store, and both Hannah and Timothy would soon be leaving their little nest.

"You should do something for yourself," Hannah said gently, putting down the wash to walk over to her sister and take her hands. "When is the last time you did that?"

Maria smiled wryly. "I cannot remember."

"Nor can I, and that's a shame. What do you want to do, Maria?"

"I don't know."

"Perhaps then you should find out," Hannah suggested. "There are any number of things you can do."

"Here?" Maria looked around again, shaking her head. "I'm part of the town, but not truly. It would be like starting over. And what of the house and the land here? I cannot maintain it by myself, and I cannot afford to hire help."

Concern moved over Hannah's pretty features, shaping her lips into a frown. "I won't leave you, then. And I'm sure Timothy will feel the same."

"No!" Maria tightened her hold on her sister's hands. "No, that isn't what I mean at all."

"But you've sacrificed so many years for us," Hannah insisted. "Only for us to leave you stranded?"

"I will figure it out," Maria promised, somehow believing her own words. "I'm sure I will. Every night, I'll pray about it, and there will be an answer. You'll see. Until then, I just want to celebrate the good things that are happening for the people I love most."

CHAPTER 2

JAMES

For the past two years, harvest time had been almost impossible for James Cartwright. Despite the fact that Montana was beautiful in the fall, with turning leaves, clear skies, and even temperatures, his farm responsibilities were overwhelming as his crop ripened and demanded harvesting. It wasn't that he didn't have enough farmhands. It was that he had too many children and no wife to raise them or manage his household. Rebekah had made sure of that two years ago, when she had left him and their twin boys on their Montana farm and fled back east where her life had been easier.

He would be lying if he said he wasn't still bitter, and for a long time, it had seemed easier to somehow manage the boys and the farm on his own rather than invite another potentially dangerous woman into his life. But he had reached the point where he wasn't sure he could go through another harvest without some change in the situation. Unfortunately, the women in Springwell had gotten more than a good look at his often-sour temper, and there wasn't one of them who wanted to take him on, much less take him on with Edward and Thomas thrown into the mix.

"Hey, boss! There ya are." Benjamin Campbell, one of James' long-term ranch hands and friends, came jogging over to him, sweating in the late August heat. The two men worked well together and had similar personalities, despite being entirely different physically. Where James was tall, lean, and strong, Benjamin was shorter and stockier. Benjamin had bright red hair, a remnant of his Scottish heritage, and a heavy beard lined his wide jaw. James, however, was a towhead, with closely-cropped dark blond hair, a face he kept clean shaven, and eyes that dominated his features. They would never be mistaken for brothers, but in many ways, that was exactly what they were.

"Whatd'ya want?" James asked, still standing by the fence, his hands braced on the solid wooden beam as he stared out at the Montana openness that stretched before him. It was his favorite place for late-afternoon contemplation, a fact that was no secret amongst his workers.

Benjamin snorted a laugh. "I see you're in as good a mood as ever."

"Harvest in just two months."

"Aye, but we always make it work, don't we?"

James shrugged, turning from the view and looking at his friend. "Like I said. Whatd'ya want?"

"Uh, well, Edward and Thomas might have gotten into the hay storage again. And they may have, you know, dumped water all over big piles of hay because that makes the hay slippery."

James closed his eyes, turning away as he once again rested his hands against the fence, this time clenching his hands around the wood. "Why wasn't Samuel watching them?"

"Bill called him to help with a sick calf."

Groaning, James let his head hang low. "They don't mean to be bad. They don't get enough trainin'. I know they don't. It can't keep goin' this way, Benjamin. Somethin' has to give."

"You thought anymore about that idea I gave you?"

"A mail order bride advert?" James let out a laugh. "One woman from out east already left me because life was too hard out here for her. Say I got another woman to travel out here, this time by herself, and she got out here to live on this farm with those two ... active boys to raise." He shook his head. "She wouldn't last half a year."

Benjamin joined him by the fence, leaning up against one of the beams. "Well, let me ask you this. What other choice you got, if you want a wife to manage your house? All the girls 'round here think you're a mean old coot, and they have reason to."

"I'm not mean."

"Didn't say you were—only that they had reason to think it," Benjamin said, scrubbing his hand along his beard. "You keep right to yerself and you don't have many kind words to sprinkle about in town."

"I didn't want any of them thinking they'd be the next missus here," James muttered, knowing that he'd been quite standoffish to the few women who, after his wife's initial departure, had made it clear that they would be happy to take her place. Now he'd built a reputation for himself. "I wasn't ready then. I have no choice but to be ready now."

Benjamin shrugged, taking his wide-brimmed hat off and running his hand around the edge. "Then you have no choice but to look east. At least try it and see who answers you."

"No woman is goin' to want to raise ready-made kids," James insisted, reaching down to dust the mud off his boots.

"Who says you have to mention them? Once she's out here, what choice does she have?"

James frowned, glancing over at his friend. "I'm not lookin' to lie."

"Don't, then. Just don't tell everything," Benjamin suggested. "When she gets here and sees the setup, she'll go along with it. What woman doesn't want to be a mother?"

"Rebekah."

"She was ... the exception," Benjamin said, clearly restraining himself from saying what he really wanted to about James' former wife. "Self-willed and selfish. You were a fool to bring her out here in the first place."

It was hard to argue with that, and James didn't even try. In fact, he gave up completely. "Fine. Write the ad and post it. With any luck, whoever shows up will be here before the heavy work of harvest sets in. Lord knows we need the help."

Benjamin clapped James on the shoulder, grinning. "I'm sure He does, and He'll send you the perfect woman. I'm sure of it."

James didn't share his friend's confidence, but he also didn't have many options, and without a good crop this year, his farm was in trouble. Having a woman around the house would be more than helpful—it would be necessary.

He didn't have to fall in love with her. If she would help him, then he would find a way to help her too. It would be all fair and equitable and utterly without personal connection. Just the way a marriage should be out west.

CHAPTER 3

MARIA

"Hannah, this is just silly!" Maria protested, half laughing, as she couldn't believe her sister might be serious. It had been two weeks since John had proposed to Hannah and she had accepted. Their wedding would be in just a few days, a small family affair with only a handful of people. They had been planning frantically so that everything would be just right for Hannah, but it seemed to Maria that all Hannah could do was worry about what Maria would do after the wedding.

Truthfully speaking, Maria was concerned about it too, but she didn't want Hannah worrying about her when she should be focusing on beginning her new life. Particularly if it led Hannah to wild conclusions about answering advertisements for mail order brides.

"It's not silly," Hannah argued, flipping the newspaper open and showing Maria the ads she had been telling her about. "Look. These are men who live out west—how exciting is that?—and they need wives. There are so few women out west and so many more men. You would have your choice of situations and plenty to keep you busy, Maria. It's different from out here."

Maria didn't even look at the advertisements, watching her sister instead. "Hannah, I would be so far away. Do you not want me here?"

Horrified, Hannah gripped Maria's hand hard. "Of course it's not that. I just ... I think that you've given up everything to take care of Timothy and me, and there's nothing much left for you here now. You can't stay unmarried forever, Maria, and I hate the thought of you married to anyone around here. If you got away, you could start all the way over, without the weight of everything that happened to our parents and your responsibility to us weighing you down. It's your turn." Hannah leaned forward intensely. "Your turn."

Still unsure, but convinced of her sister's genuine desire for her to look into this, Maria gave in. "All right, all right. I'll look. But I'm not making any promises, Hannah. This is my home, after all, and it's such an ordeal to get out west. Weeks in a stagecoach! Not to mention that it's expensive."

"We'll find the money," Hannah insisted, pulling her chair closer to the table and beginning to point out advertisements. "Look at this one. He's a trapper! Isn't that amazing? He has a home and some land and he's looking for a wife to do the cooking and cleaning and manage the house while he's away. Look—he lives in Utah! That's practically exotic, Maria."

Maria had to admit that it was certainly an interesting thought to entertain, even if she wasn't seriously considering it. "There really must be a shortage of women in the West. There are so many advertisements here. Look, this one is written by a butcher in California. And here's a baker in California. A butcher and a baker. So many choices."

"I know," Hannah enthused. "And the thing is, you can write to someone and ask more about him. Get to know him through letters. In a way, that's incredibly romantic, isn't it? Then, when you finally arrive, they've been waiting for you for so long, and they've been so lonely in a house all by themselves that they would have to adore you immediately."

"I don't know," Maria said wryly. "I don't have your beauty, my sweet."

Hannah scrunched her nose. "Nonsense. You're very pretty. People say so all the time." Reaching out, her younger sister touched Maria's dark ringlets. "Your hair is just gorgeous."

Smiling, Maria patted the younger woman's knee. "Perhaps I do all right, but you take after Mama so closely. You are the spitting image of her, Hannah, and she was always so very beautiful. I have more Smith in me than you do."

"Never you mind that," Hannah insisted, returning her attention to the newspaper. "Doesn't this sound like an adventure? And, truly, with all of the train tracks being laid, why, soon we might have one that goes all the way from this coast to that coast. And traveling would be so much easier. John and I could visit you and you could visit us. Oh, Timothy would just love to go out west someday, you know? And I'm sure there is plenty of work for carpenters. Even John talks about the idea sometimes. He doesn't know how long he wants to work in the general store, after all. We might all end up out west!"

For the first time, Maria actually contemplated the idea, biting her bottom lip as she scanned the list of advertisements. Hannah's enthusiasm was infectious, and her little sister was right in saying that there was little left for Maria to do in North Carolina now that Hannah and Timothy were grown. She had been just making ends meet for all of them for so long that she had put no effort or time into making a life for herself. And if Hannah really thought that John might want to move out west eventually ...

"Where would John want to move, if he did go west?" Maria asked, trying to sound casual. "Does he know?"

"Oh, he just talks all the time about Montana," Hannah said. "He says the pictures are so amazing."

Maria's eye landed on an advertisement from a farmer in Montana and she read through it several times. It was simple enough in what it said. A man who owned a large farm needed a wife for companionship and to manage the home while he worked the land. The town was friendly and the man described himself as financially comfortable, pleasant, and eager to make a wife happy.

Though she couldn't believe it herself, Maria was beginning to wonder if her sister's wild plan might be a better idea than she could have imagined. Maybe it was just about time that she took a leap of faith and began a life that would be her own. Aside from Timothy and Hannah, she wouldn't be leaving anything behind. Hannah's new husband, John, would take over maintaining the Smith property, and if he wanted to sell it, he could.

Maria drew the paper closer, her gaze lingering on the word "Montana."

Lord, if this isn't your plan for me, then show me now, before I make a mistake.

CHAPTER 4

JAMES

.

"OF COURSE I'M NERVOUS!" JAMES SAID, THROWING HIS HANDS UP AS HE TURNED away from Benjamin. "What kind of question is that? My new wife is arrivin' today, and I've only ever exchanged a few letters with her. But I'm about to pick her up from the stagecoach and take her to a church and marry her." He laughed in disbelief. "How could I not be nervous?"

Benjamin shrugged a shoulder, seemingly unaffected. "Listen, it's going to be fine. It happens all the time now. It's 1868, James. The West is boomin'. This is how the world works now."

"You forget that yer advertisement conveniently forgot to mention the boys."

"And your letters didn't mention them either," Benjamin pointed out, pushing off the wall and walking over to dust off the shoulders of James' shirt. "Come on now, man. Pull yourself together and get ready to make a good first impression. If she's movin' out here to marry you, she's not goin' to be turned away by two kids. She has her reasons for comin' out here."

James grabbed his hat, shoving it onto his head. "And don't think I haven't wondered about that. All she said was that she was lookin' for a fresh start, which could mean anythin'. You know, she could leave like Rebekah did. Then I'll have been burned twice."

"Ain't gonna happen," Benjamin promised, though he offered no evidence to back up his confident claim. "Come on. I'll drive you into town to meet her."

They headed toward the door, then James glanced back guiltily, having to pause for a moment to think of where the boys were and who was watching them. One of his greatest sources of guilt was the fact that he spent so little time actually with his children. Much of the time that was because he was busy out on the farm, managing every aspect of what was both his home and his business. But sometimes, and more so lately, it was because he didn't seem to be able to connect with them anymore. When they had been young, it had been easier for him to play with them and read to them. But they were getting older now, and their behavior, for a number of reasons that he could understand, was getting worse. He didn't have a handle on them, and often when he spent time with them, he only became frustrated. It was easier to just avoid the whole situation.

"Do I bring Edward and Thomas?" James asked Benjamin, stopping at the front door of his large house. "Should they be there to meet their new mother?"

"Why don't we tell her first?" Benjamin suggested, stepping out into the sunshine. "Then we'll let her meet them. Less startling that way, maybe."

James nodded, hesitated for another minute, and then followed his friend out to the horse-drawn wagon that would take them to meet some woman named Maria Smith—the woman that in just the span of a few hours, he would call his wife.

It was a short ride into the small town of Springwell, but it felt long, given what James was on his way to do. Neither man spoke much, and the silence grew, despite the birds chirping, the breeze rustling, and the wheels of the wagon bumping over the rocky terrain. It was a relief when they finally arrived in Springwell and James could swing down from the wagon and distract himself from his thoughts by greeting acquaintances and making his way toward the spot where the stagecoaches dropped off their passengers.

Without being told, Benjamin hung back, showing discretion that was quite uncharacteristic.

There were a handful of other people waiting on the stagecoach. Another man who looked like he might be in the same situation as James, and an older couple, likely waiting on family arriving from out east. They all nodded to each other, and James shoved his hands in his pockets, rocking back on his heels as he attempted to curb his nervous urge to whistle a tune.

And then all musical thoughts left his mind as the stagecoach appeared in the distance, making its way slowly but doggedly to the small group awaiting it. When the horses stopped and the dust around their feet settled, the driver of the stagecoach tipped his hat to those waiting and climbed down to open the door.

James held his breath as the first person emerged, but he doubted that the older woman with graying hair and a lined face was Maria Smith. In fact, she went to the man whom James had speculated might also be waiting on a bride, hugging him in a way that could only mean she was his mother, seeing her westward-bound son for the first time in many years. It brought a slight smile to James' face, and it was with that smile that he turned and first laid eyes on Maria Smith.

She stood there, just to the side of the stagecoach, looking straight at him. There was a slightness about her, and he estimated that the top of her head would not reach his shoulder. Her chestnut-brown hair was carefully and practically swept back at the nape of her neck, and her hat was more simple than fashionable—not that he cared about such things. Her face was pretty enough, though she didn't immediately stun him with her beauty.

But then he looked closer, and his eyes met hers. Immediately, something within him reacted to her, like an instantly forged connection. It came out of nowhere and bore with it no explanation, but it was there nonetheless. Her eyes were wide, gray, and in James' opinion, absolutely incredible. He could have fallen into them knowing nothing else about her and been perfectly content with his circumstances.

In fact, he almost felt as though he was falling into them, particularly when she cleared her throat lightly, attempted a smile, and extended her hand to him. "Are you ... James?"

There he was, lost in her gaze, and she was politely inquiring as to his identity.

So much for remaining disconnected from his wife. It seemed that ship had sailed the moment she arrived, without even pausing to drop anchor.

CHAPTER 5

MARIA

MY, BUT HER SOON-TO-BE-HUSBAND WAS HANDSOME. MARIA WATCHED HIM carefully as he gathered her bags in his hand, noting that he was tall and strong and that his face was more than averagely pleasing to the eye. She wondered briefly why he might have trouble finding a wife, even if the pool of women was not large. Surely any woman would notice him.

And the way he was looking at her ... that was something she had never before experienced. What could it mean, that look in his eyes? It made her stomach flutter, and they had hardly even spoken a word to each other.

"How was your trip?" James said, his voice abrupt. It almost sounded as though he was resentful of the need to ask the question, though Maria couldn't imagine why. His tone didn't match his gaze at all, and it confused her.

"Well," she said honestly, "It was quite long and often dusty, bumpy, and hot. But it was also quite exhilarating. I saw so many things I had never experienced before. It was the first time I had ever left the place I was born, and we saw bison and deer and these little ... chipmunks. It was fascinating. And the mountains—oh!" Without even thinking, she clutched her hands to her chest. "They're magnificent, aren't they? Or are you entirely used to them?"

He was looking at her that way again, but he said nothing at all, instead turning away from her. "They're nice, yes. Let's get to the church."

"The church?" Her eyes widened as she followed him quickly, trying to take in her new surroundings as well as keep up with his brisk pace. "Immediately?"

"Well, we can't really go on home now without the papers," he pointed out, glancing back at her.

Maria blinked at him, nodding in an attempt to convey that despite her weeks-long trip, exhaustion, and shock at arriving in a brand-new place, she was entirely ready to make their union and life together official. In reality, the switch from the slow pace of the past two months—weeks of exchanging letters, packing, and traveling —to the breakneck speed with which he wanted to get to their vows was jarring.

"What's the name of this town again?" Maria asked, attempting to get some feel for her new home to anchor her.

"Springwell."

The one-word answer was sufficient in theory, but did nothing to help situation her in time or space. All around her, she saw wooden buildings, some of which were labeled with exaggeratedly large signs advertising stores or restaurants. Horses milled about the street, carrying their owners or pulling carriages. There were dogs all around, which was quite new for Maria, though perfectly fine, and on the whole, she felt as though the atmosphere of the town was quite welcoming.

Her future husband's demeanor, however, was anything but.

"James, could we perhaps pause for a minute?" she said, stepping in front of him and attempting a charming smile. "I've traveled quite some way, you know. It would be nice to take a moment to catch my breath before we ..." She could feel her cheeks flush. "Well, before we marry."

He swallowed hard, his eyes boring into hers, then looking everywhere but her. "Of course. I'm being rude."

"Well, yes, a bit."

James looked at her in surprise, then smiled for the second time. When he had first looked at her, he'd had a smile on his lips, and then it had disappeared, reoccurring only now when honesty had slipped unintentionally from her.

"I'm sorry," he said, guiding her to a quieter spot, out of the way of traffic and setting down her bags. "If you must know, I'm feelin' a little nervous. I've never done this before. Well, not this way, anyway."

"Not this way?" Maria asked, tilting her head. "But some other way? You were married before?" He had never mentioned anything like that in his letters, and she immediately felt a strong need to know what had happened with his first wife before she became his second.

James closed his eyes, clearly wrestling with some internal war that made Maria incredibly nervous. "Yes, I was married. My wife left me years ago, though. She did not care for the life she had here."

"How terrible," Maria gasped, covering her mouth with one hand. "To just abandon you that way? How could anyone do such a thing?"

He didn't answer, once again looking at her watchfully. "Maria, there is something I have to tell you. I've felt terrible guilt over not sayin' it earlier, and just now, part of why I was rushin' was so that we could get things all squared away before you knew. But I can't do it that way."

Maria's heart thudded in her chest. "What is it?"

"I have two eight-year-old boys. Twins. Marry me, and you'll be their mother in addition to my wife."

Of all the revelations she considered he might offer, that had never crossed her mind. Children? Two of them? Twins? How could he have let her come all this way and never mentioned something so significant? It was utterly mind blowing, and on top of her arduous journey it was almost more than she could take.

She felt suddenly faint, and as she grew dizzy, the most terrible thought wormed its way into her mind.

I've already sacrificed so many years to parent children who weren't my own. I don't want to do it again.

CHAPTER 6

JAMES

He could see it in her eyes—the disapproval, the shock, and the rejection. The moment he'd made eye contact with her, James had felt something shift in him that he couldn't explain, and his first instinct had been to get them married as quickly as possible, before she could run away from him. He knew he'd been abrupt, not that he wasn't often abrupt. But it hadn't been in order to push someone away this time, but rather to draw her closer.

But she wasn't going to be drawn closer. She was already shutting down, closing him off, and he couldn't even blame her. Rebekah had walked away from him and the kids with no excuse for her behavior, but James and his children were no inherent responsibility of Maria's, and if she ran in the other direction as fast as possible, he couldn't hold it against her.

And yet he desperately wanted her not to.

"I'm sorry I didn't tell you," he said. "You're surprised."

"Quite."

"It was wrong of me. I listened to a well-meaning friend who doesn't always know what he's talkin' about."

Maria looked away from him, taking a deep breath and resting her hand against her stomach, as though trying to settle herself. "I'm not sure what to say. Had I thought children were involved ..."

"You wouldn't have come."

"No," she said, looking back at him. "Perhaps that makes me in the wrong, but no. You see, my parents passed away in a terrible accident five years ago, and I've spent those years raising my younger siblings. My youngest sibling just turned eighteen, and I decided to go and start a life for myself—for the first time, really. This is meant to be a fresh start. It's not that I resent or regret raising them. Please don't think that. But I did give up quite a lot to do it, and I just don't know how to imagine starting that process over again. With eight-year-old boys, no less."

James looked down at the ground, hearing the sounds all around them that clearly told him the world was continuing on. And, yet, he felt frozen to the spot. She had already spent so many years raising children not her own, and now he was going to ask her to do it all over again?

He couldn't. Selfish as he could sometimes be, that was too much, even for him.

"I understand," he said quietly, pulling his hat off his head and holding it awkwardly in his hands. "I'm awful sorry about all of this, Maria." His eyes lifted to hers once more, looking intently. "It looks like I'm gonna miss out on something real ... nice."

It could have just been his imagination, but he thought her breath caught in her throat. She stared back at him, both of them caught in their own mental confusion. He couldn't understand how he could feel so much for her in just moments, and she, presumably, couldn't make heads or tails of the fact that he had thrown two children into the mix.

When he opened his mouth, it was with the intention of letting her off the hook again and offering to get her back to her home somehow. Instead, something different came out. "Just meet the boys. I'll have Benjamin—he's a friend who works on the farm with me—go get them. You don't have to come to the house. But meet them and just see. Will you do that for me?"

Maria hesitated for a moment, but then, to his delight, nodded. "Of course. I shouldn't be so quick to judge. I would be happy to meet them."

He couldn't believe it. Here he had brought her out to Montana under false pretenses, and she was the one excusing her bad behavior. She was as sweet as she was pretty, and he sent up a quick prayer that the boys would, for once, be on their best behavior.

"Don't go anywhere," he said, holding a hand up as he stepped backward. "I'll be right back."

Hurrying down the street, away from her, he found Benjamin and cut his friend off before he could start asking questions.

"Go get the boys," he said. "Tell them that they're going to meet a sweet, nice, lovely lady, and they have to behave themselves. Tell them that I'll buy them treats. Tell them that I'll take a whole week off and spend it just with them. Whatever it takes. But get them clean, and get them here. Can you do that for me?"

Benjamin's eyebrows were so high in his hairline that they'd almost disappeared. "Oh my. You like her! She must be somethin' else, huh?"

James narrowed his eyes at his friend. "You know, this is pretty close to bein' yer fault, so how about you just ride back home as fast as you can and pick up my sons?"

"Aye, aye, boss," Benjamin, ever affable, chuckled, offering a salute. "Half an hour."

Benjamin swung up into the waiting wagon and took off, leaving James standing there in the cloud of dust he left behind, wondering how he could use the next half an hour to convince Maria that he was the one for her.

CHAPTER 7

MARIA

"So, as I was saying," Maria laughed, wincing slightly as she realized she'd been rambling. "Hannah's wedding was lovely. I'm sorry. All you asked was how old my sister was, and I just went on for ten minutes."

They were sitting together on a bench outside the general store, waiting for James' boys to arrive, and Maria was finding the man very easy to talk to, once she got used to his somewhat abrupt manner.

He smiled at her, his body angled toward hers and his arm stretched out across the back of the bench in a way that threatened to make her heart stutter. "No need to apologize. I enjoy hearing you so excited. You care deeply for your siblings. That's obvious."

Maria nodded, then felt a twinge of guilt again, rooted in her instinctive reaction to James' news. "Please don't think that I resent raising them after my parents passed. There was nothing else I would rather have been doing—they were everything to me."

"And then your job was done."

"Well, it changed," Maria admitted, biting her lip as she looked down at her hands. "See, I never really had time to do anything of my own. And, well, I actually love to write. I've always wanted to be able to devote myself to writing and painting, too. Oh, not that I'd ever make a living, but I love to create, and I've never had the time."

His expression was sad, and it confused Maria. Why did this man, practically a stranger to her, feel such empathy for what she was saying?

"You should have that chance to do something for yourself," James said. "Maria ... the moment I looked in your eyes, I felt you were the one for me in a way that I didn't believe existed, and I know that sounds mad, under the circumstances. But I did feel it, and it's because of that that I really want to ask you to give this a go. But when I hear you talk about a fresh start, I don't know how I can."

Maria felt a tug at her heartstrings and her hand twitched in her lap, almost as though it wanted to reach for his. She was torn, suddenly. She had been so sure of what she wanted, but now that she had arrived and found something different, she wasn't confident anymore. Did she want the total fresh start, perhaps alone, or did she want to take a risk on the man in front of her, whom she had, after all, come all this way to be with, knowing that it meant raising someone else's children all over again?

Lord, I honestly have no idea what to do. Please give me your wisdom. Give me some kind of sign.

As though in direct answer to her prayer, James' friend suddenly pulled up in the wagon, two young boys sitting in the back, eagerly leaning over the wooden slats to try to see who could find their new mother first. Maria stared at them as they pushed at each other, grinning and scrapping and generally paying no attention whatsoever to the commotion they were causing.

James had told her that one was named Thomas and one was named Edward. She had no idea which boy went with which name, but it didn't matter. As they scrambled down, Maria's eyes locked on the one in front. They looked quite similar to each other, but there were also clear differences in their faces. But when Maria made eye contact with the first boy, his green eyes and the pattern of freckles across her nose made her catch her breath.

It was exactly like looking at Timothy when he was that age, and it brought back such a flood of memories and nostalgia that Maria almost burst into tears right then and there. Surely it was the emotion of leaving her siblings for the first time and the exhaustion of travel that caused her to be so emotional, but even suspecting that, she couldn't help the words that leaped from her lips the moment she opened them, prior to exchanging one word with the twins.

"Yes," Maria said, turning to James, her voice reflecting her momentary certainty. "Yes, I still want to marry you. I want to be a family."

His eyes lit up, and he moved toward her as though he was going to sweep her up in a hug. But then the boys were there, crowding around her with more questions than she had ever heard at one time.

"Why are you here?"

"Who are you?"

"What's that color of your dress called?"

"Are you my new ma?"

"Do you know how to make cakes?"

"Can you make coffee?"

"Are you going to make us sweep the floors?"

"Do you know our real ma?"

"How did you get here?"

The questions, those and more, bombarded her all at once, and she couldn't help but laugh, caught somewhere between confusion, excitement, and the lingering memories of Timothy when he was just a boy. "My, what a lot of curiosity."

"Boys," James said, filling in for her. "This is Maria Smith, and we're going to be married. She's your new ma, and I'm sure she has all kinds of nice things she can cook for you."

"Oh yes," Maria agreed, keeping her voice bright even as her mind began to question the emotional reaction she'd had to seeing a boy so much like Timothy. "Very nice things. But only if you do the sweeping."

The Timothy-lookalike groaned. "We hate sweeping!"

"Be polite," James chided, shaking his head at his son. "Honestly, Edward, where are your manners?"

Edward put on a big smile. "Sorry, missus. We're real glad yer here to take care of us. Boy, do we need it!"

"Yeah, Papa can't bake worth anything," Thomas added, shoving his hands in his pockets. "So when is the weddin'?"

James put his arm around her waist and looked down into Maria's eyes. "It's now. The church is just across the way. Everyone is coming."

She managed a smile and walked with him and his two bouncing boys, heading for the church where she would say vows that she couldn't take back. It was what she had come here to do, and she'd had no intention of backing out until she'd heard about the children involved. Then, in the moment, even that had seemed all right.

But as she stepped inside the church building, everything happening so quickly around her, Maria couldn't deny that she still had some serious doubts as to whether she was making the right decision. The only problem was, there wasn't any going back now.

CHAPTER 8

JAMES

"Papa!" Thomas ran toward James, his little red face scrunched in frustration. "I don't want this ma anymore. I'm tired of her! Make her go away so we can get a different one."

James stopped inspecting the nearly ripened wheat and turned toward his son, an eyebrow raised. "Excuse me?"

"I said we don't like her," Thomas repeated, crossing his arms over his chest. "She isn't sweet enough, and she doesn't play with us."

"Son, Maria—I mean, yer ma—she has lots of things to do. She's only been here a few days, you know. She's settling in."

"Well, I don't want her to tell me to do anymore chores!" Thomas said, as Edward came running up behind him to chime in as well.

"She's no fun, Papa. And I don't think she likes us," Edward said, swiping the sweat from his brow. "Why can't we go play in the barn like we used to?"

James sighed, adjusting his wide-brimmed hat and attempting to kick some of the dirt off his shoes. "Because now that yer ma is here, yer supposed to be helpin' her and learnin' some schooling. Don't you want to learn numbers and letters?"

Edward scoffed. "Nobody wants to learn that, Papa. We just want how it was!"

How it was. James shook his head, thinking of how, all the years since Rebekah had been gone, he'd worried that the boys needed a mother figure in their life. Now that they had one, they didn't want anything to do with her. Wasn't that always the way?

If he was being honest, he didn't entirely blame them for their disgruntlement. Maria had been terribly moody over the past few days, sometimes seeming happy and eager to settle in and other times growing morose and withdrawn. In those darker moments, she wanted nothing to do with any of them and went to the room that he had set up for her while she was getting used to the house and her new family. He hadn't thought it was right to move her immediately into his own room, even though that was where he wanted her.

"Boys, why don't you go find Benjamin?" James suggested. "I'm gonna go talk to yer ma and figure out what's wrong, okay?"

"She doesn't want to talk right now," Thomas said. "She told us to go work outside."

"Well then, go work outside," James said, waving his sons off into the field. "Find Benjamin and help him with whatever he's doing. Go on, then."

The boys ran off, and James, taking a deep breath, headed back to the house. As he walked, he kept trying to think of ways that he could approach the situation with Maria. He still felt incredibly drawn to her. He desperately wanted her to be happy here. But he also knew that she'd had a different life planned for herself, and that she might be regretting her decision to marry him and take on his household.

Rebekah had, after all.

Strangely, it would break his heart more if Maria left him than it had when Rebekah had departed. He hadn't ever felt, even for one day, the connection with Rebekah that he felt with Maria. There was no explanation for that, and he'd given up trying to find one.

When he arrived at the house, he knocked lightly on the door to warn her that he was coming in, then stepped inside the cooler, darker area that was the front entryway of their home. "Maria?"

"I'm in the kitchen."

Her voice was pleasant enough, but impersonal, and James wasn't sure what he would find when he made his way to the center of the house, finding her standing at the counter, kneading dough to turn into bread. She didn't turn to face him, and he sighed, not knowing how to start the conversation they had to have.

"Maria, the boys feel like you might be unhappy here."

She turned then, looking at him in surprise. "Oh. I see. I'm sorry."

He sat down at the kitchen table, motioning for her to join him. "You don't have to be sorry. I feel liked I've trapped you in a life you don't want. If that's the case, I want you to tell me now. Don't wait until we're attached to leave us."

Guilt washed over Maria's face and she dusted off her hands, sitting down across from him. "Of course I'm not going to leave. I made vows to you, and I take them seriously. It's ... been a bigger adjustment than I thought. I miss Hannah and Timothy terribly, and I do question why I left them if I was simply going to be a caretaker here, like I was there. At least they were there." The words seemed to tumble out of her mouth, somewhat inelegantly. "That sounds terrible. I don't mean it that way. I guess I just got caught up in the idea of doing something grand and independent out west. It's a silly notion, I suppose."

"Why can't you do something grand and independent?" James asked, reaching over and covering her hand with his. For the past few days, he had constantly longed to hold her hand in his, and he hadn't let himself. But she was slipping away from him, and he didn't know how to bring her back.

"Because ... I need to be here. That's what you wanted. A wife to manage your home and children."

James felt his own guilt hit hard again. It was true. That's exactly what he'd wanted —a woman who would take care of that aspect of things, taking the burden off him. But the moment he had seen Maria, something in him had shifted, and he found he was willing to do whatever it took to help share the burdens of their home evenly with her so that she could follow her own passion as well.

"It is what I wanted," he agreed, squeezing her fingers to keep her from pulling her hand away. "Until I saw you. Then I realized that was selfish. Maria, if we choose to be partners who help each other, then there's no reason why we can't run a home, a farm, and have our own passions too. You can get what you need for paintin', and there's a whole world out there, waitin' to be captured by your brush. And I'll make Hank down at the general store sell your paintings. He'll do it. I know he will."

Her eyes softened, and her hand curled around his for the first time. But before she could speak, the front door of the house banged open, and then Benjamin rushed into the kitchen, out of breath and frantic.

"Edward fell down into the old well. He's not respondin' when we call to him."

CHAPTER 9

MARIA

No! Lord, please, no, don't let Edward be hurt.

All Maria could do as she ran with Benjamin and James out toward the well was pray again and again, pleading with the God she trusted in to keep anything from happening to the little boy who reminded her so much of Timothy and who, despite being rambunctious, had proven himself over the past few days to be sweet and smart. Maria had admittedly been sharp with the boys on occasion, but it wasn't because she didn't like them. It was only because of her own inner struggles. And now she couldn't bear the idea that Edward's last interaction with her had been born of frustration.

Thomas was waiting at the well along with a few of the other farmhands. The little boy was distressed, tears streaming down his suntanned face, and Maria hurried to him, throwing her arms around the boy and holding him close.

"It's all right," she whispered. "It's all right."

"We were playin'," he sobbed into her shoulder. "We were just playin' around, and he was runnin' and lookin' back at me, and then he just fell! He fell!"

"Shhh," she said, rubbing his back gently, tears in her own eyes. "It's going to be all right, Thomas. I promise."

It was a promise filled only with her faith that God wouldn't let this happen to her new family, and she clung to it as James and Benjamin tried to figure out how they were going to get down into the well. One of the farmhands had found a few coils of rope, and they were trying to fashion it into a pulley that would lower James into the well.

Maria dared a look down into the hole, and her heart sank. It was an old well and mostly dry except for a few inches of water at the bottom. That meant a further fall and a harder landing for Edward, who was lying at the bottom, curled up in a ball, unresponsive.

"I don't know, boss," one farmhand who Maria didn't know was saying. "Rope might not be strong enough to hold ya. If it breaks, all we're gonna have is two of you in that hole."

"Better to take the risk and then be in there with him," James said, intent on figuring out how to fasten the rope to his waist.

Still holding Thomas, Maria interjected. "Lower me instead."

Everyone turned to look at her uncertainly. She was still a stranger, and an Easterner at that. They would view her as a city girl, even though she wasn't really. But she just repeated herself.

"Lower me instead. I'm lighter. It's less likely to break. And I'm strong. I managed a household mostly by myself for years. I can lift him out."

James glanced down at the rope in his hands, then shook his head. "Maria, I appreciate it, but no. I can't have you fallin.'"

"Then don't drop me," she said, hugging Thomas once more then walking over to James and looking into his eyes. "Partners, right? This is what partners do. They spot each other."

"That's true," he said, staring down at her.

Then, without saying another thing, he tied the rope firmly around her waist and walked her over to the side of the well. She got into position and the men all lined up, rope in hand, to help lower her carefully. Maria didn't hesitate, lifting her skirts enough to allow her to brace her booted feet against the edge of the well. Carefully and very slowly, she began to lower herself, testing out the strength of the rope as she went until she felt comfortable that it could hold her.

As big as James was, she was probably only half his weight, and that might make all the difference.

She sank lower and lower into the well, the musty smell of water surrounding her and the air growing shockingly cooler the lower she went. It would be a lie to say she wasn't scared in the dark hole by herself, but Edward was waiting for her, and she wasn't about to let him lie down here, exposed to the elements, until he died, like her parents had.

"Edward," she called to him, looking down as he grew closer to her. "Edward, I'm coming. Can you hear me?"

To her delight, she heard a faint groan.

"Edward! Can you hear me?"

The groan came again, too faint for them to hear all the way at the top of the well. But Maria looked up at them, seeing James staring intently down at her.

"He's alive! He's responding to me."

"Oh, thank the Lord," James said, sinking to his knees, his hands gripping the edge. "Be careful, sweetheart. Go slowly. Edward, I'm here! I'm right here, son."

Again, the child groaned, and then Maria felt the water lap at her boots. Another few inches, and she was standing up to her ankles in the water. She dropped the rope, letting it hang around her waist, and turned to Edward, quickly checking him over for injuries. To her surprise, nothing appeared to be broken. She ran her hands over his limbs, and he never flinched or cried out, no matter what she pressed on.

The concern was going to be his head. It looked like he had hit it hard, and he was drifting in and out of consciousness. Her common sense told her that it wasn't the best idea to move him, but he couldn't stay down here. No doctor could see him here.

"Get the doctor here," she shouted up to the men. "He'll need his head seen to."

Then she crouched down, slipped her arms under the boy's knees and neck, and lifted him up against her. "I'm so sorry," she whispered. "You're going to be all right."

CHAPTER 10

JAMES

He could hardly believe it as he and his farmhands began to haul Maria and Edward up out of the well. Maria had been so brave, and Edward was still alive. James' heart was hammering in his chest and whispered his prayer over and over again, asking God to get them just a little further so he could grab Maria and drag them out.

"You're so close," James called down to her, as she hung, clutching Edward, two-thirds of the way up the well. "Almost here, darlin'." He wanted to say so many things to her—to beg her never to leave, to tell her that she was everything they needed, to tell her how incredible she was. But there would be time for that later.

"James—oh!" Maria suddenly gasped as the rope popped, one of its woven strands breaking as it strained under Edward's added weight. "Oh no!"

James signaled to the men behind him, then let go of the rope, lying down on the ground on his stomach so he could reach his hands down to Maria and Edward. "Reach, Maria. We're so close. Reach a little further to me, sweetheart." If he could just get Edward from her, the strain on the rope would lessen and they could pull her up.

"A little further ..." she said, one hand clutching the rope so hard that her knuckles were white and the other hand clutching Edward to her. "I can't push him. I only have one hand ..."

"Pull," James ordered the men. "Pull hard—I just need a few more inches."

His farmhands complied, and Maria moved closer to him—so close that James could brush his fingers against Edward's hair. He almost growled in frustration, so close and yet so far from his son.

"Again!"

This time when the men pulled another cord of rope popped, but James was able to grab Edward's arms and pull. Benjamin grabbed James from behind and pulled as well, and together, the two men dragged the boy to safety. For a moment, James just clutched his disoriented child to his chest, grateful to have him alive and back in his arms.

But then he handed Edward to Benjamin and turned back toward Maria, catching her arm just as the final cord of rope snapped and she began to fall. Their hands clutched at each other, and he wrapped his other hand around her arm, pulling as hard as he could. Her hand landed on the edge of the well, and together, somehow, they scrambled her back onto safe ground.

She was dirty and her chest was heaving with exertion, but James put his arms around her, kissing her for the first time ever. "My amazing wife. You did it."

Maria kissed him back without protest, her hands in his hair briefly, but then she pulled back, searching for Edward. "Where is he? Is he all right?"

"He knows me!" Thomas was crouched beside his brother, who lay on the ground under Benjamin's watch. "He said my name!"

Maria sagged against James, and he held her up, relief coursing through his whole body. "That's great, Thomas. That's so great."

Standing up with Maria, he guided her over to his son, kneeling down beside the boy's filthy, damp body and smoothing his hair back from his face. "Edward?"

"I'm sorry, Papa," Edward managed, his voice small and scared. "I fell in."

"You're not in trouble," James promised, leaning down to kiss his son's forehead. "I love you, Edward. I really do."

"Yeah?"

"Oh yes. And I'm going to get you seen by a doctor. You've got quite a knot growing on your head."

"A manly knot?"

James smiled despite the scare they'd had. "A very manly knot."

Bending down, he hugged Edward again, just holding his son for a moment. Then he stood up, letting the farmhands move around Edward to transport him back to the house as carefully as possible. Thomas tagged along beside his brother, his devotion to his sibling one of the most heartwarming things James had ever seen.

Beside him, Maria's hand slipped into his, and he looked down at her. "You were amazing," he told her again. "The rope would never have gotten him and me out."

"We're partners," she murmured. "When I knew he was in trouble, all I cared about was helping him. This is where I want to be, James. With you. With them. There will be days of doubt, but this is where I want to be."

James pulled her to him, burying his face in her hair as he held her. "I won't ever give you cause to regret it. The moment I saw you, Maria ..."

"I felt it too. I couldn't have stayed if I hadn't."

"I love you already. I want you to be happy here."

"I'm happy with you. With them," Maria murmured, looking up at him. "And I think I could love you too. I know I will."

His heart soaring with happiness, James kissed her softly, then put his arm around her as they walked together back toward his house where they would take care of Edward and start working on making a home.

EPILOGUE

MARIA

"Boys!" Maria called for the twins as she stood at the back door of her farmhouse, holding a broom. "Chore time! Come on, then. Edward! Thomas!"

The boys appeared around the corner of the house, grungy and pouty. "Ma ... do we have to? We were findin' worms!"

"Yes, you have to," Maria said with a smile, waving them inside. "But first clean yourselves off. No mess in the house! I have my painting class later."

"Oh, paint some pretty flowers," Thomas teased, but as he hurried past her, he gave her a hug around the waist. "Back in a flash, Ma!"

Edward grinned at her and hurried after his brother into their room to change clothes, and Maria laughed. Her life hadn't been boring for even one minute of the last four months, and she had grown to love every part of it. Her boys, her husband, her home, her painting classes, her articles for the local newspaper—all of it fulfilled her more than she had ever thought possible.

But at the center of it was her family. Her wild, crazy family.

"Hello, wife," James murmured, coming up behind her and sliding his arms around her waist as he kissed her cheek. "How is my beautiful Maria?"

Smiling, she leaned back against him. "Perfect."

"I agree. She is perfect."

"You are so clever," Maria teased, turning in his arms to kiss him properly. "Are you in for lunch? You're a bit early, but it'll be ready soon."

"I'm in no rush," he said, tucking her hair back from her face. "I came in a bit early so I would have time to tell you that I love you. Have I told you that today?"

Maria couldn't stop smiling, even as she pushed at him playfully. "Several times. But I love you too. So much. And I love our ..."

"Shhhh ..." he urged, covering her stomach with his hand. "Don't say. The boys have bigger ears than you'd think, and I want to surprise them with the news on their birthday."

"Me too," Maria said, covering his hand with hers as she thought of the baby that was growing beneath their palms. "They'll be so excited."

"I hope it's a girl," James whispered, patting her stomach. "And that she looks just like you."

Maria beamed, hugging her husband again. And as he held her, she knew that she had found her perfect place in the world. By the time the baby arrived, Hannah and her husband would be on their way out to Montana as well. Timothy would follow once his apprenticeship was complete.

Life couldn't get any more perfect.

God was truly good.

⊗

THANK YOU SO MUCH FOR READING MY BOOK. I SINCERELY HOPE YOU ENJOYED EVERY *bit reading it. I had fun creating it and will surely create more.*

Your positive reviews are very helpful to other reader, it only takes a few moments. They can be left at Amazon.

https://www.amazon.com/Kat-Carson/e/B01G333YP0

⊗

WANT FREE BOOKS EVERY WEEK? WHO DOESN'T!

BECOME A PREFERRED READER AND WE'LL NOT ONLY SEND YOU FREE READS, BUT *you'll also receive updates about new releases.*

So you'll be among the first to dive into our latest new books, full of adventure, heartwarming romances, and characters so real they jump off the page.

It's absolutely free and you don't need to do anything at all to qualify except go to.

PREFERRED READ FREE READS

https://katcarsonbooks.getresponsepages.com

ABOUT THE AUTHOR

KAT CARSON LIVES IN NEW MEXICO WITH HER TWO DOGS, A HORSE, AND 20 chickens. She started writing when she was a teenager and has never stopped. She loves the rich culture of the old West. Some of her stories are inspired by tales from the local storytellers in New Mexico and what her grandparents used to tell her. Others are when she travels around in her RV camping, fishing, hiking, climbing and engaging with other interesting people along the way.

She writes stories derived from actual historical facts and events and sometimes individuals with interesting characters in nature that will captivate you and leave you in awe with the twists and turns of every story. Packed with action, humor, challenge, and adventure her short stories will stretch the limits of your imagination, allowing you to marvel at the fascinating time in US history. I recommend them for anybody who enjoys an excellent feel good clean and wholesome romance story.

JENNY'S UNEXPECTED

Mail Order Bride Western Romance

RoyceCardiff
P u b l i s h i n g   H o u s e
WHOLESOME INSPIRATIONAL ROMANCE

Dear Reader,

It is our utmost pleasure and privilege to bring these wonderful stories to you. I am so very proud of our amazing team of writers and the delight they continually bring us all with their beautiful clean and wholesome tales of faith, courage, and love.

What is a book's lone purpose if not to be read and enjoyed? Therefore, you, dear reader, are the key to fulfilling that purpose and unlocking the treasures that lie within the pages of this book.

❧

NEWSLETTER SIGN UP PREFERRED READ

http://katieWyattBooks.com/readersgroup

❧

THANK YOU FOR CHOOSING A INSPIRATIONAL READS BY ROYCE CARDIFF PUBLISHING HOUSE.

Welcome and Enjoy!

A PERSONAL WORD FROM KATIE

I LOVE WRITING ABOUT THE OLD WEST AND THE TRIALS, TRIBULATIONS, AND triumphs of the early pioneer women.

With strong fortitude and willpower, they took a big leap of faith believing in the promised land of the West. It was always not a bed of roses, however many found true love.

Most of the stories are based on some historical fact or personal conversations I've had with folks who knew something of that time. For example a relative of the Wyatt Earp's. I have spent much time out in the West camping hiking and carousing. I have spent countless hours gazing up at night thinking of how it must been back then.

Thank you for being a loyal reader.

Katie

CHAPTER 1

J ENNY S IMMONS HELD HER ARMS WRAPPED TIGHTLY AROUND HER MIDDLE AS THE stagecoach hit another large hole in the road. She had no idea how this wooden contraption was staying together as it shuddered and continued rocking. All she knew was that she was ready to reach her destination.

Her queasiness had started as soon as she'd climbed aboard and had not let up since. Jenny was sure her mama would have said she was as white as a sheet on washday.

Jenny sniffed, thinking of her mama. It was her mother who had enlisted her as a mail order bride and packed her onto this rattling bucket, headed into parts unknown.

Unable to keep the tears from sliding down her cheeks, Jenny began to cry.

The woman next to her, a matronly sort, immediately began to fuss over her. "There, there now, dearie. It'll be okay," she said as she handed Jenny a piece of cloth to dry her tears. "Once we pull into Dry Gulch, I'm sure your new husband will take care of you and the wee one."

Jenny gasped and looked around her! Did everyone on board know she was with child? From their sympathetic looks, it appeared so. The tears came even harder with this knowledge.

The matron tried to take her hand, but Jenny pulled away and pressed herself up against the side of the coach, hanging onto the handle provided there.

"As I said, dearie, it'll be okay. God takes care of the innocent," the woman whispered to her.

"I'm Elsie Barnes, by the way. I'm chaperoning some of the other girls on board to meet their soon-to-be-husbands."

"Jenny ... Jenny Simmons," she said hesitantly.

"Well, Jenny Simmons, we've got some time while we bounce along here. Why don't you tell me about the babe's father?"

When Jenny began to cry again, and the tears seemed endless, Elsie asked, "Are you a war widow?"

Jenny shook her head. "No, I was a governess to two beautiful children, working in a fine house in Charlotte."

"What happened, dearie? Did you fall in love with their father?" Elsie asked.

"No, there was no love in that house," Jenny said quietly.

"Ah, he took advantage of your lowly position then, eh?" Elsie guessed.

"No," Jenny mumbled. "I was married. Briefly. The man I loved ... we'd barely been wed three months before he cut and run. My employer was less than happy when my condition started to show, claiming it embarrassed his family and confused his children. Even though I'd done nothing wrong!"

Elsie looped an arm around her. "What about your family, dearie? Were they no help to you?"

The mention of her family caused Jenny to sit up straight and dry her eyes.

"I am the eldest daughter of a very respected pastor in Charlotte." One single tear rolled down her cheek. "My parents never approved of the man I married. Father told me that I had disgraced them unspeakably and beyond measure. I was to leave and never return. I was to never say their names aloud again as they were no longer my family."

"Oh, dearie! What of your poor mother? She didn't turn her back on you, did she?" Elsie asked disbelievingly.

Jenny's shoulders slumped once again. "She's the one who made the arrangements for me to come West as a mail order bride," Jenny sobbed. "My mother said it was the only way for them to be able to hold their heads high again."

"There now," Elsie murmured, patting her knee tenderly. "It'll all come right. God will see to it, dearie. You do believe, don't you?"

JENNY SNIFFLED AND NODDED. IN SPITE OF THE PAIN OF THE LAST FEW MONTHS, her faith in God had never wavered. Nor had her love for her unborn child. It was no mistake, no matter what her husband or her parents had said.

CHAPTER 2

ABOUT THIS TIME, THE STAGECOACH CAME TO A HALT FOR ONE OF ITS SCHEDULED stops to switch horses and give the passengers a chance to use the facilities and eat a bite.

Glad for the chance to escape the cloistered interior, Jenny practically leapt off the steps and ran to the nearest water pump for a refreshing drink and a chance to splash some water on her face and throat. Several other passengers had the same idea as her, but not all, so she was able to have some privacy.

All together there were eight passengers on the stagecoach, six of whom were women.

The two men appeared to know one another, from the way they talked to each other. One was dressed in boots, jeans, and a hat. Like a cowboy, Jenny guessed. The other was dressed more refined in a suit and vest with shiny buckled shoes and a top hat.

The cowboy had started several conversations with the other ladies aboard, drawing each of them out a little bit. However, Jenny had kept to herself and not let herself by engaged in small talk. She knew better than to fall for any handsome man who looked her way.

Each time she took a quick glance in their direction, the man with the shiny-buckled shoes was looking at her appraisingly. Of course, she would quickly look away as it would be considered rude for her to be caught staring at him. She had to admit she did find him very attractive with his blue eyes that matched his cravat and his dark black hair so nicely combed.

As she'd eavesdropped throughout the journey, which was easily done in such small quarters, and listened to the other passengers' stories, she'd learned that four of the women were also signed up, or as they said, "pledged," as mail order brides.

Elsie was their chaperone, which explained her motherly attitude toward Jenny when she had begun to weep.

According to the driver, they still had another four hours to travel, so when he gave the basic "all aboard" call, Jenny almost started crying again, dreading still more hours on the coach.

When they re-boarded the coach, she found herself sitting between the two men. Slightly disconcerted, Jenny almost asked one of the other women to trade with her but didn't want to seem rude.

Jenny was accustomed to sitting by the door and being able to hold the handle there, so when the coach took a sharp turn, she automatically reached for the handle, only to grab the top-hatted gentleman's arm.

"I'm so sorry," she said. "I was trying to reach the handle, so I would have something to hang on to. I get nauseous quite easily, you see."

He smiled at her. Extending his hand, he said, "I'm Jason Hansom, card dealer extraordinaire."

Sitting nearby, the matron spoke up in a censoring tone. "He's a professional gambler. You can tell by looking at him. Best to steer clear, dearie."

Jason gave her a sharp look that had her looking away.

"Is that right, Mr. Hansom? Are you a gambler?" Jenny asked.

"Yes, I am." He reached up and tipped his hat. "And this is my traveling companion, Slim Jackson."

As she turned to him, the cowboy stuck out his big, rawboned hand and said, "Pleased to make your acquaintance, ma'am."

He seemed almost like a child trying to display his manners as taught by his elders.

"Likewise, Mr. Jackson," she murmured as she took his hand.

"Just call me Slim; everyone does," he said in his drawling accent.

"Are you two gentlemen going to Dry Gulch?" she asked.

"Yep. Me an' Jason are goin' to play in a big game there on Saturday," Slim said proudly.

Jason leaned out past her and gave Slim a look that said, "That's enough talking." Slim promptly pulled his hat over his eyes and pretended to doze.

"You'll have to forgive him, ladies," Mr. Hansom explained. "He tends to run on when he gets started, especially around such lovely young women." He gave the matron a special smile which made her titter.

"Well, y'all already know all about me; it's only fair that I should learn some more about you, don't you think?" the gambler said sweetly.

The matron spoke up first, seemingly beguiled in spite of her earlier warning. "My name is Elsie Barnes. I am escorting these young women to meet up with their betrothed husbands through the mail order bride system out of Driscoll County."

Elsie began to introduce her charges. "Sitting here beside me is Annie DeLaney. Next to her is Sarah Delaney; yes, they are sisters. Then we have Georgia Maxwell, and seated next to you, Mr. Hansom, is Naomi Fairchild."

They all turned their attention to Jenny. "I'm Jenny Simmons."

"Nice to meet you all." Mr. Hansom said. "Miss Barnes, as the leader of your group, can you tell me, do your young ladies already know the names of their betrotheds?"

"Yes, they do," she said, rather pleased with herself. "In fact, they also have pictures of their men. They've been corresponding for several months, prior to this trip. That way we ensure all matches are happy, you see."

He made sure she knew he was very impressed with the mail order bride system of Driscoll County, which made Miss Barnes puff up proudly indeed.

"What about you, Miss Simmons?" he asked. "Do you know the name of your betrothed?"

"Yes, I do, but I don't have a picture," Jenny stated matter-of-factly. "I used a different mail order service and they didn't provide such things."

"What is the name of your affianced, Miss Fairchild?" Mr. Hansom asked.

"My what?" she looked at him quizzingly. "Oh, you mean the man I'm supposed to marry? Well, it's Dalton. Dalton Darnell."

When Jenny told them, one of the other girls, Naomi Fairchild, exclaimed, "We're going to be sisters-in-law! Praise God! I already have a friend!"

"Really, Miss Fairchild! Settle yourself!" the admonishment came from Miss Barnes.

"I'm sorry. I'm just so excited that I'll be marrying into the same family as one of y'all!"

However, when Jenny looked at Mr. Hansom, she saw that he was looking at her skeptically. She also noticed that Mr. Jackson had stopped pretending to sleep and was now listening attentively.

"Miss Simmons, if you don't mind me asking so impertinently, have you and your betrothed been exchanging letters?"

Jenny squirmed in the seat as much as possible. "Well, not exactly ..." she admitted. It seemed her mother had chosen a far less thorough mail order system than the one Elsie was chaperoning.

Naomi spoke up. "I have ... we have ... my betrothed and me. He must be some relation to the fella she's promised to because their last names are the same. I'm marryin' Zeke Darnell."

She went on to ask the men. "Do you know of 'em? Our men? Can you tell us anything about them? Maybe the other girls have questions, too."

The matron quickly shut that kind of talk down. "No, ladies, we will not be listening to gossip and hearsay about your future husbands. It's not the Lord's way. Now why don't we all do a bit of embroidery ..."

❦

THEY STOPPED AGAIN IN TWO HOURS FOR ANOTHER QUICK BREAK.

Jenny noticed the two men talking and looking at her.

They seemed to come to an agreement before the driver gave the final "all-aboard" call.

Once they had reassembled on the coach, it was obvious Jason and Slim had some talking to do.

Jason started, "Now, Miss Barnes, I know you don't want to hear this, but your girls are headed for a world of trouble and me and Slim just can't stand by and do nothing to stop it."

"Why whatever do you mean, Mr. Hansom?" Elsie asked. "You are scaring these young ladies and you'd better explain yourself right away!"

"Well, first of all, I don't know what caused y'all to take such steps as leaving your homes and marrying strangers, so I don't want you ladies to think I'm judging any of you." He took a deep breath. "But, ladies, Dry Gulch is a pit of vipers."

They all gasped!

"What?" Miss Barnes shouted out. "What do you mean? Explain yourself at once!"

"I mean, Dry Gulch is no place for nice ladies such as yourselves. The men you are betrothed to are either gunmen, cattle rustlers, thieves, outlaws, or worse."

One DeLaney sister grabbed hold of the other and cried, "I want to go back home!" They both began to sob.

Miss Barnes was practically crying herself. "I had no idea! The men all came highly recommended ... What do you recommend we do? It appears our fate is in your hands, gentlemen."

Slim interrupted. "Well now, hold on, Jason! Some of these ladies may want to go on to Dry Gulch and take their chances. Let's hear them out."

"Good idea, Slim."

Georgia Maxwell and Naomi Fairchild did indeed want to meet their betrotheds and take the chance on a new life. They had nothing to return home to and no future except the one they'd set out for in Dry Gulch.

However, the DeLaney sisters didn't care to go any further. They announced they were getting off at the next stop and heading back home on the next stagecoach. Miss Barnes agreed to escort them.

That only left Jenny.

She looked at the two men. "I saw your faces when the name Darnell was mentioned. Please tell me about them. Will they be kind to me and my baby?"

Slim turned and looked out the window. Jason couldn't keep eye contact with her.

"Please, Mr. Hansom, I have to know what I'll be up against!" she pleaded.

He looked at Naomi and then at Jenny.

"There are four Darnells. There's the old man and his three sons, and they pretty much run Dry Gulch."

Naomi asked quickly, "What does Zeke do?"

"Zeke is the baby and the old man's favorite. He's pretty much run wild since their ma died eight or ten years ago. He can be mean."

Naomi looked down at her hands, clasped tightly together.

"I'm sure the old man is hoping that a wife will settle him down some, but don't count on him changing anytime soon," Jason stated plainly.

"And Dalton?" Jenny asked.

Slim sat up straighter and was rigid in his seat now.

"Dalton is the oldest. He's taken the brunt of the old man's whip for years. He's the second-in- command and nobody disputes his word, or they die. If you decide to go on to Dry Gulch and pledge yourself to him, you'll be his fourth wife in as many years."

Jenny put her hand to her mouth to keep from whimpering aloud.

"But, Miss Simmons, make no mistake. He'll never accept another man's child."

Jenny began to sob loudly.

"Dear Lord in heaven, please help me!" she cried.

CHAPTER 3

As Jason watched her fall apart, he couldn't stand it.

"Miss Simmons, I do have a suggestion that might work, but we would need everyone's help."

He looked into the eyes of everyone aboard the stagecoach.

"Everyone here would have to promise never to tell anyone, and I mean anyone, what we just discussed," Jason said solemnly.

Then he turned and looked at Jenny. "And then you'll need to agree to marry me at the next stop."

"What! What?" Everyone but Slim was surprised by the proposal.

"Don't you see? It's the only way to keep your child safe from harm," Jason explained. "If you are married to me, in name only, of course, then the Darnells have no reason to suspect you are the one they were expecting."

Elsie spoke up. "It does make sense, Jenny."

She turned and looked at the others. "What do you think, ladies? Can you help them keep this secret?"

Everyone but Naomi quickly agreed.

"Naomi? What's wrong?" Elise asked.

"I'm sad because I really wanted her to be my sister-in-law!" she sniffed.

"Well, it's going to be harder for you and Georgia to remain quiet about this since y'all will be living there in town and seeing Jenny a lot," Jason stated.

"Can you do it, Georgia?" Elsie asked.

"Of course I can! I just want my own place with some of my own kids to raise," the other girl said boldly. "Besides that, I know how to handle myself. I can fight and shoot with the best of 'em."

Everyone laughed, including Jenny, even though her heart was pounding wildly.

"So Naomi, do you agree to keep quiet about me and Jenny?" Jason asked.

"Yes, I do. But if these brothers are as bad as you say then I may be the one who is next in need of help!"

With that, Slim spoke up. "Don't worry none, Miss Fairchild. Me 'n Jason will be watchin' out for ya."

At the next and last rest stop, Elsie booked passage back home for Annie and Sarah DeLaney. However, at the last minute, she decided not to go with them.

"You understand, don't you, girls? I just can't leave these others to face the trials ahead with my guidance. I feel it in my heart that I'm needed here. It pains me deeply to let you go back alone, but God is watching out for you two. I just know it."

ALMOST BEFORE JENNY HAD TIME TO PROCESS WHAT WAS HAPPENING, SHE AND Jason were married by the magistrate.

As they took their vows, Jenny wept, and Jason remained stoic. He took a small ring from his pinky finger, placed it on her left hand, and kissed her on the cheek to seal their ceremony. He was so handsome that, for just a minute, Jenny dared to imagine their marriage might one day be more than a sham ... then Jason walked away to talk with Slim and she remembered all over again why her love story had taken such an unexpected twist.

Dear God, please let Jason at least be kinder than my first husband, she murmured.

Those in attendance, mainly those from the stagecoach who knew the whole story, gathered around to congratulate them.

They took a longer than normal break there to enjoy a few beverages and some food quickly prepared by the magistrate's wife.

However, when the driver gave the call to resume their journey, they were ready.

There were tears from the DeLaney girls, who were a little afraid to be left behind. It was a hard decision for them to make. However, in the end, they decided to wait for the next coach back home.

As the driver helped Jenny into the coach, he winked at her and said, "Mrs. Hansom, congratulations, and don't worry. Your secret is safe with me."

Jenny turned her head quickly to see if he was teasing her, but she could see he was very serious indeed.

CHAPTER 4

The remainder of the trip to Dry Gulch was relatively smooth.

Georgia and Naomi asked the two men questions about the town and its amenities which, according to Slim, were above par for some of the more remote Western cities.

He explained that the Daltons had used their "influence," as he put it, to bring in more businesses and modern facilities to attract people with more money to the area.

Of course, oftentimes, these folks met with untimely deaths, leaving their fortunes in the hands of the Daltons.

"You really don't paint a pretty picture of the Daltons, Mr. Jackson," Naomi said.

Slim smiled at her and stretched out his long legs to give them a brief respite. "Ma'am, I may not look it, but I've traveled around a lot and seen and done many things that I wish I hadn't. But I ain't never come across a group as devious as the Daltons. And that's the truth."

"What say you, Mr. Hansom? I mean, you're going there to join with them, aren't you?" Georgia asked boldly.

Jason had sat next to his new wife and tried to remain silent. He didn't really want to enter into the discussion. However, Jenny made that impossible for him.

"She's right, husband." The word sounded so strange on her lips. "Aren't you going there to play in their big tournament?" Jenny asked.

"Yes, I am," he stated matter-of-factly. "In fact, I intend to take everything I can from them." He said this while looking directly into her eyes.

She gasped and looked away.

Naomi laughed out loud. "So it wasn't just about you being a good-hearted Samaritan then, huh?"

Jason remained silent.

Naomi looked at Jenny. "Should have known, sweetheart. That's just the way men are."

Elsie reached over and patted Jenny's clutched hands. "No, that's not true. There are still some good men out there and I think you got one, dearie."

WHEN THE STAGECOACH PULLED INTO TOWN, IT WAS NIGHTTIME.

Jason turned to Jenny and said, "I'm going to walk you down to the hotel and get us a room. I'll need you to stay there until I get back, okay?"

Jenny's eyes grew large. "You're just going to put me in a room and leave me there? All alone?"

"For now, yes," he said. "You just have to trust me."

Elsie looked at Jenny and said, "Once I'm sure the others are settled, I'll come and find you."

This put Jenny's mind at ease somewhat.

Just before the stage came to its destination, Jason looked at the other ladies and said, "Ladies, get ready because this town is like nothing you've ever seen before."

Before the driver could even get the horses stopped, they could hear shouts and gunshots. The door to the carriage was thrown open and someone shouted, "Are there any women onboard this thing?"

Upon seeing Jenny first, he grabbed for her and ripped the bodice of her dress. The other ladies screamed as Jason used his boot to kick the obviously drunken man away from her.

In the meantime, the other side of the coach was opened, and an old, mean-looking character stood there, looking in.

He spit a stream to the side of the carriage before he spoke.

"Last name's Darnell. I'm expectin' one, mebbe two women to arrive on this here stage tonight for my boys, Zeke and Dalton."

No one said a word, too intimidated by the old man and the army standing behind him.

"You there, old woman. You escortin' these ladies?"

"Yes, sir. I am."

"Well then, speak up before I drag everyone out of there by their hair," he threatened. "I only want what's mine."

Elsie remained quiet, but when it appeared he might actually get violent with her, Naomi spoke up.

"I'm here for Zeke. I'm Naomi," she said meekly.

"Well come on out of there, gal!" the old man yelled out. "We been waitin' on you! Zeke'll be tickled to death that you finally made it!"

Pointing at Georgia, he said, "Who are you here for?"

"Tucker Dawson," she said plainly.

Old man Darnell took off his hat and put it over his heart, and of course, everyone else did likewise. "Sorry to tell you, sugar, but Tucker went and got hisself kilt. So it looks like you are available. You'll make my Dalton a fine wife." He sniggered.

He motioned for some rough-looking characters on the other side of the characters to pull Georgia down and out from the coach.

"Who else does that leave us with in there besides the old woman, a cowboy, and a fancy dude?"

Finally speaking up for the first time, Jason said, "There is no one else inside here available to you, sir. This lady is my wife, and Miss Barnes over there has agreed to stay on with us as a housekeeper once I am established."

This speech sent the old man and all those around him into a gust of raucous laughter.

But it suddenly stopped when the old man drew his pistol and pointed it at Jason's head. "Boy, don't nobody talk to me that way! I'm king in these here parts and what I say goes! You better git that through your head right now or I'll be puttin' a bullet there and that pretty little wife of yours can also join my family."

Darnell jerked a thumb behind him. "You see this fine man here behind me? That's my boy, Runt. His real name is Russell, but we call him Runt 'cause he's so danged big, he shore wasn't the runt of the litter. Runt, say hi to the lady."

Runt leaned into the coach and smiled at Jenny. She shrank back against the seat, wishing she could just melt into it.

Jason leaned across her, trying to position himself between them, and Runt gave him a look of pure evil.

"As far as you gettin' 'established' here, there'll be none of that without my help, which you won't be gettin' unless you play nice."

"Well, Mr. Darnell, I didn't mean no disrespect to you or your family. Your reputation is known far and wide," Jason stated humbly.

"Oh really?" the old man said. "So the name Clay Darnell has been heard of outside of Dry Gulch, huh?"

"Yes, sir."

"And just who might you be, mister, that you've gotten around different circles and heard my name?"

"They mostly just call me 'Handsome.' I dabble a bit in cards and other games of chance. Mr. Jackson here travels with me from time to time just for a little fun."

"So y'all are here for the tournament?" Clay asked.

"Yes, we are. I brought my wife along for luck," Jason said as he reached over and kissed Jenny on the temple.

"Yessir, you are a lucky man at that," Clay agreed.

"Yes, and since she's expecting our first child, I'd like to get her and Miss Barnes settled before I inspect the premises. If you gentlemen don't mind letting us disembark from here now, we'd like to get over to the hotel."

As they were finally able to step out of the coach, Jenny's legs almost collapsed under her. Jason quickly swung her into his arms He hollered at Slim to collect their bags and, with Elsie right on his heels, he ushered them to a nearby hotel and requested three rooms.

He and Jenny would share an adjoining room with Elsie, or at least that's how it would appear. In reality, Jenny and Elsie would be sharing the room. Appearances were very important in this town. If anyone suspected they were not being truthful, they would kill Jason and take her, and there was no one to stop them.

Already taken with sweet, pretty Jenny, Jason had no intention of allowing that to happen.

CHAPTER 5

Jenny was so exhausted from the ordeal of the trip and the greeting at their arrival that she slept around the clock.

When she awoke, Elsie was right there by her side.

"Where are we?" she asked.

"We're at a hotel in Dry Gulch," Elsie explained patiently.

"Did you undress me?" Jenny asked shyly.

"Yes, although Jason was so worried about you, I had to force him to leave the room." She chuckled. "He was fussing over you like a husband, if I must say so myself. He was a perfect gentleman. Once he knew you were all right and comfortably settled, he left you in my charge."

"I need to use the ladies' room," Jenny mumbled.

Elsie gave her directions and when Jenny returned, Elsie noticed her concern.

"What's wrong, dearie?"

"I just had a horrible thought! I mean, I imagined it last night when we were facing those horrible men, but here in the daylight, it occurred to me again. What if Jason gets killed? What will we do?"

Elsie answered her honestly. "Well, I've been sitting here thinking and praying about that and, if that should happen, which I don't think it will, but if it does, you and I will climb back on that stage and get out of here as fast as possible!"

"Do you honestly think those men would let us go?"

"I don't know, but we'd have to try now, wouldn't we?"

"Do you have any money, Elsie? Because I don't."

"I have a little tucked away. Don't you worry!"

"Elsie, will you pray with me?"

"Of course!"

They both knelt beside the bed.

"Dear Heavenly Father, I pray that you watch over Jason and Slim as they play their games of chance, Lord. I understand these aren't in exact accordance or agreement with your tenets but, Father, they are good men with good hearts. Please take care of them. And, Lord God, please be with Elsie and the baby and me as we try to be patient to see which path you put us on next. Amen."

After a bite to eat, Jenny dozed back off.

Elsie continued to pray. If what the men had said was true, they were all going to need God's strength and guidance to get them through these next few days.

She tried to sleep but couldn't get settled. In the back of her mind, she was worried about Annie and Sarah making it back home by themselves. Elsie felt like she'd let them down; like she'd left the job undone. She prayed extra hard for the girls to be led to safe harbor.

JASON AND SLIM WERE TIRED DOWN TO THEIR BONES. YEP, BONE WEARY. BUT they couldn't let their opponents know that. They'd been up all night, gambling, and trying to stay alert to trouble.

The saloon that the Darnells had put together was actually a fairly nice setup. If Jason had been interested in owning such a place, this was exactly what he would have in mind.

There was only one main entrance and one primary exit, which he felt was critical to any saloon worth a darn. The building itself was comprised of three stories.

The main floor was for drinking, music, and dancing. There was a small stage where, occasionally, someone would entertain the masses, but it was not often as those performers who were disliked were often killed.

The second floor was for visitors to town.

The third floor was reserved for gambling. It was high-stakes only. Those wanting to play for smaller rewards or fun were warned to play on the first floor or to go to another saloon.

The place was rather unique in design in that there were separate stairs leading down from the third floor. If someone decided to be stupid enough to rob the saloon, they'd have to make it all the way back down to the first floor to escape with the money, which would be pretty hard since the place seemed locked up tight and heavily armed.

Jason and Slim both suspected that the Darnells had the place surrounded by guards at all times. Even if they couldn't always be seen, Jason could just feel their presence.

From what the gamblers could see, there were marked decks, and cheating of all kinds taking place in favor of the house—the Darnells' house, of course. Again, no one dared call them on it or they were killed and disposed of.

Anyone who was killed while in the building was dragged out back and thrown onto a heap. No one even seemed to notice they were gone.

The more Jason took careful note of his surroundings, the more he worried about this place where he'd brought Jenny. His lifestyle might not have been entirely that of a gentleman, but he remained a man of faith.

God, help me do right by that little lady, he prayed.

CHAPTER 6

JENNY HEARD SOMEONE COME INTO THE ROOM NEXT DOOR AND ASSUMED IT WAS Jason. She slipped on her robe and knocked on the door before opening it. She was surprised when she saw Naomi sitting on a chair next to the bed.

"Naomi! What are you doing here?"

"Oh, Jenny! I'm so sorry, I had nowhere else to go!" Naomi cried.

"What's wrong? What happened?"

"They scared me so much, I ran away when they fell into a drunken sleep. Please don't make me go back, please!" she begged.

"It's okay! Come in here and lie down."

Elsie woke up to the commotion and helped Jenny get Naomi into bed where the poor girl, exhausted from her ordeal, quickly fell asleep. Her face was bruised where she had been slapped repeatedly and her arms bore stark bruises. Thankfully, those were her only injuries. She'd managed to get away before far worse could occur.

"Do you think Zeke did this to her?" Jenny asked.

"I only hope she didn't actually marry him," Elsie said grimly.

Jenny did hear Jason come in then and she rushed next door.

When he heard about Naomi, he looked ill.

"Jason, what are we going to do?" Jenny pleaded.

"There's not much we can do right now," was his only answer.

"Well, I don't believe that! There has to be an official somewhere that can come here and stop this madness! I refuse to accept that this lawlessness will just be allowed to continue!"

"You're right, Jenny. It is hard to believe, but right now, we can't do anything about it."

"Jason, I'm worried about you and Slim. What if something happens to you?"

"Don't worry, honey, I've already made arrangements for you to be taken care of if something should happen to me. You and the baby." He looked at her almost tenderly.

Jenny smiled sweetly at him. "I could almost believe you care about us."

"I do care. You're my wife, and that baby is going to be my child. I've taken an oath to look after you."

Her heart melted and she looked up into his beautiful eyes.

"Jason, please let's go away from here. Let's leave tonight!" she begged.

"I can't, Jenny! I can't explain right now. You'll just have to be patient and stay in the room. I don't want you wandering around on the streets. Things are really going to get crazy once the tournament starts. Speaking of, I've got to get back."

"Jason!" she called to him as he started to leave.

He walked back to her and pulled her to him in an embrace. He pressed his lips gently to hers. He pulled back and looked into her eyes and smiled at her. Then he left.

Jenny put her hand to her mouth. She hoped he didn't get himself killed! She would like to be able to share many more kisses with him throughout the years.

CHAPTER 7

THE BIG GAMBLING EVENT IN TOWN GAVE EVERYONE A CHANCE TO SET UP A
booth along the edge of the street and sell their wares. Some were selling food;
others had made things like baskets, clothing, household items, or things farmers
might need like lumber or feed.

Elsie and Jenny could see from looking out their window that the streets were very
crowded. Even though Jason had told them to stay in the room, they figured it was
safe to go out because no one was likely to pay them much mind with all that was
going on down there.

They needed supplies to tend to Naomi's minor wounds and a few extra clothes
since she had come to them with nothing. They also needed food for several days
so, in case they got stuck in the room, they would be able to survive without
having to go out a second time.

There was a potbelly stove in their room. They had been using it sparingly to heat
water for meals and light bathing. Elsie had also managed to make some stew with
a very tasty broth.

Giving Naomi strict instructions not to open the door to anyone and not to leave
the room, the two women left through the back door of the hotel and came up the
alleyway next to the general store.

They had made a plan beforehand. Elsie was to gather what they needed while
Jenny stayed close to the front and kept her eyes on the street. She was to let Elsie
know if she saw trouble coming their way, so they would have time to escape.

Elsie was just thanking the shop owner and gathering things together when Jenny
noticed two men ride quickly into a barn adjacent to the store. She was just able to
see one of the passengers' faces and recognized Annie DeLaney.

As one of the riders jumped off and pulled the barn door closed, Jenny waved at Elsie, trying to get her to hurry.

"I'm coming, dearie! What's got you so riled up?" Elsie whispered to her.

"Annie and Sarah! They were kidnapped! They're in the barn!" Jenny whispered back.

"Oh no!" Elsie's eyes went wide. "What are we going to do?"

"We're going to go get them!" Jenny stated.

"Jenny, no. We can't! Jason will kill me if I let anything happen to you!"

"Right now, I can't be worried about what Jason thinks, Elsie! We're got to help them and be quick about it."

"All right," Elsie agreed reluctantly. "But let me just check on Naomi quickly, first."

"Oh all right! But please hurry, Elsie! Annie and Sarah need us. Now!"

"Aren't you coming?"

"No, I'm going to stay here and make sure they don't leave with them, so please hurry back!"

Thankfully, Elsie wasn't gone long.

"I'm so glad you're back," Jenny whispered. "Are you all right?"

"I'm just fine, dearie. A little out of breath from hurrying, but I was afraid for you and the baby."

"God bless you, Elsie! You are a saint for watching out for us!"

"How was Naomi?"

"Poor child was still asleep," Elsie sniffled. "I didn't do too good a job looking out for her, but maybe I can help Annie and Sarah. Let's go get them!"

They both tried not to run as they crossed the street. When they reached the barn door, Elsie tugged as hard as she could and was unable to open it. They both pulled and moved it just enough for Jenny to slip through.

God, help me help them!

She found the girls lying in a horse stall, tied up tight. They were bound and gagged. Jenny worked as quickly as she could on the ropes and was finally able to get Sarah loose. Together they were able to free Annie and then ran for the door, where Elsie waited.

As the four women moved cautiously back to the hotel, Jenny knew not to feel safe yet. A town like this one, where women were so scarce, would surely notice four women walking around the streets. Word of this would get back to the Darnells, who would make it their business to know who the four women were.

By God's grace, they made it back to the room without anyone seeming to look their way.

Once Elsie had tended to Annie and Sarah and made sure they were all right, they got bathed and changed into clean clothes. The girls declared that the stagecoach driver must have sold them out because the two men that came for them had known their names and that they were to be mail order brides.

"Are you saying that those two men were to be your husbands? They were the ones you were supposed to meet up with here?" Elsie asked.

"That's what they said," Annie answered. "But neither Sarah nor I believed them because they didn't really look like the pictures we were sent."

"Well, you ladies were right to be suspicious 'cause this country is full of liars and thieves. That's all I can say about it!" This was from Naomi, who was sitting groggily up in bed, rubbing her bruised arms.

"There, there now. It'll be okay," Elsie said. "Why don't y'all pile up there in the bed and rest while Jenny and go in the next room and have a talk?"

WHEN THE DOOR CLOSED BEHIND THEM, ELSIE LOOKED AT JENNY WITH concern. "I think they are going to be looking for these girls pretty soon and then we're going to be in trouble."

"I know, Elsie, but what can we do? We can't turn them out into the street! We've got to hide them and give them protection as long as we can."

"You're right. I know you're right. I just wish there was another way."

"God will take care of us. I just know it. He always has, and He always will!"

"Yes, child! You are so right. *Yea, thou I walk through the valley of the shadow of death, I will fear no evil; for thou art with me; Thy rod and thy staff, they comfort me. Psalm 23:4,*" Elsie quoted.

"*God is our refuge and strength, an ever-present help in trouble. Psalm 46:1,*" Jenny quoted back.

"Oh, that's right! Your daddy was a preacher. I wouldn't want to get into a Bible verse swapping contest with you! I bet you cut your teeth on the Good Book," Elsie said.

"Yes, ma'am. He preached it and taught it every single day I can remember. I used to think he hung the moon! Until I fell from his grace." She sniffled.

"Now, now. Don't start up. You just remember this: you might have fallen from your earthly father's graces, but not your heavenly father's."

They heard a key in the door and froze. Jenny was thrilled when Jason walked through the door, followed by Slim.

CHAPTER 8

"Jason, you're okay!" Jenny cried, relieved to see him in one piece.

"Of course I am! I told you not to worry. I've got Slim watching my back."

"I know, but it's hard not to," Jenny said as she smiled at him, thinking back to his earlier, gentle kiss.

Elsie piped up. "Especially when we can hear all the guns being fired around every few minutes. It's like the fourth of July. People celebrating and such."

"It's wild out there, all right," Slim agreed.

"Honey, Slim and I need to talk in private if you and Elsie can give us a few minutes, please?"

"Of course. But then we need to talk. There's been ... uh, a new development that I need to tell you about."

Jenny and Elsie waited in the other room while the men talked. They could hear the rumble of their deep voices but could not distinguish their words. Since the three weary girls were tucked up in bed, Elsie insisted Jenny sit in the room's lone chair while she herself sat on top of a trunk. Elsie heated some water for tea, but nobody was interested in having any.

When Jason tapped on the door and stuck his head in, he caught sight of the crowded bed. "What in the world?" he asked.

"That's what I wanted to tell you. We have some new arrivals."

Jenny and Elsie went on to tell them how the ladies had come to be in their hotel room.

Jason was not happy at all. "Elsie, how could you let her go like that? She could have been taken, or worse, killed!"

Elsie smiled at him. "All I can tell you, sir, is you got yourself a strong-minded woman here. Once she makes up her mind about something, it's very difficult to change it."

Jason looked at her and shook his head. "Is that the way it's going to be the whole time we're married? You not doing what I say?"

Jenny smiled. "Well, it just depends on whether or not it agrees with what I want to do."

They all laughed at her joke, but then the two men grew very serious.

"Slim, I think it's time we told them the truth," Jason said.

Jenny frowned. "The truth? What does that mean? Jason ... have you lied to me about something?" The thought didn't sit easy with her at all. Her first husband had been a liar, through and through, and she'd made the mistake of thinking she could curb that terrible habit.

"I had a good reason," Jason told her, looking contrite, and Jenny's hopes for a future with this kind man crumbled.

"Sweetheart, don't look like that. It's not what you think. Elsie, close that door behind you," Jason instructed. "What I'm about to tell you is for your ears only."

Both ladies nodded, and Elsie moved to do as she was told.

"My real name is Jonas, not Jason. Sorry, Jenny," Jonas said sincerely. "I didn't mean to trick you. Everything happened so suddenly ... I honestly never expected to meet a beautiful woman and suddenly get married. I'm Jonas Hanstrom, and I'm a U.S. Marshal."

Both ladies gasped at this news. The twisted feeling in Jenny's stomach eased up some. It was still a lie, but at least this one had a good reason.

"So we're not really married?" Jenny asked, suddenly sad even though she'd barely started to get to know her new "husband."

"Yes, we are," Jonas said hastily. "I signed my real name on that marriage certificate. It was Jonas who married you, not Jason."

Jenny breathed a quiet sigh of relief.

"What about you, Slim?" Elsie asked.

"I'm a U.S. Marshal in training," he explained. "I go where Jonas goes until my training is completed."

"So what does this mean, Jas—er, Jonas? Why are you here in disguise, playing in this tournament?" Jenny asked.

"Because in several hours, when the tournament is almost over, this town is going to be overrun with lawmen and I don't want any of you caught in the crossfire.

While Slim and I are doing our jobs, I want to know that you are safely tucked away."

"So, I have to just stay here locked away in this room, not knowing if you're alive or dead, until you or someone else comes to tell me?"

"Yes, Jenny. Please do this for us! For the future of our family!"

He looked at her so desperately that her heart melted even further. "All right, Jonas. I'll do what you're asking. But you have to be careful. Promise me."

Leaning in, Jonas gave Jenny another kiss which made her blush to her very toes. "I promise I'll stay safe," he whispered in her ear. "And I'll come back home to you and our baby."

Whatever reservations Jenny had left evaporated at his tender words.

⚅⚄

THEY LET NAOMI, ANNIE, AND SARAH SLEEP AS LONG AS THEY DARED, THEN woke them up and instructed them to get dressed.

"What's wrong?" they all wanted to know. "Why are we getting our clothes on in the middle of the night?"

Not taking the time for a full explanation, Elsie told them to be quiet and just be ready to run if they were told to. At this point, the girls obeyed her without question.

Several hours later, they heard a commotion outside in the street. Naomi rushed to the window and looked out before anyone could stop her.

"Naomi, get away from the window!" Suddenly the window exploded as a bullet came flying through.

The other ladies screamed.

"Get down on the floor," Elsie shouted to them.

She threw blankets over them as glass kept flying. Jenny helped her, not even realizing she'd been cut on the forehead and was bleeding.

After a while, things seemed to quiet down outside. Elsie still had the other three ladies on the floor, under blankets.

They heard heavy footsteps in the hallway and quivered with fear when they recognized Clay Darnell's voice.

"I know they are here somewhere. Search every room if you have to! I want Hansom's wife!" he ordered.

Dear God, if I don't give myself up, they'll hurt us all, Jenny realized. Setting her jaw, she ignored the whispered protests of the others and got to her feet. She was starting toward the door, praying all the way, when suddenly the door burst open and there stood Dalton Darnell. Her original intended. After seeing Naomi's bruised and battered body, Jenny was terrified!

Elsie tried to get in front of her, but he pushed her out of his way to get to Jenny. "Are you Hansom's woman?"

Jenny stood tall, all five foot, four inches of her. "Yes, I am!" she said proudly, knowing she was probably sealing her death warrant. But in that moment she knew she truly was Jonas' wife. Somehow, God had seen fit to put them together in the strangest of circumstances, but Jenny knew she'd found a man she could grow to love for a lifetime. A man who would marry a woman who was pregnant with another man's child, for her safety, without thinking twice ... a U.S. Marshal who risked his life for truth and justice. Yes. That was her man. And she was his wife.

"I am his woman," she repeated boldly.

Dalton's next words shocked them both. "We've got to get you ladies out of here! You're not safe! Please come with me!"

Jenny looked at Elsie, who just stared back at her.

"I'm sorry, but I can't leave this room," Jenny said flatly, not trusting this oaf as far as she could throw him, which wasn't even a quarter of an inch, if that.

His face turned ugly, confirming her suspicions.

Clay Darnell's voice spoke up from the door. "Well you're just goin' to hafta, little lady, because if you don't come willingly, I'll drag you out there, screamin' and kickin'."

"See?" Dalton sneered. "I told you it wouldn't work. Now we do it my way."

"What about Naomi? I know she's here, too."

"You can get her later. She ain't goin' nowhere," Clay laughed. "Not with the beatin' I give her. She's likely goin' be bruised up and sore for a long time."

"That's the way you let your father treat your brother's wife?" Jenny asked Dalton. "I'm glad I chose the man I did before you and I ever met!"

"What did you just say?" Dalton demanded.

"I was supposed to be your bride but married someone else along the way." Jenny laughed, feeling somehow free in spite of the terror filling her chest.

"Why, you two-timing ..." Dalton made a move toward her, but the old man stopped him.

"Later, boy, later. Right now, we got to try to git out of town. Grab her and let's ride."

Again, Elsie tried to get between them and Dalton slapped her, hard. "Stay back, old woman. I got no problem with you unless you make a problem."

He picked Jenny up and put her over his shoulder. Elsie sat down, crying. And that's how Jonas found her.

CHAPTER 9

Jonas Hanstrom wasn't a man to be trifled with. He wasn't a big man, in terms of stature, but those who knew him, knew him to be a man of honor, and a valued friend.

After the fighting began, Jonas was in his element. He and Slim had done similar things many times. They'd ridden into some of the worst places and helped bring justice for the good people there. It was always the good people who sent for them, begging for their help.

By the time, Jonas and Slim went in, the plan was already in motion for the law brigade to ride in and reestablish law and order.

Of course, after they rode out, it was up to the townsfolk to maintain that law. Living in the West was hard, and people had to become harder and grow thicker skins to be able to adapt, or they just didn't make it.

The thought of Jenny ever growing a thick skin made Jonas slightly sick. He realized that he was already falling in love with her exactly as she was—strong, brave, but also soft and sweet.

Once the worst of the fighting was over, Jonas found Slim and assured himself his partner was okay. They then started at the top of the saloon and worked their way down, looking for the Darnells. When the search came up empty, Jonas suddenly had a very bad feeling in his gut.

He and Slim raced over to the hotel and found out his worst nightmare had come true; his wife and child had been taken by the Darnells. He almost lost his head at the thought of her in their hands; at their mercy.

God, no! Help me save the woman I'm falling in love with!

Grim-faced, he left Elsie and the other ladies with the Texas Rangers and other lawmen who had joined the brigade. By the time he rounded up a posse, Jenny had been gone at least six hours.

After interrogating some of the Darnell men and questioning the townsfolk, they had a pretty good idea where the outlaws would be holed up. It wasn't going to be easy getting in there, but Jonas was used to things not being easy.

When they got close to the hideout, they dismounted and crawled on their bellies. It was rough, going over rocks and through briars, but Jonas would have gone through worse to get Jenny back.

Sure enough, when they got to the edge of a cliff, there was a passageway heading down into the canyon. Just as they'd been told. They'd also been warned not to try and go down that way but to use another secret path, so the Darnells wouldn't suspect anything.

As the men gathered near the bottom of the rocks, Jonas gestured for them to spread out.

It would be daylight soon and he felt sure they were catching the Darnells unaware of their approach.

When Jonas got closer to the shack, the only building standing, he could hear Clay yelling.

"... never shoulda happened. Iffen you'd done what I told you to do ..." It sounded like he was hitting someone with a strap.

Jonas went absolutely white, but then he realized the female voice begging Clay to stop wasn't Jenny. His stomach unclenched slightly, even though he still felt terrible pity for whoever was on the receiving end of those blows. But had it been Jenny ...

"... and you, you just shut up," Clay ranted. "I'll get to you in a minute, when I'm done with your good for nuthin' husband." The sound of the lash struck again.

"Daddy, you can hit me all day long, but you ain't hittin' no more women. You hear?"

"Why, you snivelin', weak ..."

"He's right, Daddy. We're all agreed, even Runt. No more hittin' the women."

Jonas had heard all he could stand. Maybe some of the Darnells had had changes of heart. It made no difference to him. They'd still committed countless terrible crimes, not the least of which was kidnapping his Jenny. And she was his, by God. His by the law. His in the sight of God. And his by love, even though they'd barely met.

He motioned his men forward. He didn't see any guards, so he could only guess whoever was with Clay was inside. He had already cautioned everyone to be careful not to hit the women.

He hollered out, "Clay Darnell, come out with your hands up! U.S. Marshals and Texas Rangers are here to take you in. You, your sons, and anybody else in there with you."

Clay laughed. "Does that include your lovely bride, Mr. Marshal? We've got her in here, too. You start shootin' up the place and she just might get hit."

"It's in your best interest to see that she makes it out of there alive, Darnell," Jonas said heatedly. "Now put down your weapons and surrender."

The bullets began to fly as the people inside the cabin began to fire upon the lawmen.

It continued for about ten minutes and, as men from each side were hit, the shooting almost stopped.

Jonas hollered again. "Surrender your weapons and come out with your hands held high."

The door opened, and Zeke burst out, shooting. He was gunned down almost immediately.

"I'm gonna kill you for that!" the old man yelled out. "Only I ain't gotta kill you, exactly. It'll hurt a lot more if you're like the living dead, after I kill what you love!"

In a split second, Jonas knew what he had to do. He yelled out, "Cover me!" and charged toward the door. He knew Clay was about to kill Jenny.

When he ran inside, he saw Clay advancing on Dalton, who appeared to be protecting Jenny and Georgia. Dalton had his back turned to his father and was using his body to shield the two women. His back was cut open and bloody from taking the lashes his father had so cruelly dealt out.

Clay fired at Dalton just as Jonas yelled out. When Clay whirled toward him, Jonas shot him twice. He was dead before he hit the floor.

Jenny rushed into Jonas' arms and he held her tightly, reassuring himself that she was indeed okay.

"I was so worried when I came back and found you'd been taken, Jenny! I nearly lost my mind!" Jonas said as he held her to him and rocked her. "Please don't ever scare me like that again. I don't think my heart could take it!" he said as he kissed her hair. It was then that he noticed the cut on her face. His blood turned to furious ice. "Did they do this to you? Which one? If he isn't dead already—"

"No, no," Jenny interrupted, miraculously looking none the worse for wear. "It happened back at the hotel. A piece of glass from the hotel window cut me when it shattered."

She drew back and looked at him. "You thought you were worried! All I could hear were gunshots and shouting and screams I didn't know if you were dead or alive!"

Jonas smiled at her. "Well, that's the life of a lawman. I guess you'll have to get used to it."

Jenny looked doubtful. "I don't think I'll ever get used to that. But if it means a life by your side, I'll learn. Somehow."

Jonas cupped her cheek and kissed her tenderly. "Oh, Jenny. I do love you, beautiful girl. Already, I really do."

CHAPTER 10

After it was all over, it took a good while for order to be fully restored to the town.

With Jonas as acting sheriff/marshal and Slim as his deputy, they managed to help the town elect a mayor and city council that the few law-abiding people felt comfortable having in charge.

The first thing they did was request Jonas and Slim stay on permanently as their lawmen and make Dry Gulch their home, which the two men agreed to do. Slim had his eye on a pretty girl in town, and Jonas had quickly come to the conclusion that a more settled life could actually be appealing, so long as Jenny was in it.

It was amazing how fast time flew. Suddenly, it was six months later. Six months of happily married life, the likes of which Jonas had never dreamed possible. Every day, he fell more in love with his beautiful wife. He whistled as he worked today, even though paperwork was utter drudgery.

"Jonas!"

He leaped up in surprise as Slim slammed through the door, ashen. "Elsie says it's time. You better git!"

Going white himself, Jonas ran all the way home to the door, where Elsie stopped him. "She's doing fine. The baby is almost here."

Right about then, they heard Jenny give a loud cry and Jonas' heart almost stopped. Then a baby began to whimper and cry.

His knees turned to sheer water and he sagged against the door jamb.

Elsie patted his arm reassuringly. "Big tough lawmen just don't know what to do when they're near a birthing bed. Give us just a minute and then we'll introduce you."

Jonas waited outside, pacing as patiently as possible, until, at last, the bedroom door opened and he was ushered in.

"Come and meet your son, Jonas," Jenny said wearily from the bed, a soft smile on her lovely face.

I have a son!

As Jonas approached the bed, he thought he'd never seen anything lovelier than his wife holding the tiny newborn. His son. *Their* son. Unable to form coherent words, Jonas stopped beside Jenny, kissed her adoringly, and then hesitatingly, with his wife's guidance, stroked his little boy's downy head, full of black curls.

From the door, Slim inquire, "Whatcha goin' to name him, Jonas?"

Looking at Jenny, he smiled. "I don't know. What do you want to call him, Mama?"

"I'm thinking we'll call him Jason." She looked up at him with a beautiful grin. "After all, that's who you were when I first met you."

"Hmm. Jason. I like it." He leaned down and gathered his family into his arms, whispering prayers of gratitude.

Out of the dust of Dry Gulch, new life had sprung.

Thank you, God.

⚜

Thank you so much for reading my book. I sincerely hope you enjoyed every bit reading it. I had fun creating it and will surely create more.

Your positive reviews are very helpful to other reader, it only takes a few moments. They can be left at Amazon.

www.amazon.com/Katie-Wyatt/e/B011IN7AF0

⚜

Want free books every week? Who doesn't!

Become a preferred reader and we'll not only send you free reads, but you'll also receive updates about new releases.

So you'll be among the first to dive into our latest new books, full of adventure, heartwarming romances, and characters so real they jump off the page.

It's absolutely free and you don't need to do anything at all to qualify except go to.

PREFERRED READ FREE READS

http:/katieWyattBooks.com/readersgroup

ABOUT THE AUTHOR

KATIE WYATT IS 25% AMERICAN SIOUX INDIAN. BORN AND RAISED IN Arizona, she has traveled and camped extensively through California, Arizona, Nevada, Mexico, and New Mexico. Looking at the incredible night sky and the giant Saguaro cacti, she has dreamed of what it would be like to live in the early pioneer times.

Spending time with a relative of the great Wyatt Earp, also named Wyatt Earp, Katie was mesmerized and inspired by the stories he told of bygone times. This historical interest in the old West became the inspiration for her Western romance novels.

Her books are a mixture of actual historical facts and events mixed with action and humor, challenges and adventures. The characters in Katie's clean romance novels draw from her own experiences and are so real that they almost jump off the pages. You feel like you're walking beside them through all the ups and downs of their lives. As the stories unfold, you'll find yourself both laughing and crying. The endings will never fail to leave you feeling warm inside.

RAYNE'S MEADOW

Mail Order Bride Western Romance

RoyceCardiff
Publishing House
WHOLESOME INSPIRATIONAL ROMANCE

Dear Reader,

It is our utmost pleasure and privilege to bring these wonderful stories to you. I am so very proud of our amazing team of writers and the delight they continually bring us all with their beautiful clean and wholesome tales of faith, courage, and love.

What is a book's lone purpose if not to be read and enjoyed? Therefore, you, dear reader, are the key to fulfilling that purpose and unlocking the treasures that lie within the pages of this book.

A PERSONAL WORD FROM KATIE

I LOVE WRITING ABOUT THE OLD WEST AND THE TRIALS, TRIBULATIONS, AND triumphs of the early pioneer women.

With strong fortitude and willpower, they took a big leap of faith believing in the promised land of the West. It was always not a bed of roses, however many found true love.

Most of the stories are based on some historical fact or personal conversations I've had with folks who knew something of that time. For example a relative of the Wyatt Earp's. I have spent much time out in the West camping hiking and carousing. I have spent countless hours gazing up at night thinking of how it must been back then.

Thank you for being a loyal reader.

Katie

CHAPTER 1

RAYNE STEVENS HAD NEVER HAD HER BONES RATTLED AS COMPLETELY AS SHE had over the past few days, traveling by stagecoach from Miles City to Bozeman, Montana. Of course, before the stagecoach ride she had endured over two weeks of sporadic travel by train from her hometown of Milwaukee, Wisconsin. For at least the hundredth time in the past couple of days, she asked herself why in heaven's name she had accepted a marriage proposal from a man she'd never met.

Deep inside, she knew though. The men in Taylor's Falls didn't want her. She was too eccentric for them, or so said her Aunt Beth. Rayne certainly didn't think she was eccentric, but if that's what you wanted to call someone who spoke her mind, talked politics, and encouraged equal rights for women, so be it.

Indeed, why had she even read the Matrimonial News, designed for mail order brides, that her elderly aunt had shoved under her nose? Why was her aunt even reading such a publication? She claimed she had gotten it from a widowed friend, but Rayne didn't believe it for a moment. Her aunt wanted to see her married off before she died, which she had reiterated at least every month for the past year.

So, Rayne had taken the publication and browsed through some of the ads, lifting an eyebrow when her aunt had pointed to the first of several of the rather short requests for marriage. The ads were brief and to the point.

"Veterinarian seeking wife.
Must be young, healthy, and strong.
Respond to General delivery, Joseph Hunter, Bozeman, Montana."

The others she had read weren't much better.

"A lively widower of 40, looking much younger,

5'7" high, weighing 145 pounds would like to correspond
with some maiden or widowed lady of honor
who would like a good home, kind husband, and plenty."

And another.

"Lonesome miner wants a wife
to share stake in prospects. Please respond to..."

Despite Rayne's doubt that such proposals could be considered proper, she had to admit that her sense of adventure had kicked in, of which, there was not much in Taylor's Falls. Actually, the choices for a suitable husband in Taylor's Falls were slim pickings, and she was being generous at that.

So, to please her aunt, Rayne had penned a short letter to Mister Hunter of Bozeman, Montana, describing herself as rather petite, blond haired, blue-eyed, as well as the fact that she met his requirements that she be young, healthy, and strong. She hadn't expected a reply.

To her surprise, over the past year, at least half a dozen letters had passed back and forth between them. With their third letter to each other, they had exchanged daguerreotypes. Mister Joseph Hunter appeared thin, and his black hair was a little longer than fashionable here in Wisconsin, but she supposed that out west, such fashion was nonexistent. He had deep set eyes, a strong jaw, and a well-proportioned mouth in size with his nose. He wasn't smiling, but then, she had not been in her image either. It just couldn't be done.

Over the months, she had learned that Mister Joseph Hunter was a veterinarian who was dedicated to his profession, but had desired companionship; a helpmate. She sensed, reading between the lines, that he was in search of someone to cook, clean, and keep house for him. She had stared at this daguerreotype numerous times since it had arrived, and despite her reticence, had felt a strange and compelling attraction to the tall, lanky gentleman with the sad eyes that stared back at her.

At any rate, Rayne had decided to accept his proposal, much to Aunt Beth's delight. After all, she had nothing holding her back in Wisconsin; no family, no beaus, no prospects, and as her aunt said, what did she have to lose? What indeed.

So, after packing two trunks, she had boarded the train west, bid a farewell to her aging aunt, who escorted her to the train station, and left her with just a few words of wisdom.

"Watch your temper, Rayne, and follow your heart. Give your heart a chance. Don't just make up your mind in the first couple of days. Give it time. I'm sure Mister Hunter will make you a fine husband and provide well for you, if you just give him a chance."

Give him a chance. She nodded to herself, promising that she would do just that. Just then, the stagecoach hit a large rut in the trail and jostled her so hard she flew up off the seat and banged the side of her head against the window frame beside her with a solid *thunk*. She scowled, rubbed the side of her head, and muttered under her breath, "Tarnation!"

She clamped her lips together before her fellow passengers heard her. She would have to work on that, she thought. She'd always been one to speak her mind, and didn't typically make any bones about what she said, or who heard her. Still, this *was* the West. She wasn't sure what was acceptable out here, and what wasn't.

"Are you all right, Miss?"

The man who addressed her appeared to be in his late twenties. He sat across from her and watched her with narrow, assessing eyes, his smile hidden beneath his large, drooping mustache.

She glanced at him with a smile. "Yes, thank you...?"

"Name's Morgan Earp," he replied as he nodded, offering his hand for a gentle handshake.

"Thank you for asking Mister Earp." She lifted her gloved hands and straightened her bonnet. "It's just a little bumpy along through here, isn't it?"

He nodded. "I'm afraid to warn you that it gets a little bit worse before we get into Bozeman. I've bounced along this route many a time. I live in Butte with my wife, but often travel due to my work."

Rayne lifted her eyebrow in curiosity, prompting him to continue.

"I've been a lawman in Butte for a bit, but a few years back I joined my brother Wyatt taking jobs as security or shotgun messengers for Wells Fargo stagecoach lines."

"Sounds exciting... and dangerous," Rayne commented. He shrugged.

"Are you stopping in Bozeman, or continuing on to Butte, or perhaps even Missoula?" he asked.

Rayne nodded. "Actually, I'm going to Bozeman to meet my fiancé." There was no need for him to know that she was a prospective mail order bride. She had taken a leap of faith that everything would turn out all right. He was supposed to meet her when she arrived in Bozeman, where they would go directly to the justice of the peace to be married.

"Congratulations. Do I know the lucky groom? I often have business that takes me to Bozeman."

"His name is Joseph Hunter," she said. "He's the town's veterinarian—"

"Of course, Joe Hunter," the old man nodded. "Actually, I believe he used to be the town's doctor."

Rayne bit her lip and stifled the surprise she felt at this announcement, acting as if she already knew this. She couldn't help but wonder why Joseph had failed to mention that, but didn't want to open a can of worms by asking Mister Earp. By asking, she would imply to Mister Earp that she didn't know her fiancé very well at all. That just wouldn't do. She supposed that there was just as much of a need for veterinarians out west as there were for doctors, but couldn't he do both?

Rayne listened politely while Mister Earp became more talkative, describing interesting points in and around Bozeman. He was a nice man, and she enjoyed listening to his stories of the history of Bozeman. While he would be traveling on, she hoped that she could make friends in her new home. It had never been especially easy for Rayne to make friends, because again, to be quite honest with herself, she was pretty much a loner. She would much rather be outside enjoying nature than be cooped up in stuffy sitting rooms and engaging in idle gossip with air-headed ladies who thought only of the latest fashions, as most of her peers seemed to want to do.

The stagecoach driver let out a yell, and moments later the stagecoach came to a rather abrupt stop, causing Rayne to press herself tightly against the window frame while a cloud of dust settled over everything and made its way inside the coach. She coughed lightly.

"Bozeman!" the driver shouted.

Rayne sat frozen in the seat for several moments. This was the point of no return. She would step off his coach and come face to face with her fiancé. Was she ready? She lifted her chin and straightened her back. She'd better be!

CHAPTER 2

RAYNE WAITED NERVOUSLY AS THE DRIVER CLIMBED DOWN FROM THE STAGE, then made his way around to the door. He opened the door, then reached under the coach for a small bench. He placed it underneath the opening, and then, with a bored expression, lifted a hand to help her out of the coach.

Rayne's thoughts were still swirling with the fact that her fiancé, and soon-to-be husband, was actually a doctor. Why wasn't he practicing medicine on humans anymore? Why hadn't he told her about it? She didn't like that at all. She didn't like secrets.

One of the reasons she had avoided relationships was for that very fact. The previous, and relatively serious relationship that she had had with a young man a few years ago, had turned out rather badly. He too had kept secrets, and she was fortunate that she had found them out in time. Then again, maybe she was just overthinking it. Maybe Joseph Hunter just preferred working with animals. She wouldn't blame him a bit. She preferred animals over most humans as well.

"I'll get your trunks down in just a minute, ma'am," the stagecoach driver said as she placed her feet on the dusty main street. He gestured. "If you just wait over there on the boardwalk, it will just be a few minutes."

Rayne nodded and offered a polite smile to the stagecoach driver, brushed down her skirt, then glanced toward the boardwalk where the driver had pointed. The boardwalk fronted a corner hotel with an overhang between the first and second floors, offering shade. Several people waited there, watching passengers disembark from the coach. An elderly couple off to the left, a middle-aged woman with an expectant smile on her face, two young men talking quietly among themselves, and then, further off to the right, she saw him.

She did a double take, knowing that that tall, somber looking man standing near the hitching post was her fiancé, Joseph Hunter. For a moment, he stared back at her. He finally stepped forward, removing his beat-up cowboy hat as he did so.

"Miss Rayne Stevens?"

Rayne had to tilt her head back to look up into Joseph's face. He was well over six feet tall, and her diminutive five-foot frame made him appear a giant. "Yes, and you must be Mister Joseph Hunter."

He nodded, and after a moment of hesitation, reached for her elbow. He guided her up beneath the shade of the veranda hanging over the boardwalk. Her heart thudded in sudden panic. She thought he looked more like an undertaker than a veterinarian or a doctor. His lips curved downward in a slight frown, and while he offered her a polite nod, she didn't exactly get a sense of excitement from him. She allowed him to guide her to a wooden bench on the boardwalk while they waited for the stagecoach driver to unload the baggage. He stood next to her at the edge of the bench, watching the driver.

"Quite a lovely town you have here," she said, mainly to break the stilted silence and not because she'd had a very good view of the town from her position. There were men on horseback, wagons, and buggies appearing from here or there and then disappearing around corners, some stopping in front of the local mercantile, a couple of horses tied to hitching posts in front of the town saloon, and of course, here at the hotel. He said nothing and she glanced up, disconcerted to find him staring down at her. She lifted an eyebrow.

"Yes," he said finally, gesturing again. "As soon as your trunk is unloaded, we'll head over to the justice of the peace. Then we can head out to my property."

She shook her head. She was having none of this. They were going to be married in a matter of minutes, for Pete's sake! She quickly stood, his startled response obvious by his widened eyes. Without hesitation, she clutched at his forearm and tugged him toward the corner of the hotel building where no one stood. He could only follow, dumbfounded.

"Okay, Joseph, here it is. I'm going to be your wife in a matter of minutes, and you're going to be my husband. We'll have none of this awkwardness between us." She offered him a smile, her sense of excitement and enthusiasm burgeoning upward. "This is going to be a grand adventure, and it starts right now. If you need to change your mind, or want to, you better speak up or forever hold your peace."

She had said the words in a teasing manner, but she had meant what she said. If he was going to change his mind, he better do it quick.

"What's on your mind, Joseph?" She watched for several moments while he stared at her, as if he was considering her words.

He offered a short nod. "An adventure, you say?"

She nodded, her smile broadening. She glanced quickly right and left to make sure no one could hear. "Don't you think placing an ad for mail order bride is rather adventurous?"

He appeared to think about it before nodding once again.

"So, Joseph, let's just take this one step at a time. We'll get married and take our time to get to know each other." She thought for a moment and concluded her impromptu speech. "I'm a stickler for honesty, Joseph, so if you've changed your mind you better tell me now. I won't hold it against you."

She could tell she had taken him by surprise. From his expression, his demeanor, and his obvious hesitance to speak, she gathered that he didn't talk much. That was fine, because she did. She hoped he was a good listener. Despite her interest in his past, she figured that they could do some talking as they headed toward his property after they were married. After all, a marriage required honesty. No secrets. Ready or not, they were getting married, and she had high expectations.

"No," he said, shaking his head.

He stared down at her as if he was examining a strange bug.

"No what Joseph?" she asked, one eyebrow lifted.

"No... I'm not going to change my mind. You just... I just wasn't expecting... I'm not used to—"

"You're not used to talking much, are you?"

He said nothing, and she couldn't help but laugh.

Boy was he in for a surprise!

CHAPTER 3

Rayne sat on her side of the seat of the buggy, amazed at how hot it felt. Then again, maybe the heat was caused by the fact that she had just been married, less than a half hour ago, to a total stranger. Still, she had imagined that Montana would be a bit cooler. She knew some geography, and had done a little bit of research on the country around Bozeman. It was nearly five thousand feet in elevation, so it should have been a lot cooler, shouldn't it?

She glanced up at Mister— at *Joseph*, fanning her face with her hand. "Is it always so hot here?" she asked, surprised when he glanced down at her with a disapproving frown.

"Hot?"

"Yes, hot," she reiterated, suddenly wishing she had a fan.

"It's summertime," he said.

That was true. Heading into mid-July, she supposed it was hot everywhere, but still, he didn't have to be so grumpy about it, did he? Since they had left town less than an hour ago, they had followed the narrow dirt track northwest out of the city. She could count on one hand the number of times he had spoken to her. He *was* rather gruff, she thought, and she had yet to see him offer a genuine smile. He sat rigid on the seat next to her, his gaze straight ahead, his eyes rarely roaming from the wagon tracks they followed.

While she understood that they needed time to get to know each other, his attitude so far was aggravating. The longer the silence between them continued, the more frustrated she grew. They were newlyweds! Shouldn't they be getting to know one another?

This was not at all what she had expected. While she hadn't expected to fall in love with him at first sight, she had a least expected some indication that he was pleased by her presence. She felt her temper rising, a common fault of hers. After several more minutes of his gruff silence, she suddenly slapped both of her hands down on her knees and turned to look up at him.

"Joseph Hunter!"

He gazed down at her in surprise— again. "What?" he asked, glancing quickly around as if looking for something that had startled her.

"Don't tell me you're having second thoughts already," she said, shaking her head. "I came an awful long way to marry you. You're the one that put the ad in the paper, aren't you?"

He nodded.

"I understand that we need to get to know each other a little, and forgive me for saying so, but you act like you've just made the biggest mistake of your life!"

He stared down at her with a look of bemusement. "Are you always so outspoken?"

She stared back at him. "Is there any other way to be?" She glanced at the terrain surrounding them, admiring its beauty. "So let's talk. Let's get to know each other a little. What do you say about that?"

He made a face. "I'd say you're awfully forward," he commented. "Don't get me wrong, Miss... Rayne, I admire blunt talk. I guess I'm just not used to it coming from..."

"A woman?" she asked. She shook her head. "I have no patience for such old-fashioned ideas. A woman has a mind, doesn't she?" She didn't give them a chance to reply. "I have a brain, a rather active and intelligent one I might add, and I like to use it. I would assume that the reason you placed an order for mail order bride was for companionship, am I wrong?"

He shook his head.

"What?" She asked, prodding him with a finger to his upper arm. Her teasing smile froze when he sent her a disapproving look. "Oh pish-posh!" she exclaimed. "Why are you so grumpy?"

To her surprise he began to cough, and then she realized that he was laughing. He gazed down at her and shook his head. "I have a feeling you're going to be quite a handful, aren't you?"

She made another face. "I don't know about that, Joseph, but I can tell you one thing. We're in this together. You wanted a wife, and now you got one. You can't replace me with another one. You're just going to have to get used to me, because whether you like it or not, I'm here to stay!"

"Okay, Rayne," he finally said, then sighed. "It's summertime in Montana, meaning that it's going to be hot. Yes, we have occasional thundershowers and rainstorms, but so far this summer it's been hot and dry, and we haven't had a drop of rain since the middle of May. You do the math."

"You don't have any crops do you?"

"I have a small field of corn and a garden," he replied defensively. "As you know from my letters, I make my living as a vet. Sometimes I travel quite a bit throughout the area to take care of horses, cattle, farm animals, and even house pets."

"You only take on four-legged critters?" she asked, hoping that he would give her some indication on his own about his background. To her surprise, he turned from her, his brief and relatively pleasant mood obviously taking a turn for the worse if his scowl was any indication.

"What do you mean?"

"Never mind," she said, disappointed. Now it was her turn to gaze off into the distance. Had her stagecoach companion been wrong about her new husband? Had he mistaken him for someone else? If Joseph had been a doctor before, why would he not mention it?

"There's my property," Joseph said abruptly, pointing ahead toward a small valley that dipped down in front of them toward the northeast.

Rayne turned her head to follow the line of his finger. Her frustration was forgotten as she admired the beautiful, small valley of knee-high rolling grasses. The sky was so blue it almost hurt her eyes to look at it. The gently rolling hills bordered a large meadow, the hills capped with huge stands of pine. In the not so far distance, she saw the log cabin, sheltered on one side by a stand of aspen trees, probably serving as a wind block. To the rear of the cabin she saw a turned plot of land, probably the garden he had spoken of, beyond which was a small, stunted cornfield.

Her new home.

CHAPTER 4

THE CLOSER THE BUGGY GOT TO JOSEPH'S HOME, THE MORE NERVOUS RAYNE felt. The front door of his cabin stood wide open. To her amazement, a goat came waltzing out, apparently in response to the sound of the buggy approaching. She glanced between the goat and Joseph in surprise, but he acted like he hadn't even seen it.

She kept her thoughts to herself, but had to wonder. Goats attracted flies, and fleas. Upon closer inspection, as the buggy pulled into the yard proper, passed the glassless windowed cabin and toward a small structure that probably served as combination of barn and storage space.

She remained in the buggy until Joseph pulled the horse to a halt, stepped down, and then moved around to her side. He offered her a hand, and with a nod of thanks she grasped it, noting its strength as she stepped down and took a good look around.

"It's nothing fancy, but I built it myself, and it will hold up to the worst of the Montana winter," he stated simply. "Go ahead on in and I'll be there directly, soon as I unhitch the horse and get her taken cared of."

He gestured over her shoulder, and Rayne saw a small corral behind the little barn, assuming that he would release the mare into the corral before joining her in the cabin. Once again she felt slightly disappointed that he didn't accompany her on her first look at her new home. She didn't expect him to carry her over the doorstep or anything, but still. He acted as if her presence was nothing special, and she blinked back tears of uncertainty as she walked slowly to the house.

The goat seemed happy to see her at least, and skittered up to her, butting its small head against her leg. She reached down and gave it a gentle pat on the head, then stroked its floppy ears. "Hello there," she said. "I'm Rayne. What's your name?" In reply the goat offered a short bleat, then skittered around the side of the cabin, heading in the direction of the garden. Not sure if she had seen any fencing around the garden, Rayne followed, afraid that the goat might eat precious vegetables or leaves.

Rayne stopped stock-still when she saw the garden. It was withered and dry, the leaves of a few plants curling in on themselves. She frowned. Why take the trouble to plant a garden if he wasn't going to take the care to water it? Then again, he had just mentioned a drought. Still, she knew there had to be some water nearby. Nobody built a cabin where there was no water supply. Beyond the small garden was the small crop of corn. It also looked dry and thirsty, and many of the leaves had shriveled in on themselves.

"Drought."

"Oh" Rayne stared up at him. "You don't have a creek or a stream nearby?"

"Well of course I do," he replied, as if that were a silly question.

"Then why haven't you—"

"Rayne, I'm a busy man. Sometimes I'm gone for a couple of days at a time, sometimes more. I just don't have the time to be carting buckets full of water from the creek two or three times a day to water the garden."

She frowned. No, she supposed that's why she was here. "So what do you do about vegetables when you don't have time to garden or put up preserves?"

He shrugged. "Some of my clients who can't afford cash trade me in produce or other goods. Hay, vegetables, sometimes a chicken or two. Last winter, one of my customers gave me a side of beef. That's the way it is out here. It's a cash poor community, so bartering, trading services, and so forth is how most people around here get by."

Rayne nodded in understanding. She turned from the garden to make her way to the cabin. "Well, I'm here now, so I can certainly help with the watering."

She said nothing more as she ventured to the cabin, with Joseph following a few steps behind. When she stepped into the open doorway she paused a moment to allow her eyes to adjust to the darkness inside. What she saw caused her to shake her head. She turned to look over her shoulder, sending an accusing look toward her new husband.

Again, he shrugged. "Like I said, I'm busy."

Rayne stood in the doorway, arms akimbo, muttering under her breath as she took in every inch of the cabin. A layer of dust had settled over practically every level surface. Cobwebs hung in the corners. To the left of the doorway was a small kitchen space. On one small table stood two large, shallow tubs, obviously utilized for washing dishes. To the left of the wash buckets was another small table, upon which pots and pans, plates, and a variety of silverware was stacked.

Flies buzzed around the dirty dishes, and from where she stood, she could still see bits of food sticking to the plates. She held her peace as she glanced at the small wooden table with a short wooden bench on either side. It, like the rest of the cabin, was layered with dust. On the center wall, directly facing the doorway, stood a large stone fireplace. To the right of that, against the far right wall, was an unmade bed, the mattress filled with straw looking somewhat worse for wear.

"I'll be sleeping in the barn until we get better acquainted," he commented from behind her.

Rayne didn't turn around, not wanting him to see the blush that warmed her cheeks. She could be grateful for that, she supposed. With a sigh, she turned to look up at him. "Well, I can see that there's plenty to do in here. However, please tell me one thing, Joseph."

"What's that?" he asked, looking down at her with wariness.

"Tell me that you didn't just want a wife because you needed someone to clean up after you?"

He shifted from one foot to the other and shrugged. "Not *just* that," he admitted.

"We talked about honesty this morning, remember?" She folded her arms across her chest and gave him a steady stare. While she desperately wanted to know why he wasn't a doctor anymore, she supposed she could take things one step at a time. She didn't like it, but pressing for too much information right away might cause him to retreat completely.

"Are you always this stubborn?" he asked, crossing his own arms over his chest, mimicking her stance. "To be honest, it gets lonely out here, and yes, I do need help. I'm not getting any younger, you know."

"And that's it?" she asked, not believing it.

"Well...." He mumbled something under his breath and looked down at her. "I wanted a companion, a wife that might grow to have some affection for me, and vice versa."

He paused, looking uncomfortable. She said nothing, the silence prompting him to continue. "You sounded like a nice, young lady in the letters you wrote."

It was as if that's all he could say. Suddenly, his expression darkened and he shook his head. "You're just going to have to trust me, Rayne," he said. "I'll do right by you."

With that, he turned and left the cabin.

Rayne stood watching him, frowning once again with disappointment. How could he do right by her if he couldn't be honest with her from the get-go? She knew one thing. If he didn't tell her the truth on its own within the next few days, she was going to confront him about it. She wasn't about to enter into a relationship with a man who couldn't even be honest with his own wife.

CHAPTER 5

RAYNE STOOD IN THE DOORWAY OF THE CABIN, HANDS ON HER HIPS AND assessing her handiwork with a pleased smile. It'd been a whirlwind couple of days, and not altogether pleasant. In fact, she was beginning to wonder if she had made a terrible mistake coming out west to marry Joseph Hunter. In the past two days she'd probably seen him for about two hours. After supper that first night, he'd gone out to the barn. She had cleaned up the dishes and then looked at the bed with a wary eye. She should've taken the mattress out to shake, and at least looked for some clean beddings, but she was too exhausted, mentally and emotionally. She'd changed into her nightgown and slept on top of the bed. It was too hot to climb between the sheets anyway.

The following morning, she had seen neither hide nor hair of her new husband. She found a few eggs in a basket on one of the kitchen shelves, along with small portion of bacon. She'd placed a few small logs into the cast iron stove, lit them, and quickly moved to the front door to open it. It was hotter than blazes in here already, and the heat of the stove would only make it worse. After she had gotten the bacon sizzling and the eggs scrambled in a large cast-iron skillet, she had walked outside and made her way to the barn. The door was wide open, and the horse and buggy was gone, along with Joseph.

"Tarnation!" she had cried out, stamping her foot in frustration.

While she certainly didn't expect Joseph to tell her everything he did, he could have at least told her he was leaving for the day on his rounds, or whatever a veterinarian called them, couldn't he? She stomped her way back into the kitchen, muttering under her breath the entire way. She didn't want to let the eggs or bacon go to waste, so in a fit of pique, sat down at the kitchen table and ate them all by herself.

She had spent that entire day cleaning and scrubbing the house. The goat had wandered in a couple of times to keep her company, despite her trying to keep him out. Shutting the door only blocked out what little breeze there was, and she decided it was either the company of the goat, or the blistering heat.

She had chosen the goat.

By afternoon it was scorching hot, but she decided to try to salvage what she could of the garden. She had spent the next few hours hauling two buckets down to the creek, filling them with water, then lugging them back up the slight slope behind the cabin and watering the thirsty, struggling vegetables. After she had moistened the soil, she found a hoe in the barn and made new trenches around them. By dusk she trembled with weariness. She had just placed the buckets back in the barn when she heard the horse and buggy.

She stepped out of the barn to find Joseph turning into the meadow. Behind the buggy, a milk cow was tied. She had been ready to give him a piece of her mind, mainly because she was so tired, hot, and frustrated, but the grin on his face stopped her. She thought that he really could be quite handsome when he allowed himself to smile.

Wiping her hands on her apron, she watched as Joseph pulled the buggy around in front of the barn. The cow didn't look to be more than two or three years old, a good milker. She glanced at Joseph and lifted her eyebrow in question.

"Best trade for services I ever made," he said, nodding at his own good judgment. "Now we'll have some milk, and you can make bread and cheese."

She barely caught herself from snorting. More work. Well, she had a strong back, and idle hands were the devil's workshop, or so her mother always used to tell her. She nodded as she stepped to the back of the wagon, untied the cow, and led her into the small corral while Joseph unhitched the horse and did likewise.

"What's for supper?" he turned to ask over his shoulder.

She turned to give him a look, and then lifted an eyebrow. "I haven't even started supper," she said. "I've been at watering the garden all afternoon—"

"You've been lugging buckets back and forth all afternoon?"

"Thought maybe I could save the vegetables you planted." She shrugged, and then winced when she felt the pull of her shoulder muscles.

"Probably just a waste of time," he commented.

Rayne bit back a sharp reply. She knew she felt aggravated, and put upon, and tried to blame it on the hard work and the heat, but she knew the root cause. When would he tell her the truth? Would he ever learn to trust her? Could she learn to trust him? Was she just here to provide him with physical labor and nothing else?

"I brought some supplies from town," he said, gesturing into the back of the buggy. "Some fresh vegetables, a bag of potatoes, some flour and sugar, even some fabric if you had a hankering to make some window coverings."

Unexpectedly, tears brimmed in her eyes. They weren't from pleasure though, but from fear, frustration, and a growing belief that she had made a terrible mistake. He misunderstood the reason for her tears.

"Now, Rayne, don't start fussing. I know womenfolk like to sew things for the house, so I thought I'd get the fabric before you had to ask. I hope you like it."

Suddenly feeling ashamed of herself, Rayne looked up at Joseph's face, full of expectation, and forced a smile. "Thank you Joseph, I appreciate that. If you want to unload the supplies, I'll go in and start something for supper."

The routine had continued over the next few days. By the time Rayne woke up in the morning, Joseph was long gone. Her patience with him was growing shorter and shorter with each day. He made a few comments about how nice the house looked, and even once cast a look toward the bed. She imagined that he was getting tired of sleeping out in the barn, but until she could trust him and learn to rely on him, and vice versa, that's exactly where he was going to stay.

CHAPTER 6

THE DAYS GREW HOTTER. JOSEPH WAS AWAY FOR MOST OF THE DAYTIME, BUT Rayne kept herself occupied. She milked the cow in the morning, and if she didn't use the milk right away for baking bread, she kept it cool by placing it in the creek in a shallow alcove she had dug out of the side of the bank. Come winter it would just be a matter of sinking the bucket down into the snow.

After she finished her morning chores and had the dishes cleaned and put away, she turned her thoughts to the garden. The thought of making so many trips back and forth to the creek was overwhelming, but every morning and every evening she forced herself to do it. The vegetables looked to be surviving, but barely. If she couldn't get them thriving soon, any vegetables from the garden would be stunted. As it was, the corn in the field was barely knee-high, and the onions and carrots in the garden looked to be barely holding on.

This afternoon she had decided to focus some of her attention on the barn. It, like the house, could use some organization and cleaning. She would muck out the old hay and replace it with fresh. She might even climb the wooden ladder attached to one of the supports to see what Joseph had stored up in the loft. Maybe she could find a few things that would be useful in the house.

The day wore on and grew increasingly hot. There was not a cloud in the sky, nor any indication of rain. In addition to lugging buckets and buckets of water for the garden, she also lugged buckets to fill the water trough for the animals. After she had it filled nearly to the brim, she stared at it longingly, wishing that she could just dunk herself in it and cool off.

Why not? Joseph wasn't around, and even if he was, what difference would it make? Removing her shoes and socks, Rayne smiled with impish glee as she padded toward the now filled trough, looking forward to nothing more than cooling off. She lifted the skirt of her cotton print dress up to her knees and placed one foot and then the other into the trough. The cow and the goat stared at her, and she giggled. It felt so refreshing, so cool!

Without even hesitating, she sat down in the water, sinking in and leaning back until the water sloshed a little over the side. With a sigh of relief, she rested her head against the narrow end of the trough.

She closed her eyes, relishing in the bliss, but in the next instant her heart skipped a beat. She heard the sound of a buggy and realized that Joseph must be back. Before she could even sit upright, it was obvious that he had spotted her in the trough.

"Rayne!"

He brought the buggy to an abrupt halt in front of the barn, not far from the shade where the trough was situated in the corner of the corral.

"Rayne!"

She began to sit up, but he quickly climbed through the wood post railings and knelt beside the trough, eyes wide with alarm. "What are you doing? Are you all right?"

She had never seen him so animated. "I'm all right," she said, sitting up. Her dress clung to her skin. "I just wanted a dip, that's all, to cool off," she explained.

He stared at her, and realization dawned. "You're not hurt? You didn't fall?

She shook her head and smiled. "It's actually quite refreshing. You want to give it a try? It's so cool—"

He exploded.

"Rayne Hunter, you get out of that trough right now! Of all the—!"

With a scowl he stomped away from the trough, climbed between the fence rails, and made his way back to his buggy, muttering under his breath the entire way. He didn't once glance back at her. Rayne couldn't imagine what had gotten him so upset. She rose to her feet and stood in the trough to stare at him, hands on her hips.

"What in heaven's name has gotten into you?" she demanded. "I was just trying to cool off! I've been working hard all afternoon, and the water looked cool and refreshing!"

He turned to her as he unhitched the horse from the buggy. "Did you ever think to go take a dip in the creek?"

She frowned. "Joseph, what difference does it make where I take a dip?"

"What if someone had seen you?" he grumbled.

"And what if someone had? What's the difference if I get refreshed in the trough or in the creek?"

"It's just not seemly." He shook his head. "What will people think?"

"I don't care what people think!" She climbed out of the trough, her feet now growing muddy from the soft dirt of the corral as she too slipped between the split rails and confronted her husband. She was dripping wet, the skirt of her dress clinging to her legs and arms. Her sense of relief from only moments before was now shattered.

"It just ain't proper," he continued. "It's not seemly," he repeated.

"Not seemly? What do you mean?"

"I have a reputation around here you know," he said. With one hand on the horse's back, he turned to her, holding one of the trace lines in his hand. "What if one of my customers had come for help and saw you bathing in the trough?"

"Joseph Hunter, I wasn't bathing!" she gritted out, really angry now. "And if you want to talk about reputation, why don't you start by telling me why a complete stranger had to tell me that you used to be a doctor!"

She couldn't believe that she had uttered the words. So much for giving him time. However, she couldn't take the words back. He stared at her and she swore, if she had been so inclined, she saw the blood drain from his face.

"Who told you that?"

"It doesn't matter who told me," she said.

He said nothing, but turned away from her, his expression stricken. It gave her pause, but her temper was roiling now, almost as hot as the heat around them. Without a word, Joseph dropped the traces in his hands and walked away from the horse and the buggy, disappearing around the side of the cabin.

Shaking her head and muttering under her breath, Rayne moved toward the horse and finished unhitching her. Then she let her into the small corral with the cow.

She hadn't exactly meant to confront Joseph, but she was glad that it was out in the open. Now it was his turn to explain. Only then would she believe that she could allow herself to even feel comfortable staying here. Not wanting to argue with him at the moment, she headed for the barn as she had intended to do earlier. Still frowning and annoyed, she stared at the work that needed to be done in here and shook her head. "No, this can wait until tomorrow."

Instead, she decided to explore the loft. She reached for the wood slats of the ladder and began to climb, her bare feet carefully stepping on each rung, hoping she wouldn't get a splinter. She had made her way to the next to the last step when she reached her left hand to grasp onto one of the two by fours that rose from the bottom of the loft floor toward the ceiling.

Her left hand clasped around the wood, and she heaved herself upward, her right hand also reaching for the other support. To her dismay, however, the two-by-four suddenly snapped in half. Wood rot, termites, she didn't know which, but anything else that could have caused the wood to break escaped her thoughts as she suddenly felt herself teetering. She tried to catch her balance, tried to grasp onto something that would prevent her from falling, but her momentum propelled her backward.

Her ensuing scream was cut short as she landed hard on the floor of the barn. Her breath was knocked out of her like the kick of a mule. Pain shot through her arm and shoulder moments before she was encompassed by a great blackness.

CHAPTER 7

RAYNE DIDN'T KNOW HOW LONG SHE'D BEEN LYING ON THE BARN FLOOR. WHEN she had opened her eyes again, the shadows had grown a little longer than she recalled, but it was still daylight. What happened?

Then she remembered. She'd fallen from the top of the ladder, and landed hard. Where was Joseph? He had stomped off in a huff.

She tried to get up from the floor, but bit back a sharp cry of pain with the movement. With her good hand, she reached up toward her right shoulder, where sharp pain radiated throughout her body. Had she broken her shoulder? She couldn't tell.

"Joseph!" she cried out, but her throat was dry and her voice didn't carry very far. She tried again, and then again, but she heard nothing. Where was he? How long would it be before he found her in here? Every move she made sent waves of agony through her body, causing her to grit her teeth and close her eyes against it. Not that that did any good.

Minutes passed. Dust motes filtered down from the loft, and a fly buzzed around her. With her good hand, she swatted at it weakly. Swallowing, trying to get some moisture into her throat, she tried again.

"Joseph!"

Nothing. She turned her head and saw one portion of the buggy wheel from the open barn door way. Unless he had taken the horse out bareback, he was still around somewhere. She tried again.

"Joseph!"

Finally, she heard footsteps. She stared at the open barn door in the hopes that Joseph had finally heard her. She willed him to find her. Her disappointment was nearly palpable when she saw the goat wander into the barn and slowly make its way toward her.

"Little goat," she said. "Do you know where Joseph is?" She certainly didn't expect an answer, but talking to the goat took her mind off her pain, if only for a moment. "Nice goat, good goat... can you go find Joseph?"

The goat offered a brief bleat in reply, and gazed around the interior of the barn. The goat then lowered her head to nibble on her blouse. Rayne tried to shoo her away, without much success.

"Rayne!?"

Joseph!

A pause. "Rayne, where are you?"

"Oh thank you, God," she sighed, sending up a silent prayer to the Lord for answering in her moment of distress. "Joseph! I'm in the barn!"

Rayne watched as Joseph stepped through the open door and into the barn, his eyes widening when he saw her lying on the floor, the goat trying to eat her shirt sleeve. She saw his scowl, and could only imagine what he imagined she was up to now. Then he took in the scene. His gaze went from her lying on the floor, up the ladder, and then his eyes widened in horror.

He rushed forward and knelt down beside her, his gaze sweeping over her form. "What happened? Where are you hurt?" He made no attempt to touch her and she couldn't figure out why.

"My shoulder... and my arm," she replied.

"Anywhere else?" he demanded, his eyes boring down into hers. "You tell me, and be honest about it."

Rayne couldn't stop herself from making a face. "You're a fine one to talk about honesty."

He clenched his jaw and then reached for her, gently touching her shoulder, eliciting a sharp cry of pain from her lips. He didn't look her in the eye, but instead focused on her shoulder, running his fingers gently over her collarbone, the shoulder joint itself, and then her upper arm. Then, finally, he looked at her.

"Looks like you've broken your collarbone, and you might have fractured your arm." He reached for her. "Come on, let's get you inside where I can get a better look."

Carefully, he placed her injured arm against her waist, encouraging her to grasp the front of her skirt with her fingers.

"Now you don't move your arm," he instructed. "You hang onto me with your good arm, but don't move that injured arm."

She nodded and then reached her left arm up and wrapped it around his neck as he lowered his upper body toward her. Ever so carefully, he placed his right arm underneath her shoulders, causing a wince of pain. His left hand swept under her knees. In a matter of seconds, he had lifted her from the ground. A wave of nauseating pain swept through her, and she gasped.

"Just hang on, Rayne," he encouraged.

In moments they had left the barn, and he strode quickly toward the cabin. He carried her as if she weighed nothing. She looked up at him, saw the concern on his face, the worry and anxiety, and felt her heart softening toward him just a bit.

Inside, he quickly moved to the bed and laid her down on it. Then he stood, gazing down at her intently. She sensed hesitance. For a moment, alarm swept through her. "What is it, Joseph? Can't you fix me?"

He said nothing, but seemed to be struggling with some sort of internal dilemma.

"You are a doctor, aren't you, Joseph?" she asked gently. Even though she was in pain, she had to ask. The truth had to come out, and better now than never. She needed him, and he knew it.

He cleared his throat and then offered the briefest of replies. "Used to be."

She asked again. "Can you fix me, Joseph? Am I going to die?"

Suddenly, a sensation of dread swept through her. What if her injury *was* fatal? She'd never heard of anyone dying from a broken collarbone, but what if she had internal injuries that he hadn't told her about? Tears filled her eyes.

"Please Joseph, answer me. Can you fix me?"

He swallowed so hard that she could see his Adam's apple bob up and down. His faraway look caught her by surprise. A memory?

"What happened, Joseph?" she asked, trying to ignore the pain in her shoulder. "Why did you stop being a doctor?"

For the longest while she didn't think he would reply. Then, his voice heavy with which she could only describe as regret, he looked at her and spoke.

"Because the last patient I had, I killed."

CHAPTER 8

She stared up at him in horror, and then blinked. Her voice heavy with doubt, she asked, "You murdered a patient? On purpose?" While she wasn't doing it in a mean way, she tried to prod the truth out of them. "Did I marry a murderer, Joseph?"

That seemed to jar him out of his state. Eyes wide, he shook his head. "Of course not! Why would you think—"

"You just got finished saying that you killed your last patient." She tried to shift slightly, and winced in pain. "Who was it?"

He said nothing for several moments, but looked off into the distance through the open door of the cabin. "He was a friend of mine."

"Did you get into a fight or something? Did you kill him? What happened?"

"What?" he asked, glancing down at her with confusion.

"You're the one who said you killed him, Joseph, so I'm asking you. Did you get into a fight? Did you have a business disagreement? Was it about money?"

He began to bluster, barely getting a word out. "No... no, it was nothing like that!"

"Then you didn't actually murder him, is that right?"

He sat back, his eyes dark and angry. "No, I didn't murder him, not in the sense you mean."

Rayne bit back another surge of pain. "Either it was murder or it wasn't, Joseph, there is no in-between." She didn't think for a minute that Joseph had murdered anyone, let alone kill someone. She was tired of this foolishness. "Joseph, we need to talk about this, because... well, just because. If we're going to make our marriage work, we need to be completely open and honest with each other. However, now is not the time. I'm in pain, I've broken something, and I want you to fix me. So, Joseph, do what you need to do and fix me!"

He stared down at her, and for a moment she noticed his expression soften.

"You're very bossy, you know that?"

She knew he was teasing her, and she appreciated him for that, but she was starting to feel a little sick. Pain began to throb through her entire body, and she glanced up at Joseph with imploring eyes. Though she tried to hide it from him, he obviously noted her clammy skin, and for sure he must've seen how pale her face was. It felt pale anyway, as if all the blood had rushed out of her body and pooled in her lower extremities. Not to mention the fact that she had begun to tremble. She bit off a low cry, and that jolted him into action.

"Try not to move around. I need to gather some supplies. They're in the loft in the barn."

She said nothing, but watched as Joseph hurried outside. What were they going to do now? She would be laid up for weeks, maybe longer, she was sure. With him taking care of animals, the drought was sure to destroy any chance at all of saving the garden, or the small crop of corn that he had hoped to sell for staples that would last them through the winter. She wished her curiosity hadn't gotten the best of her, that she had taken the time to better inspect the ladder, but there was nothing to do about it now.

Joseph returned several minutes later, caring a bucket full of water and an oblong leather bag that she recognized as a doctor's kit. She watched as he poured some of the water into a basin and brought the basin to the side of the bed. He pulled up one of the kitchen benches to the side of the bed next, then looked down at her, his expression serious. He rinsed his hands in the basin, and leaving them wet to air dry, spoke to her.

"Rayne, I have to loosen the top of your dress." He reached for the quilt she had folded and placed at the foot of the bed earlier this morning. He shook it loose and covered her with it. She said nothing as he retrieved a pair of scissors from his bag, and then plucked at a portion of her sleeve, preparing to cut her dress.

"My dress, Joseph?" she protested. "Do you really have to cut it?"

"Unless you want me to roll you over so I can undo the buttons at the back," he said, shaking his head. "That's going to hurt."

"Joseph, the buttons are on the front."

"That's only part of the problem, Rayne," he explained. "Even if I got the buttons undone we'd have to peel the top of the dress off of you... and... and whatever you're wearing underneath it."

She sighed. "Joseph, you are a doctor. I'm sure you've seen—"

"Enough," he said, his eyes focused on her shirt sleeve. "I'm cutting it. I'll buy you a new one."

She lay still while Joseph cut the sleeve of her dress, all the way up over her shoulder, along the top of the shoulder seam, and up to the collar. While he gently peeled back the dress, he kept her properly covered, pulling the quilt up over her bosom, but leaving her right shoulder and arm exposed. He began to prod at her collarbone again, causing her to clench her teeth and hiss sharply.

"I'm sorry, Rayne, but I have to see where, and how badly it's broken, and if the break extends into the shoulder joint." With that, he placed both his hands on said shoulder joint and began to gently manipulate it.

It was too much.

She felt a cold sensation sweep through her until, with a low moan, she passed out.

CHAPTER 9

Rayne opened her eyes, confused. Where was she? Then she realized she was looking up at a ceiling... the ceiling of a log cabin, and it all came back to her in a rush. Joseph. The fall. Her shoulder throbbed, but now it was wrapped in swaths of torn fabric, her arm bent across her stomach and wrapped securely into place. She blinked and turned her head slightly to look around the cabin.

To her surprise, Joseph still sat on the wooden bench that he had pulled up to the side of the bed earlier when taking care of her. He sat slightly hunched over, his chin on his chest. A slight snore escaped his throat. She smiled. Suddenly, he lifted his head and stared.

"You're awake," he said, a pleased smile on his face.

Again, Rayne was stunned by the change in demeanor that such a small expression could have on her husband's face. How such a slight muscle contraction could alter his features so much amazed her, but she was glad to see it.

"Did you fix me, Joseph?"

He straightened his back, rubbed his hand over his whiskered chin, and nodded. "You have quite a bad break there, Rayne," he said. "Your collarbone is broken, you have a crack in the shoulder joint, and you have a simple fracture in your upper humerus."

She frowned in confusion. What was her—?

"Your upper arm."

He shook his head as he gazed down at her, but he didn't seem to be angry.

"What were you doing climbing up to the loft?"

She started to shrug, immediately realized her mistake, closed her eyes, and counted slowly to three as the sharp pain gradually decreased. "I was curious what was up there."

He didn't comment about that, but asked another question. "You hungry? I made some broth. It's warming on the stove."

She shook her head. "Not right now, Joseph. Maybe later." She gazed at him for several moments, and then spoke softly, but firmly. "Joseph, we need to talk."

He said nothing.

"If this marriage is going to work Joseph, we have to start with honesty. Only with honesty comes trust."

Again he said nothing.

"I know there's a lot to deal with right now with the drought and trying to save the corn and the garden. I understand all that. But in order to do that, we have to work as a team. We have to work *together*. I have to believe in you, Joseph. I have to trust you. I have to know that there are no secrets between us."

Dusk slowly began to ooze its way into the cabin, casting long shadows against the walls and floor. Joseph sat quietly on the bench, his hands folded in his lap.

"Tell me, Joseph," she said. "Tell me what happened." She wished she could reach out and comfort him, touch his hand, make a connection, but she couldn't move her right arm, and there was no way she could reach her left hand toward him.

Finally, he began to speak. "It was two winters ago. A good friend of mine was in the barn taking care of his livestock after a storm. I lived on the edge of town back then. He was supposed to come for supper that night. He did, and during supper I noticed that he occasionally grabbed at his ribs."

Joseph sat silent for a while after that. Rayne had to prod him. "What happened?"

"That's what I asked him," Joseph sighed. "He told me he had taken a good kick in the ribs from his mule. He landed hard, but thought the wind had just gotten knocked out of him. I took a quick look, felt his ribs, and didn't feel anything out of place, although I was sure that he probably cracked a few."

Rayne listened quietly, trying not to move. If she didn't move, the pain wasn't so bad. She urged him to get it out. "Then what happened?"

"His appetite was good, and he was a little stiff, but he brushed off my suggestion to wrap his ribs, saying that he'd taken worse tumbles before. Anyway, after supper he rode off back home.

He was silent after that, but this time Rayne didn't prod him to continue, knowing that he had to get it out on his own. After what seemed like a long time, but was probably only a minute, Joseph turned to her as he spoke.

"The next morning, one of his ranch hands came by to tell me that my friend was dead."

Her eyes widened in surprise. "Dead? How?"

Joseph shook his head. "He must've had more damage than we both imagined, probably some internal bleeding."

"And that's *your* fault?"

"I should have insisted on giving him a thorough examination. I should have insisted that he let me wrap his ribs. I should have kept a closer watch on him—"

"Joseph," Rayne interrupted. "Even if you had, there's no guarantee that he still would not have died. What if one of his internal organs had been damaged? Even if you had stayed with him, there was little that you could've done."

"He was my best friend, Rayne," he said, slowly shaking his head. "He was my best friend.

Rayne said nothing for several minutes. She sighed. "And because of that you quit your doctoring and focused on animals, became a veterinarian?"

He nodded.

"So to whom do the people of Bozeman and anywhere else around here go for their doctoring?"

A guilty expression passed over his features. "A new doc came into town last summer." He shook his head. "He's a quack."

Rayne felt bad for Joseph, truly she did, but he didn't seem to be the sort to wallow in self-pity and told him as much. "You made a mistake, Joseph, but you're only human. You're not God. You can't know everything. I'll tell you one thing, though," she said, her chin tilted stubbornly toward him. "You got me fixed up good and proper, didn't you?"

He glanced down at her and nodded.

"Well then," she said. "That's all there is to it, isn't there? You're a good doctor, Joseph, whether you're working on animals or people. I'm sure you were a good doctor before your friend died, and I have every confidence that you can be a good doctor again."

He began to shake his head, but she stopped him.

"Where is your faith, Joseph? I have faith in you. I believed you're a good man, and the fact that you feel so strongly about the incident proves it."

"I made a mistake that cost a man his life," he said, his voice soft.

"So learn more," she said. "We can only do the best we can with what life throws at us. You of all people should know that." She paused and looked up at him. "Am I going to be okay, Joseph?"

He nodded.

"That settles it then," she said. "You're the town's new doctor *and* veterinarian." She didn't even give him a chance to debate the issue. "Now there's another problem we need to deal with. You're busy, and I'll be unable to keep that crop or the garden watered, not to mention helping out around here. Any suggestions?"

For the first time since she'd ventured out west, she saw Joseph smile down at her with true affection in his gaze.

"I have a couple of ideas," he said. "First, you take some broth, and then try to get some sleep. In the morning, I've got some business to take care of in town."

"You're not going to sleep out in the barn, are you?" she asked, worried. "What if I need you?"

"I'll make up a bed in front of the fireplace. If you approve, of course."

She smiled up at him in turn.

"I approve, Joseph. I approve."

CHAPTER 10

FOUR DAYS AFTER HER FALL FROM THE BARN LOFT, RAYNE SAT RATHER UPRIGHT on the bed, her back against the wall, cushioned by pillows. Joseph had cared for her attentively and gently. He still had his veterinary duties to take care of, but he only left after he prepared her some breakfast, helped her outside to the outhouse, and had gotten her settled back into bed before he left.

He typically returned before noon to continue caring for her. When she asked him about it, how he was managing with his four-legged patients, he merely shrugged, but she couldn't help but notice that he smiled more often. She noted the liveliness in his step, and the sadness in his eyes had somewhat receded.

Now, close to noon, she heard the familiar sounds of his buggy turning into the yard. Several moments later his tall frame filled the doorway and he looked at her with an expression that she had never seen on his face before.

"What's happening, Joseph?"

He didn't answer her question but strode toward the bed. "How'd you like to sit outside for a few minutes, get some sunlight, and look out at your meadow?"

"My meadow?" she asked, confused.

He shrugged. "That's what I'm calling it now. Rayne's Meadow. Our home."

She couldn't help the lump that suddenly grew in her throat, the trip hammer of her heart, and the tears that began to warm her eyes. "What are you saying, Joseph?"

"Well, Rayne, I'm going to be honest with you." He smiled as he sat down on the small bench beside the bed. "You do happen to be the most obstinate, stubborn, and eccentric woman I've ever met, but I have to tell you, I've developed some pretty strong feelings for you."

Rayne felt stunned. Her eyes widened. "You have?"

He smiled. "I have. Now come on, let's go outside. There's something I want you to see."

He didn't have to ask twice. Rayne had quickly grown tired of being in the dark and stuffy log cabin. It was so stifling hot all the time that to sit outside in the shade and look out over the beautiful landscape, and the meadow— *her meadow*— brought a smile to her lips. She felt a huge swell of affection for Joseph, and believed that things would turn out all right after all. Despite the drought, despite her injury, she and Joseph had begun to form a sort of bond. She had no doubt that that bond would grow into a love.

Time. All they needed was time.

He stood, and picked up a small wooden bench, carried it outside. He returned moments later and leaned over the base of the bed and grabbed up the quilt, wrapping it around her. Then, he carefully lifted her into his arms, and for the first time since she had come west, she felt safe, secure, and protected.

Her face close to Joseph's, she smiled. He glanced down at her, and for the first time, they shared a brief kiss. It was over before she knew it, but that brief kiss promised so much for her future.

It was good to be outside, and she inhaled deeply. He placed her in the shade against the side of the log cabin, looking out over the meadow and the road leading through it to the cabin. To her surprise, she saw several wagons approaching.

"Joseph, we've got company!" She suddenly frowned. "I'm not presentable! My hair! I'm not dressed—"

"You're beautiful just the way you are, Rayne. Don't worry."

As they watched the wagons slowly make their way down the road, he sat beside her, his voice somber. "Rayne, the crop is destroyed, and so is the garden. Despite your heroic efforts, the drought has done its damage. It's too late to plant a new crop, and the almanac says is going to be a long, hot, dry summer."

She glanced up at him in alarm. "What are we going to do, Joseph? How are we going to lay in supplies for winter, or buy—?"

"Hello there in the cabin!"

Rayne turned from Joseph to watch the first of the wagons pull into the yard. The first wagon held a middle-aged couple, the second a small family, and the third two older gentleman. Tarpaulins covered cargo stored in each of the wagons. What was going on?

As the visitors climbed down out of the wagons, Joseph explained.

"Rayne, you're looking at the new town doctor, and this time it's for good. These good people are paying a part of my fee in goods. They've brought enough supplies to last us through the summer, and the women's committee from church have promised a quarter of all their canned goods and preserves to us to tide us over the winter."

Rayne stared at him in stunned surprise, and then smiled through her tears as their visitors approached, smiling and greeting her as she extended her good hand out toward them, shaking their hands and touched to the bottom of her heart by their generosity. This wasn't charity. She sensed that. This was how they did things out west.

"I can't thank you enough," she stammered, her voice cracking with emotion. The strangers introduced themselves one at a time, and though there was no possible way that Rayne could keep them all straight in her head, she knew that each and every one of them would become her friends.

The town needed a good doctor, and now they had one. Joseph would no longer be a recluse limiting his skills to animals. As soon as she was on the mend, Rayne promised herself that she would do whatever she could to help anyone in need.

She turned to Joseph, trying to hold back her tears of joy, her lips trembling.

"Isn't this wonderful, Joseph?"

He looked at her, the smile on his lips complimenting his handsome features.

"It certainly is," he agreed. "And I have you to thank for it."

EPILOGUE

THE FOLLOWING SPRING WREATHED RAYNE'S MEADOW IN HUNDREDS OF bright, colorful, purple wildflowers. Deer and elk grazed in the meadow. The goat happily chased after rabbits.

Rayne paused her chores to caress the low bulge in her belly. The winter had been long and cold, but she and Joseph had been snug and warm in their cabin. She had been busy quilting, making quilts of all sizes; some for babies, some as lap warmers, and others to cover beds. She gave every one of them away to those in need. Her sewing skills brought her compliments and attention, and before she knew it, she was also fashioning dresses for many of the ladies in Bozeman. They paid her for her troubles, and now she was even thinking of learning how to make hats and bonnets.

Joseph had laughed, shaking his head. Yes, she kept him on his toes and continually surprised him, but her impish smile and zest for life had pulled Joseph out of his shell. Every Sunday they took their buggy to church, no matter how vicious the weather, and he was now a respected member of the church community, Bozeman, and beyond.

Their love had grown and burgeoned over the months, and now Rayne couldn't imagine being anywhere else. She was active with the church women while Joseph kept busy doctoring both humans and animals. They were doing quite well for themselves, and soon the men from church would come help him add an addition to the cabin for the child that would arrive by summer.

She gazed out over the meadow, then turned to look at the cabin, the barn, and the silly little goat who came racing around the side of the cabin, bleating as it hurried toward her, gently butting its head against Rayne's leg. Her heart overflowed with love and happiness.

She was home.

⁂

THANK YOU SO MUCH FOR READING MY BOOK. I SINCERELY HOPE YOU ENJOYED EVERY bit reading it. I had fun creating it and will surely create more.

Your positive reviews are very helpful to other reader, it only takes a few moments. They can be left at Amazon.

www.amazon.com/Katie-Wyatt/e/B011IN7AF0

⁂

WANT FREE BOOKS EVERY WEEK? WHO DOESN'T!

BECOME A PREFERRED READER AND WE'LL NOT ONLY SEND YOU FREE READS, BUT you'll also receive updates about new releases.

So you'll be among the first to dive into our latest new books, full of adventure, heartwarming romances, and characters so real they jump off the page.

It's absolutely free and you don't need to do anything at all to qualify except go to.

PREFERRED READ FREE READS

http:/katieWyattBooks.com/readersgroup

ABOUT THE AUTHOR

KATIE WYATT IS 25% AMERICAN SIOUX INDIAN. BORN AND RAISED IN Arizona, she has traveled and camped extensively through California, Arizona, Nevada, Mexico, and New Mexico. Looking at the incredible night sky and the giant Saguaro cacti, she has dreamed of what it would be like to live in the early pioneer times.

Spending time with a relative of the great Wyatt Earp, also named Wyatt Earp, Katie was mesmerized and inspired by the stories he told of bygone times. This historical interest in the old West became the inspiration for her Western romance novels.

Her books are a mixture of actual historical facts and events mixed with action and humor, challenges and adventures. The characters in Katie's clean romance novels draw from her own experiences and are so real that they almost jump off the pages. You feel like you're walking beside them through all the ups and downs of their lives. As the stories unfold, you'll find yourself both laughing and crying. The endings will never fail to leave you feeling warm inside.

GOLDEN COLORADO

Mail Order Bride Western Romance

RoyceCardiff
P u b l i s h i n g   H o u s e
WHOLESOME INSPIRATIONAL ROMANCE

Dear Reader,

It is our utmost pleasure and privilege to bring these wonderful stories to you. I am so very proud of our amazing team of writers and the delight they continually bring us all with their beautiful clean and wholesome tales of, faith, courage, and love.

What is a book's lone purpose if not to be read and enjoyed? Therefore, you, dear reader, are the key to fulfilling that purpose and unlocking the treasures that lie within the pages of this book.

NEWSLETTER SIGN UP PREFERRED READ

http://katieWyattBooks.com/readersgroup

THANK YOU FOR CHOOSING A INSPIRATIONAL READS BY ROYCE CARDIFF PUBLISHING HOUSE.

Welcome and Enjoy!

A PERSONAL WORD FROM KATIE

I LOVE WRITING ABOUT THE OLD WEST AND THE TRIALS, TRIBULATIONS, AND triumphs of the early pioneer women.

With strong fortitude and willpower, they took a big leap of faith believing in the promised land of the West. It was always not a bed of roses, however many found true love.

Most of the stories are based on some historical fact or personal conversations I've had with folks who knew something of that time. For example a relative of the Wyatt Earp's. I have spent much time out in the West camping hiking and carousing. I have spent countless hours gazing up at night thinking of how it must been back then.

Thank you for being a loyal reader.

Katie

CHAPTER 1

THE HEAT WAS UNBEARABLE. SHE COUGHED. SMOKE CHOKED HER LUNGS. THE crackling and roar of the flames jarred her out of slumber. She laid on her back in the bed for several seconds, confused, staring at the undulating shapes of reddish orange patterns that lingered across her ceiling and the walls. What was it? What was happening? Her heart pounded so hard she could feel the throbbing pulse in her neck. Her instinct kicked in.

She bolted from the bed, her heavy nightgown a hindrance as she padded across the wood floor toward the bedroom door. The floor was warm beneath her feet, and when she touched the metal doorknob she jerked her hand back with a hiss.

Fire! She coughed, cried out, but heard nothing from the other side. Her parents! Her younger brother and sisters! She tried to scream, but instead she choked, doubled over in a fit of coughing. She had to get out, but the only way out was her bedroom window on the second floor of their modest home on the outskirts of Boston. In the distance she heard the cries of neighbors, men's voices shouting for water buckets. A crashing sound from below sounded like a beam falling from the roof into the sitting room beneath her parents' bedroom.

Tears from the acrid smoke filled her eyes. Choking back a sob and tamping down her rising panic, she could only hope and pray that they were already out of the house. She scrambled and reached for her sitting stool, heaving it with all her strength out her bedroom window. Glass shattered, and in the next instant, Minnie stood at the window frame, gazing down in wide-eyed horror into her front yard.

"Jump, Minnie, jump!"

The urging of several people within the crowd jolted her out of her moment of indecision. She heard another crashing sound behind her, followed by another burst of heat as her bedroom door blew open. Casting a terrified glance over her shoulder, she saw the flames licking at the door frame, seeking fresh fuel, making their way up the walls and curling and roiling along the ceiling.

She quickly snatched her night robe from the base of the bed, an arm's length away, and bundled it over the bottom of the window frame so that she wouldn't cut herself climbing through. She didn't have any time to waste. The short overhang of the porch directly below her window provided questionable footing, but she climbed through anyway, tentatively placing one of bare foot, then the other, on the porch roof. She sat down, quickly scooching herself toward the edge.

Several men stood below, arms upraised.

"Jump, Minnie! We'll catch you!" a middle-aged man with a handlebar mustache urged. He wore obviously what looked like quickly donned overalls over white long johns, gesturing for her to jump. Only one strap was fastened.

Where was her family? What had happened? How did the fire start? All these questions and a hundred more raced through her mind as she balanced on the edge of the porch roof. Dangling her legs over the side and hovering as close to the edge as she could, she pushed herself off, placing her trust not only in the men below, but in God to save her.

"My family! My family–"

Minnie jolted awake from the nightmare, one that had replayed in her mind every night since that horrible tragedy had taken her parents and her siblings. Her family was gone, the family home burned down with them. While she tried to recover, deal with the grief, the bank had coldly informed her that the land would need to be sold to pay off her family's debts. In the end, she was left penniless.

It appeared that all her dreams for her future had shattered that night. As an educated eighteen-year-old, her only desire had been to meet a wonderful man, get married, have no less than three boys, and live happily ever after. Those dreams had disappeared in the billowing smoke and ashes of what was left of her life though.

In the two weeks since the tragic fire, she had relied on the kindness of friends to provide her with daily sustenance and a roof over her head. Her friends had shared their clothes, their tables, and their beds with her, but she knew she couldn't do this forever.

She had no relatives in America. Her parents had come from England when she was but a babe and the only relatives that she knew of over there, were her mother's sister and her husband. Unfortunately, the pair had a reputation, according to her mother's not-so-kind assessment, of being rather unpleasant individuals. Her aunt was a bitter, angry woman living with a drunkard of a ne'er-do-well husband.

Minnie had despaired over what to do, when finally, the week after the fire and following the funeral of her family at the local cemetery, an old friend of the family approached her. She looked to him as a grandfather, though a distant one at that; the rich man was rather eccentric and sometimes prone to violent outbursts of temper. To her surprise... no, *shock*, he had made a rather unusual proposal to her.

Because she no longer had any assets, no dowry, and no skills to earn a living, he suggested that she marry him.

At the proposal, her stomach had turned. My goodness, he was in his sixties! She had always thought that his assessing gaze and friendly smiles portrayed a kind, old gentleman, but now she wasn't quite so sure. Neither of her two choices, the ne'er-do-well relatives in England, or the old man pressuring her to marry him, were something that Minnie was willing to consider.

She had prayed for guidance, prayed for an answer to the situation she found herself in. *Why* had this happened? She was a good girl, faithful, always doing her best to be helpful and compassionate to everyone. Why had God allowed this to happen to her? *Why?*

She woke from her nightmare, her cheeks stained with tears. She slept in the small guestroom of her best friend Florence Elmer's house, where she had stayed for the past few days.

She tried to fight back the grief, to swallow her anger, resentment, and guilt for surviving when no one else in the family had. She thought of her parents and choked back a sob. Her younger brother and two younger twin sisters... gone.

Why? Why'd she alone survived?

CHAPTER 2

MINNIE STARED AT HERSELF IN THE MIRROR, STRETCHING HER FIVE-FOOT-THREE-inch frame up as tall as she could. Maybe if she stood straighter, people would take her more seriously. Her moderately curly, chestnut hair complemented her deep brown eyes as they stared back at her. Her friends had always told her she was beautiful, but all she saw reflected in the mirror was a frightened young woman who had no idea what to do. She wore a black mourning dress that Florence's mother had quickly adapted to her small frame.

When Minnie had told Florence about the old man's proposition, she had stared at her with wide eyes, clasping a startled hand over her mouth. After Florence then telling her mother of the proposition, they had insisted that she come stay with them. As it turned out, she learned that the old man had gone through three wives in his lifetime and had a reputation of being emotionally and physically abusive. Minnie was horrified to discover the truth about him, and knew that her parents had never known or they wouldn't have had such close associations with him.

She didn't accept the old man's proposal, so it seemed that her only option was to return to England, to the relatives she had heard nothing good about, and who would likely make her life a living hell for placing an additional, and unwanted, financial burden on them.

"No more of that."

Minnie looked away from the mirror to find Florence watching her from the door-way, a gentle and commiserating smile on her face. She swallowed and blinked back her tears, forcing a smile of her own. Florence was the only person who seem to understand her and her habit of sometimes wringing her hands in indecision and confusion when faced with pressure. She was so grateful, and thanked God for such a good friend.

"I have something to show you," Florence said, stepping into the room. She sat down on the bed and patted it, gesturing for Minnie to join her.

With a sigh, Minnie turned from the mirror and sat down on the bed next to her friend, noticing that she held the classified section of one of Boston's several newspapers folded in her lap.

"What do you have there?" Minnie asked. "Did you find a job for me?" She had looked for a job as soon as she had recovered from the initial shock of the fire. Sadly, she had no specific skills on which to rely. Not only that, but she was indecisive, and always had trouble making important decisions. Since her family had died so tragically, and with such unbearable decisions in front of her, she had lost some of her trust in God.

"Not exactly," Florence admitted.

"To be honest, Flo, I don't have many things in my favor. I love to sew, but I'm certainly not a professional at it. I've never worked a day in my life. I don't particularly like to be around animals, especially horses as you know, because they scare me. I can't even earn a living as a nanny because most families have animals." Tears once more burned in her eyes. "What am I going to do?"

Before, her family had always made decisions for her. Now that they were gone, she would have to learn how to stand on her own two feet. Somehow she would need to gain more self-confidence, be more self-assured, and make her own decisions. But how would she know she was making the right ones?

"Have you ever heard of mail order brides?"

Minnie stared at Flo. A mail-order bride? "You mean agree to marry someone who placed an ad in the newspaper for a bride?" she asked, her voice heavy with shock.

Flo nodded. "It's something to consider, Minnie," she said. "After all, your only other choices, in my opinion, are much worse."

Minnie could only agree. A mail-order bride... she adjusted to the idea and realized that it just might – *maybe* – be a solution to her current problems. The thought of marrying someone she didn't know was frightening, but was this the path God wanted her to take? She definitely knew that she didn't want to travel to England. Her relatives didn't want her. The old man? Why shouldn't she grab at the only sure thing and marry the rich old man? She immediately shook her head. She'd rather die an old spinster living off the goodwill of strangers before she would agree to marry such a horrible person.

"What do you think, Flo?"

Flo shrugged. "I think you should consider it. I've circled a few of the more favorable ads. There's an interesting one from a man living in Golden, Colorado."

"Colorado!?" That was so far. So far away from Boston, her few friends, the cemetery where her beloved family was buried.

"Read this here," Flo said, pointing to one of the circled ads.

Minnie found it and began to read. "*James Thorton, seeking a wife. Consider myself clever and creative, an inventor, and not too hard on the eyes. I love chocolate, especially chocolate from Europe–*" Minnie glanced up with a small smile on her lips. "I love Belgian chocolates," she told her friend.

"I know," her friend nodded. She gestured toward the paper. "Keep reading, Minnie."

"*Loves animals. Currently a miner, but want a beautiful wife for whom I can build a wonderful home in the mountains. I would like to have three boys...*"

Minnie glanced up at Flo, her eyes wide with surprise.

"You want three boys too, don't you, Minnie?"

Could it be a coincidence? Or was this a sign from God? Her heart gave a little leap of excitement, the first since the tragedy had befallen. Did she dare? Should she take the chance? Was it possible? Did she have the strength and fortitude to leave her beloved Boston and travel thousands of miles out west to the wilderness of Colorado's mountains, just to find a man who also liked chocolates and wanted three boys?

Flo nudged her with her elbow. "What have you got to lose, Minnie?"

What indeed?

CHAPTER 3

MINNIE HAD DECIDED. FLO WAS MORE THAN EXCITED, HER PARENTS encouraging, and Minnie put a good face on her decision. She gave an outward appearance of calm, while inside her stomach churned with indecision. She lay awake for the next several nights after she replied to James Thorton's ad, staring up at the ceiling, thoughts of her upcoming so-called adventure invoking a strange combination of terror and excitement. For the first time since the fire, she didn't have a nightmare about it, although her dreams were far from settled or peaceful.

After visiting the local library, the day after Flo showed her the ad and she had impetuously responded to it and given the letter to her friend to mail before she changed her mind, she had engaged in a little research about the far west territory of Colorado. She looked for information about the growing town called the "Denver on the banks of the South Platte," close to the foothills of the Rockies. Actually, it sounded pretty bleak to Minnie. It was an area rife with Indians, hundreds of mining towns, and associated with gambling, nefarious activities, and gunfights.

Still, she had little choice.

A month later, Minnie had received a reply and invitation of marriage by James. Following her letter of acceptance, she had boarded the first of many trains that would take her to Colorado, nearly two thousand miles from everything she had ever known.

The town of Golden was approximately fifteen miles west of Denver, nestled in the foothills of the Rocky Mountains, and known as a place to stock up for supplies and rest before heading further into the mountains or overland to westward destinations in Idaho, Oregon, and California.

The journey took over a week. By the time she arrived at the purportedly new train depot at 40th and Gilpin Street in Denver (or so James informed her in his quickly penned letter along with train fare and enough money left over for incidentals along the way), she felt exhausted, both physically and emotionally. She had been fortunate. Not long ago, the Denver Pacific Railroad had linked to Denver from Kansas City. If it hadn't been for that, she likely would have had to endure yet more stagecoach rides and that jarred her to the very bone.

She stepped out of the train car, her heart thumping in nervous excitement. Her stomach was upset, and she had no doubt that upon very little provocation, she might very well lose the half sandwich she had nibbled on several hours ago. Everything here was different. It smelled different. It looked different. It *felt* different.

In a moment of weakness, she wanted to cry. She wanted to go home, back to Boston. She wanted to go back to the way things used to be. Unfortunately though, that would never be. Her home, her family– it was all gone and never coming back. She prayed to God for strength and courage and tried to hold onto her faith.

She spent several moments around the outdoor platform looking for her future husband, but had no idea what he looked like. She tried to focus on all of the gentlemen standing alone, but there weren't that many, and none of them looked in her direction. Though it was midday, the early summer temperatures were mild. She inhaled deeply, not just relishing the fresh air, but trying to restore her soul with the same breath.

"Are you Miss Minnie Andrews?"

Minnie spun around and found herself staring at a man's chest. She glanced up toward his face and saw a somber looking gentleman eyeing her closely. He was quite handsome, in a rugged kind of way. Deep set eyes, heavy eyebrows, high cheekbones, and a strong jaw. Whisker stubbles darkened his cheeks.

"Y—yes," she replied. "Might you be Mister James Thorton?"

He nodded, but said nothing. He was tall, but to someone of her slight stature, most everyone seemed tall. Heart pounding in her chest, she offered a tentative smile. He didn't return it and her stomach did a flip flop.

"Follow me and we'll head over to the church."

Minnie barely swallowed her gasp of surprise. "But my luggage! Shouldn't I freshen up first–?"

"No need for that," he said, gesturing. "Come along, the preacher's waiting."

Not knowing what else to do, Minnie stared at his back, wondering why he was so impatient. Did he think she would change her mind? Should she? She stood rooted to the spot for several moments, knowing that the second she took that first step to follow him, there was no turning back. Besides, he didn't seem overly friendly, did he?

He turned, saw that she was not following, and frowned. He gestured again, not unkindly. "Come along, Miss Minnie," he urged. "We can get to know each other after the ceremony."

Minnie was torn between running back toward the train, where she would probably get kicked off rather promptly because she had no ticket, and following the strange, taciturn, and quite impatient man, to whatever church he headed toward, to be joined in holy matrimony forever.

Indecision tore at her, and her eyes swept almost wildly over the people standing on the platform. She was alone, with no one to save her from herself or from anyone else. Stealing her nerves, straightening her spine, and taking a deep breath, Minnie took that step, praying that she was not making the biggest mistake of her life.

CHAPTER 4

As the days and weeks passed, Minnie gradually got to know her husband – but it was by bits at a time. He was of a quiet nature, and though he had intimidated her fiercely at first, she realized that he was also gentle, though he had a stubborn streak that would try the patience of a saint. Gradually, he told her about his past as a miner who had come out west to seek his fortune in gold or silver, like thousands before him during the height of the Gold Rush years.

He confided that he had managed to amass a good amount of money from his hard labors, which he then turned around and spent on the purchase of land tracts just outside the growing town of Golden. It was a beautiful area, she had to admit. The cool, crisp mountain air invigorated her senses, even as the early months of summer waned into late summer. As summer ended and fall came to the mountains, Minnie delighted in the gorgeous gold and yellow leaves of the aspen trees, trembling and quaking in the slightest breeze.

In addition to two draft horses, James had also managed to purchase a couple hundred heads of cattle. While he didn't have a proper house built yet– they lived in a small dugout or soddy built into one of the hillsides– he had finished a small barn not long before she had arrived. She stayed well away from the horses, the milk cow, and several barn cats though, even though the second morning after she'd arrived he'd asked her to milk the cow.

"I can't," she said.

"Oh, you've never milked a cow?" he replied. "Don't worry, I'll show you how."

"No, that's not it," she said. "You see James... I'm... I'm afraid of animals."

He'd stared at her for several moments, trying to imagine that.

"Horses?"

She nodded.

"Cows?"

Another nod.

He made a face. "Even the cats?"

"Especially the cats!"

He couldn't understand it and she couldn't either, but there it was. He had shrugged then and continued to deal with all the chores concerning the animals, as he had done before she arrived.

Living in a soddy was certainly a change in lifestyle for Minnie. It was small, with dirt walls and a dirt floor and only a few pieces of furniture. She washed the dishes outside in a bucket and did the same for washing clothes. She even cooked over an open campfire. She asked him what they would do in the wintertime if the house wasn't finished, and he had merely mumbled that he was hoping to have at least part of the house finished by then.

She didn't see how, as only the frame had been completed by the end of summer. One thing she had learned about James, was that he only wanted to do things his way. She had gathered that much just from watching him interact with other people. A man from church had offered to come help him work on the house one day, but James turned him down. Minnie recalled the conversation as if it had happened yesterday.

"Why did you turn down his offer to help?" she asked. "The work might go faster if you didn't have to do it alone."

He shook his head. "Everybody has different ideas and methods to building a house," he had replied, guiding the wagon back to the ranch following church services. "I've helped enough build other people's homes to know that everyone has an opinion on the way things should be done." He shrugged. "I prefer to do it my way and avoid disagreements, even if it will take me longer."

She had thought him foolish for turning down help, especially with fall coming on. Would they have to spend winter in the soddy? She was learning to stiffen her spine, so she brought that up too.

"The soddy has been fine for the last few months, but winter's coming on. I don't know how cold your winters are out here but I can imagine you get a lot of snow and freezing weather like we do in Boston." He said nothing, and she pulled up her courage and forged ahead. She had to learn to speak up for herself. "James, what we do for heat and cooking? With no stove in the soddy and no fireplace or smoke-stack, it wasn't designed for winter use–"

"You let me worry about it," he had commented.

She clamped her mouth shut, biting back a sharp retort. Why did he have to be so doggone stubborn? She had been striving for months to be patient with him. After all, patience was a virtue, wasn't it?

And so, things continued pretty much the way they were. Despite suggestions and offering ideas, he always shook his head and decreed that he knew what he was doing, and that his way was best.

Minnie wasn't happy. She missed her old life. She missed her family. She missed her dreams, even if they were the dreams of a child and not a grown woman; her dreams of a literal knight in shining armor swooping her away to a castle glistening in the sunlight.

She and James had a polite relationship, and she performed her wifely duties as expected, but they had yet to really begin communicating. Is this what God planned for her and the remainder of her life? As far as she was concerned, they were still strangers sharing a space. More often than not, in the evenings after he came in from the fields or from working on the foundation of the house, he sat outside the soddy at a small table, scribbling notes on paper and tinkering with bits and pieces of equipment.

"What are you doing?" she asked him one day.

"Working on something," he said.

"I can see that, James," she replied. "But what *is* it?"

He looked up and saw that she was genuinely interested. He pointed to the gadget he was working on, similar to an oil lamp, but with a metal cage-like device fastened to it. "I'm trying to design a safety lamp so that miners don't have to worry about open flames or candlesticks down in the mines. So many of them are filled with gaseous fumes."

Minnie was impressed. While James didn't do much active mining anymore, it was nice that he continued to think about the safety of his fellow miners.

"It might also be used to test for mine gases," he continued. "You see, the fire boss could use the lamp and determine air safety by watching the flame characteristics." He glanced up at her. "You're more familiar with coal mines back east, but out here, things like methane gas can also be dangerous for the boys."

She studied the contraption more carefully. "How does it work?"

"The basic principle is this wire gauze screen here, see it?" He looked at her and she nodded. "It has a cooling effect on the flame. If there's flammable gas inside the mine on one side, and it passes through the gauze screen, the screen will cool it down so that it won't ignite."

She smiled down at him, truly impressed. "How long have you been working on this... invention?"

He shrugged. "These kind of lamps have been around for a while, but there's no harm in trying to improve them. As soon as I'm finished, I'm going to send a set of my drawings along with a prototype to the US Patent Office." He offered her a lop-sided grin. "You never know, we might just be rich someday."

On an impulse, she leaned over and wrapped her arms around him. It was the first time that she had initiated affectionate contact with him since she arrived.

He stiffened in surprise a moment, and then relaxed. Moments later he was once again focused on his work and Minnie kept herself busy close by, preparing supper.

CHAPTER 5

Winter was fast approaching, but it wasn't the colder weather that troubled Minnie. No, it was something *much* more serious, at least as far as she was concerned, and would probably have an effect on James as well.

In all the months that she and James had been married, she had failed to conceive. She knew how much did James wanted children, and she...well, she knew how much she wanted exactly three boys. Maybe it was not *quite* as realistic as she had imagined in her dreams, but still, with every month that passed she began to grow increasingly concerned that she was... no, she wouldn't even think of the word.

Then, as the winter winds swept the russet, gold, and yellow leaves from the tree limbs, the nights grew colder, and frost covered the ground every morning, Minnie knew that it was time to bring up the topic with James. Thanksgiving was just around the corner, and he planned to go hunting the following week, boasting how he was going to find the fattest turkey he could. She had enough supplies stored in the soddy to prepare a nice meal, although she wasn't sure how she was going to roast a turkey over an open fire. James had told her not to worry, and that he would fashion a spit.

One thing she had learned about James over the past months was that, he was incredibly creative and inventive. He could create or fix anything metal. Still, the thought of cooking a Thanksgiving turkey over an open campfire wasn't exactly conducive to matching her fond memories of Thanksgiving with her family growing up. So much for a sit-down, family get-together, surrounded by friends and loved ones and a gloriously set table brimming with a turkey feast with all the fixings.

A week before Thanksgiving, Minnie finally brought up the topic she's so dreaded to discuss with her husband. Because she didn't have a winter jacket adequate for Colorado's biting chill in the air, she had donned one of her husband's older jackets and stepped outside, nervously approaching him as he sat at his table, once again focusing on a number of papers and diagrams, all held down with small rocks to keep them from blowing in the breeze.

"James, I need to talk to you."

Minnie had learned over time that James, though stubborn, impatient, and often impetuous, always meant well. He was kind, if somewhat introverted, and he didn't talk much, but when she talked, she always received his full attention. He put his pencil down and turned to look up at her.

"I... I think I may need to go to the doctor," she blurted.

He immediately frowned with concern and began to stand up. "You're ill?"

"Not exactly..." she mumbled.

"What is it, Minnie?"

All of a sudden, and quite to her surprise, her eyes filled with tears and she began to weep. "James, we've been married for nearly six months now and I haven't... I haven't been... well, I haven't yet conceived..." She glanced down at her feet in abject embarrassment while the heat of a flush warmed her cheeks. She didn't want to look up into his eyes.

He coughed in what she could only perceive as discomfort, but then he gently patted her shoulder.

"Now, now, Minnie, it will be all right. Maybe we just need to give it more time."

She looked up at him, tears shimmering in her eyes. "I don't think that time is going to help..."

He glanced from her to the house, which had come a little further in the past month. One side was already walled in, and the inside framing had finally been completed. It would be a good and proper house when it was finished, ready for a family.

She knew what he was thinking, gazing between her and the house.

"I know we don't have a lot of money, James," she said. "I wouldn't ask, but I know how important it is for you, and for me–"

"Hush," he said gently.

He stepped forward and wrapped her in his embrace. She felt his strength and appreciated it as she burrowed her head into his shoulder, allowing the tears of despair to flow through her. She wanted children so badly. It was the only dream that she could still hang on to.

"We'll head into town tomorrow, all right, Minnie?"

She looked up into his face, saw the concern in his eyes, and felt a sudden rush of affection for him.

"You're a kind man, James," she said. "Thank you."

The following day, a bundle of nerves, Minnie climbed up onto the wagon bench seat beside James to head into town to visit the doctor. She had only seen the doctor a couple of times at church before. He was a kindly, elderly man with glasses who commonly wore a dark frock coat and hat. He always had a perpetually half-sad, half-compassionate expression on his face. He spoke with a slight Irish lilt, and based on what others said about him and how busy he was, Minnie knew he was a good doctor. He would be able to either set her mind at ease, or deliver some of the worst news of her life.

As they traveled, she noticed storm clouds building to the north. Occasionally she saw streaks of lightning, and she hoped they could get to town and back before the rains came. She didn't think it was cold enough to snow, but this would be her first winter in Colorado and she had no idea what to expect.

The journey into town didn't take long, but neither of them said much along the way. Minnie's mind raced in a thousand different directions and she couldn't tell what James was thinking, as usual. Once they arrived in town, he pulled up in front of the doctor's office.

"Would you like me to come in with you?" he asked, one hand on the wagon break.

She thought about it for a minute, then shook her head. "No, James. I'm sure you have some things you can take care of while I'm in there. I don't expect it will take more than an hour."

He gazed at her for several moments, opened his mouth to say something, and then nodded. "All right, I'll go get some grain for the horses and pick up a few more supplies for the house. You'll be all right?"

While she didn't feel all right at all, she smiled and nodded gravely. "Of course, James." She began to climb down from the wagon, but he gestured her to stay put, quickly jumped down, and hurried around the wagon to her side. He lifted up his arms and she allowed him to help her down. With both feet on the ground, she kept her hands on his shoulders for a few seconds, looking deeply into his eyes.

Then, with an awkward clearing of his throat, he turned and climbed back onto the wagon seat. Releasing the brake, he drove away. She turned toward the door of the doctor's office, took a deep, trembling breath, and reached for the doorknob.

An hour later to the minute, James pulled the wagon up to the doctor's office. Minnie, leaning outside against the side wall away from the street traffic, recognized the sound of his voice as he pulled the horses to a stop. After she heard them climb down from the wagon and step toward the doorway, she called out to him.

"James, I'm over here, on the side," she said, her voice trembling. She knew she looked awful; how her face would be red from crying, her eyes most likely bloodshot, her nose red and running. She had managed to saturate her hanky, but she couldn't stop the tears. She had been standing out here for the last ten minutes or so, her spirits crushed, her dreams once again shattered.

James ventured around the corner of the building, frowning in curiosity. Her eyes met his, and she saw that he knew. At the sight of him, she let loose with a low wailing sound that shook her to the core. He rushed toward her, wrapped his arms around her, and allowed her to sob out her heartache on his shoulder.

"I'm... I'm barren, James," she shuddered. "I'm so sorry... I'm worthless to you–"

"No, no you're not, Minnie." His arms tightened around her. "We'll get through this somehow."

"But you wanted children so badly," she cried, a fresh stream of tears running down her cheeks. "So did I James! I feel... so...."

He gently nudged her away, looking down into her eyes while he grasped her shoulders in his hands. "It's a disappointment, no doubt about that, but if it's God's will–"

"Why is God punishing me?" she cried. Her heart thumped dully in her chest and she began to shiver with emotion. "First, I lost my family, all of them, in the house fire–" she looked up at him. "That's why I responded to your ad... I had nothing... no one–"

"You have *me* now," he said.

"But I can't even give you what you wanted most!" Again sobs shook her tiny frame.

"Come on, Minnie, let's get you home," he said. He wrapped his arm around her and helped her to the wagon.

As if on cue, a huge clap of thunder rumbled overhead. She glanced up, noticing several streaks of lightning brightening the now cloudy day. "Is it safe?" she asked. "I didn't think it was safe to travel in–"

"I've got supplies in the back, Minnie, and I'm going to get you home," he said. "I'm sure we'll be all right."

She didn't argue. She had no energy left to argue or disagree. After all, she knew that despite her concerns, James had made up his mind and she had no desire, at least at the moment, to debate with him. She was devastated beyond despair. *Barren*! How humiliating!

The miles passed and she barely notice them, her mind turned inward, her heart aching, bouts of weeping alternating between blank, blurry stares into the distance surrounding her. She didn't even notice when it started to rain, not until James nestled a little closer to her and wrapped his arm around her shoulder.

"We'll be home soon," he soothed.

He was right, but as they breached the rise and headed down the trail that would take them to the soddy and they're not-quite-half-finished new home, he pulled the animals to a sudden halt.

She glanced up from her hands, tightly folded in her lap, saw his face, white as a ghost, and then turned to look. The wail that escaped her encompassed disbelief, horror, and the epitome of despair.

The frame foundation of their home lay charred and collapsed in a heap, only one half of the new walls remained upright, also charred. Lightning must have struck the house.

Fresh tears flooded her eyes as she stared, gaping at what remained of James' dream house. All of a sudden she couldn't take anymore. She began to cry, sob, and shout all at the same time. She looked up into the gray, ominous, and cloudy sky and barely resisted the urge to shake her fist at it.

"Why God? Why? Haven't I suffered enough? What have I done to disappoint you so?" Her voice rose to a shriek. "What have I done for you to punish me so?"

CHAPTER 6

THE HOUSE WASN'T THE ONLY THING THAT THE OBVIOUSLY QUICK MOVING thunderstorm had damaged. Not only was the house destroyed, or at least severely damaged, but the soddy was damaged as well. One of the front sides had completely collapsed back on itself, falling into the interior. She stared in shock at it, then glanced up at James. He too assessed the damage, his jaw working furiously.

She had just opened her mouth to express her increasing panic when he turned to her and spoke.

"It'll be okay, Minnie," he said. "I can repair the soddy–"

"No," she said. "If one rainstorm can destroy it, it's not stable! I don't want to live in a soddy all winter!"

He stared down at her a moment and then nodded. "This time, I do have to agree. It was a foolish suggestion. I would not want to put you in such danger."

She grabbed his arm. "James, what are we going to do?"

Heaving a heavy sigh, he clucked the horses forward. "I guess we'll have to take up residence in the barn with the animals."

As if things couldn't get any worse, Minnie thought. The barn was small, already crowded with two horses, the milk cow, and a stack of hay in one corner, a small tack room in the back, and only one empty stall. The thought of being in such close proximity to the animals frightened her, but what else could they do? The house was inhabitable, the soddy even more so, and dangerous.

During the following couple of weeks, James had transferred most of their belongings into the barn, salvaging what cooking equipment and supplies he could from the soddy and moving them in as well.

He had made up a bed for themselves, a rather comfortable one at that, she had to admit, in the empty stall. The straw was clean and he had piled it high, covering it with blankets and their pillows. He had placed a small dresser from the soddy against one of the stall walls, and even though the horses snorted at it in suspicion for several days, they gradually got used to it.

The days she spent in the barn watching James with the animals, prompted her to begin to lose some of her fear of them. She was impressed with his gentleness, and the way he softly spoke to them as he brushed the horses every evening and milked the cow every morning, humming softly as she chewed her cud.

One evening as he brushed one of the horses, he gestured her over to his side. At first she shook her head, eyes wide with fear, but he continued to urge her. One slow step at a time, she hesitantly approached him, keeping James's body between herself and that of the huge sorrel mare. To her surprise, he handed her the brush and showed her how to slide her hand between the strap and the wood backing.

"She's gentle, Minnie," he said. "We're going to be spending the winter in here, or at least until I can get that house built, so it's probably a good idea for you to try to get over your fear of the animals."

"But–"

"But nothing," he said.

With the brush now attached to her right hand, he gently clasped her left and placed it on the mare's withers, at the base of the mare's neck. The mare turned her head slightly, glanced at Minnie with wide eyes, and then returned to eating her hay.

"A horse can sense your fear," he explained softly. "Don't be afraid. She's not going to hurt you. She loves to be brushed and stroked."

Minnie's heart pounded, but she kept her hand on the mare. With his hand, James grasped the hand holding the brush and began to stroke it along the mare's back.

"Gentle, but firm strokes," he instructed. "Always go with the grain of the hair." He showed her how to brush the mare, and then slowly released his grip on her hand.

Minnie continued to stroke the brush over the mare's back, and with each stroke, the mare offered a little shiver. After several strokes she neighed softly, then returned once again to eating her hay.

"See? She likes it."

Minnie, astounded by her bravery, smiled up at James. After several minutes of brushing the mare, growing steadily calmer, James removed the brush from her hand. She gazed up at him in question. He urged her closer to the mare's head. "Feel how soft her nose is, right between her nostrils," he encouraged. He demonstrated by running the palm of his hand down the mare's face and then over the softness of her nose.

James waited patiently for her to copy his movement. Minnie wasn't sure she wanted to get so close to the horse's mouth, but once again, stiffening her spine and strengthening her resolve, she placed her palm on the bridge of the mare's face, just below her eyes. The mare stared at her sleepily. Slowly, as James had done, she stroked her hand down the length of her face, and then over her nose, her eyes widening when she felt the soft fuzzy softness there. She giggled.

James offered a low laugh, and the sound warmed her heart.

"Watch this," he said. He pulled a chunk of carrot from his pocket, placed it in his palm, and moved his open palm beneath the horse's mouth.

Minnie watched in amazement as the horse wiggled its fuzzy lips and gently took the carrot from James, crunching on it loudly. Then the mare nuzzled her nose against James' chest.

"She wants another one," he said with a grin, glancing down at Minnie. "Do you want to give it to her?"

At first Minnie wanted to shake her head and say no, but James was looking at her with such a sense of pride and encouragement. She nodded. He dipped his hand into his pocket, and, keeping his fists clenched, placed the carrot bit into her hand.

"When you feed it to her, keep your fingers flat and pressed together. That way she won't mistake your fingers for food."

Minnie glanced up at him in alarm, and he smiled. "Don't worry. No matter what you feed her, carrots, apple bits, whatever, if you give it to her with your fingers flat, she won't bite you on accident."

Minnie clenched the carrot in her palm for several moments, working up her courage. She assumed that the mare smelled the carrot in her hand though, because she turned her attention from James to her. To her surprise, the mare gently nuzzled her chest. The horse weighed probably a thousand pounds, at least to Minnie, but she knew that the mare wasn't trying to hurt her. She just wanted the carrot.

Slowly, Minnie lifted her hand, opened her fingers, and held her palm underneath the mare's mouth. The mare's lips reached for the carrot and wiggled. Minnie giggled as the hairs on the horse's muzzle tickled her hand. To her delight, the horse snatched up the carrot, only leaving behind a thin trail of slobber. She looked down, realized that she still had all her fingers, and grinned up at James in delight, asking, "Do you have another one?"

He laughed and hugged her close, making her feel warm all over. "I think you'd better give a piece to the other one, don't you agree?"

Minnie did, and since then she had learned how to brush down the horses, keeping one hand on the horse's croup or rump as she rounded their backsides to avoid being kicked.

A week later, she had learned how to milk the cow. Watching James and his gentleness with the animals made her feel even more affectionate toward him, and her own bravery at overcoming her fears gave her a huge sense of pride in herself. James was learning patience, and she was gaining self-confidence. Before long, they were sharing conversations deep into the night, lying together on their makeshift straw bed.

The nights grew colder, but to her surprise, the barn was warmer than the soddy, for now. Still, she worried about another fire. They would need to light a fire soon to stay warm at night, wouldn't they?

After broaching that question with James, she had been surprised that once again, he nodded in agreement. An open campfire in the barn filled with straw was definitely not a good idea. One day he told her he needed to go into town, but wouldn't be gone long, and certainly be back by the midday meal.

Minnie busied herself in the barn, brave enough now to muck the stalls and put down a clean bed of hay for the horses and the cow. She even began to talk to them, and though they didn't answer back, she was feeling so much more comfortable. She still grieved over the fact that she couldn't bear children, but she had come a long way since she had first arrived in Colorado.

She had learned that she could deal with most anything now. She wondered what her friend Florence would think if she could see her as she was, living in a barn with animals. She laughed. She decided that the next time James went into town, she would ask him to buy her a tablet of paper and a pencil so that she could write a letter her old friend.

Minnie was preparing a cold lunch when she heard the wagon pull into the yard. She ventured outside of the barn as James pulled the wagon to a halt in front of the small structure, his eyes shining with excitement. He gestured over his shoulder, and she looked at the tall object covered with a tarp that he had strapped down with rope into the back of the wagon.

"What is it?"

He hopped down with a grin. "Close your eyes," he said playfully.

She laughed and did so. The laugh surprised her. It was the first one that she had allowed herself since the devastating news regarding her barren state. She realized that she was healing emotionally, and God was making her stronger.

She did as James asked and closed her eyes. She heard him untying the ropes, and then the sound of the canvas tarp being pulled away.

"Okay, look," he said.

She stared in amazement at the small, cast iron, wood-burning stove sitting so prettily in the back of the wagon. "Oh!" She looked to James, saw his prideful grin, and then quickly gave him a hug.

"It's got space enough for four skillets and a panel on the side on which you can heat an iron or keep food warm. We can put it at the back of the barn near the tack room, and I can cut a hole in the roof for the smokestack. When we get moved into the big house, I'll simply patch the roof."

Tears brimmed in Minnie's eyes. Now she didn't have to worry about freezing to death. The wood-burning stove would be a safe way to heat the barn, as well as cook throughout the winter.

She glanced from the stove, to the ground, and then back at James. "You're going to need help getting that down off the wagon bed you know," she said.

He laughed and nodded, gesturing toward the hill as another rider topped it. "I know, and that's why I asked Joe from the Mercantile to come help."

Minnie was flabbergasted. James had *actually* asked for help from someone rather than insisting on doing it alone. She was both impressed and pleased.

CHAPTER 7

Thanksgiving came and went, and soon winter came in full to the Rockies. Snow fell, then melted, and then, two weeks before Christmas, nearly a foot of snow fell around Golden. Minnie didn't really mind, as she kept nice and warm inside the barn. Actually, she had gotten quite used to the sights, sounds, and smells of the animals, and she even pitched in whenever James needed help. He had also set up what she called his invention table in the corner of the barn near the wood stove, and at night he used a lantern for light. They were careful to keep the straw or any flammable objects well away from the perimeter of the stove or lantern.

During those long nights when they listened to the wind blow outside, James and Minnie talked. She finally told him about the fire that had killed her family and consumed the only home she had ever known. He understood now why she was so concerned about fire, and bent over backwards to make sure that she knew that they were safe in the barn, despite their close quarters to the stove.

James ventured out several times during those weeks to chop enough firewood to last them through the winter. He took the team out in the morning, came back in the afternoon, most times frozen nearly solid, trace chains and hooks pulling one log at a time back to the barn. He chopped the wood and stacked it against the side of the charred wall of the house. He spent hours at this, a backbreaking and laborious chore, but by the middle of December he had a good supply gathered. He covered it with a tarp, but brought in at least two days' supply at a time to store in the barn to ensure that it stayed dry.

One day, a week before Christmas, in the midst of a snowstorm that shows no signs of ending, James turned to Minnie.

"I need to go into town. We're running low on supplies. The weather is only going to get worse, and we need to have enough to get us at least through the New Year."

By this time Minnie had grown incredibly fond of James. "You're not going alone," she had replied.

"Minnie, it's too dangerous–"

"You're *not* going alone," she stated emphatically, stamping her foot on the ground to make her point.

James had learned not to argue with her when she literally put her foot down. He grinned down at her, affection shining in his eyes as she stared up at him, her chin jutting forward, her hands on her hips, as if daring him to refute her.

He didn't. With a sigh of acquiescence, he nodded. "Put on your heaviest dress, get my old coat, and grab the blankets off of our bed," he ordered. As she gathered the necessary belongings, he put the horses into their harness, then ventured outside to hook them up to the wagon. In the brief moment that the doors were open to let the horses out, Minnie felt the bitter cold of the winter wind. For a second she almost changed her mind. Then, she decided against it.

Making sure that only glowing embers remained in the wood stove, she double-checked to make sure that everything was secure and safe in the barn, then followed him outside with the blankets.

James hitched up the horses as quickly as possible, helped her into the wagon, and then climbed up too, sitting close beside her. She relished his heat, quickly wrapping one blanket around their legs, tucking it in underneath their bottoms, and the other she draped around their shoulders. She didn't have gloves, but James did, which was good because he had to keep his hands exposed to hold the reins. She kept her hands wrapped in the blanket she clasped tightly around their shoulders.

Then knitted cap she wore over her head barely kept out the wind. She had wrapped a scarf around her face, leaving only her eyes exposed, and James had tied his hat down onto his head with a neckerchief, covering his ears. Nevertheless, they were nearly frozen solid by the time they reached the outskirts of town. It was fairly deserted and quiet, the way it always was when the snow fell, and the wind whistled in gusts.

James directed the rig over to the Mercantile, and then pulled up alongside it in an effort to block the horses from the wind. He quickly climbed out of the wagon, groaning when his nearly frozen feet made contact with the ground. He hurried around to Minnie's side, clasped her waist, and lifted her down, barely allowing her to put her feet on the ground until she reached the porch in front of the Mercantile. Together they walked inside, relishing the heat that immediately surrounded them.

Allen, the owner of the Mercantile, and his wife Jennifer, both standing behind the counter, looked up in surprise.

"Oh!" Jennifer gasped, rushing toward them.

She grasped Minnie's arm and guided her close to the cast-iron stove in the middle of the room, nearly glowing red with its heat, exclaiming, "You must be frozen solid!"

440

After she had settled Minnie and James into two chairs they pulled up as close to the stove as they dared, she bustled behind the counter and through a door to their living quarters, promising them hot tea in just a few moments.

His hand shaking with cold, James reached into his pocket and silently handed Allen a scrap of paper with a list of supplies they needed.

"You couldn't have picked a worse day to head into town," Allen commented.

Minnie held her breath, wondering how James was going to respond. To her surprise, her husband laughed in full agreement. "Don't I know it! But there's no telling how long the storm will last, or if it'll let up all winter at all. I figured we'd better get in and get our supplies before the roads became impassable."

Minutes later, while Allen prepared boxes to put their supplies in, Jennifer reappeared with two cups of tea for Minnie and James. They made polite conversation for several minutes, and then Minnie saw Jennifer capture her husband's attention. Her husband looked at her, nodded, and then stopped packing the supplies. He cleared his throat and then approached the two.

"James, Minnie," he said. "I know you two have been dealing with a few setbacks, what with the barn and... well other things."

In small towns like Golden, gossip traveled like wildfire. Minnie knew what they were talking about, and although she wasn't sure *how* they had found out, she knew that the kind couple was also speaking about her difficulty to have children. She felt the heat of a blush travel up her shoulders, all the way up her neck, and into her cheeks. Jennifer placed a friendly, comforting hand on her arm.

"We have some news, Minnie, that might interest you," she ventured. She darted a glance at James and nodded. "You too, James."

"What is it?" James asked.

"You know Jacob Shuler and his wife Maria, right?"

James nodded, as did Minnie. They had met the couple a time or two at church services before the weather had gotten too cold. The first time they'd met was just after Minnie had learned she was barren. She couldn't help but be jealous when she had seen Maria, obviously pregnant, at church.

"You haven't been in town for a while, so I don't think you've heard," Jennifer began.

"Heard what?" James asked, glancing at her over his cup of tea as he took a welcome sip.

"Maria gave birth several weeks ago—"

Minnie gasped, nearly choking on the tea she had just swallowed. How could God be so cruel? To leave her barren and yet grace Maria with the privilege of bearing children?

"She had triplets," Allen continued, his voice somber. "Boys"

Minnie's heart clenched in pain. Three boys? All at once? Tears brimmed in her eyes. She felt ashamed by the burst of envy that surged through her, but *why* was Jennifer telling her this? She knew it wasn't to be cruel.

"It's good to hear," James began graciously. "Jacob should be right proud–"

Allen shook his head. "Marie died in childbirth," he said somberly.

Minnie gasped, shame surging through her again. Oh Lord. Poor Marie. Poor Jacob! Those poor babies!

"The thing is, Jacob can't deal with it. He can hardly bear to look at the babies," Jennifer said, her voice cracking with emotion. "Oh, it's not like he blames them for Marie's death, but he can't separate one from the other. He's heartbroken." She shook her head sadly. "He hired a wet nurse, but..."

Minnie's eyes widened. "What are you saying, Jennifer?"

Allen explained. "Jacob is planning on taking the babies to Denver and placing them in an orphanage."

Minnie gasped.

"He's going to go back home to North Carolina afterwards."

"He's going to leave his babies behind?" Minnie asked, her voice filled with dismay.

Allen nodded. "He doesn't know how to take care of one baby, let alone three. Plus, with his work as a blacksmith, he wouldn't be able to watch over them well enough."

Again Jennifer placed her hand on Minnie's arm. "Minnie, I know that you and James want children... and I know it's not like having your own, but would you... would you consider...?"

Minnie realized what Jennifer was trying to ask her. Her hand trembled and the tea cup clattered against its saucer. She looked at James. Goosebumps appeared on her flesh, but they weren't caused by the cold.

She and James stared at each other for several moments, and she saw the change of expression that came over her husband's face. He gave her a smile, one filled with love, affection, and faith.

"It's up to you, Minnie," he said.

Minnie glanced from Jennifer to Allen, then again to James, and then back to Jennifer. Tears flooded her eyes and she began to weep with happiness. "We can adopt them?" she asked in disbelief. "We can adopt all three babies, all three boys?"

Jennifer's eyes also filled with tears as she gently took the tea cup from Minnie's hands and placed it on the floor. Then, she wrapped her arms around Minnie's trembling shoulders.

"They could never ask for better parents," she said, her voice choked. "I do hope you forgive the forwardness, but when we found out about the babies, Doc told us... well, he told us..."

"It's all right," Minnie assured her, leaning back to look at her. Then she looked at James. The smile that brightened his features warmed her heart to the depths of her soul. God *had* answered her prayers! He certainly did work in mysterious ways. He had taken the long way around, but then she remembered that everything happened according to God's plans, and in His own good time.

She began to laugh and cry all at once, so excited she didn't know what to do with herself. James gazed at her, love and adoration shining in his eyes. They were going to be a family!

He laughed. "It's going to be cramped quarters in the barn for a while, but if you don't mind, I don't mind," he said.

She shook her head, tears of joy spilling over her cheeks. "I don't mind, James," she said. "God has blessed us. We're going to be a *family!*"

James placed his own teacup on the floor and opened his arms to Minnie. She leaned into them, not caring that Jennifer and Allen stared at them with silly grins on their faces.

Her dreams *had* come true. Maybe not exactly the way she had envisioned them, but they had come true nevertheless.

EPILOGUE

THE WINTER WAS A LONG AND COLD ONE, BUT MINNIE, JAMES, AND THE THREE boys, John, Jacob, and Joseph, made do in the barn. It was cozy, warm, and wonderful. Jennifer had supplied Minnie with several months' worth of milk powder, and she and James kept busy taking turns feeding the babies, changing them, washing their diapers, and spoiling them rotten with kisses, hugs, and cuddles. All five of them slept in the straw bed, and Minnie couldn't have been happier.

As winter passed and the snowstorms eased, James kept himself busy working on rebuilding the house during breaks in the weather. One day, Minnie, cradling two boys in her arms while James held the third, stood outside, enjoying one of the warmer days since the onset of winter. The children were bundled up and cooing happily when the sound of wagons pulled their loving gazes from their babies and toward the rise.

Minnie's eyes filled with tears when she saw the four wagons approaching, loaded to the brim with lumber and no less than ten men ready to help James build his house. He didn't complain one bit, but shook each of their hands with a nod of gratitude and a look of wonder in his eyes. Not long after, several buggies also arrived, filled with women bearing food and blankets, curtains, and floor rugs that would be placed in the house as soon as a roof was in place.

Minnie stood beside her husband, the three babies in their arms, watching as the town pulled together to help one of their own, as James had so often done for the others. As they stood watching and listening to the joking and laughter erupting around them, followed soon by the cacophony of hammers and saws, Allen approached with a wide grin.

"I see you've got your hands full," he said, nodding at the babies.

444

James laughed. "Wouldn't have it any other way."

"I've got a letter for you, James," Allen said, pulling it from his coat pocket. "Remember that letter you sent off to the United States patent office last fall?"

Minnie glanced at her husband in surprise. His invention.

She saw him nod, and Allen wiggled the envelope in front of him. "You got a reply."

James glanced between Minnie and Allen. Minnie already had her hands full with two of the babies, so James abruptly placed Jacob in Allen's hands and reached for the envelope. Allen laughed while James tore it open, quickly scanned the contents, and then whooped.

The babies, startled by the noise he made, began to cry, but James was laughing now, dancing a small jig.

"It's patented!" he announced to Minnie. "They approved my patent!"

"My husband, the inventor," Minnie smiled, shaking her head.

He turned to her and wrapped her and the two boys she held in his gentle embrace. "This is only the beginning, Minnie," he whispered into her ear. "I'm not only going to make you the happiest woman on earth, but, with God's will, I'll make you rich!"

She smiled up at him. "I don't care about the rich part," she told him, her heart brimming with love for him. "As far as I'm concerned, I'm already the richest woman in the world."

৩৩৩

THANK YOU SO MUCH FOR READING MY BOOK. I SINCERELY HOPE YOU ENJOYED EVERY bit reading it. I had fun creating it and will surely create more.

Your positive reviews are very helpful to other reader, it only takes a few moments. They can be left at Amazon.

www.amazon.com/Katie-Wyatt/e/B011IN7AF0

৩৩৩

WANT FREE BOOKS EVERY WEEK? WHO DOESN'T!

BECOME A PREFERRED READER AND WE'LL NOT ONLY SEND YOU FREE READS, BUT you'll also receive updates about new releases.

So you'll be among the first to dive into our latest new books, full of adventure, heartwarming romances, and characters so real they jump off the page.

It's absolutely free and you don't need to do anything at all to qualify except go to.

PREFERRED READ FREE READS

http:/katieWyattBooks.com/readersgroup

ABOUT THE AUTHOR

KATIE WYATT IS 25% AMERICAN SIOUX INDIAN. BORN AND RAISED IN Arizona, she has traveled and camped extensively through California, Arizona, Nevada, Mexico, and New Mexico. Looking at the incredible night sky and the giant Saguaro cacti, she has dreamed of what it would be like to live in the early pioneer times.

Spending time with a relative of the great Wyatt Earp, also named Wyatt Earp, Katie was mesmerized and inspired by the stories he told of bygone times. This historical interest in the old West became the inspiration for her Western romance novels.

Her books are a mixture of actual historical facts and events mixed with action and humor, challenges and adventures. The characters in Katie's clean romance novels draw from her own experiences and are so real that they almost jump off the pages. You feel like you're walking beside them through all the ups and downs of their lives. As the stories unfold, you'll find yourself both laughing and crying. The endings will never fail to leave you feeling warm inside.

OKLAHOMA DESTINIES

Mail Order Bride Western Romance

RoyceCardiff

Publishing House

WHOLESOME INSPIRATIONAL ROMANCE

Dear Reader,

It is our utmost pleasure and privilege to bring these wonderful stories to you. I am so very proud of our amazing team of writers and the delight they continually bring us all with their beautiful clean and wholesome tales of, faith, courage, and love.

What is a book's lone purpose if not to be read and enjoyed? Therefore, you, dear reader, are the key to fulfilling that purpose and unlocking the treasures that lie within the pages of this book.

৩১৩

NEWSLETTER SIGN UP PREFERRED READ

https://ellenanderson.gr8.com/

৩১৩

THANK YOU FOR CHOOSING A INSPIRATIONAL READS BY ROYCE CARDIFF PUBLISHING HOUSE.

Welcome and Enjoy!

A PERSONAL WORD FROM AUTHORS

WE WANT TO THANK YOU FOR ALL YOUR CONTINUED SUPPORT FOR ALL OF OUR bestselling series. We wouldn't be where we are now without all your help. We can't thank you enough!

We had a lot of fun writing this series about adventures, hardships, hopes, loves, and perseverance. Writing this Historical Western Romance was a magical time.

We sure hope you enjoy reading it!

Ellen and Katie

PROLOGUE

ROSE

1892

"Stop fightin' against me," Rose said, frustration thick in her voice as she tended to the gunshot wound in her brother Alan's calf. "If I don't keep this clean, then it's only gettin' worse, Alan. Is that what you want?"

He grunted at her, staring out the window of their small Oklahoma home as he moped about his confinement. Rose struggled to have patience with her brother, considering that it was his own fault that he was hurt. Alan had always struggled with getting involved with the wrong people, and the last few months had been no different. As the oldest brother in the Dunn family, Rose expected Alan to be the kind of good influence that her father, Thomas Dunn, had been, but Alan had never had their father's character or their mother's work ethic. Benjamin and Matthew, both younger than Alan and Rose, often followed in Alan's footsteps, and the three of them caused so much trouble in Potomac and the surrounding area that it brought Rose to shame.

Still, she tried to be there for her brothers, keeping them fed, clothed, and tended to. Even if it did ruin her reputation in their town.

"Ouch!" Alan shouted, jerking away from Rose as she dabbed at the tender red area surrounding the bullet wound. "What's wrong with ya, girl? Don't ya know that's hurtin'?"

Rose gritted her teeth, pulling his leg back toward her and returning to her task. "Of course I know that, Alan. But this is the only way to keep you from gettin' sick, so be still while I get ya out of another scrape."

The front door slammed open, and Benjamin stalked in, filthy and reeking of sweat. That wasn't so unusual, given the summer heat in Oklahoma and the fact that, between the four of them, they did attempt to run their father's farm as best they could. But Rose knew that Benjamin hadn't been working, and she dreaded finding out what it was he'd been up to instead.

"Jack Smithson has it comin' to him," Benjamin said, ignoring Rose and speaking directly to Alan. "He just jumped me on the way home from town, sayin' we owe him money."

"We're not givin' him a penny," Alan said, pulling away from Rose again as he tried to sit up and talk to Benjamin. "He can't prove that deal ever went down, so it's his loss."

Rose poured disinfectant liquid into Alan's wound, making him shout out in pain, and she didn't feel badly about it. "Neither of you are actin' the way Ma and Pa would want you to," she snapped at them. "You're better than this life you're getting into, swindlin' and drinkin' and gamblin'. All three of you are downright shameful, and ya know it."

Alan pulled down his pant leg and stood up, hobbling away from her as he glared. "Don't get involved in what you don't understand, Rose. Who's payin' the bills around here? You or us?"

"I'd rather be in the poorhouse than an outlaw," Rose said, crossing her arms over her chest. "And I wasn't done with your leg."

"You are now," Alan snapped at her. "We have business to see to."

"Leave Jack Smithson out of it," Rose pleaded with him, following as he and Benjamin headed toward the front door. "And if you owe him money, pay it. We can still turn everythin' around, Alan. I know we can."

"That's funny, comin' from you. Isn't it all this dirty money I've made that paid you to learn to read and write? Ungrateful, that's what you are." Alan walked out the front door, making his way slowly down the porch stairs to the barren Oklahoma ground. As Rose stood there, near tears, Benjamin turned to her, sighing a bit. Though Benjamin was no angel, he felt worse for Rose than either of her brothers. Dirty though he was, he reached a hand out and squeezed her shoulder.

"Listen, let Alan do what he thinks is best, Rose. When Ma and Pa died, he had to take this family on himself, and it ain't easy supportin' four of us out here. You know that."

"I know that resortin' to some of the things he does isn't the answer," Rose said quietly. "Benjamin, you know what Pa would say."

"Pa isn't here," Benjamin told her, shaking his head. "Don't wait up."

Then he, too, was gone, leaving Rose by herself in their family's house, now rundown and falling apart. She felt close to tears, which wasn't unusual in her situation, but she was tired of crying over the family that was falling apart before her eyes. Her ma and pa had been good, godly people who had run an honest, though never terribly profitable, farm, but when they had died five years ago and Alan had taken over, everything had gotten so out of control that Rose didn't know how they could ever fix it.

She sat down at the kitchen table, her head dropping into her hands as the tears slid down her cheeks, unbidden. There was only one thing to do, and that was to pray. She whispered a verse her mother had been fond of, Psalm 84:11-12:

For the Lord God is a sun and shield; The Lord gives grace and glory; No good thing does He withhold from those who walk uprightly. O Lord of hosts, How blessed is the man who trusts in You!

Feeling comforted, Rose added,

Dear Lord, please help us. I know I've asked you this before and I trust that you will, in your time. But I don't know what to do anymore and I need help. Please show me what it is you want from and for me, because I'm lost. I don't know how to bring them back to you, Lord, but I'm here, waiting patiently and trusting despite it all.

CHAPTER 1

GEORGE

Six Weeks Later

POTOMAC, OKLAHOMA, WAS A SMALL, NONDESCRIPT TOWN THAT NOBODY WOULD ever notice if they were passing by on the road, which made it a perfect place for George Newcomb to stop and make his bed for a few days. The town inn had an opening, and he took a room that contained a bed with a simple coverlet, a chair, and a trunk for storage. There was nothing else provided, but he didn't need more than that. He was only traveling with the bag on his back, and even that was mostly empty.

George set his things in the trunk and washed up, staring out the window at the small, largely empty main street, and sighed. The past months had turned his life upside down. He had gone from being one of the leaders of the Doolin Gang, a band of outlaws famous for their wild and wicked ways, to a lone refugee with a total change of heart. And it had all happened overnight.

In his early thirties, George was hardly a young whippersnapper, and he had spent the majority of his adult years deeply embedded in the outlaw life. He was no stranger to a saloon or a prison cell, and he had stolen his fair share of money, horses, and whatever else someone had that he wanted.

And then, one day, the Doolin Gang had stopped a stagecoach, intending to rob the passengers of everything they owned, and George had seen her.

She was an older woman, bent and shriveled, with scared eyes and a lined face. The resemblance to his memories of his grandmother was so shocking that it took his breath away, freezing him in that moment so that his gang members moved around him, taking control of the horses and holding the passengers at gunpoint as George stared at her.

It wasn't his grandmother, and he knew that. She had passed many years ago, but it threw him back so completely into the days of his youth that it flipped some switch in him that had been turned off for years. It was the switch linked to his humanity, and he knew that he had to change. In that moment, he had used the element of surprise to take the stagecoach back from the Doolin brothers and had personally ridden all the passengers to safety in a nearby town, leaving his gang members in the dust.

He hadn't regretted it for a moment, and the next few days had been spent on his knees in prayer, asking for forgiveness for all of the wrong he had done and the people who he had hurt.

But if a fresh start was what he had hoped for, the Doolin gang had other ideas. They wanted revenge on him for betraying them, and they were not a group to be messed with. George had spent months on the run now, trying to stay one step ahead of the men who he had once called his family. Potomac was as good a place to hide as any, and when his time was up here, he would move on again.

This was his life now, and he had created it for himself.

George walked downstairs and left the inn, interested in exploring the few shops that made up Main Street. He nodded politely to people, tipping his hat at them as he passed by and musing about what their reaction would be if they suddenly learned who he had been just six months earlier.

"You must be new 'round here."

George turned toward the voice addressing him, seeing a tall, rugged-looking man in a wide-brimmed hat, a tight pair of pants, and a shirt that couldn't hide the fact that he was broad and muscled. He looked like he had grown up in the West, fighting tooth and nail for everything he had, and that was something George could relate to.

"I am," George confirmed. "My name is George Newcomb." He stuck his hand out to shake the stranger's.

"Alan Dunn," the man replied, shaking George's hand firmly. "What's your business in the area?"

"Just passin' through," George said, keeping it vague. "I'm in a bit of a transition, movin' from one line of work to another. I'm hopin' to take up farmin', actually. Seems like good, honest work."

Alan nodded, pursing his lips. "Well, I'll be. Where ya stayin'?"

There were a lot of questions coming at him, and George took a minute to assess the situation. He had only just arrived in town, so it was unlikely that anyone would be suspicious of him. Since leaving the Doolin Gang, he had taken his mother's maiden name as his own last name to try to avoid his past, so Alan would hardly recognize him as an outlaw.

Most likely, the man was just friendly. People were in these parts, as long as they didn't know who you really were.

"I'm staying at the inn," George said, gesturing behind him. "It seems nice enough."

"No, that place is a dump," Alan told him, shaking his head as he shoved his hands into his pockets. "And between you and me, the restaurant here isn't worth the few pennies you'll pay for the slop. But don't tell Fannie Mae I said so or she'll have my hide."

George smiled slightly. "Well, I won't say anythin' to Fannie Mae, but I'm afraid I'll be enjoyin' quite a bit of her slop."

"Why don't you have dinner with me and my brothers?" Alan asked. "My farm is just about a mile from here, and we always have hot food ready. My sister Rose sees to that. We'd be glad to welcome ya to Potomac, real proper."

Again, George felt suspicious about this man's friendliness, but he chalked it up to too many years living as an outlaw. Nobody welcomed you into their home when you were part of that lifestyle, but he wasn't anymore, and there was no reason to think that what Alan was offering was anything less than common Christian charity. If George had a nice farm to welcome strangers to, he would do it.

"That's a very kind offer," George said. "I just may take you up on it."

Alan smiled, clapping George's shoulder firmly. "It's done, then. Come on. I'm headed home now."

George started to follow Alan, then realized that the man was limping. He glanced down at the ground, but Alan's legs were covered by the thick material of his pants, offering no hint at what the problem might be.

But Alan caught him looking and patted his thigh. "Oh, got kicked by a horse the other day. Those creatures will get ya if yer not careful."

George smiled, nodding. "That they will."

As they walked back in the direction of Alan's home, George smiled to himself. It was always nice to see how people could connect to each other and help each other out without any kind of ulterior motive. Ever since he had decided to turn his life around, he had witnessed that again and again, and it made him feel good about the state of the world. There were a lot of good people out there.

CHAPTER 2

ROSE

Her kitchen was stuffy, the Oklahoma heat oppressive as she stirred a large pot of potato and cabbage stew with a few chunks of meat thrown in for flavor. Along with her stew, they would have homemade bread and fresh carrots and turnips, grown from her garden. It wasn't the most glamorous of dinners, but it was the best that she could do with the limited funds that their family had. Trying to feed three adult men who worked up appetites stirring up trouble in the town was no easy feat, but she somehow managed to do it every night—at least on the nights they were home.

As Rose began to set the plates on the table, the front door opened and she heard Alan's voice in the distance. Rose winced, hating that she dreaded hearing her older brother walk into the house, but unable to escape the fact that she did. What made her curious, though, was the strange voice that answered Alan. She hadn't been expecting company, but it seemed that company had arrived anyway.

If it was one of Alan's outlaw friends, she was going to have to put her foot down, somehow.

Rose wiped her hands off on a towel and headed out toward Alan's voice, ready for confrontation, but the man she saw standing there beside Alan was every bit the polished gentleman she hadn't been expecting.

"Hello," Rose said politely, glancing at Alan, who frowned at her. "I'm Rose, Alan's sister."

The man took his hat off, tipping it to her as he smiled. "Nice to meet you, Rose. My name is George, and your brother has kindly invited me to dinner. I sure do hope I'm not imposin' on ya."

Rose immediately took to the man, his smile warm and sweet, and his polite manners such a stark contrast to Alan's that it almost bowled her over. "Not at all," Rose assured him. "I'll set another plate."

"Where are Benjamin and Nathaniel?" Alan demanded, looking up at the staircase. "I want them down here to meet George."

"I think Nathaniel is out on the land," Rose offered. "I'm not sure about Benjamin."

Nathaniel, at least, did try to pay some attention to the farm they lived on, though he was as caught up in the outlaw lifestyle as Rose's other brothers. Out of the three of them, he was the kindest to her, maintaining some affection for his older sister.

Briefly, Rose wondered why George was connected to Alan, but then she was distracted from her musing by the smell of bread burning, and she hurried back to the kitchen, yanking the bread away from the flame as quickly as she could. The bottom was singed, but the rest of the bread was salvageable, and she set it on the counter, reaching for a knife that she could scrape the bottom with.

Behind her, George cleared his throat. "Uh, hello again."

Rose jumped, turning around quickly, the knife still in hand. "Oh! You startled me."

"Very sorry," George said, holding up his hands and stepping back. "Alan told me to come in here while he rounded up your brothers. Am I intrudin'?"

"Not at all," she assured him, feeling badly for reacting in such a jumpy way. "Sit down, please. Tell me more about yourself. How do you know Alan?"

"I don't," George admitted, taking a seat at the table and automatically beginning to set out the utensils she had put beside the plates. "We met out on the street. He was kind enough to welcome me to town with an invitation to dinner. We've only known each other for a few minutes, really."

That brought Rose both comfort and concern. It was nice to know that George wasn't one of Alan's outlaw friends, although she had already guessed that just based on his appearance. But she also knew that it wasn't like Alan to invite someone into their home for now reason. Immediately, she began to worry that George was somehow a target, and she wasn't going to let that happen to someone as nice as George seemed to be.

"Well, I'm glad you're here," Rose said, finishing with the bread, slicing it, and placing it on a plate on the table. "I'm sure they'll be in shortly. Do you know anyone in town?"

"Not a soul."

"What brings you here?"

Something flickered over his face, and Rose immediately worried that she was asking too many questions. But he didn't rebuke her. He didn't really answer her either, though.

"I'm just passin' through, hangin' about for a few days. I'm lookin' for my next place to settle down, you could say."

Rose nodded, growing more and more curious about the good-looking, well-mannered, kind man, but not wanting to push him too far with questions. She was far too used to Alan snapping at her to consider risking George doing the same thing.

Just as she was thinking of him, Alan came into the room, tossing his pack down on the floor and immediately going over to the simmering pot of stew and lifting a ladle of it out, sniffing. "Hope you made somethin' good for our guest, Rosie." He gave her a wide smile, but there was something wolfish about his eyes that made Rose unsettled again.

She just couldn't shake the idea that Alan had some ulterior motive for George, and it scared her to think what it might be.

CHAPTER 3

GEORGE

DINNER WITH THE DUNNS WAS PLEASANT ENOUGH, BUT THAT WAS MOSTLY down to Alan's sweet sister, Rose, who made sure to keep up a steady stream of conversation, though she had little help from her brothers. Alan, who had been quite charming when George had first met him, soon began to show a more sullen side to him that George found far less appealing.

But spending time with Rose was worth putting up with the less-than-ideal company of her brothers. Rose was a beautiful woman, with warm brown eyes, sandy-blonde hair, and an upturned nose that crinkled easily when she smiled. There was no doubt that, physically, she was an attractive person, but it was more than that—her sweet spirit was evident in everything she said. And George got the distinct impression that, for whatever reason, she had not had an easy life. Yet she maintained a far better disposition than any of her brothers.

They talked all through dinner, and then afterward, George helped Rose wash up. Alan lingered for a moment, but soon tired of the drudgery of kitchen work. He told George to join him in the living room for a cigar when he was done, then disappeared, leaving George and Rose alone again.

Rose gave him a small smile, which he returned as he helped to stack the dirty dishes into the waiting tub of hot water.

"It was a nice dinner," he told her. "Thank you."

"Oh, it was my pleasure."

"You seem to have things well under control around here," he observed. "You must have been runnin' this house for a while."

Rose laughed slightly. "I wouldn't say that I have things under control, no."

"No?"

She looked like she might have felt she'd said too much, though she'd hardly said anything at all. "Oh, I don't know what I'm sayin'. Where are you stayin'? Up at the inn?"

"That's right," he said, nodding as he picked up a cloth to wipe the dishes dry after she washed them. "It's a nice enough place, I reckon."

"All alone?"

"That's how I do things."

She glanced over at him, seeming shy. "No ... wife, then? Or children? I just ... I mean, you seem very familiar with ..." Rose gestured to the way he was wiping down the plate in his hand.

Chuckling, George set the clean, dry plate aside. "Oh, that's nothin'. My mama learned me right, I guess. No wife and no children. I've never had the time, though I might be interested someday if I found someone who would have me."

To George's utter delight, Rose's cheeks flushed a bright red and she looked down, not meeting his eyes. It seemed, if he was reading her right, that she was every bit as interested in him as he was in her, and that was terribly intriguing.

It wasn't as though he could do anything about that fact. Rose was a woman of good standing, and he would never take advantage of her or risk her reputation with even a hint of improper behavior. And he could hardly marry the woman, given the fact that he was only just coming out of the outlaw life, had almost nothing to his name, and no home to offer a woman. She could do far better than that, and he would want her to, even though he barely knew her at all.

But it was still nice, he thought, to realize that sweet, pretty Rose found him appealing.

"You must be betrothed," he said, digging for information. He didn't really think that she was, given how she was acting with him, but he wanted to learn more about her.

"Oh no," she said quickly, shaking her head. "Nothin' like that at all. I've never even had a beau."

"You can't be serious."

"No, but I haven't," she insisted earnestly. "People are downright afraid of my brothers, I think."

Again, she looked as though she had said too much and George wondered what she might be hiding about her brothers.

"Rose ..."

He was going to ask her if she was all right or if there was anything she wanted to tell him, but Alan walked back in, clearly growing impatient.

"You comin' out here, George? Or are you gonna fritter the night away with womenfolk? We got a cigar out here waitin' on ya."

George found that he didn't particularly care for the way that Alan spoke to or about his sister. Even when he had lived as an outlaw, he'd always had respect for women and tried to treat them well, even when their station or occupation in life didn't warrant it, according to society's standards.

But Rose seemed used to Alan's tone, and she didn't react, keeping herself busy amongst the dishes as they finished them up.

George sighed, figuring that he should show some respect to the man who had invited him into his home and that it would soon be inappropriate if he continued to linger behind with Rose. "Yes, of course. I'll be right in."

Alan nodded, then disappeared again, and George set down his last plate, giving Rose a reluctant glance. "Well, I suppose I should leave you to yourself, then."

"I suppose so," she murmured, looking up into his eyes.

In that moment, he wished away his whole past with the Doolin Gang. He wished that he'd never joined them, that he wasn't on the run from them, and that he had something that he could offer sweet, sweet Rose as she stood there, looking up at him so openly that he could see all the hope and vulnerability in her eyes. She looked like a woman who desperately wanted to be taken away from this place, and he would gladly do it if he was good enough to marry her.

But he wasn't, and so their connection, strong though it was, would have to end here, in this kitchen.

He smiled at her and dared to briefly touch her arm. "Good night, Rose."

CHAPTER 4

ROSE

After George left that first night he visited, Rose worried that she would never see him again. It was clear to her that he had not taken to her brothers, and she respected him all the more for it. And while he had been kind to her, he did not seem interested in continuing to call on her. He had made it clear that he was only in town for a short while.

But now it had been five days since he'd first visited, and Alan had come home every day talking about meeting George in town or going hunting with George or introducing George to someone. Rose wanted to ask him to bring George back around if they were going to be such fast friends, but she didn't want Alan to see that she was interested in George in the way a woman was sometimes interested in a man. Not only would he mock her relentlessly; he would make sure she never saw George again.

Besides that, there was little time to talk to Alan. Now that his leg was getting better all the time, he was out and about, often not coming home until the late hours of the night or early hours of the morning. Rose tried to carry on, running as much of the suffering farm as she could on her own, but it was a difficult burden to bear, and she was almost always tired.

It was for that reason that she was sitting out on the porch in the afternoon sun, taking a few minutes to rest and doze off as she swung back and forth. Her eyes closed and her face turned upward toward the sun, she didn't notice George approaching until he was on the porch with her.

"Miss Burns. How nice to see you again. I'm interruptin' yer nap, though."

Her eyes flew open, and Rose was on her feet in an instant. "Oh! George!"

He chuckled, clearly glad that she was glad to see him. "Hello again. I didn't mean to startle you."

468

"No, not at all," she assured him, though her heart was beating a mile a minute in her chest as she smoothed down her skirts. "What—er, what brings you by?"

"I was hoping to see you, actually." He seemed to admit it as though he might be committing a sin. "I enjoyed our chat the other night, and I was hopin' that you would fancy a walk with me. I don't suppose any of your brothers are around to grant me permission?"

"Oh no ... they're not," Rose said, trying not to let her excitement show in her voice. "But that's all right. I would love to walk with you."

He stepped back, offering her his arm, and she accepted it, her free hand lifting to straighten her hair. She did hope that she looked halfway presentable, and not as though she had been lazily napping in the sun—though she had been doing exactly that.

They walked down the path in front of the house, quiet at first until they got well on their way. Rose kept her hand tucked in the curve of his arm, her stomach doing flip-flops from even that light contact. Though she had been thinking of him often, she had forgotten how very handsome he was.

"How have you been enjoyin' yer stay in town?" she asked, searching for anything to say.

"It's been nice," he said, looking down at her. "I've stayed longer than I meant to, actually."

"Oh?"

"Yes, your brothers have been keepin' me quite busy, I must confess." He smiled at her. "Alan is a hard man to say no to."

Rose nodded. "He is that. But I hope he hasn't been ... pressurin' you?"

"Not at all," George said. "We've gone huntin', and fishin', and he's shown me around the area. It's as though he has all the free time in the world, and if he's not available, then Benjamin or Nathaniel are knockin' at my door. I'm afraid that those two have different ways than I do, though."

"How do you mean?" Rose asked, wondering again why her brothers were taking such an intense interest in George.

"Well ..." George seemed to hesitate, choosing his words carefully. "They are still young enough to give in to temptations I've put behind me. I'll put it that way, given the genteel company I'm keepin'."

Rose flushed, knowing exactly what he meant. Her brothers, when they weren't causing trouble by taking money from saloon owners or stealing horses, were often gambling, drinking, or hanging about with women whose reputations left much to be desired. She was humiliated that George was seeing that side of her brothers, and instinctively, she pulled her hand from his arm, stopping her progress along the path.

"What's wrong?" George asked, stopping beside her, his eyes searching hers.

"I ..." she shook her head, her throat working hard to keep her emotions in check.

Reaching out, George tipped her chin up with one finger, still gazing at her. "Yer not happy, Rose. I can tell."

Tears filled her eyes and she pulled away, looking anywhere but him. But she couldn't respond. She couldn't deny what he'd said.

"I know yer not," George murmured. "That's why I came back to see you. See, yer much too sweet for the likes of me, but yer also too sweet to be stuck here with those three if that's not what you want. They can be rough men, can't they, Rose?"

She looked up at him again, frowning. "What do you mean too sweet for you?"

"Oh, Rose." He took her hands in his, holding them gently. "Just trust me on that one. But that doesn't mean I can't help you. Something in me just wants to help you, sweet one."

His words were so tender, and yet they were also filled with regret that he could never be with her, which Rose was realizing, with no small amount of surprise, she wanted very much. Perhaps it was just that she wanted to be rescued from the situation she was in, but she didn't think so. From the moment she had laid eyes on George, something in her had changed. She was drawn to him, and yet it seemed she would never have him the way that she wanted to.

It was enough to finally break a girl's heart.

CHAPTER 5

GEORGE

ROSE WAS QUIET AS THEY MADE THEIR WAY BACK TO HER HOUSE. SOMETHING HE had said had upset her, and he hoped he wasn't too presumptuous if he thought that it might be the prospect of not being with him that had made her so sad. It would be a blessing and a curse if that were true. He never wanted her to be sad, and yet he would never want her to not want him either.

He wished desperately for a way that he could be with her, but Rose had had so much unhappiness in her young life, and he couldn't promise her the kind of stability and security that she deserved.

There were so many things he wanted to say to her, but he couldn't seem to form the right words to express any of this thoughts or feelings. He could only walk beside her, enjoying a few sweet moments of her presence before he had to turn her back over to her brothers. He had gotten the confirmation he'd wanted—she wasn't happy. And he would do something about it. As soon as he figured out what it was.

George was so lost in the thought that he almost didn't see Alan, glancing up at the last minute to find his newfound friend standing by the entrance to their land. Lifting a hand in greeting, George offered a brief smile. He didn't like the way Alan treated Rose or the things that the man was doing about town. But he also didn't judge him too harshly. There had been a time, and not that long ago, that George had been a similar kind of person, and just because he had managed to find his way out of it didn't mean that he looked down on other people who were still caught up in the outlaw lifestyle.

All George cared about was that it was hurting Rose.

"Rose, get inside," Alan said, his voice sharp, surprising George.

"Hey," George interjected, stopping Rose as she hurried to do as her brother had said. "What do you mean, speakin' to her that way?"

Alan's eyes narrowed. "I mean that she's my sister, and I call the shots around here. I didn't introduce you to her so you could go courtin' her."

"I'm not courtin' her," George retorted, still blocking Rose's path. "We just went for a walk. And I have to say, man to man, Alan, I don't think I like the way you speak to her. Not a bit."

"Well, thank you for yer input," Alan said, ice in his tone. "Now let my sister in the house, or I'll have to take it up with you very personally."

It was a clear threat, and for the first time George wondered just what kind of man Alan was. There were two different kinds of outlaws—those who caused trouble, had too much fun, and relegated themselves to petty sorts of crimes. Then there were those who had a mean streak in them that led to violence and power hoarding. He had thought Alan to be the first, but the look in his eyes suddenly suggested otherwise.

"It's all right," Rose said softly, touching his arm. "You'd best go. I'm fine here."

"You don't have to be spoken to that way," George said, turning toward her so he could speak quietly, just to her. "Tell me to step in for you, and I'll do it."

She shook her head, her eyes sad but resolute. "No. Thank you, George. I'll always remember your kindness. But this is my home and my family, for better or worse." Looking up into his eyes, she hesitated, then let out a resigned sigh. "You say we're not meant to be, and I guess you know best. But I wish you would stay. Not to fight my battles, but just to be by my side."

Her words cut George deeply, and he wished for nothing more than the ability to pull her into his arms, hold her, and tell her that he would never leave her again. George knew that, against all odds, he was falling hard for sweet, innocent Rose, whose very name intimated the innocence she embodied. She was beautiful, sweet, and perfect in every way, and for some reason she wanted him. And he wasn't worthy of her.

"Rose—"

Alan interrupted them, the man's large body suddenly between theirs. "That's enough now. Rose, go inside. I mean it."

Rose gave George one last look, then hurried into the house, ducking through the doorway as George grit his teeth.

"You don't have to treat her that way," George insisted. "She deserves better."

Alan turned on him, eyes narrowed. "Don't tell me how to run my family. I welcomed ya in. Know yer place."

And with that last missive, Alan followed Rose inside, and George was left outside the fence, warring internally with his inner outlaw that wanted to go and claim what he felt should be his and the man who he was trying to become—the one who followed his head instead of his gut.

CHAPTER 6

ROSE

S HE WAS ABSOLUTELY FURIOUS, PACING BACK AND FORTH IN THE KITCHEN WHEN she heard Alan walk into the house and slam the door behind him. Years of resentment and hurt and embarrassment suddenly came rushing to the surface like a Wyoming geyser, and Rose stormed into the front foyer, her hands on her hips as she stared down her much larger, much taller, older brother.

"How dare you?"

Alan moved to shove past her, uninterested in giving her even the dignity of an answer.

"Don't you walk away from me," Rose said, her voice shaking with rage as she grabbed his arm and spun him back around to look at her. "I am so tired of constantly enduring the absolute shame of your behavior, Alan Burns. Your father would be ashamed of you, and your mother would roll over in her grave if she knew the kind of things you were up to. I thought you would grow out of this phase. I thought you would stop stealin' and drinkin'. I thought you'd come back to church, like the good Christian man you could be if you'd just live yer life right. But you're getting' worse, not better. And the way you treated me out there and the way you spoke to George, who has never been anythin' but friendly to you—it's unconscionable, and if I was your mother instead of your little sister, I would find the biggest switch from the tallest tree, turn you over my knee, and whip some sense into yer stubborn hide. And don't think I wouldn't!"

The rush of words felt so good as they flew off her tongue, and so many of the things she had wanted to say for so long were suddenly out in the open, freeing her from the imprisonment of her emotions. But before she had time to really enjoy the feeling of relief, Alan took her shoulders in his hands and slammed her up against the wall behind her, his breath hot and stale on her face.

"Don't you ever speak to me like that again," he said, his voice so low it was almost a growl. "I'm the head of this house, and it'll do you well to remember that. I can throw you out if I want to and you won't have nowhere to go, will ya?"

"Do it, then," Rose said, so incensed that she didn't care anymore. "Do it, but know that you'll be the lowest kind of man there is."

A gleam of power appeared in Alan's eye and he eased away from her, letting her stand up from the wall. But he wasn't backing off or giving up. He was just switching tactics.

"So you don't have any respect for me?"

"None."

"You think I'm a bad person."

"I think you're making very bad decisions."

"You're embarrassed to even be associated with me."

"These days? Yes, I am."

Alan smirked, his eyes narrowing as he scanned them over her. "Interestin'."

"I hardly think so."

"You know that man out there? The one you're fawnin' all over?" Alan shoved his hands in his pockets, clearly enjoying himself as he leaned up against the stair railing. "That's George Mattachine. One of the leaders of the Doolin Gang, one of the biggest, baddest outlaw gangs in the area."

Rose felt her chest tighten and she couldn't breathe. "You're lying. That's George Newcomb, and he's nothing of the sort."

"Yer so naïve," Alan said, laughing at her. "He changed his last name 'cause he's runnin' from the Doolin Gang. He deserted them, and they're huntin' him down. They've put a price out on his head, little does he know. And Benjamin and Nathaniel and I are gonna get that price. All we have to do is keep him here long enough for the Doolin Gang to get here, then we point them right to him." He rubbed his fingers together, making the sign for money. "Cash right in my pocket, just where I like it. And my little sister's heart broken, to boot. This is a good day."

Tears filled Rose's eyes and she had to fight hard to keep them back. "Why are you like this?" she whispered. "Why do you hate me so much?"

"I don't hate you. You just annoy me."

The hot tears spilled down her cheeks, and Rose gave up trying to stop herself from expressing the sorrow of all the years since her parents had died—all the sorrow she felt at learning that the beloved image of George that she had built in her mind was the furthest thing from the truth. He was just like her brothers, only better at hiding it. He'd had her fooled completely, and to think that she had contemplated throwing herself at his feet and begging him to marry her and take her away.

Oh, how he would have loved that.

And yet, she still loved him. Despite it all, she still felt every bit as strongly for him, despite her great disappointment. He was an outlaw. Who knew what he had done. And yet she wasn't going to let her brothers bring about his demise—she couldn't bear it.

As Alan basked in the victory of ruining her first love, Rose thought quickly. Alan still had an injury in his leg, and he wouldn't be that fast. He also would never expect what Rose was about to do.

So she did it.

Picking up her skirts, she ran toward the front door as fast as she could, throwing it open and hurtling into the sunshine as she ran toward the fence that would mark the boundary of their land. George was long gone, but she knew where he was staying, and if she got to him before Alan did, then she could warn George away.

It was all the comfort she was ever going to have, and she wasn't going to miss the opportunity.

"Rose!" Alan's voice was just behind her, clearly infuriated. "Rose, stop right there or I'll shoot you in your tracks!"

"Do it, then," she challenged, calling over her shoulder to him. "I'm not stoppin'."

CHAPTER 7

GEORGE

SOMEHOW, POTOMAC HAD BECOME HOME WHEN NO OTHER PIT STOP HAD, AND as George packed up his little room at the inn, folding his few belongings back into his bag, he was sadder than he could have imagined. He had failed Rose, and he had learned what it was like to recognize that you could never truly have what you wanted. If he didn't leave now, he would give in and ask her to marry him, so he had to go. But he would never forget her.

As he was packing his last items, there was a knock at his door. George decided not to answer it, knowing that there was every chance that Alan was there, ready to exact revenge. He wasn't afraid of the man, but he also didn't want to get into a fight that might further hurt Rose. George was no stranger to climbing out the window to escape a building, and he would do it again if he had to.

He slung his bag onto his shoulder and began to make his way toward the window, but the sound of cracking wood had him spinning around, reaching for the gun that was usually at his side but now was tucked away in his bag.

If he had expected Alan, he couldn't have been more wrong. There, at the door of his room, was the leader of the Doolin Gang, Vince Michaelson. Large and muscled, with small, gritty eyes, Vince stared him down, a nasty smirk on his face.

"Well, well, well. If it isn't the deserter."

"How did you find me?" George asked, narrowing his own eyes. This wasn't right. Something had happened that he didn't know about. The Doolin Gang hadn't been hot on his trail—if they had been, he would never have stayed in one place for so long.

"Oh, I have my messengers," Vince said, stalking into the room, followed by his most loyal outlaw members. "You knew it would come to this, George. Nobody leaves Doolin behind. Especially not you—you were supposed to be one of us. And if you're not anymore, then you don't get to live."

George let his bag slide off his shoulder, grabbed the top of it with one hand and reached in, yanking out his gun. Before he could get it into position, though, Vince was on him, his own gun held to George's head.

"Don't even think about moving," Vince whispered. "I'm gonna take you out into the street and kill you like the dead man you already are. And all yer death is gonna do is remind people they should never mess with the Doolin Gang."

There were grunts of agreement from the others who were waiting, drooling, by the door, eager to see George, who had always been a favorite, punished for his crime of no longer wanting to commit crimes. Vince dragged George out of the room, shoving him down the stairs and entirely ignoring the frantic innkeeper. Vince had faced far worse situations, and the idea of killing a man in the street in broad deadlight didn't faze him at all.

"Vince, you're making a mistake," George said, grasping for anything that might work as Vince shoved him again, sending him tumbling into the street. "You don't have to do this."

"No, I could find my moral compass again, like you," Vince said, his tone mocking. "Get down on your knees, George. This is execution style."

Though he was terrified, George stayed on his feet, refusing to cave to the man who he had once called a friend, though now could never imagine doing so. "No. If you want to kill me, you're going to have to do it the hard way."

"You mean the fun way." Vince's eyes lit up. "You run. I'll chase."

"No. I wouldn't give you the satisfaction."

Vince raised his gun up, leveling it at George's head. "Oh, but I'm already getting satisfaction from this."

"George!"

A female voice screaming his name made George's blood freeze with terror. He knew that voice immediately, and he knew that Rose was close, her feet pounding against the pavement when everyone else who was witnessing Vince's little game had gone absolutely still.

"George, I'm coming!"

He closed his eyes, wishing with all of his might that he could will her away from this dangerous place, but he couldn't. All he could do was protect her with his life, and that, at least, would be an honorable way to die. He turned, putting his back to Vince, and ran toward Rose even as she ran toward him.

"Rose, no!" he yelled, grabbing her shoulders as they collided and using his body as a shield to protect her from the shot he heard ring out behind him. They tumbled to the dirt, landing hard, and George froze, waiting for the excruciating pain of the bullet to hit him and begin radiating through his body like it had the number of other times he had suffered a gunshot wound.

But there was no pain this time, and after a moment, when he realized it wasn't coming, he looked at Rose beside him, desperate to see if she was hurt instead. But she wasn't. She was lying there, looking back at him, and though mere seconds had passed since they had hit the ground, it felt like the world was standing still.

And then, to George's utter shock and amazement, Rose pulled a gun out from under her dress, whipped around, and from the ground, shot upward at the man bearing down on them, ready to take his second shot. George watched the bullet leave Rose's gun, and as if in slow motion, tracked it with his eyes all the way until it met its mark in Vince's gut, crumpling the man where he stood.

Vince fell with a groan, clutching his blood-soaked abdomen as he hit the ground, twitching with pain. His men stopped short behind him, staring at their fearless leader in utter shock. And then they looked up, their gazes collectively landing on Rose and George as they lay on the ground, unharmed.

In that moment, George knew that if they wanted to live, they had to run as fast as they could.

CHAPTER 8

ROSE

THERE WAS A BIG PART OF HER THAT COULDN'T BELIEVE THAT SHE HAD ACTUALLY shot a man. Granted, she had been shooting all of her life, her father having taught all four of his children to handle a gun responsibly. But the fact that she had grabbed one of Alan's guns on her way out the door and then actually used it to fell an outlaw in the middle of town to save the man she loved—all of it was more than a little overwhelming.

But there was no time to think about that now. Not when George had her hand in his and was pulling her as fast as he could toward the nearby woods that would give them some cover. The other members of the Doolin Gang had been hot on their heels, but some of the passersby had intervened, creating obstacles and holding the outlaws off so that George and Rose could get away.

She wasn't used to running so hard for such a long distance, though, and her lungs were burning, her legs threatening to give way. Just as she thought she couldn't take another step, George came to a sudden halt in front of her, and Rose gasped for breath, bending over to brace herself on her knees.

"Oh, thank you," she said. "Thank goodness. I couldn't—"

"Rose, hush," George said, warning her quietly.

Confused, Rose glanced up, and there, in front of them, standing between them and the trees they needed for cover, stood Alan, a gun in his own hand.

"You shouldn't have done that, Rose," Alan said darkly. "All we had to do was let them have him and we would have had all the money we needed for a long time. But you had to interfere. And for who? Another outlaw."

Rose looked between her brother and George, still catching her breath as the weight of the past few minutes bore down on her. Really, what had she done? She'd shot a man to protect an outlaw? That was something Alan would do—not her!

She yanked her hand away from George, remembering for the first time since she had run out of the house that he wasn't just the man she loved. He was also a criminal.

"Rose," George said, reaching for her again. "It's not like that. I left the Doolin Gang. I had changed my ways. I repented. I was making my life right. That's why they wanted me dead—for revenge. I swear, that's not the person I am. It's who I was, but it's not the man who fell in love with you. He's different. He doesn't deserve you, but he's different."

His words were exactly what she wanted to hear, which only made her that much more suspicious. "You lied to me."

"I never did," George said, pleading with her. "I didn't tell you everything, but I didn't know how I was going to feel about you. I love you, Rose. I thought leavin' was the best thing to do, so that I wouldn't interfere with your life, but I'm standing here and I have to admit that I can't live with you. I don't want to."

Alan rolled his eyes. "What nonsense. You killed a man, Rose, to save a criminal. Now you can't act like you're better than me ever again, can you?"

Rose glanced at the gun in Alan's hand—the one he didn't seem too keen on using, preferring to bask in his supposed victory. Then she glanced at George. Her whole heart wanted to believe what he was saying, not only because it would make everything right between them again but because it also meant that her brothers might stand some chance of having the same change of heart someday.

"George ..."

"Rose, marry me," George said, interrupting her. "Marry me and I'll take you away from all of this. I'll be an upstanding citizen. I'll work the land. I'll sweat in the heat. I'll build you furniture and you can quilt bedding for our kids. I never wanted that life at all. Not until I met you."

Tears filled her eyes, and her heart melted then and there. "Oh, George."

"Say goodbye, Rose," Alan said, and out of the corner of Rose's eye, she saw him move his gun to aim directly at George.

"No!" she shouted, lunging toward George.

This time, though, she didn't have to save him. He was ready, and as the bullet left Alan's gun, George tucked and rolled, ducking out of the bullets way and ramming directly into Alan's legs. Both men were on the ground, tussling, as Rose watched, holding her breath. There were limbs flying this way and that, groans of pain, dust kicked up in a cloud around them, and then finally, the triumphant call of victory.

Rose sagged in relief when it was George who scrambled to his feet, now in possession of the gun himself. He pointed it at Alan, who glowered up at him, and Rose reached a hand out.

"Don't shoot him, George, please. He's still my brother."

"I won't, only for your sake," George told her. "And because that's not who I am anymore." With the gun still trained on Alan, George took a step back toward her. "Say you'll be mine and I'll make sure you never regret it."

"Yes," Rose whispered. "Yes, I will."

"Good, then we're leaving now," George said, glancing over his shoulder.

When Rose followed his gaze, she saw that there were people approaching. She didn't know who they were or what they wanted, but neither she nor George wanted to stay around and find out.

They looked at each other, then George grabbed her hand, his other hand still firmly wrapped around Alan's gun. "Into the woods," he told her, nudging her toward the tree line. "They'll find him and help him."

Rose hurried toward the trees, then stopped and looked back at her brother, a sudden, unexplained sadness coming over her. "Do better, Alan," she whispered. "I still love you."

Then she followed George into the trees, disappearing with him into the woods. They walked for hours in the trees, until they emerged into the next small town, where they immediately got married and took a room at the inn.

That morning, Rose had woken up in her role as sister to three outlaws who weren't welcome in society, and she had ended the day having rescued the man she loved from an outlaw, having taken down one of the most infamous outlaws in the area, and having become a married woman.

"Rose Newcomb," she said, trying it out for the first time as they stepped over the threshold of their room at the inn, holding hands. "I like it."

"So do I," George murmured, and then, as he closed the door behind them, he kissed her softly. "I love you, Rose Newcomb."

"I love you, too, George Newcomb."

EPILOGUE

GEORGE

It had been a year since George had married Rose, and the Texas summer he was sweating in was every bit as the brutal Oklahoma summer he'd experienced the year before. Only this year, he had a wife, a baby on the way, and a patch of land that he could call his own.

It hadn't been easy, obtaining any of those things. Rose had almost died trying to protect him, and both of them had almost died trying to get away from her brothers and the Doolin Gang. Once they had managed that, they'd been left with nothing but the few things that George had had on him, and they'd had to start a whole new life together.

Rose had taken up some seamstress jobs and George had put his hand to whatever honest work people would provide, and over the months, they had gradually worked their way toward Texas where he'd had enough money to put down a payment on a plot of land that was about to have its first harvest.

He couldn't be prouder of all that he had accomplished in just a little over a year, and he thanked the Lord above every day for sending him that little old woman on the road to inspire him to change his life. George couldn't imagine a life without Rose and their new baby on the way. The thought alone made him so forlorn that he put down his tools and headed into the house for an earlier-than-planned lunch break.

Rose was at the stove, and he walked up behind her, slipping his arms around her swollen belly and kissing her shoulder. "Hello, dear wife."

"Hello, dear husband," she chirped back, happy as could be. "You're in early."

"I missed you."

"Well, isn't that sweet," she said, turning in his arms and giving him a proper kiss. "But you're sweaty."

"Comes from good, hard, honest labor, my dear."

Her smile was tender, her hands resting on his biceps. "That it does, my love. That it does. Sit down, and I'll serve you some lunch."

They sat down together at their little table, sharing a homemade lunch, and making small talk. George was enjoying himself thoroughly, but then Rose's demeanor changed ever so slightly.

"What's wrong?" he asked, noticing immediately.

"I've been debatin' whether to tell you," she said, biting her lip. "Alan wrote to me."

George stilled, studying her face for hints as to whether this was good or bad. "And?"

"He says that he's changed. Apparently after we skipped town, there was a hefty price for him to pay with the Doolin Gang. The doctor patched Vince up, and Vince wanted Alan's blood since he couldn't have yers."

"Oh no."

Rose nodded. "But all three of my brothers got out of town, and they've been on the run for a few months now. Apparently the Doolin Gang disbanded."

George picked up a piece of bread, pulling a chunk off it and popped it into his mouth. "So what does he want?"

"He wants to come here."

"What?" George dropped his piece of bread on the table. "Rose, we can't—"

"He says he's changed his ways. He's apologized."

"Rose."

"You were like him once, too," she said softly. "Worse, to hear you tell it. And look what a good man you are now. You're honest, hardworking, kind, generous, upstanding. You're everything I could ever want."

Her words did a lot to ease his fears, but George's protective instincts were in full swing. "The baby."

"I know," Rose agreed. "I thought we could get them a place at the inn instead of here. It seems fitting."

"You think of everything," George murmured, shaking his head.

"What I'm really thinking of is that I want for them what you found," Rose said, reaching out and taking his hand. "And that you have taught me so much about forgiveness and humility. Who am I to judge them, even after the way they treated me? If God can forgive them anything, can't I?"

He smiled, his heart growing that much more tender toward her. "Sweetheart, write back to him and tell him to come. We'll welcome him with open arms—at the inn."

Rose chuckled, leaning in to kiss him. "At the inn. Thank you, my sweet husband."

"You make me the man I always wanted to be," George whispered. "I love you, my sweet wife."

"I love you too," she whispered back.

They smiled into each other's eyes, and then the baby kicked, distracting them from more serious topics as they nibbled on bread and took turns feeling Rose's belly, their new life well on its way to joining them in a world where, at least for George and Rose, there would always be second chances.

As George left his house later that day to return to working his land, he couldn't help but send up a prayer.

Lord, thank you for getting me through the darkness and providing so much light on the other side.

◊◊◊

Thank you so much for reading my book. I sincerely hope you enjoyed every bit reading it. I had fun creating it and will surely create more.

Your positive reviews are very helpful to other reader, it only takes a few moments. They can be left at Amazon.

https://www.amazon.com/Ellen-Anderson/e/B07B8C952M

◊◊◊

Want free books every week? Who doesn't!

Become a preferred reader and we'll not only send you free reads, but you'll also receive updates about new releases.

So you'll be among the first to dive into our latest new books, full of adventure, heartwarming romances, and characters so real they jump off the page.

It's absolutely free and you don't need to do anything at all to qualify except go to.

PREFERRED READ FREE READS

https://ellenanderson.gr8.com/

ABOUT THE AUTHORS

Ellen Anderson started life near Sedona, Arizona, surrounded by the most beautiful scenery the West has to offer, along with its intricate history and myriad legends. Her favorite memories are of camping out on the family property under the vast canopy of stars, listening to her father and grandfather tell stories.

Eventually, Ellen began writing her own stories, mixing her up-close-and-personal western experiences with special characters who share her unique sense of fun and adventure. When she met her handsome husband on a horse drive, her path to writing historical western romances was sealed.

Today, Ellen and her husband still do some work on the family ranch, and their children are following in the family tradition, helping care for the Anderson horses. In her spare time, Ellen enjoys photography, swimming, trying out unique historical recipes from scratch and exploring ghost towns in the family RV.

Katie Wyatt is 25% American Sioux Indian. Born and raised in Arizona, she has traveled and camped extensively through California, Arizona, Nevada, Mexico, and New Mexico. Looking at the incredible night sky and the giant Saguaro cacti, she has dreamed of what it would be like to live in the early pioneer times.

Spending time with a relative of the great Wyatt Earp, also named Wyatt Earp, Katie was mesmerized and inspired by the stories he told of bygone times. This historical interest in the old West became the inspiration for her Western romance novels.

Her books are a mixture of actual historical facts and events mixed with action and humor, challenges and adventures. The characters in Katie's clean romance novels

draw from her own experiences and are so real that they almost jump off the pages. You feel like you're walking beside them through all the ups and downs of their lives. As the stories unfold, you'll find yourself both laughing and crying. The endings will never fail to leave you feeling warm inside.

FLOSSIE'S MOUNTAIN

Mail Order Bride Western Romance

RoyceCardiff
Publishing House
WHOLESOME INSPIRATIONAL ROMANCE

Dear Reader,

It is our utmost pleasure and privilege to bring these wonderful stories to you. I am so very proud of our amazing team of writers and the delight they continually bring us all with their beautiful clean and wholesome tales of, faith, courage, and love.

What is a book's lone purpose if not to be read and enjoyed? Therefore, you, dear reader, are the key to fulfilling that purpose and unlocking the treasures that lie within the pages of this book.

NEWSLETTER SIGN UP PREFERRED READ

http://katieWyattBooks.com/readersgroup

THANK YOU FOR CHOOSING A INSPIRATIONAL READS BY ROYCE CARDIFF PUBLISHING HOUSE.

Welcome and Enjoy!

A PERSONAL WORD FROM KATIE

I LOVE WRITING ABOUT THE OLD WEST AND THE TRIALS, TRIBULATIONS, AND triumphs of the early pioneer women.

With strong fortitude and willpower, they took a big leap of faith believing in the promised land of the West. It was always not a bed of roses, however many found true love.

Most of the stories are based on some historical fact or personal conversations I've had with folks who knew something of that time. For example a relative of the Wyatt Earp's. I have spent much time out in the West camping hiking and carousing. I have spent countless hours gazing up at night thinking of how it must been back then.

Thank you for being a loyal reader.

Katie

CHAPTER 1

Flossie stood off to the side of the town's restaurant window, the interior brightly lit with nearly a dozen lanterns, as diners sat at their tables enjoying companionship, love, friendship, and laughter. As an orphan, Flossie had always longed for that sense of belonging that never came. It wasn't like she didn't have acquaintances; she did, but she had never had a beau, and her prospects of finding one were not encouraging.

She turned away from the window and leaned against the side of the building, her gaze passing over the darkened streets of Cortez, still decorated for Christmas even though it had come and gone for her in the blink of an eye. The New Year was just around the corner. What would the year 1888 have in store for Flossie Meadows that would be any different than last year?

She slid her hand into the pocket of her long, blue woolen skirt, fingered the envelope and the telegram inside it. Her heart gave a little leap of excitement. Maybe more than she could have imagined. It hadn't been that long ago since she had replied to an ad for a mail-order bride. She hadn't expected anything to come out of it, actually felt rather silly for replying in the first place. There was no telling whether the ad was genuine or just a marketing ploy by the magazine.

Much to her surprise, a telegram had been delivered to her where she worked. In the kitchen of the very same restaurant, whose window she stood outside right now. Today was her day off, but usually she spent six days a week in the kitchen washing dishes and helping the cook prepare ingredients for her tasty dishes.

A supply train drover named Nick Richardson had actually sent a telegram. It was short and to the point, and yet gave Flossie hope. His ad had been fairly vague, but he was under fifty. At the same time, didn't specify beauty, eye color or any specific traits he was seeking. Not that Flossie had any reason to think that others found her unpleasant to look at, but some of the ads were ridiculous! No, Nick Richardson's ad had just stated fact.

Woman 20 to 35 years of age wanted. Children okay.
Must be strong, self-reliant, and know how to cook.
Reply General Delivery, Nick Richardson, Durango, Colorado

Actually, at the moment, Flossie didn't live that far away from Durango. Cortez was still a boom town, growing by leaps and bounds in only a couple of years since it'd been founded. The town had been built mainly to provide housing for men working to divert a water resource from the Dolores River into Montezuma Valley through a system of irrigation ditches and tunnels. Flossie had come to Cortez the previous summer from southern Texas, and before that, Arkansas.

Every couple of years, Flossie had moved a little further westward with money she earned at menial jobs. She stayed in boarding houses, constantly looking for something that she began to suspect never existed – for her at least. Was there a man out there for her? In all her wandering, she had never found one. Well, she had come close once, or so she had thought until she discovered that her companionship was warranted only to make the gentleman's fiancée jealous.

Actually, she hadn't intended to spend so much time in Cortez, but she had been fortunate to find a job within two days of arriving. She decided to stay for a few months and save up some money, but as it turned out, she barely made enough to pay for her room and board at the rooming house. Still the weather was nice; it was hot but not as muggy as her native Arkansas nor southern Texas. Sooner or later she had intended to pick up stakes and continue westward, perhaps Phoenix, perhaps even farther west to the Pacific Coast.

Then, around Thanksgiving time, she had seen the ad for the mail-order bride. At first she dismissed it. Outrageous! Then again, what did she have to lose? She was already alone and lonely. Maybe it was time for her to step past convention and do something a little more daring. She had responded to the ad, and then just yesterday, received the reply.

Once again she fingered the envelope containing the telegram in her pocket. She had memorized every word, not that there were that many of them.

Would like to meet you.
Have arranged for your fare on the stagecoach arriving in
Durango day after tomorrow, December 28.
Nick Richardson

No promises, no guarantees that everything would work out, but Flossie decided that she could give it a try. If she didn't like him or vice versa, she could stay in Durango over the winter and then head west come spring.

She had no idea what her fate would be. Either Mr. Richardson would turn out to be a disaster or a godsend. She had not made any promises and neither had he. She didn't know whether that was breaking the rules. After all, mail-order bride implied that she was promising to become someone's bride. Still, Flossie had a good head on her shoulders, and she wasn't about to step into a situation she knew nothing about. At her age, able to read people pretty well she felt a sense if she could trust them.

She had told Nick Richardson, in her one brief letter to him, that she would be willing to come up to Durango and travel with him on his supply train to make his delivery to Silverton upon his promise to remain a gentleman during the journey. She supposed that would give them enough time to get to know one another at least a little. If they find themselves suitable companions, she would agree to contemplate a serious proposal of marriage once they reached Silverton. If not, neither of them would be under obligation to continue with the experimental relationship.

By the time Flossie returned to her room at the boarding house, she was beginning to wonder if she really did have common sense or if she had taken leave of her senses. She was taking a chance and she knew it. Then again, a person who was unwilling to take chances never got far in the world, did they?

CHAPTER 2

NICK RICHARDSON PACED BACK AND FORTH IN FRONT OF THE STAGE DEPOT IN Durango, once again wrestling with his consciousness while at the same time insisting to himself that he had to make a living. Didn't he? He waited for Miss Flossie Meadows, arriving from Cortez. She was the only one who had responded to his mail-order bride ad this time. Marty wouldn't be too happy about that, but there was nothing he could do about it. He tried to convince himself that he was not doing anything bad, but way back in the recess of his mind, he knew better.

His three-wagon supply train ran regularly between Durango and Silverton, a remote mining town located at the top of the San Juan Mountain Range. Sometimes, he even took his pack train ticket over Red Mountain Pass and down into Ouray, another mining camp town. They were so isolated up there in the mountains that if pack trains like his didn't bring supplies on a regular basis, the inhabitants, mainly miners, would starve. Marty, a former miner in Silverton, had quit mining to expand his horizons and had approached him a year ago, to encourage in whatever way he saw fit, mail-order brides to venture up in the mountains to marry miners.

Marty charged a fee from every miner who married one of the mail-order brides that Nick brought up the mountain, and Nick also got a small 'transport fee' for his troubles. The mining town was growing, and ore came out of the mountains at a steady clip. Still, the switchback and often dangerous trail to the mining town from Durango was risky, especially this time of year. The spring rains brought landslides while winter brought avalanches.

Christmas had come and gone and a new year was just a few days away. Nick wanted to relocate, maybe closer to Colorado Springs or Denver, maybe even further north. Marty wouldn't like that, but he didn't much care. Marty's transport fee for every mail-order bride he brought with his supply train up to Silverton was nice though. Last month he had brought three.

It was an arrangement that suited Marty, the miners benefiting from the influx of women, the marriages, and of course, Nick, who could always use a few extra dollars in his pocket. Henry over at the Durango livery stable just down the street told him if he didn't make the final two payments on the last wagon and pair of horses he had bought from him soon, he was going to take them back. The bank and the sheriff would back him up too.

Nick's suppliers in Durango and customers up in Silverton paid him well enough, but he didn't want to be a drover for the rest of his life. It was difficult enough in good weather. Wintry weather was brutal, not only on his horses and wagons but on his own body. He wasn't a spring chicken anymore. Pushing thirty-five, he had to look to his future.

He wouldn't tell Flossie Meadows that he was not her intended fiancé. He had no idea who Marty would match her up with and didn't much care. His job was to bring the women up to Silverton, get paid, deliver supplies, and then go back down the mountains to get his next load. It was all about supply and demand.

How the women fared after they arrived in Silverton, whoever Marty matched them with, or whether their marriages were happy ones, was none of Nick's concern. Sometimes he felt a little guilty, sure, but he also needed to make a living, didn't he? He kept repeating that to himself. As soon as he could pay off Henry, he would be clear and free of debt and could start tucking a little money away. He had some money stashed in his rooming house at the edge of town, but he wasn't going to give that to Henry. Not unless he had to. He would make enough money from this trip to pay Henry off and have money left over, and he was anxious to make this delivery.

He wanted to put down roots somewhere. He had three wagons now and three teams of horses. In another month maybe, he would have enough money saved up to literally set up business just about anywhere he wanted. What he wanted was to set up a business where he could work relatively comfortable all year-round.

He had grown up in Durango, liked it there, but the mountains were rugged, the winter's fierce. Maybe he'd relocate along the Western Slope of the Rockies some-where, maybe even mosey over toward California where the snow wasn't so heavy and thick in the wintertime. He wasn't sure where he wanted to end up, but there's one thing he knew for sure. It wasn't Durango and it wasn't Silverton either.

His musings were interrupted by the sound of the stagecoach approaching from around the bend. Trace chains rattling, hooves pounding against the frozen ground, the creak of the stagecoach springs as it jostled back and forth along the trail. The coach driver pulled the horses to a halt in front of the depot and climbed down. He grabbed a small footstool from under the driver's seat. Nick watched as the driver moved to the door and opened it, placing the small footstool on the ground in front of it. One by one, passengers disembarked.

Nick was looking for a woman traveling alone. The first unattached woman that stepped from the stagecoach was an elderly woman, whom the driver helped down.

A middle-aged couple followed, and then a distinguished gentleman wearing a bowler hat. He began to grow nervous. If Flossie Meadows wasn't on this stage, he was going to lose his commission, and he was counting on it. Then, just when he was seriously beginning to worry, he saw a dainty foot, then a dark blue woolen skirt. His gaze drifted upward and he stared.

Was that Flossie Meadows? He frowned. Why had she not been able to find a man on her own? She was pretty enough, though a little on the thin side. Her features were pleasant enough, although her expression was hard to read. As she disembarked from the coach, she gazed around her, warily, as if not sure whether she liked being here. He could understand that. He felt the same way.

Finally, he stepped forward, pulling his hat from his head. "You Flossie Meadows?"

"Yes, I am," she replied.

She didn't smile, but he supposed she was nervous. All of the women he transported were nervous. All of them thought that they were marrying him. It wasn't until they reached Silverton and they drove up to Marty's business office that he told them that he was just the driver, served as a middleman of sorts because most of the fellows looking for brides couldn't read or write. Some of them got upset but not all of them. Again, not his problem.

"You are Nick Richardson."

She didn't ask it like a question, but a statement. He nodded. "Because it's so late in the day, you can rest up in the hotel down the street. The room has already been paid for."

The two dollars for a hotel room came out of Marty's pocket, not Nick's. "Do you have a trunk?" He gestured toward the stagecoach.

She shook her head. "Just a valise. The green one with yellow sunflowers on it."

He nodded, relieved. The last group of women he'd picked up had arrived in Durango with three or four trunks. In fact, their luggage had taken up nearly half a wagon load. He had had to leave some supplies behind, which he was taking up to Silverton with this trip.

"I'll walk you over there, and then I have to go to the livery stable, get the supplies loaded, and check on my horses. I have already arranged for a local restaurant, which happens to be just across the street from the hotel, to take a tray of supper up to your room at about seven o'clock. Is that suitable?"

She stared up at him. Her expressions varied, somewhat between curiosity, alarm, and disappointment. "You're not going to join me?"

"Sorry, Miss Meadows... Flossie, but we have to be on the road at first light if we're going to make it up to Silverton in the next couple of days. There's a snowstorm on the way, and I'd like to beat it or we may end up getting stuck. The wagons have to get through, you understand? There's folks up there waiting for food and supplies. You do understand, don't you?"

He got the impression that if anything, Miss Flossie Meadows was sensible. She nodded.

"Of course I understand. Are arrangements being made for the marriage up in Silverton?"

At least that was one thing he didn't have to lie about. "Yes." He placed his hat back on his head and extended an elbow. "Let me escort you to the hotel."

Nick always tried to be very solicitous to the ladies. He knew they were nervous, but no one had forced them to reply to the ads for mail-order brides. It's not like anything bad was happening to them. They weren't being kidnapped or sold off. Still, he knew that they assumed that he was their fiancé and he was doing nothing to clarify the situation.

"What happens now?" she asked.

She looked up at him. Something in her gaze caught his attention. He could tell she was anxious but doing her best to stifle that. At the same time, she projected a sense of bravado, but he wasn't sure whether it was genuine or she was just trying to pretend it was there.

Once again he admired her features. She wasn't a beauty, but she wasn't ugly either. Some of the women he escorted... well, Flossie Meadows was different. He couldn't quite figure out why he felt that way about her, but there it was.

CHAPTER 3

Flossie spent an uneasy night in a hotel. She wasn't quite sure what she had expected when she met Nick Richardson, but what happened yesterday afternoon when she arrived wasn't it. As quickly as possible, it seemed as if he'd shunted her to the hotel and then disappeared. Was that any way for a fiancé to act? They could've spent some time talking in the lobby, at least a little bit of getting to know one another, but as soon as he got her checked in, helped her carry her valise up to the second floor, where he had reserved a room for her, and opened the door, he had dipped his hat and left.

Of course, Flossie certainly didn't expect Nick to gush romantic expressions of devotion and love. That would've just been silly and made her very wary. Maybe he was just as uncertain about the whole thing as she was. Maybe he even regretted his decision to give her a try. Nevertheless, she was the one who had replied to his ad, so she supposed she should be the first one to take the step to develop some kind of a relationship, or at least open a dialogue with him.

Maybe they would get to know each other a little better on the trail up to Silverton. Durango, from what she had seen, looked like a nice enough town, spread out to the north and south and sandwiched between several mountains. She was up and dressed before dawn, prepared for cold weather mountain travel. She imagined it would take them at least two days to travel the distance between Durango and Silverton, especially with a pack train. She hadn't even been able to ask Nick many questions about his business. He seemed to be in such a hurry to take his leave the previous evening.

Well, they would be riding together, so she figured she had plenty of time to ask him questions. Maybe they just needed to get to know each other a little bit better and she would begin to feel better about the whole thing. They would take the journey to decide whether or not they were a good match for one another. If she didn't feel comfortable about it by the time they got to Silverton, she would figure out what to do and where to go next.

She went downstairs to wait in the lobby just after sunrise. Nick had told her he would come to fetch her as soon as the horses were hitched and he was ready to head out of town. She'd only been down in the lobby for maybe ten minutes when she saw him walk inside. He seemed surprised to see her ready and waiting. Either he expected her to be late or he was surprised by her garb.

She had substituted her dark blue woolen dress of yesterday with more practical clothing for travel. Underneath a pair of heavy canvas pants and a dark blue flannel checkered shirt she wore two pairs of long johns. She had asked about the weather up here from a couple of people down in Phoenix who had traveled through the area during wintertime. It was a bit higher in altitude than Cortez, and she hadn't been there that long. She knew that the altitude and the terrain would be quite a bit different from her typical environment in southern states and had planned, and packed, accordingly. Beside her on the settee lay her secondhand corduroy coat, a pair of gloves, and a hat and earmuffs. She may not look much like a lady at the moment, but if Flossie was nothing, she was practical.

She watched Nick approach, his eyes gazing from the top of her head down to the boots she wore and then back again. He finally grinned and nodded his head.

"Good for you, Flossie, dressing for the weather without worrying about what people might think of you wearing men's clothing. It gets cold there in the mountains, especially this time of year. I'm hoping we can beat the snow, but if we don't, I've got extra blankets." He paused and rubbed his whiskered chin. "I don't have a tent or anything, but we'll make due."

Flossie said nothing. While she wasn't too sure about the appropriateness of riding unchaperoned any distance with a man, fiancé or not, she realized that she was out of her element here. She had to follow his lead and be prepared for just about anything.

"You ready?"

She looked up at him and nodded. "How far is it from here to Silverton?"

He offered her his elbow. As they walked out of the hotel he replied. "It's about fifty miles as the crow flies, but we ain't crows. Most of the road up to the mining town is switchback. We're heading straight up into the San Juan Mountain Range. We'll be making our way past a number of peaks that climb fourteen thousand feet or higher."

"Oh?" she remarked.

"You bet. Like Mount Eolus. Silverton is sandwiched between numerous other mountain peaks including Storm Peak, Bear Mountain, Grand Turk, and Kendall Peak. It's not going to be an easy trip."

"I never expected it to be," she commented. Was he trying to intimidate her, to get her to change her mind? She glanced askance at him but his expression was stoic. What was he thinking?

On some level she felt uncertain, but that was normal, wasn't it? She was venturing into unchartered territory, and by that she meant more than just the landscape. She wasn't naïve. He didn't appear shifty, nothing quite so drastic, but it seemed to her as if he was doing his best to avoid her direct gaze. Maybe he was just nervous. She would see what would happen today on the trail. She had to give him time to adjust, just like she needed time to adjust.

CHAPTER 4

NICK HAD NOT BEEN EXAGGERATING. THE TRAIL WAS ROUGH AND THEY bounced around on the wagon seat. They followed the winding shoreline of the Animas River for a good half of the day. Winding back and forth along the base of the mountainside and following the river probably added miles as well as hours to their journey. The Animas wound this way and that like a snake in between the mountain peaks, sometimes rushing fast, at other times slower. In places, Flossie saw a good amount of ice built up along the shorelines, depending on how fast the river was running.

She doubted that she and Nick had shared more than ten words since they left Durango early this morning. He and she rode in the lead wagon. Two other wagons followed. She had been briefly introduced to the two other drovers. One was a middle-aged, portly, whiskered and unkempt looking man by the name of Travis. The other, named Alonzo, was quite a bit younger, almost a fuzzy-cheeked youngster, has sharp features and a scar shaped like a half-moon marring his left cheek. He wore a perpetual frown.

They had offered a nod to Flossie and then pretty much ignored her. Nick had helped her into the wagon seat of the lead wagon and then pointed out the direction they were going. Her heart had skipped a beat. He wasn't kidding when he said that the trail would be rough. Why it looked like they were going to wind their way upward toward heaven!

It was cold, especially at the bottom of the mountains, despite the fact that the sun struggled to show through the growing cloud cover. Those clouds were gray, some of them looking quite dark and ominous, but Nick had told her it was too cold to snow. She hadn't realized that it could ever be too cold to snow. He had warned that if it warmed up at all, they would probably get what he liked to call "powdered sugar" which he defined as a very light snowfall shaped more like pellets than actually snowflakes.

Despite the biting cold, Flossie wished it would warm up a bit, just so she could see some snow. She'd never seen a snowflake, never seen one fall from the sky. She had this childish urge to catch a snowflake on her tongue. She smiled as she thought about it, wondered what Nick would think of her if she actually did it.

"What's so funny?"

She glanced at him, surprised. He had been watching her. "I was just thinking about my first snowfall. I've never seen snow falling. I've always wanted to catch a snowflake on my tongue. Did you ever do that?" He stared at her as if she had lost her marbles. Shook his head.

"Never even thought about it," he shrugged.

"But you grew up around here, didn't you?" He nodded. "You're used to snow. Maybe for you it's more of a hindrance than a pleasure, but coming from southern climes, I have to say that I look forward to my first snowfall. It will be exciting to see something I've never seen before." She gestured around her. "Like these mountains. There's nothing like these in the places I've been."

He lifted his eyebrows. "No mountains?"

"Well, yes, there's mountains. Just east of Phoenix are the Superstition Mountains. The Spaniards used to call them Sierra de la Espuma." She shook her head. "They don't get snow, or at least when I was there."

He glanced at her. "You move around a lot. That's unusual for a woman."

"I suppose so," she admitted. "But I've been on my own since I was about fourteen—"

"Why?" he asked, astonished.

She shrugged. "I'm an orphan. After my parents died, I pretty much had to fend for myself. That was back in Arkansas. There wasn't any family around and the town was small. Any neighbors I had, already had their hands full with their own families."

Nick said nothing for several moments. "I lost my folks at a young age too, but not as young as you."

He gave her an appraising look and then a grin. She offered a grin in return. At least they had something in common. "So you've lived in Durango most of your life?" He nodded. "Do you ever want to leave? Do some exploring?" He glanced at her again, as if surprised by the question.

"Sometimes," he said. "As a matter of fact, as soon as I get my last wagon and team of horses paid off, I'm thinking of saving money and relocating."

Flossie glanced at him. He hadn't said anything about relocating before, but she supposed it didn't matter. "Where to?"

Again he shrugged. "Someplace where it's warmer, where I can run supplies year-round without having to worry about the weather." He looked up and gestured.

"Ever thought about California?" she asked. "I have." Once again he sent her a glance. She wasn't quite sure what he was thinking. Was he surprised that she expressed a certain sense of wanderlust? Did he feel the same thing but had been afraid to bring it up? "I suppose things like this are important for us to talk about, Nick. After all, we're going to be married. It makes good sense to know what each other is thinking, don't you?"

She was surprised by the look that came over his face. It was as if he had closed off all emotion. He didn't answer her question but merely looked ahead down the trail. She waited a few moments for him to answer and then realized that he wasn't going to. Had she said something wrong?

The rest of the morning hours passed relatively calmly. The horses got skittish a time or two along the narrow, winding trail. As they gained altitude, the drops grew more precipitous. It got to the point where Flossie, riding on the outside edge of the trail, clung tightly to the wagon seat, resisting the temptation to look down. In some places, the drop was hundreds of feet of steep mountainside. Other times, trees grew close. Instead, she kept her gaze focused on the horses. She sure hoped that they paid attention and didn't make a wrong step.

Growing uncomfortable with the long silences between them, Flossie tried to do her best to put Nick at ease. "Nick, there's something I would like to talk to you about."

He glanced at her, shrugged, and then nodded. "You can say whatever you have a mind to, Flossie."

"Well," she began. "I can assume that the circumstances in which we find ourselves is unique to both of us. I don't know about you, but I never expected to find a husband by answering an ad for mail-order brides."

"I can't imagine that many women do," he commented. He paused and then continued. "But it's a hard reality out here. With all the miners coming into the area, the men more than outnumber women. They're lonely. Many of them want families but, as you can realize, developing relationships this far away from city environment makes it difficult."

He glanced at her again and she wondered at his sober expression.

"You understand that in such difficult circumstances, non-traditional methods of bringing people together, such as those mail-order bride catalogs or ads in newspapers, is the only way for many couples to meet."

"But you live in Durango, Nick," she commented. "Weren't there any women in Durango that you found suitable?" He said nothing, but looked down at his hands. He seemed hesitant to look at her. "And yet you decided to take a chance on me? A complete stranger?"

He grumbled a bit under his breath and then turned to her.

"Why do you have to ask so many questions?" he said gruffly. "You answered the ad, didn't you? That implies that you're agreeable to the situation, doesn't it?"

His reply confused her. "Well yes, but I'm just curious. What was it that prompted you to place an ad?" He didn't answer right away, but merely scowled.

"There's lots of reasons why a man would place an ad like that," he muttered. "I got to pay attention to the road. No more foolish questions for now."

She was a little put off by his brusqueness. Foolish questions? Why, as far as she was concerned, these were normal questions; questions that any woman might ask. "I just want you to know Nick, that I'm going to keep my word and do my best to be a good wife for you--"

"What do you mean?"

He sounded alarmed. "Nick, I just want you to know that I don't expect you to be perfect. None of us are perfect, and I certainly don't claim to be. I don't think you do either. What I'm trying to say is that I will do my best to accept you the way you are and not try to change you into something... different. Does that make sense?" She paused, looked at him a moment, then looked ahead on the trail. "And I hope that you can accept me for the way I am and not try to change me into something you want me to be rather than who I really am."

He looked at her. "And who are you, Flossie Meadows?"

She thought about that a moment. "Well, I'm an orphan, I already told you that. I try to be kind and considerate to people, help out when I can. I'm a good Christian, or at least I try to be. I try not to hurt anybody. But the truth of the matter is, that I don't really fit in anywhere. Most people frown on a woman traveling on her own as much as I do." She shrugged. "But I've been on my own for so long that I don't even give it a second thought."

"So--"

She interrupted. "Nick, what I mean to say, is that I know that God put me with you for a reason. I always believe that no matter where I end up, God wants me there. I may not always understand it, but it's not up to me to question God's will, so I go where he tells me to go."

Nick glanced at her with a frown. "So God actually told you to come to me?"

She nodded. "I can tell. I can tell when God is trying to tell me something, to urge me to do something. Maybe that's why I move around so much. Maybe my journey, which started in Arkansas years ago, is supposed to end here, with you, in Silverton." His scowl darkened.

"I don't live in Silverton."

She made a face and smiled. "You know what I mean, Nick--"

"Enough!" he snapped.

She glanced at him wide-eyed. She was about to open her mouth to argue, then decided that now was not the time. It was obvious they had a lot to discuss, but for now he was unwilling to do so. Trying to force him to express his thoughts might only serve to drive a wedge between them. But she was not going to let it go. After all, if he was going to be her husband, they had to start off on some kind of equitable ground, didn't they?

CHAPTER 5

ONCE IN A WHILE, LOOSE ROCKS TUMBLED DOWN FROM ABOVE. FLOSSIE WOULD glance up in alarm, her body stiff with fear. Once, Nick had to pull the team up and climb down off the wagon to push the rocks away. Then, in the early afternoon, it began to snow.

At first, Flossie was delighted. She did as she always imagined herself doing. As the heavy, fat and fluffy flakes fell from the sky, she gasped in amazement. Not caring what Nick or even the other men might think of her, she stuck out her tongue, lifted her face to the sky, and waited for a snowflake to land on it. When it did, it melted immediately, but her delight was boundless. She giggled.

She glanced at Nick, staring at her with wide eyes. He certainly seemed to be in a better mood now. She hoped he wasn't predisposed to wild emotional swings. Maybe he was just stressed. Nevertheless, she was his fiancée, and she did expect a certain amount of respect and courtesy from him. If he was rude to her one more time, she was going to say something about it. She wasn't about to allow herself to be manipulated into a marriage that would not benefit both of them.

Maybe the snow was nothing new to him, but it was to her and she was enjoying it. Finally, after catching the second snowflake on her tongue, he grinned at her. She laughed, removed her gloves, and held them out in front of her, palms up. The feeling of snowflakes landing on her skin was a completely new and unique experience. As the snow fell, it seemed like a different kind of quiet settled over the mountains. The only sound was the horse's hooves striking the hard ground, the creaking of the wagon wheels, the balance of the wagon springs. Every sound echoed oddly around them.

The clouds hung low over the mountains. The heaviness and the snow dropped steadily down from the higher elevations to the lower elevations, seemingly in the matter of minutes. Soon she couldn't see more than fifty yards ahead on the trail. She glanced at Nick.

"Are we going to keep going?"

He nodded. "Until nightfall or the snow gets worse. I know some drovers who will try to navigate the roads at night with lanterns, but it's not worth it. One wrong step by the horses and not only do you lose your supplies but sometimes even your life."

She nodded. The trail was dangerous even in the broad daylight. She couldn't imagine traveling this road at night. Especially when you couldn't see more than a short distance in front of your face. At that point, one would pretty much have to trust the horses.

"It snowed last week and then warmed up a bit. This new layer of snow can cause some dangerous conditions."

She turned to him. "Like what?"

"Rock slides, downed trees worked loose from the wet soil, avalanches--"

"Avalanches?"

He nodded.

"While it's pretty early in the winter to experience an avalanche, most of them occur around February. They're relatively common up in the mountains all winter long." He shrugged. "Most of the avalanches up this way are caused by miners digging into the mountain sides, but still, Mother Nature or fools out there playing in the snow in snowshoes or on horseback can start a slide from way high up."

Flossie listened with rapt attention. She eyed the countryside around them, realized that while this rugged wilderness was excruciatingly beautiful, it could also be deadly under the right conditions.

"I almost got caught in one once, coming back from Silverton," Nick continued. "It was a couple of years ago, a bad winter all around. I lost a friend of mine that winter. He was coming up with mining equipment. An avalanche swept his wagons, the men driving them, and all the equipment off the mountainside. Didn't find hide nor hair of them until spring. I helped bury their bodies, which we found a few hundred yards down the slope next to the banks of the river. The cold, the ice and the snow had pretty much mummified their bodies."

Flossie stared at him in dismay. "Oh my goodness, that's horrible. I'm so sorry."

He glanced at her. "What you got to be sorry about?"

"I'm sorry you lost your friend," she said, surprised by the question.

"I learned a long time ago not to get too attached to anybody. Do that and you only end up getting hurt."

Flossie felt a shiver sweep down her spine that had nothing to do with the cold. If that's how he felt, what did that imply for her impending marriage? She said nothing more but sat quietly next to him on the wagon seat. She felt warm enough and focused her attention, and her pleasure, on watching the snowfall.

By midafternoon, nearly six inches had fallen. She was worried the horses wouldn't be able to find the trail, but somehow they did. She supposed it wasn't that difficult. Stay close to the side of the mountain, away from the precipices, and there was the road.

They hadn't stopped all day. She was hungry. Not only that, but she had to answer nature's call. She felt embarrassed mentioning her needs to Nick, but again, if they were to be married, she might as well get used to it.

"Nick, can we stop for a moment?"

He glanced at her. "Why?"

She felt the heat of a blush warm her cheeks. "I have to... nature is calling," she said simply.

He thought about it a moment and then nodded, pulling up the team. Where they had stopped, the trail was a little wider. Steep mountainside to their left, a drop-off to their right, but a number of trees grew close to the edge of the trail before the ground dropped away too sharply. He gestured.

"You can take care of your needs in there, but don't go too far. Just enough to shelter yourself. We'll look the other way."

Flossie waited a moment, thinking that perhaps he would help her down off the wagon, but he made no move to do so. She finally climbed down by herself, surprised to find her legs and her hips felt so stiff and sore. She glanced at Travis and Alonzo, who seemed to realize what she was doing. True to Nick's words, they glanced the other way, studied their feet or otherwise avoided gazing at her.

Flossie stepped carefully toward the edge of the trail, heading for one of the larger trees. Low hanging branches made it easier to navigate, and she hung on tightly until she could find some solid footing behind one of them. She looked back toward the wagons. None of the men looked in her direction. She stepped behind the tree, blocking her sight from them completely. She couldn't see them and they couldn't see her.

She unbuttoned her pants, crouched down, balancing herself as well as she could while grasping the tree trunk with her other hand. The cold air was frigid on her exposed derriere and she didn't waste any time taking care of her needs. In less than two minutes she was finished and her pants were hitched back up around her waist and she was making the trek back up to incline toward the wagons.

CHAPTER 6

NICK WATCHED AS FLOSSIE MADE HER WAY CAREFULLY FROM THE WAGON toward the tree line. He wasn't sure who he was more upset at - her or himself. For some reason, he was attracted to this one. That had never happened before. He tried to convince himself he was being foolish, but there was something about her, her earnestness, her attempt to assure him that she was going to do her part to make their marriage work. The problem was, she wasn't going to be marrying him. He should tell her, but he wouldn't, not until they arrived in Silverton.

He had done that once - told the truth to two women that he was carting up to the mining town. He hadn't meant to, but they both automatically assumed that they were supposed to marry him. By the time the two compared notes and figured out the truth, he realized he'd better tell them what was really happening. It hadn't ended well. After nursing a bloody nose, they had demanded he take them back to Durango. If he refused, they threatened to tell the sheriff.

He had been mad as all get out. Even after he had finally agreed to turn around and take the women back to Durango, he hadn't been sure that they wouldn't report him to the sheriff. Then again, what would he be charged with? All he had done was place the ads in the mail-order bride catalog. He had never actually - in words - promised to marry any of them.

Marty was the one who paid for travel costs, and all Nick did was transport the women from Durango to Silverton. He wasn't really doing anything illegal. He wasn't selling them into prostitution or anything. They came of their own free will. That they misunderstood what was going on wasn't his fault, was it?

Flossie emerged from the tree line. He watched as she struggled to climb up onto the wagon seat. He knew he should get down and help her, but he was hesitant to give her any indication that he wanted to have anything to do with her. It was unfair to her, he knew that, but he tamped down the feelings of guilt that surged through him as she finally made it up to the seat beside him, gave him a look, and then settled in again.

He could tell she was disturbed. The look on her face was one of confusion, wariness, maybe even a little fear. For the first time in many long months, he regretted allowing Marty talking him into this. He should've known better, should've known that eventually, someone was going to get hurt. Still, he needed the money. He wasn't doing anything illegal. Maybe if he just kept telling himself that, he would eventually come to believe it.

The truth of the matter was, that someday Nick *did* want to get married. He did want to settle down, maybe raise a family. But would anybody want him? Especially after they found out the truth about his past? He didn't think about God much, but he was thinking about God now. Would God punish him for his actions?

He scowled. So why now? Was it being around Flossie? Listening to her express her ultimate faith in God and God's wishes for her? Would her faith in God be shaken when she found out the truth?

He turned his thoughts away from such musings. It wasn't his fault what she believed or didn't or what she assumed and didn't. He refused to take the blame for her getting onto his supply wagon in Durango. She had made that choice of her own free will. He hadn't bound her, kidnapped her, or coerced her. Free will. That's something he believed in. Nevertheless, the more he tried to convince himself that he had nothing to feel bad about, the more self-doubt began to niggle at him.

It was late in the afternoon and the snow was falling heavily when he decided that they'd better stop for the night. Visibility was decreasing, the shadows deepening, and it was bitterly cold. Flossie sat silently on the seat beside him, but sometimes he heard her teeth chattering. It wouldn't hurt any of them to take shelter and warm themselves by a fire.

He knew there was a flat piece of land coming up in about another half mile. They would stop there for the night, thaw themselves by a fire, warm up the rabbit stew that he had purchased from the local restaurant - again Marty's money - and then they would bed down for the night.

He had hoped to make it up to Silverton before the heavy snow fell, but he could see that they weren't going to make it. They were at about the halfway point, so turning around wasn't an option, not that he would have anyway. Unless he got caught in a whiteout or a blizzard, he kept to his schedule. After all, if he didn't meet his delivery, he wouldn't get paid.

The supplies in the back of his wagon were mostly food provisions, canned goods, and grain for animals. The other two wagons were filled with food supplies as well, but also tools, equipment, and clothing that had been placed on order. The longer it took him to get up to Silverton, the longer the miners and inhabitants that called the town home year-round would have to wait.

Flossie hadn't said much since she climbed back into the wagon after her visit into the trees. She seemed content to keep her peace as well. Was she having second thoughts? He hoped so. As a matter of fact, he was rather surprised to realize that he didn't want Flossie to marry anyone up in Silverton. Marty wasn't too concerned about who he matched prospective brides to. Nick had yet to take one back down to Durango though. For many women, arranged marriages were their last hope. While the circumstances weren't ideal, many of them didn't want to face the embarrassment or shame of going back home unmarried.

Doing so would have irreparably damaged their reputations. Like Flossie had said, very few women traveled alone. Doing so raised eyebrows, damaged reputations, made many women downright unmarriageable. The fact that Flossie seemed to care less, rather impressed him.

Still, he didn't like to imagine Flossie with one of the dirty, old, and often uncouth miners engaging in backbreaking labor to pull ore out of the mountainsides. Many of the women he brought up here would find themselves working in those mines side-by-side with their new husbands. He didn't want to see that for Flossie. He couldn't do anything about it. She was destined to reach Silverton and what would happen to her when she got there was not up to him.

CHAPTER 7

THEY MADE CAMP. FLOSSIE OFFERED TO HELP WITH SUPPER, BUT HE HAD IT IN hand. All he had to do was start a fire, pull the heavy cast iron pot with near frozen rabbit stew out of the back of his wagon, and heat it up. The men made themselves busy taking care of the horses, getting them grain, covering them with blankets and tying them to nearby trees. Then the two disappeared into the woods to take care of their needs, emerging several minutes later to crouch down near the fire, hands outstretched toward the heat of the flames.

Flossie didn't appear to know what to do with herself. She seemed hesitant to approach too close to the fire, but instead sat on a fallen log from which he had brushed the snow before building the fire. In addition to her winter clothing, she had pulled a wool blanket he had given her when they stopped the wagons around her shoulders. Still, he could tell she was cold.

Finally, he approached. "Why don't you come warm yourself by the fire?"

She glanced at him and merely shrugged. He realized she might feel uncomfortable, and for a brief second, took pity on her. "I'll make you a small fire over here," he said. She didn't stop him, so he quickly gathered an armful of relatively dry brush from beneath a few nearby evergreen pines. Grabbing a handful of straw from the bottom of his wagon, he started it and soon it had burgeoned to life. It was smoky at first, but as the wood caught, the smoke dissipated.

"Warm yourself. I'll bring you a bowl of rabbit stew as soon as it's heated through."

She nodded but said nothing. What in blazes was the matter with her? Was she mad? Did he care? He wasn't sure. He walked back toward the other two, talked quietly with them for several moments, commenting about the worsening weather, the dangers of the trail, and once in a while cast a surreptitious glance toward Flossie.

She seemed wrapped deep in thoughts of her own, staring into the mesmerizing flames of the fire he had built for her. She had extended her hands toward it, without gloves. Her fingers were long and dainty but looked strong and capable at the same time. It took him several moments to pull his gaze away.

At this point, he knew that the sooner he got up to Silverton and delivered her at Marty's business, the better off he'd be. He would head back to Durango and these odd feelings surging through him would likely dissipate. He hadn't felt such discouragement, disappointment, or guilt over his life in quite a while, and he didn't like it, not one bit.

Making a pointed effort to ignore her as much as possible, not to be rude, but because doing so only made them feel more confused, he served her supper. He quickly left her side, muttering something about checking on the horses. He stayed by the horses for a good while. By the time he returned, everyone was finished eating.

One of the men had taken Flossie's empty wooden soup bowl and washed it out in the snow along with theirs. Each of them was now busily setting up their own makeshift beds under trees, creating warm bowers that were sheltered from the steady wintery breeze that was kicking up. The temperature had continued to drop, and Nick found himself stamping his feet several times as he walked back to the wagon to grab another couple of blankets. Flossie was still sitting on the log, hunched over the dwindling fire now.

He gathered a few more sticks, a couple of pine cones and one decent-sized small branch that he was able to snap over his thigh. After adding the wood to the fire, he cleared the snow away from the ground in front of the log and suggested that she sleep sitting up with her back resting against the log. She would still be close enough to the fire to feel its warmth, but not so close that her clothing would be in danger of catching fire. Behind her back stood a thick stand of trees that would serve to block the wind, or at least most of it. It was going to be cold and uncomfortable, but there was nothing he could do about the weather.

He had just muttered a good night to her when she looked up at him.

"Where are you going to sleep?"

He gestured. "Under the wagon."

With that, he walked slowly away, torn between wanting to sit and talk with her a while and wanting to get as far away from her as he could. This wasn't like him; this confusion, this conflict in his consciousness. He didn't like the way she made him feel. He was drawn to her but was loath to admit it.

Tomorrow he would deliver her to Marty and then she could decide what she wanted to do. No one is going to force her to stay in Silverton and marry someone. If she wanted to, she would have the freedom to leave.

The problem was when a woman wanted to leave and decided not to stay in Silverton, they often had difficulty leaving town. Transportation, either north or south, took money. Unless she had some money stashed that he wasn't aware of, she would have to get a job to earn money to hire someone, a drover maybe like himself, to take her away.

He knew one thing for sure. It wasn't going to be him.

CHAPTER 8

FLOSSIE WOKE UP, COLD, STIFF, AND SHIVERING. AT FIRST SHE DIDN'T REMEMBER where she was and felt a moment of alarm. She was outside. In the woods, under trees. In the snow. What... then she remembered. She was on her way up to Silverton with her fiancé, Nick Richardson. She made a noise in her throat. He didn't seem like much of a fiancé, at least as far as she was concerned. Still, she knew that this was a unique situation for both of them, but he had placed the ad, hadn't he?

She struggled to rise, stifling the groan that nearly erupted from her throat as her body protested not only the cold, but the movement after lying so stiff all night. A thin coating of snow covered her blanket. She had fallen asleep leaning against the log as Nick had suggested, her knees pulled up close to her body. She had been warm and comfortable enough when she had fallen asleep, but now she was anything but comfortable. She was rather surprised to discover that she had remained asleep all night despite the cold and the snow.

She chalked up her exhaustion to the stress of the journey, her concerns about Nick, and his apparently cool attitude toward her. If things didn't improve today, or he didn't give her an indication that he truly and honestly wanted to marry her, she was going to tell him so by the time they got into Silverton. There was no way in the world that she was going to yoke herself to a man who didn't want her.

But did she want Nick? She wasn't sure. He was gruff, rough around the edges, but obviously driven. The fact that he was making supply runs in this kind of weather showed her that he was a man who was determined, and one who kept his word to his suppliers and customers. Did it really matter if he wasn't the friendliest person in the world? Maybe he was just used to being alone. Maybe he wasn't sure how to act.

Once again, she decided that she would do her part to make him feel more comfortable. She wanted the same from him but realized that men thought quite a bit differently than women did. She couldn't expect him to be able to express himself the way she wanted him to. From what she gathered, he had lived a solitary lifestyle surrounded by men. Maybe he'd never courted a woman before. Maybe he didn't know how to proceed or what she might expect of him.

She wasn't sure what she expected of him either, other than maybe to act a little more pleased about her presence. As it was, she was beginning to feel that he didn't like her very much, although she didn't believe she had given him a reason not to. Maybe this was something they needed to talk about, but she wanted to do so in private, not where Alonzo and Travis, who eyed her warily, could overhear.

She also knew that due to the weather and the increasingly difficult terrain, and the fact that nearly a foot of snow lay on the ground, that Nick would have to keep his wits about him, concentrate on the trail, control the horses, and watch for signs of danger.

She rose to her feet and then slowly stretched, trying to work out some of the kinks. The wool blanket she had covered herself with seemed a little damp so she quickly shrugged it off her shoulders, shook it out, and prepared to take it to the wagon. Nick was just emerging from underneath. He frowned as he glanced at the snow on the ground, muttered under his breath, and then nodded to her.

"You doing okay, Flossie?"

She nodded, smiling. Maybe if she appeared a little more agreeable, he would too. "Is the snow going to hamper your ability to get through to Silverton today?"

He glanced up at the mountains surrounding them, at the snow on the ground, and then shook his head. "Naw, I've taken the wagons in worse weather than this, and through more than a foot of snow on the ground. We'll have to make good time today though. By the looks of the sky, we're going to get more."

With that he walked away and disappeared into the trees. She didn't see the other two drovers, assumed that they were gathering the horses and getting ready to hitch them up to the wagons. She glanced at the now cold fires, both hers and the one that had warmed the men last night. She had a sinking feeling that they weren't going to linger long. Not even long enough for a hot cup of coffee to warm their bones?

Apparently not. Seconds later the three men emerged from the trees, each leading a team of horses. She decided that now would be a good time to take care of things before they got back on the trail. Nick was busy hitching his team of horses to the front wagon, so she took the opportunity to step into the trees and take care of the calling of nature.

She emerged several minutes later to find the others already waiting in their wagon seats. She glanced at Nick, who motioned her to hurry.

"We have to get a move on," he said. He gestured toward the sky to the north. "Looks like there's a storm on the way."

She glanced in the direction he pointed and noticed the heavy, dark gray clouds spilling through the mountains. She saw the breath in front of her face when she exhaled, but it did seem just a tad warmer today than it had yesterday. Warmer temperatures meant more snow, she had learned that.

She quickly made her way to the wagon, this time a little more comfortable and sure of her steps as she climbed up onto the wagon seat. The minute she settled onto the seat, the spring squeaking beneath her weight, Nick clucked the horses into movement.

And so another day on the trail started. Nick didn't seem disposed to talk, so she didn't either, for the most part. She did want to mention one thing however, and turned to speak to him quietly so that her voice wouldn't carry back to the others.

"Nick, when we get to Silverton, we need to talk, okay?"

He glanced at her warily. "About what?"

She wiggled her finger between the two of them. "About us. And we both need to be honest about our feelings."

She hadn't said that last part as a question, but a statement. He stared at her for several moments and she lost herself in the depth of his dark brown eyes. She wondered what he was thinking. It was always hard to tell with him, but she had only known him for a couple of days. Maybe as time passed and they got to know each other, she would become more familiar with his moods and his expressions. Still, she had until the end of the day to decide whether she wanted to give Nick Richardson a chance, or if he wanted to give her one.

CHAPTER 9

Toward early afternoon, Flossie finally spoke to him. Lost in his thoughts, he didn't hear exactly what she said and turned to her. "What?"

"Can we stop for a few minutes?" she repeated.

"What for?" He frowned glancing between her, the trail, and the ever-nearing storm clouds. He had a feeling that the storm would be upon them in two to three hours, tops. He couldn't waste a lot of time. He was pushing the horses as quickly as he could so that they might reach Silverton before the storm hit, but it was going to be close as it was.

"I need to..." she gestured toward the trees.

"You can't wait?" he asked.

"Nick, I'm not a man. I haven't asked you to stop since we got on the trail first thing this morning. I just need a few minutes. That's all!"

He sighed, then nodded, pulled the horses up. He glanced back over her shoulder, made a gesture with his hand, and once again, the three of them looked in the opposite direction as Flossie quickly climbed down from the wagon and headed for the trees.

She was about twenty feet away when he heard a strange rumbling sound. He quickly looked beyond her shoulder, saw Flossie as she glanced around in alarm, not sure what it was. Nick knew that sound. He and the other men stared up at the mountainside. Acting instinctively, he slapped the reins of his horses and sharply shouted to them. They lunged forward. The other two did the same.

Then, in the next instant, the mountainside moved. Snow, debris, rocks, and parts of trees rumbled down. He heard the sharp crack as trees split and rocks slamming together. He glanced over his shoulder as he took the horses around a slight turn in the road, his heart pounding. He saw Flossie, frozen by the tree line. The look in her eyes, wide-eyed with fright and uncertainty, implanted itself in his brain, and in his heart.

"Nick!"

He heard her scream his name as she stood frozen with indecision. The ground beneath rumbled. The ensuing roar filled his ears. Then, to his horror, a wave of falling snow struck the two wagons behind him. One minute they were there, the next they were gone. He saw nothing but a wall of snow behind him. The horses panicked, tried to break into a gallop. He had to turn his attention to stopping them before they all went over the side of the mountain.

He pulled back hard on the reins, trying to soothe the frightened horses. He finally got them to stop. He glanced back over his shoulder once more, heart pounding.

"Flossie!"

He caught a flash of movement, of color, and then saw Flossie struggling to emerge from the trees. His heart leapt into his throat. She had managed to escape—

A shout of horror erupted from his throat when she was struck by another falling blanket of snow and knocked off her feet.

"Flossie!" He quickly guided the horses off the trail and toward a small flat space lined with trees, hoping that they were safely away from the avalanche. He quickly climbed from the wagon and tied the reins to a tree, all the while bemoaning the loss of his other two wagons, the horses, and of course, the drovers.

Maybe, God willing, he would find someone alive. His legs shook so badly he could hardly stand. The loss of the wagons, the horses, his men, and of course the supplies was bad enough, but the moment he had seen Flossie knocked off her feet, he had realized what was most important.

It was then, at the moment he saw her barreled over by the snow that he realized that she had made an impression on him. A good impression. Her acceptance and desire to make him a good wife shook him to the center of his being.

"Flossie!"

He ran back along the trail. The snow had stopped sliding but had left piles several feet deep or more on the trail and then spilled over the side of the mountain. He tried to pinpoint the exact location she had been standing before he saw her get hit, but everything looked different now. He glanced cautiously upslope as he scrambled his way over the mounds of snow, looking over the edge of the trail. Along here trees grew just about up to the side of the trail. With luck, those trees had stopped Flossie from being flung far downhill.

He couldn't say the same for the others. They had been close behind him, near a rather steep precipice when he'd seen them get hit. He felt sick to his stomach. His drovers, the horses, the wagons... he imagined them buried under feet of snow, slowly suffocating to death. Or they'd been hit by debris, killed instantly. He hoped it had been the latter. He hated to think of anything suffering.

Flossie. He needed to find her, or at least attempt to. In a growing panic that he couldn't quite explain, he scrambled toward the place he had last seen her. His eyes scanned the landscape, the trees broken in half, the rocks, the banks of snow where none had been before.

This close to the avalanche, he hesitated to shout too loudly. Sometimes that's all it took. Sometimes, something as simple as a stumble could cause a slide. For the first time in years, maybe even a decade, he prayed. He had allowed his faith in God to wane. He wasn't quite sure why, but over the years it had happened.

"No, not her," he muttered. "She's a good person, Lord. If you need to punish someone, punish me!" And then he realized that maybe he *was* being punished. Maybe this was his punishment for his actions, his callousness.

He knew he was at about the center of the avalanche, the place where it looked like the snow had been moving the fastest, and the most dangerous place to be now. He placed his feet carefully, tried to move sideways as he glanced upward, saw the fracture line where the snow had broken free and came barreling down. All things considered, this was a relatively small avalanche, maybe fifty feet wide, but he didn't know how deep or how far it had traveled down the mountainside. He had seen one from afar once that had appeared to take tons of snow off of a mountaintop.

He hoped Flossie had been able to grab onto something. While the center of the avalanche had appeared to rip trees from the ground, it seemed to him that Flossie had been caught on the backside of the avalanche. If she had managed to grab onto a tree, she might still be alive.

He wished now that he had told her how one of his acquaintances had survived being buried in an avalanche. He had cupped his hands over his mouth, creating a pocket of air. Luckily, he hadn't been buried too deep and had been dug out within about a half an hour. Still, the chances of surviving an avalanche were minimal at best. He knew that a person buried in an avalanche could smother to death before they froze to death.

After the last of the falling snow settled, he didn't hear a sound. Not the whinny of a horse, a call for help, nothing. He reached the location where he believed Flossie had last been, scanning the ground, looking for anything that might indicate where she was. He glanced down the slope, skimmed his eyes along the snow, seeking any sign of anything that might indicate where she was.

And then he saw it. A glove. It wasn't lying flat on the ground as if it had been pulled from her hand. No, it was standing upright. How in the world had the glove managed to land like that-- and then he realized. Maybe the glove was still attached to Flossie's hand, and her hand was reaching upward. But it didn't move.

His heart pounding in his chest, he scrambled sideways down the slope, about sixty yards down from the trail. The minute he got close to the glove, he dropped to his knees and grabbed the glove, realized that indeed, Flossie's hand was still in it. He began to dig frantically, yet taking care not to dislodge too much at once, hesitant to cause another snow slide.

"Flossie!" he called, placing his mouth close to the snow. "I'm here! I'm going to get you out!"

CHAPTER 10

FLOSSIE FELT NUMB ALL OVER. ONE MINUTE SHE HAD BEEN MAKING HER WAY back to Nick's wagon, and the next, a terrible rumbling had filled her ears. She glanced up to see that huge, massive blanket of snow rushing down the mountainside. She had watched in horror as that wave of snow had knocked the two wagons, their horses, and the drovers over the side of the mountain as if they weighed no more than a feather. Her own scream of terror had been cut short when she too had been knocked off her feet.

She had lost all sense of direction. She had been slammed to the ground, hard, knocking the wind from her. A sharp pain had blossomed in her leg, another in her arm as she had been swept headlong down the mountainside. Oh Lord! She was going to die! Despite her fear, she quickly made her peace with God. If this was her destiny, she would accept it. But until that moment when she breathed her last, she would fight for survival.

It seemed like forever before her body stopped falling. She had managed to instinctively throw her left arm over her face. She thought she had landed on her back but she couldn't be sure. She thought her right arm was extended above her, but she couldn't tell. She couldn't move. She tried to wiggle her fingers. And then she heard the voice, coming from a great distance.

Nick! And then, to her incredible relief, she felt something grasp per hand. Praise the Lord! If she could have, she would've cried but she couldn't take a deep breath, couldn't move. The arm over her face had given her a small pocket of air but she didn't know how long it was going to last. Faintly, she heard the sounds of digging and could imagine Nick up there, trying to dig her from beneath the snow. Soon, she felt his hand grasp her forearm. She must not be buried too deep, but she didn't know for sure.

Blackness began to hover around the edges of her consciousness. No! She couldn't give up! Nick was here, trying to save her. The digging sounds seemed a little closer now, and then in the next instant, she felt a hand brush roughly against her face. She opened her eyes, saw Nick's hand cast a shadow over her features. The minute his glove touched her face, he shouted with triumph.

"Flossie! I'm getting you out! Hang on!"

She wished she could smile, laugh, express a supreme joy that Nick had come back for her, had found her, but she couldn't move. She couldn't feel anything. She hoped it was just because of the frigid temperature of the snow and not because she had been terribly injured. They were still a long way from Silverton.

And then, to her surprise, she heard Nick laugh. Felt herself being lifted up and out of the snow into his arms and his embrace. One arm was around her shoulders and under her back, the other pressing the back of her head into his neck. He felt so warm! He rocked her in his arms for several moments, muttering what sounded awfully close to her prayer.

"Thank you God, thank you God, thank you God," he repeated over and over.

She opened her eyes as he shifted slightly to look down at her face. She could only stare up at him, amazed at the concern she saw in his gaze.

"Thank God, you're alive," he said, his voice trembling. "Truly a miracle!"

She agreed, but then remembered. "The others?" she asked, hoping against hope that they too had managed to escape.

He shook his head. "Not sure."

Tears filled her eyes but froze as soon as they oozed past her eyelids. And then she began to shiver. Violently. Nick pulled off his coat and wrapped it around her, and then she felt herself being lifted from the snow and cradled in his arms. She didn't know how he did it, but he managed to struggle back up the slope, holding her body close to his own. She hung on to him for dear life, wondering if she had broken bones. She couldn't tell, as frozen as she felt. She wasn't feeling any pain... yet, but that didn't mean it wouldn't come.

"I feel both Travis and Alonzo are gone but we need to go see. Maybe we can help them. Can you?"

Flossie nodded. She would do her best. Stopping by Nick's lead wagon he instructed her to grab some rags and a small pot or bowl. He grabbed some ropes and hooks and a switchblade knife. They quickly made their way over to that side of the snow covered slope of road.

"Oh, my heavens," Flossie said gasping.

While the side of the road was not a straight drop down, the incline was steep.

Nick, darting his eyes back and forth, searching for a way down several feet to another ledge like area. Then frantically turning around to see where he could tie off the rope and try to lower himself down the side.

Tying rope securely, he hoped, to a tree then wrapping it around his arm and hand he backed up and was starting his way down when Flossie yelled "Wait, the rags and more rope."

She leaned over and found pockets in his heavy canvas jacket, stuffing them quickly. Then just as quickly she brushed a kiss on his forehead.

Descending downward, holding to the rope for his life he made it to the next ledge. There Travis, the older man was. His arms wrapped around a tree trunk, scrapes and blood on his face, legs dangling with splatters of snow all over him and tears running down his face.

"Travis, thank goodness! Do you think you have any broken bones? Nick asked. Then he hollered out for Alonzo, hoping to hear a response.

Travis, shaking his head, said "no, I'm just weak. You did not give us time to eat breakfast or have coffee this morning before we hit the trail."

Nick was already scouring the area to see if he could lower himself farther down. "Sorry, sir. I was trying to save time and keep us ahead of the storm moving in. We both know all too well about avalanches but I was more concerned with the dark rolling clouds. I am so sorry. If you are not hurt, do you think we can try to find Alonzo and gather some supplies?"

Reaching one of the wagons that was turned on its side both men looked around calling out for Alonzo, the younger man. At the same time they said it appeared the horses had broke loose from the wagons.

Travis said maybe Alonzo had been able to jump on one of the horses and get out of harms way. Nick noticed the older man had a slight limp so he was probably hurt more than he let on and would try to get him to see a doctor when they arrived in Silverton.

Between the both of them they tied up a box of blankets and supplies and Flossie pulled the rope up to her, releasing and dropping the empty box back down. After several successful trips it was time for the men to crawl the rope to safety.

Nick used the side of the slope to leverage his feet and move back up to the trail. He walked over to the tree that the rope was tied to and checked its security then hurried back over to pull Travis up.

As Travis got close to the top, he looked back over his shoulder and said, "I wish you the best Alonzo, my friend, where ever you are."

Flossie let out a breath she did not realize she was holding. Overcome with happy, exhausted emotions she hugged both men.

CHAPTER 11

ALL THREE TIGHTLY BUNDLED INTO THE WAGON, FLOSSIE LEANED HER HEAD ON Nick's shoulder.

She dipped into the arms of unconsciousness, yet on the edges of it, she kept hearing his voice as he spoke to her, encouraging her.

"You hang on, Flossie!"

Darkness enveloped her.

When she next regained consciousness, she found herself leaning against something very warm. To her surprise, she realized she was half laying on the Travis' lap. She was wrapped in several blankets. She eyed the horse's rumps, felt the jostling of the wagon, and turned her head slightly to look up at Nick. He held the reins in his left hand, his other hand wrapped around her waist, holding her onto the seat beside himand Travis.

"We're almost there, Flossie," he said, smiling down at her. "We're almost in Silverton. You going to be all right. I'll make sure of it."

Sometimes, it just takes one second to change your life forever. Flossie knew that moment had occurred for Nick the minute the avalanche had struck. He told her that the second he saw her knocked down by the falling wall of snow, he had never felt so scared in his life.

After the avalanche, Flossie had learned the truth. All of it, from Nick. He was so guilt-ridden he could barely look at her. Of course, Flossie had been shocked to learn the truth, but her faith in God and her trust in Nick had prompted her to forgive him. He had come back for her. He had saved her. He had changed.

Flossie had broken one of the bones in her lower leg, and one of the bones in her forearm, but the doctor in Silverton had assured both her and Nick that they weren't bad breaks and she would mend in a couple of months. Travis had a broken ankle that the doctor bandaged up tightly and told him to try not to put much weight on it.

It was then, when she was recuperating that first week, that he had told her everything.

Travis took a room in town for a few days while Nick and Flossie sheltered in a cabin that belonged to a man named Marty. Nick told her all about him too. While she had forgiven Nick for not being honest with her, she made him promise to never do anything like that again. He assured her that he was ready to start over. Losing his wagons, his horses, and his two drovers had hit him hard. He admitted that seeing her get caught in the avalanche had hit him even harder.

He admitted to her that he had been so cold and distant because he was feeling guilty over his deception, but that doing so had been difficult because he'd been attracted to her from the moment he had seen her step off the stage in Durango.

Nick explained that he was basically a messenger and courier for Marty and his business. Marty had encouraged Nick to write letters to young ladies in hopes they would want to make a life in Colorado. As Flossie listened intently, Nick continued on saying that he wrote and signed each letter. For that, he shared with her that he was sorry for misleading the mail-order brides. As they arrived in Durango and he transported them to Marty's business in Silverton then he explained to the ladies it would be a miner that they would be able to marry.

Most were grateful for the chance to be free from their previous life and the place they had called home. They were eager to start a new life, full of hope, in a beautiful land that did keep most in Silverton and the small surrounding communities. Although some did not want to stay....so Marty, being the kind soul he was would give them a small bit of money and Nick would take them to the next town.

EPILOGUE

Now, four years later, living in Montrose County, about sixty miles north of Silverton near the Gunnison River next to a mountain, Nick had taken up farming. He'd wanted to start completely over. A new chapter in his life, one that included a wife, a stable lifestyle, and someday, children.

He had worked hard to earn Flossie's trust, and she had learned to love him with everything in her heart and soul. He was a good man. He had just had to find himself, had to learn what was most important in life. It wasn't money. It wasn't material things. It was something that you couldn't touch or physically embrace. Nick Richardson had learned the importance of, and the impact, that love and affection could have on his life. After that, he was a changed man.

"You ready?"

Flossie smiled as her husband called her from the yard. They were heading to town to attend church services. After that, he would teach Sunday school class while she attended the women's meeting, deciding how to distribute this year's supply of extra grain, corn, flour, and other goods to outlying residents scattered throughout the Western Slope.

While Nick and Flossie weren't rich in material ways, they had been blessed in others.

"Come on children!" she called out. She smiled as her three-year-old twins, George and Minnie, raced out of their room, laughing and giggling.

Flossie stared down at both of them, amazed at how much George took after his father, while Minnie took after her. Her wanderlust had been satisfied, and Flossie was more than happy to put down roots here in Montrose with Nick. She reached out her hands and her children clasped them. Together, they walked out to the yard, where Nick waited beside the wagon. The children raced to their father as he laughed, lifting each of them into the wagon bed before turning to her.

"Ready, Flossie?"

She stepped into his embrace, snuggled her cheek against his shoulder, and nodded. Her destiny - her fate - had been decided. She smiled.

"Thank you God," she breathed. "For every second of it."

ॐ

THANK YOU SO MUCH FOR READING MY BOOK. I SINCERELY HOPE YOU ENJOYED EVERY bit reading it. I had fun creating it and will surely create more.

Your positive reviews are very helpful to other reader, it only takes a few moments. They can be left at Amazon.

www.amazon.com/Katie-Wyatt/e/B011IN7AF0

WANT FREE BOOKS EVERY WEEK? WHO DOESN'T!

Become a preferred reader and we'll not only send you free reads, but you'll also receive updates about new releases.

So you'll be among the first to dive into our latest new books, full of adventure, heartwarming romances, and characters so real they jump off the page.

It's absolutely free and you don't need to do anything at all to qualify except go to.

PREFERRED READ FREE READS

http:/katieWyattBooks.com/readersgroup

ABOUT THE AUTHOR

KATIE WYATT IS 25% AMERICAN SIOUX INDIAN. BORN AND RAISED IN Arizona, she has traveled and camped extensively through California, Arizona, Nevada, Mexico, and New Mexico. Looking at the incredible night sky and the giant Saguaro cacti, she has dreamed of what it would be like to live in the early pioneer times.

Spending time with a relative of the great Wyatt Earp, also named Wyatt Earp, Katie was mesmerized and inspired by the stories he told of bygone times. This historical interest in the old West became the inspiration for her Western romance novels.

Her books are a mixture of actual historical facts and events mixed with action and humor, challenges and adventures. The characters in Katie's clean romance novels draw from her own experiences and are so real that they almost jump off the pages. You feel like you're walking beside them through all the ups and downs of their lives. As the stories unfold, you'll find yourself both laughing and crying. The endings will never fail to leave you feeling warm inside.

JOSEPHINE

Mail Order Bride Western Romance

RoyceCardiff
Publishing House
WHOLESOME INSPIRATIONAL ROMANCE

Dear Reader,

It is our utmost pleasure and privilege to bring these wonderful stories to you. I am so very proud of our amazing team of writers and the delight they continually bring us all with their beautiful clean and wholesome tales of, faith, courage, and love.

What is a book's lone purpose if not to be read and enjoyed? Therefore, you, dear reader, are the key to fulfilling that purpose and unlocking the treasures that lie within the pages of this book.

NEWSLETTER SIGN UP PREFERRED READ

https://ellenanderson.gr8.com/

THANK YOU FOR CHOOSING A INSPIRATIONAL READS BY ROYCE CARDIFF PUBLISHING HOUSE.

Welcome and Enjoy!

A PERSONAL WORD FROM AUTHORS

WE WANT TO THANK YOU FOR ALL YOUR CONTINUED SUPPORT FOR ALL OF OUR bestselling series. We wouldn't be where we are now without all your help. We can't thank you enough!

We had a lot of fun writing this series about adventures, hardships, hopes, loves, and perseverance. Writing this Historical Western Romance was a magical time.

We sure hope you enjoy reading it!

Ellen and Katie

CHAPTER 1

KANSAS TERRITORY, JUNE 1866

JOSEPHINE MILLER HAD DAWDLED TOO LONG FETCHING WATER THAT MORNING. She knew it had been a mistake, but hadn't been able to resist a few extra minutes of peaceful reflection on the beauty of a prairie sunrise as it lit up the purple larkspur and golden sunflowers. She'd spotted an unfamiliar insect that her fingers had itched to add to her sketchbook though there was no time during the busy mornings on the Santa Fe Trail. Now, she needed to hurry back and prayed that her father would be too busy with the wagon and the oxen to notice her tardiness.

"Where have you been?" he hissed into her ear the moment she rounded the back of the wagon.

Jo's stomach sank and clenched at the same time. To avoid sloshing too much water out of the pails, she'd had to walk slower than her increasingly worried mind had liked. The dilemma had pulsed through her. Pa disliked tardiness, but he also disliked wastefulness. Which would earn her the least of his ire? She'd been walking on a balancing wire as she always did.

"I'm sorry, Pa," she said meekly, eyes down. Jo had mastered meek repentance long ago. It was the only chance she had of soothing her father's ruffled feathers. There was no use in explaining the fantastic colors of the sky, the way the dew had lit up and sparkled, or the way the fields of grass had waved their greeting to the sun. Pa didn't hold with such flights of fancy. Besides, Jo couldn't bring herself to open up her innermost thoughts only to have them ripped apart by her father's cruelty.

"Were you talking with one of them railroad fellers?" Pa leaned over her.

Jo looked up into his eyes and relaxed slightly. The dark monster that sometimes took him over was still hibernating. So long as he was missing, Pa could be mollified.

"Of course not, Pa. I was by myself the entire time. I just had trouble getting the pails full in the shallow stream." It wasn't a lie, though it wasn't the whole truth; another careful balance to be maintained. "I took my time coming back so I wouldn't waste water. I remember what you said about that."

Earl Miller rubbed his left arm in what was fast become a characteristic odd motion and leaned back, appraising his daughter. Jo knew that he liked being right and he loved it when she pointed it out.

"All right then, girl. Go get breakfast on and don't dillydally this time."

Jo let out the breath she'd been holding and went on her way.

ALL OF THE MEN HEADING TO SANTA FE TO WORK ON THE NEW RAILROAD WERE uncomfortable about the father and daughter traveling with them. The wagon master had been hesitant to allow a lone woman along. Despite his worries that this would cause trouble with the other men, he'd agreed. After all, Earl Miller had been adamant that he would keep his daughter away from the others.

It hadn't taken long for them to understand that he meant it. Even the most remote of civilities were growled at. No one dared do so much as bid the girl good day now, knowing that they'd be accused of trying to take liberties with her. After three weeks traveling together on the Santa Fe Trail, the girl was given a wide berth.

Of course, the men talked about it when they were out of earshot of the pair. Hiram "Tom" Thomas was part of a circle that felt sorry for her and wished they could step in and help. He'd noticed the longing in her eyes at times when the men were laughing and talking together. Tom had never met a sadder-looking female in his life. Her occasionally bruised face made something inside of him burn with anger.

But what could he do? Tom had taken the job to help build the Atchison Topeka and Santa Fe Railway Line gladly. His parents had both passed away and his only sister had married and moved away years ago. Back in Saint Louis, Tom had worked his way to a fine job in a building company. The company was family owned and there was little more room for advancement. When the opportunity for adventure had come along, Tom had snapped it up.

He watched Jo struggle to carry both buckets of water and fill the cistern on the back of their wagon. Early on, he'd made the mistake of offering to help her and he'd barely avoided an altercation with her father, who seemed to think that Tom had ulterior motives.

Sipping his coffee, Tom squinted, trying to read her face. He couldn't see any new bruises there and she didn't seem too upset. His shoulders relaxed slightly and he chastised himself for the motion.

Why did he care? That woman was none of his concern. He needed to stay focused on helping protect the wagon train through Indian Territory. Once they got to

Santa Fe, they would go their way and the Millers would go theirs. If he kept on watching her like this, he was sure to get himself into a whole heap of trouble that he didn't need.

"She's looking real pert this morning, don't you think?" Ned Harkiss leered as he took a spot next to Tom. "I'd like to get her alone for a few minutes." He snickered lewdly and Tom gritted his teeth.

In every group there was always someone like Ned Harkiss. It never failed. Ned's group of flunkies was the very reason that Earl Miller had to watch his daughter so closely. Ned was crude, vile, and not ashamed of it at all. He was also the biggest man in camp as well as being in charge of the railroad workers until they arrived at their destination.

Ned gulped the last of his coffee and got to his feet. "Better get to work," he said shortly and strode away.

Sven Anders was checking the harnesses when Tom joined his friend.

"How's Ned this morning?" Sven asked. "Foul as always?"

Tom grunted his answer. "One day he's going to say too much and ..." he trailed off, shaking his head. It wasn't wise to make threats against the bigger man.

"God will judge him," Sven said quietly. "Don't you doubt that."

Tom wished he had Sven's faith in the Almighty. His acquaintance with the man upstairs was nowhere near as strong. It was one more thing that drew him to his Swedish friend. There was just something about a man who had that kind of confidence in what he couldn't see.

He glanced up and watched Jo struggle to light the fire. Her long brown braid kept slipping over her shoulder and she repeatedly threw it back into place without even realizing she was doing it. She was just too pretty for her own good, Tom grumbled inwardly. Why wasn't she a plain girl or a stocky girl or missing her teeth? Even Ned Harkiss would leave a toothless hag alone, wouldn't he?

CHAPTER 2

ALL DAY, TOM COULDN'T GET JO OFF HIS MIND. SHE WAS LIKE A TICKLE HIS brain couldn't turn off. As he rode his horse alongside the wagons and plodding oxen, he checked on her. Earl wouldn't let her out of her sight, so she was stuck bumping along on the wooden bench all day long. At noon, she fixed lunch for her father and Tom heard him scolding her for overcooking the bacon. Though she flinched back, Earl never did more than yell and Tom felt his tense muscles relax slightly.

Tom also noticed Ned watching her as he ate. At one point, Jo looked their way and caught Ned's gaze. The big man leered at her from his spot several wagon-lengths away. The poor girl blushed, forehead furrowing, and snapped her eyes back down. When Ned caught Tom watching the exchange, his smile broadened and he waggled his eyebrows up and down suggestively.

Even Sven noticed that Tom was preoccupied. The two men paused to water their horses that afternoon at the same time as the Millers' wagon rolled past. Edoardo Mancelli, another good friend, whistled softly and patted his drinking horse on the neck.

"I've never seen anything like it," he muttered. "I wish there was something we could do to help."

"Unfortunately, staying away seems to be the biggest help," Sven replied.

The tickle in Tom's brain grew into an idea. He snapped his fingers, brown eyes lighting up. "Maybe there is something we can do. If one of us could just talk to her, be friendly, you know, it would probably keep her from feeling so alone."

Sven shook his head. "Her father would never allow it."

"He wouldn't know about it if someone keeps him busy elsewhere," Tom looked between the two men. "One of us could talk to her and the other two could engage her father in a conversation."

"Which of us should talk to her?" Edoardo asked.

Tom grinned at this question. At least it wasn't a refusal.

THE TROUBLE WITH THE PRAIRIE, JO THOUGHT, WAS THAT IT OFFERED NOWHERE to be alone. Sure, the prairie grass could be as tall as six feet, but there were no hills and few trees. What Jo wouldn't have given for a shady tree by a brook where she could sit and cool her feet without worrying that someone was watching her. Being surrounded by new plants, animals, birds, fish, and insects thrilled her, but she was too timid to pull out her small, worn blank book and try to capture their likenesses where anyone could see her.

She missed their lonely farm back in Missouri. It felt funny to say that after all the years she'd spent wishing she was anywhere else, but back there she'd had her favorite spots. She'd known where to hide when Pa was in one of his tempers. There had been the peaceful pond with the birds and fish where she'd drawn everything that crossed her path in the one gift her father had ever given her: her sketchbook.

Now she had nowhere to go. Pa wouldn't let her go to relieve herself unless he was on high alert, protecting her from danger at a respectable distance. What would she give to have even ten minutes each day when she could be free from worry that one of those railroad men would catch her alone? Most of them seemed fine, but there were a few that frightened her. But whether the men had nefarious intentions or not, Pa would be sure to cause another humiliating scene. It destroyed any chance of respite whenever Jo was out of her father's sight.

This evening, she knelt at the brook and filled her buckets. While one regular worry was slightly lessened—Pa wasn't feeling well, so he would be less likely to notice if she was slow getting back—another concern surfaced. It was futile trying not to think of the man who'd been watching her at noon. He was big, which made him especially dangerous. Jo knew that his name was Ned Harkiss and she'd gathered enough from the way he looked at her to give him a wide berth. Though she'd had little enough experience with young men, Jo had a lifetime of knowledge of ominous expressions.

Rustling in the tall grass behind her made Jo tense. *Please don't let it be Ned*, she prayed. To her relief, another man parted the grass and stepped out to the stream, bucket in hand. She let out her breath, though Jo was now alert for signs of her father. If he came upon her here with this man, they'd both be in trouble.

The young man smiled at her timidly. She knew his name was Tom Thomas and that he was well liked around camp. He was of average height and build, and sported a beard that wrapped from one ear to the other under his chin with no mustache. Jo had thought his round spectacles made him look serious and intelligent. It was enough for her to dare a small smile in return.

He glanced over his shoulder and then said, "I'm Tom."

"I know," Jo replied. "My name is Josephine. Jo."

Tom's smile grew steadier. "It's strange that we've been out here so long and haven't introduced ourselves."

Jo's eyes dropped. It wasn't strange at all. It was her father's fault and they both knew it.

The two focused on filling their buckets and the silence stretched.

"It's been hot lately, hasn't it?" Tom finally asked.

Jo's eyes grew wider. He still wanted to talk to her? She could hardly believe it. "Yes, it's been very hot."

Tom's eyes lifted to the skies. "We'll probably have a big thunderstorm before long. I've heard the storms out here are nothing like back in Missouri."

"I don't know if I'd want to go through one, even if it does bring cooler weather." Jo pursed her lips for a moment. "Are you from Missouri, then?"

"Mostly," Tom said with a crooked grin. He stepped closer and set his full bucket down. "My family came from Tennessee when I was a little tyke. We farmed in the northern part of the state for most of my life. I've been in St. Louis the past six years, though."

Jo nodded. It felt wonderful to have a normal conversation with a young man. All her life, she'd imagined what she would say and what he would say in return. Living it out was both as good as she'd hoped and nothing at all like her imaginings.

"Can I help you with that last bucket?" Tom asked, stepping even closer.

Jo was so surprised by his nearness that she relinquished the pail without even thinking about it. He leaned forward, one foot in the water, and let the water rush in. With much less struggle than she usually had, Tom rose and placed the now-full bucket on the ground.

Jo studied him intently for a long minute. Then, realizing she was just staring at him, she blushed and hurried on to say, "I should get back."

"I'd offer to help you carry your buckets, but ..." Tom mercifully didn't finish.

Jo was more grateful than she could say. "If you don't mind, I'll go first."

"That's probably best." The man went back for his own pail. "It was nice talking to you, Jo."

She smiled shyly, picked up her buckets, and began the trek back to the wagons. Later that night, she would lie in her bed and give herself a firm talking to about getting her hopes up about a man. But, for now, Jo's imagination spun a fine story about Tom standing up to her father and asking for her hand in marriage.

CHAPTER 3

For the next five days, Jo went to get water when the wagons stopped for the night and hoped that Tom would arrive. And, for five days, he did. Their conversations were always short and never delved deeply into any important topics, but they quickly became the best part of her days.

Perhaps the ever-present risk of Earl finding out about their clandestine meetings fueled the romance for Jo. She told herself again and again that it was silly to dream of Tom at night and create elaborate stories about their possible life together. Still, a tiny spark of hope lit in her heart and she was all too eager to huddle around its feeble warmth.

Tonight, though, there was no water. The wagon train was too far from the river to benefit from even the most meager of tributaries. Instead, Jo spent the time looking for dried grasses that would fuel their fire. Pa was feeling poorly again and needed even more heat than usual to ward off the evening's chill. She ranged farther and farther from the wagons and began to despair that Tom wouldn't be able to find her. The thought of missing their few minutes of friendly conversation was enough to punch a hole through Jo.

Finally, the sound of someone moving through the grass pulled her to her feet and she held her breath as she waited to see who it was. Now, though, the prayer had become, *Please let it be Tom.*

And then he was there. His dark eyes twinkling behind his glasses, his bowler hat in place as always, and his friendly grin instantly dissolved the dark cloud of despair that had been growing inside Jo.

"Looks like a storm's coming," he said without preamble.

This was how it was now. They acted as though they were continuing one long conversation. Jo smiled at Tom before scanning the western sky. Sure enough, tall, dark clouds were marching towards them. "We'll have to put out the cisterns," she replied.

"Did you hear that Edoardo's horse threw a shoe?" Tom reached for a clump of dead grass and joined her in twisting it into a tight bundle before tossing it in the burlap sack thrown over her shoulder.

"No, I didn't. Is he all right? Is the horse hurt?" Jo reveled in the feeling of being included in the bigger group.

Tom began to tell the tale and Jo was so drawn in that she failed to notice the sound of someone else moving through the grass. The grass around them was so tall that it wasn't until he was right upon them that either of them knew they were no longer alone.

But, in a horrible moment, the stalks parted and Earl Miller crashed into view, shattering the cozy gathering.

Jo jerked up and her heart froze. The look on her father's face was one she knew far too well. The irrational, furious monster had taken possession of him. There was nothing she could do but brace herself for the coming storm and let her mind drift away to a safer place.

❦

TOM'S HEART SANK AT THE SIGHT OF JO'S FATHER. TOM WAS NOT A BIG MAN, BUT he had enough experience in schoolyard scraps that he could hold his own. The man facing him, chest heaving and eyes swinging accusatorily between the two of them, was not large. He rubbed his upper left arm almost without thinking, which made him seem like he'd lost his reason. It made Tom reluctant to do anything rash.

Tom knew that he should step in front of Jo and shield her from danger. The thought flickered through his mind and he made to move. However, almost instantly, he knew that this would only make matters worse. Past interactions with Earl had taught the men of the camp that Jo's father's biggest fear was one of them corrupting her.

"What are the two of you doing?" Earl hissed. His shoulders hunched, his hands balled, and he took a slow, menacing step towards them. "You're hiding out where no one will see your illicit behavior!"

A quick glance at Jo made Tom's heart pound harder. She stood perfectly still, eyes glassed over, and offered no defense against these ridiculous accusations. More than the man in front of him, this sparked fear in Tom. Jo knew what was coming and was bracing herself to withstand whatever came. Tom felt himself growing hot with anger.

"Mr. Miller, we haven't done anything of the sort. We were both just collecting grass and I thought I'd make sure your daughter was safe from wild animals or snakes." Tom tried a soothing voice.

"The only snakes that are a danger to my daughter are the two-legged kind," Earl snarled. "If I catch you near her again, I'll make sure you don't live to tell the tale. I'm her father and it's my duty to ensure she's not hurt."

And in direct contradiction to that statement, Earl reached out and grabbed Jo roughly by the arm. He shot one last poisonous glare at Tom before dragging his daughter away.

Tom waited a full minute, chest heaving, before going back to the camp. Immediately, Edoardo and Sven hurried to him.

"What happened?" Tom asked.

Edoardo shook his head. "He got away from us." The two men had been taking turns to ask advice or share a smoke with Earl. The three men had believed that this was a foolproof way for Tom to have a few quiet minutes with Jo.

"He grew suspicious," Sven admitted, rubbing the back of his neck. "I guess we weren't as smart as we thought we were."

"Where are they?" Tom's eyes scanned the camp.

"In their wagon," Sven pointed grimly. "Earl looked like one angry mother bear."

A low, intense mumbling could be heard even from across the camp. Tom gritted his teeth in frustration. This was ridiculous! How could they stand here and listen to Jo being chastised for innocently talking to someone?

At that moment, the sharp crack of a slap snapped all heads up. Instantly, Tom was on his feet. Edoardo was up beside him only a beat later and put a hand on his shoulder.

"Wait, Tom. You can't step into this. He has every right to discipline his daughter as he sees fit. The law's on his side." Edoardo's voice was resigned, but reasonable.

Ned Harkiss got slowly to his feet and loped over. He swaggered, crossing his arms and said, "Looks like Miller knows how to keep his women in line." Ned's cruel laugh dared Tom to make a move.

The sounds of further hitting reached out to the men. Some shifted uneasily while Ned's gang of reprobates grinned and nudged each other.

Tom registered that he'd yet to hear a sound from Jo. She was taking this unearned beating without even a cry of pain. Never in his life had he felt more impotently furious.

Ned must have read some of this on his face because he leaned forward and poked Tom's chest. "Stay out of it, Thomas. We're not going to risk the railroad's good name by getting ourselves involved in a domestic dispute."

His fists balled and Tom ground his teeth, his eyes shooting daggers up at Ned.

"You step in there and you won't have a job when you get to Santa Fe. In fact, I'll make sure you don't work anywhere. You understand me?" Ned's hot, foul breath scalded Tom's face.

Tom channeled all his rage through his eyes and into Ned's. The other man only leered at him, waiting. Finally, Tom allowed one curt nod.

Ned swaggered away and Sven and Edoardo were able to pull Tom to the stewpot. Even though he was sure he couldn't eat while knowing what was happening to Jo, Tom accepted the plate and hunk of bread. Thankfully, the sounds from the wagon quieted and Tom found himself praying for the first time in many years that Jo was all right. He also found himself imagining how good it would feel to take out his anger on both Earl Miller and Ned Harkiss.

CHAPTER 4

THOUGH HE KNEW IT WAS UNWISE TO MAKE ANY ATTEMPT TO TALK TO JO again, Tom watched her carefully over the next few days. She sported a swollen lip and black eye that made his stomach clench whenever he saw it, but otherwise she seemed about the same. She'd always been a bit timid, with a tendency to daydream, and that hadn't changed.

There was nothing to do but continue on down the trail. The wagon train was deep into Indian Territory now and the men had to keep a careful watch all the time against attacks. Unlike the Oregon Trail, the Indians in this territory did not allow intruders willingly and had developed a habit of stealing horses and other livestock from anyone who dared cross their land.

Tom wasn't sure if it was the constant threat of Indian attack, the situation with the Millers, or Ned Harkiss' dark presence, but the entire wagon train seemed to be walking under a dark cloud at all times. There was an invisible *something* that made all of them glance around uneasily every few minutes and tense their shoulders. It felt as though they were all waiting for something big to happen.

So, it wasn't a surprise when one of the men spotted a pair of Indian scouts on a distant bluff just sitting on their horses, watching the train go past. The cry passed through the train and everyone reached for their guns.

"Don't do anything rash," their trail guide, Ronald Nash, called. "We're within a day's ride of Fort Union and they'll let us pass this time."

"We could take 'em," Jethro Moffat, one of Ned's cronies, boasted. "No Injun can stop us."

Tom and Sven exchanged a disbelieving look and shook their heads. Tom thought longingly of the time when they would be able to escape the likes of Jethro and Ned, as well as Indian attacks and the Millers.

The guard that night was extra vigilant and the sense of impending danger followed them into the next day. Still, not a single thing happened until the next day at noon.

It had become the habit of most of the train to eat a quick meal when the train stopped for dinner each day and then lie down for forty winks. Most of the men stretched out on the ground, covered their faces with their hats, and were snoring in under a minute flat.

Tom usually took advantage of the quiet to pull out one of his books and read a few pages. The one trunk of belongings he was allowed was full of his worn, mostly secondhand favorites. Today, as he looked around for an empty patch of ground away from most of the noise, he watched Jo and Earl head off into the high grass. After that, try as he might, Tom couldn't keep his mind on his reading.

Finally, he closed his book and huffed a sigh of frustration. What was it about Josephine Miller that got under his skin? Sure, she was awful pretty, but she wasn't the sort of girl that he usually liked. His last sweetheart had been a plump, teasing young woman who had laughed at his quiet ways and drawn him out into the crowd. He'd liked that about Ella. Jo, on the other hand, was like a little mouse who was constantly being chased by a ferocious cat. When he'd first started talking to her, he'd expected her to be a bit simpleminded, but had found that to be far from the truth. She was quick and curious and remarkably kind, considering the treatment she'd suffered all her life.

The thought of that treatment, and how much Tom wished he could change it, was moving through his mind as Joe and her father suddenly stepped back out of the grass and Tom watched them walk back towards their wagon. Jo's eyes darted briefly his way, but never made contact with is. Her father, his complexion a sickly gray, stalked along beside her as though daring anyone to talk to his daughter. Upon closer inspection, Jo sported a fresh cut on her cheek and Tom gritted his teeth.

૭୪୬

THE NIGHT WORE ON, HOT AND HEAVY WITH THE PROMISE OF RAIN, BUT TOM couldn't sleep. He tossed and turned in his spot by the fire, thoughts of Jo keeping his eyes from closing. He replayed every one of their meetings, imagined the soft lilt to her voice and husky laughter, on the rare occasion he'd managed to draw it from her. He thought of her beautiful laughter and the way her eyes glowed with excitement whenever they lit on a new flower—

A scream pierced the night and Tom bolted upright, a chill racing down his spine. The scream came again, but he was already on his feet, racing toward the Millers' wagon. Jo screamed and screamed and screamed as Tom swung himself up and darted inside, regardless of whether it was proper or not. The terror in her voice was a live thing that ate at him like a burning coal.

"Jo?"

He stumbled into the darkness of the wagon, seeing Jo silhouetted in the light of a candle that was flickering not from wind, but because her hand was shaking so much.

"Jo." Tom moved over to her, averting his eyes from her nightgown and following her own gaze to where Earl lay prone on a sleeping pallet. "Jo—" He'd scarcely reached out an arm, following an automatic instinct to draw her close and try to offer comfort, in spite of the fact that Earl would likely break every bone in his body, when the screaming stopped and Jo whispered,

"He's dead."

CHAPTER 5

THEY BURIED EARL MILLER WRAPPED IN AN OLD QUILT, IN A HOLE THAT TOM helped dig. As Sven said a few compassionate words in regards to the soul of the cruel, twisted man who God had seen fit to take in his sleep, Tom watched out of the corner of his eye as Jo stood like stone.

Her face was the color of chalk, so white he was afraid she might faint. But she was alone now, with no chaperone, and walking over to rest a gentle hand on her back the way he desperately wanted to might be a gesture misconstrued by all the wrong people. The last Jo needed was to be looked upon askance in this terrible time of need. So Tom stood by, grim-faced, as Jo suffered in silence through the short funeral, then walked back to her wagon and disappeared inside.

"We've got to keep moving," Ned demanded shortly thereafter. "There's no time to stay here."

The fear of Indians was upon them all, so none argued. Tom was about to volunteer to drive Jo's wagon, when she emerged from cover and took a seat on the buckboard. Her slender shoulders were ramrod straight as she sank into the seat previously occupied and took up the reins, staring straight ahead, leaving the men around in awe at her strength, one man in particular.

Tom watched her throughout the day, riding up alongside the wagon frequently to check on Jo, but she never said a word, not as they covered long, dusty miles and her shoulders and back must surely ache. Not as they briefly stopped for lunch, which she did not eat, even when Tom placed a bowl beside her. Not when they continued on into the night.

He was riding up again to do another check, beginning to realize as he did that he was doing it almost as much for himself as Jo—he *needed* to know she was all right —when a snippet of conversation drifted over to him.

"Now that her watchdog is gone, I'm going to enjoy getting to know that little filly better," Ned crowed and his slimy compatriot snickered appreciatively.

Tom's blood ran cold. He switched directions, kicked his horse into a trot, and rode up to the wagon that Sven was driving. "What do you think of pitching our bedrolls near the Millers' wagon tonight?"

Sven glanced over his shoulder to where Ned was riding. "That's a good idea."

When the wagons circled for the night, Tom filled Edoardo in on the plan and the Italian man was quick to agree to it. Without saying anything, the three friends got their bedrolls from the supply wagon and spread them out around the back of Jo's wagon then went about their usual chores.

Ned didn't notice until supper was dished up and Tom, Sven, and Edoardo made their way over with their bowls and mugs. The big man's eyes narrowed, but he kept his distance, much to Tom's relief.

Tom didn't sleep much that night, for more than one reason. Every sense strained toward the wagon, listening for any sign of the grieving young woman within. But her silence now was as stoic as every time she'd endured a beating.

❧

THE DAY PASSED FOR JO IN A STRANGE HAZE. SHE'D ELECTED TO DRIVE THE wagon because sitting in the quiet, hot back, lost in her thoughts would have driven her utterly mad. She thought back over the years, remembering Pa's anger, his slaps, his cutting words. But even as those ugly thoughts cut her deep, she also remembered the occasional moments as a little girl when Pa had been kind, had lifted her up on his shoulders and given her a perch to view the world. The moments when he'd seemed to actually be proud of her budding artistry.

Lying in the hot darkness she'd been trying to avoid all day, Jo's hand closed over the sketchbook and drew it close to her heart. It was the one thing Pa had given her, and thus her one remaining physical connection to the man she'd never understood. And yet she'd loved him, even if the pain of his loss was likely far less than daughters of kinder men.

All of a sudden, Jo felt the full weight of how alone she was and the tears finally came. There was no one to keep an eye on her when she went off alone. And what would become of her in Santa Fe? Her father had been a cruel man who was impossible to live with, but he had protected her from all other danger and provided for her.

When the urge to relieve herself finally became urgent, she rubbed at her eyes and stepped out of the wagon. She could feel eyes watching her, but no one spoke as she walked resolutely to the tall grass and stepped through. To her great relief, no one followed and she was able to take care of her personal needs without any difficulty.

Stepping back into camp a few minutes later, she felt an immediate tension in the air. Jo looked around and saw that Tom, Edoardo, and Sven were casually leaning against her wagon, shining their rifles. Tom's kind eyes watched her as they had all day, but she couldn't bring herself to meet them just yet. She'd received such little kindness in her life, she truly had no notion of how to respond to the well-meaning young man who'd gone out of his way all day to keep an eye on her.

Across the camp, Ned and a few others were watching them with glittering eyes. A bad feeling unfurled in the pit of Jo's stomach. Jo didn't know what was going on, but she knew that she wanted to be back in her wagon and out of sight, however suffocating it might be.

She was reaching up to open the canvas when a voice from behind her said, "Pardon me, Miss Miller, but may I have a word?"

Turning, Jo saw Theodore Humphrey wringing his hands and looking decidedly uncomfortable. She'd never spoken to the man before but knew that he represented the railroad that had hired the men and was tasked with caring for the money and getting the men to Santa Fe. Where Ned Harkiss was in charge of the workers, Humphrey was in charge of Ned.

Jo nodded and Humphrey took her arm, leading her to a quiet spot down the line. Once they had found a place that seemed to satisfy him, Humphrey began to hem and haw, clearing his throat and fiddling with his collar.

"Miss Miller, first let me say that I'm sorry that your father passed on," he finally said. "I know that this leaves you in a very difficult situation."

Jo nodded slightly.

"Unfortunately, having an unmarried woman in a train full of men is not something that the Atchison, Topeka, and Santa Fe Railroad Company finds acceptable, regardless of how it happened. You have no chaperone and no one to protect you."

Jo shifted uncomfortably. There was no argument for his words.

Humphrey was now pacing in front of her. "We'll be at Fort Union tomorrow and I would recommend leaving you there under normal circumstances. However, Fort Union has very few women and I doubt they would let you stay. I understand that it's a very wild place due to the dangerous nature of the Indian situation in these parts."

Her heart sank. If the fort was dangerous and wouldn't allow her to stay, what other option was there?

"I do have a solution that I hope you will find acceptable." Humphrey stopped pacing. "A single man in our train has offered to marry you tomorrow at the fort and take care of you."

Jo's eyes widened and she felt her heart begin to pound, a faint thread of hope touching her. Had Tom maybe ... she hadn't dared to believe the connection she felt was more than a daydream, but could it possibly—

"Would you consider his offer of marriage?" Humphrey took her hand with fatherly concern.

It would be inappropriate to look too happy on the day her father died, so Jo kept her nod as stately and serious as she could manage.

"I don't know that there are any better choices," she added.

"I couldn't agree with you more." Humphrey stood back and clapped his hands. "Well, I'll send Ned your way to discuss his offer."

Jo went cold in spite of the sultry heat. "Did you say Ned?"

"Yes, of course," Humphrey blinked at her in confusion. "Ned Harkiss suggested that the two of you marry. He's the foreman, you know, and that makes him quite a good catch."

All the breath left Jo's body and she leaned hard against the wagon, weak-kneed and faintly sick.

CHAPTER 6

NED HARKISS SHOWED UP A FEW MINUTES LATER AND JO FOUND NO WAY TO deny him his request for a walk around the perimeter of the camp. They walked in silence for a few minutes before Ned finally spoke, not bothering to offer condolences for her loss before going straight to the matter at hand.

"I guess Humphrey told you what I was thinking," Ned said loudly as the two walked slowly around the ring of wagons.

Jo was glad they were out of sight of everyone's eyes, but that was the only thing she could think to be glad about at the moment. She hadn't been this close to the big man before and couldn't help but keep her arms crossed over her chest and lean slightly away from him.

"When we get to Santa Fe, you can find a job until we start having kids. I expect we'll stay with the railroad and move from camp to camp. They usually give married men tents for their wives and kids to sleep in."

Jo's stomach roiled. She wasn't sure if it was due to the thought of Ned Harkiss himself, raising children in a tent camp, or the way he acted as though she'd already agreed to marry him. There was no way that she would ever agree to that, she promised herself. Somehow she would find the courage to refuse him.

"We'll find the chaplain when we get to the fort tomorrow and get hitched then. Don't worry about your dress," Ned looked her up and down and Jo cringed. "I don't need no fancy bride."

He gave her braid what was probably supposed to be a friendly tug, but Jo's head was pulled back slightly and she froze. It was the sort of thing her father had done so many times. Having a husband who touched her that way would mean miseries that Jo couldn't imagine.

Without another word, Ned winked at her and strode away, chest out and grin fixed on his smug face. Jo watched him go, brow furrowed, and finished walking back to her wagon.

Tom joined her, worry carving lines across his handsome face. "What was that about?" he asked, putting a hand on her arm as soon as she got back.

Jo looked up at him, an idea beginning to form in her mind. Tom's hand on her arm was gentle and he had never spoken to her in a cruel way. Perhaps she could marry him after all and be saved from Ned. Maybe Tom hadn't thought of it because she didn't inspire such ideas in men—she was nowhere near as pretty or vivacious as other women—but perhaps he might consider the idea given their previous friendship?

Mustering her courage, Jo squared her shoulders. "Theodore Humphrey says I shouldn't stay with the wagon train after tomorrow unless I marry someone," she summarized. "Ned Harkiss gave him the idea and says he wants to marry me."

"What?" Tom took a step closer, alarm spreading over his features.

"I don't want to marry Ned. He's just like my father," Jo mumbled, waiting, but still, Tom didn't take the hint.

The two stood in awkward silence. Finally, Jo decided there was nothing else for it and said, "They're right that I shouldn't stay here by myself."

"Could you stay at the fort?" Tom was quick to ask.

Her hopes were fading quickly, but she tried again. "Mr. Humphrey says it's too rough there and that there wouldn't be much work for me. I'm going to have to marry someone."

Tom looked uncomfortable. He wouldn't meet her eyes and shifted his rifle from hand to hand.

Oh God. Guide me, Jo prayed fervently, and blurted out, "I was thinking that you and I could maybe get married."

Tom's face went slack. "Uh—Jo—um. I—Jo—" He sputtered and stammered, turning beet red, and as she watched him, Jo felt her hopes crushing under his shuffling feet. What a fool she had been to think fantasies could ever become reality.

Quickly, she backpedaled. "Never mind, Tom. It was just an idea. I'm sorry I said anything. It was ... terribly forward of me." She turned to make a fast escape into the wagon.

"Look, Jo," Tom touched her arm once more and Jo flinched back. "I don't know if I'm the sort of man you ought to marry."

"What does that even mean?" Jo whispered under her breath, head bowed, refusing to looking at him.

"Just, let me have some time to think, all right?" Tom said gruffly.

"No, don't worry about it. It was a foolish idea. Please forgive me." Jo dived into her wagon before he could see her hot, broken-hearted tears.

CHAPTER 7

Tom felt like an idiot. A better man would have known what to say when Jo had suggested they marry. A better man would have said ... something. Anything. God, the hurt on her pretty face! Even now, hours later, Tom didn't know what he should have said.

He rolled over in his bedroll and punched the bag of clothes he used for a pillow. If he refused, Jo would have to marry Ned Harkiss. Ned Harkiss! But Tom knew marriage ... and he had no intent of ever embarking on that path ever again.

Frantically, Tom's mind ran from possible solution to possible solution. She could stay at the fort. No, it was full of rough Indian-fighting soldiers. Perhaps one of the other men on the train would make a better husband. He ticked each man off. Sven? No, Sven had a wife and kids back home. Edoardo had a sweetheart waiting for him. Who else would he trust to marry Jo? Not Jethro, of course. Harry? Pete? John? No, no, no.

His brain went back over each of the men of the wagon train. Surely one of them would make an acceptable husband for Jo. But no matter how many times he thought through the list, no one was right.

It left Tom tired and cranky the next morning. The sun was too bright. The horses were contrary. Everyone was entirely too cheerful.

And the worst of all was Ned. Today, the foreman swaggered around the camp, laughing heartily and slapping others on the back. Tom spent so much time with his teeth clenched that his jaw ached by breakfast.

"What's eating you?" Sven asked.

Tom shrugged. "Humphrey thinks Jo ought to marry Ned."

"Come again?" Edoardo demanded.

"He says a single woman isn't safe in a wagon train full of men and that the fort is too dangerous. There's no choice but for her to marry and Ned offered." Tom stabbed at his oatmeal viciously.

He could feel Sven and Edoardo exchanging a look.

"Don't even suggest it," he barked. "I'm not going to marry her."

"Why not?" Sven asked, his voice far more surprised than Tom thought it should be. "We both thought you were sort of sweet on her."

"Doesn't matter if I am," Tom said curtly, giving Sven a hard look. "You know why I can't."

Always a man to be trusted, Sven said nothing of the secrets Tom had once revealed to him. Instead, he commented, "Well, we can't let her marry Ned. He'd be worse than her father."

The thought made Tom sick. "I know. I was up all night trying to figure out what to do," Tom admitted.

"There's only one thing I can think of," Edoardo said meaningfully, and took a swig of coffee.

Throughout the long day, Tom ruminated over and over his past history, but couldn't find a way to make it so that he could wrap his mind around ever marrying, no matter how beautiful and sweet Jo Miller might be.

Sven rode up briefly to offer words of unsolicited advice. "Your past can't define you, Tom. If you allow it to, two lives might be destroyed today." He rode away before Tom had the chance to snap an irritable reply.

By the time he was sitting with his friends near her wagon, eating their supper, Tom felt like he was chewing on nails, so torn was he. He'd never considered himself a fearful man, but tarnation, what if he was worse than Earl in the end? Jo deserved more than that. So much more.

"One more night of freedom, boys!" Ned's voice rang out through the camp. "By this time tomorrow, I'll have a regular ball and chain!"

The rough crowd surrounding him hooted and jeered.

"We'll need to go to the fort tonight to celebrate. Tomorrow night I'll be busy teaching my wife how to submit to her new husband!" Ned's friends cheered and the group tromped off towards the fort.

Tom glanced up to see Jo climbing, white-faced, from her wagon. Their eyes met and he knew she'd heard every word. Tom didn't like how distant her expression was. It reminded him of the way she'd looked after her father had caught them talking. He felt like he'd been punched in the gut as he realized that she was bracing herself to endure something highly unpleasant.

He followed her as she walked to find a secluded place and until she emerged from the high grass. She walked right by him, face blank, shoulders stiff.

"Jo—"

"Please don't," she said so quietly he almost didn't hear her. "I'm humiliated enough already, Hiram. The only things I have left are my wagon and my dignity. In a short while, I'll have neither left. Allow me a few minutes with both before I bid them farewell forever. Please."

From another woman's lips, the words might have sounded whiny or manipulative. From Jo, they were soft, stoic, and so strong that Tom's gut turned her over. He took her arm and didn't let go even when Jo pulled back. When she raised her head and he saw the flash of anger in her eyes, he dropped her arm quickly, surprisingly glad to see that she had some kind of temper, even if it had never before been on display.

"I understand. I'm not the woman you want to marry," Jo said simply, her emotions slipping back under her usual stoic façade. "I should never have asked. Now let me go. Please, Hiram."

"Stop calling me that," Tom begged. "We're friends, Jo. I want what's best for you."

Her smile was sad. "I believe that."

He shook his head vehemently. "You don't understand. I have reasons for not wanting marriage—" he hurried on at the look on her face. "Personal reasons, Jo. They have nothing to do with you at all. Nothing! I don't want to marry any girl, honestly. If I had to, you would be the one though."

Jo frowned. "Personal reasons ... I don't understand." She tugged her arm away. "You don't need to explain. I really must get back, though. My fiancé will ... be unpleasant if I linger with another man."

Hearing the word *fiancé* on her lips did something to Tom. Protective rage and simultaneous jealousy surged within him. He stepped in front of Jo, grasped her shoulders, and spoke without thinking.

"I'll marry you."

Jo blinked in shock and the blank expression disappeared. "You ... you will?" She sounded as surprised as he felt.

"I can't let you marry Ned Harkiss." He took a deep breath as a plan began to come together in his mind. "We should go tonight and find the chaplain while Ned's busy. By the time he finds out, it'll be too late for him to do anything."

"You just said you don't want to marry anyone," she pointed out. "The last thing I need is to be in a marriage with a man who resents me, Tom. I've had that. I'll have it again soon enough."

"I don't resent you." Desperate, Tom cupped her lovely face in one rough palm and tilted it to look up at him. "Like I said, it if I was going to marry anyone ... it's you, Jo. I'll marry you. Yes. Right now. Come one."

Not even affording her the courtesy of awaiting a reply, Tom grasped her hand and started toward the chaplain's quarters. Jo said nothing, but didn't resist him, and her hand in his felt so right that Tom had a faint notion, a wondering, of whether he could do this right in spite of his past history.

CHAPTER 8

AN HOUR LATER, JO STOOD IN FRONT OF THE CHAPLAIN, HARDLY DARING TO believe that she was marrying Tom instead of Ned. She'd prayed so hard that God would save her without any real hope that He would actually come through. And now, here she was, becoming Mrs. Hiram Thomas.

Jo peeked shyly at Tom and noted his stony face. His earlier words replayed over and over in her mind. She knew that he didn't really want to marry her, that he was just doing it to protect her. Her eyes fluttered back to the bouquet of wild purple larkspur she was holding. She'd briefly wondered if she'd entrapped him, but no. She'd given him every chance to back out after her initial foolish offer. She didn't understand why he'd changed her mind, but he had.

And it didn't really matter that he didn't love her. Maybe friendship would grow into something. Or maybe that would be all that ever lay between them. Either way, it was better than any other hope Jo could ever have had after her father's death, and she was deeply grateful.

She squared her shoulders and turned her mind back to the chaplain's words. She would do everything in her power to show Tom that she was grateful and capable of being a good wife. She wouldn't complain or nag or be too demanding of him.

"Do you, Hiram Thomas, take Josephine Miller to be your lawfully wedded wife?" the chaplain asked.

Jo's heart leaped as Tom answered, "I do," even if his voice was slightly strained.

The chaplain turned to her, smiling. "Do you, Josephine Miller, take Hiram Thomas to be your lawfully wedded husband?"

"I do," Jo whispered.

"I now pronounce you man and wife."

Jo looked up at Tom and offered him a shaky smile. He leaned down and very gently kissed her, Jo's first-ever kiss, and she trembled slightly at the soft touch. Then Tom was shaking hands with the chaplain and the marriage certificate was completed. In no time at all, the pair was walking back through the dark fort towards their camp. Jo was glad to have her bouquet to keep her hands busy.

"Thank you for marrying me," she said into the awkward silence.

Tom shrugged. "It was the right thing to do." He sighed heavily. "I've never liked bullies like Ned."

"Or my father," Jo agreed.

"Was your father always like that?" He'd wondered but hadn't felt he had the right to ask before.

Jo reflected. "Almost always. My mother died when I was very young. I hardly remember her. I don't know if he treated her like that or not. Sometimes I wonder if he was angry that she died and took it out on me. But I suppose I'll never really know."

"Was he ever kind to you?"

"I remember one time when a trapper came and asked to stay at our farm for the night. Papa let him sleep in the barn, but he came in the house when Papa was out doing chores and tried to hurt me." Jo hugged herself with one arm as she remembered how afraid she'd been and how glad she'd felt when Papa had come home. "Papa was like a mama bear protecting her cub when he came in and saw me cowering in the corner. I was so grateful that he'd come home when he did. And he bought me a blank book each year for Christmas along with two new pencils. So he could be kind. Occasionally."

Jo bit her lip and shot Tom a sideways glance. Had she said too much? Tom had always been friendly, but their conversations had been short. What if he was the sort of fellow who didn't like too much noise? Or the sort who preferred to talk about himself?

"What is your family like?" she asked quickly.

Tom put his hands in his pockets. "My parents worked hard on the farm. They were always sort of tired. It sometimes felt like they had children in order to get free labor. My sister married when she was sixteen and moved a ways off. I haven't seen her since. Dad died in the winter and Mother died the following spring. I've been on my own for the past four years."

"And your ... past history?" she asked, thinking that they shouldn't have secrets from one another. It didn't seem like a good start to a relationship.

Tom looked away and shook his head. "I can't, Jo. Not yet."

The pain in his voice was evident and Jo didn't press him. She nodded, tucking away this new information about her husband. She intended to think about it more when she was alone, but soon realized that was not to be. No sooner had they arrived at the wagon than Tom began rubbing the back of his neck and refusing to meet her eyes.

"I sure don't want to invade your privacy," he hedged. "It's just that Ned might question if we're really married if we don't ... share the wagon ... at night."

Her cheeks instantly flushed and Jo managed a small, "Oh."

"Why don't you go ahead and get ready for bed and I'll be in ... later." Tom waved vaguely at the wagon.

After hurrying to change into her nightgown and dive under the quilt, Jo's nerves thrummed and she couldn't get her mind to settle on anything for long until Tom called quietly from outside.

"May I come in?"

"Yes," Jo whispered, then realized he wouldn't hear and spoke louder, "Yes. Please."

A moment later, Tom climbed in. "I ... generally change into a different shirt to sleep," he said awkwardly, holding out a small bundle in his arms that he'd obviously retrieved while she changed. She noticed his dark hair was also wet and his arms and face were damp. "I wash up at night. So's I don't have to rush around changing first thing in the morning, when there are other chores to be done."

For a moment, Jo couldn't figure out what he was telling her, and then her cheeks flamed and she hastily turned to her side and reached for her pillow to press over her face. "Please. Go ahead."

She heard his shuffling movements as he changed, her cheeks burning bright as candlelight as he finished and slid under the blanket as far as he could from her. They lay in tense, stiff silence, until Tom finally murmured, "Good night, Mrs. Thomas."

Jo smiled very slightly, in spite of the terrible awkwardness and wondering if it would always be like this between them. "Good night, Mr. Thomas."

CHAPTER 9

WHEN JO OPENED HER EYES THE NEXT MORNING, SHE WAS SURPRISED TO SEE that Tom was still lying there. From the light outside and the noise in the camp, it was later that she usually slept. She'd imagined that Tom would have wanted to get busy with the day's work. Instead, he was reading a thick book, his spectacles in place.

"Morning," he said softly when he noticed her watching him. He raised his book and smiled a little sheepishly. "One more reason I like to change at night. Gives me a few minutes I don't get otherwise."

"Morning," Jo echoed, smiling back. There was something so intimate about having a man see her sleep and she felt even more shy than normal. Even so, the closeness of the early morning conversation warmed something frozen deep inside her and she dared to hope yet again that they could make something good of this unexpected union.

Tom put a placeholder between his pages and put the book down then propped himself up on his elbow and turned to her. "You're going to want to put on enough clothes to be decent because, when I step out of this wagon, Ned's going to make a scene. I think it might be a good idea for you to still be in your nightgown, but you'll want to put on ... other things too."

It was a good point and Jo hadn't thought about Ned's reaction. Yet again, here was Tom protecting her. She didn't know what to say, so she nodded and Tom went back to reading, turning so his back was to her as she pulled on some underclothes and wrapped a shawl around her shoulders.

"I'm ready," she said quietly.

Tom rolled over again and sat up. He pulled on his boots and nodded at her. She took a deep breath and nodded back, noting that he had yet to put on his shirt and carried it with him as he climbed out of the wagon.

She waited with bated breath. Almost instantly, the noise of the camp stilled.

"Thomas, what the ..." Ned's voice sounded truly shocked. "What are you doing in the Millers' wagon?"

"Well, that's the interesting thing, Ned." Tom's response was loud enough to be heard by all. "As of last night, it's now the Thomas' wagon."

"What are you talking about?" Ned's voice was growing dangerous.

"It just so happens that Jo and I got married last night."

A murmur swept the camp. Jo knew it was her cue and she climbed out of the wagon in her nightdress, clutching her shawl around her shoulders. As she walked to where Tom stood, she felt all eyes watching her.

"You did what?" Ned growled.

Tom reached into his back pocket and pulled out their folded marriage certificate. He held it up for all to see. "We got married last night."

Ned rounded on Jo. "You two-timing, traitorous, unfaithful ..."

But his insult was cut short as Tom said, "Better watch what you say to my wife, Harkiss."

The bigger man looked between them and turned on his heel and stalked away. Jo let out her breath and looked up at Tom gratefully.

"You can get dressed now," he said in a voice that told Jo he was pleased with himself. "I've got some chores to do."

THEIR BUSINESS AT THE FORT WAS SOON CONCLUDED AND THE WAGON TRAIN WAS rolling away early the next morning, with Tom driving the wagon this time. Maybe it was the satisfying way that Ned had taken the news, but Tom felt downright good about his marriage today.

He studied his wife out of the corner of his eye as they rode along. Jo was really very pretty. If only he could think of something to say that would get a conversation started, the ride would be downright enjoyable.

"Do you enjoy reading?" Tom asked.

Jo shook her head. "Papa taught me to read, but we never had any books."

"Did you go to school?"

"No."

Tom frowned, feeling stymied. "Oh, I see." He thought back over their previous conversations. "You said your father gave you a blank book every year. Do you write in it?"

"I like to draw plants and animals that I haven't seen before," she said as quickly as possible.

"I'd love to see your drawings someday," Tom said eagerly.

"They're not very good," Jo said quietly. "I doubt they're worth your time."

Tom slumped. Clearly, she wanted to keep her drawings private and he couldn't really force his way into her privacy without offering up something private of his own. But telling her about Elsie ... he shook the thought furiously away. It was a full five minutes before he thought of something else to ask her. "What do you enjoy doing?"

Jo gave him a look that made him think she was weighing her answer carefully.

After a pause she said, "I like to cook and clean."

"No one likes to cook and clean," Tom laughed. He swallowed his mirth as he began to think about her life. Maybe Earl had been the sort of man who didn't let her do anything except care for the house. Maybe she really did like cooking and cleaning and he'd just insulted her.

The rest of the long morning passed in silence. Tom was glad when the stopped for the noon hour. Jo jumped down and was a whirlwind of activity as she prepared their lunch, collected fuel for the fire, and gathered water. He wondered briefly if he should tell her to stop, but then Tom remembered their conversation from earlier. Maybe she really did like cooking and cleaning.

Thankfully, Edoardo and Sven joined them for lunch. The three men enjoyed the rest, though Tom began to be a bit annoyed over the way that Jo kept jumping up and trying to care for their every need. He could tell that his friends found her behavior odd as well.

When it was time to roll out, Tom touched her arm and said, "Wouldn't you rather walk for a while? That bench isn't any too comfortable."

Jo's blue eyes studied him silently and she nodded.

"Don't get too far from the wagon," Tom cautioned as she set off on foot.

As he watched her go, Tom wondered what it was that was making her so quiet and what in the world he was going to do about.

CHAPTER 10

OVER THE NEXT FEW DAYS, JO DID HER BEST TO BE WHAT SHE BELIEVED WAS THE perfect wife. She did every task without a word of complaint and kept her mouth shut even when she saw a bird soaring that made her heart sing. Tom stopped trying to talk to her and she was rather disappointed, missing their previous conversations. But he hadn't wanted this marriage, so perhaps he needed time to adjust to the idea. Out of respect, she quieted whenever she was around him, trying to give him the space that he seemed to need to mull things over.

As for Jo's own ideas of their impromptu wedding—being married to Tom was still much better than living with her father. She found she enjoyed waking up beside him and falling asleep with his slightly ragged breathing a few feet away. She like the brief intimacy in the morning, before the day took over and so did awkwardness along with.

Unlike her father, Tom didn't mind when she asked to go for a walk on her own. Jo would walk until she found a little pond or a bit of a hill or even a dead tree. Then she pulled out her sketchbook and drew careful likenesses of the plants she didn't recognize. She even was able to capture several butterflies she'd never seen before in her drawings and Jo's heart sang with pleasure every time she looked at them.

It was here in nature when she felt closest to God. Her father had never taken her to church but he had read from the big family Bible to her. In fact, it was one of the few things she had to use to learn to read. Even though there were places where she thought that God was like her father, there were other places where He was nothing at all like Earl Miller.

Jo's favorite verse was Psalm 27:10 which said, "When my father and mother forsake me, then the Lord will take me up." Years ago, she'd memorized it and whispered it to herself when she was especially sad or her face ached from yet another slap. She knew that a good father wanted what was best for his children and even disciplined them when they needed it, but he didn't berate them or call them stupid or hit them for no reason at all.

Now that she'd been married to Tom for almost a week, she was beginning to wonder what sort of father he would be if they ever had children. Even though he was very quiet, she hoped that he would laugh with them like he did with Edoardo and Sven. Perhaps he would teach their children to read from all the books he had tucked in his trunk.

The thought of children and Tom always made Jo blush and she decided it was time to make her way back to the wagons. She didn't want her husband to be inconvenienced by having to come looking for her.

She paused to drink from a stream and wetted her handkerchief to press against her too-hot neck. A large shadow loomed over her and Jo blinked up in surprise. As soon as she realized that it was Ned Harkiss standing over her, Jo's body reacted instinctively. Her muscles tensed, her pupils dilated, and she sat as still as she could. All the tricks she'd learned for keeping her father from growing angrier might work on Ned.

"You thought you were so clever when you sneaked off and married Thomas," the big man growled down at her.

Jo got slowly to her feet, careful to keep from meeting his eyes. There was no response that would placate him, she knew. He wanted to have his say and perhaps she'd be allowed to escape unharmed.

Ned laughed mirthlessly. "But I'm going to enjoy taking his woman from that little bookworm even more now." His hand shot forward and grabbed her elbow so tightly that Jo cried out. Ned's head dropped closer to hers. "If you say anything to him about this, I'll make sure he never walks again."

"Leave Tom alone," Jo pleaded, twisting so that Ned's face wasn't so close to her own.

He shook her violently to quiet her. "You're going to do exactly what I say or else I'm going to find the sheriff in Santa Fe and tell him how suspicious it was that your father died one day and you married a man he wouldn't have approved of the very next day. I'll bet he'll think you and Thomas poisoned your old man."

Jo's heart constricted. She couldn't bear it if Tom went to jail for something he didn't do. It was the one threat Ned could have levied that actually worked on Jo, because it held a ring of truth to it, however much it was an utter lie.

"What do you want?" she whispered.

Ned ran a finger down her cheek and Jo had to fight not to pull away instinctively. "Oh, I want all sorts of things. But I'm not going to rush this. I'm going to enjoy every minute of it."

His slap came so fast that Jo didn't have time to react. One moment his hand was at his side and the next it was crashing into her face. Jo fell to the ground, shocked at the pain that had come out of nowhere.

Ned laughed and left her lying in the dirt trying not to cry.

⚜

Tom had worried when he saw Ned disappear into the grass, but he'd been reluctant to charge after him. It would have been too reminiscent of her father to go charging after him. Still, Tom didn't relax until the foreman returned alone a few minutes later.

In fact, he'd put it entirely from his mind and when Jo appeared, he didn't notice that she was nervous and watchful. She'd taken to walking behind the wagons when she needed a rest and, since the silence was painful when they sat together on the seat, Tom encouraged her. It was no longer uncommon for Jo to swing down from the moving wagon or climb up without needing him to slow down at all.

Her wide-brimmed bonnet kept him from noticing her black eye until they'd been traveling for several hours. She'd joined him after walking only a short time, but been as quiet as always and Tom had hardly spared a glance. It wasn't until Edoardo rode by on Tom's horse that they both turned to look and he'd seen her face.

"*Jo!*" Tom exclaimed. "What happened to your face?"

Jo lifted her fingers and touched the edge of the purply-green area so carefully that he knew it had to hurt her greatly.

"I fell," she said quietly, her eyes not meeting his exactly. "It was silly. I was by the stream and I slipped and hit my head on a rock."

He understood her reluctance to say more. Such a clumsy accident was embarrassing. Making a fuss over it would only make things worse. "We'll put a damp cloth on it later tonight and that'll help. I've had my share of shiners in my day."

His words seemed to calm her as Jo's shoulders relaxed. Tom gave himself a mental pat on the back for finally doing something right.

CHAPTER 11

THE SOUNDS OF DRUMS IN THE DISTANCE DIDN'T HELP ANYTHING. EVERYONE kept guns close at hand and the night watch was doubled. It meant less sleep for all and tempers were shorter than ever.

Tom's own temper was sorely frayed from a combination of confusion and worry. Jo's initial black eye had turned into a mashed thumb from when she smashed it between two buckets. She'd twisted an ankle stepping in a gopher hole. She'd cut her lip when she tried to break a stick and it had sprung back and surprised her.

Under the cover of eating, Tom watched her surreptitiously. Jo was definitely in some sort of pain. She sat and moved as if the skin on her back hurt by even the lightest touch of her dress. The more Tom watched her try desperately not to flinch, the more it felt like a rock was growing in his stomach.

He hadn't wanted to jump to conclusions, but only a fool would fail to see that something was terribly wrong. His beautiful, strong, courageous wife—every day he liked the sound of the word more—had fallen utterly silent, even more so than when Earl was alive. She attended Tom and his friends diligently, ensuring their coffee mugs were full and their plates always heaped, but beyond that she was a bruised, silent wraith.

What is happening?

Confronting her about it would be a mistake, but Tom planned to follow her closely. If someone was hurting her, he would know and he would stop it.

Jo moved painfully as she cleaned up and Tom pretended to read his book from his usual spot in the scant shade of the wagon. When she slipped her notebook into her pocket, Tom scanned the camp. He clenched his jaw when he saw Ned slink off in the same direction. He'd wondered, but had tried desperately not to jump to conclusions.

Tom waited only the briefest of moments before following the pair. He parted the grass and stepped carefully, trying not to make a sound. Their voices reached him and Tom felt his ears strain to catch their words.

"You're happy to see me, aren't you?" Ned's oily voice prompted.

"Of course," Jo replied, and Tom's stomach turned over.

Without thinking, he bolted through the grass, into the clearing, finding his small wife wrapped in a bruising kiss with Ned. Tom stopped and stared and Elsie flashed through his eyes, his cheating first wife's face eclipsing the terror on Jo's face so he didn't even see it as his fists clenched.

৩৩৩

"DON'T HURT HIM!" JO CRIED OUT IN FEAR FOR TOM, AS NED RELEASED HER and she stumbled back, flinching at the pain of her wounded ankle when her weight shifted so abruptly.

But her husband misunderstood. "Protecting your lover?" Tom snarled.

Jo was completely nonplussed and only gaped wordlessly between the two of them. She needed to step in and stop what was coming, but knew that she couldn't possibly do anything. Running for help would be the only way she might have a prayer of saving Tom.

Unfortunately, Ned threw an insult at Tom who responded in kind. They circled each other menacingly, waiting for some mysterious sign. Then Tom threw himself at the bigger man and Jo screamed.

The men rolled on the ground, fists connecting with flesh, grunts and curses flying, and Jo scrambled to stay out of their way.

"Stop it! Stop it!" she yelled, tears flowing down her cheeks.

It didn't take long for the noise to awaken the men back in camp and the two men were pulled apart with a great deal of effort.

Theodore Humphrey looked between the two in astonishment. "I don't know what is going on here, but the two of you are in most serious trouble."

Tom wiped carelessly at his bleeding nose. "Ned Harkiss has been hurting my wife. I want to press charges against him at the next fort. Until then, he needs to be kept under guard."

Jo watched the men tie Ned's hands behind his back and lead him away. Then Tom turned slowly and gave her an exhausted look. The disappointment in his eyes broke something in her right down the middle. She should've been stronger. She should've been braver and resisted—

"I'm so sorry," she breathed and stepped forward.

Tom shook his head, turned, and walked away. Jo watched the empty spot where he'd just been, feeling hollow. She made to follow him on legs that were suddenly so heavy. The sun glinted off something and she noticed Tom's spectacles lying on the ground. Somehow, they'd survived the fight with only a bent arm.

Jo reached down and picked them up, hugging them to herself and wondering if this was the only part of him that she'd ever get to hold close.

CHAPTER 12

TOM WOULD HAVE THOUGHT THAT FINALLY SEEING NED HARKISS TIED UP would have been a reason to cheer. Throughout the afternoon, most of the men on horseback rode up to check on him and those who'd been driving wagons made sure to ask after his health once they'd circled the wagon for the night. With the exception of a handful of men, everyone was glad to have the bully shut up once and for all.

It would have been a reason to smile despite his injuries. But Tom couldn't. His mind replayed the kiss over and over again and it was far worse than the cracked rib he'd gotten from Ned's boot.

Everything he'd feared about Jo had to be true. He couldn't spend his life checking in on her constantly to make sure she was being faithful.

Not again!

Tom decided he would have their marriage annulled when they reached Santa Fe. It was the only way. He'd give her some money and help her find a job, but that was it. Even as the though settled uneasily on his mind, he forced the uncertainty away, replacing it firmly with his past history.

The talk around the campfire was too cheerful, too carefully avoiding the fight. Tom felt that everyone had to be speculating about Jo and Ned and what they were doing in the tall grass. Had they pieced together all Jo's injuries and realized that this had been going on a long time? Why she would want to be with a man who was hurting her—a man she had not wanted to marry at all? It made no sense to Tom, and that made it all even worse.

All the eyes around him made Tom restless and he said good night sooner than he would have. Jo had been hidden in the wagon all afternoon, not even showing her face at dinnertime. Tom would get his bedroll and sleep with Sven and Edoardo outside the wagon.

His mind on his plan, Tom didn't stop to knock. He pulled back the canvas and had one foot thrown over the back before he even noticed that Jo was in the middle of changing into her nightclothes. It was the first time he'd seen her in just her chemise and Tom felt a blush rush up his neck and into his ears.

Hoping she hadn't heard him, he tried to back out. But then the light from the lantern caught the markings on Jo's back and Tom froze, sick to the marrow of his bones.

"Don't move, Jo," he cautioned.

🌚🌝🌚

Jo gasped and clutched her nightgown to her chest. She'd been so deep in misery that she hadn't heard him until Tom was already in the wagon. They'd slept next to each other for many nights, but he'd never seen her in her underwear and she was mortified.

She threw a frightened look over her shoulder at him. What could he want from her? But Tom had his hands out and was looking at her as though she was a wounded animal he was trying to gentle.

"I'm going to look at your back," he said in a careful voice. "I'm not going to hurt you."

Jo nodded, her heart pounding. She felt his fingers trace the old scars from her father's belt that peeked up over the edge of her chemise. He pulled her arm out and examined the fading bruises that almost didn't hurt anymore from when Ned had grabbed her roughly. Thankfully, Tom's fingers avoided the worst of the places that gave testimony to Ned's last beating with a stick.

Finally, he sat back and sighed sadly. Jo pulled her nightgown over her head, ignoring the pain as she did so.

"Why, Jo?" Tom sat down heavily beside her, staring at his hands. "You asked me to marry you. Why would you do that, if you were really interested in him? And my God—why *him*, of all men?"

Jo stared in shock at her husband. "You ... you think I ... like Ned Harkiss?"

He raised one shoulder. "I don't know what to think. You chose not to marry him, yet I found you kissing him. He's hurt you badly. You allowed that without ever once coming to me. I don't understand, Jo." Tom's voice cracked a little and he raised his head briefly.

The look her husband gave her was so full of raw emotions that Jo had to look away. "I don't like him, Tom. We're supposed to love our enemies, but I don't like or love, Ned. He's a vile, cruel man." Her mouth was like sand, starting to understand Tom's earlier anger. It hadn't been solely in her defense. "Ned said that if I told anyone he'd say we killed Pa on purpose. He promised to make sure you'd go to jail."

"So—" his voice was so ragged that Jo was forced to turn to look at him and saw a look of sheer anguish on Tom's face. "You weren't cheating. You were being abused … in order to protect me."

All the piece of her husband's mysterious past fell into place like a puzzle and Jo couldn't even find it in herself to be more than a little angry. "You were married before," she said softly. "And she was unfaithful. Right, Tom?"

He nodded once, his jaw set in stone. "With a cruel man like Ned, yes. He eventually killed her. I had no idea until it was too late. How am I so blind?"

"It's not about you," Jo said with fierceness that startled them both. "I didn't cheat, Tom. And I'm not your previous wife. I'm very sorry you were hurt so badly. But I am not that woman. I would never do anything to hurt you. I was trying so hard to stop you from being hurt—" her own voice cracked and then somehow she was in Tom's arms, sobbing, and he was holding her tight.

Her bruises ached, but it didn't matter because of the words he was frantically whispering. "I'm sorry, Jo. I'm so sorry, sweetheart. I was the biggest kind of fool, not only for misjudging you today, but for not realizing faster that there was a problem. I allowed you to be hurt. I don't know if you can ever forgive me, but I'll spend a lifetime making it up to you, I swear. I love you, Jo."

She lifted her tearstained face to his in awe. "You love me?"

"So much," Tom said raggedly, wiping the tears from her damp cheeks. "I've been nothing but a fool around you almost from the first day. I should've been the one to propose. I should've seen the danger you were in. I should've realized that kiss was nothing more than Ned's cruelty."

Tentatively, he reached out and skimmed a thumb over her cut lip and Jo trembled. "I'll earn your love, Jo, somehow. Forgive me."

"I forgive you," she whispered. "And I love you, you foolish man. I have from that first day."

The look of awe on Tom's handsome, swollen face was one Jo would carry with her to the end of her days, just like his kiss.

EPILOGUE

SANTA FE, DECEMBER, 1866

Jo knew that Tom was disappointed not to spend their first Christmas together in their own house. They were still living in the same boarding house where they'd rented rooms when they'd finally pulled into the rough town months before. Tom's work for the railroad was keeping him busy and pleased. He'd wanted to buy land in town right away and begin construction on their own house made of the red clay bricks that had delighted them both when they'd first arrived.

But they didn't know if they'd stay long. The company was considering who would follow the railroad as it was built and Tom was on their list of candidates. Despite what Ned had said, families with children weren't usually accommodated, though some wives did trail along with their husbands.

Jo smiled a happy, secretive smile to herself. Only a few days ago, she'd received confirmation from a local midwife that her suspicions were accurate. There was no way that she and Tom would be following the railroad now. He'd be so excited to know that they could go ahead with their plans to build a home of their own.

The door opened and Tom burst through, Sven and Edoardo not far behind. The three men laughed and chattered about work. Tom gave her an unembarrassed kiss and his friends followed with quick greetings, punctuated with a hug.

"We heard some interesting news today," Edoardo said. "Ned Harkiss was caught trying to rob a bank at gunpoint. He'll get hard time for that."

Jo's hands flew to her lips and she gasped. It had been a disappointment to have the man released after only a week on the chain gang for his attacks on her. She'd watched over her shoulder constantly. Now, thanks to his own foolishness, the brute would be put away for a long time.

"Thank God," she said fervently.

"Amen to that," Tom grinned. He and Sven had begun studying the Bible together while still on the wagon train. Their nightly sessions had drawn several other men. The group had been glad to find that Santa Fe had several good churches and now they never missed a Sunday meeting.

It was one more reason for Jo to be grateful. The couple who owned the boarding house were friendly and kind. They were happy to let Jo share in the cooking of the holiday meal. Pies, cakes, potatoes, rice, and a roasted pig were all ready downstairs. Jo had only to change her dress and pin her hair up again and they'd be ready to eat.

Sven and Edoardo headed back to their own rooms to change and Jo was left alone with Tom. He watched her as she changed her dress and Jo smiled at him, so thankful for the happy marriage they had built.

"I have a present for you," Tom said suddenly.

"Really? I have one for you."

"Open mine first." He went to a drawer and pulled out a book wrapped in brown paper.

Jo pulled the paper off impatiently and held up a black journal. She flipped the pages and saw that they were blank. Her heart filled and she looked at Tom with damp eyes.

"I know your father wasn't a kind man, but you told me he gave you one of these each year. I wanted to carry on the good things he did for you."

"Oh, Tom, thank you," Jo broke down into tears and threw her arms around his neck. It was exactly the thoughtful sort of thing she was coming to expect from him. What had she done to deserve such a wonderful husband?

"All right, enough of that. I want to open my present," he teased her gently.

"Well, I didn't wrap it," she said, brushing away her tears.

"Is it a house?"

Jo smiled shakily. "In a way."

Tom's expression became puzzled and Jo took pity on him. "The railroad won't let us go with them when they learn that we're going to have a baby next summer."

Jo felt that she'd given her husband the world. His face lit up and he hooted happily, pulling her into his arms and twirling her around.

It was a long time before the Thomas family made their way down to Christmas dinner and when they finally arrived, everyone wondered at their silly grins.

THANK YOU SO MUCH FOR READING MY BOOK. I SINCERELY HOPE YOU ENJOYED EVERY bit reading it. I had fun creating it and will surely create more.

Your positive reviews are very helpful to other reader, it only takes a few moments. They can be left at Amazon.

https://www.amazon.com/Ellen-Anderson/e/B07B8C952M

৩৯৫৩

WANT FREE BOOKS EVERY WEEK? WHO DOESN'T!

Become a preferred reader and we'll not only send you free reads, but you'll also receive updates about new releases.

So you'll be among the first to dive into our latest new books, full of adventure, heartwarming romances, and characters so real they jump off the page.

It's absolutely free and you don't need to do anything at all to qualify except go to.

PREFERRED READ FREE READS

https://ellenanderson.gr8.com/

ABOUT THE AUTHORS

ELLEN ANDERSON STARTED LIFE NEAR SEDONA, ARIZONA, SURROUNDED BY THE most beautiful scenery the West has to offer, along with its intricate history and myriad legends. Her favorite memories are of camping out on the family property under the vast canopy of stars, listening to her father and grandfather tell stories. Eventually, Ellen began writing her own stories, mixing her up-close-and-personal western experiences with special characters who share her unique sense of fun and adventure. When she met her handsome husband on a horse drive, her path to writing historical western romances was sealed.

Today, Ellen and her husband still do some work on the family ranch, and their children are following in the family tradition, helping care for the Anderson horses. In her spare time, Ellen enjoys photography, swimming, trying out unique historical recipes from scratch and exploring ghost towns in the family RV.

KATIE WYATT IS 25% AMERICAN SIOUX INDIAN. BORN AND RAISED IN Arizona, she has traveled and camped extensively through California, Arizona, Nevada, Mexico, and New Mexico. Looking at the incredible night sky and the giant Saguaro cacti, she has dreamed of what it would be like to live in the early pioneer times.

Spending time with a relative of the great Wyatt Earp, also named Wyatt Earp, Katie was mesmerized and inspired by the stories he told of bygone times. This historical interest in the old West became the inspiration for her Western romance novels.

Her books are a mixture of actual historical facts and events mixed with action and humor, challenges and adventures. The characters in Katie's clean romance novels

draw from her own experiences and are so real that they almost jump off the pages. You feel like you're walking beside them through all the ups and downs of their lives. As the stories unfold, you'll find yourself both laughing and crying. The endings will never fail to leave you feeling warm inside.

BE MINE, VALENTINE

Contemporary Western Romance

RoyceCardiff
Publishing House
WHOLESOME INSPIRATIONAL ROMANCE

Dear Reader,

It is our utmost pleasure and privilege to bring these wonderful stories to you. I am so very proud of our amazing team of writers and the delight they continually bring us all with their beautiful clean and wholesome tales of, faith, courage, and love.

What is a book's lone purpose if not to be read and enjoyed? Therefore, you, dear reader, are the key to fulfilling that purpose and unlocking the treasures that lie within the pages of this book.

రీస్తూ

NEWSLETTER SIGN UP PREFERRED READ

http://brendaclemmons.gr8.com/

రీస్తూ

THANK YOU FOR CHOOSING A INSPIRATIONAL READS BY ROYCE CARDIFF PUBLISHING HOUSE.

Welcome and Enjoy!

A PERSONAL WORD FROM BRENDA

Dear Readers,

You read about the Wild West because of the romance, the adventure, the spirit of possibility that filled those frontier days. I write these books for the same reasons. I love the stories of the pioneer women who crossed the country to build new lives in what must have felt like a totally foreign land. With courage, faith, common sense, and a good dose of humor, many of these courageous women married their true loves and became the Old West's literal founding mothers!

Many of my books draw directly from history, using the real-life stories of those women to tell the story of the birth of the western half of our nation. As I look around my southwest backyard, I often take a moment to think about what it might have looked like before we all moved in. These stories are my attempt to share that wonderful adventure with you.

Happy reading,

Brenda

PROLOGUE

"*WHOA!*" ANDIE WHITE-KNUCKLED THE STEERING WHEEL OF HER BATTERED Honda Civic as a sixty-mile-per-hour gust of wind sent it lurching sideways.

"Andie?" Brianna yelled on the other end of the line. "Andie? Are you okay?"

"Yes. No. Call you back."

Andie didn't bother to cut the phone connection. No sooner had she managed to get back in her lane than a gale from the opposite direction shoved the vehicle up against the worn shoulder of the deserted Vegas highway. Hail bounced off the roof of the old car, probably adding to its already substantial collection of dents, and the Civic groaned ominously as she reluctantly brought it to a stop.

Sagging back into her seat, Andie stared bleakly out at the desert landscape, watching a stand of scraggly cacti vanishing under the onslaught of the storm. Water lapped at her tires, courtesy of the oversaturated land, unable to absorb the full measure of the sudden winter squall.

She shivered and sank lower, rubbing her arms, buried beneath several layers of usually warm sweaters. They couldn't compete with the chill, however, anymore than the car's dying heater could keep up with the sudden overall Fahrenheit drop.

"How is this my life?" she muttered, eyes drifting to the manila envelope riding shotgun in the passenger seat. She didn't open it a second time. Even though she had only picked it up a few hours earlier, the words might as well have been tattooed on the insides of her eyelids.

Date of Dissolution: 02/14/07

Regarding the contested divorce suit by petitioner Andrea Merrill against Ethan Bainbridge. Be it resolved that the agreement is approved in its entirety by petitioners and the bonds of matrimony which united said petitioners are hereby declared dissolved ...

The phone vibrated in the cupholder and Andie answered without looking at it, the ache in her chest so big and raw that she couldn't even cry. "Didn't crash and burn. Not on the highway, anyway."

There was a silence before Brianna replied, "That's a positive attitude ..."

The hollow sensation was something Andie didn't know if she'd ever wrap her emotions around. By now it was vaguely familiar. Since she and Ethan had gone their separate ways many months back, she'd been existing in a half-numb state that served to protect her at least slightly from the pain.

"Hello?" Brianna pressed. "Say something to reassure me the car really isn't in flames and you're not huddled on the side of the highway, hoping the rain fixes things so you don't have to call somebody."

Rain wouldn't fix things. Not the things Andie needed fixed, at any rate. She and Ethan had done a great job of 'fixing' them beyond any chance of repair. The proof was sitting ride beside her.

"I'm divorced." Her voice rang uncomfortably loud in the car, the very word itself ugly and consonant, seeming to echo and rumble with the thunder. *Divorced.*

"You are," Brianna replied, ever pragmatic, even when her tone was edged with empathy. "And I'm really sorry. I love you, and I wish I could be with you right now, sis."

They weren't actually sisters, but from the day they'd met as little kids—Andie shy and uncertain, Brianna bent on conquering the world even at age five—the two had formed a bond that ran as deep as family, and deeper than legalities, Andie mused, still staring at the envelope that had officially ended her dreams. It had been a long time coming, but that didn't make it any easier to accept. She'd been in love with Ethan for almost as long as she and Brianna had been best friends. It wasn't supposed to end this way. It wasn't supposed to *ever* end.

"Don't ever divorce me," Andie muttered.

Bri laughed. "You wish you could get rid of me that easily. Really, though. Is the car okay?"

"Yeah." She rested her cheek against the cold window, feeling the damp chill seep into her bones. "This storm turned out way worse than predicted, sort of like my life, but the car's fine. I think."

"Stop," Bri warned. "Your heart is broken on Valentine's Day. I get it. But that's no reason—"

"Valentine's what?" Ever since she and Ethan had filed for legal separation, days had blurred into mere pages on a calendar, filled with what felt like meeting after meeting, even when their divorce had apparently been extremely simple, according to lawyers. Neither of them had wanted anything but to go their separate way.

And I didn't even want that.

Andie sat up and looked at the date on her phone, then at the intricate little red heart emblazoned on the corner of the envelope, the coveted Valentine, Nebraska, Valentine's Day stamp.

Feb 14, 2007

"Valentine's Day," she said in disbelief. "I didn't even realize it. My divorce came through on the most romantic day of the whole year." The words still felt strange on her tongue. *My divorce.* Those two words were never supposed to be in the same sentence, much less any part of her life.

"Is Valentine doing its usual?" Her hometown was nationally known for its year-round romantic flair, but it pulled out all the stops on Valentine's Day.

"What do you think?" Bri asked wryly. "I'm about to head to the teddy bear vote."

One of Valentine's myriad Feb. 14 traditions was a teddy-bear-decorating contest where participants each decorated a stuffed toy with a V-Day theme. The bear with the most votes won a prize and then the other bears were distributed to kids at the hospital.

"Go," Andie told her, knowing Brianna would stay on the phone with her until the event was long over, if necessary. "I'll be home in a couple days. Let Bruce know." At least her cat would be waiting at home, so she wouldn't be returning to a totally empty house. Ethan had been his usual gracious self and had let her keep practically everything, including their one-year-old tabby. Everything except her heart.

"Will do. Call me when you get to the hotel."

"Yeah. Love you. Bye." Andie hung up and picked up the envelope at last, slowly tracing the postmark that thousands of people applied for every single year. When she'd worked in the Valentine post office, she'd seen letters come from as far away as Japan, seeking that small bit of old-fashioned romance for their special someone on that special day.

Anger curled around her heart and she tossed the envelope away before restarting the car and squaring her shoulders as the tires spun, working to gain traction on the road that was slick with the oil which always seeped out during the first ten minutes or so of such weather.

God, keep me safe, she prayed, thinking of her parents' accident and holding the steering wheel more tightly still.

She turned up the radio loud enough to drown out her thoughts, and stared straight ahead. There was a gas station about thirty miles away that she'd hole up in until the danger of flashfloods passed. Then she'd drive cross-country, sleeping in the car overnight as needed, until she got home. Eventually, life would return to some kind of normalcy, even if her dreams were as drowned out as the landscape flashing past her windows now.

No Valentine's Day for me this year. No Valentine's Day ever again, if I have anything to say about it.

CHAPTER 1

JUNE'S GIFT

JAN 3, 2014

"Ms. MERRILL?"

Andie swiveled in her chair, the wheels snagging as always on the library's frayed green carpet, so she kind of staggered right at the end as she turned to face her customer. Sometimes people commented on that last little lurch, but in this instance, six-year-old Nicole Castañeda, beaming a hopeful gap-toothed smile in her direction, didn't notice. Oddly, her parents didn't seem to be nearby, but Andie dismissed the immediate question. They were probably in the stacks, watching their independent-minded firstborn do her thing.

"Ms. Nicole," Andie said with an answering smile. "How may I help you?"

"I'm doing a project," Nicole confided, standing on her toes to see over the counter, small hands clutching the lip of the desk.

"A project," Andie repeated. "That's impressive. Do you need some library resources?"

Nicole nodded vigorously, red-gold braids bouncing against her freckled cheeks. "Mrs. Yao says I need a book. This one." She pushed a Post-it as far as she could and Andie picked it up, easily reading Brianna's chicken scrawl.

"*Valentine Traditions Around the World.* Okay. Do you remember what the first step for doing research is?" Usually she'd have guided Nicole on the computer, but the old monitors were on the fritz yet again.

"Look it up," Nicole said eagerly. "And then you tell me what section of the library. And then what number. And then I can find it."

"Exactly," Andie agreed, doing a search on the library's ancient database. Like everything else in the Lohman Branch, it badly needed an update, but still did the trick. "Here we go." She wrote down the information and handed it over to Nicole. "It's too early for us to have pulled the Valentine's Day books yet, so you'll need to go searching. Want help?"

Nicole scrutinized the paper, already an excellent reader at her ripe young age. "Nope. I got it!" she declared, and darted off, calling "thank you!" in a decidedly non-library voice as she disappeared into the stacks.

Chuckling, Andie started to sink back into her chair when another voice piped up, coming from about waist level.

"Ms. Merrill?"

Startled, she turned and then smiled as she spotted Jeremy Washington in his wheelchair, liberally decorated with football stickers. The boy might have been born with cerebral palsy, but his parents had made sure from day one to support him in every possible way. The result was a determined, goofy seven-year-old, who let nothing stand in his way. Curiously, she didn't see Jeremy's mom or dad anywhere.

Hmm ...

"Mr. Washington. How may I help you?" she inquired, walking over to where he waited at the small desk she'd installed for him several years back. One of her dreams, along with overhauling the library from top to bottom, was to have half of the counter modified specifically so people in wheelchairs could roll right up and see her without straining.

"I need a book," he informed her, waving a Post-it just like Nicole's.

Andie took it. "*A Story of Roses*, huh. Not your usual reading material." The boy was sports mad to the extreme. Smelling the literal roses wasn't something he'd usually do.

He wrinkled his nose and scrunched his shoulders almost to his curly black hair. "For Valentine's. I'm making something for my mom. Roses are her favorite."

Eyebrows raised—Jan 11th was early for Valentine's requests to start filtering in, even in this crazy town—Andie nevertheless nodded and retrieved the information for him. He needed a little more help than Nicole in finding the book, because he was less familiar with the library.

When Andie got back to the desk, she found four more youngsters lined up all in a row, not quite by height, no parents in sight. Kenya, Hugo, Malcolm, and Veda all beamed as they spotted her. The self-designated spokesperson in any group, Veda spoke for them, her wide smile flashing wide against her beautiful copper-colored skin.

"We need books!"

"Valentine's books?" Andie guessed ruefully, by now fully aware of what was happening. Two parentless children, okay. Six? Brianna's hand in the game was becoming more visible by the minute.

She helped the four find their individual reading assignments, then sat back and waited. It wasn't long before children seven, eight, and nine, walked in the door, seemingly right off the street. By the time kids nineteen and twenty disappeared into the stacks, and Brianna sauntered in innocently, Andie was laughing. The local school where Bri was a first grade teacher was adjacent to the library, and the setup was now entirely clear.

"A little early in the day for an ambush, don't you think?" she accused, sitting back in her chair and waiting as her best friend rounded the counter and made herself right at home, as though she was a library employee.

"I could use some help on Valentine's this year," Brianna began, reaching for Andie's empty coffee mug. "We're doing an unusually big project—"

"Already made reservations in Custer," Andie interrupted. "No dice, Bri. Nice try."

Every year since she had moved back to Valentine, Andie had made very sure that she was out of the way for at least two days before and after the big romantic holiday. She saw no reason to subject herself to the onslaught of happy couples on prominent display every which way in the lead up and aftermath to Valentine, Nebraska's, huge celebration.

"It's a total waste of your sick days," Brianna informed her irritably, helping herself to a mocha from the Keurig she'd gifted Andie with on her birthday. "I need the help, Andie. Come on."

"You'll survive," Andie promised. "Someone else has said that plenty to me ..." Her eyes flickered to the library doors as June LeShawn hobbled in, leaning heavily on her cane. Knowing better than to try to help the independent octogenarian, even though the doors were a pain even for able-bodied people, Andie just waved and started collecting her things.

"How are you making ends meet, with your hours cut?" Brianna asked bluntly.

That the Lohman Branch, an offshoot to the main library, was struggling financially was no secret. If the chipped brickwork and faded library sign weren't enough evidence, the way the front door stuck, the sometimes-dangerous fray of the carpet, and the outdated carousels were all giveaways. Then there were the computers, so old they might as well have grown pterodactyl wings and flapped away, and the books themselves. Try as Brianna and June did, they could barely squeeze enough money out of the ultra-lean budget to keep up with current reading material. So when Andie's hours had been cut last month and divided fifty-fifty with June, once the other full-time librarian, it had been no surprise.

Andie shrugged. "It's only been a month, so I'm not in trouble. Yet. Hey, June."

June eased her painfully thin frame around the counter and made a beeline for the chair Andie had vacated. "Hi, honey." She winced as she slowly sat down and leaned back, exhaling thankfully once the weight was off her painful knees and hips. "You know I'd be happy to give you my hours. It's high time that I head for greener pastures."

"Absolutely not," Andie said firmly, as she did every time June brought up the subject. June lived on a meager pension and Andie wasn't about to add to the old woman's financial burdens. "This just means I have more time to write my great American novel," she joked, giving June an affectionate hug before nodding at Bri and spotting the kids starting to filtering out of the stacks, headed for the checkout counter. "Your minions are on their way back. I'll catch you later."

"Wait." June leaned forward and caught her wrist as Andie reached for her purse. "I have something for you."

Andie frowned. "June. You don't need to get me things. I told you that already." Ever since the change in their work schedule, June had been bringing in everything from homemade bread and coffee mugs to little sachets of bath salts.

"And I told you I want to." June pressed a folded paper firmly into Andie's hand, closing her fingers around it. "Read it at the opportune moment. Hello, Joshua!" She turned her attention to the first kid at the counter, the struggling library, of course, having no self-checkout station.

Exchanging curious looks with Brianna, Andie looked down at the folded paper, shook her head in confusion, and shoved the gift in her pocket as she headed for the front door, prepared to wrestle it open.

CHAPTER 2
CASTING CALL

THE FRESH AIR, SCENTED WITH PINE NEEDLES, FELT GOOD ON HER FACE, EVEN IF the temperature was just shy of forty degrees. Andie snugged her coat tighter, wound her fuzzy green scarf more closely around her neck, and started down the sidewalk without a particular goal in mind. She had yet to fully figure out a new schedule, so she was often at a loose end at times when she previously would have been working.

Gotta figure something out. Soon.

Her wallet was suffering, and so was her mood. It was way too easy for thoughts of Ethan to creep up when she wasn't kept busy. Banishing that dangerous train of thought, Andie walked unhurriedly past the different buildings, ranging from brick, to Western wood fronts, to sleek, modernistic metal and glass. It was the unique Valentine touch that helped bring the varied styles together: hearts painted on the sidewalk; street signs punctuated with cardinal directions in little white hearts; green lampposts with signs that had hearts emblazoned with "Welcome to the heart of the Sand Hills."

Before he'd died, Andie's father liked to joke Valentine was a "hearty city," and it really was. When she'd been a kid, Andie had despaired at what she'd melodramatically called "living in a cliché." Now, though, she looked around at the tourists cuddled up on cheerful red benches, taking a picture under yet another heart sign. Across the street, by Gail's Hardware Emporium, little Tony Wright was teasing Cassidy Jones, the tots already so besotted with each other that their parents joked they'd get married before they were out of Pull-Ups. Jennie and Arthur Castaneda strolled past a mural depicting the history of Valentine's Day, Arthur guiding his heavily pregnant wife with an arm around her shoulders.

It occurred to Andie that the theme was less hearts than it was love. Valentine loved love. So the world loved it. What a notion.

She skirted a sculpture of an eagle—no heart accoutrements on this one—freshly cleaned by the busy chamber of commerce, and was about to step into Lewis' General Store when she heard,

"Andie!"

She turned to find Carter Laramie hurrying toward her. Masking a sigh, Andie smiled instead. Carter was just about the nicest guy in Valentine, and with his friendly smile and clear green eyes, he was easy on the eyes. Unfortunately, he seemed to think the same thing of Andie, and she hadn't managed to dissuade him.

"Hey," he said, grinning as he joined her. "There's a band playing at the Miller Brewery tonight. Would you go with me?"

It was all she could do not to wince. The Miller Brewery had been one of Ethan's favorite hangouts and she'd shared her first kiss with him in one of the dark corners suited just right for a young couple newly in love.

Obviously reading her expression, Carter switched gears seamlessly. "Okay. Scratch that. How about this instead. There's a casting call happening right now. Come with me for moral support. Please?"

Andie laughed in surprise. As many times as he'd asked her on a date, a casting call was a new one, although Valentine had its fair share. "I didn't realize you were set on Hollywood."

He chuckled and ran a hand self-consciously over his crewcut. "I'm not. This is just for bit parts. Background people and stuff, you know. Not even any lines, probably. It's on my bucket-list. You could do it, too ... this one doesn't even require you be registered with central casting or anything. You don't need to rehearse or wear certain clothes or be a certain look. It's just basically background in the crowd."

She was about to tease him that he was way too young for a bucket-list, but then again, she'd just hit the big 3-0 two weeks back and she knew he couldn't be far behind. Her smile faded as she thought of all the things she hadn't accomplished, which she'd always just assumed would be automatics before her third decade. A book published. A master's degree. A house of her own. Marriage. Kids.

"Okay." She shocked herself, and by the looks of it, Carter, too, as she suddenly made up her mind. "Yes. Why not? Let's go be movie stars for a day!"

"Yeah?" Carter broke into a dazzling smile that would have melted any woman who wasn't Andie. "Wow. Really? Wow."

Feeling immediately guilty at leading him on, Andie opened her mouth to try to explain, but he cut her off, his own smile fading.

"Don't. I get it, Andie. I do," Carter said quietly. "I figured it out a while back, honest. Doesn't mean I'm not hoping, but if you never feel for me ... that way ... it's fine. Not really fine, but fine, you know? No, you don't know." He sighed. "We were friends in high school. I'm good with us just being friends like that again. Can we do that? Maybe?"

Feeling a weight lift off her shoulders, Andie smiled in relief. "Yes. Absolutely, definitely, yes. Carter, you *are* my friend. You always have been. I'm just sort of a mess. I'm sorry."

"Don't be." He touched her shoulder lightly and immediately dropped his hand once more. "I'm the one who's sorry for whatever happened. You and Ethan were good together, Andie. I never messed with that then. I won't now."

"If we'd been that good together, we wouldn't have split," she answered with a trace of bitterness, before pushing aside the lingering hurt and smiling again. "So. Where is this fast-track to the big screen?"

⁂

"I DIDN'T REALIZE THERE WERE THIS MANY PEOPLE IN ALL OF VALENTINE," Jeannette Malloy whispered in Andie's ear as they waited for their cue in the vast basement of Sal's Books 'n Wine. All around them, people bustled about doing different things. Never having been at a casting call, Andie didn't know half of what was happening. There were lights, what looked like a possible costume department, someone frazzled looking who might have been a director ... did movie extra auditions have directors? ... not to mention hopeful 'actors' by the dozens.

In the two hours or so since she and Carter had arrived, and then been separated, much to Carter's dismay, the scene hadn't changed much. They'd all been given a series of directions and had done a few test runs. Turned out that even casting calls for movies required precise coordination. Now it was just a waiting game.

"I hear it's like this on big movie sets," Jeannette went on, leaning up against the cool concrete walls of the increasingly stuffy basement. "More waiting than anything else. People say it's not exciting. But how can it not be, right? I mean— it's a *movie!* Big or small, that's not something everybody can say they've been and done."

Andie nodded absently, still looking around at the crowd, wondering if she'd spot Carter. It seemed like he might be up for a slightly bigger role, he'd said, where he actually got to do something like brush by the lead actor. Of course, there were no big names here today, just stand-ins.

"Sorry for the delay, folks."

The wind went out of Andie's lungs as she heard the deep, slightly husky voice from somewhere within the crowd.

No.

"Having a few technical glitches," the voice went on, its tone at once comfortably in command and apologetic. "We'll be up and running in a minute or seven."

No, no, no, no!

"Help yourselves to the doughnuts," the man, hidden by the crowd, continued.

Andie stared in utter disbelief, spotting the hint of a dark head and a broad shoulder, innocuous to anyone, probably, unless you'd seen those same physical attributes every single day for a decade.

The shoulders and voice turned toward another unseen person. "Carl, do you know if we have refills on the coffee coming?"

She'd first heard that voice when she was eight, turning the corner to PE and bumping smack into another kid. Wiry, lean, with a shock of hair so blond it was almost white, he'd complained loudly at first, then dusted himself off and teased her for turning bright red. She'd always blushed easily. Ethan had been a master at making that happen.

That voice had followed her into PE, and then it had followed to class, where a teacher had assigned Andie to show the new boy around. It had grown up alongside her, changing from high and squeaky to today's low rasp, and she'd heard it happen, just as she'd seen the physical changes that accompanied the shift, starting with the inches in height that suddenly separated them, hair darkened with sun highlights after days of working for his dad's roofing company, stubble that gradually began to roughen a previously baby-smooth jaw ...

"Andie?" Jeannette asked. "Andie, what are you doing? They told us to wait right here!"

She shoved through the crowd, fighting against the press of confused bodies, seeking out the exit even as the voice echoed in her mind. That voice had followed her from elementary to middle to high school. It had whispered tender words in her ear at their graduation dance and, that very same night, had proposed marriage in the bleachers in a shaky, atypically shy voice, down on bended knee with his grandmother's ring.

The voice had laughed with her, sung with her, comforted her when her mother and father passed in a car accident. It had declared its love for her at an altar and been beside her for twelve months and six days before it had agreed with her that this wasn't working ... the last time she'd heard that voice, up until today, had been when it whispered goodbye, cracked and strained with the weight of grief.

He can't be here. I'm imagining things. I have to be. She spotted a gap in the crowd and made a beeline for it, her vision tunneling so she saw nothing but that all-important escape route.

"Watch out!"

Doughnuts and steaming coffee rained every which way, but she didn't stop. The pain of the burns wasn't nearly as bad as what she knew she'd feel if she laid eyes on Ethan. Head down, feet burning where the coffee soaked through her shoes, Andie ducked and ran.

CHAPTER 3
STILL GOT IT

"IT WAS CHILDISH. DON'T EVEN DENY IT." BRIANNA DRIED HER HANDS ON A dishtowel and scowled as Andie finished rinsing the last of their lunch dishes.

"Why would I? I know it was. You can quit reminding me," she retorted, reaching for the remains of the lasagna and folding a sheet of tinfoil around the pan.

"You're both adults," Brianna went on in her best teacher voice. "Divorced adults see each other. Sometimes they even have dinner together. They—"

"I get it!" Andie snapped, startling Bri, since Andie rarely lost her temper. One more reason the suddenly endless fights with Ethan had been so strange. "I get it," she repeated more quietly, reaching for her cappuccino. She folded her fingers around the cozy mug and held it close to her chest as her cat wound anxiously around her legs and meowed, wondering at the yelling. "It's okay, Bruce."

Andie fixed Brianna with a look before heading for the living room, where she sank into the comfortable old couch and Bruce promptly joined her in his usual spot on the armrest. She scratched his scruff with one hand as Brianna hovered in the doorway.

"There are a dozen ways that I could've and should've behaved," Andie acknowledged. "But I didn't. So you can quit scolding me. I'm not six years old, even if sometimes I act like it."

Brianna opened her mouth to say something, when the doorbell rang. Andie groaned. "Carter, probably, coming to check on me. I shouldn't have told him about the coffee when I called to apologize for ditching him. Can you get it?"

Brianna vanished and Andie turned her attention to her cat and her coffee. Anything to keep her mind off the other direction, where it had wandered all night. Hearing Ethan's voice yesterday had been straight out of a combination nightmare and daydream. She'd just about managed to convince herself that she'd been imagining things—there was no way he was back in Nebraska. None whatso-ever.—when, out of the blue, the voice came again.

"Hello, Andie."

Her head jerked up and the lukewarm coffee tipped toward her pajama-clad legs. She'd barely registered the oh-so-familiar warm brown eyes and strong, stubbled jaw when both were suddenly diving toward her. Brianna yelled. Bruce yowled and ran. And Andie just sat there stupidly as Ethan Bainbridge literally jumped back into her life, using a nearby sweater to mop up the tepid cappuccino.

"Are you okay?" he asked again and again, as he patted her down, sopping up liquid, clearly thinking she'd been scalded.

"Why are you here?" she blurted, staring up at him. He stared back, his gaze, usually edged with mischief, now dark with worry, and his full lips pressed into a tight line. They were so close that she could see the tiny crinkles at the corners of his eyes. They gave him depth, she thought vaguely. Made him look distinguished. So now she'd seen that transition too, from innocent kid to fully grown man, with the hallmarks of everyday life imprinted upon him. *Life looks good on him.*

Somewhere in the room, Brianna made a disgusted noise and a door slammed, telling Andie her best friend had made her exit.

Ethan stepped back, still holding her soggy sweater. "Carter told me about what happened at the casting call," he explained, warming her from head to toe with that deep voice. "I was worried."

"Carter?" Andie echoed, finally coming to her senses and getting up to take her dripping sweater from him. When their fingertips brushed, she told herself the warmth she felt was solely from the coffee, even while she knew that was a lie.

"Yeah. I bumped into him at the Miller Brewery."

Right. The band that Carter had asked her to go see with him. Andie started for the laundry room and was almost there when she heard the creak of the floor behind her and realized Ethan was following. He knew where everything was in the house, of course. He'd bought this house with her. They'd made the first payments together.

Shoving the sweater into the washing machine, she turned to face her ex, arms crossing defensively across her chest. As she did, she realized what a mess she really was. Sopping pajama pants. Stained retro T-shirt. Her hair not even combed. No makeup.

Her cheeks flamed.

"I've still got it," Ethan said quietly, and she knew he meant the blush.

"I had no idea that—" she said at the same time that he said,

"Listen, Andie. Just now, I didn't mean to—"

They both stopped, and awkward silence filled the laundry room, broken suddenly by a peremptory yowl. Ethan looked down and Bruce reared up, placing his paws on Ethan's knees. His orange head butted into Ethan's thigh insistently before the cat looked up at him once more.

"He remembers me," Ethan said in wonder, reaching down and lifting the cat into his arms. Bruce snuggled right into his big chest, burrowing deep just like he used to when he was a kitten and Ethan and Andie had first rescued him off the street. He purred so loudly that Andie could hear him a few feet away, feeling an irrational surge of jealous at how much she wanted to be where Bruce was.

"You're hard to forget," she said unthinkingly, cursing herself as the words escaped. "Oh God. I didn't say that. I am such a mess. Ethan—"

"Andie—"

Again, they spoke over another and again, they stopped, caught in an awkward silence born of a love that hadn't ended for any of the reasons Hollywood ever made movies. A love that for Andie, frankly, had never ended at all. Why bother denying it at this stage? She'd loved this man when he was eight, eighteen, and she loved him now, just a few months shy of thirty. She was the older woman, they'd always joked.

"Can we talk?" Ethan finally said, looking at her over Bruce's furry head. "I have to run to a meeting today, but soon. Please?"

She knew he'd be gone again in a couple days or less, and then she'd be left alone once more. Hollow. Aching. And yet, saying no didn't even cross her mind.

"How about tomorrow, around 3:30?" Andie asked, as he walked with her back down the hall, for a moment making it feel like the last ten years hadn't happened and this was just another day in their happy ever after.

"You get out of work that early?"

"Library budget cuts." They stopped at a linen closet, where she grabbed a clean towel, and then veered into the living room, beginning to mop up the mess.

"I'm sorry. That stinks." He frowned, trying to put Bruce down to help her clean. The cat protested volubly and Andie waved him away.

"Don't bother. Bri made the cappuccino, so it was sweet enough to bring roaches running in the middle of winter. I'll have to mop the floor and wash the couch cover. This is just momentary damage control."

It occurred to her then, and maybe to him, given how things suddenly got awkward all over again, that she'd just described their whole relationship. Once so sweet it made their friends pretend to gag. Then a puddle on the floor to be mopped away, followed by their conversation today, attempting some kind of damage repair.

"I missed you," Ethan said quietly.

"Don't," she whispered, scrubbing fixedly at the couch. "Not now, Ethan. Give me a chance to get my head around things. Please?"

When he didn't answer for a long time, she finally looked up and saw Bruce sitting forlornly in the middle of the living room, Ethan nowhere to be seen. Walking toward the kitchen, Andie saw there was a note on the whiteboard in the hallway, where she kept her to-do list and other things she needed to keep track of day-to-day.

3:30 tomorrow. Meet me at Sal's? – E.

CHAPTER 4
FIGHT OR FLIGHT

IT FELT GOOD TO PUSH HERSELF HARD TO FINISH THE THREE-MILE RUN, HER lungs burning as Andie jogged the last few hundred yards to her home. Running always cleared her mind, and even with Ethan's sudden reappearance and their looming 'meeting'—definitely not a date, she told herself over and over again—Andie felt better as she jumped into the shower and scrubbed off, mentally reviewing her to-do list, including researching an article for the local paper, which she often freelanced for. Then she had a scheduled oil change for her car, followed by a class for library programming for kids on the autism spectrum. And then, of course, Ethan.

She had just finished pulling on a soft green sweater dress and was reaching for the hair dryer when her phone rang. Now, who would be calling at 7:30 in the morning?

"Hello," she said without looking at the phone, switching gears and walking into the kitchen instead to whip up a smoothie.

"Andie, it's Nick Lamas."

She stopped in front of her fridge, surprised to hear the chairman of the board of commerce. "Hi, Nick."

"I'm sorry for calling you on your day off. Could we meet in an hour or so? I understand if you already have plans."

"I do actually have plans," she replied, worry edging in quickly. The last time she and Nick had talked, her hours had been slashed. "Can we talk over the phone?"

"I'd much prefer you come in," he answered. "What time would be convenient for you today?"

She pulled out a carton of yogurt and some frozen berries. "Will two be okay? I have something going on at 3:30." She looked over at the whiteboard, to Ethan's message written in handwriting that hadn't changed much from their high school days. She smiled faintly, then realized Nick had been talking. "I'm sorry. What?"

"Two is fine," he repeated.

"Okay, thanks. See you then." Andie ended the call and shelved her worries about it. It was a busy day, and those were her favorite kind.

It took Nick Lamas less than ten minutes to wipe away the smile that had been Andie's face all day. Her article was shaping up well, her car was still hanging on somehow, and the class had had all kinds of practical, immediately applicable information. Now all those things felt moot, especially the class. No point in designing library programs for kids if you were suddenly no longer a librarian.

"I'm sorry, Andie," Nick said, his gray head bowed as if in contrition. "If there was anything at all we could do differently, we would."

She sat in stunned silence across from him, his words echoing through her mind on a loop pedal. *We're going to have to let you go due to budgetary constraints.*

A thousand questions roared through her mind, none of which she asked because of June. She could survive this, somehow, so long as she knew June still kept her position.

"Will I get severance?" It was the one thing she had to know.

"Nebraska law doesn't require us to provide it."

Andie stood up, her legs slightly shaky. "This is wrong, Nick. I understand that June needs the job far more than I do, so I won't fight, but you're turning me out on my ear after nine years, when I've never had an employee review that wasn't five-starred."

"I realize that, and—"

"And yet you're still firing me."

"Terminating your employment due to lack of funds to pay your salary. Firing is a different thing altogether," he said hastily.

"I don't see it that way." She started for the door. "What I see is that I have no idea how I'll be paying my bills, and that you didn't bother to let me know this could be coming, so I would have a chance to prepare. I could have offered ideas that might have saved both money and my job."

She let the door to his office thud shut behind her and walked down the hallway of the chamber of commerce's office building, ignoring the sympathetic looks she got from everyone who knew her well, including old classmates. Their pity left her feeling queasy. It reminded her of the looks when she'd driven in from Vegas after the divorce had gone through.

Sitting in a stiff blue chair near the exit, June looked up as Andie appeared, and struggled to her feet. "Andie—"

"It's not your fault." Andie hugged the old woman as tightly as she dared. "Don't you dare do anything to jeopardize your own job. They're keeping you on because you're the best at it; you know every in and out. Plus, you're a tradition, June. Valentine loves its traditions, and seeing you behind that desk is something most people have gotten used to since childhood. They need you even more than you need them, so don't you let them forget it."

She pulled back and looked down into June's anguished face. "I love you, Junie B. I'll be okay," she promised, easing June back into the chair. "It's for the best. I promise. For the best," she repeated, walking out the door and onto the street.

⊙⁂⊙

To her surprise, Ethan was standing right outside, his hoodie pulled up against a light mixture of sleet and rain that must have started while she was in the meeting. The day had been beautiful up until that point.

"I heard. Andie, I'm so sorry."

"Who told you?" Andie demanded. She wanted to walk straight into his arms and let him hold her until some of the anger and hurt ebbed away, but those days were long gone. The thought piled anger upon anger, so her tone came out edged with barbed wire.

"Molly," Ethan replied, nodding at the café down the street that one of their classmates owned. "I stopped in for coffee and she pulled me aside. I don't know who told her. You know how it is around here."

"I do," Andie agreed. "I know all too well. And it's time I got out of Dodge. I can't do this anymore."

Ethan frowned and gestured at a Ford pickup parked nearby, probably his rental while he was in town. "It'll be warmer to talk in there."

"I don't want to talk," Andie snapped. "What I want is to be somewhere where everybody doesn't know my business almost before I even know it myself. After you and I split, I couldn't move on because every time I turned a corner, there was a pitying face. Even today, I hear about how sad it is that we went our separate ways." Her fists clenched. "Now I'll hear about this from here till Judgment Day."

Ethan shoved his hands in his pockets, the rain dripping down his hoodie, dampening the shoulders. "So you're angry that people care about you? That doesn't make much sense. Whatever happened to your New York dreams, anyway? Nobody would have known your business in that city."

Knowing ears were straining from every direction, it was all Andie could do not to shout in frustration. Instead, she started down the street, walking at a fast clip. In school, her long legs had served her well on the basketball team. Now they carried her across downtown swiftly and furiously. Unfortunately, Ethan had even longer legs, which had won him a football scholarship to university, and he kept up without breaking a sweat.

"This is your problem, you know," he informed her as they nearly sprinted through the heart of Valentine.

"What? Being fired?" Andie rounded on him incredulously, halfway across Centennial Hall's lawn. Behind her, the oldest standing high school in Nebraska, rumored to be haunted, stood stark and proud against the gray day. But right now the only thing Andie knew was haunted for certain was her heart. And one of its ghosts was standing a few feet away, couched in a damp maroon hoodie that looked frustratingly good, especially when paired with jeans that fit exactly right, proving that Ethan was in shape as good, or even better, as he had been in high school.

"Tell me, Ethan," she spat in disbelief. "What is my problem, exactly?"

"Running away," Ethan retorted, eyes flashing. "You insisted we run away to get married, instead of fighting your parents for their approval."

Stung, Andie gaped at him. "*I* insisted? As I recall, you were fully onboard with avoiding that conflict!"

"Because I knew that if I fought you, you might change your mind entirely, which is exactly what eventually happened!" Ethan snapped, sending an arrow right through Andie's heart, and not one of Cupid's. "You ran from that casting call. You're running instead of fighting for your job. You're running from the feelings we obviously both still have now. You ran from the problems in our marriage."

"I ran from the problems in our marriage?" Andie yelled, so incensed that she didn't even stop to absorb his confession. "You filed the papers! I tried to talk to you about them every which way, and you avoided me like I was trying to tackle you on the field! Who's the one who caught the first flight out of Nebraska? How can you say I ran when I obviously—" she waved her arms in every direction —"never left?!"

"You don't have to catch a plane to be a fugitive," he said grimly, yanking his hoodie down farther as the rain picked up. "Are you gonna run now, Andrea? Or will you stand and fight for something for once in your life?"

"There's nothing to fight for," she reminded him, feeling like the very marrow of her bones was icing over, and not from the rain. "You left. Even if I fought now, Ethan, how would it work, huh?" She took a step toward him. "Huh? I don't even know what you do or where you live, but I'm thinking California is a big probability. How do we fight if you're there and I'm here?"

"You just got fired," he pointed out coldly. "Seems like at the very least your career ties have been severed here. If you're going somewhere here in Valentine, I'm not seeing it, Andrea. Seems like you're at a total dead end, actually." Even as he spoke, the anger in his eyes faded and Andie could see the remorse setting in fast. "Wait. I shouldn't have said that. That was going too far—Andie. You're running again, see? *Andie!*"

She walked away, her shoulders hunched against the rain, her eyes glazed over with what she told herself were just tears created by the wind. And just like before, she ran, and he let her go.

CHAPTER 5

OPPORTUNE MOMENT

"Nice job!" Andie high-fived Tameka Lowry and the little girl ran proudly to her cubby, carrying the spelling worksheet she and Andie had just gone over together. She put it carefully away, pulled on a puffy purple coat, and then raced out the door to the playground, where she still had fifteen minutes left of recess.

"I worry about that kid," Brianna admitted from the front of the class, where she was standing on a desk, taking down a few Christmas decorations that remained after the winter break. "She's too young to worry so much about every little thing. There was no need for her to take time away from recess; I could've helped her in class. But you saw me try to convince her otherwise."

Andie walked over to take the bits of tinsel and snowflakes from Brianna as her friend finished, then handed up strips of tape, along with the newest set of decorations. Valentines, of course. She stifled a sigh.

Brianna pressed the first heart firmly into the wall. "I worry about you too."

"Don't start," Andie warned.

"You're not exactly earning any money helping me out in the classroom."

"You asked me to help!"

"I need the help, with my usual aide out sick," Brianna agreed, artfully stringing decorative strands between each new heart, so the decorations looked like a candy necklace. "But I've taught with no aide plenty of times. Mostly, I want you out of your house, Andie. Ever since the library thing, and then Ethan, you've vanished from polite society."

"It's only been two weeks," Andie said dryly, putting a hand out to steady the desk when Brianna stepped too close to the edge and it wobbled.

"Bri, can I get some help out here?" The playground monitor, Carl Gottfried, stuck his head in the door, looking frazzled. "Royce and Jeneca are at it again. Fighting over a jump rope this time."

"Those two!" Brianna exclaimed in frustration, hopping down from the desk and making a beeline for the door. "Go grab some lunch, Andie."

Andie stood in the empty, silent classroom, looking around at the evidence of busy, cheerful little minds. Brianna was an outstanding teacher, and her hard work was reflected in her students' projects. She modeled a great work ethic, and they emulated her in everything from worksheets to tests to in-class art projects, all decorating the walls.

As a librarian, Andie had also prided herself on being the very best at her work. She'd attended seminars, taken online classes, sought out mentor figures, and devoted herself entirely to making the library the best possible resource for her community, within the tight financial constraints of her position. Beyond the job itself, she'd especially loved spending time with her youngest customers. Her chances of having a child of her own were fast slipping away, so spending time with little ones made her as happy as it did sad.

Thoughts of children invariably turned to thoughts of Ethan and Andie scowled and shoved that particular face to the recesses of her mind. She wasn't going to think about his face that last fight. Or about how she'd prayed he'd show up on her doorstep, since she didn't even know his phone number. No, she was definitely not thinking about either of those two things.

The cafeteria was in the next building, so she pulled on her coat. As she did, a paper fluttered to the ground. Surprised, Andie leaned down to pick it up and remembered, as she unfolded the pale blue stationery that June had given it to her.

Is this an opportune moment? she wondered, reading what was written on the paper out loud. "Dear Andie, I know you still pray, in spite of the heartache you've suffered, and I'm so glad. But don't give up on love, because God is love, honey. Give up on it and you're also giving up on Him, whether or not you realize it. Love, Junie B." After the note there was a Bible verse which Andie didn't remember ever having read.

Many waters cannot quench love; rivers cannot wash it away. If one were to give all the wealth of his house for love, it would be utterly scorned. – Song of Solomon 8:7.

"Oh, Junie," Andie muttered, tucking the note carefully away. "Hard not to give up on love when it hurts so much most of the time that I can't sleep."

This January afternoon wasn't as cold as some, and Andie enjoyed the sun on her face as she walked to the cafeteria. Classes had been busy decorating, and all manner of Valentine's décor, from chubby cupids to love haikus, was plastered in and out of the building.

Thank God I have reservations in Custer already. She made a mental note to double-check them that night. She didn't really have the money for a weekend getaway, but staying around for Valentine's Day ... *Nooooo. Not happening.* The usual frenzy had started to overtake Valentine, decorations going up a mile a minute and the annual greeting card contest currently in full swing, the whole town competing for the prize of creating the town's official annual Valentine's Day missive.

She stopped and conversed for a few moments with a couple other teachers she'd come to know in the last two weeks while she'd been spelling Brianna's aide, who was recovering from an appendectomy. They headed back to their classrooms and she glanced at the monthly menu, posted on a bulletin board opposite the door.

"Jan 18 …" She scanned the menu for today. "Baked chicken with dinner roll, sweet potato, applesauce, zucchini coins, gingerbread."

"Better than what we used to get fed."

Andie jumped in shock, spinning to find Ethan a few feet away. Her heart lurched at how handsome he looked in a brown leather bomber jacket that made his eyes— gazing intently in her direction—twice as deep and dark.

"What are you doing here?" Andie stammered, and watched his face fall. "I didn't mean it that way," Andie said hastily. "Please—please don't leave again. I mean, not, like, ever. Well, yes, actually, ever—" she broke off and watched, relieved, as Ethan smiled slowly. "I'm blushing again, right?"

"Like a sunset," he informed her. "You have the prettiest blushes I've ever seen. Always have. As for your question, I was here giving a talk for sixth grade career day. I'm a casting director, by the way."

"I thought you were gone for good," she said softly, stepping aside to let a class exit the cafeteria.

"I thought I was too," Ethan admitted soberly. "You made me about as mad as I've ever been at you." He held up a hand to forestall her argument. "And I made you just as angry. I get it. I had to come back." Ethan reached for her hand and she let him take it, feeling a spring-like thaw as his long fingers wrapped around hers. "Because this isn't over, Andie. Not that fight. And not this thing between us. Not by a long shot. No way. We've been fooling ourselves. It's time to quit, don't you think?"

"Yes," she said instantly. "Yes to all of that. I'm sorry. You were right. I just had refused to see that part of myself."

"I'm no innocent." He tugged her on her hand, drawing her a little closer, and a pack of butterflies—a herd? A clowder?—did loop-the-loops in her chest. "You ran, and I should have followed. We're repeating the same old patterns that did us in the first go 'round."

Andie's mouth went dry. "First go. Are you saying you could potentially be inter-ested in a second?"

Ethan pulled her closer still, until he was gazing directly into her eyes. "I am more than interested. I asked you before if we could talk, and we never did. Any chance we can still make that happen?"

"If you try to put him off by saying I need you, I don't," Brianna said from behind Andie.

Still holding Ethan's hand tightly, Andie looked over her shoulder and found her best friend smiling from ear to ear from just inside the cafeteria. "Get out of here, Merrill. And don't come back until there's a permanent smile on that gorgeous face. And on yours."

"Hey!" Andie burst out laughing as the door swung closed between them. She turned back to Ethan, who was grinning widely. "You heard the orders. Brianna is never to be disobeyed."

He shuddered. "Not in this lifetime. I still remember when I didn't follow her instructions for how to decorate for that seventh grade Valentine's Dance!"

Andie smirked, walking beside Ethan, their fingers tightly intertwined, toward the parking lot. "It was just a plastic snake." Rattlers were common on the prairie and to get revenge for his refusal to deck the entire elementary school gym in neon pink, Brianna had exploited Ethan's ophidiophobia.

"Thanks for the sympathy," he said dryly. "I screamed so loud, people probably heard me in the next county. Not good for a tough-guy rep!"

"Poor baby," she teased, and he hip-checked her in rebuttal.

"The usual place?" Ethan asked, as they reached the truck.

She smiled at the familiarity newly reestablished between them. "Where else would we go to solve all the problems of the world?"

He opened the door for her and waited until she was settled in the passenger seat, then leaned in impulsively and brushed his lips over her cheek, and the laughter died on her lips, replaced by butterflies again. Or more like hummingbirds, given the speed at which her heart now beat. Then he was gone, walking around the truck to climb in the other side, and Andie was temporarily left with a flock of birds taking wing in her chest, along with her hopes.

Many waters cannot quench love; rivers cannot wash it away, she whispered to herself. *Please, God. Let us figure it out this time.*

CHAPTER 6

I'LL CATCH YOU WHEN YOU FALL

THE BUFFALO LUMBERED PLACIDLY ALONGSIDE THE PICKUP TRUCK, UNPERTURBED by their presence on its home turf in the Niobrara Wildlife Refuge. Even so, Ethan gave the massive beast a wide berth. He made sure they were a safe distance away before giving Andie a roguish grin.

"Remember?"

In the passenger seat, Andie laughed. "How could I forget? My car is still missing paint in places."

Once upon a time, they'd picnicked by a waterfall and a buffalo had decided to use her car to scratch an itch. Its coarse fur had done a real number on the paint job which, back then, had been almost new.

"I still can't believe it didn't do more damage," he commented, guiding the car down a dirt road. Remnants of snow crunched beneath the tires.

"My car's a tough beast in its own right," she reminded him, and enjoyed his answering chuckle.

Around them, the boreal forest made of paper birches, box elders, and ponderosa pines whispered with an early-afternoon wind. In the distance, the silhouette of a lone deer could be seen against the clear blue horizon.

"Remember?" Ethan finally said, as they passed a prairie chicken feasting on a patch of withered poison ivy berries that had somehow not been devoured yet.

Andie wagged a finger at him. "I warned you."

He'd been sixteen and as stubborn then as he still was now. They'd gone for a hike, and she'd dropped her keys at some point. They'd spotted them in a thicket of native grasses and Andie had noticed the telltale poison ivy leaves, but Ethan had been intent on being her hero, rather than waiting for her to figure out a solution that didn't involve definite urushiol poisoning.

"I itched for days," he said ruefully.

"You looked so cute with calamine spread every which way," she teased.

"Having you put it on me made the itch bearable."

She didn't have time to blush before he stopped the car and was moving around to her side. "I might have a little surprise for you."

Andie looked at him curiously as she got out and shut the door behind her. "If you have a surprise, then you assumed I'd agree to this ... whatever this is."

"Not assumed," he corrected. "Hoped. Sometimes you have to give hope a fighting chance." He reached into the bed of the truck and held up a pair of ice skates, dangling them an inch from Andie's nose. "Remember?"

Delight mingled with memories of every time he'd ever tried unsuccessfully to teach her to ice skate. "But—I'm the worst!"

"I'll catch you every time you fall."

If his words had the same impact on the frozen river as they did on Andie's heart, they might be going for a swim instead of a skate.

⁂

"How can you not have improved in the slightest?" Ethan teased as Andie lurched around the ice, doing a credible imitation of a deer trying its legs out for the very first time.

"People pretty much gave up on teaching me—oh no. Help!" She floundered, feeling the ice rush up to meet her and then Ethan was there, catching her exactly as he'd promised. For a long moment he held her close and she sank into him, happy for any excuse to be in his arms once more. Then he took her hands and began to skate backward with smooth, even strokes, drawing Andie along with him.

Somehow, she managed to keep up, so long as he held her upright. "I don't know why I'm so bad at this," she groused. "Basketball, swimming, soccer—I have *some* athletic abilities."

"It's payback for you knocking me off my feet that very first day," Ethan said with a wink, doing a slow circle before releasing one of Andie's hands. "And ... twirl ..." He spun her around and before she could fall, pulled her back into his chest, then sent her spinning out again.

Laughing so hard she almost staggered sideways, Andie followed his lead, trusting him to keep her upright at least ninety-five percent of the time. On the rare occasion that she did take a bad stumble, Ethan always caught her before she hit the ice.

Finally, they made their way back to solid ground, both red-cheeked from the combination of laughter and cold wind.

Helping her to the big boulder, the one with their initials carved into it in a place that was unnoticeable unless you looked for it, Ethan settled Andie on the rock and then knelt to help her with her skates. She didn't even try to protest as he carefully unlaced them, too lost in the sight of his smile and the words on the rock behind them.

E & A 4-evr.

Ethan looked up and gently brushed the hair back from her face. "Prettiest blush. Prettiest smile. Prettiest everything, Andie Merrill. Close your eyes for me?"

Andie did as he asked and waited. And waited. And waited so more.

"Any day now ..."

A moment later, she heard Ethan approaching. "Okay, open 'em."

Her eyes flew open and landed immediately on the blanket spread across the ground, a small battery-powered heater set up along with a spread of her favorite picnic foods, everything from smoked salmon to potato salad.

"Ethan," she whispered, pressing a hand to her mouth.

He sank down beside her on the boulder and drew her into his arms. "Remember?" he whispered as he wrapped her up tight in his warm embrace.

"Senior prom," Andie murmured into his jacket. "We partied with everyone for a while and then snuck away. You had this all set up for us."

"I loved you then." Ethan tipped her chin up and gazed into her eyes. "I love you now. I never stopped. I shouldn't have filed those papers, Andie. The truth is, I didn't understand the commitment I was making when we got married, and I definitely didn't understand the divorce any better. I was at my wit's end, hating waking up angry and going to bed even angrier. I just gave up on us, for no reason at all. I broke our marital vows, and I've spent the last ten years kicking myself for it ever since. Can you ever forgive me?"

She swallowed the huge knot in her throat and laced their fingers, squeezing tightly. "I didn't fight you when you filed. I didn't fight for us or do anything to try to save the marriage. Yes, I forgive you. Absolutely."

"Can we try again?" he asked, freeing one hand and sliding it through her hair until it cupped the back of her neck.

"Yes. Please, yes." She nodded over and over again, tears streaming down her face. "I love you too. Whatever we did wrong last time, I want to learn from it so it never happens again."

His lips found hers and there was no more cold, no more wind, no more winter. It was just the man she loved holding her close once more, and the terrible great divide between then beginning to finally mend as he kissed her again and again and again.

CHAPTER 7
FROM BAD TO WORSE

By the time they made it back to Andie's house, the heart shadows were long on Valentine's sidewalks, cast by the many decorations already in place for the big parade. Floating on something far greater than cloud nine, Andie walked with Ethan to her door and reached for her keys.

"You want some hot chocolate?" she offered, not wanting him to leave just yet. They'd talked for hours, trading stories about everything from Ethan's wildly successful casting company, providing thousands of actors to movie sets around the world, to Andie's adventures in New York City before obtaining her library sciences degree. Even with a full evening of conversation under their belt, they'd barely scratched the surface of their time apart, but it was a start.

"You don't have to ask twice," he said with a grin.

She pushed the door open just as an old brown sedan drove up right alongside Ethan's truck.

"Who—" he began, but Andie was already hurrying over to June's car, reaching for the old lady as she tried to ease her way out without falling on the slick street.

"You have to take my job," June muttered, clutching both her canes and glaring up at Andie. "I mean it, Andrea. This arrangement is no longer acceptable."

"It's too cold to talk out here. Come inside," Andie urged as Ethan walked over.

"Hi, Junie," he smiled, leaning down to give her a warm hug. "No homework for you to help me with today."

She chuckled and patted his cheek before resuming her grip on her cane. "You were just about the worst speller I have ever worked with, Ethan Bainbridge, but I still always knew you and Andie would do great things."

Andie and Ethan exchanged worried glances as they walked beside June, being careful not to hover but making sure she didn't slip.

She doesn't look good, Ethan mouthed with a slight shake of his head and Andie nodded in agreement as they reached her house.

In spite of her struggles with arthritis and diabetes, June usually was rosy-cheeked and bright-eyed. But today she was almost gray, her eyes faded and weary. She seemed to struggle to walk more than usual, clutching the canes so tightly that her gnarled hands went white.

When they finally got inside and settled her in an armchair, she exhaled a low, relieved wheeze and closed her eyes. That gave Ethan and Andie the chance to confer silently again, trading worried looks once more.

"Will you make her some tea?" Andie asked. "In the cabinet on the left. She likes passionfruit."

"On it." Ethan squeezed her hand and vanished in the direction of the kitchen.

"You were gone all day," June rasped, and Andie turned back toward her.

"Did you need something?" she asked worriedly. "I'm sorry. I—"

June waved her silent. "You were spending time with your husband. Don't apologize."

"He's not exactly—"

"Yes, he is," June said flatly. "That divorce decree only means something if you both want it to. If neither of you do, it's still a marriage with everything but the official stamp on it. Now. I have some terrible news, Andie. You may want to sit down for this."

Confused and alarmed, Andie sank into a nearby chair. "Okay ..."

June took another deep breath, coughed for a long spell, then leaned forward as she spoke. "They're closing the library."

"What!" Andie stared in disbelief at her friend. "What—when—"

"They held an emergency board meeting today. If you ask me, they waited till they were sure you weren't around, because they knew you'd kick up a fuss."

"But—but—by cutting my job, surely that frees finances up enough to at least keep the doors open!" Andie exclaimed.

"It will for six months only," June rasped, coughing to clear her throat. "And you must take my job for that time, so you can save up a little money for the future. Look at me, Andrea. I'm in no shape to work any longer."

Thoughts reeling, Andie sat back, aghast. "It's not about my job or even yours. This town needs that library. Yes, there's the big shiny main branch, but ours has all the events for children. The reading circles. The children's theater. The homework helpers and visits from local authors."

"Their argument was that one fully staffed, high-tech library is sufficient for a town this size."

"They can't do this," she said fiercely. "We won't let them, June." Andie paced back and forth, muttering under her breath, searching for any possible solution.

"Andie?"

She looked over to see Ethan standing in the doorway, a steaming mug in his hands. "Andie, I couldn't find the—look out!"

Andie whirled to see June in some kind of a seizure, limbs akimbo, sliding from the chair. Her skin was the color of oatmeal. "*Junie!*"

CHAPTER 8

SAYING GOODBYE

Jan. 25, 2014

THE PASTOR'S FINAL WORDS FADED AWAY, ALONG WITH THE REMAINING PEOPLE at the snow-dusted gravesite. Ethan held Andie's hand as she stood and stared at the place where June had been laid to rest less than a week after she'd collapsed at Andie's place.

"It's like I'm losing my mom for the second time." Andie leaned into Ethan and he wrapped his arm around her waist, bending to kiss her hair. They'd both lost their parents young, yet another life event that had bound them irrevocably.

"She loved you like the daughter she wished she had," he replied. "I don't know if it helps, but at least she didn't suffer long." His own mother had undergone multiple rounds of chemotherapy before passing away the summer Ethan turned thirteen. The loss had destroyed his father and he'd taken to drinking, dying of cirrhosis of the liver shortly before Ethan and Andie divorced.

"It helps a little." Andie wiped her eyes with her sleeve. "It was the news about the library that finished her off. I'm sure of it."

He nodded. "I don't doubt it. That would've been quite a shock, knowing a place she'd worked at for sixty years was being shuttered. Without biological kids, she probably saw it as her legacy."

Andie thought of her final conversation with June, and the Bible verse. "She said you were still my husband."

"Did you agree?"

"I'm afraid to," she said bluntly, too tired to pull punches. "I still don't understand what went wrong with us. What if it happens again?"

They started back toward the car, passing graves with valentines set out in front of them, stuffed animals, even the occasional box of chocolate.

"It sounds simplistic, but I think we were just too young," Ethan said, after they were in the truck, the heater going full blast in spite of the sunshine, which today seemed to afford no warmth. He didn't drive them anywhere, neither one of them having a place they needed to be. The solitude and quiet of the car suited them both at the moment.

Andie held her hands in front of the vent, watching color return to them. "Some people make it when they're young."

"Well, we kind of got married when we were twelve," he reminded her, and she smiled slightly, thinking of the mini ceremony they'd held for themselves at an age when no one else thought there was any possibility it would last. "It was like we defaulted to one another from the day we met. And I love that, don't get me wrong, but maybe we needed to grow up a little. The things we fought about ..."

She rolled her eyes. "You have no idea how many people have asked me why we ended. They want to know if you cheated, if I cheated, if you were abusive."

He nodded. "I've heard it all myself. They want a reason. And the only reason I can give is that we suddenly fought about absolutely everything."

"Everything," she echoed, thinking back to the fights about sock folding, TV, how to wash dishes, what music to play ... "We never did that before we were married."

"Never," he agreed. "So I don't know. The one thing I do know for sure is that there was nothing inherently wrong. We just up and quit, basically, maybe because we'd never before had our relationship tested and eighteen-year-olds are moody and impulsive on the best of days."

"What did you do when you got the papers?" Andie looked over at him.

A pained look crossed his handsome face and he glanced out the window at the graveyard. "You drove to Vegas to get them, right?"

"Sort of. The legal requirements didn't mandate that, so I drove there more to clear my head. I was hoping twenty hours on the road would do ... something. Not really sure what. Twenty hours there, twenty back ..." She winced at the memory of what had eventually felt like an endless drive, nothing but her whirling thoughts and broken heart keeping her company. "My head was no better when I got home. Frankly, it was worse."

"I visited Mom and Dad." Ethan nodded at the low hill where he and Andie had visited his parents earlier that day, before June's funeral. She'd also spent time at her parents' grave site the previous day, with Ethan waiting patiently in the car when she'd asked for some time alone with them to think and talk and pray.

"Did it help?" Andie asked, reaching over to touch his knee. He covered her hand with his own.

"No. I wanted them to give me advice on how to get over you. Realized later that they would never have offered that. They loved you." Ethan looked over at her. "Even on his worst days, Dad still talked about you like you were a queen. They both probably think I'm an idiot for letting you go. Because I was."

Andie slid across the bench seat and he lifted her onto his lap, gathering her into a soft kiss first, then holding her tight.

"I'm afraid of screwing things up again, Ethan."

He tipped her chin up to look into her eyes. "Honey, I'm flat-out petrified. My heart won't survive losing you a second time. So I figure the failsafe is making sure it never happens again, whether that involves counseling or, I don't know, sumo wrestling."

Andie laughed, the sadness of losing June still present, but now somehow eased. "Sumo wrestling could be one way to work out arguments about dishwashing, I guess."

He grinned, then sobered. "Seriously, though. This time, if we do this, we're going to go the distance, Andie. There's no Plan D."

She nodded. "I agree completely. But, Ethan ..." she asked the question that had most been troubling her since their reconciliation. "What about your job?"

"You want to stay in Valentine, right?" he asked, and she nodded.

"This place drives me crazy sometimes, but I can't imagine living anywhere else. Mind you, I need to find a job, but once that's settled, this is home. It always will be."

"How about a compromise?" Ethan asked. "I can't ask you to split your time between two places, because your career likely won't allow it."

She snorted. "Career? I don't think the other library is likely to hire me after the fuss I raised about them shutting down the Lohman Branch." After June's heart attack, Andie had written an editorial for the local paper, eviscerating the board for its underhanded tactics to destroy an old woman's legacy and a source of learning for so many young children.

"Assume they do. You won't be able to take six months off and work remotely. But I can," Ethan said. "All those years we were apart, I burned the midnight oil to try and forget you. Now I own the agency and it's financially in the black. If I want to work six months out of the year from an office here, that's my prerogative. I'll still have to travel during that time, but this will be home base."

"You'd do that for me?" Andie asked, kissing him lightly.

"What was that cheesy line of poetry Mr. Halman read us in ninth grade lit one year? Something about shooting down the moon and gathering stars for my love?"

Mystified, she shrugged. "No idea. But I did spend half of his class doodling *Mrs. Bainbridge* over and over again ..."

Smiling, Ethan kissed her and as always, the world outside, and all its highs and lows, faded away.

CHAPTER 9

A RAT REVEALED

FEB. 7, 2014

"Not those. Ethan!" Brianna snapped in exasperation, stalking over and prying the fuchsia streamers from his hands. "What is this, seventh grade again? *These*." She handed him a bundle of ivory-colored ones instead, and hurried off to read someone else the riot act.

From a few feet away, stapling decorations to the side of valentine queen's float, Andie waggled her eyebrows at Ethan. "Watch out for snakes ..."

He rolled his eyes and grinned good-naturedly, resuming the decorating task he'd been assigned at the front of the car, but not before blowing Andie a kiss. She smiled from ear to ear and ducked her head, laughing as she heard him whisper, "Cheeks the color of cranberries ..."

The two weeks since June had died had been the strangest mixture of sad and elated. Andie still had a hard time getting around the collision of emotions, but with each day that passed, with each moment that she and Ethan spent reconnecting, things were starting to fall into place once more. She looked around at the organized chaos, thoroughly orchestrated by Brianna for maximum efficiency, which she hadn't been a part of since her divorce. She hadn't realized how much she missed seeing the decorations go up all over town, the tourists descending en masse to join the many Valentine's Day festivities, the wedding parties that came in specifically to take advantage of the holiday in a town like no other.

Yesterday had been the annual greeting card contest, with Molly Harold carrying off the top prize of a weekend stay for two at the Whispering Pines lodge, the nicest hotel in town. Today was the final prep for the annual parade. Tomorrow there was something else on the agenda—Andie couldn't remember exactly what, but Bri would be sure to remind her about thirty times.

"You missed a spot," Carter called as he walked by, followed closely by Molly herself, who he'd turned his attentions to. "Bri will have your guts for garters if you don't fix that," he teased, and she found herself glad again that he'd been sincere about being happy that she and Ethan had reunited. He was a good man, and she prayed that he and Molly would find happiness together.

Reunited ... Andie straightened, stretching out the kinks in her neck and taking a minute just to watch her ex work, his long, lean frame curled around the float doing something or other. Except he wasn't her ex anymore. She wasn't sure what to call him—boyfriend sounded so strange, when they'd been married—but all that mattered was that he was here. He'd taken time off work to be with her for her first real Valentine's Day in a decade, and somehow, they were going to find a way to make it work this time. A quiet feeling of peace filled her and she whispered a prayer of thanks for this second chance.

As she watched him work, she spotted a camera being trundled past, pushing through the various decorating teams. "Is that a camera like the ones at the casting call?" she said curiously.

Ethan sat up and ran his fingers through his dark, sandy hair, strewing bits of tinsel throughout it. "That is," he agreed, following her gaze. "Huh. Didn't know another crew had arrived in town after mine left."

"Looks like they're headed for the library," Andie said in confusion, walking over to him and watching as the camera was joined by another, from the opposite direction.

Frowning, Ethan laced his fingers through hers and they started toward her old workplace, shuttered ever since June's death. Though the chamber of commerce had promised six more months, their excuse for closing had been a lack of staff. Irony of ironies.

"Hey," Ethan greeted a lighting tech. "What's going on?"

"Just getting some shots for the video," the man replied from behind the rig.

"Video?" Andie repeated. "What video?"

"The one for the ad."

Ethan and Andie exchanged looks before Ethan walked over toward another guy and held a brief conversation. He returned to Andie, a grim expression on his face. "You might want to hear this ..."

⚜

"You rat!" Andie snarled at Nick Lamas, her rage having grown by the minute since she'd learned about the real reason for the library's shuttering. "You good for nothing, lowdown *scumbag!*"

Nick stared at her stolidly, utterly unperturbed. "It made the most financial sense."

"So much sense that you chose not to disclose your backdoor dealings to the town," Ethan pointed out, standing with his arms crossed in the doorway to Nick's office.

"We made a decision based on sound financial analysis and the town will ultimately benefit from it," Nick said with a shrug. "The library is a landmark, but it did nothing for Valentine in terms of a bottom line. Using it as a studio makes sense on all kinds of levels. Crews come here all the time and need a base of operations. They can store their equipment, and we'll charge them for rent, at rates comparable to large cities."

"Nobody will pay that!" Andie exclaimed, even though it was entirely beside the point. When she'd learned that the Lohman Branch was going to be gutted, its insides turned into headquarters for visiting scouts, directors, casts, and crews, everything had fallen into place. The library had always struggled financially, but it was only in the last few years that the pressure had really come down to slash costs. There was no doubt whatsoever in her mind that Nick had engineered the setup bit by bit, first cutting the money they had for facility upgrades, then for general library programming, then for staff, and finally, for the building itself.

"They'll pay," Nick promised, so comfortable behind his big desk, clearly secure in the knowledge that he technically hadn't done anything illegal, that it made Andie physically sick. "You don't understand, but this was all for Valentine. Look into it. I'm not turning a personal profit on the matter. It's all legit. Andie, that library has been a financial blackhole for way too long. This will do far more for everyone, including the kids."

She clenched her fists, wanting to spew curses and venom, but whenever it came to confrontations, she'd always been someone who got tongue tied, and then thought of all kinds of strong comebacks later. "So it's a done deal? This is just it then. Sixty years of teaching kids to love all the wonderful things about reading, and it's just over?" She snapped her fingers. "Like that?"

"It's not a done deal until we find someone who will buy the property and renovate it to our specifications, but it will be." He finally stood, smoothing his preppy patterned tie and his khakis with their knife-creased pleats. "If you'll excuse me, I have another meeting now. Feel free to follow up with me at a later date with other questions."

"Oh, I will," Andie promised furiously, as Ethan touched her shoulder in wordless support. "You better believe there will be many, *many* questions."

CHAPTER 10
NOT QUITE A BULL'S-EYE

THE DART SAILED THROUGH THE AIR, EMBEDDING ITSELF SOLIDLY ON THE OUTER rings of one of the Miller Brewery's three dart boards.

"You've lost your touch," Molly teased, as Andie sat back down at the table where they were hanging out, largely avoiding Brianna on her latest Valentine's Day rampage. "Back in the day, that would have been a bull's-eye."

Andie said nothing and leaned back in her seat, toying with the lid of her beer.

"You've said about five words all evening," Molly observed. "Still fuming about the library? Or did you and Ethan have an argument?"

Leave it to Molly to be blunt as an old butter knife.

"No, Ethan and I are fine," she muttered, tracing the rough edges of the table, carved by one of Valentine's home ec students several years back. "I don't know what we are, exactly, but whatever place we're in, it's good. He wanted to be here tonight. It's his favorite hangout. Always has been. He just had stuff to do."

"And that bugs you," Molly guessed, waving a waiter down and ordering another drink.

"No. Yes. I mean," Andie sighed, irritated at herself far more than she was with Ethan. "I get why that's totally unfair. He's taken weeks off his job for us to be together and figure out what went wrong so we can try again. I just ... with the library, I'm moody, I guess." That was putting it mildly. In the days since her meeting with Nick, her mood had yo-yoed from mourning June, to joy over Ethan, to seething with rage, to grieving the loss of the library and everything it had provided for so many generations. "Ethan has been beyond patient. I wouldn't want to be with me right now."

Molly nudged her foot beneath the table. "It's okay to be human, you know. Major life changes can throw anybody for a loop, and you've had several back-to-back, in under a month."

"Don't make excuses for me," Andie said tiredly. "I just have to pull myself together." She picked up a dart and twirled it around and around between her fingers. "I've been racking my brain, trying to figure out any possibility whatsoever to save the Lohman Branch, but nothing has come to mind. I was hoping that article I wrote for the paper would trigger something, but people are so neck-deep in Valentine's prep that they probably barely even read it. And even if they had, it's just a library. It probably means more to me because of my history. Nobody else is going to care that much."

"That's at least somewhat true," Molly agreed. "Except that this is Valentine. We've never been a place to let our history get bulldozed over by so-called 'progress.' Like you said, it's the holiday. Once that simmers down, you can write another article, and that'll probably have more impact." She accepted her beer from the waiter and took a long sip that left foam on her upper lip.

"By then it may be too late. Nick might have a buyer." Andie spotted Carter walking in, and stood up. "Your guy's here. I'll leave you two alone."

"You don't have to," Molly protested.

Andie laughed a little. "You're a brand-new couple, right around the corner from Valentine's Day. You don't need me hovering around spoiling the newly romantic vibes. Hey," she greeted Carter as he joined them. "You two behave now."

Carter sank into the seat beside Molly and looked up at Andie in surprise. "You don't have to—"

"Yeah. I do." She pressed his shoulder, gave Molly a quick hug, and hurried out of the dark, crowded bar.

Halfway to her car, the phone rang. Andie answered without looking, having been ignoring her best friend's nagging all evening. Much as she was enjoying seeing Valentine decked out in its very best red and white, she'd reached a saturation point when it came to decorating. Even so, it would be a good way to keep her busy. "Okay, Bri, you found me. I'm all yours. What's next?"

"You're all Bri's? I'm jealous. Here I thought you were mine."

Andie's irrational anger thawed and she smiled into the phone. "I'm yours. Even though that's something straight off a candy heart—which I'm totally sick of right now, by the way—I am so yours. What are you doing? I thought you said you were busy today."

"I was," Ethan replied, the impact of his low voice doubled when it was straight into her ear, rasping over her senses. "I took care of things. Meet me somewhere?"

"Sure. The usual?" It wasn't a very cold night, and the thought of walking through one of the wildlife reserve's forests, holding hands with the man she loved, made Andie smile for the first time all evening.

"No, not this time. The Lohman Branch, in fifteen." He hung up before Andie could ask why.

She stood there staring at the phone for a long moment before reversing course. There was no point in driving, when the library was just a few blocks away.

CHAPTER 11
LOVE'S SURPRISE

"Hey." Ethan jumped out of his truck and walked over to where Andie was sitting on a bench, staring forlornly at the building she no longer even had keys to, even though she knew its ins and outs better than some people knew their children, from the way to get the rickety old furnace going when it kicked up a fuss, to how to reboot the glitchy internet connection on one computer without messing up all three, to how to get the water to stop running in the handicapped bathroom.

Seeing him eased the heaviness in her heart and she stood up, arms already opening to hug him tight. To her surprise, he leaned in for a quick kiss, but didn't walk into her embrace. Instead, he gestured at a man climbing out of the Ford's passenger seat.

"Andie, meet Carl. Carl, Andie," Ethan introduced, as the guy, a short, stocky man who Andie vaguely recalled from the casting call, joined them.

"Hi," she said uncertainly, shaking hands with Carl.

"Carl's a location scout for Paramount Pictures," Ethan explained. "He and I have been doing some talking tonight, along with a lot of walking around this old place." He nodded at the library.

Andie's brow furrowed. "Uh ... why?"

"Because Paramount just bought the place," Carl replied.

Stunned, Andie stared at both men. "Wha—so—" Reality felt like it had smashed her across the back of the head, all her hopes for coming up with some kind of a plan sliding straight down the drain. On the heels of that pain came a feeling of utter betrayal.

"Whoa." It was Ethan's turn to frown. "Carl, give us a few."

He took Andie's elbow and drew her, still shell-shocked, a short distance away. "I can read you like one of the books inside this library, Andie. Tell me you know I'd never sell you out like that."

Just like that, a different reality returned, one where she knew—she *knew*—this man she loved would never do anything like this. "I'm sorry." Andie teared up and turned her face away. "I'm an idiot. Of course I know that. I guess you know him since he's in the business."

Tenderly, Ethan touched her cheek and turned her back to him, his thumb brushing away the hints of tears. "Hey." He leaned down to rest their foreheads together. "That's why I know him, yes. But there's way more to the story than that. Give Carl a chance to explain?"

Drawing a slow, ragged breath, she nodded wordlessly. If she spoke, she was afraid she'd cry, and she'd shed way too many tears recently. *Way* too many tears.

Sliding his arm around her waist, Ethan walked with her back to where Carl was standing, texting. He looked up and pocketed the phone.

"Hey. So I take it she doesn't know the details yet."

Ethan shook his head.

Carl rubbed his hands together and nodded. "Right ... so, Andie, here's how this is going to go down. Paramount bought the building. They paid a pretty penny for it, let me tell you, because even though this is Nebraska, this is exactly the kind of 'look' movies are always aiming for." He pointed at various parts of the building, elaborating. "The stairs—perfect for movie kisses. The brick—just right for 'college' buildings, without all the hassle of filming on an open campus. Ethan and I did a walkaround. The grounds themselves will be great for background shots for things like chick flicks—"

"I get it," she interrupted. "It's a gorgeous building, in all respects. I've always said it would be great in movies. But how does that change anything?"

"Paramount bought it," Carl repeated. "But they're not going to gut it, Andie. It's not entirely ideal—a compromise had to be struck—but basically, they'll use the library as a bought-in film location. That means that whenever they need outside shots, or occasional inside shots, for everything from movies to documentaries to occasional advertisements, they'll use the place. Those will be disruptive events, depending on the size of the production. I'm not denying it. But the rest of the time, the library will stay open."

"Open, Andie," Ethan said in her ear, as Andie's jaw dropped, understanding finally dawning. "As in, books. Kids. And you, back behind that desk, walking young minds through their first literary adventures."

"Does that sound okay?" Carl asked. "Not that it matters if it is or not, unfortunately. The paperwork's signed. But it'd be nice if you were on board. I know that would mean a lot to—"

"Okay?" Andie cut in. "*Okay?* You're keeping my library open!" She threw her arms around the short man and squeezed him so hard that Ethan joked,

"Easy there. I'm getting jealous."

Turning from Carl, Andie wrapped her arms around Ethan and kissed him fiercely, oblivious to Carl standing behind them watching. Tears streaming down her cheeks, she held him tight and whispered, "Thank you. Thank you. Thank you."

Ethan gathered her closer and smiled into her teary eyes. "All I did was talk to a few contacts. The building sold itself. But you're welcome. It's great for Valentine, but more importantly, it makes you happy. That's my goal from here on out, Andie. Nothing but happy for the woman I love."

Thank you, God, Andie whispered as she kissed him fervently. *Thank you. Thank you. Thank you.*

EPILOGUE

Feb. 14, 2014

THE LAST FLOAT IN THE PARADE RUMBLED PAST, AND ANDIE WATCHED HER BEST friend collapse against the side of a building, almost knocking over a stand of colorful heart-shaped helium balloons in the process.

"Finished," Brianna sighed happily, fanning herself with a bit of decorative cardboard. "Every year I wonder if it'll happen."

"And every year it goes just fine," Andie pointed out, looking around as the huge crowds began to disperse, some on their way to Valentine's Day brunch, others to more festivities, still others to do some shopping and take home some Valentine, Nebraska-branded memorabilia to their homes, wherever those might be.

"Where's Ethan?" Bri asked, unzipping her coat, now that the early afternoon sun had broken fully through the clouds.

"Doing something or other with Carl," Andie answered, unwinding her own scarf and running her fingers through her curly black hair, making sure no parade confetti lingered in the soft strands.

"So you two are good, huh."

Andie smiled. "Maybe the best we've ever been. I don't know why we ever let each other go in the first place, Bri. We were just dumb kids, I guess."

"This dumb kid still loves you," she heard from behind her.

Andie turned and found Ethan suddenly there, kneeling amidst the parade debris. Surrounded by hearts of every shape and color and size, with their hometown's bedecked Main Street as their backdrop, the man she'd married at eighteen looked up into her eyes and held out a beautiful ring.

"I still love you," Ethan said softly, gazing at Andie with so much devotion that her heart expanded to fill her entire chest. "I never stopped, and I never will. We have a lot of ground to cover before we get to 'I do' again, because this time it has to stick."

Obviously expecting this, Brianna gave a shell-shocked Andie a nudge in Ethan's direction, as their friends appeared and formed a half circle around them.

Tears blurring her vision so much she could barely see Ethan, Andie managed to stumble over until she was close enough where he could take her hand. He held it tight and went on,

"Like I said before, Plan D isn't an option this go 'round. But I want to make sure that while we're figuring everything out, everyone knows you're with me. I love you, Andrea Merrill. Will you marry me? Again? Forever this time."

"Yes!" she cried, her mascara instantly running every which way. "Oh my God, Ethan. Yes!"

As the people they'd grown up with cheered loudly, Ethan slid the ring onto Andie's finger and drew her into a deep, sweet kiss that outshone every other celebration on this most romantic of days.

Years later, even Brianna would admit Ethan's proposal and Andie's acceptance completely blew away her vaunted Valentine's parade. And their Valentine's Day wedding in 2015, choreographed by Brianna, of course, took its place in the annals of Valentine's most romantic stories.

THANK YOU SO MUCH FOR READING OUR BOOK. WE SINCERELY HOPE YOU ENJOYED every bit reading it. We had fun creating it and will surely create more.

Your positive reviews are very helpful to other reader, it only takes a few moments. They can be left at Amazon.

https://www.amazon.com/Brenda-Clemmons/e/B07CYKVVRT

It's absolutely free and you don't need to do anything at all to qualify except go to.

PREFERRED READ FREE READS

http://brendaclemmons.gr8.com/

ABOUT THE AUTHORS

On a college road trip down the "Mother Road," Route 66, Brenda Clemmons fell in love with the beauty of the southwest and promised herself that one day she'd return. After graduating with a history degree, Brenda fulfilled that promise and moved to Arizona, where she met her future husband, who was teaching literature in the classroom several doors down from her own social studies class. Today, she, her husband, and their two kids love to explore the Southwest's beautiful mountains and deserts every chance they get. Brenda's habit of pulling over at every historical marker eventually led to her husband suggesting that she combine her love of romance novels with her in-depth historical knowledge. She put pen to paper and has been writing ever since, filling her stories with the landscapes, legends, and unique local characters that she wants everyone else to share in!

Katie Wyatt is 25% American Sioux Indian. Born and raised in Arizona, she has traveled and camped extensively through California, Arizona, Nevada, Mexico, and New Mexico. Looking at the incredible night sky and the giant Saguaro cacti, she has dreamed of what it would be like to live in the early pioneer times.

Spending time with a relative of the great Wyatt Earp, also named Wyatt Earp, Katie was mesmerized and inspired by the stories he told of bygone times. This historical interest in the old West became the inspiration for her Western romance novels.

Her books are a mixture of actual historical facts and events mixed with action and humor, challenges and adventures. The characters in Katie's clean romance novels

draw from her own experiences and are so real that they almost jump off the pages. You feel like you're walking beside them through all the ups and downs of their lives. As the stories unfold, you'll find yourself both laughing and crying. The endings will never fail to leave you feeling warm inside.

ANNABEL AND ERNEST

Mail Order Bride Western Romance

RoyceCardiff
P u b l i s h i n g   H o u s e
WHOLESOME INSPIRATIONAL ROMANCE

Dear Reader,

It is our utmost pleasure and privilege to bring these wonderful stories to you. I am so very proud of our amazing team of writers and the delight they continually bring us all with their beautiful clean and wholesome tales of, faith, courage, and love.

What is a book's lone purpose if not to be read and enjoyed? Therefore, you, dear reader, are the key to fulfilling that purpose and unlocking the treasures that lie within the pages of this book.

☙❦❧

NEWSLETTER SIGN UP PREFERRED READ

http://katieWyattBooks.com/readersgroup

☙❦❧

THANK YOU FOR CHOOSING A INSPIRATIONAL READS BY ROYCE CARDIFF PUBLISHING HOUSE.

Welcome and Enjoy!

A PERSONAL WORD FROM KATIE

I LOVE WRITING ABOUT THE OLD WEST AND THE TRIALS, TRIBULATIONS, AND triumphs of the early pioneer women.

With strong fortitude and willpower, they took a big leap of faith believing in the promised land of the West. It was always not a bed of roses, however many found true love.

Most of the stories are based on some historical fact or personal conversations I've had with folks who knew something of that time. For example a relative of the Wyatt Earp's. I have spent much time out in the West camping hiking and carousing. I have spent countless hours gazing up at night thinking of how it must been back then.

Thank you for being a loyal reader.

Katie

CHAPTER 1

"I'M SO SORRY FOR YOUR LOSS, ANNABEL. RICKY WAS SUCH A GOOD MAN. A good, hard worker, and a friend to us all. He will be sorely missed at Elton House," Annabel's employer, Mrs. Hedron, said as she placed a posy of flowers on the freshly dug grave.

Annabel Winters still couldn't believe it. Three days ago, she and Ricky had been laughing together on their day off, snacking on sweets from the local apothecary, and walking through Druid Hill Park. Then, as they were crossing the road, Ricky had been hit by a phaeton traveling at unconscionable speed. He had pushed Annabel out of the way, and as she'd fallen to the ground, she had seen her beloved best friend and betrothed get knocked to the ground and trampled. He had lain there, unmoving, and even before Annabel had gotten up and run to him, she had known he was dead. Her best friend and the man who, the week before, had proposed marriage to her, was gone forever.

And now, as Annabel looked at the grave before her, it sank in once again that she would never wander up from the kitchens of Elton House to find Ricky polishing a mirror or silverware, looking up from his work to give her his signature big smile and crack a joke or two. He was dead, and Annabel had lost any desire to continue to exist.

But she had to. She had work to do. Mrs. Hedron had given her the day off for the funeral, but the next day she would be back in the kitchens, whipping up biscuits and pastries and mousse like nothing had happened. And Annabel simply couldn't stand it. She needed to leave Baltimore, leave this place where every street corner seemed to hold another memory of her dear Ricky.

"It's all right, Annie," Leticia Erickson told Annabel, lacing an arm through hers and leading her through the gates of the graveyard and back to the carriages that would take the household staff back to Elton House. "He's gone, but he won't be forgotten. Of that, I can promise you. We all loved him so, and we'll talk and reminisce about him every chance we get."

Annabel tried to be fortified by her best friend's words, but though she knew that Leticia meant well, she also knew that even if they spoke of Ricky every minute of every hour, it still wouldn't be enough.

"I think I need to leave, Letty," Annabel whispered to her friend as they neared the carriages.

"Well, of course," Leticia replied. "We're nearly out of the graveyard and then we'll be back home and away from this sorrowful place."

"No, I mean, I think I need to leave Baltimore," Annabel said.

Leticia stopped walking and turned to face her friend. "Whatever do you mean, leave Baltimore? This is your home!"

Annabel shook her head sadly. "Not anymore, it isn't. Not without Ricky." And then, for the first time that day, she let the tears fall silently down her cheeks. Leticia hugged her close and they stood there, at the gates of the graveyard, Annabel letting her grief drip down into the grass and seep into the ground full of so much death. She knew in her heart that she needed to leave, and so, as she dried her tears and allowed her friend to lead her to the carriage, she began to plan.

⊙⁂⊙

"Nevada! What could there possibly be in Nevada?" Letty whispered a few weeks later as they stood at the large kitchen table kneading dough for bread. Annabel had spent her days off scouring *The Sun* for any opportunity that would allow her to escape Baltimore, and two weeks ago, she had found one. A rancher in Ely, Nevada, named Thomas Michaels, was looking for a mail order bride.

In return, Annabel would be able to live on the ranch in peace, managing the house while her husband worked the fields. While she certainly didn't relish the idea of marrying a man other than Ricky, Ricky was dead, and she had no other choice if she wanted to leave Baltimore. She didn't make enough as a kitchen maid to afford any other kind of escape. As it was, she was going to have to spend all her savings on the stagecoach fare to Nevada because Thomas had told her all his money was in the ranch and he couldn't send her cash for the journey.

"A new life. A chance to heal away from this place where every candlestick and banister reminds me of Ricky," Annabel said, punctuating her statement with a rough pound of dough.

"But you don't even know this man, Annie. He could be a liar or a crook or worse. Stay here and you'll heal in time. I'll help you. Please don't leave."

Annabel didn't want to leave her best friend, but, in spite of her grief, she was excited by the prospect of a new place. She had never left Baltimore, and the trip alone would take her through far-flung grassy plains she had only read about in books.

641

"He's good and kind and God-fearing, I know that from his letters. That's all I need in a husband. And it's a chance to start over for me, Letty. Maybe after a while you could come join me. Maybe I'll meet a man who is right for you, and together we can start a new life out west. Wouldn't that be exciting?"

Leticia looked at Annabel with worry and fear, shaking her head. "You know I could never leave this place. It was where I was born. My mother, God rest her soul, told me if I work good and hard here, Mrs. Hedron will set me up with a small cottage in Albany when I'm old, and I can live out my days among the cows and pigs and fresh grass and sunshine."

Annabel nodded her head resignedly, understanding her friend's reticence but sad that the plan she had been forming in her head for the two of them wouldn't come to fruition. She had to forge on alone.

Sensing Annabel's sadness, Letty looked around to make sure that no one was watching them, then she brushed the flour from her hands on her apron and dove into the small pocket of her dress, handing a small square object to Annabel.

"What's this?" Annabel asked. Letty had handed her a small book, obviously well-loved, if its cracked spine and torn cloth cover were any indication.

"It's the Bible my mother gave me when I was a child. I want you to have it."

"But Letty! You have so few things of your mother's! I could never take this from you." Annabel tried to hand the book back, but Letty refused.

"You need it far more than I do, Annie. I know you've lost your faith since Ricky died, but you'll need God's guidance for this trip. Take it and think of me when you read it," Letty said, placing her hands over Annabel's and squeezing them around the book.

Tears formed in Annabel's eyes as she carefully put the book in her pocket. Both girls turned back to their work, and Annabel lost herself in the rhythmic motion of kneading dough, thinking about her upcoming trip. Her stagecoach was set to leave in two days, which meant she had little time to prepare herself for the weeks-long journey.

CHAPTER 2

NINE PEOPLE WERE PACKED INTO THE STAGECOACH THAT LEFT FROM
Baltimore's busy Charles Street. Annabel was squashed in between two men, an
old, graying man of indeterminate age who fell asleep the moment the horses
started moving, and a young, attractive man about Annabel's age who was reading
what looked like a novel.

"Is it good?" Annabel asked him, gesturing towards the book.

"Oh yes. It's a satirical account of English upper-class society. Very humorous.
Have you read it?" the man asked, showing Annabel the title. *Pride and Prejudice*,
By a Lady, the cover said.

"No, I don't believe I have. Up until very recently, I didn't have much time for
reading, I'm afraid," Annabel told the man. She couldn't help but notice the ice
blue of his eyes, offset by the sandy brown of his hair. He had an open, honest face
and a kind smile that seemed to appear rather easily, as though his face were
predisposed to break into a grin. Lately, Annabel had felt her face was inclined to
do the exact opposite; since Ricky's death, she'd noticed new lines around her
mouth and eyes, frown lines that made her look worn and tired.

"Oh, and why is that?" the man asked, then said, "Oh, how rude of me! I haven't
introduced myself. I'm Ernest Blom."

Annabel took the man's proffered hand and shook it. "I'm Annabel Winters.
Pleased to make your acquaintance, Ernest. The reason I didn't have time to read
is that I was working as a kitchen maid."

"How fascinating!" Ernest said, sitting up straighter in his seat and turning to face
Annabel more fully. "I myself worked in the Blom Bakery up until very recently.
Well, actually, up until yesterday. My family owns the bakery, you see."

"Blom Bakery! I love your cakes! My best friend Letty and I spent most of our wages on the *apfeltaart*," Annabel said. She and Letty had spent many of their days off sampling various sweet treats and freshly baked loaves at the bakery. It was a Dutch bakery and sold the most delectable cinnamon-spiced cookies.

"My handiwork! My father wouldn't let me graduate to bread until I'd mastered that. What is sending you out west?" Ernest asked. For a moment, Annabel didn't hear him, distracted as she was by the sights of Baltimore going by. This might be the last time she'd ever see the carriage house on Preston Street; her last glimpse of the neighborhood she had called home for eighteen years.

Annabel turned back to Ernest and decided to be honest with him. After all, she most likely wouldn't see him again after they got to Ely. "I'm marrying a man I've never met who owns a ranch in Nevada."

"Mail order bride?" Ernest asked.

Annabel was surprised that he knew the term; before she had read the advertisements for mail order brides in the newspaper, she hadn't realized that such a thing existed. "Yes. Yes, his name is Thomas Michaels. He seems very nice from his letters."

Ernest smiled at Annabel. "Well, any man deserving of your love and devotion must be a saint." Annabel smiled at the compliment.

AS THE MILES AND DAYS FLEW BY, ANNABEL AND ERNEST SETTLED INTO AN EASY rapport, discussing their childhoods in Baltimore, their dreams for their future out west, and their fears of homesickness.

"I loved the bakery, but it was never my passion. I've always loved the outdoors and animals, and when I saw the advertisement in the paper for a ranch hand, I couldn't pass it up," Ernest explained. "It took a while for my parents and brothers to get used to the idea of me leaving, but by the end I think my older brothers were happy to get me out of the house so our mother would stop crying. I'm the baby of the family, so she took it really hard."

"That's understandable," Annabel said and took a bite of the biscuit in her hand. They were now somewhere near Kansas and had been in the stagecoach for close to three weeks. All the passengers were achy and tired and greatly looking forward to their final stop in a week's time, weather permitting. "My best friend Letty, the one I told you about, she was heartbroken when I told her I was leaving. I was hoping she'd come with me, but she couldn't bear to leave Elton House. Her parents worked there too, so it really is like home for her."

Ernest nodded, and as they settled into a companionable silence, Annabel thought, and not for the first time, that she wished she was to marry Ernest, not Thomas. Ernest was kind and funny and sweet. He told her hilarious stories of mishaps at the bakery, read passages from his book to her, and even prayed with her the few times she'd woken up in the middle of the night and had gotten scared by the seemingly endless darkness. He was a good man, a man she knew, unlike Thomas, who she was becoming more and more certain couldn't possibly measure up.

CHAPTER 3

ANNABEL WAS SO SICK OF THE STAGECOACH DESPITE ERNEST'S COMPANY THAT when they finally arrived in Ely, she had to hold back the urge to leap to the ground and kiss it. Her back was sore from so much sitting, she had grown thin from the sparse rations eaten on the road, and she was desperate for a bath. Still, all those concerns had to be set aside, because when she looked up and saw the town of Ely in front of her, she remembered that she was finally here. Home, or rather, what would soon become her home.

"Looks like a nice place, doesn't it?" Ernest said from behind her.

Annabel turned and looked at him anew, really seeing for the first time just how handsome a figure Ernest cut. She hadn't realized how tall he was, sitting down as they had usually been in the stagecoach, and his eyes seemed even bluer in the sunlight. He was breathtaking.

Annabel was speechless, staring at him openly until Ernest gave her a look that told her she hadn't answered his observation. "Yes!" she cried, louder than she had meant to. "It looks like a very nice town. I can't wait to explore it." Annabel turned around and began looking for Thomas, who had assured her that he would meet her at the stagecoach stop. *"I'll wait all afternoon for you, my dear,"* he had written in his letter.

According to the coach driver, it was three o'clock when they all alighted from the coach, so Thomas should be waiting. Yet as the minutes passed and Annabel walked back and forth from one end of the main street to the other, with no sign of a man fitting the way Thomas had described himself, she began to worry. Shops were flipping their signs from open to closed, and the late winter sun was beginning to set, still with no sign of Thomas.

"Is your betrothed not here?" Ernest asked from where he was perched on a nearby wooden bench. He had offered to wait for Annabel to meet Thomas, and despite her protests, had stayed on the bench, guarding her trunk as well as his own. As she had continued her pacing, he had begun to express his concern. A woman, even one as strong as Annabel, shouldn't be out by herself past dark.

"I cannot see him. He said he would be here! I have it here, written in his own hand in his last letter. Do you think something has happened? Perhaps he's been in some sort of accident, or worse!"

Ernest stood and came forward until he was in front of Annabel, blocking the late-afternoon sunlight from her eyes. "I'm sure he has a perfectly good reason for being late. Do you have the name of the ranch? Perhaps we can ask one of the shop owners for directions and I can walk you there and see what's happened. Maybe something happened with the cattle that he had to attend to."

Annabel smiled despite her anxiety. Ernest really was such a kind man. She nodded and gave him the piece of paper on which Thomas had written the name of the ranch. Ernest glanced at it and laughed. "Ha! Well, what do you know, we're heading to the same place! Green Pastures Ranch is where I've been hired as a ranch hand!"

"No! Really? How delightful!" Annabel cried. The anxiety she could feel creeping up her stomach and into her throat immediately dissipated once she knew that she would have a friend, someone she knew and trusted, at her new home.

While Ernest went to ask the owner of the nearby apothecary for directions to the ranch, Annabel adjusted her hat and checked her trunk for scratches. She remembered the Bible Letty had begged her to bring and resolved to take it out that night and read a few chapters, saying a prayer of gratitude to God for looking out for her. Maybe she was still in His thoughts after all.

The walk to the ranch was a short one, and in just ten minutes, they were at the gate. The ranch house was further inland, and as they approached it, Annabel was appalled by the state it was in. There was a broken window, slats missing from the roof, what looked like a giant hole in the porch, and the rank smell of rotting vegetables coming from a large heap of rubbish to the right side of the structure. She only hoped it looked different inside.

But inside, Annabel and Ernest found something even worse, for there, lying on the floor, drunk and snoring, was none other than Thomas Michaels. From her vantage point above him, Annabel could tell that Thomas was a good twenty years older than he had described in his letters. His hair was completely gray, and a ratty beard covered the lower half of his face. He was gaunt, so thin she could see his cheekbones and the sockets of his eyes as he lay supine on the uncarpeted, rough wooden floor.

This man was nothing like the husband Annabel had spent hours picturing in the stagecoach. She had imagined a kind man with an easy temperament, but the man lying before her looked mean, sickly, and, judging from the bottle gripped in his left hand, alcoholic. What had she gotten herself into?

CHAPTER 4

"What do we do?" Annabel whispered. She had backed away and was now standing with her back against the door, fearful that Thomas would wake up and get a fright at the strangers in his home.

"Go wait outside and I'll see what I can do to wake him up," Ernest said, and Annabel obeyed. She found an old but sturdy rocking chair on the porch and sat, watching the sunset and listening for sounds of her husband-to-be stirring. An hour later, Ernest put his head out and told her it was safe to come back in.

Annabel walked with cautious steps back into the house and, for the first time, got a good look at its interior. The walls were bare, dark wood, and the furniture was sparse—only a table with a bottle lying sideways on it, and one small chair occupied the room. The woodstove was small and there didn't seem to be any crockery or cutlery, or even mugs, anywhere in the space. It was cold and dark, no candles lit. It wasn't a home, not for Thomas, and Annabel couldn't imagine herself considering it so either.

"He's awake and sobering up. There's a well out back so I've given him some water, and I'd like to get some food in him, but there doesn't seem to be anything edible in the house. All I could find was a collection of empty whiskey bottles," Ernest said as he left the bedroom off to the right of the main room, shutting the door behind him.

"Yes, the house does seem to be ... lacking in necessities," Annabel said, looking around worriedly. Ernest opened his mouth, no doubt about to offer her some words of comfort, but then the bedroom door banged open and out walked Thomas Michaels.

"Lottie? Lottie, is that you?" Thomas said, rushing toward Annabel and grabbing her hands in his. She jumped with fright, trying to back away from the man who was looking at her with confused love in his eyes.

"Lottie? No, I'm ... I'm Annabel Winters. Your mail order bride. I've come from Baltimore. We're to be married. Remember?" she whispered.

Thomas leaned toward her, peering at her eyes and face. "But you look just like her. Just like my Lottie. The same lovely brown hair, the same beautiful green eyes," Thomas whispered, and then, to Annabel and Ernest's surprise, Thomas began to cry.

Annabel looked to Ernest for help, but he shrugged, unsure what to do. Leading Thomas to the table and seating him in a chair, Annabel crouched down next to him. "Thomas, who was Lottie?" she asked, though she had a sneaking suspicion she knew.

"My wife," Thomas whispered, tears still falling down his face. "My beautiful wife. She's gone. Gone three years this Sunday. You looked so much like her, my dear. I thought my prayers might have been answered, that perhaps she had finally come back to me."

Annabel's heart broke at the pain evident in Thomas' voice. "I'm so sorry, Thomas," she said, then took his hands in hers and squeezed them tight.

Thomas looked down at her through glassy eyes and smiled. "I forgot you were coming, my dear. It's been ... it's been a hard week, and I'm sorry to say I've been drinking more than I should. I don't have anything ready for you. The small house out back is bare of firewood and furniture and I haven't been to the market in months. All the ranch hands used to handle my errands for me, but they seem to have deserted me."

Ernest stepped forward then and stuck his hand out to Thomas, who shook it weakly. "Well, sir, I'm Ernest Blom, and I'm here to help you. Leave it all to me and Annabel here and we'll have the ranch back up to snuff in no time."

FOUR HOURS LATER, ANNABEL COLLAPSED INTO THE COT ERNEST HAD MADE FOR her out of old, but clean sheets and a bale of hay. The house out back was indeed sparse in its furnishings, but Thomas promised that the next day they would go to the market and buy her furniture and enough food to keep the three of them fed for the next few weeks.

Ernest had brought Annabel's trunk into the house, and as she sat up to get out her nightgown, she noticed Letty's Bible sitting on top of her lace fichu. Removing the book, she opened it up. It fell open to a page that was marked with a small piece of lace, one Annabel recognized as a scrap from one of Mrs. Hedron's dresses. Annabel lifted the piece of lace to her nose and inhaled, smelling the lavender scent of Letty's soap that always seemed to hang in the air of Elton House.

Tears ran down her face as a wave of homesickness hit her so fast and hard that she doubled over. The stark realization that she was here in Ely, about to spend her first night in her new home, shocked her. Her adventure had officially begun, but for the first time, Annabel began to wonder if this was truly what she had bargained for.

A knock sounded on Annabel's door, and she shot up from bed.

"Who is it?" she whispered as her fingers grasped the cold metal handle of the house's front door.

"It's me, Ernest," a deep male voice said.

Annabel opened the door to find Ernest outside on her porch. He had changed clothes and, if his wet hair was any indication, washed. Annabel caught the scent of cedarwood and mint in the air, an intoxicating smell that soothed her fractured nerves. Ernest's presence also did much to calm the anxiety that had been building in her, and as he stood in the doorway, she realized he was exactly what she needed to distract her from her homesickness.

"I know it's not proper for me to come in, but I just wanted to check that you were all right. I know today was a bit different than you had probably expected."

Annabel nodded as she walked through the doorway and onto the porch, wrapping her shawl tighter around her shoulders.

"That it certainly was. I don't know, Ernest. I'm having second thoughts. I came here to escape all the pain and hurt I experienced in Baltimore, but marrying a man who is still so lost in the same grief I'm dealing with just feels like I'm digging myself even deeper into a hole. Does that make any sense?" Annabel asked, dropping her head in her hand, the weight of it all becoming too much.

Ernest reached out and lifted Annabel's chin. "Of course it does, but perhaps you and Thomas can help each other heal. And when you have a bad day like this, I'll be there to support you. I promise I won't leave you, Annabel. I'm afraid that you're stuck with me," Ernest said, a grin quirking the corners of his mouth. Annabel's skin tingled at his touch, and a warmth spread in her belly as she looked into his deep blue eyes.

"That's all right with me," she whispered. They said their goodnights, and Annabel walked into the house and opened her Bible again, realizing that the page Letty had marked was one about fate and chances and good things coming to those who deserve them. She thanked God for Ernest, for his strength and friendship and the way he made her feel both totally at ease and a little bit nervous, like his very presence sent bolts of electricity through her belly.

CHAPTER 5

"WE'LL NEED PLENTY OF COFFEE AND CORNMEAL, FLOUR, SUGAR, BACON ..."
Annabel said, reading off the shopping list she had made on a scrap of paper she
found on the table at the ranch house. She, Thomas, and Ernest had gone to the
town center in Ely early that morning, and after stopping at a store selling well-
made wooden furniture, the tailor, and the apothecary, they were now on their last
stop at the grocer.

"I'll just take that to Jones and see what he can find for us," Thomas said, indi-
cating the man behind the long wooden counter at the front of the store. Annabel
nodded and began walking through the aisles, admiring all the different foodstuffs
on offer.

"It's very different to Baltimore, isn't it?" Ernest said, coming up behind where
Annabel was admiring the largest glass bottle of soda water she had ever seen.

"Yes, it is!" Annabel said. "Back east, we always had our shopping delivered to the
house. I don't think I ever went to the market unless it was on one of my days off,
and even then, Letty and I didn't go often. But this is amazing. The food is so
different!" Annabel was glad to be able to reminisce with Ernest. Though they had
come from different backgrounds, he knew exactly which market she spoke of,
recalling the cakes he would buy in secret on his way to buy flour and yeast.

They spent a few more minutes talking about home while walking through the
store, and then Thomas came to find them. "All done. One of the shop boys is
bringing our purchases to the horse and cart."

Annabel couldn't help but marvel at the furniture, food, and cloth as Thomas,
Ernest, and one of the new ranch hands brought in the new purchases. A new
feeling of power overcame her as she realized that this was her first act as lady of
the house, choosing her own furniture and kitchen supplies.

"THAT SHOULD SET YOU UP NICELY FOR THE TIME BEING," ERNEST SAID, WIPING his brow as he deposited the last of Annabel's new kitchen chairs in the front room of her house later that afternoon. Annabel had hung the curtains she had purchased earlier that day, and now, with the table and chairs and carafes of coffee and sugar lining the shelf above the stove, her house was finally starting to look like a home.

"Thank you so much, Ernest," Annabel said, handing him a glass of water from the well. She couldn't help but notice the enticing sheen of sweat coating his brow. She hadn't realized how strong he was, or how nice the smell of exertion would be as it radiated off him, filling her nostrils with his particular scent of soap and musk. "Why don't you and Thomas go tend to the cattle while I make us a special supper?" Annabel was dying to get into the kitchen and experiment with the food she had bought. She wanted to make a good meal for the men. She hadn't been out of the kitchen for so long since she was a child.

"Excellent! I'll see you in a few hours, then. We'll bring our appetites!" Ernest said as he walked out the door. Annabel caught herself watching him leave, admiring his strong stature, and scolded herself as she turned back around and busied herself refolding a napkin. Ernest wasn't her betrothed, hers to look and stare at with affection and admiration. Thomas was.

In town, Thomas had run into Robert, the son of one of his old neighbors. The boy had been working in a neighboring town's cattle ranch, but after cattle rustlers had stolen the ranch's herd, Robert had been let go from his position as a ranch hand. "Well, you must come work for me, then!" Thomas had said, and just like that, Robert was hired.

Annabel was glad to see that Ernest and Thomas wouldn't be handling the ranch by themselves; Thomas was too frail for much of the hard labor, and Ernest was so new to cattle ranching that it would take him some time to settle into the role of ranch hand. Robert would be a real asset to Green Pastures.

"MUSHROOM RAGOUT ON GROUND CORNMEAL WITH FRESHLY BAKED HERBED bread and corn pudding for dessert," Annabel said, setting the meal out in front of the three men.

"This looks mighty good, Miss Annabel," Robert said, grinning shyly at her. Annabel smiled at Robert but noticed Ernest giving the man an angry, almost defensive look. She wasn't sure what had sparked it but hated the way the scowl marred his fine, chiseled features.

"Yes, yes it does, Robby. Now, let's say a quick grace and dig in. All that work with the hay has me starving," Thomas said. He led the prayer, his voice soft and reverent as he thanked the Lord for the fortune to have a good home and kind people and food with which to fill it.

The four of them ate hungrily, the men eliciting the occasional groan of "my, but this is good" and all of them asking for second helpings. Annabel had foreseen this, and made more than enough, though by the end of the meal, there was hardly any ragout left and only a spoonful of corn pudding still in the pot.

Robert patted his belly with satisfaction, then rose with Ernest to help clear the plates. "I can do it myself," Ernest snapped, but Robert still went around the table collecting forks and spoons and the butter dish and beginning to wash them.

Annabel was about to get up and help them when Thomas placed his hand gently on her arm. "Would you mind sitting here with me for a few minutes, my dear? There's something I'd like to ask you."

Annabel nodded. Though she'd only known Thomas a day, she could tell he was a kind man. His sadness had seemed to dissipate slightly, making her think that perhaps he had been lonely before she and Ernest arrived, and that the company had served to distract him from his sorrows. She knew he would have more bad days—months later, she still woke up crying in the middle of the night, the weight of Ricky's death weighing heavily upon her—but she hoped that together, they could get through them without the aid of whiskey and whatever other vices Thomas had been using to numb the pain.

"Annabel, would you still like to marry me? I know I'm not the man you corresponded with in your letters, but I can still take care of you and give you a good home. I'd like to do that if you'll let me."

And there was no other answer Annabel could give than yes. Marrying Thomas was what had brought her to Ely, and now that she knew him better, she knew that while he wasn't the young, handsome, charming man that Ernest was, he was still kind and loving and would make a good partner. Together, they could have a good life, and right now, that's all she wanted.

"Yes, of course I will," Annabel said, covering Thomas' hand with her own. As she looked into Thomas' eyes, she didn't miss the scowl Ernest was giving her, and her heart broke a little knowing that her silly stagecoach dreams of marrying Ernest wouldn't come true.

CHAPTER 6

The wedding was to be two weeks from that day, and so Annabel set to making her wedding dress. She went back to town one afternoon and selected a bolt of beautiful light blue cloth that reminded her of the color of Ernest's eyes, though she swore to herself that wasn't why she chose it. She bought the pattern from the tailor and, after threading her needle and setting herself up on her porch, spent happy afternoons stitching a garment fit for a queen or, in her case, a former kitchen maid turned rancher's wife. Annabel took the lace Letty had left in her Bible and sewed it into her bodice, hoping that having something of her friend's close to her would help calm the wedding-day nerves that had begun building as the day drew closer.

Sitting on the porch, Annabel was able to watch the men work, walking the herd from one field to another, digging out the fence and repairing the broken slats, riding the horses for their daily exercise. She saw Ernest grow stronger and surer of himself with the animals, handling the cattle with more confidence. Robert fell easily into the role of Ernest's second-in-command, teaching the man what skills he didn't know but allowing Ernest to take the lead when necessary. The easier tasks were given to Thomas, who, despite good, filling meals three times a day and a nap every afternoon, was looking even thinner and gaunter than when Annabel and Ernest had first arrived.

"Thomas, why don't I make us all another special meal tonight? We'll need a hearty meal for tomorrow's festivities," Annabel said to Thomas the afternoon before their wedding day. They were sitting on his porch drinking coffee and watching the sun set, the sky turning a beautiful watercolor of pinks and golds and vibrant reds.

"That sounds ... that sounds just lovely, my dear Annie," Thomas said, his words halting and slow. He'd been lethargic all day, and Annabel was worried that even with his decreased workload, thanks to Ernest and Robert, he was still doing too much.

"Excellent. Why don't you go rest while I start cooking?" Annabel led Thomas into the house and helped him to his room, shutting the door gently behind her. She could hear his soft snores as she padded back into the kitchen and took out the good, sharp knife to start chopping.

Two hours later, supper was ready. The men were seated at the table, anxiously awaiting the meal as Annabel spooned portions of the thick meat stew into their bowls.

"There's fresh bread as well. I had a bit of trouble with the baking at first, but I think it turned out fine in the end," Annabel said, placing a basket of freshly sliced white bread on the table.

Thomas took a bite and hummed appreciatively. "I must say, Annie, my dear Olivia, God rest her soul, was a mighty fine cook, but I think you just might surpass her in ability. She never made anything quite like this. That old mistress of yours must've been sorry to lose you, but I sure am happy you're mine, or about to be, anyway."

Annabel smiled at Thomas, pleased at the compliment. She looked across to Ernest and saw him scowling at Thomas. He'd been doing a lot of that lately, and Annabel suspected it had something to do with the wedding. Ever since Thomas had asked to marry her, Ernest had been short and gruff with the man, only saying the bare minimum of words to him and speaking to him only when necessary. Thomas had been nothing but kind and supportive of Ernest from the moment they met, and Annabel didn't know what had happened between the two men to cause Ernest's animosity.

Still, despite the tension, the meal was enjoyable, with Robert entertaining all of them with stories from his previous job, including one tale that involved him being woken up by a cow standing at his window, mooing mournfully.

Thomas was laughing good-naturedly, clutching his belly in that way people do when the laughter is clenching their insides, when suddenly, he doubled over, spilling his beer all over the table.

"Thomas!" Annabel cried, standing from her chair and rushing to his side. Thomas' face was beet red, and he clutched his chest and breathed hard. "What's wrong, what hurts, what can I do?" Annabel cried, but before she could so much as touch him, Thomas collapsed, falling from his chair and onto the hard wooden floor. His body twitched for a few seconds, writhing back and forth on the ground, and then he relaxed, the light going out of his eyes and the breath leaving his lungs.

"I don't understand ... What just happened? Ernest? Ernest?" Annabel said, looking up and meeting Ernest's eyes. His expression said it all, the resigned look of sadness marring his beautiful features, and Annabel knew. Thomas was dead.

Dear God, no! Not again!

THE NEXT HOUR HAPPENED AMONGST A FLURRY OF ACTIVITY. ROBERT RAN TO the horse barn and saddled one of the fillies, riding with great speed to the sheriff's house. Ernest stayed with Annabel, holding her as she cried over Thomas' body, her tears dropping onto the soft leather of his vest. She couldn't believe that not four months after losing Ricky, she had lost yet another man she loved. Sure, it wasn't the same kind of love, but it was affection nonetheless, and the grief that wracked through her was remarkably similar.

I don't understand, God. Why me? Why again?

By the time Robert returned with Sheriff Paxton in tow, Annabel had dried her tears and made a pot of coffee. As she listened to the men discussing what to do with the body and when to have the funeral, Annabel retreated to her house and opened her Bible. She was angry with God but took solace in His Word, and she fell asleep with the book clutched against her chest, as though it could guard her from further pain.

CHAPTER 7

"AND WHILE WE CANNOT ATTEMPT TO UNDERSTAND THE HANDS OF FATE, LET US take solace in the fact that God is watching over us, comforting us in times of grief and raising us up. Turn to Him in times of despondency and let Him be the balm to your wounds," the priest said as they all stood looking over the freshly dug grave. In it lay a large wooden coffin, the best money could buy, and inside that lay Thomas.

Annabel had long since stopped being able to cry. She had shed seemingly all the tears she was capable of in the first few days following Thomas' death, and now, her face was dry, but drawn and haggard, more lines having appeared around her mouth and eyes in the days since Thomas had passed. On either side of her stood Ernest and Robert, each clothed in the dark black suits typical of a funeral.

But to Annabel, this was no typical funeral. Though she had known Thomas less than two weeks, she had loved him and cared for him like he was her own family, and his loss left a gaping hole in her life. The wedding dress she had so looked forward to wearing for him was now packed away at the bottom of her trunk, and the ring he had bought her had been returned to the jeweler at Annabel's request. All evidence of their impending nuptials was gone, allowing Annabel to wallow fully in her grief.

"Miss Annabel," a voice said from behind her, and Annabel turned. A young, solemn man stood in front of her, wearing a long coat and faded gray top hat. Small spectacles were balanced on his nose, and in his hand he carried a small leather case.

"Yes?" Annabel said questioningly. Ernest and Robert looked over their shoulders, Ernest's eyebrows rising in a silent question, but Annabel nodded and gestured for them to turn back around and help the priest fill the grave, a task she most certainly was not up to.

"I'm Mr. James, Thomas' solicitor. I wondered if perhaps we could speak soon, as there is a matter I wish to discuss with you," the man said, adding, "About Thomas' will, I mean."

Annabel nodded. She had meant to look into Thomas' will, to see what would happen to the ranch now that he'd died, but between planning the funeral and canceling the wedding, there had been so little time. Still, her own livelihood, as well as that of Ernest and Robert, depended on it.

"Yes, of course. Could I meet you at your office tomorrow afternoon, say at two o'clock?" That would give her enough time to get ready; her sleep had been erratic as of late, and she was lucky if she fell asleep before dawn, resulting in her lying in bed well into the late morning.

"Of course. I shall expect you then," Mr. James said. "My condolences. Thomas was a good man, a great business owner, and an excellent client. He will be missed greatly."

At those kind words, the tears that had been briefly absent in Annabel's eyes suddenly sprang forth, and she nodded at the man before turning around and letting the sobs out. Ernest put down his shovel and turned, gathering her in his arms and holding her as she wept into his coat, wept for all that she had lost, for the life she had imagined for herself which once again had been shattered by fate and its absurd and twisted way of snatching the men she loved from her.

❦

"But ... that can't be possible. I'm a woman, a woman he wasn't related to or even wed to!" Annabel said, shocked at the words Mr. James had just spoken.

"Be that as it may, Thomas still left Green Pastures Ranch to you. It says so right here in his will. 'And to my dearest Annabel I leave the whole of my livelihood, Green Pastures Ranch, and all the land and livestock therein,'" Mr. James read from the large sheet of paper in front of him.

Annabel couldn't believe it. She was a ranch owner. Green Pastures was hers to do with as she pleased. It didn't seem plausible, and yet there it was, in Thomas' own writing. Some of her anger at God abated and she sent up a prayer of thanks that He had provided for her, in spite of allowing her yet another terrible grief.

"Well, thank you, sir. I accept that responsibility." Annabel worried that running the ranch would be too much on her own, thinking perhaps that she needed a partner. And suddenly, she knew exactly what to do. Sitting up a little straighter in her chair, she said, "Mr. James, I do wonder, is it possible to share the ownership with someone if I so choose?"

Though the idea had just come to her, she knew that it was a good one. Ernest would be her partner. Ernest had worked so hard on the ranch, had learned so much about the cattle, and there was no one else she would rather work with to make Green Pastures the most successful cattle ranch in all of Ely. Because that's what she would do with the gift that Thomas had left her. She would make Green Pastures the best it could be, in Thomas' honor. And to do that, she needed

Ernest's help. There was no one else as smart and strong and caring as he. She wanted him by her side.

"Yes, that is absolutely possible. If you give me the man's name, I can have the papers drafted and ready to sign tomorrow."

"ARE YOU SURE? THOMAS LEFT THE RANCH TO YOU FOR A REASON, ANNIE," Ernest said that night over cups of coffee after dinner. Robert had retired early to bed, so it was just the two of them at the kitchen table, a candle burning between them and illuminating the strong lines of Ernest's jaw, the stubble growing there. Even in her grief, Annabel still hadn't stopped noticing that Ernest seem to grow even more handsome with every passing week, as though the fresh air and hard labor were turning him from boy to man.

"Absolutely. I know I have the management skills necessary for this endeavor, but I need your knowledge of ranching to help me succeed. Together, I truly think we could do something great with Green Pastures," Annabel said, hoping Ernest could see from the look in her eyes that she meant her words. And it appeared that he could, because after a moment's deliberation, Ernest stuck his hand out for Annabel to shake.

"Well then, it's settled. To our partnership," Ernest said, shaking Annabel's hand and lifting his cup in a toast. They clinked their tin mugs together, and that night, they stayed up till dawn, laying out the plans that in the months to come would make Green Pastures Ely, Nevada's, most successful cattle ranch.

THEIR DISCUSSION RESULTED IN THE HIRING OF FIVE MORE RANCH HANDS AND the purchase of seven more cattle, ensuring that the ranch had more than enough staff and resources on hand to increase business tenfold. By the following winter, Annabel and Ernest had a thriving ranch full of healthy cows that turned a pretty profit at the local market.

"I can't believe it," Ernest said to Annabel one night as she helped him brush down one of the mares they had used to ride into town that day. "We did it, Annie. We really did it. Thomas would be so proud."

Ernest put down the brush and reached for a carrot, leaning into the bucket by Annabel's side. She caught a whiff of his particular scent and breathed in deeply, letting the fragrance wrap itself around her like a warm, comforting hug that sent shivers down her back.

In the past year, Ernest had grown stronger, filling out the linen shirts and cotton trousers he had adopted as his uniform of sorts. He now stood before Annabel, his hair streaked blond and his face and arms tanned from the sun. He was even more beautiful than when Annabel had first seen him on the stagecoach what felt like years ago, back when she'd daydreamed that they would get married and live happily ever after. While it hadn't quite worked out that way, she was not unhappy with their arrangement, working so closely together as business partners and best friends. She did her best to ignore the moments when she wished for something more from him.

"I can't believe it. It's been hard work, but we've really done it, haven't we?" Annabel said, wiping the sweat from her brow. She'd spent most of the day in the kitchen, making baskets of bread and preserves to treat the ranch hands that had worked solidly all through the summer and fall. Her arms were sore from so much stirring and kneading and she was looking forward to a long, peaceful sleep.

"We have," Ernest said. "And now, we rest. Tomorrow we start again."

CHAPTER 8

ANNABEL WAS HAVING ONE OF HER FAVORITE RECURRING DREAMS, ONE WHERE she sat at the kitchen table, telling Thomas about her day as they sipped from a large pot of coffee, when a shout woke her from her slumber.

Thinking it was just one of the cows at first, she settled back down into her pillow and closed her eyes, drifting back into sleep, but when the shouts continued, she woke again and sat up, grabbed her robe, and headed to the door.

It must just be the cows, she thought again to herself as she tied the sash of her robe.

But the sight that greeted her when she opened it was not the sight of a few disturbed cows. No, the sight that greeted her was like something out of one of her worst nightmares.

The moon that night was full and the sky clear, meaning that despite the darkness, Annabel could clearly see the cattle rustlers herding the cows in the field in front of her out toward the road. They wore dark pieces of cloth over their faces, no doubt so ranchers couldn't identify them. The cows were groaning in distress, clearly aware that something bad was afoot. Though Annabel had never come in contact with rustlers, she had heard about them, and knew she needed to act quickly. Turning, she grabbed Thomas' old shotgun, which she kept near the front door, checked to make sure the magazine was full, and opened the door.

She didn't stop to think about what she was doing as her bare feet traveled quickly and quietly over the land. All she knew was that she had to get to those men before they finish herding the cattle onto the road. Those cattle were everything she had, and she wouldn't let those men steal everything she had worked so hard for. She cared not a wit for own safety at that moment; just then, all she cared about were her cattle.

Lord, help me save this dream. Thomas' dream. My dream. And Ernest's.

Annabel neared the fence that lined one of the fields, the men just to her left. She paused, watching the men as they slapped one of her cows on its flank, urging it forward. The violence made her blood boil, but she took deep breaths, knowing she needed to rein in her temper if she had any hope of success.

Annabel heard muttering and stepped closer, grateful that the men seemed so wrapped up in their conversation that they did not hear her approach. The rustlers were muttering about what route to take out of town, arguing over whether to turn right or left. Annabel shook her head and nearly laughed at the idea of rustlers stealing cows with no idea how to get them away. These men must be amateurs or sorely out of practice.

She was creeping closer, her gun cocked and ready, when one of the cows looked over at her and began mooing loudly. A rustler turned toward Annabel and began to draw a knife from his belt, but Annabel was faster. She raised her loaded gun and didn't hesitate as she pulled the trigger. She braced herself for the blowback, feeling the force as it rocked through her shoulder muscles. She was glad she had let Ernest give her shooting lessons last spring; at the time, she hadn't been sure whether they were useful, but now she was grateful for his insistence.

The bullet seated itself in the man's knee and he fell to the ground screaming. She didn't have time to be shocked at what she had done to another human being; the other rustlers would be upon her if she paused even for a second.

One of them turned and began making his way toward her, picking up the knife his friend had dropped. Annabel had plenty more bullets in her magazine and knew she could take out every one of the rustlers if need be, but that didn't make the sight of a man advancing toward her with a dagger in one hand and the other fist cocked any less nerve-wracking.

Annabel was just preparing to shoot again, eager not to let the man get any closer, when footsteps distracted her. She turned and raised her gun, worried that one of the other rustlers had snuck up behind her, but the person running toward her was not a rustler, but Ernest, a shotgun in his hand as he sprinted toward the rustlers to Annabel's right.

"Stop right there!" he shouted at the man in front of Annabel. At the sight of not one, but two ranch owners with guns, the man dropped his weapon, curled his fist, and backed away, his hands up in surrender.

"Weapons on the ground, now!" Ernest shouted at the rustlers, who were now standing in a cluster again. They hesitated, and Ernest raised his gun, letting them no he would brook no arguments. Annabel's eyes flicked from Ernest to the ranchers and back, amazed and yet not at all surprised that they were afraid of him. Standing with his hair wild, his shirt half buttoned and a gun in his hand, Ernest looked like a crazed lunatic, and Annabel herself nearly put her gun on the ground at his words.

But then he turned to her, and he was Ernest, her Ernest, her friend and partner who had just protected her from harm. "Are you all right?" he whispered, keeping his eyes on the rustlers as he spoke from one side of his mouth.

"Yes, just fine. Though I did have to shoot one of the rustlers," Annabel told him, her gaze also floating over to the men emptying their pockets of multiple knives, rocks, and one unloaded shotgun.

The rustlers were tall, burly fellows who looked like they could snap Annabel in half like a twig without so much as a blink, but they treated Ernest with the respect he deserved. Annabel wished they had been as afraid of her, but then again, she was probably the only female ranch owner they had ever met.

Ernest was just lowering his gun, satisfied that the men had relieved themselves of all possible harm-inducing implements, when one ran toward him suddenly, his arm cocked in a fist. The man aimed for Ernest's jaw, but he easily deflected the hit, spinning the man around and pinning his arms behind his back.

"For goodness' sake, gentlemen. The fight is over. You're not getting our cattle, you're not punching me, and there is no way on God's green earth that you are leaving this ranch in anything other than the sheriff's company." Annabel shivered slightly at the devastatingly forthright way Ernest said this, but recovered enough to look at the men and mimic his scowl.

The men looked back at them with scowls of their own, but they stayed where they were, leaning against the fence, the cows they had been trying to steal now looking at them suspiciously, when the thumping sound of horse hooves came from somewhere in the distance.

The figure of a short man atop a large gray horse erupted onto the horizon, and Ernest laughed, realizing it was Sheriff Paxton.

"Sheriff! You're just in time!" he said, walking over to greet the man. The sheriff and his horse had slowed to a clop and came to a stop in front of the rustlers, the horse sniffing disinterestedly at the men as Sheriff Paxton hopped down from his saddle.

"Well, if it isn't the Austin rustlers, here all the way from Texas. That's a long way to travel for so little success, gentlemen," Sheriff Paxton said, eyeing the rustlers with a grin on his face.

"They were trying to steal the herd right out from under our noses, but Annabel over here set them to rights, didn't you, Annie?" Ernest said, turning back from where she was standing with the sheriff and giving her a grin. Annabel nodded, blushing at the compliment and the steady stare Ernest was giving her.

"Well thank you kindly, Miss Annabel. It's made my work quite a bit easier. I'm getting too old to give chase, you know," Sheriff Paxton said.

Ernest stepped back to give the sheriff room to deal with the rustlers, coming to stand beside Annie, and they watched as Sheriff Paxton rounded up the rustlers, tying their hands together with rope he had on his belt. The men didn't make it easy, dodging the rope and, at one point, running behind him to try and escape, but Sheriff Paxton was good with a lasso, and he had all the men tied up and subdued before Annabel was able to catch her breath from all the excitement.

"I'm glad I got here in time. Of course, I know you folks can handle yourselves and your cattle just fine, but these men were the bane of my existence a few years ago, terrorizing ranchers up and down these parts. Last time they came through I arrested what I thought was the whole gang, but one got away and must've started a brand-new operation. A short-lived one, too, right boys?" Sheriff Paxton said, turning and grinning at the rustlers, who spat in the dirt and cursed under their breath in response.

"As soon as I heard the shot, something in me told me they must be back and had found your herd," Sheriff Paxton said to Annabel and Ernest as they stood, watching him as he secured the rope holding the men together onto a loop on his saddle, pulling it extra tight for good measure.

"I knew there used to be rustlers here, but until I saw them, I never imagined we'd have them here at Green Pastures. I didn't even think ..." Annabel whispered. She looked at Ernest. "We could have lost everything. Everything we've worked for."

She immediately thanked God, realizing He'd come through and saved the day in spite of her doubts.

Ernest put his hands on her shoulders and turned her to face him, the feel of his hands on her shoulders warming her and calming the anxiety she was feeling. "But we didn't. Thanks to you. You're a marvel, Annabel Winters. A right ol' cowgirl, I'd say."

Sheriff Paxton laughed at that. "I'd surely say so. All right, I'll take these men over to the county jail and see they get locked up in a cell for a good long while. You two go check on the ranch hands and then get some sleep. And be good to those cows in the morning. They'll have had a good fright just now with that gunfire."

Annabel nodded and watched Sheriff Paxton ride off, the rustlers in tow. "You go check on the ranch hands," she said. "And I'll get the cows settled, Ernest, while you brew us up a big pot of coffee. I know I definitely need a hot drink after all that ruckus."

CHAPTER 9

GETTING THE COWS TO CALM DOWN TURNED OUT TO BE MORE OF AN ORDEAL than Annabel had initially thought. By the time the herd was all back in the same field and resting, the sun was just coming over the horizon, lighting up the sky and reminding Annabel that it was time to turn in, because in a few hours, she would need to be up again, tending to the chores that were the daily life of a ranch owner. Annabel took a last look at the sunrise and then began slowly walking back to the main ranch house, so tired she could have laid down right there in the grass and fallen asleep, were it not for the scent of coffee carried on the air.

"Coffee?" Ernest asked, turning around from where he stood at the stove, just finishing making enough coffee for an army. A better sight Annabel had never seen as she crossed the threshold of the house and walked toward the table.

"Yes, please!" Annabel said, collapsing into a chair. "I don't know that I've ever been so tired. Those cows took ages to settle down. Of course, if I were them, I'd never want to sleep again, worried that men would be coming in the night to steal me away to parts unknown. I never even considered that we'd be at risk of rustlers out here. I knew it was possible, knew enough to know I needed my gun, but ... I just can't believe it."

Ernest came over to the table and planted a large china cup full of coffee in front of Annabel, part of the tea set he had given her for Christmas the previous year. Though they tried to save most of their profit to put back into the ranch, Christmas was the one time of year they allowed themselves luxuries. Annabel had always wanted a tea set like the one Mrs. Hedron had. She couldn't believe Ernest had remembered that, but then, he was always so attentive to her. He knew her better than anyone else in the world, made her feel better than anyone else, too.

"Don't trouble yourself, Annie. I'd forgotten about them, too. This town has so little crime, and I haven't heard any mutterings of rustlers any of the times I've gone to the market. I thought they'd been long since gone from this area. There was no way we could have known they would come for our herd, and in any case, you did a mighty fine job of fighting them off. You should be proud of yourself," Ernest said, reaching across the table to cover one of Annabel's hands with his own. He squeezed her palm in his, showing her without words that all was well. She relished the contact.

"I certainly have changed since I've been here. I couldn't have imagined I'd ever have cause to fire a gun back when I was working as a kitchen maid for Mrs. Hedron."

Ernest smiled at Annabel. "But even when you first left Baltimore, when I met you on that stagecoach, there was something about you, Annie. It takes a certain kind of person to have the courage to leave the only home they've ever known and go somewhere totally new and different. You've always been a strong, brave woman."

Annabel squeezed Ernest's hands and took a sip of her coffee. "And you're the same! That boy who left the bakery in Baltimore and was itching with adventure has grown into quite the cowboy while we've been out here." Ernest chuckled.

"Do you ever miss it?" Annabel asked suddenly.

Ernest quirked an eyebrow up. "Miss what?"

"Baltimore, of course!" Annabel said.

Ernest contemplated the question for a few minutes, idly stroking his stubbled jaw before replying. "Yes, but if I went back there now, it wouldn't feel like home. Ely feels like home. You ... you feel like home."

Annabel looked up at those words, shocked by the weight of feeling in them. She had caught glimpses of such emotion in his gaze at various points over the last year, but she had never let herself believe that Ernest felt anything close to the deep love and respect for her that she felt for him.

"I do?" she asked, her voice quiet and hopeful. Though she had only spoken two words, those words meant so much more. They meant "tell me how you feel"; they meant "do you love me?" They meant "let me know I'm not the only one who feels this way."

And Ernest, astute man that he was, read through those words and gave Annabel the exact answer she had been hoping for, and so much more. "You do. Annabel, you're my home, my partner, my love. Everything I have, everything I am, is because of you and your belief in me. I know these last few years have been trying —losing Ricky, losing Thomas, getting the ranch back up and running—but those hardships have turned you into the woman I admire. The woman I love. Because I do love you, Annie. I love you with all my heart. I always have, and I expect I always will."

Ernest was looking at her intently, a question in his eyes, begging her to respond, and there was really only one answer that Annabel could give: "Ernest, I love you too."

And then, suddenly, though they'd had the most eventful night of their lives and it was dawn and there was sleep to get and work to do, Annabel knew it was the perfect time to ask the question she'd been ruminating on for the last few months. There was no better time than right this minute.

"Ernest, will you marry me?"

"Will I ... will I what?" Ernest asked, shock and confusion clear on his face. He clearly hadn't expected that, but a moment later he recovered, a smile beginning to work its way on his lips and in his eyes as he looked at her with plain affection and, she realized for the first time, love. The same look he had been giving her all this time.

"Will you marry me? Will you be my husband and run this ranch with me and give me children and live out your life with the cows and the ranch hands and plenty of coffee and cornmeal with me here at Green Pastures Ranch in Ely, Nevada?"

Ernest stared at Annabel a moment, then shocked her by jumping up from his seat and coming around the table to her. He leaned down and lifted her into his arms, twirling her around the kitchen, her nightdress billowing out beneath her feet like the petals of a tulip.

"Yes! Yes, I will marry you! Haha! Yes!" he shouted, then leaned down and captured Annabel's lips in the sweetest, softest kiss she could have ever imagined.

Annabel broke away and smiled up at Ernest, at her newly betrothed, her best friend, and business partner. "It's always been you, you know," she whispered.

"What do you mean?" Ernest asked.

"Even when we were in that stagecoach and I knew I was on my way to marry Thomas, God rest his soul, it was you I was dreaming of say 'I do' to. Don't you see, Ernest? It's always been you. I've loved you from the first time you spoke to me, and I've kept loving you all this time. I just didn't quite know how to tell you."

Ernest set Annabel down, his hands still on her waist. "Well, thank goodness for that, because I've been smitten with you since that first day, too. I don't mind telling you now that I was mighty jealous of Thomas when he proposed to you. I couldn't believe he got to be with you instead of me. He was a great man, a kind and honest one who would have treated you like a queen, but God rest his soul, he didn't love you like I do."

Annabel stepped back, finally putting the pieces together. "Is that why you were always glaring at him? Because he was marrying me and not you?"

Ernest nodded sheepishly. "Yes. I should have swallowed my pride, but I was so jealous. I want to be the only man who holds your heart."

"And now you will be."

EPILOGUE

"I NOW PRONOUNCE YOU HUSBAND AND WIFE. MR. BLOM, YOU MAY KISS YOUR bride," the priest said, and Annabel whooped in surprise as Ernest grabbed her by the waist and laid a soft kiss on her lips. Clapping sounded from the crowd behind them, and they broke apart to see all their friends smiling at them with joy clear in their eyes and their smiles.

The wedding was held in the same chapel where Annabel and Thomas had planned to get married. For a long time, whenever she passed by the heavy wooden doors of the chapel, her heart would fill with sorrow for Thomas and the marriage they would never have, but now, she knew that the chapel would hold a happier place in her heart, for inside it was the altar when she had pledged her troth to the love of her life, with the town watching.

The dress she had sewn for her wedding to Thomas still fit, and Annabel found herself often rubbing her fingers on the delicate square of lace from Letty during that happy day. She had received a letter a week before the wedding from Letty saying she was planning a trip out west. "Baltimore just isn't the same without you, and you have made me brave, Annie. I want to have my own adventures out west, and I hope you won't mind if they start in Ely."

Annabel couldn't wait to be reunited with her best friend, though she was glad that she and Ernest would have a few weeks to themselves first, to ready the house for Letty and attend the last of the year's cattle markets. She hoped to make an even better profit than last year and put some money away for the crib she hoped she would need soon. She wanted a big family, with enough children to fill the ranch house with laughter and joy at all hours of the day and night. Ernest wanted the same, and Annabel couldn't wait to see him as a father. She knew he'd be kind and gracious and teach their children everything they needed to know about being good people and good ranch owners. Annabel hoped their children would keep the ranch going long after she and Ernest were gone. She wanted Green Pastures to thrive for many years to come.

"You two sure do make a good couple," Sheriff Paxton told Annabel later that day as they all gathered back at the ranch for a post-wedding party.

All the ranch hands, their wives, and children were gathered on the porch and yard outside the main ranch house, and Annabel had placed candles in all the windows and along the steps, lending a romantic glow to the occasion. Sheriff Paxton was there with his wife, who had offered to cook for everyone as a gift to Annabel for finally ridding Ely of those pesky rustlers. Annabel could smell the sweet scent of corn and the tang of bacon coming through the kitchen window.

Annabel looked over at Ernest, clad in his best suit and talking to Robert, and smiled. He looked over at her and caught her eye, giving her the grin that she couldn't wait to see every day for the rest of her life. "We sure do, don't we?"

Thank you, God, for this life you have given me!

ROYCE CARDIFF PUBLISHING HOUSE PRESENTS OTHER WONDERFUL CLEAN, wholesome and inspiring romance short stories titles for your entertainment. Many are value boxset and as always FREE to Kindle Unlimited readers.

Sweet Frontier Cowboys Complete Series Collection (A Novel Christian Romance Series)

Mega Box Set Complete Series By Katie Wyatt

Katie Wyatt Mega Box Set Series (12 Mega Box Set Series)

❦

THANK YOU SO MUCH FOR READING MY BOOK. I SINCERELY HOPE YOU ENJOYED EVERY bit reading it. I had fun creating it and will surely create more.

Your positive reviews are very helpful to other reader, it only takes a few moments. They can be left at Amazon.

www.amazon.com/Katie-Wyatt/e/B011IN7AF0

❦

WANT FREE BOOKS EVERY WEEK? WHO DOESN'T!

BECOME A PREFERRED READER AND WE'LL NOT ONLY SEND YOU FREE READS, BUT you'll also receive updates about new releases.

So you'll be among the first to dive into our latest new books, full of adventure, heartwarming romances, and characters so real they jump off the page.

It's absolutely free and you don't need to do anything at all to qualify except go to.

PREFERRED READ FREE READS

http:/katieWyattBooks.com/readersgroup

ABOUT THE AUTHOR

KATIE WYATT IS 25% AMERICAN SIOUX INDIAN. BORN AND RAISED IN Arizona, she has traveled and camped extensively through California, Arizona, Nevada, Mexico, and New Mexico. Looking at the incredible night sky and the giant Saguaro cacti, she has dreamed of what it would be like to live in the early pioneer times.

Spending time with a relative of the great Wyatt Earp, also named Wyatt Earp, Katie was mesmerized and inspired by the stories he told of bygone times. This historical interest in the old West became the inspiration for her Western romance novels.

Her books are a mixture of actual historical facts and events mixed with action and humor, challenges and adventures. The characters in Katie's clean romance novels draw from her own experiences and are so real that they almost jump off the pages. You feel like you're walking beside them through all the ups and downs of their lives. As the stories unfold, you'll find yourself both laughing and crying. The endings will never fail to leave you feeling warm inside.

LOVING THE WRONG BROTHER

Mail Order Bride Western Romance

RoyceCardiff

Publishing House

WHOLESOME INSPIRATIONAL ROMANCE

Dear Reader,

It is our utmost pleasure and privilege to bring these wonderful stories to you. I am so very proud of our amazing team of writers and the delight they continually bring us all with their beautiful clean and wholesome tales of faith, courage, and love.

What is a book's lone purpose if not to be read and enjoyed? Therefore, you, dear reader, are the key to fulfilling that purpose and unlocking the treasures that lie within the pages of this book.

ふふ

THANK YOU FOR CHOOSING A INSPIRATIONAL READS BY ROYCE CARDIFF PUBLISHING HOUSE.

Welcome and Enjoy!

A PERSONAL WORD FROM ADA

I LOVE WRITING BOOKS ABOUT THE HARDSHIPS AND STRUGGLES OF WOMEN WHO turn around their hopeless situations and in the end found true love and happiness is something that she enjoys bringing to the readers.

I wishes that the readers will once again learn to believe in love and develop trust through reading her books, and be inspired by the characters in her novels who through perseverance, in spite of very tough harsh obstacles that tested their faith, overcame the hurdles in the end.

If you love Western Romance and Mail Order Bride stories about the courageous women who traveled alone to the Wild West with nothing but hope and strong faith in God. Now's the time to grab it!

Thank you for being a loyal reader.

Ada ..

CHAPTER 1

Colorado, Late June 1871

Susan Lockhart watched without a display of emotion as the red dust from the cart filled the air. Late. She had missed the last cart that was to take her to the ranch. A large, frustrated groan rushed from the depths of her belly to her throat as she turned to the other end of the track.

Nothing.

She marched to the other side of the tracks. Squinting her eyes, she looked along the abandoned, dusty route down the valley. Silent. The path lay still and impassive as though the last means of transportation that had traveled on it had done so a very long time ago. Centuries before, actually.

Thank God it was almost sundown; otherwise she would have been standing under a scorching sun with absolutely no idea of what to do next.

Susan closed her eyes briefly and whispered a prayer for help, wishing she could blame this on the recent happenings in her life. But that would not explain the other times she had made the same mistakes.

Never double-checking before leaping.

Just like she had testified against Ted without considering the consequences. Like she had applied for a mail order bride ad without thinking it through first.

It was bad enough she had agreed to marry a man she had only met through the few letters they shared. A man whose looks and character she had no knowledge of. As usual, her impulsivity had ruled the day and she'd just jumped right in when the opportunity presented itself.

But Susan believed she had stumbled upon that ad by sheer providence. She had prayed fervently after the last attack on her life and asked the Lord what to do.

Two days later, she'd been outside the estate she had inherited from her father in Philadelphia, at a loss, when she had seen the newspaper on the street. She'd picked it and, without giving it much thought, had applied to the first mail order bride request.

She'd waited the next day, and the next for a response. When she had given up hope and was pondering the next action to take, she'd finally gotten a response from the man, Jake Jacobs.

Susan rubbed the dull ache gradually building between her eyes. Why had she decided to take the train instead of using the stagecoach her fiancé had paid for?

Because she was terrified, she reminded herself.

She had been so terrified someone might track her down to the coach station after the last attack that she had decided to take the train at the last minute. Now, here she was. Lost. No means of transportation. A fast-approaching nightfall. And probably mountain lions in the hills, with no help should the worst happen.

There was only one thing left to do, she determined. Walk. There was only one problem with that: her shoes weren't made for such terrain. Not even a little bit. But then, she hadn't been planning on trekking to the ranch.

A lone tear escaped and ran down her cheek; she swiped at it angrily with the back of her hand. Jake was probably at the coach station, waiting for her arrival, wondering where she could possibly be.

Stop wallowing in self-pity, Susan, she admonished herself.

Standing on a lonely, deserted road and waiting for a knight in shining armor to come to her rescue was a waste of precious time.

With that, she picked up her suitcase with a mixed feeling of helplessness and tiredness. She took a step forward with a little surge of determination. And just like a cord that had exceeded its elastic limit, the heel of her shoe bowed and snapped. Astounded, Susan glared down at her foot and wiggled it a little, watching the now useless shoe flop about.

Ludicrous.

That was what this whole situation was. What else could go wrong? Where could she go from here?

She looked heavenward and offered a brief prayer. *Dear Lord, please send me help on this lonely road. Don't let me be dinner for a mountain lion.*

As the final words passed her lips, the faint whinny of a horse sounded behind her and increased. She turned just in time to see a brown stallion stop beside her. With one finger, the tanned, lean cowboy astride the large animal pushed his hat back and gave her a wide smile.

"Hello, miss. Can I give you a ride?"

Susan shifted in her tracks, her mind doing a hasty calculation. *What if he's one of the men who are after me?* She considered running, but there was her shoe. And the fact that he was on horseback. Also that she had nowhere to run *to.*

"I er ... missed the cart that was to connect this ... station to the next town."

The cowboy smiled, revealing his white teeth against his nicely tanned face as he swung down from the horse. "This ain't no station, miss. It's just the place the mail gets dropped off. But that wasn't what I asked."

Handsome, tough, and *fearless,* were the three words that came to mind as she stared at him.

He removed his hat and held it in his right hand, revealing golden hair. His eyes, the bluest blue she had ever seen, twinkled as he gazed down at her from his considerable height. She prided herself in being tall at five feet nine, but this cowboy must be at least six three.

Susan clamped her mouth shut, realizing she had been staring. The stranger grinned even wider.

"Tell you what, ma'am; since it's almost nightfall, why don't you let me help you on your way? This ain't no place for a lady all by her lonesome."

CHAPTER 2

THIS WASN'T WHAT BILL JACOBS HAD ANTICIPATED WHEN HE'D HEADED TOWARD town to send one last letter to his brother's mail order bride.

Why Jake had gone searching for a wife in the paper was beyond Bill. It didn't surprise Bill in the slightest that Jake had gotten cold feet at the last minute and gone on to abruptly marry his childhood sweetheart—all without the knowledge of his mail order bride, of course.

Jake had pleaded with Bill to drive into town and deliver a letter to the other woman to tell her of the changes that had occurred since they last communicated. Bill only hoped the lady in question would get the letter on time and not hop a train to Colorado. How terrible would it be for a woman to arrive in an unfamiliar town, expecting marriage, only to discover she'd been jilted by mail?

While his thoughts had been wrapped around the mail order bride, he'd come upon this young lady. That had been a surprise far greater than Jake's poor behavior. Lone women didn't wander these parts—with good reason. For a brief moment, Bill wondered if she could possibly be bait for outlaws hiding nearby, then dismissed the notion as absurd. He was well aware that he had a tendency to mistrust women, given his past experiences.

He studied the woman standing before him. She had a simple natural beauty to her that he liked, including the way her green eyes flashed with fire and her dark curls tumbled every which way, lightly coated with trail dust.

"I don't know you," she pointed out unnecessarily.

Bill hid a smile, assuming it would be poorly received.

"No. You don't," he agreed. "And I know you're worried about accepting a ride from someone you hardly know. I can't say I blame you. But by the time you walk into town, it'll be dark. There'll be no cart then, I assure you. And there'll be plenty of men about who are far less trustworthy than I am."

Bill watched her pretty face crease into a scowl as she turned things over in her mind. "Wild animals are pretty bad in these parts. I sure wouldn't want to be out here after dark," he added.

Her eyes narrowed suspiciously. "I ... think I'll walk," she informed him.

He raised an eyebrow and folded his arms over his chest. "Suit yourself."

The woman took a few steps and then stopped, muttering under her breath. "You can go on your way. Don't stand there watching me."

"My horse needs a rest," Bill blatantly lied. She whirled and directed such a glare at him that he had to swallow a laugh. Feisty, this one was! He liked it. A lot. Too much, as a matter of fact. When she turned away again, his thoughts moved to Isabella, as they often did. And when she took center stage in his mind, there was nothing Bill could do to stop it.

He closed his eyes to the unwelcome emotions that surged through him whenever he thought of her. As always, he wondered, had he not been loving enough? Was that why she had betrayed him, not once, not twice, but several times? His mind retreated to the last fight they'd had, where Isabella had flung her unfaithfulness in his face.

The pain was still searing even after all this time. Gritting his teeth, Bill brought himself back to the present day and watched the woman as she stomped along. Her gait was a little off, he realized after a minute, and then his eyes fell on the shoes discarded by the side of the tracks where she'd been standing a few moments ago.

Barefoot. The woman thought she could make it ten miles barefoot, through rattlesnake and cacti country, all the way to town. And that wasn't even taking into account the big cats that prowled the area or the far more dangerous outlaws who made a home of the various caves and canyons.

Bill watched a little while longer, seeing how the suitcase was obviously getting heavier and harder to handle with each step the woman took. He couldn't help but admire her stubborn courage as she charged along, regardless of obviously being exhausted. At one point, she pitched forward and he fought the urge to rush headlong to catch her—not that he was anywhere close enough for such an instant rescue. She righted herself, stared at her suitcase, stuffed it into some shrubbery, and continued forward.

She's got some grit.

With a sigh, Bill swung back on his horse and caught up with the woman. "Miss," he called.

"Stop following me," she snapped, not looking his direction.

Even though he was a patient man, his feathers were ruffled. He hadn't been anything but gentlemanly!

"Miss, you don't understand. You won't make it into town," he insisted. "That ain't just because you're a lady. A man on foot out here, with no shoes and no weapon, would be in just as much danger."

"I could have a weapon."

Bill rolled his eyes. "Sharp as your tongue is, it won't do any good if a bear decides you'll make a good dinner. Or if an outlaw reckons the same."

She kept stomping along. Bill kept following. He couldn't just leave her, confound it. It wouldn't be Christian.

Suddenly, she whirled, and a shower of stones flew his direction. His horse shied and Bill shouted in surprise, barely keeping his seat. It wasn't as though the pebbles were any danger. They'd just caught him off guard. As his mount bucked, the woman started off at a dead run.

That was when Bill realized the look he'd seen in her eyes a moment ago wasn't just stubbornness. It was fear. He knew mistrust when he saw it, given how little he chose to share his trust with anyone.

Dismounting, Bill tied his horse to a nearby tree and walked at a safe distance from the woman, whose running had forcibly slowed because of her bare feet and the rough terrain. "I know you're afraid," he said quietly. "I won't hurt you, ma'am. My name's Bill Jacobs. All I want is to help you safely get wherever it is you're going."

She stopped then and slowly turned to him, huge eyes widening even further. "Jacobs? As in Jake Jacobs?"

Just like that, Bill's heart—what remained of it after Isabella's drubbing—sank to his toes. "Yes, ma'am. Are you ..."

"Susan Lockhart. Are you related to my fiancé?"

He removed his hat and clasped it awkwardly to his chest, feeling like a heel for having to deliver the news even though it wasn't any fault of his own. "I'm his brother. But miss ... I hate to tell you this. Jake's gone and got himself hitched already."

CHAPTER 3

ON HER ARRIVAL AT JAKE JACOBS'S HOUSE, SUSAN HAD A DISTURBING FEELING that coming west was the worst decision she had made in a while. And she'd made plenty of poor decisions. When Bill had told her about Jake's recent marriage, she'd been inclined not to believe him. But then he'd produced the letter from his saddlebag.

It had taken all she had left in her to climb up behind Bill and let him escort her to Jake's home even though she knew she was no longer welcome there.

"How could you?" she demanded of Jake yet again as she sat in his sitting room, avoiding eye contact with his pretty new wife. It wasn't the woman's fault, but Susan couldn't help but be furious at her anyway. She wasn't sure where Bill had gone off to since they arrived, but as humiliated as she was, she was glad he wasn't here to witness her further mortification.

"I'm sorry, ma'am. I honestly believed my letter would catch you before you left." Jake at least had the decency to look remorseful as he spoke.

"I have nowhere to go!" she exclaimed, fighting back desperate tears. True, she could be in worse straits. She had money. But there was a matter of the men following her. "I sold everything I owned to come out here. What am I to do?"

Jake stared a bit at her and then sighed, rubbing his neck and looking over at Erica. His wife shook her head and disappeared from the room.

His wife. That was supposed to be Susan's title!

The woman, as Jake had explained earlier, was the daughter of one of his foremen and they had been friends for a long time before he had placed the ad. When Erica had learned he'd placed the ad, she'd apparently broken down and confessed her feelings to Jake. Jake had then realized his feelings for her ...

Susan swallowed a lump in her throat. It wasn't Erica's fault that this cozy-looking home should have been hers. The three-room house with a fireplace freshly lit at one end of the room and a table with a lantern neatly placed in the center of the room. She would've been the one in the kitchen, bustling about as she could now hear Erica doing. Love was love ... and it seemed Susan would never find it.

Jake sat quietly and studied Susan. She studied him right back, seeing the similarities with Bill in terms of his hair color and overall build. But Bill was taller and more muscular. His eyes had more of a blue fire to them, and his dimples—

"Did you travel down here all alone?" Jake interrupted her thoughts.

Susan glared at him. Had he not listened to anything she said? "Yes."

"You made no arrangements for a chaperone?"

"No, I felt there was no need for one." She couldn't very well tell him she hadn't had time to locate a chaperone, what with her life on the line!

"What about your parents? Are they back east?"

It occurred to Susan then how little this man she had been meant to marry knew about her. And how little she knew of him. "I lost my parents when I was very little. My aunt raised me. She died recently."

"I'm sorry," Jake muttered, looking away.

"You're sorry my aunt died. You're sorry you got married and left me in a bind. Sorry isn't helping me, Mr. Jacobs!" she exclaimed, then ducked her head, horrified at the tone of her voice. Angry she might be, but there was no need for her to sound like a harpy.

Feeling the tears she'd been holding back for far too long start to roll down her face, Susan jumped to her feet and rushed blindly out of the room. Thankfully, she remembered the way out and managed to stumble onto the porch. As she did, she collided with a massive, muscled chest.

Her head jerked up and she stared into Bill's clear, gentle eyes. "Easy there," he said quietly, offering a handkerchief.

Susan snatched it up and covered her face with it, shoulders shaking uncontrollably. It was all too much.

"I'm so tired," she whispered. She felt a big hand on her shoulder and then Bill guided her to a seat and eased her down. "What am I to do?" Susan asked plaintively again, wrapping her arms around herself.

There was an extended silence before she heard a low sigh. "You ain't alone, miss. Jake's thoughtless, but he ain't a bad man. We'll make sure you're taken care of."

"Of course I'm alone," Susan retorted, wringing her hands. "I have nothing and no one. You don't understand. I'll move into a hotel in town, I suppose—"

"There ain't no hotel."

Frustration boiled up inside her and Susan squeezed her eyes shut once more. "Of course not. Your brother may not be a bad man, but he's put me in an absolutely untenable position." Truthfully, she'd contributed to that by jumping without looking. As always. But she wasn't inclined to be charitable just now.

"No hotel. No husband." It seemed the only thing left to do was to go back. But to go back meant—

"I have an idea."

There was such resignation in Bill's voice that Susan risked a look, wondering what could be going through his mind. His handsome face was pale beneath the golden tan and his eyes were blank as he murmured, "You can marry me instead."

"What!" Susan gaped at him in utter shock. Whatever she'd expected from Jake's brother, that wasn't it.

Bill lifted a broad shoulder and toyed with the brim of his hat. "I won't lie to you. Marriage is the last thing I've thought of in ... quite a few years. But you're in a bad way. And I think we might suit one another as companions."

She blinked. "Companions."

He nodded once, curtly. "I don't hold with romance. I want you to know that. But I'd be a good husband to you. Respectful. Hardworking. You'd want for nothing. The only thing I'd ask in return is honesty."

She swallowed hard. She might have missed the cart, but it sure felt like she was on one right now, veering off the tracks at high speed. Engaged to one man. Proposed to by another. A murderous mob on her heels.

"Yes," she whispered. "All right. Yes. I don't know you any better than your brother. I can promise honesty. Yes. I will ... marry you."

CHAPTER 4

Susan sat stiffly beside the man she hadn't given the time of day when he had offered to help her the first time they had met. The man who'd followed her even when she'd warned him not to. Who'd persisted even when she tried to stone him. Who'd calmed her fear and escorted her to his brother's house. The man who had married her ten minutes back.

How had that happened? It was all a blur. After she'd accepted his proposal, Bill had driven them into town. In short order, he'd found a pastor. There had been vows—there must have been, even though Susan could barely remember them. Was there a kiss to seal them? No. She thought she'd recall that. Vows and a confirmation by the priest that they were husband and wife and ...

Now this silent wagon ride, both of them desperately awkwardly. Bill's face had remained an utter blank from the moment he'd suggested the idea.

Susan released the breath she had no idea she had been holding. What did one say in such circumstances?

"Thank you, Bill," she heard herself say. Those were the right words, she was sure. It had been an incredible kindness for him to make such a proposal when it was clear marriage wasn't anything he wasn't interested in. If he hadn't, she'd have been forced back east and straight into the path of those following her.

At the thought of the attackers, Susan shivered slightly and rubbed her arms.

"You needn't thank me for anything." He didn't look at her as he spoke. "Just remember our agreement. We're companions, Susan. Partners. Nothing more. And all I ask is honesty."

Susan shifted uncomfortably. It was obvious something in Bill's past was rearing its head as he repeated his odd request. Of course a spouse expected honesty. You wouldn't ask for such a thing unless you'd been hurt at some point. But she had a past too, and she didn't appreciate people prying, so she didn't press him with questions.

She looked out the moving wagon and stared at the landscape. Someday it would be as familiar to her as Bill's face would become. But for now, it, and he were strangers. Silent and forbidding.

"Do you mind critters?"

His voice startled her, as did the question. "I beg your pardon?"

Bill clicked his tongue at the horse and guided it around a sharp corner before repeating himself. "Critters. Do you mind them? Animals, I mean. Big ones like cows and horses. Smalls ones like chickens and the occasional snake."

She frowned. "I've never had anything to do with animals, truthfully, other than the odd dog or cat. I suppose if I need to get comfortable around livestock or barn animals then I will. Snakes, on the other hand ..."

He stared out across the vast landscape, looking even more distant than he had been when he was silent. "You're bound to run into one of them at some point. Learn this rhyme. *Red on yellow, kill a fellow. Red on black, venom lack.*"

Susan repeated the odd little rhyme to herself. "All right ..."

"That's strictly for coral snakes," Bill explained. "You might occasionally see one. Mostly though, it's rattlers. For them it's just a matter of common sense. They're most active in the morning. Don't go stomping around in tall grass. Check before sitting down on any big boulders. If you hear a rattle, freeze. Figure out where the sound is coming from. If possible, retreat very slowly. If not, stay still until the snake settles. They're not out to get ya. Just defendin' themselves."

Susan rubbed her arms nervously. "Freeze. Retreat," she murmured vaguely, suddenly feeling more out of her depth than ever. She'd come west to escape predators, but it seemed like there were plenty waiting here for her already. "All right."

For the first time, Bill spared her a glance. His sharp eyes seemed to soften slightly. "Don't be scared. This land is wild but full of beauty. It's God's own country, Susan. Truly."

She liked the way he said her name, and even more she liked the hint of warmth that eased the hard lines of his handsome face. "I want to learn about it. The more I know, the better partner I can be to you."

He nodded and looked away once more, focused on the horizon again. "We can build a good life together. Long as you keep in mind the rules."

Susan stared down at her feet. The rules. Snake rules. Rules about catching feelings. About honesty. She didn't object to any of them ... it just all felt so prescribed, and she was someone who had a bad tendency to buck against boundaries.

Dear Lord, help me honor my new husband, she whispered silently before asking, "So you were raised here? You and your brother, I mean?"

Bill nodded. "Never known any other place. Never wanted to—look over there!"

Her head swiveled at his exclamation and she spotted a large animal hopping swiftly from boulder to boulder along a craggy hillside. "What on earth?"

"Bighorn sheep," he informed her. "They're not good for much in the way of hunting, but they sure are fascinating animals to watch. No matter how steep a hill is, I've never seen one slip. Not even the babies."

The amazement in his voice made Susan smile a little. So there was a hint of softness in him somewhere, at least. "What other animals are out here?" she asked.

"Oh, everything. Bear. Moose. Deer. Elk. You name it, it probably roams these parts."

"And mountain lions too," she recalled from their first meeting.

"Big ones, yes. Ever catch one of those stalkin' you, draw yourself up as tall as you can and holler louder than you ever have," Bill said seriously. "It's the only chance you stand—frightening it away."

Susan's smile grew improbably wider. "But I shouldn't be afraid, huh."

He looked sideways at her for a brief second, and maybe—just maybe—that was a smile that hovered at the corner of his lips. Then it was gone as he responded, "Not afraid. Just respectful. No different than in a human relationship, really. Lack of respect will get a person eaten alive."

She had the strangest feeling that, though Bill bore no outward scars—none that she'd seen so far anyway—he was badly scarred anyway.

The awkward silence between them resumed as he drove them to his house, and it persisted long after Bill had shown her around the spartan two-bedroom structure and then left Susan to wash up and bed down for the night. Alone.

Partners, she reminded herself over and over after she climbed into bed and huddled under the covers, feeling lonelier than ever before. *Not husband and wife outside of the legal aspect of things.*

The thought rang hollowly through her tired mind until she finally drifted off to troubled dreams.

CHAPTER 5

Two weeks later

"What are you doing, Bill?"

Bill threw his brother an irate glance as he shoveled up another gob of stable muck and tossed it expertly into a waiting wheelbarrow. "What does it look like?"

Jake shrugged and leaned against one of the stalls. His baby brother wasn't quite as tall as him, but a life of hard work had packed him with muscles and the wooden framework protested at the heavy weight. "Looks like you're avoiding your new wife."

"Break that gate and I'll tan your hide," Bill snapped, digging more ferociously into his task. "I oughta tan it anyway. She was supposed to be *your* wife, need I remind you? And I'm not avoiding anything. I'm doing my work. Why aren't you doing yours?"

At least Jake eased back a little so the wood quit groaning quite so much. But he didn't ease up with his pestering. "I got my chores done a little earlier than usual. That's what happens when you let someone help you. You know. Like your wife."

Bill rolled his eyes. "You're telling me you have Erica helping you in the barn?"

"Well, why not?"

"Because she's five feet tall and weighs a hundred pounds soakin' wet," Bill pointed out unnecessarily. "Any livestock decides to lean on her or throw a kick—"

"The one who's gotten kicked is you," Jake cut in. He picked up a shovel, let himself into the neighboring stall, whose resident horse was outside in the pasture with Bill's three other animals, and started mucking out at a speed similar to Bill's.

The brothers had grown up doing this kind of work. It was as much in their blood as it was ingrained in their muscle memory.

Bill scoffed and stepped out to grab a fresh bale of straw to lay as clean bedding. It felt good to feel the heavy pull of the bale as he hefted it upwards with a pitchfork and tossed it just outside the stalls he and Jake were working in. "I haven't been kicked since that steer did a number on my ribs when I was sixteen because I was fool enough to turn my back on it. What are you yammerin' about?"

Only Jake's blond head was visible as he leaned over his shovel. "I'm sayin' your ribs are still plenty bruised, especially right above your heart, courtesy of Isabella."

Bill froze with his pitchfork stabbed into the bale. The soft, sweet hay fragrance lingered around him, but he didn't even notice it as all the pleasure he usually took in his work was chased away by Jake's words.

"You know better than to bring up her name."

"But you apparently don't know better than to break a heart of your own," Jake shot back with uncharacteristic aggression. It was usually plenty difficult to rile Bill's laconic brother.

"What are you talking about?" Bill demanded, tossing straw into the stall but not enjoying the task like he usually did. Typically it was nice to see the fresh bedding cover the wooden slats and to know his horses would spend their nights in comfort. But right now he derived no pleasure from the task.

"I'm saying she broke your heart. But that little lady you up and decided to marry, well, she has one too. And I can see it leanin' your way, Bill. If I hadn't noticed how she looks at you, well, Erica's pointed it out more than once. What're you doing, brother?" Finally, Jake straightened and looked him right in the eye.

Bill felt the tension build in his neck and shoulders until they fairly ached with each swift jab of the pitchfork. "She knew the deal when we got married."

"Never figured you for a fool."

Bill saw red and dropped the fork, his big hands clenching into tight fists. "You lookin' for a fight, *brother*? Because I can provide one if you keep this up. You brought her out here and left her with few alternatives. Poor woman had no place to go. Marrying her was the Christian thing to do."

Jake snorted and stepped out of the stall. "Keep telling yourself that. It's very Christian to—"

A gunshot cut through his words like a knife in fresh butter, followed by a high-pitched scream. Argument forgotten, Jake and Bill locked eyes for one long second and then both bolted from the barn, running with all they had toward where the sound had come from.

As they raced over the hard-packed yard, Bill's heart pounded. The scream had been so utterly full of fear—something in him rebelled at the notion that Susan could be hurt. Sure, he'd been avoiding her as much as humanly possible ever since their wedding. He'd even stopped eating breakfast because watching her cook and then having to endure sitting across from her at the table while she tried to initiate conversation left him empty inside. She was a beautiful, intelligent, kind woman, but Bill just didn't have it in him to dare to allow himself to care again. Even so, the notion that she could be hurt made his chest ache, just like when that steer bashed him.

The scream came again and Bill veered off toward the chicken coop. He spotted Susan standing just inside and lunged for her. "What? What is it?" he shouted, dragging her backwards from her place and spinning her around to look at him. Frantically, Bill looked her up and down, searching for some kind of injury. When he found none, he grabbed her by the shoulders and shook her slightly, looking down into her ghost-white face. Her beautiful eyes were the size of saucers and filled to the brim with tears. "Susan! Confound it, Susan. Talk to me! What happened?"

She bit her lips and the tears started to flow silently down her cheeks. He could feel her trembling and hated the way it made him feel inside. "Susan," he tried again, gentling his voice. "Tell me what happened."

"Snake," Jake snapped behind him, and Bill's heart dropped to his toes. But she had no injury! He was sure of it!

Keeping a tight grip on Susan's slender shoulders, trying not to notice the way her dark curls tumbled askew all down her back, he turned toward his brother. "What'd you say?"

Jake stabbed a finger at a revolver lying in the dirt, then jabbed a finger inside the henhouse. "Big ol' rattler was having dinner on your breakfast eggs. She shot his head clean off, Bill."

Bewildered, Bill looked back at Susan. "But—if that's the case—why are you cryin'?"

For the first time since he'd reached her side, Susan spoke. Her voice was a raw whisper. "I've ... never killed anything in my life."

And then she collapsed.

CHAPTER 6

SUSAN STARED INTO THE STEAMING CUP OF COFFEE, HER NERVES STILL ENTIRELY too fired up for her to dare to try and hold it without scalding herself. Peripherally, she was aware of Bill conversing with Jake at the far end of the kitchen in low whispers, but she was too ashamed to take any interest in whatever they were saying. It was true the snake had terrified her, and she had reacted utterly instinctively to protect the eggs. Rushing back into the house to grab Bill's gun, she'd bolted straight back to the coop and killed the rattler. And that was what had undone her—the sound of the gunshot, so reminiscent of the incident that had forced her to flee out west.

"Susan."

She looked up from the coffee and found Bill looking down at her. Oh why did he have to be so handsome? They had such a strained relationship already; it was enough to make her want to cry all over again to imagine what this incident would do to their 'marriage.' No matter how she'd tried in the two weeks since her wedding, she couldn't seem to get Bill back to that place they'd briefly been in the wagon where they'd actually conversed pleasantly for a moment. Instead, he actively avoided her from morning until dinner. She'd halfway decided to give up eating, mealtimes were so unpleasant. And yet she still wanted him to like her for some reason.

"Susan, don't cry."

The rasp in his voice startled her almost as much as the realization that tears were once again skating down her face. Irritated at herself, she swiped them away. "I'm fine. It was a bit of a shock, that's all. I'm sorry I disturbed you."

He frowned and took a seat in front of her—his usual seat, the one where he usually glared at his eggs or oatmeal like they'd done him wrong. But this time his clear blue eyes were trained on hers, worry shadowing them.

"I'm fine," she began again, only for him to cut her off.

"You didn't disturb me."

It was Susan's turn to frown, even as the tears fell faster and she dropped her head to mask her humiliation. "Of course I did."

When he covered her hand with his, she almost jumped out of her seat, it startled her so much. The warmth of his touch was one she'd inexplicably been craving though she didn't understand why, since he clearly had no interest in her whatso-ever. To feel it now, when she was laid so low ... she jerked her hand away.

"Go back to your chores, Bill. I'm fine. Please. Just let me gather myself and I'll get back to my own work," she mumbled, staring at her fingers, still warm from his big hand.

"Where'd you learn to shoot like that?"

It was another shock to realize Jake was still in the kitchen. Susan turned, almost grateful for the interruption. "My daddy taught me," she explained, sniffling a little and wiping her cheek with her sleeve. "He was a crack shot himself. Always wanted a son. But when I was the only child that came along ..." she shrugged and wiped her face again. "He decided he'd teach me what a boy should know."

Jake approached and, to Susan's surprise, held out a handkerchief. It looked creased and more than a little dusty. "It's clean," he promised.

Gratefully, Susan took the square of fabric and dabbed her cheeks.

"You can go on home, Jake," Bill rumbled, and she looked over at him, curious at the edge to his tone. His features remained neutral but there was an odd warning light in his eyes.

Jake chuckled. "I'll see myself out. Hope you get to feeling better, Susan." Nodding at her, he walked away and slipped out the kitchen's back door.

That left her and Bill alone. Not knowing what else to do, Susan wrapped her hands around the cup of coffee, letting its heat seep into the cold spaces that her past history and the last two lonely weeks had left inside her.

"You, uh, want some sugar with that?"

She blinked and dared a glance at her husband. "Excuse me?"

He shuffled to his feet and returned a moment later with a pitcher of cream from the icebox and a container of sugar. "I've seen how you take your coffee. It's more like a cup of sugar with a little coffee for color."

Was that a hint of teasing in his tone? she wondered in amazement, accepting the cream and sugar with a muted, "Thanks." It was hard to believe he'd paid enough attention to her to realize how she liked her coffee.

"You didn't disturb me," Bill said after a long moment of silence. "I'm sorry if I've made you feel that calling on me for assistance is something I frown upon. You *are* my wife, Susan. My job is to protect you."

Susan sighed and stirred cream in with unnecessary vigor. "But you regret marrying me," she pointed out with characteristic candor. "Don't deny it. We both know the last two weeks have been painful."

More silence. Just when she thought he wouldn't say anything, Bill spoke again. "I don't regret it."

Anger flared in her and she raised her head and set her jaw. "Don't lie to me. You were the one who made that rule. Remember? You couldn't be more obvious if you tried, Bill. You married me out of some ... some impulsive kindness to try and mend Jake's mistake. And ever since, you've regretted it."

"I'm not lyin'." Bill leaned back in his chair and rubbed his jaw. "You're a good woman, Susan. There's no missin' that. You're as capable a housewife as you are headstrong, intelligent, and lovely."

Her jaw almost dropped at the compliment. She honestly didn't care much if he thought she was lovely. Plenty of men did. But for him to have watched her enough to learn about her temperament?

He smiled a little, apparently reading her mind. "Yes. I've noticed. And while I still hold to what I said at the beginning—this is a partnership, not a romance—I would like the chance to start over on a better foot. Will you give me that chance, Susan?"

The way he was looking at her ... there was something both hopeful and guarded in his eyes. Like he had a secret. Well, she had one too. Who was she to hold that against him?

"I'd like that," she said quietly. "I'd like that a lot."

This time when he placed his hand over hers, it was a little awkward, yes, but there was a slight tenderness to the touch that made Susan's heart hammer with sudden hope.

CHAPTER 7

"Thanks, Max." Bill nodded at the mercantile owner. "Just have your boy load the wagon for me, will ya? I have a few other errands to run while I'm in town."

The burly old store owner chuckled. "Better watch yourself, Bill. Women like nothing better than shiny trinkets and new clothes. If your new missus is anything like mine, she's probably in the new fabric store."

His missus. It still sounded strange to Bill. And yet ... it was growing on him. As he walked out of the mercantile and started in the direction of the blacksmith, he reflected on the last few weeks. Ever since Susan had had that strange reaction to shooting the snake—and it still seemed off, no matter how many different ways Bill tried to look at it. But then again, what did he know about women?—and they'd conversed in the kitchen, things had gotten markedly better between them. Something about realizing she honestly thought he didn't like her, followed by her easy rapport with Jake, had sat deeply wrong with Bill. When his brother had been the one to offer Susan a handkerchief—the idea had never even occurred to Bill—that had been the last straw.

He'd made a concerted effort ever since to be kinder to Susan, albeit still trying to keep his distance enough to prevent a repeat of Isabella. While he knew by now that was unfair—nothing in Susan remotely suggested she'd betray him similarly—he couldn't help but keep his guard up. Even so, it had been nice to start to get to know his wife. She was a spitfire, for sure. They argued half the time, about everything from politics to his plans for the farm, but it was always in good fun, and he appreciated a woman who stood her ground, regardless of societal notions that the "fairer sex" should be meek.

Bill snorted at that notion. Susan was no more meek than she was stupid. The woman quoted famous authors as easily as she dished up a pot pie or put the cantankerous livestock in their place. Even the rooster was slightly in awe of her and had quit being so ornery whenever she walked past its territory. That was after Susan had warned it repeatedly that a soup pot was waiting if it didn't learn some manners.

"Afternoon, Bill," Joseph, the blacksmith, greeted him as Bill entered the heat of his shop, immediately hit with a blast from the furnace. "Got that wagon wheel for you right here." He jabbed a thumb at the wheel with its repaired axle, leaning against the far wall.

"Thanks, Joseph." Bill tipped his hat. "What do I owe you?"

Joseph wiped his hands on his leather apron and shook his head. "Nothing. Your Susan did my girl a big favor the other day. I don't rightly know what it was, but Laura had been mighty blue. Then Susan come along and suddenly my girl's chipper again." He looked baffled, but delighted. "She's a gem. Don't you be forget-tin' that."

Bill smiled. "I won't. Thanks. I'll bring the wagon around in a little while and pick up the wheel."

"Before you do," Joseph said, reaching for a towel to wipe his sweat-slicked bald head. "I heard you were in the market for another farmhand?"

Surprised, Bill nodded. "The farm's doing well enough that I'm going to need extra help before too long. Figured I'd hire someone on before the harvest, so he knows the general run of the place by then. Did Susan mention that?"

"Naw." Joseph shook his head. "You know what this town is like. Tell anyone anything and 'fore sunup ..." he trailed off. "Anyway, there's a man just arrived in town a few days back. Name of Ted. Looks like he might fit the role, if you're interested in sounding him out. He's at the saloon right now, I think."

"Thanks," Bill said. "Much appreciate that, Joseph."

He ducked out of the shop and was immediately grateful for the cool blast of air that hit him as he made his way to the saloon. How Joseph stood that heat day in, day out, Bill did not know.

Entering the saloon, he nodded at various friends and walked over to the bar to consult with Rusty, the owner. "Hiya, Rusty. Joseph said there's a man by the name of Ted 'round these parts?"

Rusty jerked a thumb at a man with his back to them, seated toward the far wall. "Yessir. Came in about an hour back. Nice fella."

Thanking the barkeep, Bill walked over, making enough noise as he walked to ensure he didn't startle the stranger. You never knew how people in these parts would react to being snuck up on. Having a gun pulled on you wasn't unlikely.

But when Ted turned toward him, there was no wariness on the man's face. Bill assessed him swiftly. He was short and compact, more wiry than muscled, but with the definite look of an individual who'd done work with his hands. A long scar wound down from his left temple to his jaw, suggesting he'd done some rough living at some point.

The man gave him a friendly smile and touched his index finger to his forehead. "Howdy, boss. I take it you're Bill?"

Bill nodded and extended a hand. He was pleased at the stranger's firm grasp. The callouses on his hands were further indication of an individual accustomed to hard work. "I'm in the market for a farmhand. Word has it you might be able to help me out."

Ted waved at Rusty. "Barkeep, bring us two beers," he called, before returning his focus to a surprised Bill. "It's only polite to offer your new boss a drink."

Bill raised an eyebrow. "I ain't hired you yet."

Ted shrugged. "But you will. And if you don't, a good drink is never a waste. But you will," he repeatedly confidently as their drinks arrived and he took a long slug almost immediately, then wiped the foam off his upper lip with his forearm. "You need help on your farm. And I aim to deliver, boss. Give me a couple weeks' trial. If you don't like my work, you can let me go. I'll sign papers sayin' I won't kick up a fuss. But I ain't never had anyone send me packing once they learn how valuable a hired hand I am."

Impressed, if mildly wary, Bill clinked his beer against Ted's. "All right, then. It's a deal. The only thing I need is some kind of a reference from the last person you worked for."

Ted smiled. "I'll talk to my old boss first thing tomorrow."

Bill nodded and quickly downed his drink. "That would be great. Now, if you'll excuse me, I don't mean to be rude, but my wife will be wonderin' where I am."

Ted's smile widened. "Go right ahead, boss. Not good to keep the womenfolk waitin'. I'll find my way to your place as soon as I get that letter from my old boss. Might take a few days."

They shook hands and Bill made his way toward the fabric store. Halfway there, he bumped into his wife, her arms full not of fabric but of ... lumber? Hastily, he lifted the heavy load from Susan's arms. "Susan, what on earth ..."

"The chicken coop needs to be strengthened so snakes can't slip in so easily," she informed him, a happy light in her eyes that made Bill's heart do dangerous things.

"Crazy woman," he muttered affectionately, and she bumped her hip playfully against his as they started toward the wagon. Again, his heart did strange things that Bill knew he shouldn't be allowing to happen. But how was he supposed to resist? There was just something about his new wife. Something he liked. A lot.

"What'd you help the blacksmith's wife with?" he inquired after they finished loading the wagon and started back toward home. It occurred to him that he liked having Susan sitting beside him, looking curiously around at the passing landscape as though she hadn't seen the same thing every time they came to town. She always seemed to find something new to point out, which made Bill thank God for things he often took for granted like the river or the fresh fragrance of a juniper or even the amusing antics of a cottontail gamboling by.

Susan laughed. It was a warm, soft sound that wrapped its way around Bill and held on tight. "Nothing, really. She was feeling a little ignored by her husband. This is his busy season, apparently. I made a few suggestions about ways to get him to be slightly more attentive, starting with not waiting around at home doing nothing and showing up instead at his shop with a picnic basket. That apparently shocked the heck out of him ... but I hear he liked it."

Bill raised an amused eyebrow. "I wouldn't doubt it. You do beat all, Susan Jacobs. Are picnics something you enjoy?"

In response, Susan grinned from ear to ear and reached behind her. A moment later she lifted a large hamper into her lap, her eyes twinkling. "I was wondering, Mr. Jacobs," she drawled. "If you'd have time to indulge in a small repast by the river."

He let out a whoop of laughter. "I don't even know what a re-past is. But I'm willin' to learn!"

It was a dangerous game indeed, he reflected, as Susan took the reins of the horses and guided them to a spot she'd apparently already predetermined. But Bill found that, though his rules were being badly broken, he couldn't bring himself to object.

CHAPTER 8

Susan hummed happily to herself, moving about the day's business with a new lift in her step. With each chore, she whispered another prayer of thanks for this new life she was suddenly living. It was like Bill had become a different person ever since that day with the snake. In the weeks since, they'd actually become close. They were having meals together. Sometimes he'd stick his head in during the day and just say hello. He invited her into town with him more often than not. And though Susan was trying hard to keep from breaking his blasted rule, she knew in her heart that she was more than a little in love with her husband already. Erica Jacobs had told her as much yesterday. She and the other woman had struck up a friendship of sorts. It wasn't Erica's fault that Jake had jilted Susan, after all.

Erica had dropped by several days after the picnic and Susan had eagerly told her all about how she and Bill had ended up spending several hours just talking, skipping rocks on the water, getting to know one another better. When she'd finished telling the story, Erica had given her an odd look and had informed her that, "The man is falling hard for you. That's bound to scare him. Be careful."

But she'd refused to say *why* it would scare Bill, and Susan had come to the conclusion that she had to ask. It was time they both came clean about their respective secrets. Thankfully, hers were thousands of miles away. Nevertheless, she still wanted Bill to know about them. And whatever was weighing his heart down so badly ... she couldn't help with that unless she knew his story.

Stifling a small sigh, she finished emptying the laundry water into the garden patch and walked back to the house, debating whether she'd set to work on the chicken coop today, walk into town to have tea with Mrs. Hutchison, the minister's wife who was quickly becoming a dear friend, or start on the fresh coat of paint the porch badly needed.

To her surprise, as she walked up the weathered porch, the kitchen door opened and Bill stepped out. "Hello, Mrs. Jacobs."

She wasn't sure if it was his smile, his drawl, or his use of her married name—of *his* name attached to hers—that made her heart immediately speed up a little. It also could have been that the man was just a sight to behold, no matter if he was sweaty and dusty or fresh as a daisy after a shower.

"Hello, Mr. Jacobs," she replied, miming a tip of an imaginary hat and hovering on the porch steps. "What brings you home from your chores so early? It's not even close to lunchtime."

"A good friend said something to me the other day," he replied, folding his arms across his broad chest. "About how her friend was feeling neglected by her hard-working husband."

Susan's mouth went dry. "Uh ... yes. Laura and Joseph—"

Bill held up a hand, interrupting her. "I may not be the sharpest knife in the drawer, but I've still got an edge." Ducking back inside, he reemerged a moment later with a bucket of paint in one hand and a bouquet of wildflowers clutched clumsily in the other.

Susan gaped. She couldn't help it. "Wha—wha—" she stammered. "I—"

"Put the flowers in water," Bill directed, waving them at her. "And then you and I will start on this porch together. I have a new hire coming on board soon, so I'm a little less pressed for time in terms of getting everything done by myself."

Stunned and delighted, Susan took the pretty red and yellow flowers and pressed them to her nose, inhaling deeply before hurrying inside and finding a nice cup to tuck them into. They looked lovely sitting in the center of the kitchen table and she beamed before rushing back out to join her husband.

He held out a brush already dipped in paint, pale blue droplets dripping onto the porch steps. "You said you like this color a lot. I ordered it special."

A lump formed in her throat and it was all Susan could do to avoid tearing up. Since that was sure to put a literal damper on Bill's lovely gesture, she covered it up with a pretend sneeze, wiped her eyes, and turned determinedly toward the porch, assessing it.

"I'll start on this end—" she waved the brush, "and you start on that one."

Bill saluted with his own brush and nearly painted a blue streak into his blond hair. Grinning, Susan set to work.

"So, a new hire?" she inquired as they went about their task, various farm animals wandering past behind them curiously, inspecting whatever was happening and then wandering away once more.

"I've been thinkin' for some time that I need one," he replied, swiping the paint on in smooth, even strokes that quickly covered the dingy white paint from who knew how long back. Ordinarily it would probably need to have been scraped off, but there was so little of it left. "Joseph referred me to a recent arrival in town. Name of Ted. Seems like a good man for the job."

Susan was glad that her face was turned away when she heard the name. Of course it wasn't *her* Ted. Nevertheless, it wasn't a name she liked hearing.

"When does he start?"

"Soon as he gets a reference," Bill answered. "Might take a bit. I don't mind waitin'. Say, I heard the ladies in town have been discussing plans for Christmas, even though that's ages away. Somethin' or other about a pageant and dance. You wouldn't have had anything to do with that little idea, would you?"

She flushed. "No ..."

Bill laughed. "Liar! You just broke our honesty rule!"

Her flush deepened until Susan was certain she resembled a tomato. "I mentioned it was something our church did back home and they ran with the idea!"

"Leave it to you to upend our town's staid traditions of doing pretty much nothing to celebrate our savior's birth," Bill teased. "Truthfully, we've needed something like that for a long time. Just don't drag me into the preparations!"

"I'll make you play one of the angels in the pageant!" she threatened.

They worked like that for several hours, bantering comfortably as they each completed their respective side, moving closer and closer until they finally met in the middle. As they did, Bill looked down at her, a huge smile on his face.

"Mrs. Jacobs, you have paint on your nose," he informed her.

She beamed up at him and dabbed her brush on his own nose. "Now we match."

"Hey!" Bill protested, lunging for the brush. She danced away, down the as-yet unpainted steps, and he gave chase. With his longer legs, he quickly caught up, and Susan squirmed and laughed as he tried to pry the brush from her fingers, getting more and more paint all over him in the process. Nearly doubled over in laughter, Susan finally gave up the brush, only to see him swipe it down her cheek.

"Hey!"

It was her turn to lunge, only she was unsteady on her feet from having laughed so hard a minute earlier and Bill caught her, keeping her on her feet. He lifted her back up and raised his hand to her unpainted cheek, tucking her hair back behind her ear. Just like that, the laughter fled and Susan felt heat rise inside her as his gentle fingers lightly stroked her cheek.

"Susan ..."

He leaned toward her and the intent warmth of his eyes washed over, leaving her feeling like her knees were weak. But his arm was still around her waist and he was holding her up ... then his lips brushed hers and Susan melted into him, stunned by how tender and sweet his kiss was.

Just as her eyes drifted shut and she lifted a hand to covers his where it still rested on her cheek, Bill jerked back. Susan's eyes flew open and met his. Where a moment ago there'd been passion, now there was outright fear. Her heart sank to her toes.

"Bill—"

To her dismay, he yanked away as though she'd burned him. "No. No. This was a mistake. I can't."

Eyes wide, she watched him rush away toward the barn, shoulders slumped, fists clenched, looking for all the world like she'd struck him. But Susan didn't feel any better as she stared after her fleeing husband, her heart feeling like it was in a million pieces at her feet.

CHAPTER 9

THREE WEEKS LATER

"WHAT ARE YOU DOING, BILL?"

This time it was Bill who asked himself that question as he hammered home the final boards in a new hog pen. There was no real need for one. The old one was only a few years old. But there also hadn't been a need to construct a brand-new chicken coop. Or to dig a new well. Or to spend hours reconsidering his usual crop rotation scheme. But the more chores he could come up with, the better he could avoid Susan.

There was no point in lying to himself—he'd kept as much distance as humanly possible between them since that kiss. Just the thought of it was enough to make him want to rush to wherever Susan was, drag her into his arms, beg for forgiveness, and then kiss her senseless. He knew he was in the wrong. The woman was pure gold and he was treating her like she had the plague.

Because he was scared. No denying that fact. Isabella had done a number on his heart, just like Jake had said. Only problem was, Bill couldn't figure out how to fix that. No matter how he tried, there seemed to be this invisible wall he couldn't scale to get back on the same side that he and Susan had briefly been on.

Every time he tried to find the courage to give love another try, the memory of Isabella knocked him flat. What if it happened again? What if Susan turned out to be the same kind of person? What if—

"What if I'm an idiot?" Bill straightened, staring at the house with its pale blue porch. The rest of the building now looked twice as bad, but neither he nor Susan seemed to have the heart to tackle that project.

You are an idiot, he heard a quiet voice say, and he wouldn't have been surprised if it was God himself admonishing him. *So fix it.*

"How?" he said out loud, his eyes fixed on the kitchen window, where Susan could usually be seen at this time. He didn't see any sign of her now, though.

Talk to her. Explain about Isabella. Apologize.

Apologize. Bill took a deep breath. Okay. Yes. He should do that. He could do that. He *would* do that. Before his treacherous heart talked him out of it, he hurried to the house and stepped inside. "Susan," he called. "Susan ... I need to talk to you. I'm sure you don't want to hear it, but I owe you an apology."

He walked through the house, growing more and more confused when he found no sign of her. It was dinnertime. No matter how awful things had been between them, Susan had yet to miss a dinner. She'd eventually given up trying to talk to him, but still she made his meals and sat with him at suppertime, watching silently as Bill gulped down her delicious food and then rushed away.

You are a fool, the little voice inside Bill whispered as he stopped by her room and his brow furrowed in confusion when he knocked, received no response, peered in and saw that it had been stripped of all her possessions.

A nagging fear started low in Bill's belly and only grew as he stepped inside and stared at the empty nails on the wall that previously had held some of Susan's paintings. The Bible was gone from her nightstand. Heart now firmly in his throat, he peered into her closet and found her clothing gone.

"Oh God," he whispered, realization setting in. Even as he began to understand, his eye fell on a tiny scrap of paper on her pillow. Rushing over, he plucked it up and read,

I can't do this anymore. I deserve better. So do you. Goodbye, Bill.

A kind of film seemed to descend over his vision and Bill sank down onto the bed, feeling like he'd been gut shot. He'd done it. He'd well and truly done it. He'd fallen in love with a woman—why bother denying it? He loved Susan from the top of her beautiful head to the tip of her rather long toes, which he teased her about whenever she went barefoot—and she'd smashed his heart to smithereens again.

Only ... *that's not what happened*, he told himself. No. Susan had tried and tried, day in and day out. He was the one who had driven her to this.

"Boss?"

Vaguely, he heard Ted calling to him from the front door. Feeling like he was in some sort of trance, he stumbled along the hallway and found his new hire eyeing him worriedly. The man would never take a step inside the house without a direct invitation, Bill had quickly learned.

"What is it?" he murmured, though he could barely find it in himself to care about whatever problem had presented itself on the farm. He'd lost Susan. God had sent her to him as a second chance at happiness—a first chance, really, since he'd never been happy with Isabella in the first place—and he'd not only squandered it; he'd pushed it away as hard as was humanly possible.

"Boss, I saw Mrs. Boss ride out here like a bat out of h—" Ted checked himself, having quickly adapted his language when he'd learned there was a woman on the farm. It was another thing Bill liked about the man. "Mrs. Boss rode out of here right quick. Everything okay?"

Slowly, Bill lifted his head from where he'd been staring at his shoes. "No, Ted. It's not," he replied, a plan forming in his mind. "It's not at all. But it might be ... it might still be if you can help me."

Ted squared his shoulders. "Just say the word, boss!"

"Saddle the fastest horse in the stable."

"Uh ... she took that one."

Bill scowled. "Then the next one. Never mind. I'll saddle it myself. Ted—you ride like the wind into town in the carriage and see if you can stop the train!"

Bewildered, the small man stared at him. "Train?"

"I'm sure that's where she's headed," Bill yelled as he ran for the barn. "We have to stop her, Ted! I can't let her go!"

There was a confused silence before Ted snapped, "On it, boss!"

As Bill saddled up Pete, he thanked God that Ted was undoubtedly already tearing towards town. One of them was bound to reach the train before it left. Then Bill could get on his knees and beg Susan for forgiveness and a second chance. And he wouldn't quit until she knew he adored her and would turn the world upside down to right his foolish mistake and mend her broken heart.

CHAPTER 10

Something wasn't right.

Susan jolted awake, woken by some unknown noise, and opened her eyes briefly, expecting to be in the comfort of her bed. She closed them again at the thickness of the darkness that seemed to rush towards her face and shivered with the fear that suddenly suffused her mind.

She opened her eyes again, confused, and tried to figure out what had happened. The room was cold, dark, and silent. It smelled of horses and cow dung. Darkness, thick as an angry cloud, rose up all around her, suffocating in its intensity. As it did, Susan gradually remembered, the ache in her head clueing her in to the memory.

She'd been in the kitchen making dinner. Even though Bill would probably have scarfed down woodchips, so long as he could get them down fast and get away from her, she continued to try to mend what had once been between them. Sometimes she cried at night, thinking she might as well call it quits and leave ... but she loved the man, darn him. She couldn't just up and leave. No matter how badly he was hurting.

So she'd been making his favorite stew, thinking about how tonight she was going to force him to listen, when she'd heard a creak in the floorboards behind her. Before she could turn, wondering why Bill, who made a point never to startle anyone from behind, would have snuck up, something heavy had struck her temple and the world had gone black. And now ...

Susan tried to sit up and realized that she was tightly bound, hands and feet tied to some immovable object.

"Help!" she shouted. "HELP!"

From the darkness, a low, dry chuckle came, so cold that she trembled in fear.

"No help's coming, sunshine," the voice rumbled, and from the shadows, Susan saw half of her nightmare emerge as a candle flared to life and revealed Andrew Manheim.

Gasping, she instinctively tried to squirm away from the treacherous banker who was partially responsible for the destruction of her life back east.

The malevolent man chuckled, but thankfully didn't take another step toward her. "We told you you'd pay," he lectured in that whiny, nasally voice that had always set Susan's nerves on edge even before she realized he was a monster.

"You'd better let me go before my husband gets here!" she cried. "He has quite a temper when provoked!"

Manheim sneered, the flickering light making him look that much more sinister. "Your husband's not going to be causing us any trouble now or ever, little woman."

Her blood ran cold. "What have you done? If you've hurt Bill, I'll kill you!"

Again, Manheim chuckled. "I haven't done anything to anybody. Ted, on the other hand ..."

Susan's heart all but stopped as the door to wherever she was being held creaked open and in walked Theodore 'Ted' Milstaff. Manheim's thieving accomplice whom she'd had the misfortune of catching in the act of murdering an innocent bank teller, with Manheim standing guard.

"You're in jail," she whispered. "This is all a bad dream."

Ted's sneer was like ice cutting through her. "It's a bad dream, all right. And you're going to wake. I told you the day you testified and got Manheim and me locked away that we'd come find you eventually. You must've known I meant it, because you fled town like a scared rabbit right after testifying. But I have eyes and ears everywhere. Took me a while to bribe us out. Took more time to find you. But I did ... and here we are at last, Susan Lockhart."

"What have you done to Bill?" she demanded, fighting back the desire to weep and instead praying for strength. Her mother's favorite scripture, Psalm 46:1-3, drifted through her mind and she clung to it. *God is our refuge and strength, an ever-present help in trouble. Therefore we will not fear, though the earth give way and the mountains fall into the heart of the sea, though its waters roar and foam and the mountains quake with their surging.*

"Bill? You mean the boss?" he mocked.

Susan took a shallow breath. "You. You're the man he hired."

Ted grinned cruelly. "Didn't even disguise myself or change my name. All I had to do was keep out of your sight till I figured out the farm routine. You never showed any interest in meeting me. If you had, things might've got interesting."

She swallowed a groan of dismay. It was true that she hadn't made time to meet Bill's new hire. She'd been too busy trying to figure out to get past the walls Bill had built around his heart—

"Where is he?" she repeated, struggling to sit up even though she knew it was useless.

"Dead," Ted said simply, and Susan's already bruised heart cracked cleanly in half.

"No."

"Oh yes." He took a menacing step toward her. "He thought I was 'helping' him, you see, to chase you down after you left him."

"I would never leave him!" Susan cried out, fighting the ropes with everything in her. "Where is he? What have you done to him! BILL! BILL!"

Abruptly, Ted lunged forward and backhanded her across the face so hard that Susan very nearly lost consciousness again. She clung to the very edges of awareness, refusing to give in to the darkness again. Blood trickled from her split lip and she tasted salt tears.

Dear God. Help me, she prayed, cracking an eye to see where Ted was now.

He and Manheim were pacing around the room and Susan realized with horror what was happening. The smell of kerosene quickly permeated her senses as they poured the fuel all around her bed. Dazed, she watched as Manheim left the room and returned, and that was when Susan's senses came back in full force and she resumed fighting, shouting, struggling against her bonds with fresh fury.

"*Bill!*"

Manheim dumped her husband's motionless form beside the bed and he and Ted exchanged a look before they started for the door.

"I'd say it was nice knowing you, Susan," Ted drawled mockingly from the door. "But that would be a lie. And the boss has such a thing against lies."

Then he struck a match and hurled the lit wooden stick to the floor before he and Manheim rushed away.

CHAPTER 11

BILL. BILL. BILL, PLEASE!

Groggily, Bill forced his eyes open, every muscle in his body aching. Somewhere close by, a familiar voice was screaming.

"Bill! Wake up! You have to wake up! Dear God, let him hear me!"

"What ..." he mumbled, his head pounding so much that he could barely hear, much less see straight.

"Bill," the voice said again. "I don't know what they did to you, but you have to listen. The flames are almost on us!"

For the first time, he felt the fierce heat licking at him. Vague awareness permeated him and he remembered something about saddling a horse ... being struck from behind ... something about Susan ...

Susan!

That memory sent him bolting upright in spite of the pain. As he sat up, consciousness returned in full force and he took in the horrific scene before him. It was a small room, illuminated solely by orange and blue tongues of flame licking their way toward him at a vicious pace. The flames painted a brilliant circle around where he lay and around where Susan was tethered to a cot, fighting furiously to break free.

"Oh God." Bill's eyes widened. "Susan!"

"Get up," she pleaded. "It's only by the grace of God that the room hasn't exploded yet!"

But moving required muscle coordination that Bill seemed to have lost when he was struck. He fought to regain control of his arms and legs, eventually realizing crawling would have to. So he crawled over to Susan and fumbled with her bonds, his fingers refusing to do as he commanded.

"You have to get out," Susan insisted over and over. "I'm done for, Bill. Go!"

"Not going anywhere," he rasped, his mouth like sandpaper. "We're both gettin' out of this. I love you."

Tears poured down her face. "I love you too. But because I love you, you have to leave!"

Giving up on the ropes, Bill hauled himself to his feet by using the side of the bed. Then he switched tactics and grabbed the head of the cot. With all his strength, he yanked at it. To his relief, it wasn't very heavy and it immediately moved an inch. So he pulled it again. And then again. Never mind that he was dragging it straight toward the flames. This was the only way.

"What are you doing?" Susan cried, staring up at him. She should have looked vulnerable, bound the way she was, completely at the mercy of the fire, but to Bill she looked like the strongest, most beautiful woman he'd ever known.

"I'm getting us out of here," he croaked, pulling determinedly. "And then I'm gonna marry you again."

"Oh, Bill," she whispered. "I just don't think there's any way—"

A tongue of flame broke from the circle and rushed forward. Bill stamped at it furiously, ignoring the pain of immediate burns,

"Gonna marry you again," he repeatedly dizzily. "And you're not giving up, Susan Jacobs. No way. You just sit tight. I'm gonna get us out of here, even if we get a little cooked in the process."

"The mattress," Susan suddenly said. "Bill, the mattress! You can use it—"

"The flames," he realized before she finished her sentence. "Sit tight, sweetheart."

"What choice do I have?" she shot back, but there was laughter through her tears.

Bill hauled the flimsy cot as far as he could before connecting directly with the now leaping flames that were sending tiny embers to sear through his clothes and making his eyes water to where the entire world was a blur. Then he reached beneath Susan and yanked the mattress out from under her. Almost in the same motion, he used the mattress to block the flames standing in his path to the door. It would only work momentarily, but that was long enough for Bill to push and shove the cot the remainder of the way. By the time the flames burst through the thin mattress, Bill had Susan, still tied to the cot, out in the open.

The threat was by no means over—the flames now came at them through the open door, but now Bill at least knew where they were. The loft.

"Hold on, sweetheart!"

Rushing away, he rummaged in the loft, knowing exactly where certain things were kept. A moment later he was back with a knife he used to cut twine for hay bales. In a few swift slashes, he cut Susan free and hauled her into his arms.

She clung to him, but there was no time to waste. Already, the flames were eating into the hayloft. The barn was a lost cause, Bill knew.

He rushed them to the ladder. "Hold on tight. Don't you dare let go," he warned Susan as he started down with her holding onto his back for dear life. Around them, tongues of fire began to race along the barn's old beams, eating into every surface, beginning to already hollow it out like a pumpkin.

A moment later they were in the barn and Bill scooped Susan up, about to run for the door and safety, when she stopped him. "The animals, Bill."

"God, I love you," he whispered fervently, stealing a swift, fierce kiss before dropping her outside and rushing to let the frantic horses and cows out of their stalls. They all rushed to the exit, the livestock thundering past along with several frightened barn cats, and then Bill was in the farmyard with Susan, carrying her once more, racing to get as far from the building as he could before it was completely consumed by flames.

She insisted they free the hogs and the chickens, in case the flames reached their pens, and it wasn't until every animal at least had the chance to run for safety that Susan finally allowed Bill to carry her far away toward the river.

There, he finally put her down and they held each other close, watching the destruction of their livelihood and, undoubtedly, their home, along with everything else in the path of the relentless flames.

"It's all gone," Susan whispered, and Bill looked down at her.

Her cheeks were raw and burned. Her clothes had gaping holes in them. Her voice sounded like she'd smoked multiple pipes in quick succession. Her eyes were red and watery. He undoubtedly looked the same. And yet she remained the most beautiful woman he'd ever seen.

"You're still here," he told her. "The woman I love is still here and alive and well. That's all that matters."

Susan dragged her eyes from the farm and looked up at him. "I would never leave you. Ever. No matter how crazy you make me."

Bill kissed her softly. "We'll rebuild everything, including our marriage. Will you give me the chance to do that, Sue?"

She smiled up at him. "That's the first time you've ever called me that. And yes. So long as you let go of whoever it was who broke your heart before. I can't compete with a ghost, Bill, no matter how much I love you. Speaking of ... you don't even know who Ted is, do you."

"Nope."

"I caught him and his accomplice murdering someone to rob a bank. I testified against them and got them locked away. Then I answered Jake's letter to get away from town, in case they ever came after me."

Bill nodded. "My story's less dramatic. I was in love with a woman who cheated on me repeatedly. Nothing more to the story than that. She broke my heart. And you rebuilt it."

This time she kissed him. "No more secrets after this. No more misunderstandings. And from now on, Mr. Jacobs, I expect this marriage to be *far* more than a mere partnership!"

He chuckled and held her tight. "Yes, ma'am. You better believe it. Yes, yes, ma'am."

EPILOGUE

THREE MONTHS LATER

"I'll get you!" Ted snarled as the US Marshal frog-marched him in the direction of the prison cell. "I swore I would before and I would've done it, too, if Manheim hadn't been incompetent!"

Standing off to the side, Susan's fingers curled tightly around Bill's as they watched one of the two men who'd tried to kill her be taken back to prison. This cell would only be a temporary pen. He was destined for Utah, and likely for the gallows.

After the fire, she and Bill had walked into town and told the sheriff everything. A massive manhunt had taken months before it finally flushed Ted out of the hovel he was hiding in deep in New Mexico territory. Manheim remained on the run.

She leaned into Bill and he held her close as Ted continued to scream and curse before he was led inside the building and his shouts faded away.

"What if Manheim carries out Ted's threat?" she asked quietly.

Bill kissed the top of her head before guiding her through the assembled crowd, starting toward the buggy they'd ridden from Jake's farm, where they were temporarily staying. "We're on our guard now. They'll catch him one of these days soon. I promise you, Sue. He won't get his hands on you again."

"Promise?" she asked as he helped her up into the buggy and then climbed up beside her.

"On my life. On my second wedding vows. On my love for you," he replied, tilting her chin up and kissing her tenderly.

She gazed up into his eyes. Though the past few months had been chaotic as they began to try and rebuild everything they'd lost, Jake had been more than a help, and the townspeople had all come together to offer assistance. Truly, they were blessed by all the kindness they'd received. And now they had one more blessing to look forward to.

Reaching out, Susan drew Bill's hand to her stomach. "Bill ... we need to finish our new home in the next, oh, seven or eight months, I'd say. Otherwise Jake's house will start to feel a little crowded."

He stared down at her, his brow furrowing. "Wha—the—I—" Then realization hit home and the biggest smile she'd ever seen darted across Bill's face, cutting through the weary lines of many months of laboring to get back on his feet. "You're ..."

"That's what the doctor told me this morning when I stopped by before the trial." Her smile more than matched his own.

"Sue," he whispered, wrapping her tightly in his arms and leaning down for a long, slow kiss. "Oh, Sue. I couldn't love you more if I tried. Thank you. Thank you."

She was lost in his sweet kiss when an unfamiliar female voice called, "Bill Jacobson?"

Susan blinked and pulled back, looking around. Her eyes fell on a petite blonde waving wildly from a few feet away. She was lovely, no question about it, with big green eyes and full lips that more than one man probably glanced at sideways. The rest of her was probably equally appealing to the male eye. Interestingly, though, Susan noted, not one man was actually giving her the time of day.

Nor was Bill, Susan realized suddenly. He glanced over in the woman's direction, his eyebrows shot up, and then he laughed and guided the horses forward. It wasn't until they were a good distance away, the woman's increasingly incensed shouts of, "Bill? Bill. Bill!" finally having faded, that Bill pulled the wagon to a stop, still chuckling.

"What?" Susan demanded, poking him.

He leaned down and kissed her stomach gently, unexpectedly, and she stroked his blond head, waves of love moving through her slowly. Then he sat back up and shrugged.

"That, my love, was Isabella."

Susan's eyebrows shot up. "What!"

Again, Bill shrugged. "She'll try and cause trouble, no doubt. But I don't love her, Sue. She isn't my wife. She isn't the mother of my child. She isn't the woman I'll build a new life with and spend my days beside. Can you live with her being a mild bother in the background of our lives until she gets bored and moves on, at least, so long as you know that my heart belongs solely to you?"

Susan frowned, turning that over in her head, and then laughed. "Why not. Life would be boring without some kind of madness!"

This time when Bill kissed her, there was no interruption. Not from outlaws. Not from Isabella. And not from the man Susan loved, who had finally conquered his demons and was decidedly uninterested in ever looking back over his shoulder again.

When they finally broke apart, it was solely because they were both breathless. Laughing like two teenagers, they cuddled up together in the buggy and set out for Jake's place, where Susan had first arrived all those months ago. Jake hadn't been the man for her, but Bill certainly was.

"God knows what he's doing," she whispered happily, and her husband kissed her, drew her closer, and wholeheartedly agreed.

ROYCE CARDIFF PUBLISHING HOUSE PRESENTS OTHER WONDERFUL CLEAN, wholesome and inspiring romance short stories titles for your entertainment. Many are value boxset and as always FREE to Kindle Unlimited readers.

COMPLETE SERIES
Sweet Western Romance

KATIE WYATT, BRENDA CLEMMONS AND ELLEN ANDERSON

katie wyatt box set complete series

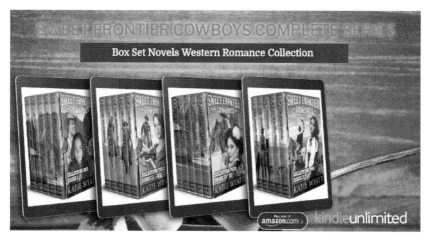

Sweet Frontier Cowboys Complete Series Collection (A Novel Christian Romance Series)

Katie Wyatt Mega Box Set Series (12 Mega Box Set Series)

Brenda Clemmons Box Set Sweet Clean Contemporary Romance Series

THANK YOU SO MUCH FOR READING MY BOOK. I SINCERELY HOPE YOU ENJOYED EVERY bit reading it. I had fun creating it and will surely create more.

Your positive reviews are very helpful to other reader, it only takes a few moments. They can be left at Amazon.

www.amazon.com/Katie-Wyatt/e/B011IN7AF0

WANT FREE BOOKS EVERY WEEK? WHO DOESN'T!

BECOME A PREFERRED READER AND WE'LL NOT ONLY SEND YOU FREE READS, BUT you'll also receive updates about new releases.

So you'll be among the first to dive into our latest new books, full of adventure, heartwarming romances, and characters so real they jump off the page.

It's absolutely free and you don't need to do anything at all to qualify except go to.

PREFERRED READ FREE READS

http:/katieWyattBooks.com/readersgroup

ABOUT THE AUTHOR

ADA OAKLEY IS AN AMERICAN-BORN ITALIAN, WHO HAS LIVED MOST OF HER life in Dallas Texas and has traveled to many countries. She has been an avid reader and a lover of western movies since her teenage years, so she decided to pursue a writing career.

Ada loves writing Western Romance and Mail Order Bride stories about the courageous women who traveled alone to the Wild West with nothing but hope and strong faith in God.

Her inspirations are her dogs and three lovely cats! So if you're up to reading an excellent feel good clean romance story, her stories are highly recommended.

Printed in Great Britain
by Amazon